Altermundos

AZTLÁN ANTHOLOGY SERIES

AZTLÁN ANTHOLOGY SERIES, VOLUME 4

Altermundos
Latin@ Speculative Literature, Film, and Popular Culture

Edited by

Cathryn Josefina Merla-Watson and B.V. Olguín

UCLA Chicano Studies Research Center Press
Los Angeles
2017

CSRC Director: Chon A. Noriega
Senior Editor: Rebecca Frazier
Business Manager: Connie Heskett
Manuscript Editor: Catherine A. Sunshine
Design and Production: William Morosi

Cover image: Laura Molina, *Amor Alien*, 2004. Oil, fluorescent enamel and metallic powder on canvas, 35 × 47 inches (89 cm × 120 cm). Permanent collection of the National Museum of Mexican Art, Chicago. Image courtesy of the artist.

Library of Congress Cataloging-in-Publication Data

Names: Merla-Watson, Cathryn Josefina, editor. | Olguín, B. V., 1965- editor.
Title: Altermundos : Latin@ speculative literature, film, and popular culture
    / edited by Cathryn Josefina Merla-Watson and B.V. Olguín.
Description: Los Angeles : UCLA Chicano Studies Research Center Press, 2017.
    | Series: Aztlán anthology series ; Volume 4 | Includes bibliographical
    references and index.
Identifiers: LCCN 2016059829 | ISBN 9780895511638 (pbk. : acid-free paper)
Subjects: LCSH: American fiction--Hispanic American authors--History and
    criticism. | American fiction--Mexican American authors--History and
    criticism. | American fiction--Women authors--History and criticism. |
    Speculative fiction, American--History and criticism. | Hispanic American
    women--Intellectual life. | Mexican American women--Intellectual life. |
    Women and literature--United States. | Motion pictures and women--United
    States.
Classification: LCC PS153.H56 A59 2017 | DDC 813.009/868--dc23
LC record available at https://lccn.loc.gov/2016059829

⊠ This book is printed on acid-free paper.

CONTENTS

Front cover of Love and Rockets, no. 5 (March 1984). Reproduced by permission of Jaime Hernandez and Fantagraphics.

The Time Machine
From Afrofuturism to Chicanafuturism and Beyond

Catherine S. Ramírez

Octavia Butler's 1993 novel *Parable of the Sower* brought me back to science fiction. I had been a science fiction fan when I was growing up, but had drifted from the genre with age. Perhaps my interest began to wane when I decided that, for all its emphasis on newness, the typical science fiction hero was a messianic white boy. Think Anakin Skywalker in *Star Wars* and Ender Wiggin, the prodigy-protagonist of Orson Scott Card's *Ender's Game* series. Or perhaps I decided I was done with sci-fi when I attended back-to-back screenings of *Star Wars*, *The Empire Strikes Back*, and *Return of the Jedi* at the 1,300-seat UC Theater during my freshman year at the University of California, Berkeley, and saw that I was one of but a handful of women in the audience (to say nothing of the dearth of women on the screen). Or maybe the last straw was Jar Jar Binks, George Lucas's pitifully anachronistic sci-fi rendition of Stepin Fetchit.[1] Whatever the source of my alienation and discontent, I had pretty much written off science fiction by my mid-twenties. The genre was for immature white male nerds with dubious politics, I concluded; I was a feminist woman of color.

Then I encountered *Parable of the Sower*. It was the mid-1990s and I was supposed to be preparing for my PhD qualifying exam. I was looking for a distraction when I picked up the yellow and orange paperback. More than a mere diversion, Butler's novel proved to be a compass and inspiration. Its troubled and powerful heroine, Lauren Olamina, is a black teenage girl who experiences others' physical sensations as if they were her own and who manages to lead a motley group of survivors out of a postapocalyptic

Southern California to a northern haven. This extraordinary young woman cast new light on the theories of double consciousness, intersectionality, *malinchismo*, and cultural identity that I had been struggling to grasp in the classroom. I had no idea science fiction could be so smart, pleasurable, and politically down.

Parable of the Sower also introduced me to feminist science fiction and Afrofuturism. *Wikipedia* defines the latter as "a literary and cultural aesthetic that combines elements of science fiction, historical fiction, fantasy, Afrocentricity, and magic realism with non-Western cosmologies in order to critique not only the present-day dilemmas of people of color, but also to revise, interrogate, and re-examine the historical events of the past."[2] I present this definition not only because it is accurate and pithy, but also because the very existence of a Wikipedia entry for Afrofuturism speaks to the term's significance and circulation since Mark Dery coined it in 1993. Like other terms that brilliantly name that which is before us but is seemingly invisible, natural, immutable, or permanent—for instance, capitalism and heteronormativity—Afrofuturism had surrounded me long before I knew the word for it. Take, as an example, the music of my childhood and adolescence. More than just the freak-a-zoid and atomic dog, Afrofuturism was the desire and audacity to imagine an alternate reality and alternative ways of being. It was Afrika Bambaataa's Planet Rock, Marvin Gaye's funky space reincarnation, and the need to travel through time by renarrating the past and striving for a brighter future.[3]

Afrofuturism and the work of New Mexican artist Marion C. Martinez brought the concept of Chicanafuturism to me. I first saw Martinez's mixed-media Catholic icons in 2001 at the Museum of International Folk Art in Santa Fe as part of *Cyber Arte: Tradition Meets Technology*, a bold and innovative show that explored some of the ways in which four Latina artists—Martinez, Teresa Archuleta-Sagel, Elena Baca, and Alma López—used technology in their work. Like good science fiction, Martinez's nine pieces in *Cyber Arte* were both familiar and new to me: they depicted the Virgin of Guadalupe and Christ with his crown of thorns, yet they were made of discarded computer parts, like wires, chips, and disks. These luminous works brought the high-tech and rasquache together and prompted me to define Chicanafuturism as "cultural production that attends to cultural transformations resulting from new and everyday technologies (including their detritus); that excavates, creates, and alters narratives of identity, technology, and the future; that interrogates the promises of science and technology; and that redefines humanism and the human" (Ramírez 2004, 77–78).

With its clear ties to Afrofuturism, Chicanafuturism is itself a chimera concept, a suturing of Butler's fiction, theories of Afrofuturism, Gloria Anzaldúa's notion of alien consciousness, and Martinez's cyber arte. It is by no means pure, and as one of many alternative futurisms, to use Sherryl Vint, Rob Latham, and Nalo Hopkinson's term, it is not original. Vint, Latham, and Hopkinson's work highlights the ubiquity and capaciousness of alternative futurisms and the need for peoples across time and space to scrutinize the present, reexamine the past, and envision the future.[4]

Using the time machine, a staple of sci-fi, Aamer Rahman's *Fear of a Brown Planet* offers an alternative narrative of the past to cast new light on the present.[5] In this sharp and sardonic stand-up routine, Rahman, an Australian comedian of Bangladeshi descent, responds to criticism from whites that his comedy is reverse racist and to the assertion made by some people of color that reverse racism does not exist. "I don't agree with that," he remarks. "I think there is such a thing as reverse racism. I could be a reverse racist if I wanted to. All I would need would be a time machine." He then proceeds to retell the last five-hundred-plus years of world history. However, in his version of the story, African, Asian, Middle Eastern, and Central and South American nations invade, colonize, and plunder Europe. Black and brown powers set up a "trans-Asian" slave trade in which whites are forced to "work on giant rice plantations in China." Above all, they establish "systems that privilege black and brown people at every conceivable social, political, and economic opportunity [so] white people would never have any hope of real self-determination." "If, after hundreds and hundreds and hundreds of years of that," Rahman concludes, "I got on stage at a comedy show and said, 'Hey, what's the deal with white people? Why can't they dance?' *that* would be reverse racism."[6]

Not just a simple revenge fantasy or reiteration of clichés, *Fear of a Brown Planet* exposes the absurdity of the very notion of reverse racism by bringing into relief profound historical injustices and social inequalities in our world. By invoking Public Enemy's 1990 LP *Fear of a Black Planet*, and bearing more than a wee resemblance to George S. Schuyler's speculative fiction novel *Black Empire* (1993), Rahman's joke both draws from Afrofuturism and pushes it in new directions.[7] The contributors to this dossier do the same as they rethink Chicanafuturism. I defer to their expertise, commend their labor and creativity, and can't wait to see where they'll take us.

Notes

1. Stepin Fetchit was the stage name of Lincoln Theodore Monroe Andrew Perry (1902–85), an African American comedian and film actor who exploited and helped popularize racist stereotypes of the lazy, freewheeling, "Negro" simpleton over the course of the twentieth century.

2. "Afrofuturism," *Wikipedia*, https://en.wikipedia.org/wiki/Afrofuturism (accessed December 30, 2014).

3. "Freak-a-Zoid" is from Midnight Star's 1983 album *No Parking on the Dance Floor*, and "Atomic Dog" is from George Clinton's *Computer Games* (1982). "Planet Rock" is a 1982 song by Afrika Bambaataa and the Soulsonic Force, and "A Funky Space Reincarnation" is from Marvin Gaye's *Here, My Dear* (1978).

4. For more information about Vint, Latham, and Hopkinson's alternative futurisms project, see Miller (2014).

5. Rahman developed *Fear of a Brown Planet* with fellow comedian Nazeem Hussain and performed it at comedy festivals for several years beginning in 2004.

6. All quotes are from Rahman's performance at http://www.youtube.com/watch?v=dw_mRaIHb-M.

7. *Black Empire*, about the creation of an independent and menacing nation on the African continent, was originally published under Schuyler's pseudonym, Samuel I. Brooks, and ran as a serial in the *Pittsburgh Courier* from October 1937 to April 1938.

Works Cited

Butler, Octavia. 1993. *Parable of the Sower*. London: Women's Press.

Dery, Mark. 1993. "Black to the Future: Interviews with Samuel R. Delany, Greg Tate, and Tricia Rose." *South Atlantic Quarterly* 92, no. 4: 735–78.

Miller, Bettye. 2014. "Science Fiction Through Lens of Racial Inclusiveness." *UCR Today* (University of California, Riverside), July 14. http://ucrtoday.ucr.edu/23789.

Ramírez, Catherine S. 2004. "Deus ex Machina: Tradition, Technology, and the Chicanafuturist Art of Marion C. Martinez." *Aztlán: A Journal of Chicano Studies* 29, no. 2: 55–92.

Schuyler, George S. 1993. *Black Empire*. Boston: Northeastern University Press.

Altermundos

Reassessing the Past, Present, and Future of the
Chican@ and Latin@ Speculative Arts

Cathryn Josefina Merla-Watson and B. V. Olguín

We began this anthology project by curating and editing two thematic
dossiers on the Latin@ speculative arts published in *Aztlán: A Journal of
Chicano Studies* in fall 2015 and spring 2016. In doing so, we sought to
recover an element of vernacular culture that has always been a mainstay
of the Chican@ and Latin@ literary, visual, and performing arts but that
has not been fully appreciated or theorized, despite Catherine S. Ramírez's
(2004) prescient call two decades ago to recenter the speculative in theories
of Chican@ poetics. We also simply like speculative fiction, particularly
its boundlessness and its unabashed insistence on the utopian as a real
possibility. What has emerged from the myriad dialogues, discoveries,
recoveries, and theories of the Latin@ speculative arts is a profound, and
profoundly productive, disorientation. Time travel—the old trope of the
speculative arts—has merged with shape-shifting: virtually nothing of
what we thought we knew about Latin@ literary, theatrical, cinematic, and
visual arts genealogies and histories has remained intact. The possibilities
for theorizing Latinidades are again boundless and endless.

Building on the two dossiers, this expanded anthology presents criticism of Latin@ speculative arts along with original creative production
of speculative fiction and visual art. Screening approximately five dozen
proposals and stewarding the development and revision of the pieces
that are included in this anthology prompted a radical reassessment
of what constitutes the speculative in terms of generic boundaries and

1

substance. Contributing authors such as Shelley Streeby have answered Ramírez's visionary call to refocus our lens to recover the speculative in the interstices of genres. Gregg Barrios reminds us that Chican@ theater was toying with the speculative alongside foundational utopian struggles in the Chican@ movement, such as the one in Crystal City, Texas, that began with a student walkout to protest racist school practices in 1969. Seven years later, Chican@ youth in Barrios's high school classes produced *Stranger in a Strange Land*, a performance that riffed on David Bowie's Ziggy Stardust period, with *The Rise and Fall of Ziggy Stardust and the Spiders from Mars* forming the sound track of the production. The play explored the trope of aliens and alienation in a racist capitalist society. The speculative arts thus stretch the contours and horizons of what we thought we knew about Chicana/o culture, identity, and politics far beyond standard generic boundaries and cultural nationalist paradigms.

The history of the Latin@ speculative arts has yet to be written, though numerous contributors to this anthology offer major inaugural interventions in this regard. The collection includes references to at least 100 Latin@-produced literary texts, films, plays, and artworks, as well as non-Latin@-produced speculative cultural productions that involve Latin@s in one way or another. In the course of excavating speculative pasts and the unrecognized speculative present, we found leads to dozens more works, most of which have yet to be examined by scholars. Who would have known that award-winning *Def Poetry Jam* poet Amalia Ortiz starred in *Mexicans on the Moon*, a rasquache punk knockoff of *Star Trek* by Jorge Solís, in 2010? Numerous ephemeral local productions described as "Chican@ Star Trek" apparently have been staged in local theaters throughout the increasingly Latinized United States. Local theaters have also hosted the always provocative work of Guillermo Gómez-Peña, whose speculative gamut runs from *The Couple in the Cage*, performed with collaborator Coco Fusco, to solo works such as *El Naftazteca: Cyber-Aztec TV for 2000 AD* (1995). Latin@ independent film festivals are rife with short speculative works that vanish immediately after their screening, as if through a wormhole, only to emerge later as feature films such as *El Mariachi* (1992), *From Dusk Till Dawn* (1996), or *Spy Kids* (2001). While this anthology disinters heretofore buried or "inter-American" (Alemán 2006) genealogies of the speculative, it simultaneously serves as a call for scholarship that further unearths and reassesses Latin@ speculative aesthetics.

Several contributing authors undo and discombobulate the very generic and historical parameters that have traditionally delineated the speculative,

those defining science fiction and fantasy as well as horror. Linda Heidenreich, Luz María Gordillo, Amalia Ortiz, and Cynthia Saldivar, for instance,
emphasize that horror, the gothic, and the post-apocalyptic are not foreign
notions to Chican@ and Latin@ subjectivity but rather powerful and enduring structures of feeling. As they show, horror and related genres are apropos
for interpreting Latin@ social life and subjectivity, not only because Latin@s
have been continually figured as the monstrous other in US popular culture
but also because horror and terror have been endemic to and have textured
Latin@ lived experience and history. Indeed, the histories of Chican@s and
Latin@s in the Americas have been punctuated by graphic forms of violence,
both banal and apocalyptic—the very stuff of horror. Though contributors to
this anthology largely engage works of fiction and performance art, they point
to how we might use the lens of horror as a mode of reading that illuminates
Latin@ affect within various states of terror, including the "intimate terrorism" that Gloria Anzaldúa describes in *Borderlands/La Frontera*:

> The world is not a safe place to live in. We shiver in separate cells in
> enclosed cities, shoulders hunched, barely keeping the panic below the sur-
> face of the skin, daily drinking shock along with our morning coffee, fearing
> the torches being set to our buildings, the attacks in the streets. Shutting
> down. Woman does not feel safe when her own culture, and white culture,
> are critical of her; when the males of all races hunt her as prey. (2007, 42)

Through this mode of feeling, seeing, knowing, and reading, real horrors are
brought into relief: they range from the atrocities of the Spanish conquest to
the historical spraying of Mexicans with toxic chemicals at the US-Mexico
border, from the systematic lynching of Mexicans in South Texas in the
nineteenth and early twentieth centuries to the more recent appearance
of rape trees throughout the Southwest, marking spots where immigrant
women are violated.

The discoveries and theorizations of new (and not so new) Latin@
speculative works in the two *Aztlán* dossiers have morphed into a rhizom-
atic creative, critical, and hybrid creative-critical speculative anthology.
It contains essays, stories, visual arts, manifestos, and testimonios, as well
as myriad fusions and sui generis speculative works that have not yet been
named in extant criticism. These include Christopher Carmona's borderlands horror, Debora Kuetzpal Vasquez's speculative testimonio, Gregg
Barrios's barrio space opera, and Linda Heidenreich's Chicana lesbian
vampire alternative history tale. Together, these works threaten to dislodge
the certainty of Latin@ literary and cultural studies, Latin@ historiography,
sociology, anthropology, and Latin@ epistemology in general. Like the

fabled Pandora, the call for proposals for the two dossiers and the anthology has given rise to a series of reclamations, declamations, and declarations, so that—as Ernest Hogan assures us when he writes, "Chicano is a science fiction state of being" (406)—it might be impossible to see Chican@ and Latin@ cultural production the same way again. As we noted in the dossiers, the perspectival shifts are myriad, complex, and convoluted, and they begin with the very definition of the speculative.

To be sure, the super-genre of speculative fiction (SF) is a notoriously porous and slippery one, encompassing sci-fi and fantasy as well as their subgenres, which continue to proliferate. Yet as Shelley Streeby underscores in this anthology, the category of SF enables readers to flesh out vital connections between texts and genres and to refuse pitched Pyrrhic battles concerning the integrity of genres. Streeby also demonstrates how the broader category of SF enables us to excavate, remap, and recenter the Chican@ and Latin@ contributions to sci-fi, fantasy, and intersecting categories and genres.[1] When we refer to the "Chican@ and Latin@ speculative arts" here, however, we do not intend to denote mimetic acts or simple permutations of what has historically been a largely white, male, Eurocentric, and heteronormative genre. Rather, we want to bring into view the creative and resilient ways in which Latin@ cultural producers since at least the 1970s have continued to repurpose and blend genres of sci-fi, horror, and fantasy to defamiliarize the ways in which the past continues to haunt the present and future. Latin@ speculative arts also make space for texts not normally included within the discrete generic bounds of sci-fi, horror, and fantasy, effectively questioning the constitutive parameters of these genres and remapping them. Extending and diversifying Catherine S. Ramírez's foundational prism of "Chicanafuturism" (2008), the broader Latin@ speculative arts continue to show how various forms of Latin@ cultural production obscure colonialist boundaries between self and other, between the technologically advanced and presumed "primitive," between the human and nonhuman, and between the past and future. Perhaps most saliently, the Latin@ speculative arts remind us that we cannot imagine our collective futures without reckoning with the hoary ghosts of colonialism and modernity that continue to exert force through globalization and neoliberal capitalism.

Such persistent and palpable specters engender what Cathryn Josefina Merla-Watson terms *altermundos* in her chapter titled "(Trans)Mission Possible: The Coloniality of Gender, Speculative Rasquachismo, and Altermundos in Luis Valderas's Chican@futurist Visual Art." Altermundos, Merla-Watson explains, make sensible "'third space' visions that are at once grounded in concrete realities while looking toward the decolonial and utopian" (355). She elaborates that this "neologism is inspired by the utopian spirit of the global justice movement's 'altermondialism' and by Alicia Gaspar de Alba's (1998) 'AlterNative' and Laura Pérez's (2007) 'altarity,' both of which index decolonizing aesthetic practices" (355). Protean and always evolving, altermundos are "speculative rasquache" compositions that are as diverse as they are contradictory and dissensual, as our contributors amply show. And so we have chosen *Altermundos* as the anthology's main title, for if there is a unifying thread to be parsed out within the emergent and seemingly scattered field of the Chican@ and Latin@ speculative arts, it is that of the creation of altermundos and, consequently, productive dissensus, polyvocality, and "pluriversality" (Mignolo 2011).

Topologies of Chican@ and Latin@ Sci-fi

In formulating the highly influential framework of Chicanafuturism, Catherine S. Ramírez has forged a keen methodology for recuperating the Latin@ speculative arts, asking, "What happens to Chicana/o texts when we read them as science fiction?" (2008, 190). Ramírez (2002) earlier takes up this question in her rethinking of Gloria Anzaldúa's new mestiza, elaborated in *Borderlands/La Frontera* (2007), as a queer borderlands subject who embodies a particular cyborgian and oppositional consciousness. Ramírez's work on Chicanafuturism has provoked scholars to reclaim texts not conventionally included within the generic parameters of sci-fi or the broader category of SF and to reconceptualize generic boundaries altogether. In his contribution to *Latinos and Narrative Media*, Christopher González (2013) has also addressed issues of excavation in his assessment of narratology for analyzing Latin@ speculative film. He insists that the apparent lack of a Latin@ sci-fi cinematic tradition has been due to a narrow focus on "narrative technique or design," and he calls us to recuperate this cinematic subgenre by shifting our attention to the "thematics" or "narratological components of sci-fi" (212). The "narrative blueprint" of sci-fi (223), González emphasizes, furnishes an apt vehicle for articulating the lived experiences of Latin@s, particularly those related to "immigration, employment, and both political and economic clout" (212), as illustrated in his exegesis of Peruvian American filmmaker Alex Rivera's film *Sleep Dealer* (2008). Ramírez and González both signal the need to rethink and redefine generic and subgeneric boundaries associated with SF for the purposes of more fully engaging the Latin@ speculative arts.

Another methodological thread stitching together this nascent field of study is the use of a trans-American or hemispheric approach to recovering genealogies of Latin American and US Latin@ SF. Miguel López-Lozano's 2007 monograph *Utopian Dreams, Apocalyptic Nightmares* not only gives focused attention to Chican@ dystopian fiction but also traces connections between US Latin@ speculative letters and those of Mexican writers. López-Lozano draws from Latin American philosophies of coloniality to understand how, at the turn of the millennium, "dystopian fiction provides the means for Mexican and Chicano authors to question fundamental tenets of Latin American culture such as the Western model of industrialized capitalism as the only possible pattern for the economic development of the hemisphere" (2007, 3). These Mexican and Chicano authors, López-Lozano contends, construct imaginative spaces in which they reveal the fissures in the supposedly smooth surface of economic globalization and development in Latin and Latin@ America, particularly after enactment of the North American Free Trade Agreement (NAFTA) in the early 1990s. In her germinal 2012 article on Latin@ cyberpunk and its critique of globalization and late capitalism, Lysa Rivera, a contributor to this anthology, also demonstrates the importance of using a hemispheric approach to apprehend the local and global sociopolitical import of Latin@ speculative fiction and film. Although Rivera takes a cue from geographer David Harvey in conceptualizing neoliberal economic hegemony, her analysis of borderlands texts dovetails with those of López-Lozano and draws on theories of coloniality as she foregrounds how globalization in the US-Mexico borderlands operates as an "enduring extension of colonial relations of power between the United States and Mexico" (2012, 416). Rivera's and López-Lozano's hemispheric approach, we would add, falls in line with José David Saldívar's hermeneutic of "trans-Americanity," illuminating how narratives from the global South and subaltern segments of the global North demarcate a contrapuntal hegemonic space "in which their stories of global coloniality of power seek to create an epistemological ground on which coherent versions of the world may be produced" (2011, xx).[2]

As these scholars affirm, Latin@ sci-fi and the speculative arts—even the most bleak, terrifying, and dystopic—project a utopian spirit through the genre's capacity for incisive social critique that cuts to the bone of our shared pasts and presents. For this reason, John Morán González observes, "Chican@ writers have increasingly turned to science fiction . . . to articulate their most pressing aesthetic and social concerns" (2010, 176). In the introduction to *Black and Brown Planets: The Politics of Race in Science Fiction*, Isiah Lavender III (2014) writes that "skin color matters in our visions of the future" and that sci-fi is uniquely poised to imagine beyond the color line to "build a better, more progressive world" (6). This relation between sci-fi and utopian possibility is also underscored by Frederick Luis Aldama, who says that despite dominant sci-fi's lack of a more liberatory imagination, science fiction as a genre is promising in that it "can go beyond its historical situatedness *and* its generic limitations" (Stavans and Aldama 2013, 63). It could well be argued, moreover, that the very notion of Aztlán and of Chican@ identity is predicated upon the utopian, as evident in texts ranging from the 1969 "Plan Espiritual de Aztlán" to Cherríe Moraga's watershed essay "Queer Aztlán: The Reformation of Chicano Tribe" (1993).

One of the most powerful theorizations of hope and utopian possibility within Latin@ studies comes from José Esteban Muñoz in his work on queer futurity. In his 2009 monograph *Cruising Utopia*, Muñoz redeploys the critical idealism of philosopher Ernst Bloch to articulate queer "utopian feeling" that functions as an "educated mode of desiring," connecting the past and present to imagine the future (1). Adamantly resituating the utopian as a collective "concrete possibility" informed by intersectionality and queer of color critique so as to unbind the "hamstrung pragmatic gay agenda" (10), Muñoz rejects what he perceives to be the political pessimism of the left and refuses the anti-relational turn myopically focused on notions of singularity and negativity. His emphasis on the utopian as a collective project of concrete possibility will serve, we are quite certain, as a conceptual and political touchstone for Latin@ SF scholarship. Kristie Soares (2014), for example, has elaborated Muñoz's concept of hope and his "utopic approach" to enrich and open up feminist and queer theory to the utopic imagination, which, she posits, tends to focus solely on present forms of activism and struggle. Redirecting Muñoz's utopic approach toward Latin@ sci-fi and the speculative more generally invites this question: How might this comprehensive genre, often organized around the projection of brown bodies into the future—"a future with a past," in the words of *Sleep Dealer*'s protagonist Memo Cruz—always already be a project of queer futurity?

Yet institutionally, Latin@s and people of color have been conspicuously absent as writers, creators, and producers of sci-fi and SF literary canons and cinematic productions. They have also been largely missing from representation, except as "structured absence" or as "narrative subtext or implicit allegorical subject" (Nama 2008, 2). William Nericcio (2007) points out that "Latina/o Americans have represented a subject[ed] population—that is, until quite recently, they have not contributed to mainstream, mass cultural textual and cinematic representations of their own communities" (17). Charles Ramírez Berg (2002) and other film and media studies scholars have further noted that Latin@s are often merely alluded to or figured through the alien in popular film and culture—or they are simply not present at all. Colombian American actor John Leguizamo, in his one-man stand-up performance in *Freak* (1998), directed by Spike Lee, remarks humorously though aptly, "There were no Latin people on *Star Trek*," adding that this omission "was proof that they weren't planning to have us around for the future." In other words, being discursively *cut out of* the future is tantamount to being *cut off from* the future, with the specter of genocide lingering. Such representational aporias in sci-fi and the speculative arts, then, raise questions about social transformation and about the realization of more emancipatory and inclusive presents and futures. To reckon with such absences, we, the editors of this anthology, assert that Latin@s and allies must dare to shake off hegemonic "investments in deferring various dreams of difference" (Muñoz 2009, 11) and instead reclaim our own futurity. We must insist, through the cultural production that Catherine S. Ramírez began to map over a decade ago, *¡Latin@futurism ahora!* The speaker of Rodolfo "Corky" Gonzales's 1967 epic poem *I Am Joaquín* pointedly declares, "I WILL ENDURE!," and the speculative arts enable us to make this survivance into a visionary and potentially revolutionary force.

As contributors to this anthology highlight, Latin@ cultural producers since at least the late 1970s have taken up this revolutionary call, composing what we call the Latin@ speculative arts, a complex and even contradictory genre that reflects the diversity of Latin@ concerns and experiences. It is a genre articulated through the grammar of the subjective and subjunctive, which culls from the past and present to visualize other kinds of emancipatory futures. The anthology begins with "The Time Machine: From Afrofuturism to Chicanafuturism and Beyond," by Catherine S. Ramírez, who codified and authorized "Chicanafuturism" as a legitimate movement and field of study. Tracing her own complicated encounters with sci-fi, Ramírez assures us that this genre is not solely reserved for middle-class whites and that indeed there exists a corpus of Chican@ sci-fi that is, in her words, "smart, pleasurable, and politically down" (x). Ramírez insists that Chicanafuturism, Afrofuturism, and alternative futurisms more generally force us to reckon with the past and reengage our present milieu to conceive other futures, however terrifying they may be.

Refiguring Fantasy, Horror, and Monstrosity

On any given day or night in San Antonio, Texas, especially around Halloween and el Día de los Muertos, one can witness the ritualized crossing of the "Ghost Tracks" of the old Southern Pacific Railroad on the city's Southside, an area that is predominately Mexican and Mexican American. According to urban legend, sometime during the 1930s or 1940s a school bus full of children stalled over the tracks and was hit by an oncoming train, killing all inside. *Se dice que los niños* now haunt the tracks to prevent travelers from meeting the same tragic fate.[3] At the crossing, motorists, predominately working-class Mexican Americans, sprinkle their back bumpers and windshields with baby powder, turn off their headlights (if it is night), and shift their cars into neutral. According to popular lore, the car will move forward slowly and then pause over the tracks, where the ghost children will push it to safety. Afterward, the driver restarts the car, pulls over to the side of the road, and examines the back of the car for ghostly imprints. Inevitably, they appear—the past impressing upon the present. The ritualized crossing of the Ghost Tracks is replayed in myriad ways throughout Aztlán and everywhere Mexican Americans have laid down roots. It illustrates how Mexican American vernacular culture (perhaps like all vernacular cultures) performs alternative truths, with tropes such as *se dice que* introducing alternative epistemologies where the real and unreal, fiction and truth, natural and supernatural blend.[4]

However, a recent slew of popular cultural productions misrepresent and mistranslate the Ghost Tracks for a heteronormative white audience. The horror mystery film *Fingerprints* (2006), for instance, deracinates and whitewashes the urban legend. Directed by Harry Basil, the film was shot in Oklahoma and stars white actress Kristin Cavallari. The cast consists mainly of white middle- and upper-class teenagers, with the exception of Lou Diamond Phillips and a racially ambiguous teenage actor, both of whom are depicted as sexual predators, perpetuating racist and colonialist Hollywood scripts and stereotypes.[5] Such misrepresentations bespeak not only the deeply subjective and contested nature of horror and fantasy—the cultural specificity giving form and content to what haunts and resonates with us—but also the relationship between the speculative and social power. Several essays and creative works included in this collection explore these tensions by continuing to foreground the generative and complex ways in which Chican@s and Latin@s engage with and reconceive horror, fantasy, and the speculative through our own differential and cultural prisms.

From the glosses of "true crime" genres in biopics of pathological human killers to supernatural forces of evil to fantasy horror fusions such as the proliferation of zombie cultural production and spectacles (e.g., zombie walks), horror has required suspension of belief while reminding us of the always already real possibility of these dystopic nightmares coming to pass in our own world. Horror also is a mode of reading that enables us to access nuances in established genres, including war literature, subaltern women's discourses such as the testimonial literature about border femicides, African American slave narratives, and prisoner literature, to name but a few. Such a merging of fantastical horror spectacles with mundane Chican@ barrio realities is dramatically rendered in the hit television serial *The Walking Dead*. In an episode titled "Vatos" (season 1, episode 4), a cholo character remarks of the new dystopian reality: "It's the same as it ever was . . . We can take it." He thereby conflates real existing poverty and violently carceral barrio realities with cataclysmic tragedies that threaten the very existence of humanity. The essays and creative writing included in this volume similarly bring to the fore the subjective nature and situatedness of horror and fantasy. They also interrogate the revolutionary potential and ideological complexities and contradictions of the Latin@ speculative arts. Linking these essays and stories, then, are questions that explore the differential aesthetics, poetics, and politics of horror, fantasy, and the speculative in general.

While sci-fi is able to radically defamiliarize the past and present, the companion genres of fantasy and horror hold a similar potential to re-represent the seemingly mundane as terrifying, horrific, or even sublime. This is a fundamentally political act, with writers and artists illuminating the power of ideological state apparatuses and the culture industry to make carceral, militarist, and exploitative realities seem "normal." While different from sci-fi, fantasy and horror frequently intersect with sci-fi through multiple topoi, particularly their myriad depictions of dystopias, which always carry a subversive potential even if this potential frequently remains underarticulated and unactualized. In *Fantasy: The Literature of Subversion*, Rosemary Jackson (1981) shows that while fantasy is often unleashed from the confines of the real, it is ultimately undergirded by the material, yet often invisible or repressed, realities shaped by class exploitation. Robin Wood (1986) similarly notes that the horror genre functions as a vessel for the "return of the repressed," including the phantasms of racism, sexism, xenophobia, and homophobia. Yet conceptions of—or of what is *perceived as*—the monstrous, horrific, and fantastic are striated by difference; that is, they are culturally, socially, and historically constructed as well as geographically specific. Farah Mendlesohn observes that fantasy seeks to make difference and deviance believable and normative within the fictional world created, and the very efficacy of a fantasy text thus relies on a "dialectic between author and reader for the construction of a sense of wonder"—that is, on the "consensual construction of belief" (2008, xiii). It is no surprise, then, that much of the fantasy and horror penned by Latin@s is grounded in the Southwest and draws upon familiar folkloric figures such as La Llorona, El Cucuy, and *lechuzas*.

José David Saldívar (1991) and Ramón Saldívar (2011) theorize that Latin@s and minority writers have retooled fantasy by forging hybrid formal strategies to reckon with racial oppression and collective traumatic histories. These strategies consciously move away from or wholly reconfigure magical realism, historically a staple of Latin American as well as Latin@ letters. In "Postmodern Realism," José David Saldívar (1991) identifies a new phase of magical realist fiction inaugurated by a wide range of pan-American and US ethnic writers, including Arturo Islas, Helena María Viramontes, and Jamie and Gilbert Hernandez. According to Saldívar, these authors' diverse works continue to call upon magical realist narrative strategies in new, postmodernist ways so as to defamiliarize and make acute the oppressive lived experiences and histories of minorities. In contradistinction to other kinds of historical fantasy, these narratives do not revel in ludic postmodern play or apolitical musings on the death of stable referents (1991, 534). Collectively these authors differentially engage crises in representation and create speculative historiographies, thereby maintaining "a more active relationship to resistance and the politics of the possible" (534).

In a more recent essay, Ramón Saldívar (2011) foregrounds the inadequacy of magical realism as a means to portray racial oppression and traumatic histories. A new generation of twenty-first-century Latin@ and minority writers have inaugurated a genre of "postrace" fiction, including what he alternately terms "neo-fantasy" (575), "historical fantasy" (594), or "new world fantasy" (596)—fiction that, seemingly paradoxically, is concerned with the real and with racial formation as a result of imperialism and racism, thereby charting "a new province for the ethnic novel" (595). Citing as examples Salvador Plascencia's *People of Paper* (2005) and Junot Díaz's *Brief Wondrous Life of Oscar Wao* (2007), Saldívar argues that through its redeployment of "parabasis," postrace fiction moves beyond magical realism and postmodernism to create novel formal conventions deeply involved in social justice and transformation. He further explains that "historical fantasy is not merely phantasmal depiction of deep ideological mystifications. Rather, it works also as a basis for recognizing and understanding the construction of the new political destinies we may witness taking shape among diasporic groups in the US today" (595). This new world genre does not necessarily give full transparency to or insight into the real, but it

11

explores the symbolic construction of race and the desire for social change. Both Saldívars underscore new outgrowths of the magical realist genre and the articulation of new forms of fantasy, horror, and the speculative as they pertain to Latin@ and minority letters and aesthetics.

Both Saldívars additionally show how fantasy and horror manifest in ways specific to the trans-American imaginary. Many contributors to this anthology build on this premise, demonstrating that Latin@s need only look to our own history to locate and envision the speculative, which contains disappeared structures of feeling that are in turn made sensible in true tales of horror, the gothic, the dystopic, and the apocalyptic and post-apocalyptic. In his article on descriptions of the apocalypse in contemporary Mexican science fiction, Samuel Manickam (2012) observes that the Spanish conquest itself was an apocalyptic event within the Mexican national imaginary. He writes, "For the Aztecs the Spaniards who rode in on strange four-legged beasts and donned seemingly unassailable shiny armor and wielded fire-throwing weapons might as well have come from another planet. The clash of these two incompatible civilizations, which in turn gave birth to modern Mexico, seems the fantastic stuff of a sf tale" (97). It perhaps is no accident that the genre of Latin@ horror and related genres begin to take shape around the same time that scholars are moving to excavate and document these and other previously invisible historical atrocities. For example, in 2013 historians William D. Carrigan and Clive Webb published *Forgotten Dead: Mob Violence against Mexicans in the United States, 1848–1928*, and in 2016 John Morán González, Trinidad Gonzales, Sonia Hernández, and others collaborated to create the project and traveling exhibition *Refusing to Forget*.[6] Both the book and the exhibition document state-sanctioned violence in the Texas-Mexico borderlands in the late nineteenth and early twentieth centuries, including the rampant lynching of Latin@s by the Texas Rangers.

The aspect of gothic horror attending state-sanctioned violence against brown bodies in that historical period is also captured by filmmaker John Valadez in *The Head of Joaquin Murrieta* (2015), a part-fiction, part-documentary film produced for broadcast on PBS. The film's premise is that the filmmaker receives in the mail, from an anonymous sender, the head of Murrieta, the legendary Mexican outlaw who was decapitated in 1853 by bounty hunters who then put his head in a jar. The decapitated head in the film becomes a synecdoche for the buried history of lynchings of Mexicans throughout the Southwest and the complicated ways in which the past impinges upon the present as a spectacle of horror requiring response and responsibility. Valadez uncovers, in other words, what writer Myriam Gurba

(2015) describes as "America, the horror" in her Chicana gothic short story "How Some Abuelitas Keep Their Chicana Granddaughters Still While Painting Their Portraits in Winter" (15). It is within this longer and differential historical trajectory that writers including Marta Acosta, Adelina Anthony, Gloria Anzaldúa, David Bowles, Christopher Carmona, Terri de la Peña, Rudy Ch. Garcia, Xavier Garza, Myriam Gurba, Yuri Herrera, Joe Jiménez, Cherríe Moraga, Amalia Ortiz, and Ito Romo are brought into full sensibility. Importantly, the coalescing of Latin@ gothic horror opens up critical vistas for tracing the intersectional and overlapping ways in which racial formation in the United States has been experienced as nothing less than apocalyptic or world-ending for people of color. In this manner, this diverse cultural production clamors for concrete interventions and coalitional praxis.

Yet while there is a robust body of scholarship dedicated to articulating the African American gothic,[7] there remains a dearth of culturally and ethnically specific theoretical lenses for understanding Latin@ horror, gothic, and fantasy cultural productions. Within current whitewashed theoretical frameworks, the San Diego–based "cholo goth" band Prayers, San Antonio–based queer Chican@ dance troupe Zombie Bazaar, and East LA–based Morrissey cover band El Mariachi Manchester—to cite just a few examples—are rendered nothing more than curious or quaint anomalies.[8] What we need, and what this anthology begins to provide, are more sophisticated theoretical tools for analyzing this rich cultural production, turning our attention to its particular contexts and histories. Syndicated columnist Gustavo Arellano ("¡Ask a Mexican!") and others have hypothesized as to why Mexican Americans are drawn to the gothic music of Morrissey, an English singer-songwriter who hails from a working-class Irish family.[9] Meanwhile, Alexandro Hernández, an ethnomusicologist and vocalist with El Mariachi Manchester, explains simply, "Singing lyrics about the underdog, singing lyrics of tragedy, I think has ways of mediating oppression."[10] The Irish, after all, are among England's first colonial subjects. In an episode right out of a speculative tale, they occupy a revered space in the pantheon of Mexican American saints for the role of the San Patricios, the beleaguered Catholic US Army conscripts who suffered discrimination and who defected to the Mexican side during the US-Mexico War from 1846 to 1848. The gothic aspects of this epochal conflict are featured in Antonia Bird's black comedy and horror-suspense film *Ravenous* (1999), which features cannibalism by US soldiers. Hernández's incisive comment about why Mexican Americans are attracted to Morrissey, we suggest, resonates with the Chican@ gothic for these and many more reasons.

Understanding the Chican@ gothic as a mode of "mediating oppression" opens up space for delineating alternative literary periodizations and hermeneutics. Using this thematic rubric, we can trace the origins of the Chican@ gothic to myriad cultural texts that emerged in the mid-to-late nineteenth and early twentieth centuries, after the signing of the Treaty of Guadalupe in 1948. They include, among others, the 1885 gothic romance novel *The Squatter and the Don*, by María Amparo Ruiz de Burton, and the fiction of Américo Paredes, most notably his early 1950s novel *The Shadow* (1998), which is set in postrevolutionary Mexico. Literary scholar Jesse Alemán has already done significant work toward refashioning lineages of the gothic in the Americas by arguing that early-nineteenth-century accounts of the Spanish conquest of the Aztecs authored by white men, including works by Robert Montgomery Bird and William Prescott, as well as the anonymous 1826 novel *Xicoténcatl*, most likely penned by a Mexican, a Cuban, or another Latin American, in various ways map out "a trans-American gothic space haunted by the specters of empire" (Alemán 2006, 410). As well, in *Buenas Noches, American Culture: Latina/o Aesthetics of Night*, Maria DeGuzmán (2012) shows how representations of the nocturnal in Latina/o letters symbolize the Other America. She contends that nocturnal imagery must not be subsumed within traditional literary frameworks of European and US gothicism but rather must be interpreted through its own cultural confluences and contact zones. DeGuzmán elucidates that the topic of night in Latina/o literature "crosses borders along with the people and cultures employing these tropes, as with the case of the Renaissance and early modern conquistadores, missionaries, and colonizers from Spain who brought their Baroque poetry to the New World, where it mixed with the nocturnal imagery of Mesoamerican cosmologies. Night as a topic and tropes of night are *transfronterizos*, border-crossers" (16). Like Alexandro Hernández, Alemán and DeGuzmán discern vital connections between histories of violence, oppression, and deterritorialization, on the one hand, and the manifestation of the Latin@ gothic, on the other.

However, discussions of Latin@ identity and cultural production in relation to horror, fantasy, and the monstrous are riddled with minefields. Too often, Latin@s and people of color have been dehumanized in dominant visual culture, as exemplified in the aforementioned film *Fingerprints*. We frequently are figured as monstrous, threatening, or beastly through stereotypes of the bandido, drug dealer, or gang member, and as actual *monsters*. These vexed filmic representations can be found as early as 1915, when D. W. Griffith's *Martyrs of the Alamo* portrayed Mexicans as "sexually hungry subaltern men, predators devouring the [white] angelic female with their looks" (Fregoso 2003, 51). Chon A. Noriega (2000), Rosa Linda Fregoso (2003), and William Nericcio (2007) have variously addressed how Chican@s and Latin@s are perpetually cast in film as the monstrous other. In his semiotic analysis of what he terms "the Tex[t]-Mex project," or dominant white fantasies of the Mexican and Chican@ other, Nericcio observes "the wily retinue of animated, conjured, fabricated, costumed 'monsters' that pass for 'Mexicans' in the popular imagination of the United States" (2007, 173). Such monsters include "the posed corpses from the US-Mexico military skirmishes that find their way onto postcards" or "the 'half-breed' in Orson Welles's *Touch of Evil* that drives its Falstaffian anti-hero . . . to murder and more" (173).

Calling upon cognitive metaphor theory and examining public discourse, Otto Santa Ana (2002) also points out that various popular media such as newspapers from the 1990s onward painted Mexican Americans and Mexicans in apocalyptic strokes of infestation, plagues, and floods. Concretely tracing how these racist metaphors have influenced public policy—he cites as an example California Proposition 187, a draconian anti-immigrant ballot initiative in 1994—Santa Ana underscores that metaphors, and representation more broadly, *matter*. Thus we must tread cautiously and critically when both concocting and theorizing our monsters. We must produce our own culturally specific hermeneutics for interpreting and reckoning with our collective "ghostly matters"—that is, the spectral presence of past horrors that Avery Gordon (1997) insists continue to shape the present. Furthermore, it is imperative to recognize that Chican@ and Latin@ studies scholars have long theorized and provided complex theoretical models for interpreting the differential experiences of the horrific and fantastic as well as the dystopic and utopic.

Many Latin@ studies scholars have produced nuanced and culturally attuned accounts of the monstrous and ghostly, paying particular attention to how these creatures have served as important vehicles of the socially symbolic and as a site of scathing social critique. María Herrera-Sobek shows that the Dancing Devil functions as a disciplinary figure of "defilement" and "shame" for working-class Chicanas, consonant with misogynist Catholic values (1988, 154–55). José Limón extends her analysis in *Dancing with the Devil* by arguing that this figure operates in South Texas and beyond as "a register of the society's initial and shocking encounter with the cultural logic of late capitalism" (1994, 179). In other words, the Dancing Devil

15

embodies the contradictions and uneven rollout of late capitalism in the borderlands, effecting "race and class domination" (14). More recently, William Calvo-Quirós continues Latin@ deployments of horror as political critique by locating the monstrous within political economy, arguing that the Chupacabras, a vampiric "goatsucker," is birthed within and generates a nuanced social critique of the devastating repercussions of NAFTA. Calvo-Quirós asserts that "the Chupacabras is more than just a naive livestock-blood-sucking creature, but rather, it represents a sophisticated entity that carries within it the violent struggles lived by communities of color, because of the local impact of global neoliberal policies, as manifested by late capitalism, during the last quarter of the twentieth century" (2014, 212). Our monsters, these scholars signal, are more than just superstitious or naive figments of the "primitive" imagination: they are sophisticated articulations of how late capitalism and neoliberal globalization brutally and palpably exert force upon the lives of Chican@s and Latin@s.

The most developed body of scholarship dedicated to conceptualizing ghostly matters within Chican@ and Latin@ studies consists of Chicana feminist theorizations of La Llorona, including the innovative scholarship of Norma Alarcón, Gloria Anzaldúa, Cordelia Candelaria, Ana Castillo, Rosa Linda Fregoso, Alicia Gaspar de Alba, Cherríe Moraga, Domino Renée Pérez, Emma Pérez, Tey Diana Rebolledo, and Sonia Saldívar-Hull, among so many more. Taken together, this corpus powerfully unveils how vexed binaries of virgin/whore or active aggressor/passive victim invisibly—though tangibly—inhere in and texturize the fabric of daily social life for Chicanas and Mexicanas. These scholars emphasize that La Llorona's figure is a composite one, embodying and situated within a "long line of vendidas" (Moraga 2000) who include the specters of the Aztec goddess Coyolxauhqui and of Cortés's translator and lover Malintzin, or Malinche.[11] Not only do these misogynist colonial imaginaries affect how Chicanas and Mexicanas are seen and therefore treated, they also haunt Chicana and Mexicana sexuality and desire. While Emma Pérez notes that these related colonial imaginaries undergird a "desiring economy" of "patriarchal Chicano nationalism" (1999, 107), Norma Alarcón (1999, 68) similarly explains that these cognate figures function as, quoting Gayatri Spivak, "regulative psychobiographies," controlling Chicana sexuality through shame and guilt. For these reasons, Chicana scholars, writers, and artists have reenvisioned this fraught figure, unfettering her complex figure from the stranglehold of patriarchal colonial and neocolonial imaginaries. In Domino Renée Pérez's estimation, "the most radical repositionings" within literature in particular "involve abandoning traditional elements of the lore or changing the outcome to challenge its social conventions and the dominating forces at work in it: forces most often cited as heterosexual Mexicanos and Chicanos, Catholicism, and other patriarchal institutions" (2008, 72).

And while Chicanas have reimagined the Llorona figure, the very need to continue doing so shows how gendered, sexualized, and racialized colonial imaginaries continue to haunt in material ways the Chicana and Mexicana social body. It also underscores that these figures continue to invoke horror or enact the horrific, as demonstrated, for instance, by the ongoing femicides in Ciudad Juárez and greater Mexico (Fregoso 2003). Several of the essays in this anthology thus explore questions regarding the affective texture and tenor of terror, the fantastic, and the speculative more generally, with particular attention to the tensions between the dystopian and utopian impulses of science fiction, fantasy, and horror.

Overview of Sections and Chapters

Dialogue was central to the book's conception. We sought to include a wide range of authors and artists as well as diverse genres and discourses, but we could not include all proposals or all scholars who work on the Latin@ speculative arts, given limitations of time and space. Under these constraints, we sought to avoid too much overlap in article content in order to highlight underexamined trajectories and texts. While we made extra effort to include the many authors and producers of primary works as central to the dialogue, notable absences remain. To all the authors and artists whom we were not able to accommodate, we apologize deeply; but we would also emphasize that this project is just the beginning. We are committed to extending the ongoing dialogues, which, we hope, will lead to more panels, roundtable discussions, symposia, colloquia, conferences, articles, anthologies, books, and above all else, utopian collaborations that keep expanding the network of dreamers and dreams made manifest.

The first section, "Reassessing Chican@ and Latin@ Speculative Aesthetics," provides culturally attuned theoretical tools, methodologies, and genealogies for navigating and conceptualizing the Latin@ speculative arts. Taken together, these essays chart out new constellations and reorient more generally what we think of as the speculative. In "The Emancipatory Power of the Imaginary: Defining Chican@ Speculative Productions," William Calvo-Quirós extends his previous work on the Chupacabras by discussing how horror, the monstrous, and the speculative are culturally situated. In outlining what he understands as the definitive though overlapping characteristics of Chican@ speculative production, Calvo-Quirós argues that the monstrous operates as a sophisticated mode of knowledge production and social critique, blurring putative boundaries between the real and the imaginary. Importantly, this essay exhorts us to go beyond sclerotic notions of the archive and to look also at diverse sites such as police records, economic data, and ephemera.

Susana Ramírez extends Catherine S. Ramírez's groundbreaking recuperation of Gloria Anzaldúa as a speculative writer by examining the Anzaldúa Papers at the Benson Latin American Collection at the University of Texas, Austin. In "Recovering Gloria Anzaldúa's Sci-Fi Roots: Nepantler@ Visions in the Unpublished and Published Speculative Precursors to *Borderlands*," she argues that Anzaldúa's one published and two unpublished sci-fi short stories challenge the misogynist and heteronormative impulses of early Chicano science fiction. She shows how Anzaldúa's sci-fi substantially develops a pre-*Borderlands* "nepantlera" paradigm to conceive the possibility of "transspecies, transspatial, and transtemporal" (56) subjects, moving us through and beyond the new mestiza.

The next two essays are similarly attuned to the utopian possibility of the speculative. They build on extant scholarship by piecing together innovative approaches and methodologies for excavating, energizing, and reloading the many genres and subgenres that constitute Chican@ and Latin@ sci-fi and speculative arts. Shelley Streeby, in "Reading Jaime Hernandez's Comics as Speculative Fiction," and Lysa Rivera, in "Chicana/o Cyberpunk after el Movimiento," tackle questions of genre boundaries in their reclamations of Chican@ sci-fi and concomitant recoveries of Chicanafuturist genealogies. In her analysis of the various comic book series by Los Bros Hernandez, especially the visual semiotics of *Love and Rockets* and *Ti-Girls Adventures*, Streeby underscores the need to refuse the generic apartheid of sci-fi, fantasy, and realism. She instead places these genres within the broader category of the speculative to forge vital connections between them and to chart out new "constellations" of the Latin@ speculative arts. Her new hermeneutic is dramatically illustrated in an image that shows Los Bros Hernandez's Maggie, from their series *Maggie the Mechanic*, cruising her Hoppers barrio in Oxnard, California—in a hovercraft! (73). Extending her 2012 essay, Rivera further traces how Chican@ cyberpunk emerges as a post-*movimiento* phenomenon. She investigates how, ironically yet presciently, a select cadre of Latino male writers such as Enrique Chagoya, Guillermo Gómez-Peña, Ernest Hogan, Alejandro Morales, and Roberto Sifuentes commandeered the metaphors of cyberpunk to forge new hybrid subjectivities that rejected myopic, nostalgic, and masculinist iterations of cultural nationalism.

The second section, "Cyborgs, Networks, and Posthumanism," interrogates questions of communications technology and interconnection in our increasingly globalized milieu. "Posthumanism," a term associated with the fiction of H. P. Lovecraft, especially his 1936 novel *The Shadow Out of Time*, does not, for us, index a moment of being beyond or after the human; rather, taking a cue from feminist science studies, critical posthumanism studies, and related fields, we redeploy the term to signify that ever-evolving engagements with various forms of technology enable different and differential understanding of the human, one striated by intersectional categories of race, class, gender, and sexuality, among others.

In "From Code to Codex: Tricksterizing the Digital Divide in Ernest Hogan's *Smoking Mirror Blues*," Daoine Bachran analyzes the gendered and sexualized facets of Ernest Hogan's 2001 speculative dystopian/utopian novel. Hogan says he wrote it with the goal of "outraging the country's religious conservatives." He adds:

> The book was a desperate act by a frustrated Chicano janitor who spent a lot of time cleaning toilets, drinking beer, and watching bizarre Mexican action films. I wasn't sure if it would ever be published. Maybe if I made it like those sleazy sex paperbacks they used to have in racks in the dark corners of liquor stores, it might stand a chance . . . besides the only people who were publishing me were a short step from being in the porno business.[12]

The next two analytical essays consider the role of technology in Latin@ fantasy and sci-fi, particularly in the dystopian/utopian dyad that animates much of the speculative arts. In "Contrapuntal Cyborgs? The Ideological Limits and Revolutionary Potential of Latin@ Science Fiction," B. V. Olguín pushes back against what he argues are overly celebratory discourses about the counterhegemonic resonance of the Latin@ speculative arts. He investigates the dissensus and attendant ideological complexities and contradictions in various models and renderings of the Latin@ cyborg and explores what he terms a "neo-Luddite" portrayal of technology in Latin@ dystopian/utopian sci-fi. In placing Alex Rivera's 2008 dystopian feature film *Sleep Dealer* in dialogue with Sánchez and Pita's 2009 novel *Lunar Braceros 2125–2148*, Olguín deploys a Marxist hermeneutic to map the salient discourses animating the different revolutionary theories of praxis operative in each text. His mapping of the vexed relationship between technology and the utopian ideal in the Latin@ speculative arts ultimately calls for more skeptical materialist critical readings in this growing subfield of Latin@ studies.

In "Machete Don't Text: From Genre Textualities to Media Networks in *Machete*," William Orchard examines how the film *Machete* (2010) reaches and activates a Latin@ body politic through its manifold engagements with technology. Drawing upon Bruno Latour's actor-network theory, Orchard shifts our critical gaze, so that instead of viewing the film solely through traditional genre criticism, in which we examine how cultural producers deploy particular conventions and to what end, we also look at the relationship between human and nonhuman objects within and beyond the film. Doing so, Orchard argues, reveals that women in *Machete* are in fact agentic figures of futurity through their relationship to technology, and that representations of technology and the medium of film itself cooperate to galvanize diverse Latin@ publics. Taken together, these two essays offer innovative interpretive lenses for approaching representations of and engagements with technology in the Latin@ speculative arts, thereby allowing us to reconsider how the technological may be used in service of social transformation pursuant to revolutionary syntheses.

Michelle Habell-Pallán's essay, "Girl in a Coma Tweets Chicanafuturism: Decolonial Visions, Social Media, and Archivista Praxis," looks at how San Antonio–based indie rock band Girl in a Coma uses social media to engage with Chicanafuturism. The band's social media practice activates a "feedback loop" connecting them with the 2009 exhibition *American Sabor: Latinos in US Popular Music* at the Museo Alameda in San Antonio (of which Habell-Pallán was a curator) and with the Women Who Rock Digital Oral History Archive, an open-access networked archive. This digital interchange, Habell-Pallán contends, propels a radical archivista praxis and shows how "Chicanx music serves as a resource to speculate on how new media can transform Chicanx scholarship in its production and delivery" (161). She concludes that Chicanafuturism encompasses an arsenal of vital tools for advancing not only Chican@ studies but also the digital humanities into more decolonial futures.

Essays in the third section, "Latin@ Horror and the Politics of Monstrosity," heed Calvo-Quirós's call to rethink the generic parameters of the horrific and monstrous in relationship to Chican@ and Latin@ identity and lived experiences. While Cynthia Saldivar and Luz María Gordillo show how Chican@ short story writers fundamentally rewrite the horror genre, Linda Heidenreich actually *rewrites* the horror genre and conceptions of the monstrous by penning an alternative narrative. Her story centers on two queer Chicana vampires who survive colonial violence and whose subjectivities and futures are not tied to the sanctity and integrity of the nation-state. In chorus with Calvo-Quirós, the writers in this section reveal that the horrific is indeed constituted in the eye of the beholder; it is an envisioning that is collective, experiential, and differential.

Cynthia Saldivar's essay, "#rapetreesarereal: Chican@futurism and Hybridizing Horror in Christopher Carmona's 'Strange Leaves,'" bridges the previous section to this one by examining how Carmona (2014) uses the hashtag and communications technology within his award-winning short story to convey the horrific plight of undocumented Central American Latinas in South Texas. Rising to the challenge we posed in the second *Aztlán* dossier—to consider how various works of Chican@ and Latin@ fiction, including those usually categorized as realist, might be read through the lens of horror and might upend traditional definitions of horror—Saldivar shows that "Strange Leaves" offers new ways of thinking about horror that are not confined to the supernatural or the explicitly graphic or gory. Indeed, Saldivar argues that through his deployment of communications technology, Carmona effectively hybridizes horror, merging the subgenres of body and domestic horror as well as collapsing putative distinctions between terror and horror.

Luz María Gordillo, in "Contesting Monstrosity in Horror Genres: Chicana Feminist Mappings of de la Peña's 'Refugio' and Hamilton's Anita Blake, Vampire Hunter Series," also explores the way in which horror and the monstrous are conceived along the mutually reinforcing axes of race, class, gender, and sexuality. She analyzes the remarkable short story "Refugio" (de la Peña 1996), showing how it subverts racialized, classed, and gendered notions of monstrosity through the figure of a Chicana lesbian vampire, thus challenging the racism and heteronormativity of hegemonic horror and fantasy genres.

Linda Heidenreich's "Colonial Pasts, Utopian Futures: Creative and Critical Reflections on the Monstrous as Salvific" offers an original contribution to this anthology. She intertwines the speculative dimensions of recent Chican@ studies historiographies, which tell stories of people whose existence persists in whispers and faded corners of archival records, with the inherently speculative enterprise of fiction to create an alternative history in the form of a lesbian avenger vampire tale. Part of a larger project, her excerpt draws upon various archaeologies of historically abject yet recently recovered Chicana victims of US heteropatriarchal settler colonialist violence, particularly Josefa, also known as Juanita, who was lynched in Downieville, California, in 1851 for killing a man who attempted to assault her. Heidenreich prefaces her alternative historiographic fiction with a critique of hegemonic vampire master narratives, and she invokes feminist warrior archetypes to explore the banalities of life and love in the story of

Josefa, who in this rendering has a lesbian partner, Jesusa. The vampire sub-text enables Heidenreich to conceive of these women's agency as extending far beyond extant recoveries of nineteenth-century Latin@ lesbian subjects, which ultimately enables a new mapping of counterhegemonies in the present and future Southwest and in the Americas more broadly.

The fourth section, "From the Dystopic to the Utopic," tracks the tension between the two horizons that animate much of the speculative arts: dystopias and utopias. The articles explore a range of speculative subgenres and themes that enable fresh insights into the enduring ideological dimensions and potential counterpower of art in general and the Latin@ speculative arts in particular. The first two essays tackle Latin@ speculative texts that do not fit squarely within discrete subgenres of horror, fantasy, and sci-fi, but rather draw upon conventions from each to carve out space for what Darko Suvin (1979) has termed "cognitive estrangement." In "The Future of Food? Indigenous Knowledges and Sustainable Food Systems in Latin@ Speculative Fiction," Gabriela Nuñez examines the novels *Lunar Braceros 2125–2148*, by Rosaura Sánchez and Beatrice Pita (2009), and *Atomik Aztex*, by Sesshu Foster (2005), both of which engage food systems in relation to futurity and survival. These novels bring attention to the fact that Latin@s and people of color disproportionately lack access to healthy food, and they spotlight the exploitive economic systems that continue to buttress inequitable food systems. Analyzing these novels as trenchant social critique, Nuñez shows that they imagine and call into being alternative, more desirable food systems to secure a future for Latin@s. In "Narrating the Right to Health: Speculative Genre in Morales's *The Rag Doll Plagues*," Andrew Uzendoski traces how Alejandro Morales (1992) advocates the universal right to health for Latin@s through cognitive estrangement. In particular, Morales deploys this concept to connect pandemics to the dissolution of the sovereignty of the nation-state and to the global takeover by transnational corporations, which Michael Hardt and Antonio Negri (2000) have identified as the central feature of the new Empire. Uzendoski shows how Morales demands participation from his readership and how he underscores the collective aspects of social movements. Both Nuñez and Uzendoski tease out the taut interconnections between health, survival, and futurity in Latin@ sci-fi and emphasize that reading Latin@ speculative fiction is participatory and potentially transformative.

In the next two essays, José R. Flores and Isabel Millán examine the uses of cyberpunk in Latin@ utopian, dystopian, and speculative aesthetics. In "'Waking the Sleeping Giant': Mestizaje, Ideology, and the Postcyberpunk Poetics of Carlos Miralejos's *Texas 2077*," Flores shows that this 1998 self-published novel marshals a postcyberpunk sensibility to explore the role of race and politics in imagining culturally and geographically situated utopian possibility. The Miralejos novel plays on the metaphor of the Latin@ population as a political "sleeping giant," teasing out its utopian potential by imagining a "new era" in which Latin@s have united on the basis of presumed shared cultural backgrounds and mestiz@ identities, realizing *la raza cósmica* of José Vasconcelos. While Flores suggests that Miralejos's Latin@ political utopia is perhaps overly simplistic, he shows that the novelist pushes the limits of speculative fiction by daring to imagine a future shaped by an empowered Latin@ public. Next, questioning the putative distinctions between Chicanafuturism and Afrofuturism, Millán identifies intersections between Afro-Latina, Chicana, and Mexican immigrant heroines in sci-fi and fantasy. In "Engineering Afro-Latina and Mexican Immigrant Heroines: Biopolitics in Borderlands Speculative Literature and Film," Millán analyzes how the character Loup Garron in the speculative fiction of Jacqueline Carey and the character María Isabel "Isa" Reyes in José Néstor Márquez's science fiction film *ISA* (2014) both critique real violence in the US-Mexico borderlands and throughout the Americas. Through their very survival, Millán argues, these characters embody a critique of the biopolitical and emphasize the alternative imaginaries that may dismantle oppressive systems of power, pointing to the liberatory potential of Chicanafuturist and Afrofuturist texts.

In "Decolonizing the Future Today: Speculative Testimonios and Nepantlerx Futurisms in Student Activism at the University of California, Davis," Natalia Deeb-Sossa and Susy J. Zepeda explore dystopian realities and defiant utopian yearnings among youth. Taking as a point of departure the proto-fascist response to student protests over tuition increases at a University of California campus, where black-clad police attacked students with chemical agents, the authors map student invocations of the utopian impulse of Chican@ and Latin@ testimonial practice. Their case study not only imagines a new paradigm for a decolonial university but also deploys testimonio to address in-group threats and political contradictions that must be collectively confronted and transformed for true liberation to occur in the real world.

The fifth section, "Charting Chican@futurist Visual Art," weaves together contributions that reflect this emergent genre, including creative and critical works, an interview, and a curator's communiqué. Connecting these diverse Chican@futurist visions are decolonial perspectives that question and move beyond colonial, Eurocentric binarisms of the so-called primitive and technological and that offer glimpses into more liberatory futures by drawing upon the past and present. This section begins with "Juventino Aranda and

23

Chican@futurism," Margarita E. Pignataro's interview with Washington State visual artist Juventino Aranda regarding his incorporation of Chican@futurist themes and tropes. The interview focuses on two of Aranda's sculptures, *All Is Not Quiet on the Southwestern Front* (2011) and *The Neo-Middle Passage* (2010), probing their explicit engagement with Chican@futurism and Afrofuturism as well as with the utopian and dystopian. Aranda points to eclectic and unexpected influences on his work, from Guillermo Gómez-Peña and Roberto Sifuentes to David Bowie and even his father's white barber. This interview also suggests another vital element of Chican@futurist art: determined attention to the past and present in the construction of the future today.

In her speculative testimonio, "For Those Seeking Signs of Intelligent Life: Xicana Chronicles of the Original Alien Ancestors," visual artist and Xicana comic book author Debora Kuetzpal Vasquez similarly imagines a queer Chicana-centered future informed by Mayan cosmology. Written in the first person, this narrative extends and further synthesizes the profound legacy of testimonio by taking it into the realm of the speculative and vice versa. The story traces the genesis of Citlali, La Chicana Super Hero, a character Vasquez created "who is a guerrillera of justice for mujeres, animales and her raza" (2015). Citlali was conceived in 1998 while the artist was earning her master of fine arts degree at the University of Wisconsin, Madison, and has appeared in various exhibitions, publications, and social protests in the Southwest and throughout the United States. For Vasquez, Citlali represents a novel expression of *la raza cósmica*, embodying not only US and Mexican cultures but also extraterrestrial culture (2015). Vasquez radically repurposes hegemonic genres of sci-fi and fantasy by boldly refusing what Ramírez describes in the opening of this anthology as sci-fi's "messianic white boy" complex (ix). Vasquez's 2015 painting, *Interstellar Love: The Conception of Citlali* (acrylic on canvas), features Citlali's two mothers, Ixchel and Koyol, in an erotic embrace during Citlali's conception. It illustrates that neo-Chican@futurism not only exemplifies a queer reimagining of sci-fi and fantasy but also defiantly rejoices in what white heteronormative right-wing America fears and renders as horrific and abject: brown queer futurity replete with new hybridities redefining categories of human and nonhuman. *Interstellar Love*, moreover, gestures toward the core impulse of this anthology by inviting viewers and readers to reconsider the contours and substance of the science fictional, fantastic, and horrific or monstrous.

Following Vasquez's speculative testimonio are images and a communiqué, "The Mission Manifesto: Project MASA," by San Antonio–based visual artist and art educator Luis Valderas, who originally hails from the Rio

Grande Valley in South Texas. This Chican@futurist manifesto accompanied four Project MASA (MeChicano Alliance of Space Artists) exhibitions held from 2005 to 2007. Embodying what Cathryn J. Merla-Watson terms "speculative rasquachismo" (355), Project MASA homophonically suggests both NASA, the space agency, and *masa*, corn dough for making tortillas, thereby blending the high and low, the modern and the so-called primitive, concatenating new chains of associations and meanings and going beyond Western dualisms. Valderas highlights this recombinatory sensibility in his manifesto and connects it to more liberatory futures: "The intermingling of cultures in a more tolerant society is the future of the Chicano family. Adaptation and transformation require a foot in the past and present, a familiarity with transitions between borders, and a flexibility that is conducive to a reimagination of realities" (349). Accompanying the manifesto is the Project MASA logo, along with glimpses of Valderas assembling one of his solo exhibitions, *The Sky Is Brown* (2014), as well as the installation *Black Dream Place* (2015). Like fellow Tejan@ writer Carlos Miralejos in the novel *Texas 2077*, Valderas implicates mestizaje in visions of the future predicated upon racial as well as political-economic egalitarianism.

In the next essay, accentuating the complex visual codes undergirding the Latin@ speculative arts, Merla-Watson analyzes how the Chican@futurist art of Valderas intervenes within the "coloniality of gender" by visually confusing images associated with the ostensibly feminine and masculine and, relatedly, the primitive and modern within the neocolonial geography of San Antonio and South Texas. The altermundos created by Valderas and Project MASA, Merla-Watson contends, show that coloniality is animated by a dualistic and gendered mode of seeing, and they creatively reassemble speculative and more holistic "third space" visions that truss together the past, present, and future. In doing so, Merla-Watson maintains, Valderas draws out the visionary aspects and potential of Chican@futurist cultural production.

In a curator communiqué, "Mundos Alternos: A Skylab for Speculative Curation," Robb Hernández critically reflects on the development of *Mundos Alternos: Art and Science Fiction in the Americas*, which is slated to open on September 16, 2017, at the University of California, Riverside ARTSblock. Co-curated with Tyler Stallings and Joanna Szupinska-Myers, this exhibition examines the interconnections between Los Angeles and Latin America with respect to science fiction imaginaries. In assembling the exhibition, the curators undertook intensive research in several Latin American countries and ten US cities. In this essay, Hernández "explicates curating as a translation of interpretative processes" (373). He reflects specifically on his fieldwork in

Puerto Rico, which he describes as "a site little regarded within Latino/Latin American science fiction studies" (373) that has nonetheless "produced a strikingly decolonial SF visual vocabulary" (376). His research uncovered a science fiction vernacular already present in the Caribe and also enhanced visual definitions of SF in the Americas at large.

The sixth and final section, "Latin@ Literary Altermundos and Multiverses," features an interdisciplinary *diálogo* among creative writers and performance artists who represent the far reach and eclecticism of Chican@ speculative letters and performance. These writers engage and blend the genres of utopian/dystopian, sci-fi, horror, apocalyptic, and post-apocalyptic discourses. They also speak to how Latin@s differentially engage these genres, conceive and deploy them on their own terms, and explore their liberatory possibilities that are grounded in the intersectional lived experiences and histories of Latin@s.

John Phillip Santos opens this section with an author communiqué, "Intimations of Infinite Entanglement: Notes toward a Prolegomena to Any Future: Repudiatory Postscript to *The Farthest Home Is in an Empire of Fire*." His meditation on the radical indeterminacy of reality in quantum physics as a template for decentering our notions of the real and unreal, of fiction and nonfiction, insists on the indispensability of the arts to contemporary intellectual, cultural, and political life. Immersed in the Internet age while simultaneously informed by the continued salience of ancient oral histories and epistemologies, Santos's speculative autobiography, and his reflection on the writing of it, offers another variation on mestizaje: the family ghosts who haunt the machines we have invented to get away from the past in pursuit of a new future. Santos shows us that this future, ironically, is already inscribed with the past through these cyborgian ghosts—specifically Cenote Siete, his ancestor from the future, who had a hand in producing the family autobiography.

In "*Becoming Nawili*: Utopian Dreaming at the End of the World," Cordelia Barrera discusses the inspiration drawn from her own lived experiences as a South Texas Chicana and the conceptual underpinnings of her newly completed speculative novel, which revolves around environmental racism and environmental justice paradigms. Her reflection is followed by three excerpts from the yet-unpublished "new adult" novel that center on the coming of age of the central character, Pepa. Barrera explains, "*Becoming Nawili* is a speculative Latin@ fantasy—part Aztec creation myth and part queer Latin@ bildungsroman. It takes place in the mid-twenty-first-century borderlands, on the cusp of a new world order that reaches back to an indigenous, matriarchal past to imagine a social and environmentally just future" (393). This experimental novel traffics in the metaphysical and uncanny, inspired by Gloria Anzaldúa's speculative concept of the *cenote*, a cavernous limestone sinkhole filled with water that Anzaldúa (1995) identifies as a "dreampool" to "access my culture's collective history," a place where "memories collide, conflict, converge, condense and negotiate relationships between past, present and future." Barrera's work exemplifies a nascent and promising body of Latin@ children's and young adult speculative fiction, which includes authors such as David Bowles and Xavier Garza, that reconceives horror and fantasy through our own terms and terrains.

Next, Latin@ artist Ernest Hogan presents his "Chicanonautica Manifesto." Aware of widespread unfamiliarity with the Chican@ speculative arts, and particularly with his genre of choice, speculative fiction, Hogan insists on its normalcy and its centrality to Chican@ culture. He proclaims that this genre intimately entwines the barrio and the world within a universe of possibility that transgresses and recombines boundaries of race, science, and technology. He also points to how the Chican@ speculative arts refuse boundaries established by the publishing world, which previously had been incapable of registering and encompassing the hybrid, mestiza/o voices of the emergent "Chicano planet." This is the "crazy" and "bizarre" visionary terrain of the "Chicanonaut," which he also imagines in visual form as a "Calacanaut" (fig. 1). After all, as Laura Pérez has averred, "to

Figure 1. Ernest Hogan, Calacanaut, 2002. *Crayola crayon and grease pencil manipulated in GIMP, 290 × 420 pixels. Image courtesy of the artist.*

27

reoccupy Aztlán, the oppressed hallucinate—and that practice has no borders" (1999, 39). In a related pan-Latin@ context, Junot Díaz's *Brief Wondrous Life of Oscar Wao* presents an unreliable postmodern narrator who rhetorically asks, "What more sci-fi than Santo Domingo?" (2007, 6), illuminating the otherworldliness and horror of the US-sponsored dictatorship of Rafael Trujillo from 1930 to 1961. In a similar vein, Hogan provocatively announces that "Chicano is a science fiction state of being" (406). This affirms that Chican@ identity is rooted in the strange and sublime, evoking (science) fiction and its dystopian and utopian subgenres—from white European aliens descending upon *la tierra madre* and colonizing its brown hosts, to a border wall between the United States and Mexico that acts like a force field powered by the US Empire, to the 2006 immigration protests embodying the utopian spirit of "another world is possible," or rather, "otro mundo es posible." Noted for his robust vocabulary of neologisms, Hogan underscores his speculative credentials with a portfolio of satirical, surrealist rasquache drawings (figs. 2, 3) that navigate between the visual poetics of Laura Molina (fig. 4) and the magical realist imaginary of Gabriel García Márquez, to name but a few of his interlocutors.

In "Flying Saucers in the Barrio," Gregg Barrios offers insights into the long legacy of the speculative in Latin@ letters by reflecting on the Chican@ high school staging of his play *Stranger in a Strange Land* in

Figure 2. Ernest Hogan, Invading Kafkazona, *2010. Uniball manipulated in GIMP, 261 × 414 pixels. Image courtesy of the artist.*

Figure 3. Ernest Hogan, Western Vision, *circa 1979. Pen and ink manipulated in GIMP, 589 × 428 pixels. Image courtesy of the artist.*

Figure 4. Laura Molina, The Green Lady, *2007. Oil on canvas, 28 × 22 inches. Image courtesy of the artist.*

Crystal City, Texas, in 1976. This speculative performance was put on by the author's students just seven years after student boycotts heralded the electoral victory of the Raza Unida Party in the city's government. Riffing on David Bowie's futuristic character Ziggy Stardust as a trope for the extraterrestrial, Barrios meditates on how the play and the student actors offer incisive political critiques of the draconian policing of those whom the US Border Patrol terms "aliens." Barrios closes his reflection by noting the canny similarities between the student play and Bowie's final Broadway production of *Lazarus*, his sequel to *The Man Who Fell to Earth*, the year before the artist's death in 2016: forty years later, inspiration has come full circle through the speculative arts.

Similarly driven to the utopian possibilities of speculative fiction, San Antonio–based queer Chican@ writer Joe Jiménez contributes a new short story that reflects fresh and resolutely queer directions in the Latin@ speculative arts. "Sexy Cyborg Cholo Clownz" bridges the genres and subgenres constituting the speculative, articulating novel, queer hybridities, and forms of mestizaje that are intimately connected with the human and nonhuman. Read to an audience at Trinity University in San Antonio in 2014, the story was published for the first time in the second *Aztlán* dossier that preceded this anthology. In the story, Jiménez imagines queer cyborg cholo *cariño* amid the chaos of the post-apocalypse, a setting in which drone fire pierces the sky and brown cyborg bodies alike, with pandemics looming large. A cyborg vato "with the plastic bones and the lithium corazón" attempts to revive his "fallen camarada," a cyborg cholo clown who has been impaled by a drone through the chest and back (416). These queer brown cyborgs engage in erotic and penetrating acts of *cariño* as radical actions of healing, reconnection, and resistance, thereby reconnecting to a longer, collective history of what Jiménez figures as "mamando" (419). Of this short story, Jiménez (2015) muses:

> So when I think of a queer Chicano erotics, I testify to this truth about the brown clown cyborg self as ganas, as resistance against domination. In this case, war. In this case, policing by drones. In this case, environmental decimation. For me, the cyborg cholo clownz are a way to "bludgeon aloneness," how through cariño we make do with what we have, an erotic rasquache, how the body becomes the word to heal another using what is available to it, particularly, in this story, a body with parts missing and added and damage and want. For me, nothing is as powerful as want—a want linked to others' wants.

This section concludes with an artist statement and excerpt, "*The Canción Cannibal Cabaret*: A Post-apocalyptic Anarcha-Feminist Revolutionary Punk Rock Musical," by spoken word artist Amalia Ortiz. Ortiz refashions familiar tropes of the apocalyptic and post-apocalyptic to lay bare structures of feeling that color the lifeworlds of women of color. She states,

> The prose tells the story of a post-apocalyptic anarcha-feminist revolution fueled by the teachings of La Madre Valiente, who has "cannibalized" thoughts and rewritten them into repurposed "folk" songs from the pre-apocalyptic world. While the revolutionary figure remains in hiding, her poem songs are performed by her emissaries, Las Hijas de la Madre, in traveling propaganda rallies aimed at secretly educating and galvanizing allies into joining the Mujerista Resistance against the State. (422–23)

A hybrid "poetry/theater text," this speculative performance piece is meant to be "fully staged as a punk rock musical" (422). Incorporating and merging multiple texts, voices, and influences, such as those of Gloria Anzaldúa, Ramón Ayala, P. J. Harvey, Toni Morrison, Marilyn Manson, The Clash, and Patti Smith, the piece embodies a decidedly rasquache aesthetic and multicultural perspective. It also stretches and enriches what Arturo J. Aldama, Chela Sandoval, and Peter J. García (2012) have termed "de-colonial performatics" or "perform-antics," by which they mean the "mestizaje, the hybridity, the bricolage, the rasquache interventions organized around de-colonization" (1). Through its decolonial, anarcho-feminist aesthetics, *The Canción Cannibal Cabaret* emphatically gestures toward a future that is not simply gender-neutral or gender-free but is contoured by an intersectional praxis that strives toward horizons of possibility grounded in a global collective, as declared in Ortiz's speculative rasquache lyrics: "Let's fuck the divisions and put them to bed" (448).

In an afterword titled "Rewrite the Future!," Matthew David Goodwin discusses the creation of *Latin@ Rising: An Anthology of Latin@ Science Fiction and Fantasy*. An outgrowth of Goodwin's dissertation work, this groundbreaking collection is set for publication in late 2016 by San Antonio–based Wings Press, which has a long and distinguished history of publishing Latin@ authors. The project is based on the principle of reciprocity, whereby authors participate in shaping the collection and volume editors pursue creative Internet-based approaches to raising funds to compensate artists for their labor. Meditating on the politics of publishing and particularly Latin@ publishing, Goodwin raises compelling questions for research scholars and artists even as the release of *Latin@ Rising* signals the vitality and bright future of the Latin@ speculative arts.

31

The Future Is Now: The Speculative as Praxis

In this vein, we extend Catherine S. Ramírez's exhortation to analyze through the lens of sci-fi many texts that are not conventionally designated as such, including the companion genres of horror and fantasy as well as all the hybrid genres recovered by the scholars and artists in this collection. When we use a sci-fi lens, we believe, new monsters are brought into the distribution of the sensible, and differential experiences of terror are brought to the fore. In late 2016, as we conclude this anthology, new monsters take the form of an elected xenophobic US president, Donald Trump, who reminds us that monsters can assume benign and quotidian guises that appeal to the masses. And the homophobic murder of forty-nine people, predominately queer Latin@s, in the gay nightclub Pulse in Orlando, Florida, reminds us that monsters can also surface in complicated, contradictory, and graphically violent manifestations. The exposés, critiques, and utopian alternatives modeled within the Latin@ speculative arts promise to combat these old monsters with newer ones that might help set us all free.

Notes

1. Our use of the "@" ending in this anthology corresponds to Sandra K. Soto's privileging of this symbol as a recognition of the complex, fluid, and queered dimensions of identity and ontology, which the Latin@ speculative arts synthesizes in complex ways. Soto writes that her "queer performative 'Chican@' signals a conscientious departure from certainty, mastery, and wholeness, while still announcing a politicized collectivity" (2010, 2). Our own use of Chican@ and Latin@, and especially Chican@futurism and Latin@futurism, is intended to allow for the fullest range of speculative theorizing of Chican@ and Latin@ ontologies that the essays in this anthology explore.

2. Saldívar builds on the concept of "Americanity," elaborated by Aníbal Quijano and Immanuel Wallerstein, which claims that the creation of the Americas enabled the consolidation of capitalism and not the other way around.

3. "They say that . . ." *Dichos* and *cuentos* (sayings and stories), which are key parts of Mexican American folklore, often begin with this phrase, signaling oral transmission and a collective and intergenerational form of meaning making.

4. For further discussion of the Ghost Tracks, see Merla-Watson (2011) and Lindahl (2005).

5. Phillips identifies as a mixed-race Filipino–Native American–Anglo.

6. On *Refusing to Forget*, see https://refusingtoforget.org.

7. See, for example, Maisha L. Wester's 2012 monograph *African American Gothic: Screams from Shadowed Places* and Mehtonen and Savolainen's *Gothic Topographies: Language, Nation Building and "Race"* (2016).

8. On Prayers, see José Anguiano, "Voicing the Occult in Chicana/o Culture and Hybridity: Prayers and the Cholo-Goth Aesthetic," forthcoming in *Race and Cultural Practice in Popular Culture*, ed. Rachel V. Gonzalez-Martin and Domino R. Perez.

9. See, for instance, "¡Ask a Mexican! Why Do Mexicans Like Morrissey So Much?" https://vimeo.com/95478437.

10. "From UK Rock to Latin Folk," AJ+ video available on Twitter, https://amp.twimg.com/v/2c7ebaed-98a0-4ab3-9c5a-7316924fd3cd.

11. In her forthcoming article "Evoking the Shadow Beast: Disability and Chicano Advocacy in San Antonio's Donkey Lady Folktale" in the online journal *Contemporary Legend*, Mercedes E. Torrez shows how the figure of the Donkey Lady extends and gives fuller dimension to the composite figure of La Llorona through embodying collective heteropatriarchal fears around disability and motherhood.

12. Ernest Hogan, email to B. V. Olguín and Cathryn J. Merla-Watson, February 15, 2015 (ellipsis in original).

Works Cited

Alarcón, Norma. 1999. "Chicana Feminism: In the Tracks of 'The' Native Woman." In *Between Woman and Nation: Nationalisms, Transnational Feminisms, and the State*, edited by Caren Kaplan, Norma Alarcón, and Minoo Moallem, 63–71. Durham, NC: Duke University Press.

Aldama, Arturo J., Chela Sandoval, and Peter J. García. 2012. "Toward a De-Colonial Performatics of the US Latina and Latino Borderlands." Introduction to *Performing the US Latina and Latino Borderlands*, edited by Arturo J. Aldama, Chela Sandoval, and Peter J. García, 1–27. Bloomington: Indiana University Press.

Alemán, Jesse. 2006. "The Other Country: Mexico, the United States, and the Gothic History of Conquest." *American Literary History* 18, no. 3: 406–26.

Anguiano, José. Forthcoming. "Voicing the Occult in Chicana/o Culture and Hybridity: Prayers and the Cholo-Goth Aesthetic." In *Race and Cultural Practice in Popular Culture*, edited by Rachel V. Gonzalez-Martin and Domino R. Perez. Austin: University of Texas Press.

Anzaldúa, Gloria. 1995. "Nepantla: The Theory and Manifesto." Manuscript draft. Box 61, folder 21, Gloria Evangelina Anzaldúa Papers, Benson Latin American Collection, University of Texas, Austin.

———. 2007. *Borderlands/La Frontera: The New Mestiza*. San Francisco: Aunt Lute.

Berg, Charles Ramírez. 2002. *Latino Images in Film: Stereotypes, Subversion, and Resistance*. Austin: University of Texas Press.

Calvo-Quirós, William A. 2014. "Sucking Vulnerability: Neoliberalism, the Chupacabras, and the Post-Cold War Years." In *The Un/Making of Latina/o Citizenship: Culture, Politics, and Aesthetics*, edited by Ellie D. Hernández and Eliza Rodriguez y Gibson, 211–34. New York: Palgrave Macmillan.

Carmona, Christopher. 2014. "Strange Leaves." *Texas Observer*, September 29. https://www.texasobserver.org/short-story-contest-christopher-carmona. Forthcoming in *The Road to Llorona Park*, by Christopher Carmona. Nacogdoches, TX: Stephen F. Austin State University Press.

Carrigan, William D., and Clive Webb. 2013. *Forgotten Dead: Mob Violence against Mexicans in the United States, 1848–1928*. New York: Oxford University Press.

Cisneros, Sandra. 1991. "Woman Hollering Creek." In *Woman Hollering Creek and Other Short Stories*, 43–56. New York: Vintage.

DeGuzmán, María. 2012. *Buenas Noches, American Culture: Latina/o Aesthetics of Night*. Bloomington: Indiana University Press.

de la Peña, Terri. 1996. "Refugio." In *Night Bites: Vampire Stories by Women*, edited by Victoria A. Brownworth, 165–78. Seattle: Seal.

Díaz, Junot. 2007. *The Brief Wondrous Life of Oscar Wao*. New York: Riverhead.

Foster, Sesshu. 2005. *Atomik Aztex*. San Francisco: City Lights.

Fregoso, Rosa Linda. 2003. *MeXicana Encounters: The Making of Social Identities on the Borderlands*. Berkeley: University of California Press.

Gaspar de Alba, Alicia. 1998. *Chicano Art Inside/Outside the Master's House: Cultural Politics and the CARA Exhibition*. Austin: University of Texas Press.

González, Christopher. 2013. "Latino Sci Fi: Cognition and Narrative Design in Alex Rivera's *Sleep Dealer*." In *Latinos and Narrative Media: Participation and Portrayal*, edited by Frederick Luis Aldama, 211–40. New York: Palgrave Macmillan.

Gordon, Avery F. 1997. *Ghostly Matters: Haunting and the Sociological Imagination*. Minneapolis: University of Minnesota Press.

Gurba, Myriam. 2015. "How Some Abuelitas Keep Their Chicana Granddaughters Still While Painting Their Portraits in Winter." In *Painting Their Portraits in Winter: Short Stories*. San Francisco: Manic D. Press.

Hardt, Michael, and Antonio Negri. 2000. *Empire*. Cambridge, MA: Harvard University Press.

Herrera-Sobek, María. 1988. "The Devil in the Discotheque: A Semiotic Analysis of the Devil Legend." In *Monsters with Iron Teeth: Perspectives on Contemporary Legend III*, edited by Jillian Bennet and Paul Smith, 147–58. Sheffield, UK: Sheffield Academic Press.

Hogan, Ernest. 2001. *Smoking Mirror Blues*. La Grande, OR: Wordcraft of Oregon.

Jackson, Rosemary. 1981. *Fantasy: The Literature of Subversion*. London: Methuen.

Jiménez, Joe. 2015. Email to authors, August 19.

Lavender, Isiah III. 2014. "Introduction: Coloring Science Fiction." In *Black and Brown Planets: The Politics of Race in Science Fiction*, edited by Isiah Lavender III, 3–12. Jackson: University of Mississippi Press.

Limón, José E. 1994. *Dancing with the Devil: Society and Cultural Poetics in Mexican-American South Texas*. Madison: University of Wisconsin Press.

Lindahl, Carl. 2005. "Ostensive Healing: Pilgrimage to the San Antonio Ghost Tracks." *Journal of American Folklore* 118, no. 468: 164–85.

López-Lozano, Miguel. 2007. *Utopian Dreams, Apocalyptic Nightmares: Globalization in Recent Mexican and Chicano Narrative*. Bloomington, IN: Purdue University Press.

Manickam, Samuel. 2012. "Apocalyptic Visions in Contemporary Mexican Science Fiction." *Chasqui* 41, no. 2: 95–106.

Mehtonen, P. M., and Matti Savolainen, eds. 2016. *Gothic Topographies: Language, Nation Building and "Race."* New York: Routledge.

Mendlesohn, Farah. 2008. *Rhetorics of Fantasy*. Middletown, CT: Wesleyan University Press.

Merla-Watson, Cathryn. 2011. "Spectral Materialisms: Colonial Complexes and the Insurgent Acts of Chicana/o Cultural Production." PhD diss., University of Minnesota.

Mignolo, Walter. 2011. *The Darker Side of Western Modernity: Global Futures, Decolonial Options*. Durham, NC: Duke University Press.

Moraga, Cherríe. 1993. "Queer Aztlán: The Reformation of Chicano Tribe." In *The Last Generation: Prose and Poetry*, 145–74. Boston: South End Press.

———. 2000. *Loving in the War Years: Lo que nunca paso por los labios*. Cambridge, MA: South End Press.

Morales, Alejandro. 1992. *The Rag Doll Plagues*. Houston: Arte Público.

Morán González, John. 2010. "Aztlán @ Fifty: Chican@ Literary Studies for the Next Decade." *Aztlán: A Journal of Chicano Studies* 35, no. 2: 173–76.

Moya, Paula M. L. 2002. *Learning from Experience: Minority Identities, Multicultural Struggles*. Berkeley: University of California Press.

Muñoz, José Esteban. 2009. *Cruising Utopia: The Then and There of Queer Futurity*. New York: New York University Press.

Nama, Adilifu. 2008. *Black Space: Imagining Race in Science Fiction Film*. Austin: University of Texas Press.

Nericcio, William. 2007. *Tex[t]-Mex: Seductive Hallucinations of the "Mexican" in America*. Austin: University of Texas Press.

Noriega, Chon A. 2000. *Shot in America: Television, the State, and the Rise of Chicano Cinema*. Minneapolis: University of Minnesota Press.

Paredes, Américo. 1998. *The Shadow*. Houston: Arte Público.

Pérez, Domino Renée. 2008. *There Was a Woman: La Llorona from Folklore to Popular Culture*. Austin: University of Texas Press.

Pérez, Emma. 1999. *The Decolonial Imaginary: Writing Chicanas into History*. Bloomington: Indiana University Press.

Pérez, Laura Elisa. 1999. "*El desorden*, Nationalism, and Chicana/o Aesthetics." In *Between Woman and Nation: Nationalisms, Transnational Feminisms, and the State*, edited by Caren Kaplan, Norma Alarcón, and Minoo Moallem, 19–46. Durham, NC: Duke University Press.

———. 2007. *Chicana Art: The Politics of Spiritual and Aesthetic Altarities*. Durham, NC: Duke University Press.

Plascencia, Salvador. 2005. *The People of Paper*. San Francisco: McSweeney's.

Ramírez, Catherine S. 2002. "Cyborg Feminism: The Science Fiction of Octavia E. Butler and Gloria Anzaldúa." In *Reload: Rethinking Women and Cyberculture*, edited by Mary Flanagan and Austin Booth, 374–402. Cambridge, MA: MIT Press.

———. 2004. "Deus ex Machina: Tradition, Technology, and the Chicanafuturist Art of Marion C. Martinez." *Aztlán: A Journal of Chicano Studies* 29, no. 2: 55–92.

———. 2008. "Afrofuturism/Chicanafuturism: Fictive Kin." *Aztlán: A Journal of Chicano Studies* 33, no. 1: 185–94.

Rivera, Lysa. 2012. "Future Histories and Cyborg Labor: Reading Borderlands Science Fiction after NAFTA." *Science Fiction Studies* 39, no. 3: 415–36.

Ruiz de Burton, María Amparo. 1885. *The Squatter and the Don*. Reprint, edited by Rosaura Sánchez and Beatrice Pita, Houston: Arte Público, 1997.

Saldívar, José David. 1991. "Postmodern Realism." In *The Columbia History of the American Novel*, edited by Emory Elliot, 521–41. New York: Columbia University Press.

———. 2011. *Trans-Americanity: Subaltern Modernities, Global Coloniality, and the Cultures of Greater Mexico*. Durham, NC: Duke University Press.

Saldívar, Ramón. 2011. "Historical Fantasy, Speculative Realism, and Postrace Aesthetics in Contemporary American Fiction." *American Literary History* 23, no. 3: 574–99.

Sánchez, Rosaura, and Beatrice Pita. 2009. *Lunar Braceros 2125–2148*. San Diego: Calaca.

Santa Ana, Otto. 2002. *Brown Tide Rising: Metaphors of Latinos in Contemporary American Popular Discourse*. Austin: University of Texas Press.

Soares, Kristie. 2014. "The Political Implications of Playing Hopefully: A Negotiation of the Present and the Utopic in Queer Theory and Latina Literature." In *The Un/making of Latina/o Citizenship: Culture, Politics, and Aesthetics*, edited by Ellie D. Hernández and Eliza Rodriguez y Gibson, 121–44. New York: Palgrave Macmillan.

Soto, Sandra K. 2010. *Reading Chican@ Like a Queer: The De-Mastery of Desire*. Austin: University of Texas Press.

Stavans, Ilan, and Frederick Luis Aldama. 2013. *!Muy Pop! Conversations on Latino Popular Culture*. Ann Arbor: University of Michigan Press.

Suvin, Darko. 1979. *Metamorphoses of Science Fiction: On the Poetics and History of a Literary Genre*. New Haven, CT: Yale University Press.

Torrez, Mercedes E. Forthcoming. "Evoking the Shadow Beast: Disability and Chicano Advocacy in San Antonio's Donkey Lady Folktale." *Contemporary Legend* (International Society for Contemporary Legend Research).

Vasquez, Debora Kuetzpal. 2015. Email to authors, May.

Wester, Maisha L. 2012. *African American Gothic: Screams from Shadowed Places*. New York: Palgrave Macmillan.

Wolff, Elaine. 2005. "The Green Lady Is Back: Laura Molina Finds a Heroine in the Kitsch of Calendar Paintings and '60s Sci-Fi." *San Antonio Current*, October 20.

Wood, Robin. 1986. *Hollywood from Vietnam to Reagan*. New York: Columbia University Press.

PART I

Reassessing Chican@ and Latin@ Speculative Aesthetics

The Emancipatory Power of the Imaginary
Defining Chican@ Speculative Productions

William A. Calvo-Quirós

> In many ways, you need to turn yourself into a monster,
> willing to deconstruct and dismantle history,
> trying to be free from the constraints of history
> in order to study the monsters of history
> and the history of monsters.

Monsters and the phantasmagoric have long been central to the Chican@ experience as reminders of our unresolved haunted histories of violence and oppression. Furthermore, the speculative has been a valuable source of epistemic information about those histories of subjugation. The substantial list of Chican@ speculative authors includes Gloria Anzaldúa, Aristeo Brito, Ana Castillo, Sandra Cisneros, Alicia Gaspar de Alba, Emma Pérez, and Tomás Rivera, among others. While Chican@ speculative production is not new, as Sabrina Vourvoulias (2015) points out, the process of decoding these productions is only now getting under way in the emerging field of Chican@ speculative studies.

In this essay I first provide a definition of how I understand and approach the area of Chican@ speculative production (CSP), a definition that centers on the concept of proposing (and producing) a new world. It is a world first constructed in the imagination but never completely disassociated from the "real." Here, the real is perceived as temporal, as a stage toward a world that is based on the premise of equality and social justice. In this way, the real world is the world in the future, not the one in which we now live. In other words, our current world, the one *in* the present, is only a phantom; the real world is the one in which we were meant to live as full humans. CSPs are concerned both with this end product and with the process of constructing it.

Second, I discuss four main characteristics that define CSPs and differentiate them from mainstream speculative works. In particular, I explore how CSPs enact what performance artist and scholar Guillermo Gómez-Peña defines as one of the central challenges of cultural productions by Chican@s, that of finding a language that articulates their unique experiences (1986, 11). To support this argument, I cite several examples of how Chican@s have consistently developed speculative productions as tactics for emancipation and self-governance. The Chican@ speculative imaginary deeply intertwines sociopolitical and historical oppressive experiences and engenders a unique typology of speculative productions that emerge from the margins for the margins.

Finally, I discuss how Chican@ speculative production is foremost an epistemic endeavor. I frame CSPs as part of a larger interconnected system of Chican@ cultural productions that grant access to the complex ways in which Chican@s make sense of what is happening around them and interpret their histories of resilience and intellectual resistance. As scholars Atsuko Matsuoka and John Sorenson explain,

> Looking at ghosts and shadows helps us to understand both ontic and epistemic aspects of diaspora experience. . . . [They] are not merely the spectral recurrences that haunt individual experiences; they often become the source of a structure of feelings, the basis of the mythico-history that allows groups to analyze their collective experience and identity. They are neither objective nor subjective. (2001, 5)

CSPs provide fertile ground for understanding how a community under siege is capable of developing collective epistemological tactics for survival even as it envisions a future free of oppression. These communities are not passive victims but rather active agents constantly trying to make sense of their reality. I contend that border communities understand their oppressed condition, the limitations imposed on them, and the absurdity of their subjugated position. It is precisely because they know "their place" and "their status" within the structures of power in our society that they are capable of developing *clandestine* intellectual maneuvers to retain collective memory and in situ knowledge to navigate the conditions that oppress them. My point here is that the study of Chican@ speculative arts gives us tools to recognize the power of the fantastic, the phantasmagoric, and the imaginary as unique instruments for the pursuit of emancipation, dignity, and social change.

Defining Chican@ Speculative Productions

As P. L. Thomas (2013) explains, quoting Maxine Greene (1995), one of the functions of science fiction and speculative fiction is to "move readers to imagine alternative ways of being alive" (4). This quality of speculative fiction is particularly relevant to analyzing Chican@ speculative productions. For many Chican@ communities, the monstrous real world they experience every day is one defined by extreme violence—a world where, in Ruth Wilson Gilmore's words, racialized groups are subjected to the "production and exploitation of group-differentiated vulnerability to premature death" (2007, 28). Under these conditions of extreme everyday violence, Chican@s strive to "imagine alternative ways of being alive," because in many cases this is the only way to remain alive and endure the challenges of day-to-day existence. Speculative productions for Chican@s are essential components of their survival, allowing them to envision, enact, and work toward an alternative world as they bridge into a world of possibilities.

For Gloria Anzaldúa, the imagination "has the capacity to extend us beyond the confines of our skin, situation, and condition so we can choose our responses. It enables us to reimagine our lives, rewrite the self, and create guiding myths for our time" (2002, 5). As she writes, the imagination works as a powerful tool with which the oppressed can actively liberate and decolonize themselves and foresee a world outside the norms of subjugation. Here, imagining an alternative world becomes a strategic, political, and epistemic tactic for survival. It is first in the imagination that a community can see itself free from a cruel reality defined by poverty, lack of job security, poor heath care access, limited social mobility, historical erasure, and mass incarceration or deportation.

For those at the margins, the realm of the imaginary becomes a medium to envision and put into practice an "alternative" world, one that emerges both from lived experiences and from aesthetic stipulations, language provisions, and cultural categories. I argue that CSPs epistemologically materialize a unique borderland standpoint as they embody what Américo Paredes identifies as "sabidurías populares" (1982, 2), the vernacular wisdom of the borderlands. However, they do not stand alone, as they are part of a vast network of other Chican@ cultural productions (Saldívar 2006, 56) invested in proposing and enacting new possibilities of being. Furthermore, the processes of imagining and creating speculative worlds manifest Renato Rosaldo's concept of "cultural citizenship," putting into practice Chican@s' "right to be different and to belong" fully as members of society, demanding

41

control over their own destiny (1994, 402–10). For Chican@s imagining a new self, collectively and individually, CSPs become a political project of self-affirmation, valorization, and emancipation.

It is not coincidental that Karl Marx, writing in 1867, described capitalism's greed as a "vampire thirst for the living blood of labour" (1976, 367) and capital as a "vampire-like" creature that "lives the more, the more labour it sucks" (342). It is precisely because of the normalization of this atrocious vampire world of racial exploitation, division, and segregation that the future proposed by the "real" world is as monstrous and dangerous as the present. Therefore, the imagination emerges as a principal means to envision an alternative non-vampire world and to visualize the steps required for emancipation. Imagining a world free from racism, oppression, discrimination, and bigotry within a "real" world that manipulates differences to perpetuate exploitation is almost an act of madness. It is one that forces individuals and communities to navigate the world of the unknown, and to hope.

As Cherríe Moraga explains in *The Last Generation*, "The Chicano scribe remembers, not out of nostalgia but out of hope. She remembers in order to envision. She looks backward in order to look forward to a world founded not on greed, but on respect" (1993, 190–91). In this sense, the speculative is a cultural genre that fulfills the need to create a world where a new reality can be drawn and new possibilities can coexist. The fight to create a space for the recognition of Chican@s' knowledge as a valid foundation for their world rests on the speculative. For subjects not meant to survive outside the constructs of exploitative labor or the exotic other, life existence is a brave, tangible demonstration of a new world already in the making. Therefore, for Chican@s the experience of the speculative is intimately linked to the terrains of desire and longing for a future meant to come.

Nevertheless, I refuse to define speculative arts exclusively within the realm of the imaginary. We should avoid the trap of interpreting the speculative solely within the terms of a rejection or reaction to the real; rather, we must acknowledge that the speculative and the real are interwoven. As Jacques Lacan notes, the real and the imaginary, as well as the symbolic, are deeply interconnected although they occupy distinct spaces (Gallop 1987, 167). Because of the sociopolitical location of Chican@s as racialized subjects—as occupants of a racial category that is in itself fictional, since there is only one human race—their speculative productions do not only move from the real to the imaginary, as both spaces are inscribed within a continuum between oppressive imaginaries and emancipatory imagination. CSPs emerge from a real world dangerously polluted by the effects of racism, a fictional ideology that turns the falsehood of race into uncanny flesh and then into "premature death" (Gilmore 2007, 28). CSPs reckon with the absurd of the present world constructed and haunted by the deadly legacies of colonialism and the violence of modernity. Here, to be haunted, as Avery Gordon underscores, is to be "tied to historical and social effects" (1997, 190). Inspired by Gordon, I argue that in order for Chican@s to be free from the haunting of their colonial past, we must collectively exorcise or drive out those ghosts until a new world based on equality and justice is in place. This decolonial exorcism has both corporeal and incorporeal components. The Chican@ movement has consistently worked on both fronts. Corporeally, it includes the fight for new laws that ensure equal access to education, housing, job opportunities, health care, and so on. Incorporeally, the movement has focused on cultural dignity, historical pride, epistemic relevance of our experiences, aesthetics and beauty, as well as on the power of the imagination. In this case, CSPs work as reminders of what is missing, interconnecting the corporeal and the incorporeal, the real and the imaginary. CSPs share, in this case, the qualities of the uncanny ghosts described by Gordon, as they are "symptom[s] of what is missing" (63) but at the same time represent "a future possibility, a hope," and "a concern for justice" (64).

The relational tension between being haunted by the ghosts of colonialism (what is missing and taken away) and the desire for change and emancipation is powerfully articulated by Emma Pérez as she describes how the "colonial imaginary" has "influenced" and "circumscribed" Chican@ historiography (1999, 5). As Cathryn J. Merla-Watson explains, to be a colonial subject implies being "haunted by an invisible net of history and embodied memor[ies], specters of colonialism and misogynist transnational imaginaries" (2013, 236). Furthermore, as Merla-Watson notes, in the context of subjected colonial oppression,

> The ghost is also a social figure, an absent presence that also functions as a marker of hope and reconstruction. . . . The specterly also functions . . . as an entanglement of loss and desire, past traumas and present yearnings, the embodied and disembodied, or, to restate, structures of lived experience that coalesce in sometimes unexpected and previously unthinkable ways that are not necessarily antithetical or mutually exclusive. (230)

Therefore, the process of speculating and imagining a different world is foremost a method of action. This is how feminists, Chicanas, queers, and people of color (and their allies) were able to first imagine and then bring into life new worlds and norms, new forms of thinking and knowledge for their communities. In this sense, although CSPs are born of this world, they are not enslaved by it. They question and redefine the normativity of this world as they propose a different one: a new reality where the Chican@ experience is recentered and where the possibilities of unity are realized. In this light, CSPs can be read as intentional productions that utilize the tools of the imaginary and the fantastic to move the viewer toward a new and different world and new ways to be alive outside the everyday oppressive limitations of the "real."

Leading by Difference: Characteristics of Chican@ Speculative Productions

Chican@ speculative productions include a diverse array of visual art forms, literary productions, and academic interventions, from short stories to novels, murals and graffiti, cartoons, imaginary monsters, legends, and music. Despite this diversity, they have, I would argue, four defining characteristics that relate them to each other and differentiate them from mainstream speculative productions: CSPs are (a) politically subversive, (b) alter-Native, (c) transformative, and (d) epistemic. Let us consider each in turn.

POLITICALLY SUBVERSIVE

Chican@ speculative productions are by their nature deeply political. They are tangible manifestations of Gloria Anzaldúa's "*haciendo caras*," making face, which she interprets as "making *gestos subversivos*, political subversive gestures, the piercing look that questions or challenges, the look that says, 'Don't walk all over me,' the one that says, 'Get out of my face'" (1990, xv). In other words, CSPs not only propose a new world, they also valorize and center Chican@ identity. They are not passive but actively engage in challenging the sources of oppression. As Anzaldúa (2002) explains, one of the central purposes of the imagination for Chican@s is to transform society.

One example of the subversive nature of CSP is Laura Alvarez's Double Agent Sirvienta (DAS). In this series, done in cartoon/comic soap opera style, the artist plays with the real and the imaginary (fig. 1). As Laura E. Pérez explains, "While creating an imaginary landscape that in its improbability is often humorous, [Alvarez's DAS project] brings attention to the ways in which the social space of the home is inhabited, gendered, and racialized" (2007, xv). The central character in the series is a female Mexican immigrant turned into an "undercover agent posing as a maid on both sides of the border" with the mission of "stealing secrets and blackmailing authorities for the demands of the less fortunate" (182). The absurdity of the labor exploitation experienced by Latina maids in California is subverted in such a way that the racialized female subject becomes a spy agent, dethroning assumptions about maids. Here, fears of the racialized others rebelling against their masters become reality. As Pérez

Figure 1. Laura Alvarez, Blow Up the Hard Drive, 1999. *Silk-screen print, 26 × 18 inches. Image courtesy of the artist.*

proposes, DAS is "able to penetrate class and cultural barriers and retrieve otherwise inaccessible information" precisely because the "spy and [the] servant are both phantas(ma)tic, only partly visible social figures" (182). In this fictional world, both characters are merged and utilize their social position of *invisibility* to navigate, and in this case subvert, the system, at least momentarily. The artist creates a fictitious parallel world, a space that mirrors the world in which she lives, but she envisions a different way of being, where the rules defined by the market are subverted and a servant is able to navigate with new agency.

This speculative quality of subversion can also be identified in many other cultural productions: murals, artworks, and corridos that map this new world, as well as in the ephemeral performance and spoken word pieces created by Chican@s. This is the case of Asco, the art collective from East Los Angeles (1972–87). It is not coincidental that the group's name appropriates the Spanish word for nausea and disgust, placing the undesirable at the center. In this case, their new real emerges as a series of ghost-like performances, where the artists challenge the normativity of the ruling-class real and reframe what has been dismissed as absurd or kitsch as the new norm. Many of Asco's performances were short-lived and done on the move, with monster-like masquerades and gothic costumes. Their No Movies series questions Hollywood's exclusion of Chican@s, a pointed commentary by artists who live and work so close to, yet so far from, Hollywood. Also a comment on rejection is their famous *Spray Paint LACMA* (also known as *Project Pie in De/Face*), a graffiti piece that comments on the refusal of the Los Angeles County Museum of Art (LACMA) to exhibit the work of Asco and of other Chican@ artists. In this act of rebellion and self-affirmation, Asco turned LACMA into a canvas. By painting their names on an outside wall, they publically declared the "first Chicana/o art exhibition in LACMA" (Latorre 2008, 258–59). In their new world, the museum escapes the limitations of the museum and becomes a site of both political decadence and reaffirmation.

ALTER-NATIVE

For those under siege, speculative productions do not exist merely as recreation or an escape from reality; that is a luxury not possible for those who occupy the fraught space of the borderlands, where resources are limited. In response to the normalized, everyday reality of horror, CSPs propose a new world that heals the effects of violence and simultaneously creates a space where the self is defined outside subjugation: an "alter-Native" world to the one dominated by greed and racial exploitation. I use this term following Alicia Gaspar de Alba's notion that "Chicano/a culture is an alter-Native culture within the United States, both alien and indigenous to the landbase known as the West" (1998, xvi). In this sense, the new alter-Native world is also a project of resignifications, where articulations and meanings are reassigned and regenerated. Just as Jonathan Inda has illustrated in the case of the term *Chicano* (2000, 74–99), this process of resignification moves beyond the perpetuation of traditional models of subjugation and toward something that is simultaneously new and alien.

The figure of Joaquín, as constructed by Rodolfo "Corky" Gonzales (1972) in his famous poem *Yo Soy Joaquín*, is an example of a speculative hero who emerges from the ashes of a world in decadence. Joaquín is a new type of human who can only live in a new world that is at once both utopian and real. Despite the poem's male-centered heteronormative limitations, at its writing in 1967 it was understood as proposing a plan of action for the construction of Aztlán, the original mythical land of the ancient Mexica/Aztec people that turned into a speculative model of the Chican@ community in the United States during the 1960s. I frame the reemergence of the myth of Aztlán, during the same period, within this speculative theoretical context and as an example of a CSP, not only because it reimagines a unifying past for a very diverse community but also because it works as a prototype for a different future world. Aztlán eventually became a central symbol for Chican@ epistemic discourses about self, the politics of space, and the reconstitution of a diverse community under a common umbrella for citizenship rights, emancipation, and self-definition.

"El Plan Espiritual de Aztlán" (The Spiritual Plan of Aztlán) and "El Plan de Santa Bárbara" (The Plan of Santa Barbara), foundational texts for the Chican@ movement, build their pedagogical and political discourses around their speculative interpretations of the myth of Aztlán. Here, the new Aztlán is envisioned as a point of both departure and arrival of a new egalitarian world, one that is centered on Chican@ experiences and struggles for equality. Logistically, the reconstitution of the myth of Aztlán by Chican@s during the 1960s demonstrates what I call the "sticky" nature of speculative productions, or their tendency to introduce multiple points of access or adhesion to a community. As a result, the members of a heterogeneous group such as Chican@s can relate personally to the narrative of Aztlán as an unifying element despite their differences with regard to language, citizenship, immigration status, religion, and their identity as members of *la raza*. As Rudolfo A. Anaya and Francisco Lomelí explain,

"For Chicanos the concept of Aztlán signaled a unifying point of cohesion through which they could define the foundations for an identity" (1997, ii). The myth of Aztlán allows very diverse Chicano/Latino individuals to unify around one origin myth, with one set of common ancestors and with a shared past of oppression and segregation. As Anaya and Lomelí write, "Aztlán brought together a culture that had been somewhat disjointed and dispersed, allowing it, for the first time, a framework within which to understand itself" as an unified historically subjugated social body (ii). Consequently, Aztlán enabled Chican@s to understand their past, to make sense of their present, and to have hope for the future (iii–iv).

However, Aztlán, as proposed by the Chicano nationalist project of the 1960s–70s, was not immune to the faults of patriarchalism. As early as the 1980s, Chicanas and queer Chican@s denounced the heteropatriarchy inscribed within this nationalist project and called for a new Aztlán, a more inclusive type of political speculative production. This task was made possible only by those who were both within and outside the Chicano movement, those who were not afraid of losing Aztlán, in part because they were never fully included in this project. They were able to inscribe a new Aztlán because they were not tied to or constrained by the one already in place. Cherríe Moraga (1993) contextualizes this extraordinary speculative project in her essay "Queer Aztlán." This imagined new Aztlán exemplifies both Emma Pérez's (1999) concept of the decolonial imaginary and Gloria Anzaldúa's (1987) methodology of a mestiza consciousness. In her essay, Moraga applies Anzaldúa's methodology, moving from a critical "inventory" and the reinterpretation of history to the "shape [of] new myths" (Anzaldúa 1987, 104) and simultaneously creating a new reality toward an emancipated future, one beyond the norms of coloniality of today. Queer Aztlán emerges, according to Moraga, as a new "nation strong enough to embrace a full range of racial diversities, human sexualities, and expressions of gender" (1993, 164). Built from the raw materials of the previous Aztlán project, Queer Aztlán rejects those aspects understood as oppressive. This new alter-Native world, a new semiotic myth, is presented as a path of action for inclusion.

Transformative

One of the characteristics of Chican@ speculative productions is their atemporal nature, or their capacity to move between times and places without being constrained by the aesthetic limitations imposed by discourses on rigor or purity characteristic of each period. In this regard they can be interpreted as examples of Michel Foucault's concept of heterotopias, or spaces of otherness, where the imagined and the real coexist simultaneously. This is possible because, as Foucault explains, a "heterotopia is capable of juxtaposing in a single real place several spaces, several sites that are in themselves incompatible" (1986, 25). This transformative atemporal characteristic can be visually represented by the custom paint job on a lowrider car. These artistic productions encompass different elements from different periods, coexisting without apparent conflict, because the emphasis is not on the individual aesthetic elements but rather on the overall visual narration, the interconnection between the images. The power of CSPs (and many other Chicana/o cultural productions) depends heavily on the ability of an artist to collect and select images in order to build a narration. This plurality of symbols, images, and treatments can be overwhelming for the untrained eye or for viewers fixed on puritan aesthetic discourses of historical lineal progression. CSPs hold these atemporal qualities in ways that allow their communities to pick and choose and to relocate an element into the present. Furthermore, according to Foucault, the role of heterotopias is to "create a space that is other, another real space, as perfect, as meticulous, as well arranged as ours is messy, ill constructed, and jumbled" (25). Therefore the new imaginary worlds created by CSPs are deeply detailed and intentional.

Another example of the transformative resignifying enacted by CSPs can be found in the work of Los Angeles artist Alma López, who utilizes the highly charged semiotic image of the Virgin of Guadalupe to propose a new world, in this case one where queer love is accepted and normalized. She follows the tradition of other Chicana artists, such as Yolanda M. López, Ester Hernandez, Guadalupe Rodriguez, and Isis Rodriguez, in giving a new set of meanings to the image of the Virgin of Guadalupe. For Alma López, the love affair between Guadalupe and another popular image, La Sirena, places queer love at the same level as heterosexual love. This queering of the Virgin of Guadalupe works as a tool to denounce sexism, homophobia, and the limitations of patriarchy from a Chicana perspective. Alma López frees the Virgin and unveils the woman behind the mandorla, in this case one made of flesh and human emotions. This Guadalupe lives with her lover La Sirena in a *another* world, one that is too close to be unreal but is simultaneously impossible for many to see or recognize. Paradoxically, because of the effects of homophobia in the "real" world, Guadalupe is also forced to live as a double agent, both as a devoted virgin mother and as a human being with sexual desires and the need for affection and intimacy; both Guadalupes are merged in the same city, Los Angeles, as one single being. In the works of Alma López, the Virgin of Guadalupe is more than a religious icon; she holds a Nepantla passport between our ancestral past and our hopes for a speculative future of equal love.

EMANCIPATORY

One of the most important characteristics of Chican@ cultural productions, including Chican@ speculative productions, is their epistemic value and function. This occurs because of a combination of factors such as the marginalization experienced by this community, their limited access to resources, the guarded access to mainstream sources of knowledge distribution, and the formal and informal colonial policing of knowledge. As we know, the process of colonization of Chican@ communities is manifested partly in the sanctioning, silencing, and marginalization of their knowledge (Santos 2006). It is in this context that speculative productions emerge as venues for the transfer of information about how to survive, decentering power and transforming lived worlds. This transformation happens at the epistemic level, certainly by imagining a new world, but also by questioning and refusing both the assumptions about what it means to be a Chican@ and the binaries created by oppressor/victim paradigms. Even more important, Chican@ speculative productions create new knowledge about the world, about Chican@s, and about their communities.

James Scott (1992), analyzing African American production of gospel music during slavery, observes that behind the obviously religious nature of many of these hymns were concealed discourses of emancipation, social justice, and hope for a world beyond oppression. These hymns spoke about the forthcoming of a new world order defined by justice. Similarly, CSPs are sophisticated knowledge productions that bespeak the possibilities of a new order. Ironically, it is precisely because vernacular speculative productions are dismissed by society that they can be used to clandestinely share knowledge in ways that pass undetected by the mainstream. Behind the apparently innocent nature of these speculative fantasies, fictional worlds, and monsters are concealed the knowledge and experiences of these communities. In this sense, CSP manifests what Rossana Reguillo defines as "critical social knowledge" (2004, 40) and Walter Mignolo refers to as "subaltern modernities" (2000, 13), or sophisticated productions that subjugated communities use to deal with the effects of modernity in their everyday lives.

It is precisely because of the epistemic nature of CSPs that their forms, qualities, and modus operandi are never random. The characteristics of a given CSP correspond to a specific time, social context, and economic threat. For example, the Chupacabras, a blood-sucking monster, emerged in the mid-1990s as a sophisticated metaphor for the behavior of late capitalism during that period. As policies of market expansion and global deregulation ravaged rural Latin@ communities, the Chupacabras can be understood as neoliberal ideology turned uncanny flesh. The atrocities generated at the "crossroads of a new millennium require[d] an even more complex system of uncanny signifiers to accommodate a new set of hyper-realities" imposed by neoliberalism (Calvo-Quirós 2014b, 230). Confronting the devastating transformations required by the North American Free Trade Agreement (NAFTA), members of rural communities understood that their livelihoods as small farmers were under threat, being sucked away by transnational corporations, international banks, and global markets. The Chupacabras thus emerges as a sophisticated epistemic product rendering visible the invisible economic policies whose deadly effects were being felt in vulnerable communities. Moreover, the Chupacabras fulfilled a crucial function by transferring information to rural and Latin@ communities under siege. Surviving the attacks of the Chupacabras was synonymous to surviving a wave of apocalyptic economic policies linked to NAFTA in Mexico, Texas, and Puerto Rico during the decade of the 1990s:

> Clearly, for those on the losing end, the experience of land dispossession, forced migration, and the loss of their sources for maintaining their families and preserving their culture, could have been perceived as the effects of a monster that was attacking them, one that little by little, was sucking their lives away. In those days, just as today, there were more than just livestock animals dying and succumbing, there were also communal histories, and traditions at stake. (Calvo-Quirós 2014a, 98)

The form and shape of CSPs, as multilayered social texts, tell us about the characteristics of the threats and anxieties afflicting Chican@ communities. Furthermore, the power of a speculative production is not limited to its literary or artistic form, but also derives from its relationship with the community involved. The significance of the Chupacabras is as much about the communities it ravages as it is about the creature itself. Creating a sophisticated "imaginary" creature such as the Chupacabras requires an understanding of the monstrous real.

Finally, because Chican@s use the speculative to create new paths for knowledge and knowledge transfer, researching and theorizing CSP requires unique tools. These include traditional disciplines such as anthropology and history, but also a solid engagement with critical race theory, gender, and sexuality. The integration of multiple methods and analytic processes is essential. For example, while researching CSP I found it essential not only to do interviews, oral histories, and ethnography visits to saints' shrines and sites of spectral sightings but also to analyze governmental archives, newspaper coverage, demographic data, police reports, and economic data as well as other cultural productions such as films, jokes, murals, and corridos. Since these cultural objects are not always what they seem, it is imperative to develop what Emma Peréz calls a "decolonial queer gaze" (2003, 124) or Laura Pérez calls a critical investigative eye that can see between the lines (2007, 128) and beyond what is apparent. This is particularly essential because of the limited official archives available about oppressed communities and because of their limited access to traditional media.

Final Thoughts and Continuing Questions

The development of this essay has been fascinating and provocative. It started with the task of explaining how I understand the area of Chican@ speculative productions, their unique characteristics, and the epistemic relevance of a field of study that has been an important and consistent component of the Chican@ experience in the United States. Simultaneously, this essay also became an intellectual effort to emphasize the significance of Chican@ speculative research within Latin@ studies, Chican@ studies, cultural studies, and American studies, as a medium to study the experience, struggles, and resilience of a community.

Several questions have emerged during this project, and some of them may be central for the future development of CSP as an area of investigation and analysis. For example, how do we deal with CSPs that are obscure because of their producer or topic? How do we deal with those speculative productions that reproduce colonialist violence against women and nonnormative subjects? How does the area of speculative studies justify its existence and differentiate its analysis from more traditional fields of study, like folklore, anthropology, and literature? What are some of the specific decolonizing methodologies required for approaching, analyzing, and studying CSPs? What are the next steps required to advance the development of Chican@ speculative studies?

Certainly, these are exciting times to be a part of Chican@ and Latin@ studies as new and more refined areas of research take shape. As the field grows and matures, the forces that militate against its transformative and epistemic nature are also becoming more sophisticated, toxic, and threatening. More than ever, the need to imagine a new world outside the norms of oppression is imperative for the survival of all. If we cannot use imagination to create change, what is left behind for humans?

Works Cited

Anaya, Rudolfo A., and Francisco Lomelí, eds. 1997. Introduction to *Aztlán: Essays on the Chicano Homeland*, edited by Rudolfo A. Anaya and Francisco Lomelí, ii–iv. Albuquerque: University of New Mexico Press.

Anzaldúa, Gloria. 1987. *Borderlands/La Frontera: The New Mestiza*. San Francisco: Aunt Lute.

———. 1990. *Making Face, Making Soul/Haciendo Caras: Creative and Critical Perspectives by Feminists of Color*. San Francisco: Aunt Lute.

———. 2002. "(Un)natural Bridges, (Un)safe Spaces." In *This Bridge We Call Home: Radical Visions for Transformation*, edited by Gloria E. Anzaldúa and AnaLouise Keating, 1–5. New York: Routledge.

Calvo-Quirós, William A. 2014a. "Chupacabras: The Strange Case of Carlos Salinas de Gortari and His Transformation into the Chupatodo." In *Crossing the Borders of Imagination*, edited by María del Mar Ramón Torrijos, 95–108. Madrid: Instituto Franklin de Estudios Norteamericanos, Universidad de Alcalá.

———. 2014b. "Sucking Vulnerability: Neoliberalism, the Chupacabras, and the Post-Cold War Years." In *The Un/Making of Latina/o Citizenship: Culture, Politics, and Aesthetics*, edited by Ellie D. Hernández and Eliza Rodriguez y Gibson, 211–34. New York: Palgrave Macmillan.

Foucault, Michel. 1986. "Of Other Spaces." Translated by Jay Miskowiec. *Diacritics* 16, no. 1: 22–27.

Gallop, Jane. 1987. *Reading Lacan*. Ithaca, NY: Cornell University Press.

Gaspar de Alba, Alicia. 1998. *Chicano Art Inside/Outside the Master's House: Cultural Politics and the CARA Exhibition*. Austin: University of Texas Press.

Gilmore, Ruth Wilson. 2007. *Golden Gulag: Prisons, Surplus, Crisis, and Opposition in Globalizing California*. Berkeley: University of California Press.

Gómez-Peña, Guillermo. 1986. "Border Culture: A Process of Negotiation toward Utopia." *La Línea Quebrada/The Broken Line* 1: 1–6.

Gonzales, Rodolfo "Corky." 1972. *I Am Joaquín/Yo Soy Joaquín: An Epic Poem*. New York: Bantam.

Gordon, Avery F. 1997. *Ghostly Matters: Haunting and the Sociological Imagination*. Minneapolis: University of Minnesota Press.

Greene, Maxine. 1995. *Releasing the Imagination: Essays on Education, the Arts, and Social Change*. San Francisco: Jossey-Bass.

Inda, Jonathan Xavier. 2000. "Performativity, Materiality, and the Racial Body." *Latino Studies Journal* 11, no. 3: 74–99.

Latorre, Guisela. 2008. *Walls of Empowerment: Chicana/o Indigenous Murals of California*. Austin: University of Texas Press.

Marx, Karl. 1976. *Capital*, vol. 1, *A Critique of Political Economy*. Translated by Ernest Mandel. New York: Penguin. First published 1867.

Matsuoka, Atsuko, and John Sorenson. 2001. *Ghosts and Shadows: Construction of Identity and Community in an African Diaspora*. Toronto: University of Toronto Press.

Merla-Watson, Cathryn J. 2013. "Haunted by Voices: Historical Im/materialism and Gloria Anzaldúa's Mestiza Consciousness." In *El Mundo Zurdo 3: Selected Works from the 2012 Meeting of the Society for the Study of Gloria Anzaldúa*, edited by Larissa M. Mercado-Lopez, Sonia Saldívar-Hull, and Antonia Castañeda, 225–41. San Francisco: Aunt Lute.

Mignolo, Walter. 2000. *Local Histories/Global Designs: Coloniality, Subaltern Knowledges, and Border Thinking*. Princeton, NJ: Princeton University Press.

Moraga, Cherríe. 1993. *The Last Generation: Prose and Poetry*. Boston: South End Press.

Paredes, Américo. 1982. "Folklore, lo Mexicano, and Proverbs." *Aztlán: International Journal of Chicano Studies Research* 13, nos. 1–2: 1–11.

Pérez, Emma. 1999. *The Decolonial Imaginary: Writing Chicanas into History*. Bloomington: Indiana University Press.

———. 2003. "Queering the Borderlands: The Challenges of Excavating the Invisible and Unheard." *Frontiers: A Journal of Women's Studies* 24, nos. 2–3: 122–31.

Pérez, Laura E. 2007. *Chicana Art: The Politics of Spiritual and Aesthetic Altarities*. Durham, NC: Duke University Press.

Reguillo, Rossana. 2004. "The Oracle in the City: Beliefs, Practices, and Symbolic Geographies." *Social Text* 22, no. 4: 35–40.

Rosaldo, Renato. 1994. "Cultural Citizenship and Educational Democracy." *Cultural Anthropology* 9, no. 3: 402–11.

Saldívar, Ramón. 2006. *The Borderlands of Culture: Américo Paredes and the Transnational Imaginary*. Durham, NC: Duke University Press.

Santos, Boaventura de Sousa. 2006. *The Rise of the Global Left: The World Social Forum and Beyond*. London: Zed.

Scott, James C. 1992. *Domination and the Arts of Resistance: Hidden Transcripts*. New Haven, CT: Yale University Press.

Thomas, P. L., ed. 2013. *Science Fiction and Speculative Fiction: Challenging Genres*. Rotterdam: Sense.

Vourvoulias, Sabrina. 2015. "Putting the I in Speculative: Looking at U.S. Latino/a Writers and Stories." Tor.com, February 2. http://www.tor.com/2015/02/02/looking-at-us-latino-latina-speculative-writers-and-stories.

Recovering Gloria Anzaldúa's Sci-Fi Roots

Nepantler@ Visions in the Unpublished and Published Speculative Precursors to *Borderlands*

Susana Ramírez

First published in serial form in 1975, Reyes Cárdenas's nineteen-episode novella *Los Pachucos y La Flying Saucer* featured a spaceship erotically shaped like a woman with huge breasts that are sucked by two stoned picaresque pachuco warrior heroes who time-travel to refight the Mexican Revolution and other wars (Cárdenas 2013). Such early Raza science fiction (sci-fi) inserted brown bodies into the realm of science and technology in highly problematic ways.[1] Flash forward twenty-seven years to the nation-wide multimedia art exhibition *Chicano Now! American Expressions*, which ran from 2002 through 2008.[2] The show opened in the Alameda's Museo Americano, a Smithsonian Institution affiliate in San Antonio, Texas, and was billed as an attempt to neutralize the lingering negative connotations surrounding the politicized and highly racialized identity symbolized by the moniker "Chicano."[3] Yet upon entering, guests were greeted with a brightly painted Chicano border mural "juxtaposed against an orange rocket ship and cheese-like moons, as well as a [sci-fi-esque] video montage produced by performance art group Culture Clash" (M. Soto 2003, 93). According to literary critic Michael Soto, the pieces offered readily consumable representations of an apolitical version of Chicano culture as opposed to "the cutting political message traditionally found in Chicano art" (94). Like its Chicano sci-fi predecessor, the *Chicano Now!* exhibition fell short of its politicized potential; instead it replicated stereotypical imaginaries of Chican@ identity, with the futurist allusions rendered kitsch masquerading as utopian. While Catherine S. Ramírez, the forerunner of Chican@ science fiction scholars, struggles to find herself reflected in early mainstream sci-fi of the 1970s such as *Star Wars* (2008, 185), we Chicanas, specifically queer Chicanas, also struggle to find ourselves in early Raza sci-fi. These polemics inspired me to ask: What are other early Chican@ sci-fi texts? And what might locating the earliest Chican@ sci-fi texts offer to our attempts to extend and reconstruct the genealogy of Raza sci-fi?

Inspired by Ramírez's excavation of alternative Chican@ sci-fi roots that would speak to a political consciousness that does not elide questions of gender and sexuality, I returned to Gloria Anzaldúa, particularly the rich archive contained in the Gloria Evangelina Anzaldúa Papers, 1942–2004, housed at the Benson Latin American Collection at the University of Texas, Austin. Recently opened to the public, the Anzaldúa Papers offer exciting new opportunities to reconstruct and continue reassessing the unique contributions of Chican@s, particularly Chicana feminists, to the speculative arts. Many people familiar with Gloria Anzaldúa's work are unaware that she was an avid reader of science fiction and also wrote science fiction herself. In fact, one of her earliest drafts, variously titled "Dreaming la Prieta" and "Los Entremados de PQ," dates to 1970, which makes her possibly the first Chican@ science fiction writer![4]

Through preliminary close readings of some of Anzaldúa's published and unpublished sci-fi stories—"Reading LP," "Werejaguar," and "Puddles"—I argue that her science fiction challenges the heteronormativity found in many early Raza sci-fi texts. More important, her sci-fi introduces new cosmologies through her unique concept of "nepantlera," which challenges material-versus-spiritual dichotomies. In Anzaldúa's sci-fi, the nepantlera subject functions as a transspecies, transspatial, and transtemporal agent who moves in between and beyond the mestiza paradigms made famous by Anzaldúa's *Borderlands/La Frontera: The New Mestiza* (1987). Nepantlera thickens her mestiza consciousness, which has always been a simultaneously material and spiritual praxis and theory, though its spirituality—or "historical im/materialism," to use the term of cultural theorist Cathryn Merla-Watson (2013)—is left largely undertheorized. According to Merla-Watson, historical im/materialism refers to the psychological, spiritual, and socially spectral that valorizes what is not readily seen, for the purpose of formulating and enacting oppositional consciousness and social transformation. Already renowned for transforming the Chicana/o canon and revolutionizing Chicana/o epistemologies and ontologies, Anzaldúa, who donated over 1,000 sci-fi books from her private collection to the Benson

Collection, also helps us reimagine and reconstruct the Chicana/o sci-fi canon with her stories.

Reconstructing Chicana/o Science Fiction Genealogies: Gloria Anzaldúa as Sci-Fi Writer

In her foundational text *The Decolonial Imaginary*, Emma Pérez reminds us that it is not enough for Chicana/os to rewrite ourselves into historical narratives; we must develop different lenses, methodologies, and technologies with which to read the in-between spaces of resistance to oppressive power relations. She suggests that these spaces can be found within collective heterogeneous stories of our collective pasts, presents, and, I would add, *futures*. Pérez further explains:

> Chicana/o historiography has been circumscribed by the traditional historical imagination. This means that even the most radical Chicano/a historiographies are influenced by the very colonial imaginary against which they rebel. (1999, 5)

Parallels can be drawn to early Raza sci-fi, in which Chicano cultural nationalists erased brown female, queered bodies even as they wrote some Chicanos into this genre. When members of marginalized communities attempt to revise master narratives, they often still replicate exclusionary or colonial practices of erasure. While some instances of early Chicano satire, such as Teatro Campesino's speculative satirical play *Los Vendidos* (Valdez 1971), do not fit this mold, others such as Cárdenas's *Los Pachucos y La Flying Saucer* involve caricature and sexist signifying practices, which continued to be evidenced up to the *Chicano Now!* exhibition.

Following Pérez, I advocate for a sci-fi decolonial imaginary that contends with and counters discursive formations and practices that always already shape how we retell historical narratives, including our collective Chican@ sci-fi stories. Many of the growing number of women of color science fiction writers are making meaningful interventions that disrupt colonial ideologies and offer decolonial alternative *conocimientos*.[5] More specifically, Anzaldúa, as a sci-fi writer, radically transforms the genre of science fiction by pushing its generic limits and engaging with alternative cosmologies and epistemologies. Research in the Anzaldúa Papers, which include Anzaldúa's unpublished and published sci-fi stories, enables this new hermeneutic that offers profound interconnected worldviews and alternative familial/communal networks.

Catherine S. Ramírez (2002a, 2008) has already done some heavy lifting in this search to locate queer and women of color sci-fi writers. She is likely the first to read Gloria Anzaldúa as a sci-fi author, specifically as a Chicanafuturist author. Inspired by Afrofuturism and the sci-fi-esque artwork of Chicana artist Marion C. Martinez, Ramírez coins the term *Chicanafuturism* to talk about the relationship between Mexican Americans and technology, progress, and humanism (2008, 186). Her scholarship centers on women of color sci-fi writers who are grappling with notions of the "alien" and who appropriate the technologies of science fiction to critique the status quo that demarcates such alienations. Ramírez aptly asks:

> What happens to Chicana/o texts when we read them as science fiction? To Chicana/o cultural identity? And to the concepts of science, technology, civilization, progress, modernity, and the human? (2008, 190)

Accordingly, Catherine Ramírez revisits and rereads *Borderlands* as a sci-fi text. She poignantly reclaims the sci-fi figure of "the alien" in Anzaldúa's writing to refer to the history of struggle over the borderlands that splits the land and the racialized, sexualized, and colonized subject for whom it was and continues to be home (2002a, 389). Moreover, Ramírez makes the bold assertion that potentially every Chican@ text can be read as sci-fi because the recurrent themes of alienation, misrecognition, and estrangement felt by many communities of color in the United States invite readers to read other (typically nondesignated) sci-fi texts with this lens.

While Ramírez introduced Anzaldúa as a sci-fi writer through rereadings of *Borderlands*, Lysa Rivera applies Anzaldúa's *Borderlands* theory to sci-fi texts on both sides of the US-Mexico geopolitical border. In "Future Histories and Cyborg Labor: Reading Borderlands Science Fiction after NAFTA" (2012), Rivera places Guillermo Lavín's short story "Reaching the Shore," the sci-fi films of the US filmmaker Alex Rivera, and Rosaura Sánchez and Beatrice Pita's novel *Lunar Braceros: 2125–2148* in conversation to critique global capitalism and NAFTA agreements that created unique historical borderlands sites. Rivera asserts that borderlands sci-fi reflects this violence on the US-Mexico border. Ramírez and Rivera, in brief, offer powerful readings of Anzaldúa as indirectly writing to the sci-fi genre, but I am also interested in how we can frame her more directly as a sci-fi writer. This search for a way in which to conceptualize Anzaldúa's queer and Chicana feminist sci-fi leads me to Erin Ranft's (2013) excavation of feminist sci-fi authors who expose bodily issues that affect women of color in the United States, such as reproductive control and sterilization procedures, and who utilize conventions of sci-fi to portray these women's resistance and survival.

In her dissertation, Ranft reads Anzaldúa as a sci-fi writer and utilizes Anzaldúa's spiritual activist theory of nepantla to explicate two of her archived sci-fi stories: "Reading LP" and "Sleepwalkers."[6] Ranft proposes an intersectional nepantla approach toward reading black and Chican@ feminist science fiction that portrays the resistance of women of color as they fight against institutional bodily oppressions. Ranft defines intersectional nepantla as a term that merges feminist theories of intersectionality and nepantla to "denote a framework that addresses individual confrontations with institutionalized oppressions based on the intersections of different elements of identity, but also the internalized oppressions and emotional struggles that women, particularly women of color, experience in a white (hetero)patriarchal society" (2013, 139). Like Ranft, I am concerned with the specific multidimensional, intersectional material struggles imposed on the bodies of women of color, and with how they respond to them. However, I build on Ranft's discussions by centering materiality and more pronounced readings of metaphysical or spiritual properties that are found in Anzaldúa's archived sci-fi stories. Anzaldúa's spirituality includes profound interconnections that go beyond relations with people to include relations with the environment, land, animals, and the cosmos. She has creatively turned to science fiction to portray alternative complex worlds, interrogating fixed, constructed notions of race, gender, class, sexuality, and nation to stress the urgency of creating alternative coalitions based on profound interconnectedness and alternative familial/communal networks.

Gloria Anzaldúa's Speculative Nepantler@ Cosmologies: Toward Transspecies, Transspatial, and Transtemporal Subjectivities

In *Borderlands*, Anzaldúa introduced "the new mestiza" and mestiza consciousness to synthesize different cultures. The Spanish word *mestizaje* refers to the violent mixing of peoples and cultures as a result of the Spanish *conquista* of México. In Norma Alarcón's interpretation, "the Mexican nation-making process was intended to racially colligate a heterogeneous population that was not European" (2006, 122). Because of European classifications of racial superiority and purity, this hybrid subjectivity often privileged the Spanish element of mestizaje while erasing the indigenous and African presence. Inspired by José Vasconcelos's *raza cósmica*, Anzaldúa proposed that the new mestiza creates new epistemologies in that she is "alienated from her mother culture, [and] 'alien' in the dominant culture" and thus adopts an "alien" consciousness as a result of straddling both cultures (1987, 42). Anzaldúa further asserts that "the *future* will belong to the *mestiza*" (102, emphasis in original). While the concept of the new mestiza was useful in reclaiming all parts of a plural identity, and arguably invites readings of *Borderlands* as sci-fi and speculative literature, many have critiqued Anzaldúa's appropriation of an indigenous identity. Indeed, I submit that Anzaldúa moves away from some of the limitations of the "new mestiza" subjectivity with her pre- and post-*Borderlands* theories—particularly her controversial use of a trope of race, mestizaje, that necessarily involved genocide as the precondition for the mixture of European, indigenous, and African.

One of the leading scholars who speaks to the importance of examining Anzaldúa's later theories is her writing *comadre* and friend AnaLouise Keating. In her essay "From Borderlands and New Mestizas to Nepantla and Nepantleras: Anzaldúan Theories for Social Change," Keating states:

> Perhaps not surprisingly—given the multifaceted nature of *Borderlands* and the diversity of Anzaldúa's other writings—readers have overlooked additional, equally important dimensions of her work, leaving what Anzaldúa might call "blank spots" that prevent us from grasping the radical nature of her vision for social change and the crucial ways her theories have developed since the 1987 publication *Borderlands*. (2006, 5)

Anzaldúa's oversimplication of indigenous identity within her conceptualization of the new mestiza represents such a blank spot in her long trajectory toward imagining more radical and inclusionary worldviews.

However, before Anzaldúa prematurely passed away, she introduced the spiritual activist theories of nepantla and nepantleras to describe cosmic borders between the material and metaphysical and the visionary agents moving across them. Following Cathryn J. Merla-Watson's essay "Haunted by Voices: Historical Im/Materialism and Gloria Anzaldúa's Mestiza Consciousness," I agree that for Anzaldúa, materiality is animated by the seemingly immaterial (and vice versa) and in this sense offers a more holistic alternative interpretation of Latina/o cultural productions (2013, 9). I extend Merla-Watson's analysis of the material/immaterial divide to explore how nepantla more fully breaks from this dichotomy. Anzaldúa's nepantlera offers a more fluid subjectivity, troping the ancient Nahuatl etymology of a term for anomie and hybridity and organically bridging the material with the immaterial. For Anzaldúa, nepantla, and particularly nepantlera subjectivity, denotes significant shifts and departures in her imagination of and desire for a more complex and inclusive worldview; in this sense it may be even more reflective of the vision for social transformation that she articulates in her writings after *Borderlands*. Following Catherine S. Ramírez's call for a rereading of Anzaldúa as a sci-fi artist, and drawing on my own encounter with Anzaldúa's speculative short stories, I seek to locate nepantlera in the realm of sci-fi to challenge the (hetero)normative parameters of both Raza and mainstream science fiction.

Inspired by the complex Náhuatl concept of nepantla, which signifies in-betweenness, or as Keating proposes, "chaotic thresholds" (2013, 12), Anzaldúa invented the word *nepantlera* to refer to cultural visionaries engaging in spiritual activism. These subjects "work from multiple locations" and "try to overturn the destructive perceptions of the world that we've been taught by our various cultures" (2009d, 293). Nepantleras understand that boundaries are more malleable than Anzaldúa's conceptualization of the new mestiza suggests. Keating writes, "Anzaldúa coined the term *nepantlera* in her post-*Borderlands* work as she developed an expansive alternative to Chicana lesbian identity politics" (2013, 12). Anzaldúa's profound yet still undertheorized nepantlera represents new sacred subjectivities that both embrace and question cultural, ethnic, philosophical, and other classifications. I submit that Anzaldúan nepantleras are agents constantly moving in between time and space and beyond the material body to challenge, expand, and reimagine the "reality" of these constructs.

Moreover, I propose that Anzaldúa's use of nepantleras in her sci-fi thickens her theory of the new mestiza. Indeed, in these stories nepantleras function as transspecies, transspatial, and transtemporal subjects who create new perspectives from the often-painful process of negotiating different worlds and existing within "cracks between worlds" (2000d, 255). In "Speaking across the Divide," an essay included in *The Gloria Anzaldúa Reader*, Anzaldúa writes:

> Las nepantleras, modern-day chamanas, use visioning and the imaginal on behalf of the self and the community. . . . They change the stories about who we are and about our behavior. They point to the stick we beat ourselves with so we realize what we're doing and may choose to throw away the stick. They possess the gift of vision. Nepantleras think in terms of the planet, not just their own racial group, the U.S., or Norte América. (2009d, 293)

To answer Sandra Soto's call to complicate simplistic gender readability, I build on Anzaldúa's concept of nepantlera by adding the "@" symbol. Soto writes, "I like the way the nonalphabetic symbol for 'at' disrupts our desire for intelligibility, our desire for a quick and certain visual register of a gendered body the split second we hear the term" (2010, 2–3).[7]

Notably, nepantler@s do not dismiss material and historical specificity, but expand on its importance. Through these painful movements, nepantler@s forge commonalities across differences. Nepantler@s borrow from different strategies to survive multiple realities; they do not remain fixed on one strategy. In different contexts, different parts of our identities will be more salient than others. However, all identities are present at all times; they cannot be separated. Just as nepantler@s can sometimes move beyond oppositional frameworks, Chela Sandoval's model of oppositional or differential consciousness—a materialist nepantler@ synthesis that still accounts for the subjective aspects of consciousness and agency—helps map the salience of a nepantler@ paradigm. As Sandoval explains:

> Differential consciousness represents a strategy of oppositional ideology that functions on an altogether different register. Its powers can be thought of as of mobile—not nomadic, but rather cinematographic: a kinetic motion that maneuvers, poetically transfigures, and orchestrates while demanding alienation, perversion, and reformation in both specta-tors and practitioners . . . it permits functioning within, yet beyond, the demands of dominant ideology. (2000, 44)

Nepantler@s understand the usefulness of oppositional practices when necessary. They simultaneously work toward newfound possibilities for the world that move us from *reacting* subjects to more active and even proactive agents.

As a preface to my explications of Anzladúa's published and unpub-lished speculative stories, it should be noted that spirituality has always been an important part of Anzaldúa's work, and it is infused into her science fiction. Indeed, spirituality is integral to the political consciousness of the texts and subjects of her speculative stories. Her nepantler@ cosmologies intersect with Theresa Delgadillo's (2011) model of spiritual mestizaje, which Delgadillo defines as a process of critiquing all forms of oppression (including their material forms) that provides a path toward personal and collective transformation. While Delgadillo centralizes Christian spirituali-ties in her readings of Anzaldúa's spiritual mestizaje, Anzaldúa adamantly moved away from Christian-based spiritualities. She states in an interview with Christine Weiland, "To me religion has always upheld the status quo, it makes institutions rigid and dogmatic" (2000e, 95). Christian spirituality is not the spirituality that Anzaldúa is articulating in her science fiction stories. AnaLouise Keating emphasizes that Anzaldúa's spirituality focuses on both the material and metaphysical and sees their interconnection as integral: she is concerned with the fusion of spirituality (contemplation, meditation, and private rituals) with the technologies of political activism (protests, demonstrations, and speakouts). Anzaldúa's thinking pushed beyond reductionist ways of understanding borderlands theory and toward more inclusionary, relational worldviews rooted in spirituality.

Lastly, Anzaldúa's sci-fi critiques notions of "reality" and asks why alternative realities, such as dream worlds, cannot also be seen as legitimate realities. As she noted in the foreword to the second edition of *This Bridge Called My Back*, the world of dreams can potentially impel us to "break with routines and oppressive customs" (2009a, 73). Playing with the idea of the "real" and "fiction," Anzaldúa turns these worlds upside down and brings them together to create alternative spaces and agents moving across them. By appropriating the genre of science fiction that lends itself to such questioning, Anzaldúa asks us to deconstruct dominant reality and the status quo—to look at the cracks between realities such as rigid notions of identity, the linearity of time, and the boundaries of the body. In an interview with Andrea Lunsford, she explains,

> You can recreate reality. . . . When we're born we're taught by our culture that this is up and that is down, and that's a piece of wood, and that's a no-no. To change the tree, the up and down, and the no-no, you have to get the rest of your peers to see things in this same way—that's not a tree and that's not a no-no. We all created this physics, this quantum mechanics; now we all have to recreate something different. . . . One of the members of the tribe has to start making that aperture, that little hole, that crack. . . . And once you have this consensual view of reality, along comes Anzaldúa who says, "No, that's just the reality of your particular people—who are Indo-European, or Western, or Inuit, or whatever. Here's a different way of looking at reality." (2000d, 270)

Guided by this vision, Anzaldúa's sci-fi articulates notions of "fiction" and "reality," decentering the status quo and centering alternative realities. These include metaphysical realities rooted in what AnaLouise Keating calls a metaphysics of interconnectedness, which "posits a cosmic, constantly changing spirit or force which embodies itself in material and nonmaterial forms" (2012, 62). That is, through this political move,

Anzaldúa asks: Who constructs these politicized worlds, and what are their material implications?

Recoveries and Readings of Gloria Anzaldúa's Published and Unpublished Sci-Fi Short Stories

Anzaldúa's science fiction introduces the unique dimensions of her nepantler@ paradigm that I have outlined above. "Reading LP" (2009c), included in *The Gloria Anzaldúa Reader*, is one of her two published science fiction stories and contains scenarios that involve teleporting across and in between time, space, and the material body. Anzaldúa consciously wrote it as a sci-fi piece, and several drafts of earlier versions can be found in the Benson Latin American Collection under multiple titles, including "Entremados de LP." The story takes place in a contemporary rural setting, on a Texas ranch formerly owned by the main character, La Prieta (a diminutive for "dark-skinned one"), who inherited the ranch and renamed it La Tigresa. The two main characters are LP (short for La Prieta), a Tejana dyke graduate student, and her racially ambiguous lesbian partner Bar-Su. This coupling resists exotifications of brown bodies or lesbian couples; even in their "sex scene," the characters speak in code to deflect the male gaze.

In this story we see traces of Anzaldúa's new mestiza in the character of Bar-Su; however, LP pushes us in new directions. Every time LP picks up the book *Entremados*, for instance, it triggers strong teleportations through painful "entremados," a state of being in between walls, where realities of everyday life converge with the reality of "that other place" (Anzaldúa 2009c, 269). As LP teleports from one space to another, she finds herself literally between two walls and feels herself yanked into the "reality" of the book. In this entremados space, the quintessential liminal space, she loses sense of time and feels herself part of a continuum. Even her body expands beyond its physical confines, illustrating the nepantler@ challenge to, and reimagining of, the "reality" of, false constructs such as time, as well as the boundaries of the body. Each time she teleports, LP gains new understandings of the "real."

When the story opens, LP suddenly finds herself in a well, surrounded by water, with no tools for navigating this space, and she must travel up the shaft of the well to catch her breath. The closing scene of this speculative narrative, along with its ethereal setting, also brings her back to water, and again she finds herself in a tunnel-like space she must navigate to reach the other side. The narrator describes this shift:

> She's in some kind of tunnel. Or she's inside a serpent—yeah, she's been
> devoured by the earth serpent. No, this is more like a birth canal. (267)

Anzaldúa later develops the significance of such a passageway through her
theory of the Coatlicue state:

> In the midst of the Coatlicue state—the cave, the dark—you're hibernat-
> ing or hiding, you're gestating and giving birth to yourself. (2000a, 226)

The serpent is also significant as symbolic image of "counterknowledge"
(Anzaldúa 2000d, 266). Through these constant teleportation experiences
triggered by the reading of the book *Entremados*, LP comes to realize that
there are other realities beyond the boundaries of time, space, and body,
but that she must first make painful crossings through this figural "birth
canal" to reach them (2009c, 267). In so doing, Anzaldúa calls attention
to the elusiveness of reality and the potential to expand on the material
body and become part of a larger cosmos.

However, this *conocimiento* requires letting go of imposed social narratives that limit our existence. As the narrative progresses, LP states:

> The book. It's opened up some kind of passage. And now I don't even
> need the book to get to the other place. When I'm en ese otro lugar I'm
> not the same as the me here and now. (269)

Opening the *Entremados* book offers LP wider awareness and opens locked
knowledge systems, much as does the "red pill of truth" in the popular
sci-fi film *The Matrix*. Echoing Foucault's concept of power/knowledge,
Anzaldúa has noted elsewhere that the notion of what is "real" is fed to
us over and over, so that at some point one no longer needs policing to
maintain these realities; instead they become "The Truth." An example is
the historical narratives taught by the public school system (2000b, 163).
Anzaldúa's depictions of nepantler@s in this story, and in her other sci-fi
stories, remind us that there are realities and other truths beyond dominant
realities that privilege the few, but that we must be willing to make painful
spiritual crossings through Coatlicue states to discover them. Significantly,
in "Reading LP," this process involves embodiment and the simultaneous
transcendence of it in ways only speculative literature allows.

Anzaldúa's theory of nepantler@ consciousness also is poignantly
depicted in a transembodied and transspecies embodiment in "Werejaguar"
(1991), an unpublished science fiction piece found in the Anzaldúa Papers.
In this story, La Prieta, a recurring semi-autobiographical character in

Anzaldúa's sci-fi stories, begins teleporting between her material world and dream world. In her dream world, she meets a half-female, half-animal entity and begins to fantasize with this hybrid species. Finding herself caught between the realities of her dream world and her waking world, LP begins to blur the line between the two. Anzaldúa speaks to this in an interview with Christine Weiland: "I think that process happens naturally when you sleep. You leave your body. You go out in the astral" (2000e, 99). By the end of the story, La Prieta herself transforms into a werejaguar, and she, like the reader, cannot tell in which world this is happening.

Shape shifting is a recurring concept in Anzaldúa's sci-fi stories, one that she carries over to her theorizing about social change. In an interview with AnaLouise Keating, she states:

> I don't see why in the future I can't literally transform my body into a jaguar. But right now such transformations are limited to the beliefs of the majority of people and they don't believe it can be done. I think this is the great turning point of the century: we're going to leave the rigidity of this concrete reality and expand it. (2000c, 285)

Anzaldúa introduces shape shifting as a viable reality in her science fiction and understands that current notions of "reality" are what limit her holistic spiritual potential. In a blurring of sci-fi with the fact of her existence, she continues:

> In actuality I don't think that my hands can become flesh-and-blood claw and my mouth a jaguar mouth. I can't do it in my flesh-and-blood body but in my other body, I can. I also think that you can lose that body, just like people can misplace their souls. It can stay in the jaguar reality, in the jaguar form. (284)

In thinking through a transcorporeal ontology, Anzaldúa acknowledges the limitations of the physical realm as far as shape shifting into different hybrid forms such as a "werejaguar." She proposes expanding our concepts of reality in order to expand our cosmos, and our spiritual agency within it.

Anzaldúa's "Puddles" (1992) is a shorter, published bilingual science fiction piece, with many unpublished edited drafts, before and after the published draft, contained in the Anzaldúa Papers. This story also engages with transspecies ontologies, as characters convert into lizard-like beings after coming into contact with a contagious disease suggestive of the AIDS epidemic of the 1970s. Those afflicted see their skin transform into a green, reptilian wrinkled armor, which spooks people away. At times they emit a green liquid. Significantly, when characters experience these green "puddles," they begin to feel a profound hyperempathy toward "the other." Here, shape-shifting elements enact a critique of the ongoing AIDS epidemic and discrimination against HIV-positive and AIDS patients as yet another group of outcast, marginalized people. For Anzaldúa, however, the transspecies metaphor—already endowed with positive and empowering significance in her speculative stories—presents a scenario in which this "disease" creates a sense of interconnectivity rather than estrangement. In this short story, instead of the "disease" being demonized, it offers the potential for learning and empathy. This allows those afflicted to gain a new awareness, which is emblematic of Anzaldúa's theory of *la facultad* that she further develops in *Borderlands*. According to Anzaldúa, *la facultad* is

> the capacity to see in surface phenomena the meaning of deeper realities, to see the deep structure below the surface. . . . Those who are pounced on the most have it the strongest—the females, the homosexuals of all races, the darkskinned, the outcast, the persecuted, the marginalized, the foreign. (1987, 60)

Characters afflicted with "puddles" embody this newfound *facultad*, a form of knowledge that shields them and equips them for survival as they are shunned by their communities.

Prieta, a Tejana dyke waitress and the main character of "Puddles," contracts the disease from a customer, a gay man who always leaves a green puddle on his chair. Though he never speaks, he exchanges "a knowing look" with her (Anzaldúa 1992, 43). The third-person omniscient narrator describes the gradual change in Prieta's body: "se convertía en cuerpo de lagarto" (she transformed into the body of a lizard) (44). Interestingly, this metamorphosis equips her with extra intuitive knowledge. By the fourth day, she knows customers' orders before they even open their mouths. Equipped with this intuitive knowledge or *facultad*, Prieta discovers that one of her customers intends to sexually assault his daughter. She threatens to turn him green, like herself, if he does anything to his daughter, thereby exploiting the fear of contagion even as she deploys this difference as subaltern counterhegemonic power. Soon after, she loses her job, but she discovers her bigger calling as a nepantler@, which in this context is fundamentally transspecies. Prieta decides she will move from town to town, keep her knees covered, and "let slide a puddle of tears" (44), thereby troping yet again the operative term and title of the story. In this story, we are reminded that nepantler@s are agents constantly moving in between time and space and beyond the material body to challenge and reimagine the "reality" of these constructs. Significantly, Anzaldúa's reimagining offers a speculative world in which difference is power, which she would later synthesize in similar yet also different ways in *Borderlands*.

Anzaldúa's sci-fi resists traditional heteronormative readings, and her nepantler@s introduce new cosmologies. I add that nepantler@ visions teleport us between the past, present, and *future* to demonstrate more expansive notions beyond colonial imaginaries. Nepantler@s belong to many worlds simultaneously, refusing to entirely adopt or belong to any one worldview or identity; they find themselves in the "cracks between worlds." Anzaldúa's science fiction begins by asking us to consider whose reality we are privileging. Currently, we center a concrete material reality in the dominant Western world that is devoid of spirit (or one in which spirituality often is rendered as highly politicized organized religion). But through the reclamation of conventional sci-fi technologies such as transtemporal locations, teleportation, and transspecies characters, Anzaldúa constructs alternative in-between realities. In her subsequent interviews and other writings, Anzaldúa asks us to consider whether these in-between spaces might also be potential and actual realities.

It is important to reiterate that for Anzaldúa, nepantler@ visions are not simply an amalgam of different realities but a critical analysis of these realities. In her science fiction, she extends arguments about a synthesis of the borderlands and moves beyond an overemphasis on the materiality of the borderlands. As she states in *Interviews/Entrevistas*, borderlands theory was not meant to be an exclusively material phenomenon, but academics and scholars refused to see the strong politic of spirit infused in her borderlands theory (quoted in Keating 2000, 7). So she offered her theories of nepantla and nepantleras with more pronounced spiritual resonance to resist such readings.[8] In so doing, she invites us to consider spiritual and metaphysical dimensions of existence that are interconnected with material realities and earth-centered worldviews, thereby enabling us to speculate on how transspecies, transspatial, and transtemporal nepantler@ subjectivities can also become a powerful praxis.

The preliminary readings of Gloria Anzaldúa's sci-fi writings invite further study. Similar attention should be given to nepantler@ authors and artists who have yet to be discovered or fully examined. By recuperating these sci-fi stories by Anzaldúa, I am in conversation with work on the recovery of Chicana lesbian texts being done by scholar Catrióna Rueda Esquibel, who emphasizes the need to "gather lost stories and tell them to new generations of women and men who never knew what came before"

(2006, xvi). Without such stories, we are left with an incomplete genealogy of Raza sci-fi that leaves out "the females, the homosexuals of all races, the darkskinned, the outcast, the persecuted, the marginalized, the foreign" (Anzaldúa 1987, 38). This work continues.

Notes

I would like to thank Ben V. Olguín and Cathryn J. Merla-Watson for their ongoing support through the long editing process. Thank you for supporting my work, and for believing in me. Special thanks to the editors of *Aztlán*, particularly Cathy Sunshine. Your patience and generosity helped push my essay to the next level. I could not ask for better editors. Mil gracias a mis papás, que aunque a veces no entienden lo que hago, siempre me apoyan completamente. I owe special thanks to Elizabeth Rodríguez, whose unconditional love nourished me throughout the writing process. Additionally, I am grateful to the spirit of Gloria E. Anzaldúa, whose writing continues to inspire me in profound new ways throughout the years.

    1. I describe speculative fiction that centers on *la raza*, the broad category of people of Mexican descent and primarily from working-class communities, as Raza sci-fi.

    2. *Chicano Now!* was a collaboration with the comedian Cheech Marin, who provided paintings from his personal collection. It was underwritten in part by the department store Target and was directed at both Latino and mass audiences.

    3. I use *Chicano* deliberately to demonstrate the absence of gender and sexuality in early discussions of science fiction.

    4. The most recent version is titled "Reading LP" and can be found in *The Gloria Anzaldúa Reader*, edited by AnaLouise Keating (Anzaldúa 2009b).

    5. In a glossary appended to *The Gloria Anzaldúa Reader*, AnaLouise Keating defines *conocimiento* as a "nonbinary, connectionist mode of thinking. . . . Conocimiento underscores and develops the imaginal, spiritual-activist, and radically inclusionary possibilities implicit in these earlier previous theories" (Anzaldúa 2009b, 320).

    6. According to Anzaldúa, spiritual activism is the amalgam of "inner works" and "public acts." Spiritual activism urges us to respond not just with the traditional practices of spirituality (contemplation, meditation, and private rituals) or with technologies of political activism (protests, demonstrations, and speakouts), but with both.

    7. When speaking directly about Anzaldúa's "nepantlera," I omit the "@" symbol in deference to her orthography. When speaking about my own expansion of the concept, I include the "@" symbol as a reflection of the productively disruptive inclusiveness that Sandra Soto proposes and that the editors have affirmed in their introduction to this dossier.

    8. According to Anzaldúa, "The 'safe' elements in *Borderlands* are appropriated and used, and the 'unsafe' elements are ignored. One of the things that doesn't

get talked about is the connection between body, mind, and spirit. Nor is anything that has to do with the sacred, anything that has to do with the spirit. As long as it's theoretical and about history, about borders, that's fine; borders are a concern that everybody has. But when I start talking about nepantla—as a border between the spirit, the psyche, and the mind or as a process—they resist" (from a 1993 interview, quoted in Keating 2000, 7).

Works Cited

Alarcón, Norma. 2006. "Chicana Feminism: In the Tracks of 'the' Native Woman." In *Cultural Representation in Native America*, edited by Andrew Jolivétte, 119–30. Lanham, MD: AltaMira.

Anzaldúa, Gloria E. 1987. *Borderlands/La Frontera: The New Mestiza*. San Francisco: Aunt Lute.

———. 1991. "Werejaguar." Manuscript drafts. Box 82, folders 1–6, Gloria Evangelina Anzaldúa Papers, Benson Latin American Collection, University of Texas, Austin.

———. 1992. "Puddles." In *New Chicana/Chicano Writing*, vol. 1, edited by Charles Tatum, 43–45. Tucson: University of Arizona Press.

———. 2000a. "Doing Gigs: Speaking, Writing, and Change: An Interview with Debbie Blake and Carmen Abrego (1994)." In Anzaldúa 2000b, 211–33.

———. 2000b. *Interviews/Entrevistas*. Edited by AnaLouise Keating. New York: Routledge.

———. 2000c. "Last Words? Spirit Journeys: An Interview with AnaLouise Keating (1998–1999)." In Anzaldúa 2000b, 281–91.

———. 2000d. "Toward a Mestiza Rhetoric: Gloria Anzaldúa on Composition, Postcoloniality, and the Spiritual: An Interview with Andrea Lunsford (1996)." In Anzaldúa 2000b, 251–80.

———. 2000e. "Within the Crossroads: Lesbian/Feminist/Spiritual Development: An Interview with Christine Weiland (1983)." In Anzaldúa 2000b, 71–127.

———. 2009a. "Foreword to the Second Edition (of *This Bridge Called My Back*)." In Anzaldúa 2009b, 72–73.

———. 2009b. *The Gloria Anzaldúa Reader*. Edited by AnaLouise Keating. Durham, NC: Duke University Press.

———. 2009c. "Reading LP." In Anzaldúa 2009b, 250–73.

———. 2009d. "Speaking across the Divide." In Anzaldúa 2009b, 282–94.

Cárdenas, Reyes. 2013. *Los Pachucos y La Flying Saucer*. In *Reyes Cárdenas: Chicano Poet, 1970–2010*. San Antonio: Aztlán Libre.

Delgadillo, Theresa. 2011. *Spiritual Mestizaje: Religion, Gender, Race, and Nation in Contemporary Chicana Narrative*. Durham, NC: Duke University Press.

Esquibel, Catrióna Rueda. 2006. *With Her Machete in Her Hand: Reading Chicana Lesbians*. Austin: University of Texas Press.

Keating, AnaLouise. 2000. "Risking the Personal." Introduction to Anzaldúa 2000b, 1–15.

———2006. "From Borderlands and New Mestizas to Nepantlas and Nepantleras: Anzaldúan Theories for Social Change." *Human Architecture: Journal of the Sociology of Self-Knowledge* 4, no. 3: 5–16.

———. 2012. "Speculative Realism, Visionary Pragmatism, and Poet-Shamanic Aesthetics in Gloria Anzaldúa—and Beyond." *WSQ: Women's Studies Quarterly* 40, nos. 3–4: 51–69.

———. 2013. *Transformation Now! Toward a Post-Oppositional Politics of Change.* Urbana: University of Illinois Press.

Merla-Watson, Cathryn J. 2013. "Haunted by Voices: Historical Im/Materialism and Gloria Anzaldúa's Mestiza Consciousness." In *El Mundo Zurdo 3: Selected Works from the 2012 Meeting of the Society for the Study of Gloria Anzaldúa,* edited by Larissa Mercado-López, Sonia Saldívar-Hull, and Antonia Castañeda, 225–42. San Francisco: Aunt Lute.

Pérez, Emma. 1999. *The Decolonial Imaginary: Writing Chicanas into History.* Bloomington: Indiana University Press.

Ramírez, Catherine S. 2002a. "Cyborg Feminism: The Science Fiction of Octavia E. Butler and Gloria Anzaldúa." In *Reload: Rethinking Women + Culture,* edited by Mary Flanagan and Austin Booth, 374–402. Cambridge, MA: MIT Press.

———. 2002b. "Deus ex machina: Tradition, Technology, and the Chicanafuturist Art of Marion C. Martinez." *Aztlán: A Journal of Chicano Studies* 29, no. 2: 55–92.

———. 2008. "Afrofuturism/Chicanafuturism: Fictive Kin." *Aztlán: A Journal of Chicano Studies* 33, no. 1: 185–94.

Ranft, Erin. 2013. "Black and Chicana Feminisms, Science Fiction, and US Women's Bodily Oppressions in the Past, Present, and Future." PhD diss., University of Texas, San Antonio.

Rivera, Lysa. 2012. "Future Histories and Cyborg Labor: Reading Borderlands Science Fiction after NAFTA." *Science Fiction Studies* 39, no. 3: 415–36.

Sandoval, Chela. 2000. *Methodology of the Oppressed.* Minneapolis: University of Minnesota Press.

Soto, Michael. 2003. "*Museo* Without Walls." Review of *Chicano Now: American Expressions* by Cheech Marin, at Museo Americano, San Antonio. *American Quarterly* 55, no. 1: 89–102.

Soto, Sandra K. 2010. *Reading Like a Queer: The De-Mastery of Desire.* Austin: University of Texas Press.

Valdez, Luis. 1971. *Los Vendidos.* In *Actos y El Teatro Campesino.* Fresno, CA: Cucaracha.

Reading Jaime Hernandez's Comics as Speculative Fiction

Shelley Streeby

When Los Bros Hernandez's *Love and Rockets* first appeared in the early 1980s, one of its most eye-catching elements was the comic's play with the icons and codes of science fiction and fantasy (SFF). A striking example is the third issue. Gilbert's front cover features a masked female superhero holding a baby, from whose eyes stream rays of green light bisecting the darkness of the nighttime cityscape, while on the back cover Jaime's dystopian, near-future, bad-ass punk girl with a "Mi Vida Loca" tattoo fights a giant killer robot in a post-apocalyptic war-world (fig. 1). Jaime's most famous character, Maggie, who started out fixing robots and rockets all over the globe, is depicted on several covers in full sci-fi glory. In issue no. 5, she glamorously pilots her own ship while two other rocket ships hover in the background, sharing the puffy white clouds (fig. 2). Issue no. 7 finds her in the arms of a giant golden robot, wrenches hanging off her belt, amid a crowd of strange smaller robots and robot parts (fig. 3). Clearly these gorgeous SFF covers were a huge part of *Love and Rockets'* visual appeal to the readers who clamored for the comic.

Featuring stories written by Jaime, Gilbert, and occasionally Mario, *Love and Rockets* opened the door to a new wave of alternative comics that began to flourish in the wake of the Hernandez brothers' success. But I argue that it is also important to see the comic as part of a constellation of Latina/o speculative fiction and speculative arts, which significantly distorts, denaturalizes, and thereby reimagines racialized hierarchies of space, race, gender, and sexuality since the long 1970s (Rosenberg and Rusert 2014). Much of the best of the relatively scant scholarship on Jaime's stories in *Love and Rockets* has explored how they document and imaginatively respond to Southern California spaces and movements, such as the punk Latina

Figure 1. Back cover of Love and Rockets, *no. 3 (Summer 1983). Reproduced by permission of Jaime Hernandez and Fantagraphics.*

Figure 2. Front cover of Love and Rockets, *no. 5 (March 1984). Reproduced by permission of Jaime Hernandez and Fantagraphics.*

73

Figure 3. Front cover of Love
and Rockets, no. 7 (July 1984).
Reproduced by permission of Jaime
Hernandez and Fantagraphics.

world of late twentieth-century Southern California. In *Loca Motion*, for
instance, Michelle Habell-Pallán situates *Love and Rockets* in relation to
the emergence in the late 1970s and early 1980s of "a punk 'Do It Yourself'
Chicana grass-roots feminist cultural production" (2005, 149) that was a
significant source of feminist theory. A few years later, Jessica Jones ana-
lyzed the 2005 anthology of Jaime's Maggie and Hopey stories to support
her argument that they dramatize "the production of bodies in space" and
thereby help to "reimagine the barrio as a queer world" (2009, 42, 44). In
what follows, I build on this work but also insist that the genres of science
fiction and fantasy are not extraneous nor an obstacle to the more serious
project of imagining nonnormative worlds, bodies, and ways of living that
unsettle and transform hierarchies of gender, sexuality, class, and race in
Southern California spaces. Instead, I argue, the codes of SFF have always
been and continue to be central to Jaime Hernandez's speculative fictions
of alternate Chicano worlds, histories, and futures.

World Building in Chicana/o Speculative Fiction

Here I deliberately choose the term *speculative fiction*, an umbrella category
that draws genre boundaries expansively to encompass heterogeneous forms
and genres of writing, notably including science fiction and fantasy, as well

as work by people of color. At the same time, however, I want to hold on to the genre terms *science fiction* and *fantasy* rather than abandoning them or replacing them with other terms that have enjoyed more literary prestige, such as *magical realism*. Science fiction and fantasy are subsets of speculative fiction and two of its main motors, but like comics they have been greatly underappreciated and often misunderstood when not maligned as hopelessly low forms of culture. In contrast, I suggest that in Jaime Hernandez's comics, SFF has always provided crucial tools that shape the greatness of his art, and that it is precisely the juxtaposition and convergence of the codes of SFF and realism that makes possible the transformation of normative spaces and ways of living and the building of nonnormative worlds. As well, I argue that the codes of SFF interrupt sociological clichés about barrio life and working-class Latina/os that only reproduce damage, as Jaime speculates on the quotidian by distorting his present and thereby imagines other worlds and futures.

The great SFF writer Samuel Delany defines science fiction as, among other things, a genre that uses the future as a narrative convention to produce significant distortions of the present (2012, 26–27). Jaime Hernandez, in the alternate comic worlds that he imagines, plays with SFF conventions to distort the present in multiple ways.[1] In what follows, I argue that reading Jaime's work as speculative fiction helps us see him as a major contributor to this genre, which has become increasingly important for writers and artists of color since the 1970s. It also helps make visible a longer history of Chicana/o science fiction and fantasy production that is almost always ignored by those telling the story of the SFF genres in the United States.

In thinking about how speculative fiction encompasses the genres of SFF and about how Jaime plays with those codes to imagine alternate worlds, it is useful to consider Delany's theory that science fiction is a reading practice involving particular protocols and codes around world building: "If we read in an SF story about a person who wakes up transformed into a bug, we are certainly concerned with how the person will react; but the underlying question that guides even that concern is this: What *in the world of the story* caused it to occur?" (Delany 2012, 136, emphasis in original). In other words, people and bugs may figure in a range of cultural forms, but the SF reader knows she must work from the start to figure out the rules of the story's world, which is not our world, though it should be a significant distortion of our present. Thus there is a certain imaginative world building required of the reader as well as the writer of SFF. Delany concludes that "*How would the world of the story have to be different from our world in order for this to occur?* is the question around which the play of differences in the

SF text is organized" (136, emphasis in original). That is, readers of SFF will expect the world of the story to swerve away from their own world even as it references that world in distorted form, and figuring out the play of differences is part of the pleasure and creative labor of reading science fiction.

Fantasy, on the other hand, is often what narrow definitions of science fiction are laboring to exclude. Fantasy as the Other of science fiction reinforces hierarchies of gender, race, and nation, partly because fantasy tends to be associated with women and science fiction with men, and also because Eurocentric ideas about what count as magic, science, and nature undergird most exclusionary definitions of science fiction. Therefore, in order to make visible the contributions of women, people of color, and those from outside Europe and the United States, it can be helpful to consider continuities between science fiction and fantasy, which the umbrella term SFF seeks to encourage. The related term *fantastic* is also salient in Mexican contexts, as Eduardo Jiménez Mayo, one of the editors of *Three Messages and a Warning: Contemporary Mexican Short Stories of the Fantastic* (2012), suggests in his opening remarks to that volume (xvii–xx). In the reading of Jaime Hernandez's work that follows, we will need many terms that, in the scholarship on his comics, tend to be relatively devalued or disappeared in favor of realism. Science fiction, fantasy, and the fantastic, as well as the umbrella concept of speculative fiction, are all crucial building blocks of his Chicano alternate world building.[2]

Robots, Rockets, and Realism

Critics too often belittle or deem incidental or extraneous the science fiction, fantasy, and speculative elements of Jaime's comics, with some claiming that he experimented with SFF icons, codes, and genre conventions only to later transcend them in favor of a more complex and mature realism. Historically, both SFF and comics have been devalued within dominant cultural hierarchies, so it makes sense that those wanting to endow *Love and Rockets* with more cultural capital would fear SFF's degrading contamination and would suggest instead that Jaime's comics were like realist novels. But even though Jaime has said that for a while in the 1980s and 1990s he tried to take a "harder, grittier path" and "put reality in front of my readers as best I could" (Aldama 2009, 186), more recently he has added, "I'm really not worried about ruining the reality of it. Maybe because it's just something I grew up with in comics. That the real life and fantasy go together" (Champion 2012). In other words, instead of settling on a progress narrative in which a movement from SFF to realism is crucial to claiming greatness for his art, Jaime argues that the convergence of "real life" and "fantasy" is one of the distinctive aspects of comics, which inspires his own juxtapositions and combinations of SFF elements. He also reminds us that such convergences and juxtapositions are not exceptional but in fact are part of the long history and the grammar of comics.

The history of comics and the history of science fiction and fantasy are in many ways inseparable, since they emerged from the same world of sensational newspapers, dime novels, and pulp magazines of the late nineteenth and early twentieth centuries. While female mechanics were relatively unfamiliar figures in popular culture at the time that Jaime's Maggie the Mechanic appeared, there is a long history of female adventure stories in which "female" is added as an adjective to an occupation (implicitly understood as normally male) in the title, such as *The Female Land Pirate*, *The Female Marine*, *The Female Criminal*, and so forth. By the turn of the twentieth century, the boy inventors and mechanics of dime novels and serialized story-paper fiction in newspapers, and, later, the engineers and pilots of pulp science fiction and early comics, sometimes had "female" counterparts—tomboyish girls who challenge the rules of gender and sexuality by wanting to do what is usually reserved for boys, even as their beauty and appeal to men suggest that their tomboy status is a transitional stage, like a butterfly's cocoon (Streeby 2002, 83–135).

Science fiction as a genre is deeply entangled with this history of cheap stories of invention, engineering, transport, and mechanics. Maggie's persistent love for Hopey, along with Jaime's many other changes to the usual story, fundamentally transforms the popular conventions of female adventure, which often pivot on the whiteness of the heroine. Yet Maggie's character type—the plucky and gender-transgressive girl or woman who takes on a "male" occupation—is familiar from the subgenre of female adventure first popularized in dime novels, cheap newspapers, and pulp science fiction magazines. Jaime thus brings together the histories of female adventure, science fiction, and comics, juxtaposing dinosaurs with rocket ships as Maggie travels the world "to fix rockets and robots and have adventures" (Hernandez 1983c).

In *Love and Rockets*, the rockets and robots blast Maggie out of her usual space-time continuum, juxtaposing the realist details that make up her life at home with other worlds where things are dramatically different and where almost anything is possible, notably including revolution in the first stories. This female adventure story transports its heroine across the globe to help fix a rocket that crashed into the jungle years ago. Stuck in the mud next to the rocket is a giant dinosaur, a fantastic juxtaposition that is another example of Jaime's imaginative mixing of different temporalities, another way he puts pressure on realist notions of time. While in Zymbodia, Maggie comes under the tutelage of Rena Titañon, a former superhero and female world wrestling champion from whom Maggie's Aunt Vicki stole the title. Rena ostensibly came to Zymbodia to do research on why dinosaurs were still alive there and why ones from so many different times existed, but she was actually there to covertly help incite revolution, a project that ends up succeeding. When Rena "wasn't in the ring she was trotting the globe fighting monsters and crooks, starting revolutions and all other types of heroics" (Hernandez 1983a, 13). At the end of this story, it turns out that "the people of Zymbodia planned to destroy their self-appointed leader" all along and had thus called in Rena, who "shows the people how to think free then moves on" (40). In these ways, Jaime's strange juxtapositions and convergences open up the possibility that the scene of the static "real" can be reimagined and transformed, partly by playing with and unsettling realist notions of time and temporality.

Chicano SFF Speculations on the Quotidian

At the same time, the juxtaposition of the quotidian and mundane with the fantastic and the science fictional also makes us look differently at what gets reified as the real; it denaturalizes and changes our perspective on what we thought was familiar and forces us to look again. One of the most memorable aspects of *Love and Rockets* is Jaime's time-capsule capturing of key details of turn-of-the-twenty-first-century working-class life in Southern California, including its low-rise sprawl; architectural styles such as dingbats and stucco apartment complexes; the look of the streets from the perspective of those who walk as well as those who drive; neighborhood restaurants, thrift stores, and barber shops; the particularities of style and fashion, especially those of the punk world; lettering and icons on signs, posters, and billboards; the creative interior decoration in working-class apartments; the inside of clubs; party scenes; and so on. Because of these oft-remarked layers of detail, comics scholar Scott McCloud classifies Jaime as an artist who combines "very iconic characters with unusually realistic backgrounds," allowing readers to "mask themselves in a character and safely enter a sensually stimulating world" (1993, 43). Jaime both embraces and swerves away from the mundane, however, by imagining sensually stimulating alternate worlds that do not reproduce static, sociological conceptions of barrio life. The codes of science fiction and fantasy are indispensable to this project.

Many *Love and Rockets* readers appreciated that the convergence of SFF and realism was one of the things that made the comic great. Thus Fantagraphics editor Gary Groth's periodic references to the demise of science fiction in the comic caused some readers to write in and argue that *Love and Rockets'* unusual take on science fiction was a big part of its appeal. In one of the first published letters from a female fan, which appeared in *Love and Rockets* 1, no. 9 (November 1984), the author, "Karen Weiss and her friends," wrote that she especially appreciated the combination of realism—the layers of details depicting the lives of these "amazing chicks"—and fantasy in Jaime's stories:

> It's incredible that Jaime, by all accounts a male, should have such insights into female friendships, feelings, and fashions. The excellence of the plot and plight of these amazing chicks is rivaled only by the artwork involved in their depiction. Every weird angle, reverse negative, bizarre shadow, piece of graffiti, rip in the sleeper-sofa, visible panty-line, ace bandage all enrich this very real fantasy.

Although many artists have used detailed depictions of working-class neighborhoods to suggest that the lives of their inhabitants are fixed, static, and defined by loss and pain, Jaime's juxtaposition of realism and SFF, this fan suggests, interrupts these clichés that only reproduce damage. The comic not only sees beauty in what others' limited imaginations render as simply ugly and lacking but also speculates on the quotidian in light of the fantastic and science fictional, thereby putting pressure on dominant, static framings of the "real."

In the fourth issue, for instance, the narrator begins to characterize Maggie and Hopey by stringing together a list of stereotypical sociological details, but then the sentence takes a surprising turn: "They live in a small run-down apartment in a Mexican neighborhood, always without food, months behind on rent, and rumor has it that they're lesbians. How perfect can you get? The only thing she doesn't have is superpowers. But wait, she has a job" (Hernandez 1983c, 1). While the first four details sound like a predictable litany of working-class deprivation, Jaime humorously transforms lack into plenitude and abundance, deeming Maggie's and Hopey's arty, marginal, nonbourgeois, possibly lesbian life "perfect" rather than aberrant or insufficient. Revising the initial claim that the only thing Maggie lacks is "superpowers," Jaime suggests that Maggie manifests superpowers in her daily life, in her job as a mechanic, which cracks the deficit lens through which urban working-class worlds and queer lives and times are often viewed.

And these realist scenes of Maggie and Hopey in the neighborhood streets, in a car packed full of *locas*, in bed, at the barbershop, and so forth share space with other stories in which Maggie is transported to other worlds or in which she is a superhero, such as "Maggie v. Manniak." The superhero storylines in Jaime's comics are important from the beginning, especially in the narrative arc of Penny Century (Beatríz García), a character from back home who somehow turns up across the globe in Zymbodia. Beatríz is also an avid comic book reader who longs for superpowers, and it is her desire that provokes the telling of Maggie's own story about how she was a superhero once. Following a familiar pattern, Jaime explains the birth of superheroes and super-villains by telling a story about science run amok. While fixing a highly delicate mini-transporter as part of her first job as a pro-solar mechanic, Maggie plays with the machine and ends up inadvertently liberating Manniak, "voyager of the cosmic stream" and "possessor of the infinitesimal [sic] power of the universe," thereby enabling him to return to our world, which he plans to dominate and rule (Hernandez 1983b, 25). To avert disaster, Maggie researches superhero comic history and finds an old Ultimax comic, which explains how Ultimax once defeated Manniak. Before Ultimax will agree to save the world, however, he requires Maggie to join him as a superhero sidekick in this endeavor. The alternate worlds that Maggie and Penny Century inhabit are connected because Jaime's characters appear in both, miraculously recognizable, as one reader commented, despite dramatic changes in setting and in how the characters look. This juxtaposition and convergence of the codes of realism and SFF transports and transforms Jaime's characters, unsettling familiar stereotypes about barrio life to insist that other worlds are possible, both within and outside the everyday working-class spaces of greater Latino Los Angeles.

Another unusual story of transport and mobility that adapts SFF codes in the early issues features a young black woman, Rocky (short for Rocket), and her robot Fumble, who inhabit a near-future world. Jaime introduced Rocky and Fumble in the fourth issue, along with the story about Maggie's and Hopey's "perfect" life that's better than having superpowers; Rocky and Fumble also appear at the bottom of the front cover, juxtaposed to Jaime's *locas* and female figures from Gilbert's stories. The beautiful space scenes and the unusual characters are the most striking aspects of these stories, which are episodic and do not unfold in a linear progression. A later issue travels backward in time to provide Fumble's origin story: the garbage man, who had previously given Rocky wonderful unexpected presents like a copy of "Dennis the Menace in Mexico," gifts her with a cast-off robot which, with her dad's help, soon comes to life, making her the happiest little girl in the universe. (So rasquache![3] In Jaime's world, trash is something potentially valuable and generative.)

Rocky lives on a farm and longs for mobility and freedom. During a visit to her cousin in the big city, she finds a strange portal in the backyard that opens up onto the galaxies, which Rocky and Fumble decide to explore. The art is especially stunning in these sequences as Rocky climbs the backyard fence and stands looking at the universe, breathing in the smell of outer space; ascends into the stars, spinning around while holding the hand of her faithful robot; and balances on an asteroid with worlds behind her and Fumble on her shoulder. Such fantasies of transport and mobility, of not being fixed in place, interrupt the stereotypical, sociological "real" that black characters are more typically used to support. But the story ends abruptly and unexpectedly when the hole in space closes up while Fumble is away, and Rocky is forced to settle on the planet of Mako Mato, hoping that Fumble will return and that together they can find their way home.

Instead of remaining lost in space, however, Rocky later turns up in Hoppers as a friend of Danita Lincoln, one of Maggie's co-workers who briefly dates Ray, thereby further entangling realist and SFF worlds.[4] And in a recent interview, Jaime says he initially imagined the Weeper, one of the female superheroes in his post-2006 Ti-Girls stories, as one of his "old characters"—namely Rocky—in a "different dimension" (Hernandez 2012a).

Despite Rocky's return, in different forms, to the realist and SFF worlds of Jaime's later comics, the closing up of the hole in space in this 1986 issue resonates with what has become a critical commonplace: that Jaime eventually turned away from SFF to embrace a deeper realism. But the more I studied Jaime's work, the more I became convinced that this transition never fully took place. Yes, there is a deepening of the gorgeous rasquache realism of the Hoppers world, but it is striking that even when there is an explicit and self-conscious statement that the comic is moving away from SFF, its codes and conventions are still quite evident. As early as the eighth issue, for instance, editor Groth claimed that the comic was starting to lean "more toward love than rockets." He added, however, that "the rockets are still there, of course—symbolically, at least, in Jaime's adroit mixture of realism and fantasy—but the emphasis is clearly on the drama and humor found among ordinary lives." And yet, despite this professed greater attention to ordinary lives, Maggie and Rena Titañon look far from ordinary on the cover of the very next issue, where they are shown trapped in a tunnel and thigh-deep in a weird, oozing black and yellow liquid after an explosion in a robot warehouse.

But midway through the 1980s, Jaime does shift the Maggie and Hopey stories toward a more finely elaborated vision of everyday life in Hoppers and its surround. As Jaime has suggested, this was partly a response to Gilbert, who continued to create science fiction and surreal stories but began to be bolder and more experimental in imagining the characters and complex worlds of Palomar, a fictional town located somewhere south of the US-Mexico border that soon became the main setting for Gilbert's comic world. Thus it is not surprising that Jaime, working closely with Gilbert, would feel challenged to be more ambitious and serious in imagining his own art and would produce stories such as "The Death of Speedy," a 1987 tragic tale of the demise of one of the male Hoppers characters, which has been acclaimed as a masterwork and as indicating a fundamental shift in Jaime's art.[5]

Jaime's interest in exploring more facets of Maggie's character, especially her aging and her struggles with weight, also led to the deepening of his depiction of life in Hoppers. This is especially evident in the Ray Dominguez and Maggie storyline, introduced in 1987 and persisting through his latest work, which includes lush renderings of many details of their everyday lives. The June 1988 issue, for instance, features an opening full-page picture in which Maggie is curled, spoon-like, around Ray, whose penis is shown despite the usual ban on it in US popular culture. Other details, such as the records and album covers on the floor, the posters on the wall, the plaid and floral blankets, and the stripes on the rugs all add to what is in some ways a revitalized, deeper realism. But at the same time, what comics scholar Charles Hatfield characterizes as the achievement of "a startling degree of realism" (2005, 72), comparable to the "deep focus" (73) of photography and cinema, coexists with Jaime's continuing interest in female superheroes and SFF codes.

Rena Titañon is just one member of the extensive multigenerational female superhero crew that Jaime has drawn so lovingly from the earliest days of the comic to the present. Penny Century/Beatríz García is another significant SFF character who inhabits the *Love and Rockets* mix from the beginning. Penny eventually marries billionaire H. R. Costigan, whose prominent horns are one sign of this character's distance from a realist

universe. During the five-year hiatus (1996–2001) between the two volumes of *Love and Rockets*, Jaime even made Penny the star of a new comic
bearing her name. On the cover of the first issue in December 1997, she is
resplendent in a superhero costume, complete with cape, boots, and tiny
purse. Inside are stories that connect her superhero world to the many other
worlds that Jaime imagines.

It is important to note that Penny moves back and forth between Maggie's, Hopey's, and Ray's worlds. In other words, she is not isolated in her
SFF world but brings SFF elements with her when she crosses over into the
Hoppers world. For instance, in a one-page episode called "I Am From Earth,"
sandwiched in between stories about Maggie and Hopey, caped superhero
Penny walks the rocky terrain of an alien planet with two other female
superheroes, telling them about the strange ways of Earth and about two of
her friends who are hopelessly in love with each other but are constantly
on the run from each other—an allusion to Maggie and Hopey that further
entangles these converging universes (fig. 4). Jaime's juxtaposition of a kind
of quotidian working-class Latina/o Southern California realism with SFF
thus continues in these late 1990s stories rather than being left behind by
the great artist who, some suggested, had finally learned to use his gifts in the
service of realism. And after 2000, in the second series of *Love and Rockets*
and in the brothers' *New Stories*, published since 2008, the SFF elements
become, if anything, more prominent than they were in the 1990s. In the
conclusion, I suggest that when these SFF elements move to the foreground
and collide with the Hoppers universe, Jaime's converging worlds open up
new possibilities for displacing and transforming the usual "realist" chronologies of the aging female body's physical decline and irrelevance.

World-Changing Bodies Defying Space and Time: Superheroes and Wrestlers

During the 1990s, in the years before Jaime's post-2000 proliferation of nonnormative female superhero stories, the world of wrestling, which overlaps
in many ways with the superhero world, was Maggie's main connection,
along with her relationship to Beatríz/Penny, to Jaime's more fantastic
stories of female adventure. You may recall that Rena Titañon was introduced in the first issues as both a wrestler and a superhero and that Rena
had the world wrestling title stolen from her by Maggie's Aunt Vicki. In his
1990s *Whoa Nellie!* comic, Jaime brings Maggie back into Vicki's world in a
dramatic way. Among other things, Aunt Vicki teaches Maggie important

Figure 4. "I Am From Earth," Penny Century, no. 5 (1999). Reproduced by permission of Jaime Hernandez and Fantagraphics.

lessons about their illustrious lineage as the offspring of Mexican wrestlers, including a female forebear who wrestled both women and men in Mexican sideshows: "I could feel it in my bones . . . you were the one," Vicki tells her niece, disappointed that Maggie is unwilling to step into the ring and alluding to her mighty untapped powers (Hernandez 1996, 11). Throughout *Love and Rockets* and its related texts, the wrestling world and the superhero world are connected in multiple ways. For one thing, "All superheroes from Mexico started out in the ring" (Hernandez 2012b, 27). For another, there are the costumes, which Jaime loves to draw. If you're just looking at the pictures and not reading the text, it can be difficult to decide whether a given drawing shows a wrestler or a superhero—the boots, belts, elaborate outfits, and dramatic poses are the same (fig. 5). Both the superhero and the wrestler do wondrous, heroic things with their bodies—and physical action is central to stories about both superheroes and wrestlers.

This is another process that connects Jaime's work to Chicana/o working-class culture and the world of Mexican wrestling: the working body, the body that mostly labors or suffers in realist representations, instead becomes

Figure 5. "Pro Wrestling Legends Series, no. 1062." Whoa, Nellie! no. 2 (1996). Reproduced by permission of Jaime Hernandez and Fantagraphics.

superhuman, world-changing, invincible. These kinds of heroics around the physical body and the transformative possibilities of physical action are commonplace in stories about men but still relatively rare for female characters, let alone older female characters. But in Jaime's Maggie and Vicki stories, we encounter female wrestlers such as the Birmingham Lady bashers, the greatest female tag team of all time, who appear to be quite elderly and are "so awesome that they haven't changed their hairstyles since they won the belts in '72." Their advanced age meets with no derision and does not even provoke any commentary in Jaime's world, where it is not at all unusual to encounter middle-aged and elderly women whose bodies are capable of amazing things and who defy normative narratives of female aging.

In the second volume of *Love and Rockets* that began in 2001, Jaime continues to play with the codes of SFF and to juxtapose them with realism, especially by focusing on the converging worlds of multigenerational superheroes and an aging Maggie. In doing so, he puts pressure on realist notions of time and also makes fun of and upends orthodoxies around age and aging. On the one hand, Jaime has devoted much thought and talent to representing Maggie as she ages. Twenty years ago, in a *Comics Journal* interview with Neil Gaiman, he said, "Maggie I can see growing old with" (Hernandez 1995), and one of the main pleasures of reading Jaime's work through the years has been following the unpredictable and creative ways he imagines Maggie's aging. These representational methods refuse the usual timelines of female bodily decline and sexual irrelevance as well as conventional highlights of the normative female life such as childrearing. On the other hand, the realist project devoted to documenting Maggie's daily life over the decades, with its the artful accretion of telling details, is juxtaposed throughout the 2000s with SFF stories featuring Penny Century and Rena Titañon as well as female superheroes such as Space Queen and Cheetah Torpeda. These characters are straight out of the comics that Maggie reads obsessively after she stops fixing robots and rockets and instead uses her mechanical skills in her new job as a Valley apartment manager. Once again, SFF worlds and realist worlds are not separate worlds; instead they converge to create new possibilities.

These SFF comics play a significant role in Maggie's everyday life, which is only one of many ways that realist and SFF worlds continue to collide in Jaime's post-2000 work. These convergences are both imaginary and material: the comic world is an alternate world that gives Maggie strength, yet it is also a product of the imagination that does not stay in the realm of the imaginary but comes to life, affording opportunities for some characters, such as Maggie's friend Angel, to move back and forth between worlds. In a 2001 story, for instance, Maggie says the "lucky comics" that Hopey gave her when they "first started hanging out" got her through some of her "toughest bouts" of depression (Hernandez 2001, 10).

In the *New Stories* of 2008 to the present, Space Queen and Cheetah Torpeda figure in a new storyline, "The Ti-Girls Adventures" (fig. 6), which foregrounds the codes of SFF and disrupts normative narratives of the aging female body. This SFF storyline involves Penny Century, Maggie, and Angel, Maggie's new roommate and best friend, who joins the Ti-Girls after her mother reveals that she, too, used to have superpowers. "All women are born with it but most lose it at a really early age," Angel's mother tells her. She emphasizes, however, that women who access superpowers later in life make even more of an impact, since the most impressive powers tend to "blossom" when women are "much older." This account derails the usual heteronormative story in which females blossom when they're young, ripe for reproduction, and then begin their long decline. Here all females are born with superpowers: guys "gotta go out and have lab accidents and other stuff to get their cojones but we got it born right into us" (Hernandez 2012b, 82). Although many females lose these powers at an early age, perhaps as a result of the disciplinary social process of "girling," as Judith Butler

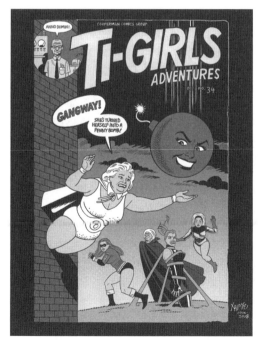

Figure 6. "Ti-Girls Adventures, no. 34." Mock cover. Love and Rockets: New Stories, no. 1 (2008). Reproduced by permission of Jaime Hernandez and Fantagraphics.

87

(1993, xvii) calls it, superpowers tend to emerge in their strongest forms when embodied by older women. Thus in Jaime's comic worlds, the aging woman's body is the site of plenitude and the locus of amazing, generative powers rather than a phobic, diminished, sad object.

The series is strongly multigenerational, especially when the first generation of Ti-Girls comes out of retirement to help, which is another way Jaime reimagines and transforms the usual chronologies of the aging female body's physical decline. Suddenly a bunch of senior citizen women are kicking serious ass, notably Fuerza/Espectra and the Weeper, the character Jaime originally based on Rocky, who wears a mask that "goes back to when her great great grandmother wore it to battle the Ku Klux Klan after the Civil War" (Hernandez 2012b, 36). Although the clueless Space Queen thinks Espectra is "just a housekeeper," she is actually the leader of the Ti-Girls, and she even has to help defeat her own evil double from the "dark depressing future" in one episode (fig. 7). There are extensive sequences of middle-aged and septuagenarian female physical action here that recall Jaime's great female wrestling sequences featuring Vicki, Rena, the Birmingham Lady Bashers, and others. At the end of the story, the Ti-Girls head off to look at photos of the Weeper's great-great-grandchild, thereby emphasizing their advanced age in a story that celebrates their heroics and that must be seen as a kind of running SFF complement and counterpoint to the realist narrative of Maggie's aging.

When these serialized stories were collected under the title *God and Science: Return of the Ti-Girls* (Hernandez 2012b), Fantagraphics advertised it as a "rollickingly creative super-hero joyride featuring three separate super-teams and over two dozen characters" and ranging "from the other side of the universe to Maggie's shabby apartment." The excerpted strip above also makes that connection, as scenes of Espectra kicking the ass of her double from the future are linked in the final frame to Maggie's and Angel's everyday lives in their Valley apartment. Angel hints that Maggie also may have the superhero "gift," and though Maggie replies, "Oh right, Angel," the reader can imagine all the ways in which it's true: Maggie is indeed a superhero, no matter what world she lives in. By bringing the other side of the universe into Maggie's apartment, Jaime and the Fantagraphics team called attention to a juxtaposition and convergence of SFF and realist worlds that has characterized Jaime's entire career. It is at the heart of his speculative brilliance, not only as one of the greatest cartoonists of all time but also as a major contributor to the Latina/o speculative arts and the SFF genres, which are key to imagining alternate worlds and futures today.

Figure 7. Love and Rockets: New Stories, no. 2 (2008). *Excerpted strip from "Part 4: Mothers of Mercy," page 9. Reproduced by permission of Jaime Hernandez and Fantagraphics.*

Notes

Thanks are due to my Comics group, funded by the Center for the Humanities at the University of California, San Diego, especially Erika Cheng, Pepé Rojo, and Emily York, for reading a draft of this article and giving me excellent comments. This piece was also much improved by the feedback of Ben Olguín and Cathryn Merla-Watson. Finally, I'm grateful that Curtis Marez put up with my fangirl mania through the fall and winter of 2014–15 as I reread everything by Jaime. I'm also lucky that he often enthusiastically joined in when I couldn't stop talking about it. Many of the ideas here emerged from our dialogue.

1. Jaime's distorted present is inspired by Oxnard, California, the city north of Los Angeles where he and Gilbert were born. They were part of a large family of five brothers and one sister whose mother, Aurora, raised them alone after her husband, Santos, died before Jaime turned eight.

2. Other work on Los Bros includes Aldama (2006, 2009), Chang (2012), Creekmur (2013), Hatfield (2005), Merino (2009, 2010), Nericcio (2002), Saldívar (1991, 2011), Saxey (2006), Scott (1995), Tullis (2014), Vargas (2010), and Wolk (2007a, 2007b).

3. Building on the work of Mesa-Bains (1999) and Ybarra-Frausto (1990), Jason Bartles suggests that "a rasquache sensibility arises among those who live the reality of the 'down but not out' and who make use of everyday materials. Instead of throwing away 'trash,' they reuse and transform those materials to get by, but also to create and embellish" (2014, 108).

4. Another example of the convergence of fantastic and realist worlds is the case of Maggie's friend Izzy Reubens, whose world includes ghosts and strange dreams that Pepé Rojo has reminded me underline the significance of a Chicano version of the Mexican fantastic in Jaime's *locas* stories.

5. See Clough (2012), McDonald (2010), and González (2013).

Works Cited

Aldama, Frederick Luis. 2006. "Jaime Hernandez of Los Bros Hernandez." In *Spilling the Beans in Chicanolandia: Conversations with Writers and Artists*, 119–28. Austin: University of Texas Press.

———. 2009. *Your Brain on Latino Comics: From Gus Arriola to Los Bros Hernandez*. Austin: University of Texas Press.

Bartles, Jason. 2014. "A Queer Chicana/o Ethics of Representation: Rasquache Camp in the Novels of Rechy and Luna Lemus." *Aztlán: A Journal of Chicano Studies* 39, no. 1, 105–32.

Butler, Judith. 1993. *Bodies that Matter: On the Discursive Limits of "Sex."* New York: Routledge.

Champion, Edward. 2012. "Gilbert and Jaime Hernandez (The Bat Segundo Show)." *Reluctant Habits*, October 11. http://www.edrants.com/gilbert-and-jaime-hernandez-the-bat-segundo-show.

Chang, Jeff. 2012. "Locas Rule." *Colorlines*, March 15. http://colorlines.com/archives/2002/03/locas_rule.html.

Clough, Rob. 2012. "A Tribute To Jaime Hernandez." *High-Low*, September 2. http://highlowcomics.blogspot.com/2012/09/a-tribute-to-jaime-hernandez.html.

Creekmur, Corey. 2013. "What It Feels Like: Childhood in Gilbert Hernandez's *Marble Season*." Afterword to *Marble Season*, by Gilbert Hernandez. Montreal: Drawn and Quarterly.

Delany, Samuel R. 2012. *Starboard Wine: More Notes on the Language of Science Fiction*. Wesleyan, CT: Wesleyan University Press.

González, Christopher. 2013. "Turf, Tags, and Territory: Spatiality in Jaime Hernandez's 'Vida Loca: The Death of Speedy Ortiz.'" *ImageTexT: Interdisciplinary Comics Studies* 7, no. 1.

Habell-Pallán, Michelle. 2005. *Loca Motion: The Travels of Chicana and Latina Popular Culture*. New York: New York University Press.

Hatfield, Charles. 2005. *Alternative Comics: An Emerging Literature*. Jackson: University Press of Mississippi.

Hernandez, Jaime. 1983a. "Mechanics." *Love and Rockets* 1, no. 2: 1–42.

———. 1983b. "Maggie vs. Manniakk." *Love and Rockets*, 1, no. 3: 25–33.

———. 1983c. "100 Rooms, Part One." *Love and Rockets* 1, no. 4: 1–6.

———. 1995. "The Hernandez Brothers." Interview by Neil Gaiman. *Comics Journal*, no. 178: 91–123.

———. 1996. "Whoa, Nellie, Part Two." *Whoa, Nellie!*, no. 2: 1–20.

———. 2001. "Maggie." *Love and Rockets* 2, no. 2: 9–20.

———. 2012a. "The Gilbert and Jaime Hernandez Interview." By Tim Hodler, Dan Nadel, and Frank Santoro. *Comics Journal*, December 13. http://www.tcj.com.

———. 2012b. *God and Science: Return of the Ti-Girls*. Seattle: Fantagraphics.

Jiménez Mayo, Eduardo. 2012. "When Fixed Ideas Take Flight." In *Three Messages and a Warning: Contemporary Mexican Short Stories of the Fantastic*, edited by Eduardo Jiménez Mayo and Chris N. Brown, xvii–xx. Easthampton, MA: Small Beer.

Jones, Jessica. 2009. "Spatializing Sexuality in Jaime Hernandez's *Locas*." *Aztlán: A Journal of Chicano Studies* 34, no. 1: 35–64.

McCloud, Scott. 1993. *Understanding Comics: The Invisible Art*. New York: Harper Collins.

McDonald, Jennifer. 2010. "Junot Díaz's 'Run, Don't Walk' Books." ArtsBeat (*New York Times*), October 19. http://artsbeat.blogs.nytimes.com/2010/10/19/junot-diazs-run-dont-walk-books/?_r=0.

Merino, Ana. 2009. "The Bros. Hernandez: A Latin Presence in Alternative U.S. Comics." In *Redrawing the Nation: National Identity in Latin/o American Comics*, edited by Héctor Fernández L'Hoeste and Juan Poblete, 251–69. New York: Palgrave Macmillan.

———. 2010. "Feminine Latin/o American Identities on the American Alternative Landscape: From the Women of *Love and Rockets* to *La Perdida*." Translated by Elizabeth Polli. In *The Rise of the American Comics Artist: Creators and Contexts*, edited by Paul Williams and James Lyons, 164–76. Jackson: University Press of Mississippi.

Mesa-Bains, Amalia. 1999. "'Domesticana': The Sensibility of Chicana Rasquache." *Aztlán: A Journal of Chicano Studies* 24, no. 2: 157–67.

Nericcio, William A. 2002. "A Decidedly 'Mexican' and 'American' Semi[er] otic Transference: Frida Kahlo in the Eyes of Gilbert Hernandez." In *Latino/a Popular Culture*, edited by Michelle Habell-Pallán and Mary Romero, 190–207. New York: New York University Press.

Rosenberg, Jordana, and Britt Rusert. 2014. "Framing Finance: Rebellion, Dispossession, and the Geopolitics of Enclosure in Samuel Delany's *Nevèrÿon* Series." *Radical History Review* 118: 64–91.

Saldívar, José David. 1991. "Postmodern Realism." In *The Columbia History of the American Novel*, edited by Emory Elliott, 521–41. New York: Columbia University Press.

————. 2011. *Trans-Americanity: Subaltern Modernities, Global Coloniality, and the Cultures of Greater Mexico*. Durham, NC: Duke University Press.

Saxey, Esther. 2006. "Desire Without Closure in Jaime Hernandez's Love and Rockets." *ImageTexT: Interdisciplinary Comics Studies* 3, no. 1.

Scott, Darieck. 1995. "Love, Rockets, Race and Sex." *Americas Review* 23, nos. 3–4: 73–106.

Streeby, Shelley. 2002. *American Sensations: Class, Empire, and the Production of Popular Culture*. Berkeley: University of California Press.

Tullis, Brittany. 2014. "Constructions of Femininity in Latin/o American Comics: Redefining Womanhood via the Male-Authored Comic." PhD diss., University of Iowa.

Vargas, Deborah R. 2010. "Representations of Latina/o Sexuality in Popular Culture." In *Latina/o Sexuality: Probing Powers, Passions, Practices, and Policies*, edited by Marysol Asencio, 137–49. New Brunswick, NJ: Rutgers University Press.

Wolk, Douglas. 2007a. "Gilbert Hernandez: Spiraling into the System." In *Reading Comics: How Graphic Novels Work and What They Mean*, 181–92. Cambridge, MA: De Capo.

————. 2007b. "Jaime Hernandez: Mad Love." In *Reading Comics: How Graphic Novels Work and What They Mean*, 193–202. Cambridge, MA: De Capo.

Ybarra-Frausto, Tomás. 1990. "Rasquachismo: A Chicano Sensibility." In *Chicano Art: Resistance and Affirmation, 1965–1985*, edited by Richard Griswold del Castillo, Teresa McKenna, and Yvonne Yarbro-Bejarano, 155–62. Los Angeles: Wight Art Gallery, University of California.

Chicana/o Cyberpunk after el Movimiento

Lysa Rivera

Just over a decade ago, the US military invaded the oil-rich nation of Iraq with a ferocious display of "shock and awe," a US military tactic that relies on, among other things, "decisive" and "overwhelming" force in order to render one's adversary "entirely impotent" before, during, and after battle (Ullman and Wade 1996, xxiv). As one supporter of the war commented days after the invasion, the ultimate goal of this "techno-spectacle" is to "make everybody on the other side feel that resistance is hopeless and quit" (Safire 2003). A year later, scholar Catherine S. Ramírez would prompt her colleagues in Chicano studies to think more critically about the fraught relationship between technology and Western imperialism and about their dubious impacts on Americans of indigenous Mexican descent living in the United States. More specifically, she asked us to reconsider how twenty-first-century technologies are a site of power *and* of resistance to that power by American mestizas and mestizos, primarily those who identify as Chicana or Chicano.

The umbrella term for this new point of inquiry, *Chicanafuturism*, encompasses all Chicana/o art that situates itself at the intersection of technoscience and Chicana/o culture.[1] This is art that, although interested in questions of form, genre, and style, is deeply attuned to the impacts of new technologies (in the past, present, and still undetermined future) on Chicana/o and Mexican indigenous cultures and communities. Similar to Afrofuturism, which Ramírez herself cites as a theoretical inspiration, Chicanafuturism is a type of cultural production—in literature, film, visual art, and music—that repurposes the "familiar memes of science fiction" to imagine, interrogate, and invent not only new political realities but also new cultural identities (Hopkinson 2004, ii). Now more visible than ever,

93

in both the academy and pop culture, today's Afrofuturist and Chicana-futurist artists and writers embody the potent fusions made possible when science fiction sets its imaginative sights on the experiences, conditions, and political demands of people of color.

My particular interest in Chicanafuturism homes in on Chicano science fiction produced in the 1990s, a particularly dark and tense time for people of color living in Southern California, where virtually all of the writers and texts spotlighted in this essay are based. By the 1990s Southern California was in deep economic and racial turmoil. Although Los Angeles was no stranger to racial tension, this particular decade saw a sporadic resurgence of racial conflict and white xenophobia. Many will of course recall the justice riots of 1992 following the Rodney King verdict. Fewer will remember that during the decades leading up to the riots, Los Angeles's Latina/o community had become an object of intense fear, a menacing encroacher upon a dwindling white racial majority. In his extensive study of journalistic coverage of immigration in the United States from 1965 to 2000, cultural anthropologist Leo Chavez notes that in 1994 an unprecedented number of magazine covers depicted the fearful "specter of multiculturalism," signaling pervasive US cultural anxieties over the impending demise of the white US majority (2001, 174). This "new nativism" rigorously "criminalized Mexican migration" and sought to police brown bodies by militarizing the US-Mexico border and hardening the internal borders that relegate people of color to the margins of society and culture (Jacobson 2008, 136). This anti-immigration sentiment culminated in the 1994 passage of California Proposition 187, also known as the "Save Our State" initiative, which drew support from those who were "tired of watching their state run wild and become a third world country," in the words of a former regional immigration official (Wood 1994, 1). While proponents of the measure insisted the issue was not a racial one, dominant representations of the debate, in print and on television, regularly framed it as a patriotic fight to preserve white America from an all-out "alien" invasion, one that brought the Third World dangerously close to the First.

What interests me most is how a handful of Chicano writers and artists responded to this period with the critical and transformative gaze of science fiction (SF), by which I mean they availed themselves of the genre's ability to both interrogate and transform (albeit imaginatively) the political or social status quo of their time.[2] I am specifically interested in Chicano texts from this period that reworked the SF subgenre known as cyberpunk, which emerged forcefully in the mid-1980s in response to both globalization and the information or "cyber" technologies that propel it. Frequently set in familiar near futures and concerned with the social, economic, and ecological impacts of globalization and information technologies, cyberpunk has received an abundance of recent scholarly attention; yet, within this body of scholarship, a sustained conversation about its Chicano participants has yet to fully materialize. Thomas R. Foster's impressive *Souls of Cyberfolk* (2007) argues that cyberpunk "didn't so much die as experience a sea change into a more generalized cultural formation" (xiv). Working with a diverse mix of cultural theorists, including at one point Gloria Anzaldúa and Chela Sandoval, Foster insists that far from being culturally and politically irrelevant or outdated, cyberpunk continues to probe the malleability of embodiment and identity formation and therefore offers its writers and fans more complex models of selfhood and subjectivity. In fact, a central aim of *Souls of Cyberfolk* is to explore how "cyberpunk opens a potential space for the development of models of historical existence other than the white, middle-class male paradigm of individual freedom" (73). Yet, despite this aim, Foster spends very little time looking specifically at Chicana/o cyberpunk texts.

Similarly, the second half of *Beyond Cyberpunk: New Critical Perspectives* (Murphy and Vint 2010) attends primarily to the genre's historically problematic treatment of gender and race, at one point referring to Movement-era cyberpunk (1980s cyberpunk) as an anxiety-prone attempt to preserve a white, masculine cultural dominance in the face of an increasingly diverse authorship and reading base. The very end of the collection works to counter this by exploring not the demise of the subgenre but rather its invigorating afterlife in texts heretofore overlooked in cyberpunk scholarship. However, as with the case of Foster's excellent study, *Beyond Cyberpunk* does not offer any sustained critical study of Chicano and/or Chicana practitioners of cyberpunk.

More recently, a 2012 article of mine in *Science Fiction Studies*, the genre's most widely read scholarly journal, observes that US-Mexico borderlands science fiction enlists the dystopian motifs and sentiments of cyberpunk to militate against the ways in which global capitalism starves the indigenous to fatten the capitalists. In that essay, I argue that dystopian SF produced in and around the borderlands region interrogated the problems of globalization and neoliberalism as they relate to indigenous communities in the Americas, specifically in Mexico and the US-Mexico borderlands.[3] Texts like *The Rag Doll Plagues* (Morales 1992) and *High Aztech* (Hogan 1992), discussed further below, redirect the critical dystopian gaze of cyberpunk to probe how technological innovation and global capitalism have created a vast North American underclass—Chicana/os in the United States and mestiza/os in Mexico—whose labor feeds the consumer class and whose land serves as its dumping ground.

My aim here is to redirect that previous conversation ever so slightly by considering Chicano cyberpunk as a post-movement literary phenomenon that both reflected and produced new identity paradigms that resisted the nationalistic and homogenizing impulses of an earlier era. I begin by historically situating the emergence of Chicano cyberpunk within a distinctly post–Chicano movement context. I trace the ways in which Chicano writers and artists, such as Ernest Hogan, Alejandro Morales, Guillermo Gómez-Peña, Enrique Chagoya, and Roberto Sifuentes, made use of cyberpunk's rich inventories of metaphors and motifs to fashion new hybrid cultural identities. These often flew in the face of the nationalist logics of *el movimiento*, whose writers and artists largely aimed to recover and preserve a core, essential, and pre-Columbian cultural identity erased by centuries of colonial oppression and exploitation. As I hope to show, Chicano cyberpunk, while equally invested in an antiracist politics, engages concerns that are more unique to the new millennium, including the rise of globalization and information technologies and the new hybrid identities made possible by both.

Utopia and the Chicano Movement

Two important contexts, political and aesthetic, helped animate Chicano cyberpunk: the nationalist utopian project of the Chicano movement (late 1960s–70s) and the DIY (do-it-yourself) Chicana/o punk movement of the 1980s. Looking closely at those two periods will help us understand the emergence of 1990s Chicano cyberpunk. The Chicano movement, to start, was a brief and electrifying period when Mexican Americans began to vocalize demands for education reform, labor rights, and political self-determination. Shrugging off the assimilationist impulses of the post–World War II period, this younger generation refused to be "absorbed" by the Anglo cultural dominant, as Rodolfo "Corky" Gonzales famously declared in the movement's signature poem, *I Am Joaquín* (2002, 199). Although relatively short-lived, *el movimiento* was an important catalyst for raising national awareness about the oppressive material conditions of the vast majority of Mexican Americans living in the United States. Its 1969 foundational document, a collaboratively written manifesto called "El Plan

Espiritual de Aztlán," illustrates in no uncertain terms how *el movimiento* was at its core not only a nationalist project but also a utopian one as well:

Chicanos (La Raza de Bronze) must use their nationalism as the key or common denominator for mass mobilization and organization. Once we are committed to the idea and philosophy of El Plan de Aztlán, we can only conclude that social, economic, cultural and political independence is the only road to total liberation from oppression, exploitation, and racism. (Anaya and Lomeli 1989, 2)

This new generation of students, activists, and artists believed strongly that a racially and culturally distinct national identity was the fundamental first step toward political "mobilization and organization." They favored the self-chosen moniker *Chicano*, a word with indigenous origins, over the more compromised and assimilationist term *Mexican American*. To cultivate this new cultural identity, movement writers turned to their pre-Columbian, indigenous history and proclaimed the myth of Aztlán as a unifying symbol for all Mexicans living north of the border. Aztlán, the imaginary (or utopian) ancestral homeland of the Aztecs, provided disillusioned Chicanos and Chicanas with an arsenal of provocative images, symbols, and metaphors with which to forge a collective national and cultural identity. Like many homeland imaginaries, the "idea" of Aztlán offered dispersed Chicana/o communities throughout the United States a "way of imposing an imaginary coherence on the experience of dispersal and fragmentation" (Hall 2003, 227). In other words, it offered them a foundation for the development of a distinct and sovereign Chicano nation—a "bronze" nation.

This type of cultural nationalism found a corollary in movement-era Chicano science fiction that rejected assimilation outright. Here, I am thinking of Luis Valdez's 1967 play *Los Vendidos* (The Sellouts), which takes clear aim at Chicana/os who opt to "sell out" their ethnic identity for social, economic, and/or political gain. One of the earliest-known pieces of Chicano science fiction, the play enacted the political vision of Valdez's agitprop theater collective, El Teatro Campesino: "Inspire the audience to social action. Illuminate specific points about social problems. Satirize the opposition. Show or hint at a solution" (Valdez 1994, 12). Merging the conventions of science fiction with this political and aesthetic vision, *Los Vendidos* presents the SF icon of the humanoid robot (or "type") as a metaphor for the ways in which ethnic and racial stereotypes—malicious or benevolent—dehumanize their Chicano and mestizo subjects (Valdez

1994, 41). The *acto* takes place in "Honest Sancho's Used Mexican Lot and Mexican Curio Shop," a fictional California store that sells robotic "models" of various Mexican and Mexican American stereotypes, including a docile, hardworking farmworker, a knife-wielding, maladjusted pachuco, and a romantic Mexican *revolucionario*. The story is set in motion when Governor Reagan's secretary "Miss JIM-enez," a fully assimilated Chicana who intentionally mispronounces her name to distance herself from her ethnic identity, visits the shop to procure a "Mexican type" for the conservative state administration—it is an election year, after all (41). After examining a few models, none of which proves to be "American" enough, Miss JIM-enez finally settles on a "bilingual, college educated" model named "Eric García," a fully assimilated "Mexican-American" who "represents the apex of American engineering" (51). Soon, the robots begin to gesticulate wildly, spewing out pro-Mexican, pro–labor rights phrases, and scare the secretary out of the store. Eventually, it is revealed that Sancho himself is a robot, and the supposed robots are real Chicanos who are simply performing their stereotypes. They keep Miss JIM-enez's money and decide, after she leaves, to celebrate their successful heist. Here, Valdez's role reversal—a motif that pervades his *actos* during the 1960s—underscores the victory at the heart of the story: those who deny their ethnic roots will, like Miss JIM-enez, pay a price.

Valdez's allegorical satire is a prototypical Chicano cyberpunk text. For although he is not interested in making either a scientific or technological statement, Valdez does put science fictional tropes in the service of cultural and social critique. In fact, the *acto* delivers on one of the central projects of Chicanafuturism, which is to "defamiliarize the familiar" in order to bring "into relief that which is generally taken for granted" (Ramírez 2004, 190). In the case of *Vendidos*, familiar Chicana/o and Mexican cultural stereotypes or identities are rendered strange ("defamiliarized") by being depicted as robotic "models" instead of actual people. Valdez manages to expose how these racialized "types" are, in the end, socially engineered, entirely performative, and fundamentally ideological machines that Anglo-Saxon hegemony uses in order to police, contain, and exploit Mexican and Mexican American bodies. As such, they anticipate Gómez-Peña's "ethno-cyborgs" of the 1990s, which also function as highly charged cyborg-like symbols of what is essentially a "non-existent, phantasmatic Mexican/Chicano identity, [a projection] of people's own psychological and cultural monsters—an army of Mexican Frankensteins ready to rebel against their Anglo creators" (Gómez-Peña 2000, 49).

Chicana/o Punk and the Transnational Turn

The rebellious spirit of movement-era texts like *Los Vendidos* and the movement's "call to action" gave rise to the era's many antiwar demonstrations, student walkouts, and national youth conferences. Yet as others have observed, *el movimiento* was not without blind spots and oversights, particularly with respect to its nationalist tendencies and rhetoric, which many Chicanas, in particular, began to recognize during the movement proper. For them, *el movimiento* not only muted gender issues; it was also seen as too nationalistic and precluded the possibility for cross-racial and cross-ethnic alliances and solidarities. As one movement-era Chicana feminist observed, "To meet with people from other struggles makes one aware of the meaning and the [effects] of systemic genocide, personally as well as within our descendant family trees. It makes one further aware of the meaning of the sufferings and turmoil of Vietnam, Angola, Puerto Rico, Latin America and the whole of Asia" (Vasquez 1997, 172). Anticipating the coalition politics of US Third World feminisms, Vasquez calls for a more global liberation movement, one that includes not only Chicanas but all colonized or oppressed women of color, regardless of national affinities and allegiances. Her insistence on a more globalized approach to liberation clearly suggests that even during the movement there were stirrings of more transnational and cross-cultural political alliances. If we look ahead to the 1980s, we begin to see these bear fruit, most notably in the DIY aesthetic of Chicana/o punk rockers in Los Angeles.

Chicana/o punk rockers in the 1980s, most of whom were too young to have participated directly in the movement, found punk to be "an alternative oppositional movement to the Chicano movement" (Habell-Pallán 2005, 165). It allowed room for more self-fashioned (again, DIY) cultural identities that departed from the strict nationalism of the movement in favor of more complex, nuanced, and culturally hybrid forms. For these younger artists, the movement's "desire for a time before oppression . . . necessarily suppressed the historical reality of cultural fusion (*mestizaje*)," which in turn reinforced traditional gender, sexual, and cultural identities of Chicana/os who came of age after *el movimiento* (39). Chicana/o punk and pop music artists like Teresa Covarrubias, Alicia Armendariz Velasquez, and El Vez shared a penchant for a more transnational and cross-cultural approach to political resistance. In one sense they simply appropriated, repurposed, and interrogated imagery and sounds from other cultures, including (and especially) the underground punk movements popular in both Britain and the United States. In another, arguably more important sense, though, these artists resisted the grand narrative of the movement by focusing less on recovering a lost history and more on remedying the political exigencies of their present (the 1980s) and the rising tide of neoliberalism that had overcome it. In other words, while clearly attuned to racial, gender, and class inequities, these younger artists sought to locate the source of those injustices within the broader context of neoliberalism (globalization), which plagued urban lives in the 1980s through economic privatization of social spaces and services. As Habell-Pallán insists, "Theirs is a story of transnationalism told from the bottom up, in the years leading up to accords like NAFTA, from the point of view of working-class women" (156).[4]

One example of Chicana/o youth culture putting the "punk" in cyberpunk in the 1980s can be found in the music and performances of El Vez, a US-born Chicano who has made a career out of appropriating and translating Anglo-American pop culture into a Chicana/o milieu. Similar to *punkeras* like Covarrubias and Velasquez, El Vez had no formal training and relied on a DIY aesthetic to present to his fans a type of self-fashioned Chicano identity marked not by ties to an ancestral past, but rather by cultural hybridity and syncretism. His music drew as much from an Anglo-European punk aesthetic as it did from an East Los local cultural milieu. The ultimate "transculturator of popular culture," El Vez destabilizes traditional definitions of nationhood and masculinity by refusing to reduce Chicana/o identities to rigid nationalist, sexual, or even gendered categories (Habell-Pallán 2005, 183). As a result, although not exactly a presence in the genealogical history of Chicana/o speculative arts, El Vez and his transnational, culturally hybrid aesthetic gestures toward a reinvigorating new politics that makes visible the possibility for coalitions of resistance that are not bounded by nationalist logics and notions of racial or cultural purity.

1990s Chicano Cyberpunk

Whereas we can say that the decade of the 1980s brought with it a new Chicana/o *punkera/o* subculture, the 1990s witnessed another iteration of this aesthetic, albeit with a technoscientific inflection: the Chicano cyberpunks. Take, for example, Guillermo Gómez-Peña's "ethno-cyborgs." In ways strikingly similar to Valdez's movement-era Chicana/o humanoid robots, the ethno-cyborgs recycle popular science fiction themes of their time to allegorize the dehumanization of Mexicans and Chicanos in the US cultural imaginary. They also inhabit a curio shop, the "Ethno-Cyberpunk

Trading Post & Curio Shop on the Electronic Frontier." In this large room, "computer screens, video monitors, neon signs and digital bars flashing taxonomic descriptions" of the ethno-cyborgs on display "added a sci-fi flavor to our techno-tribal environment," calling to mind "a Catholic temple from a cyber-punk novel" (Gómez-Peña 2000, 46, 39).

These uncanny ethno-cyborgs are the product of what Gómez-Peña has called "reverse anthropology," an aesthetic critical practice that reverses the museum's ethnographic gaze back onto the spectators, who stand to learn "more about America's cultural projections and its inability to deal with cultural otherness than about the Latino 'other'" (40). Through the construction of a "techno-confessional" website, the artist asked Internet users to "share their projections and preconceptions about Latinos and indigenous people" (30). He then used the data to construct various performance personae—the ethno-cyborgs—who both embodied and performed the fears and fantasies shared anonymously online. Like Luis Valdez's robot "types," these ethno-cyborgs embody Mexican and Chicana/o cultural stereotypes. And like the robots, they are more satirical than serious—at least most of the time. Yet rather than dwell for long on questions related to cultural authenticity and the selling out of that authenticity for monetary profit or political gain, Gómez-Peña is decidedly more interested in the mechanics of stereotyping itself and in the role technologies play in those mechanics. His ethno-cyborgs reverse the critical gaze onto the white cultural dominant. In critiquing the stereotypes on display in this post-movement updating of Valdez's satirical SF, Gómez-Peña focuses on the engineers of the stereotypes, the Anglo-American Frankensteins, if you will, of his "engineered Mexicans" (46). Far more than Valdez's robots, they invite a social-constructionist reading of stereotypes, one not much interested in preserving authentic Chicana/o or Mexican cultural identities that have been subject to colonial erasure or distortion, but concerned, above all, with exploring how Chicana/o cultural identities are technologically mediated. The effect is to shift the "problem" more explicitly onto the technological apparatuses of white racial fears rather than letting it rest on the shoulders of Mexicans and Chicana/os themselves (47).

In other words, Chicano cyberpunks like Gómez-Peña merge the creative and practical features of new information technologies to continue many of the cultural and political projects of their punk predecessors, but with an eye toward the rise of globalization, neoliberalism, and the new technologies that enable both. Unlike robots, cyborgs are uncanny precisely because they defy easy categorization. They are at once human (real) and machine (artificial), and their hybridity defies easy categorization and binary thinking. As powerful symbols, they embody "the multiple fears and desires of a culture caught in the process of transformation" (González 1995, 267). Whether they are responding to radical social, political, or technological changes, cyborgs emerge most forcefully when "a hybrid model of existence is required to encompass a new, complex and contradictory lived experience" (270). For Gómez-Peña and his 1990s ethno-cyborgs, and for other Chicano cyberpunks during this time, this "new, complex and contradictory" experience is due largely to the rise of both global/transnational capitalism and the computer and information technologies that enable it.[5]

While Gómez-Peña was busy repurposing the cyborg metaphor, fellow Chicano SF writers Ernest Hogan and Alejandro Morales intervened in cyberpunk by reenvisioning the subgenre's familiar near-future cityscapes— those bleak "*Blade Runner* scenarios" that dominated the genre, in print and film, throughout the 1980s.[6] Whereas many if not most Anglo-cyberpunk cityscapes appear as dystopian enclaves overrun by "Third World" refugees, the cities in Chicano cyberpunk, though not without conflict and tension, thrive on multiculturalism and cultural syncretism. In other words, what were "ominous" "*Blade Runner* scenarios" in the 1980s become vibrant, multicultural heterotopias in 1990s Chicano cyberpunk (Davis 1992, 82). Hogan's *High Aztech* and Morales's *The Rag Doll Plagues*, both published in 1992, for example, speculate on the future of globalization. Evoking the cyberpunk cityscapes in *Neuromancer* (Gibson 1984) and *Metrophage* (Kadrey 1988), both Chicano writers depict near futures where traditional national borders are fluid and porous, which is in keeping with the unique look and feel of cyberpunk. Their protagonists are male hackers at odds with the state; the narratives take place in near futures inundated with new cybernetic technologies; and both protagonists must navigate their lives within dense urban cities where low-tech subcultures and a techno-elite mix and collide in a fast-paced, largely lawless underground community.

High Aztech features Xólotl Zapata, a thirty-year-old mestizo from Mexico City who writes comic books and poetry for the city's "electronic underground" (Hogan 1992, 6). As the novel opens, the city, renamed "Tenochtitlán" to commemorate its colonial past, is on the brink of a massive riot. At war are two competing religious ideologies—Aztecan and Christian—that are represented in the novel by the "Neliyacme" (True Aztecan Warriors) and the "quixtianome" (non-Aztecans). Xólotl learns that he and thousands of other city dwellers have contracted new synthetic viruses that rewire deep structures in the basal ganglia to control their religious beliefs and allegiances (171). As one character puts it, this new "faith virus" actually rearranges brain cells and "download[s] the Aztecan religion into a person's mind" (171, 198). Xólotl is apprehended first by a North American Christian fundamentalist band of spies who infect him with a Christian virus. Subsequently, his own mother, in the name of science, infects him with multiple mind viruses to test a hypothesis: that one religion will cancel out another until none is left, leaving the host with the ability to "think for him[self]" (171, 234). Throughout the novel, it is clear that Hogan is interested in a more syncretic model for the future, one that leaves behind the binary logic represented by the warring factions and enters the murkier realm of cultural syncretism and mestizaje. Xólotl sees himself as being both culturally and racially mixed, and he prefers cultural syncretism and heterogeneity to the uniformity of thought and mind demanded by religious fundamentalisms.

Hogan's take on the cyberpunk cityscape appears in one of the novel's most lyrical chapters, "Tenochtitlán." Totally "high" on the viruses (he is, after all, a "high" Aztec), Xólotl wanders the city streets, hallucinating visions of complete cultural, racial, and ethnic fusion:

> Marilyn Monroe zoomed by like a jet-propelled Earth Mother/Sacred Virgin. Mao Zedong, Karl Marx, Thomas Jefferson and Frankenstein's monster—who looked very much like Boris Karloff—discussed the problem of modernization and introducing advanced technology to feudal and agrarian societies. Mohammed had Salman Rushdie autograph a copy of the first edition of *The Satanic Verses*; the Prophet told the writer that he got all the jokes. (214)

Here, Hogan imagines a global city where national and literary icons collide to create a type of urban postnational tableau. In this passage and others like it throughout the novel, Hogan's narrative resists notions of cultural, racial, and linguistic purity, fascinated as he is with the cultural collision and intermixing that results from globalization. Hogan's commitment to this vision appears in the very texture of the language itself as he incorporates over one hundred "Aztecanisms," words from a fictionalized language called "Españahuatl," a new creole vernacular made up of Spanish and Nahuatl. Even the language of the text reflects its message.

This brief discussion of Chicano cyberpunk would be incomplete without a nod to Alejandro Morales's novel *The Rag Doll Plagues*. Simultaneously historical and speculative, *Plagues* recasts three distinct periods of indigenous Mexican history, treating them in three "books" within the novel: the colonial period (fifteenth century), the present day (1990s), and the future (2079). Book Three is aptly titled LAMEX in reference to a new North American geopolitical formation, one in which Mexico City and Los Angeles (along with San Diego) form one large metropolis, as national boundaries have entirely collapsed. The inhabitants of this sprawling, futuristic city do not pine for a bygone world, and those who thrive most in the novel are those who have learned to adapt to the borderless, transnational new world order. In fact, the model for the future envisioned in *Plagues* comes directly out of Morales's call for new cultural identities in his essay "Dynamic Identities in Heterotopia":

> People are learning to live in heterotopia and must constantly develop new survival strategies. Southern California, from Tijuana to Santa Barbara, is a perplexing urban area constituted by a continuum of shapeless cities with no center, no core of a single identity. Southern California is a profusion of cultural enclaves, a multitude of othernesses, developing together and creating literal and metaphorical borders. It is an unending, unfinished process of continuous movement, of ceaseless change, of always becoming, of perpetual transformation. (1996, 24)

This heterotopic imperative emerges from an acute awareness of having to "develop new survival strategies" to accommodate the shifting topographies of an emergent postnational world—a world with "no core of a single identity." We see this world in Book Three's depiction of the new middle class in future Los Angeles, which has become a "center for Mexican/Asian culture. Chinese, Japanese, Koreans, and Southeast Asians had migrated in great numbers . . . In order to survive and coexist, the Mexicans and Asians united economically, politically, culturally and racially" (Morales 1992, 148). Clearly a futuristic model for a type of coalition politics, this seemingly incidental description reemerges at the novel's end as Gregory contemplates the birth of a child conceived in a mixed-race marriage. "That child," he notes, "represents the hope for the new millennium" (199). As in Book One, the novel ends "pregnant" with the possibility of novel hybrid identities born of the heterotopic future Morales effectively imagines.

Conclusion

As we have seen, these engagements with hybridity and cultural syncretism represent a departure from *el movimiento*'s push for Chicano cultural nationalism, which, while perhaps a necessary first step in resisting white hegemonic dominance, also problematically reproduced gender hierarchies and stifled the possibility for cross-cultural formations (mestizaje). But they accomplish more than that: in embracing the transnational, culturally syncretic potential made possible by globalization and transcultural dialogue, these Chicano cyberpunk writers also refuse to submit to the dystopian racial anxieties prevalent in classic, Anglo-American cyberpunk. They frame their multiracial and multicultural futures as sites of possibility, not pessimism.

As their high-tech, exploratory enterprises make clear, Chicano cyberpunk texts from the 1990s, the decade of NAFTA, turn to the rich metaphors of this SF subgenre because doing so enables them to speculate on the impacts of globalization from marginalized and muted perspectives. These new social, political, even environmental realities—these new dystopias—certainly demand scrutiny and the possibility of transformation. The early Chicano cyberpunks were relatively uninterested in nationalist logics that aim to preserve a fixed, immutable core identity to which all Chicana/o artists are connected and through which their work must be interpreted. Instead they turned to the malleable metaphors of science fiction, cyberpunk in particular, to imagine, stage, and even produce alternative models for identity. These models, both individual and communal, defied easy categorization and rejected models of cultural and racial purity. In ways similar to the DIY Chicana/o punks before them, Chicano cyberpunk writers of the 1990s selectively appropriated various tropes and motifs of Anglo culture to comment critically on that culture (in this case, to throw into relief the reactionary tendencies of cyberpunk) and to fashion new, post-movement cultural identities that recognize and dramatize the historical, present-day, and potential future histories of mestizaje.

Notes

1. Throughout her early work on Chicana/o speculative arts, Catherine Ramírez (2004, 2008) uses the feminine-gendered neologism *Chicanafuturism* to refer to various male and female artists and writers, prompting me to follow suit. In this essay, then, the term refers to both male and female artists, although my specific interest here is in Chicano cyberpunk writers.

2. There are Chicana cyberpunk writers and artists, and I have written about two of them elsewhere, but for this conversation the moniker Chicano applies as I focus entirely on male writers and artists, with the exception of the *punkeras* of the

1980s, whose influence, I argue, is important in thinking about the development of a clear Chicana/o cyberpunk aesthetic.

3. My understanding and use of the term *neoliberalism* to refer to the political and economic underpinnings of globalization derives from David Harvey's (2005) work in this area. Harvey argues that neoliberal economic theory, which emphasizes deregulation, privatization, and withdrawal of the state from its role as guardian of labor, consumer, and environmental protections, took root in the 1970s and has continued to dominate not only the so-called First World, but developing nations as well.

4. Strong aesthetic affinities and genealogical strands connect this *punkera/o* DIY subculture and the Chicana/o working-class sensibilities of both *domesticana* and rasquachismo, which are vernacular forms of cultural production that emerge from having to make do with very little. Rasquachismo was central to Valdez's aesthetic sensibility—it was, after all, farmworker theater—and as such it must be seen as central to the development of Chicano cyberpunk. Perhaps even more fascinating is how both rasquachismo and Chicano cyberpunk, while honoring the antiracist impulses of *el movimiento*, appear to privilege cultural syncretism over cultural nationalism. As Tomás Ybarra-Frausto notes with respect to rasquachismo, it "engenders hybridization, juxtaposition, and integration. Rasquachsimo is a sensibility attuned to mixtures and confluence, preferring communion over purity" (1991, 156).

5. I would be remiss in failing to acknowledge Chela Sandoval's subsequent reinterpretation of this "power symbol." In "New Sciences," for example, she elaborates on the concept of "cyborg consciousness," which refers to "a particular and specific form of oppositional consciousness" that colonized peoples of the Americas "developed" in response to Anglo-European colonial and hegemonic dominance (Sandoval 1995, 408). Emerging out of a "set of technologies that together comprise the methodology of the oppressed"—including things like appropriating, subverting, and working simultaneously within and outside of dominant ideology to construct alternative models of existence and survival—this new "cyberconsciousness" is at once a metaphor and a reality for Sandoval (409).

6. This telling phrase first appeared in *L.A. 2000: A City for the Future*, a thin and glossy pamphlet prepared and distributed by a Los Angeles planning committee in 1988. Itself a speculative text, *L.A. 2000* peers into the future and warns Angelinos of a multiethnic future marked by polyglottism and unharmonious cultural differences.

Works Cited

Anaya, Rudolfo A., and Francisco Lomeli, eds. 1989. *Aztlán: Essays on the Chicano Homeland*. Albuquerque: University of New Mexico Press.

Chavez, Leo R. 2001. *Covering Immigration: Popular Images and the Politics of the Nation*. Berkeley: University of California Press.

Davis, Mike. 1992. *City of Quartz: Excavating the Future in Los Angeles*. New York: Vintage.

Foster, Thomas. 2007. *The Souls of Cyberfolk: Posthumanism as Vernacular Theory*. Minneapolis: University of Minnesota Press.

Gibson, William. 1984. *Neuromancer*. New York: Ace.

Gómez-Peña, Guillermo. 2000. *Dangerous Border Crossers: The Artist Talks Back*. New York: Routledge.

Gonzales, Rodolfo "Corky." 2002. *I Am Joaquín*. In *Herencia: The Anthology of Hispanic Literature of the United States*, edited by Nicolás Kanellos, 195–99. New York: Oxford University Press.

González, Jennifer. 1995. "Envisioning Cyborg Bodies: Notes from Current Research." In *The Cyborg Handbook*, edited by Chris Hables Gray, 267–80. New York: Routledge.

Habell-Pallán, Michelle. 2005. *Loca Motion: The Travels of Chicana and Latina Popular Culture*. New York: New York University Press.

Hall, Stuart. 2003. "Cultural Identity and Diaspora." In *Theorizing Diaspora: A Reader*, edited by Jana Evans Braziel and Anita Mannur, 233–46. Malden, MA: Blackwell.

Harvey, David. 2005. *A Brief History of Neoliberalism*. New York: Oxford University Press.

Hogan, Ernest. 1992. *High Aztech*. New York: Tor Books.

Hopkinson, Nalo. 2004. Introduction to *So Long Been Dreaming: Postcolonial Science Fiction and Fantasy*, edited by Nalo Hopkinson and Uppinder Mehan, 7–9. Vancouver, BC: Arsenal Pulp Press.

Jacobson, Robin Dale. 2008. *The New Nativism: Proposition 187 and the Debate over Immigration*. Minneapolis: University of Minnesota Press.

Kadrey, Richard. 1988. *Metrophage*. New York: Ace.

Morales, Alejandro. 1992. *The Rag Doll Plagues*. Houston: Arte Público.

———. 1996. "Dynamic Identities in Heterotopia." In *Alejandro Morales: Fiction Past, Present, Future Perfect*, edited by José Antonio Gurpegui, 14–28. Tempe, AZ: Bilingual Review Press.

Murphy, Graham J., and Sherryl Vint, eds. 2010. *Beyond Cyberpunk: New Critical Perspectives*. New York: Routledge.

Ramírez, Catherine S. 2004. "Deus ex Machina: Tradition, Technology, and the Chicanafuturist Art of Marion C. Martinez." *Aztlán: A Journal of Chicano Studies* 29, no. 2: 55–82.

———. 2008. "Afrofuturism/Chicanafuturism: Fictive Kin." *Aztlán: A Journal of Chicano Studies* 33, no. 1: 185–94.

Rivera, Lysa. 2012. "Future Histories and Cyborg Labor: Reading Borderlands Science Fiction after NAFTA." *Science Fiction Studies* 39, no. 22: 415–36.

Safire, William. 2003. "Shock and Awe: A Tactic, Not a Law Firm." *New York Times Magazine*, March 30.

Sandoval, Chela. 1995. "New Sciences: Cyborg Feminism and the Methodology of the Oppressed." In *The Cyborg Handbook*, edited by Chris Hables Gray, 407–22. New York: Routledge.

Ullman, Harlan K., and James P. Wade. 1996. *Shock and Awe: Achieving Rapid Dominance*. Washington, DC: National Defense University.

Valdez, Luis. 1994. *Los Vendidos*. In *Luis Valdez: Early Works: Actos, Bernabé, and Pensamiento Serpentino*. Houston: Arte Público. *Los Vendidos* was first performed in 1967.

Vasquez, Enriqueta Longeaux. 1997. "Third World Women Meet." In *Chicana Feminist Thought: The Basic Historical Writings*, edited by Alma M. García, 172–73. New York: Routledge. First published in *El Grito del Norte* in 1973.

Wood, Daniel B. 1994. "Ballot Vote on Illegal Immigrants Set for Fall in California." *Christian Science Monitor*, June 1, 1.

Ybarra-Frausto, Tomás. 1991. "Rasquachismo: A Chicano Sensibility." In *Chicano Art: Resistance and Affirmation, 1965–1985*, edited by Richard Griswold del Castillo, Teresa McKenna, and Yvonne Yarbro-Bejarano, 154–60. Los Angeles: Wight Art Gallery, University of California.

PART II

Cyborgs, Networks, and Posthumanism

From Code to Codex
Tricksterizing the Digital Divide in Ernest Hogan's *Smoking Mirror Blues*

Daoine S. Bachran

Adam J. Banks's *Race, Rhetoric, and Technology* (2006) deploys the digital divide, a term that arose in the mid-1990s to describe the class gap in access to digital technologies, as a metonym for the racial divide in the United States. Focusing on how "an entire group of people have been systematically denied the tools, the literacies, the experiences, the codes and assumptions behind the design choices, [and] the chance to influence future designs," Banks argues that digital access and authorship shape "people's educational success, employability and thus their incomes, roles in the society, and their political power" (xxi). He reveals the material ramifications of being left out of technological advancement for people of color generally, and for black Americans specifically, and the far-reaching consequences of a lack of digital representation and literacy. Lisa Nakamura similarly finds that the Internet promulgates a "discourse of color blindness in terms of access, user experience, and content" that deliberately erases people of color (2007, 4).

The digital divide is particularly sharp for Latina/os in the United States. Latina/os have lower Internet use and literacy than white people do, and a disproportionately small number of them earn degrees in STEM subjects; thus the digital divide leaves Latina/os behind as both creators and users of digital spaces (Hauschild 2012).[1] Because of the gap in literacy, education, and access, cultural representation of Latina/os in digital and mainstream media is also unequal and is heavily shaped by non-Latina/os.[2] Consequently, Latina/os are absent from these spaces or saddled with stereotypes such as "laziness, the siesta, tequila, banditry" (Nericcio 1996, 196). These characters serve as "vivid synecdoches for a particular and peculiar sensually charged form of evil potentiality" (192), so that portrayal of Latina/os serves interests not their own. The lack of Latina/o representation in the fields involved in creating and mediating digital technologies indicates that the trend will continue without intervention.

In this essay I argue that Ernest Hogan's third novel, *Smoking Mirror Blues* (2001), challenges the erasure of Chicana/os in mainstream media and explores how the appropriation of digital technologies can combat capitalist exploitation. The novel is set in a cyberpunk future Los Angles—"El Lay" in the narrative—during Dead Daze, an amalgamation of Halloween, Día de los Muertos, and a massive street party. It begins when Beto Orozco, a Chicano video game designer, returns from Mexico with a "god-simulating" computer program stolen from its Mexican author, Xochitl Echaurren. Beto uses the program to simulate the Aztec trickster god Tezcatlipoca.[3] The newly digitized god hypnotizes Beto, possessing his body as Smokey Espejo, and takes over the mediasphere.[4] In this bifurcated form, as digital Tezcatlipoca and embodied Smokey, the trickster appropriates a corporate-sponsored gang, commandeers a band, and composes the song "Smokey Mirror Blues" in an attempt to hypnotize the world. In a narrative overflowing with violent confrontations and explicit sex scenes, Xochitl, Caldonia (a black lesbian), Madam Tan Tien (an Asian detective), and Zobop Delvaux (Tan Tien's black partner and lover) careen through El Lay's Dead Daze to thwart Tezcatlipoca's plot. The story evokes cyberpunk's legacy of technology gone awry, but it is rooted in recovered myth and history alongside more traditional genre conventions of fantasy and science fiction.

While the digital divide threatens to leave Latina/os in the past, Hogan invokes Mesoamerican, specifically Aztec, mythology and images to rupture the codes of technologized racism. Just as Catherine Ramírez theorizes that Chicanafuturism "questions the promises of science, technology, and humanism for Chicanas, Chicanos, and other people of color" (2008, 187), Hogan's novel interrogates the promise of Chicana/o visual and digital representation in US society. In particular, he traces the lack of access to digital spaces for Chicana/os as authors and consumers to earlier disparities in Hollywood film and network news. Advocating for digital, transcultural nationalism, Hogan highlights the future's dependence on mass media for culture as he creates space for Chicana/o techno-signification "to tricksterize the mediasphere, and even tricksterize the real world" (Hogan 2001, 22).[5] In *Smoking Mirror Blues*, Hogan seeks to reclaim mass media to recover Chicana/o histories, from Aztec myths to the zoot suit riots, recasting Chicano nationalism's practices for a new digital era. However, the novel's radical conscription of visual media uncritically replicates problematic representations of women, limits women's characters to familiar stereotypes, and reinscribes women's presence primarily as objects for the scopophilic male gaze. Even as the novel refuses Chicana/os' erasure and seizes control of their commodification, its return to Chicano nationalism replicates *el movimiento*'s privileging of masculinity, unintentionally revealing problems with an otherwise imaginative digital mestizaje.

The Celluloid Divide and the Symbolic and Material Violence of Erasure

Smoking Mirror Blues deploys a metanarrative in which the author traces the digital divide and exclusion of Chicana/os to the signifying practices in mainstream media, particularly early film. It re-creates what is arguably the most important locus in Hollywood's history and connects it to contemporary digital representation through the novel's "mythic" setting at the "fabled corner of Hollywood and Vine" (Hogan 2001, 18). The massive Dead Daze street party centers on this intersection; Tan Tien and Zobop's office is in "the building that used to be the Bank of America on Hollywood and Vine" (9); and Beto's apartment is located nearby. The old Bank of America building that is mentioned fourteen times in the novel most likely references the Hollywood Guaranty Building. Built in 1923, it housed Guaranty Savings, a bank that helped finance the rise of Hollywood, and whose owner, as the building's application for historical status claims, was vital in "establishing Hollywood and Vine as the city's central district." Subsequently, the bank played "a starring role in the demise" of Hollywood's prosperity through the owner's embezzlement of investors' funds.[6] The building was sold in 1931 after the crash, and Bank of America moved into the lower floors. (It was bought in 1988 by the Church of Scientology and continues to house their main offices.)

By setting the novel in the context of Hollywood and Vine, with the gloss of Guaranty Savings, Hogan evokes a legacy of movie representation shot through with financial, political, and religious scandals in addition to problematically racialized political legacies. The location evokes Hollywood's boom of the 1920s, its financial corruption during the Great Depression, and film's rising dominance of mass culture. Significantly, the rise of the Hollywood film industry was accompanied by the decline of Latina/o presence in film. During the silent movie era, Charles Ramírez Berg reminds us, Latina/os were some of Hollywood's biggest stars, but after the addition of sound most film stars with "ethnic" accents moved to

113

the margins (2002, 263–66). This began the process of codifying images of Latina/os in film to a small set of roles including "*el bandito*, the harlot, the male buffoon, the female clown, the Latin lover, and the dark lady," stereotypes persisting to the present (66). As Latina/os' roles in cinema changed and Hollywood actors became whiter, Charles Dobbs argues, "mass culture helped replace individual ethnic culture" and "Hollywood-produced movies" became "the dominant popular culture" (2009, 208). Thus the cinemascape delivered a limited version of Americanness just as the United States' mass culture replaced individual ethnicity; to be American was visually encoded as being white. This telos became a "celluloid divide" that provided a framework for the current racialized digital divide that the novel seeks to challenge and transform.

While Hollywood was disappearing Latina/os from visual representation, Los Angeles was the hub of a federal repatriation program that, through forced removal or the threat of it, resulted in the return of thousands of Mexican nationals (and some US citizens) to Mexico between 1929 and 1939, effectively disappearing Mexicans from physical representation in the United States. Thus the setting of *Smoking Mirror Blues* recalls the rise and fall of Latina/o representation in early-twentieth-century California. The Bank of America collapse in El Lay parallels the fate of Guaranty Savings, the omnipresence of digital media in the United States reflects Hollywood's presence as the arbiter of mass culture, and the digital divide becomes the de facto representational hurdle for Latina/os in Hogan's future. Beto's invented god steps smoothly into this space, an embodiment Ti-Yong/Hoodoo detective Zobop predicts when he calls Tezcatlipoca's electronic machinations "the spirit of Hollywood manifesting itself in the mediasphere" (2001, 43). Tezcatlipoca's construction heralds a shift in representation—one rooted in Hollywood's history, the digital present, and an Aztec past.

While Hogan recovers the history of Chicana/o representations and subsequent exclusions in Hollywood film, *Smoking Mirror Blues* uses vignettes of late-twentieth-century network news and documentary film to demonstrate how "factual" reporting sensationalizes Los Angeles's legacy of police violence, racially motivated rioting, and gang warfare. From the news media's reporting on the 1943 zoot suit riots to coverage of the Rodney King verdict and subsequent uprising, ratings-fuelled representations of violence, especially violence related to Chicana/os, Mexicans, and blacks, terrified Anglos. The National Association of Hispanic Journalists' annual report, *The Portrayal of Latinos and Latino Issues on Network Television News*, consistently finds that news presentations depict Latina/os as mired in violence, gangs, drugs, and other illegal activity (Subervi, Torres, and Montalvo 2005). Couple the biased reporting about Latina/os with networks' rising coverage of crime (even as crime rates have decreased drastically since the early 1990s), and Los Angeles becomes "factually" presented as a city rife with "dangerous" people of color: a situation Hogan (2012) equates to "a world gone mad on the evening news." *Smoking Mirror Blues*, too, reflects the unsubstantiated fear of racial violence, as the previous year's Dead Daze riots loom menacingly over El Lay. The opening paragraph's newscast warns Angelinos, "You wouldn't want to get caught in any riots like there were last year" (Hogan 2001, 6). These riots are mentioned repeatedly in the novel without explanation, but always hinting at the possibility of a repeat performance. Hogan's archeology of the digital divide, which involves reclaiming the celluloid divide, is both a critique of technoracism and a proposed intervention.

Smoking Mirror Blues next connects news depictions of Chicana/os to legislation and police action against them, reinforcing the material importance of media control. The violent representations of Dead Daze, by a documentary director who narrates vignettes in the novel, reflect what Sara Beale contends are actual media practices of adjusting the level of violence in program content in order to attract viewers and, in turn, meet the demands of corporate sponsors (2006, 421–22). Smokey's rise to stardom begins when the gang called Los Olvidadoids confronts him as he sits in the street playing the *teponaxtle*. Hogan's trickster reacts violently by killing the gang's leader: "Without a pause, Tezcatlipoca took the drumsticks and forced them through the soft flesh under the Olvidadoid's chin all the way up into his brain" (2001, 35). The director catches the act on camera and exclaims, "It's great! We caught a SoCal citizen exercising his legal right to kill a certified gangster in self-defense! Every network on the planet will want it!" (35). Smokey kills the gangster under the "Sepulveda law," a name echoing the Langdon Street Injunction against gang members along the Sepulveda corridor of LA in 2000, the year before the novel's publication. One of a cascade of injunctions against gangs in Los Angeles and surrounding suburbs and barrios, the legislation banned members of the Sepulveda "gang" from "associating in public, hanging out on private property, flagging down cars, using walkie-talkies and other activities" (McGreevy and Larrubia 1999). Hogan's narrative demonstrates how media violence against Chicana/os at the end of the century caused police violence. The "war" on drugs and gangs in Southern California at the turn of the century, Beres and Griffith assert, encouraged people to view "young minority males as the enemy," thus fostering "illegal police conduct" (2001, 747). The demonizing of youth "can lead voters to pass draconian anti-crime measures directed against young offenders" (748). Hogan's camera captures how the news media's sensationalization of racially coded violence promulgates police violence and harsh legal action against people of color. The emergent digital divide, he makes clear, is a function of violence against people of color that involves visual effacement and even physical erasure.

Smoking Mirror Blues also critiques the commodification of Chicana/o bodies and the reification of Chicano males as always already gang members by parodying how increased police violence and corresponding rises in media ratings generate advertising dollars for news corporations. The death of the Olvidadoids' leader, for instance, demonstrates how El Lay's Chicana/os are trapped by the corporate search for capital. His mother protests:

> How can they let this maniac kill my son, and then say it's all perfectly legal! There's something wrong here!
>
> People are still thinking in old stereotypes. It's not like gangs are what they were thirty years ago! Nachito worked his way up through the gang to leader honestly, and the corporate sponsors had their eyes on him. (Hogan 2001, 49)

In addition to humanizing the gang leader through familial connections and showing his "forgotten," or *olvidado*, heritage, the mother's speech demonstrates the lack of opportunities afforded marginalized men in El Lay. Ironically, gangs provide one of the few "legitimate" ways that Chicana/o youth can make money in the novel, providing a path into the corporate world that would otherwise be inaccessible: Nachito's mother was "sure he would have ended up an executive in a few years" (49). However, as gangs gain corporate sponsorship, they remain illegal, allowing the creation and destruction of gang members to provide money for corporations. The gangs serve corporate interests while alive, "enforcing corporate fashion laws" (62) and fueling consumer spending, and their members' deaths are sold as spectacle by media networks. By contrast, nonviolent media representations of Chicana/os in El Lay (and LA) are part of the *olvida*, or forgetting, as they are not profitable. Hogan's dystopian futurescape thus resonates allegorically with the contemporary disenfranchisement of and systemic violence against Chicana/os, both mediated by digital and media violence.

Looking through the Smoking Mirror

Hogan's critique of Chicana/o erasure reveals how the media distort their depictions of the real, in some cases substituting simulations that have "no relation to any reality whatsoever" (Baudrillard 1994, 6). Tezcatlipoca counters mainstream media's skewed reflections with the metaphor of the *tezcatlipoca*, a smoking mirror made of obsidian that recovers Aztec vision. Capitalism's denaturing of the real leaves an empty space where a trickster god, a simulation himself with no relation to reality, can manipulate culture's empty signifiers. While mainstream media provide limited entry for Chicana/os as active agents, the novel presents art, particularly digital narratives and music, as sites primed to formulate Chicana/o identity and presence in the digital age of the present and not-too-distant future. The novel does this by connecting Aztec mythic history and digital representation to offer a new space for signification. Tezcatlipoca's first act once he posseses Beto, for instance, showcases the connection between digital art and representation. Smokey Espejo sees himself in Beto's bathroom mirror and notes that it makes "everything look so unnaturally bright and clear. You could stare into this mirror for days and all you'd see would be this sharp reflection of what things looked like, no visions would come" (Hogan 2001, 26–27). Conversely, the "the obsidian mirror attached to the monitor screen" (26) promises something different. Computer monitors, televisions, and other screens when powered down provide a surface similar to a flake of obsidian: a distorted, muted reflection. However, when turned on, the screens provide "visions" of anything a programmer or camera can capture. From capitalist-driven advertisements to a simulated god flashing his name at a user, these visions emphasize the power inherent in digitized content, a power rife with artistic possibility. The novel exploits the linguistic connection between mirror and god, both *tezcatlipoca*, metaphorically transferring the god's trickster impulse to the computer when Beto adheres his *tezcatlipoca* to the monitor.

The computer games Beto designs demonstrate the potential revolution that digital art provides and the resistance it enables against mass media's gatekeepers. Beto's adherence to a Mesoamerican aesthetic—involving Aztec warriors, ritual sacrifice, and traditional Aztec art—in his virtual reality games threatens his access to mainstream production and employment, but this exclusion is also liberating. His games are unique: the scenery is photorealistic, but the light doesn't fall where it should, and the game's Aztec characters look "like drawings from codices" (17). Beto literally turns code to codex, flashing Aztec imagery on the computer's smoking mirror screen. By adding pictograms to digital technology, Beto begins the process of creating Chicana/o presence in the future's technologies—all based in the past. However, his business partner Ralph, exemplifying white corporations, interprets Beto's programs as lacking "a sense of the appropriate" and delving "too far into Aztec culture" and "postpostmodern art" (16). In other words, Beto's work moves beyond the "appropriate" role for Chicana/os in video games, which Frederick Luis Aldama marks as a "nonplayable character, obstacle to overcome, or simply part of the backdrop" (2013, 241). This narrative tension reflects Hogan's own experience in the publishing world: in an interview, he describes "New York publishers" refusing his "noisy minority" writing because it "wasn't 'commercial' enough for them" (2003). A lack of access to mainstream publication (for Hogan and Beto) polices representation, ensuring that Chicana/o depictions in the present are "appropriate," which ultimately maintains the erasure of Chicana/os in the future.

Ralph also considers Beto's deviations from the norm as not acceptable to a "contemporary audience," a phrase he immediately imagines Beto would clarify as an "Anglo audience" (Hogan 2001, 16). Conflating ethnicity and temporality—screening "Anglo" as "contemporary"—removes all racially "other" subjects from the novel's present (our future). To be white means existing in the present and future. The novel treats representation of Chicana/os in digital space as tantamount to cultural survival, and given that mainstream news representations of marginalized subjects threaten their physical survival, the stakes are nothing less than continued Chicana/o existence. Ralph's contradictory consideration of the game rests on a refusal to allow Chicana/o history into the present, and it is Beto's insistence on representing ethnicity and refusing the color-blind racism endemic in digital spaces that hinders his ability to break into digital markets. Hogan's novel is animated by the author's rejection of the dual edict that one cannot have Aztec traces in the present and one cannot allow Chicana/o history to be integrated into the digital future.

Even as Beto's revolutionary and disruptive art is denied market representation, the novel establishes the potential of this art to influence people and illustrates the wealth of possibility repressed by the mainstream media. Its power is demonstrated when Beto's games invade Ralph's dreams. Ralph sees Beto burst through his door and hand him

> a human heart that didn't have a speck of blood on it—it was still beating. Ralph put it down next to his computer. Blood-red wires wormed out of the heart's venal and arterial openings and, with crackling sparks on contact, worked their way into Ralph's computer. The monitor flickered. Then there was a nuclear blast. (33)

The prescient image of Beto taking over a computer with his heart, his blood, demonstrates Beto's digital potential as it remembers Chicana/o and Mexican artists such as Marion C. Martinez, who blend technology and traditional calendar art. The digital heart also invokes the Mexican Sacred Heart, a symbol bridging Aztec and Catholic cultures that remains a powerful image in Chicana/o art. The dream foregrounds the invasion of the digital realm by the heart and soul of Chicana/o culture—a cybernetic blending that reflects the biological and cultural mixing of Mexico's colonization. Beto's art works its way into Ralph's unconscious, reflecting the presence of Chicana/os in capitalist culture and representation: repressed, but not lost or erased.

Tezcatlipoca provides Chicana/o art with its audience, exploiting the future's need for a route out of the maze of media simulations and capitalist signification. Dead Daze conscripts ethnic identity as capitalist product through recomboculture, and this commodification attenuates ethnic history and cultural significance, leaving people open to the influence of media as the arbiter of morality, culture, and thus reality.[7] People are "crying out for gods" in the new world (44). Tezcatlipoca is an amalgamation of "trickster beings, all over the planet" (160), from Henry Louis Gates's signifying monkey to Gerald Vizenor's trickster as "semiotic sign" of "agnostic imagination and aggressive liberation" (1989, 13). As such, he can provide a path to salvation and liberation. When introducing his music on the radio—the cue containing subliminal messages that were to hypnotize the masses—Tezcatlipoca claims, "You need me to sing the blues for you. To jolt you out of the prison you call your self. To heal you. To allow you to dance the ecstatic, chaotic dance of life" (Hogan 2001, 160). Using the blues as a tool for signification, upsetting order and fostering chaos, Tezcatlipoca promises freedom from mass media violence. He takes over the mediasphere: every station in the novel presents interviews, music videos, or promotional ads starring Smokey Espejo. Tezcatlipoca controls the industry to conquer the world. According to Hogan's speculative novel, the revolution *will* be televised. And Chicana/o culture will be central.

Hogan's god thus creates a digitized Chicana/o nationalism reveling in its own contradictions to fight erasure in a commodified, recomboculture world. A simulation himself, Tezcatlipoca denies his fabrication and demands a biological link back to the real. This is either a playful contradiction or, as Sheila Contreras (2006) notes of Chicano nationalism's reappropriation of Aztec identity, a modern primitivism that ignores the actual Natives of Mexico and belies the colonial impulses girding Chicana/o history. Unlike Contreras's critique of Alurista and Gloria Anzaldúa, Hogan's nationalism undermines the very history it constructs, replacing the nostalgic conscription of the Aztec past with digital copy, underscoring its own constructedness. For example, Tezcatlipoca pushes Beto into his own unconscious to discover an ironic, essentialized link to his Mexica ancestry. After having a direct neural link to the computer implanted in Beto's body, Tezcatlipoca locks Beto into his own brain, claiming that he

> was alive and well and living in your DNA long before you had any claim to it, long before you were even born, back when your ancestors crossed the land-bridge from Asia, and later when you searched the deserts and mountains of Mexico for Lake Texcoco where you would build the glorious city of Tenochtitlán; I was running your brain the way you run your computer. I gave you all your ideas Beto. . . . I made you conjure me out of the god-simulating program. (Hogan 2001, 111)

The naturalization of a biological Aztec identity by a clearly manufactured computer program redefines Chicano nationalism with postmodern trickster play, as this naturalized identity arises in a simulated god who revels in a cultural milieu incorporating all cultures (modern primitive to technophilic) as equal contributors to mestizaje.

Control of the future means control over both access to digital media and development of digital content. Tezcatlipoca embodies representational possibility and synthesizes the contradictions involved with creating ethnic identity in a culture of color-blind racism. His mastery of the mediasphere allows him to inject Chicana/o history into digital representation. Hogan's gods actually take over Aztlán, and Hogan naturalizes this control by projecting that all American technologies, histories, and cultures were built from Mexican/Aztec code(x), even as he demonstrates the fabrication of the construction. The possibilities and problems for the future are most clear in how the digital version of the trickster god lives on, a recombo of what has been his body and soul through the novel, alive and well in the digital realm. Far from being vanquished, Tezcatlipoca becomes the mediasphere. The message is clear. We are everywhere. We are timeless. You cannot make us disappear. We are inside you.

Gender, Scopophilia, and the Smoking Mirror's Limits

As the novel demands space for Chicano authorship, it simultaneously erodes women's claims to authorial agency and relegates women to accoutrements of men's art. For over a quarter century, Chicana feminists have critiqued the Chicano movement for its uncritical display of hetero-normative and patriarchal ideals, which relegate women to positions as heterosexual mothers and lovers. The novel's nationalism replicates these problems even as it addresses the complications involved in creating a neonationalist identity as a challenge to the digital divide.

Beto's video game represents the raw artistic material that the main-stream media refuse to promote, but the truly powerful digital content in the novel is the god-simulating program itself, written by Xochitl and cloned without permission by Beto to animate Tezcatlipoca. Xochitl receives little textual credit as author of the chip, but overwhelming attention is given to her as the body holding the program, as a mother figure. She "births" the program before the novel's opening, writing the lines of text that allow gods to be formed and laboring through the creative process. Yet the reader is first introduced to the program through Beto's "crazy, mumbo jumbo ceremony" (Hogan 2001, 12–13) that allows the code to come alive and become a powerful force. Beto stands on Xochitl's labor, shaping the trickster force that allows digital Chicano nationalism to exist; she births the art, he shapes it. What recognition she gets is erased when Tezcatlipoca insists that his origin predates the chip's. Moreover, Xochitl has no control of the code once Beto lets it loose into the mediasphere. She can create a "truncated version of her god-simulating program" (183) to affect goddesses with Tan Tien's help, but Xochitl is powerless against her textual creation. In bringing Tezcatlipoca to life on women's labor and simultaneously marginalizing women's work, the novel inadvertently reveals broader problems with women's authorship in digital spaces.

To keep control over someone who would otherwise be an excellent scholar and a strong, independent Mexicana, the novel frames Xochitl as a "decent, practical Mexican woman" (10)—what Isabel Molina Guzmán calls one of the "long-standing US archetypes of Latina immigrant femininity and domesticity, that of the self-sacrificing, almost-virginal, always-religious ethnic mother" (2005, 183)—then punishes her for being sexually unavailable. The novel forces Xochitl through a gauntlet of eroticized violence: she is chased, manhandled, and molested for the reader's pleasure. For example, an extremist religious organization wants the program to create the "One True God" (Hogan 2001, 163), and their disciples accost her several times: "The ghosts carried Xochitl through the streets of University City. Two figures . . . carrying a kicking and screaming, nightgown-clad woman just wasn't anything unusual" (30). Even though the novel's commercial documentary director focuses his attention on gang violence in El Lay, he also captures the violence against Xochitl. The camera leers at her, providing a scopophilic entry into the scene: "try to get some closeups—she doesn't have any underwear on and there may be the chance for some nudity, which always ups the salability. Ah, yes, one of her breasts has popped out—be sure to get as close as you can, and in focus!" (31).

Hogan seeks to critique the scopophilia of the digital age, which is a continuation of Hollywood's practices. But the camera's lens, coupled with Hogan's overly graphic descriptions, ultimately eroticizes the physical and visual violence against Xochitl, inviting readers to take pleasure in "controlling" and "punishing" her (Mulvey 1988, 64). Xochitl's body becomes a site of violence as she denies what patriarchy demands be given to men (the chip and her body). She is sexually molested, too. On the bus from Mexico to the United States she is accosted by nonchalant assailants while sleeping: "An asio man in a Chinese National Corporation uniform was in the seat next to her, with a hand on one of her breasts; before she could figure out what was going on, he grinned sheepishly and turned away" (Hogan 2001, 60). The sheepish grin of her attacker diminishes the assault's impact, and the casual tone of the text reinforces the normalcy of the behavior—an attitude that contrasts starkly with empathetic depictions of the gang members through Nachito's mother. The novel replicates the visual media's eroticization of violence against women without providing a focused critique of the patriarchal abuse of women.

The women not controlled by violence are instead presented as overly sexual objects for male consumption and as the very stereotypes the novel otherwise refutes. The male gaze directs the visual media's depictions of women; they are filmed, placed, dressed, and otherwise presented for men's pleasure (Mulvey 2003, 58). Ralph's description of Tan Tien exemplifies both the limitations of women's roles in the novel and the text's exoticization of Asian women. When Ralph first sees Tan Tien, she is at her detective agency. He notes, "She was barefoot, and wearing a short kimono and loose jeans—her tiny feet were gorgeous. Her overpowering feminine presence bowled him over instantly. She was so small and delicate, yet strong and powerful; she could be lover, mother, sister, daughter as the moment demanded" (Hogan 2001, 92). She is defined by her potential relationship to men (as lover, mother, sister, daughter), a move that reflects Xochitl's typing as the "almost-virginal" mother and limits women's agency outside male influences. Celine Shimizu reminds us that "popular [representation] for Asian/American women is infused with a particularly powerful and perverse sexuality in U.S. cinema and performance in the twentieth century" (2007, 12), and women of color are constructed as "pathological: excessive, aberrant, and deviant" to normalize white women's sexuality (279). Tan Tien is described as an exotic Asian other (a generic "asio" in fact), and her sexual escapades, from tantric yoga to sex as "healing magic," provide an outlandish entry into an imagined sexuality (Hogan 2001, 205). In addition to providing several graphic sex scenes where "tiny" Tan Tien contrasts with her black partner, "gigantic" Zobop, emphasizing the depictions of Asian women as small and delicate, she is unfailingly proper, polite, and mysterious with her "Mona Lisa half-smile" (39). Either sipping tea or engaging in outrageous sex with Zobop, she is limited by the submissive and polite Lotus Blossom stereotype in which she is cast. Tan Tien, like Xochitl, is an intelligent woman; however, the novel's presentation of her oversexed body focuses the reader's gaze on her fetishized flesh.

Furthermore, the novel uses Phoebe Graziano, a white woman, to provide an idealized figure of womanhood that reinforces women's positions as objects for the male gaze and signifiers for masculinity. The most fetishized person in the text, she embodies La Malinche, a legendary Mexican betrayer and whore based on Malinalli, the indigenous woman sold into servitude whose claim to agency involved helping Hernán Cortés conquer the Aztecs, and who subsequently bore his child. Phoebe is an empty shell, a hedonistic woman driven solely by desire for sex, attention, and drugs. Phoebe thinks that "the whole world should want inside her vagina!" (134). Her need for attention, particularly sexual attention, leads her to switch sides several times in the text, playing either Smokey's prized groupie or Caldonia's lover. She becomes a symbolic prize for the characters: Tezcatlipoca wants her because her presence keeps Beto under control, and Caldonia wants her as a lover. The pull and push for control of her body drives the second half of the narrative, and conquering the white woman sexually becomes Caldonia's primary and Smokey's secondary objective. Smokey reinforces his machismo by possessing Phoebe, keeping her locked in a hotel room under guard and his hypnotic command, substantiating Mulvey's contention that the female body is "a signifier for the male other, bound by a symbolic order in which man can live out his fantasies and obsessions" (1988, 58). Phoebe's desire for Smokey as well as her desirability elevates Smokey's status, and her hedonistic bisexuality functions as a heterosexual male fantasy.

Just as the camera focuses on the violence against Xochitl's body, these images and the novel's descriptions indulge heavily in voyeurism of lesbian sex, framing the novel's queer subjects for the male gaze. When the director sees Phoebe and Caldonia, he demands, "Zoom in on the two women kissing—they're dressed as an angel and a medusa on that motorcycle that's blocking traffic. This is perfect!" (Hogan 2001, 21). Rosalind Gill argues that lesbians in mainstream media are visually "packaged . . . primarily for a straight male gaze" (2009, 152), and Lisa Diamond contends that "the most desirable and acceptable form of female–female sexuality is that which pleases *and* plays to the heterosexual male gaze, titillating male viewers while reassuring them that the participants remain sexually available in the conventional heterosexual marketplace" (2005, 105; emphasis in original). Hogan seeks to weave this type of scopophilia into his critique of Chicana/os' commodification, but he falls into the trap of inviting the very gaze he critiques. Phoebe's relationship with Caldonia ultimately provides soft-porn graphic images that denature lesbian identity. For example, the novel recollects a vacation the two had: "Caldonia had the big, black, strap-on dildo that Phoebe had picked out," and they "screwed until Phoebe's vagina, anus and mouth were raw and the surface of the dildo was buffed as smooth and shiny as an obsidian mirror" (2001, 102–3). The novel's reminiscence eroticizes their bodies for male fantasy, privileges the phallus as an intermediary between the women, and assaults Phoebe, replacing what might be a description of pleasure with a violent image of "raw" flesh. The novel depicts lesbian sex as equivalent to violent, heterosexual encounters and equates Caldonia to a heterosexual man in search of a penis, one compared to a *tezcatlipoca*, linking the phallus to male trickster power.

In the novel, men's lack of access to all women is also critiqued through Caldonia, and men's ownership of female sexuality is reinforced. The only group of lesbians the novel presents is at "Lesbos West," where "homely dykes whose fat, lumpy asses seemed to be permanently grafted to the barstools up front" eat tiger penis soup, devouring the very phallus they should be worshipping (78). Because they are inaccessible, the novel makes them undesirable, ugly man haters, whereas Phoebe's bisexuality increases her value, as men can partake of lesbian scopophilia without being excluded from sex with the objects of their desire. The novel reinforces male ownership of women's sexuality as Phoebe, bisexual, continually turns toward heterosexuality via Beto and Smokey. The two women who do not actively participate in their own sexualization for men, Caldonia the lesbian and Xochitl the virgin mother, are forced into heterosexual spectacle to reify their availability for the male gaze. To put program "control elements" (204) on Tezcatlipoca and push him from

Beto's body, the two women use a truncated version of the god-simulating program that transforms them into goddesses, allowing them to contain Tezcatlipoca within a digital bed of phallocentric erotics. Choosing the women unavailable to conventional voyeuristic pleasure to play in the simulation clearly marks their position in patriarchy: you can say no unless we need/want you.

Smoking Mirror Blues transmutes *all* women's power to their heterosexual prowess and turns queer woman straight, but it does not enact sexual inversions on men in the same manner. Male heterosexuality is instead deified through Smokey and reinscribed through women's actions. Hogan's contradictory recovery and digitization of Aztec mythology is powerful, defying Anglo definitions of Chicano and Mexicano subjectivity and using postmodern play to contain, but not resolve, modern primitivism and the socially constructed nature of Chicana/o identity. As Hogan says in this dossier, his heroes are "Chicanonauts" who "explore, but since they carry the complex Chicano cultural baggage, they aren't cool or detached. The stories they generate crackle with conflict in the new environments." However, the novel re-creates patriarchal essentialism without critiquing it, duplicating the digital absence of Chicanas instead of exploring and challenging it. This future denies women the authorial agency Tezcatlipoca's revolution creates, refusing them the access that digital representation provides.

While Hogan provides a radical paradigm for upsetting the digital divide in relation to Chicanos, the ways in which the novel reproduces the dominant media's reflection of women occludes its otherwise visionary intervention. The novel calls for, albeit unintentionally, a queering of Chicano nationalism, bringing intersectional conceptions of identity into the digital age. *Smoking Mirror Blues* inadvertently points to its own shortcomings, invoking other marginalized groups' struggles and highlighting the need to queer Aztlán more fully than Tezcatlipoca's machinations manage to do. Enfolding a critique of gender and sexuality in addition to race and class within the novel's tricksterizing of the digital divide would have allowed the deconstruction of "dominant ideological signs" and their transformation into "a new, imposed, and revolutionary concept" (Sandoval 1994, 78). In short, this lacuna in the text demarcates not only an absence of Latina/os from the digital landscape but also an absence of women and queer subjects from a nationalized space in which visual representation shapes digital media.

Notes

1. STEM fields include science, technology, engineering, and mathematics.

2. In this essay I use the term *media* to refer to mainstream US news, television, film, Internet, and video games.

3. Tezcatlipoca is leader of the Aztec pantheon, who takes his brother Quetzalcoatl's place after tricking Quetzalcoatl into getting drunk, sleeping with their sister, and leaving the continent on a raft of snakes. The novel draws from Aztec codices and calendars such as the Florentine Codex and the Codex Borgia to link Chicana/os to their Mesoamerican past. For more on Tezcatlipoca's stories, see Olivier's (2008) *Mockeries and Metamorphoses of an Aztec God*.

4. Smokey Espejo is an English-Spanish translation of Tezcatlipoca.

5. The future's mediasphere refers to the United States' agglomeration of mainstream film, television, music, advertising, and the Internet (Hogan 2001).

6. The National Register of Historic Places inventory-nomination form for the Guaranty Building, with a statement of the building's historic significance, was submitted in 1979 by Solendar & Company to the National Park Service. http://pdfhost.focus.nps.gov/docs/NRHP/Text/79000481.pdf.

7. Hogan (2013) defines his globally inclusive mestizaje as "recomboculture," which alludes to "recombinant DNA" and "the cultural mutations that happen when cultures come together, fuck & fight, damage chromosomes, and generate fascinating new monstrosities."

Works Cited

Aldama, Frederick Luis, ed. 2013. "Getting Your Mind/Body On: Latinos in Video Games." In *Latinos and Narrative Media: Participation and Portrayal*, edited by Frederick Luis Aldama, 241–58. New York: Palgrave Macmillan.

Banks, Adam J. 2006. *Race, Rhetoric, and Technology: Searching for Higher Ground.* Mahwah, NJ: Lawrence Erlbaum.

Baudrillard, Jean. 1994. *Simulacra and Simulation*. Translated by Sheila Faria Glaser. Ann Arbor: University of Michigan Press.

Beale, Sara Sun. 2006. "The News Media's Influence on Criminal Justice Policy: How Market-Driven News Promotes Punitiveness." *William & Mary Law Review* 48, no. 2: 397–481.

Beres, Linda S., and Thomas D. Griffith. 2001. "Demonizing Youth." *Loyola L.A. Law Review* 34, no. 2: 747–66.

Berg, Charles Ramírez. 2002. *Latino Images in Film: Stereotypes, Subversion, and Resistance*. Austin: University of Texas Press.

Contreras, Sheila Marie. 2006. "Literary Primitivism and 'the New Mestiza.'" *Interdisciplinary Literary Studies* 8, no. 1: 49–71.

Dobbs, Charles M. 2009. "Hollywood Movies and the American Community." In *Great Depression: People and Perspectives*, edited by Hamilton Cravens and Peter C. Mancall, 207–25. Santa Barbara, CA: ABC Clio.

Diamond, Lisa M. 2005. "'I'm Straight, but I Kissed a Girl': The Trouble with American Media Representations of Female–Female Sexuality." *Feminism and Psychology* 15, no. 1: 104–10.

Gill, Rosalind. 2009. "Beyond the 'Sexualization of Culture': Thesis: An Intersectional Analysis of 'Sixpacks,' 'Midriffs' and 'Hot Lesbians' in Advertising." *Sexualities* 12, no. 2: 137–60.

Hauschild, Alexander. 2012. "Digital Resources: Developing Chicano/a Latino/a Digital Resources." In *Pathways to Progress: Issues and Advances in Latino Librarianship*, edited by John L. Ayala and Salvador Guerena, 139–49. Santa Barbara, CA: Libraries Unlimited.

Hogan, Ernest. 2001. *Smoking Mirror Blues*. La Grande, OR: Wordcraft of Oregon.

———. 2003. "Interview: Ernest Hogan." By James M. Palmer. *Strange Horizons*, February 10. http://www.strangehorizons.com/2003/20030210/hogan.shtml.

———. 2012. "Guest Post: I Didn't Know I Was an Alien, or: How I Became a Recombocultural Sci-Fi Guy." *News + Opinion from the Future Fire*, May 15. http://djibrilalayad.blogspot.com/2012/05/guest-post-i-didnt-know-i-was-alien-or.html.

McGreevy, Patrick, and Evelyn Larrubia. 1999. "Suit Seeks to Limit Langdon Street Gang Activity." *Los Angeles Times*, March 30.

Molina Guzmán, Isabel. 2005. "Gendering Latinidad through the Elián News Discourse about Cuban Women." *Latino Studies* 3, no. 2: 179–204.

Mulvey, Laura. 1988. "Visual Pleasure and Narrative Cinema." In *Feminism and Film Theory*, edited by Constance Penley, 57–68. New York: Routledge.

Nakamura, Lisa. 2007. *Digitizing Race: Visual Cultures of the Internet*. Minneapolis: University of Minnesota Press.

Nericcio, William Anthony. 1996. "Autopsy of a Rat: Odd, Sundry Parables of Freddy Lopez, Speedy Gonzales, and other Chicano/Latino Marionettes Prancing about Our First World Visual Emporium." *Camera Obscura* 37 (January): 188–237.

Olivier, Guilhem. 2008. *Mockeries and Metamorphoses of an Aztec God: Tezcatlipoca, "Lord of the Smoking Mirror."* Boulder: University Press of Colorado.

Ramírez, Catherine S. 2008. "Afrofuturism/Chicanafuturism: Fictive Kin." *Aztlán: A Journal of Chicano Studies* 33, no. 1: 185–94.

Sandoval, Chela. 1994. "Re-entering Cyberspace: Sciences of Resistance." *Dispositio/n* 19, no. 46: 75–93.

Shimizu, Celine Parreñas. 2007. *The Hypersexuality of Race: Performing Asian/American Women on Screen and Scene*. Durham, NC: Duke University Press.

Subervi, Federico, Joseph Torres, and Daniela Montalvo. 2005. *Network Brownout Report 2005: The Portrayal of Latinos and Latino Issues on Network Television News, 2004 with a Retrospect to 1995*. Austin: National Association of Hispanic Journalists.

Vizenor, Gerald, ed. 1989. *Narrative Chance: Postmodern Discourse on Native American Indian Literatures*. Norman: University of Oklahoma Press.

Contrapuntal Cyborgs?
The Ideological Limits and Revolutionary Potential of Latin@ Science Fiction

B. V. Olguín

> Not all new art is revolutionary, nor is it really new. . . . The Russian Futurists have affiliated with communism; the Italian Futurists have affiliated with Fascism.
> —José Carlos Mariátegui, "Art, Revolution, and Decadence"

The speculative arts have always been part of the fabric of Latin@ literature and popular culture, as demonstrated in the scholarship on Latin@ science fiction and fantasy (SFF) genres in the two *Aztlán* dossiers dedicated to this topic. Catherine S. Ramírez's testimonial reflections on being a science fiction "nerd" (2002) and her groundbreaking theoretical interventions to recenter writing by women of color, especially Gloria Anzaldúa, in the genealogy of SFF were an invitation for more speculative "coming outs," dialogues, and research into the revolutionary potential of this multi-genre category (Ramírez 2002, 2004, 2008). The scholarly excitement following Ramírez's interventions led to the discovery, recovery, and celebration of Latin@ SFF, which on the surface appeared to pose revolutionary alternatives to the hegemonic exercise of power. But is it accurate to assume that all Latin@ SFF is counterhegemonic? Do the Latin@ speculative arts break from the colonialist and xenophobic genealogy of SFF and from the equally troubling colonialist nostalgias, salient chauvinisms, and ideological contradictions undergirding much of Latin@ literature and film? How "revolutionary" is the growing body of Latin@ speculative work, and exactly what constitutes "revolution" in these texts? Is it a Trotskyite vision of armed autonomous workers' councils, the privileged peasant revolutionaries of the Maoists, anarchist communitarian affinity groups, neo-Luddite anti-technology paradigms, mystical spiritualisms, combinations of these, or something else altogether?

The goal of both *Aztlán* dossiers on the Latin@ speculative arts has been to recover and critically assess this growing body of work. In her essay in the first dossier, Daoine Bachran (2015) explicates important contradictions in the gendered and racialized signifying practices in Ernest Hogan's otherwise visionary speculative novel *Smoking Mirror Blues* (2001). Her trenchant analysis invites further candid interrogations of the ideologies being performed by specific Latin@ speculative artists and texts. In this essay I offer additional contrapuntal readings of the signifying practices of select Latin@ speculative film and fiction works that propose radical critiques of power and alternative theories of praxis. I believe that they are successful in only a very few cases. I am especially concerned with the ideological differences undergirding various models of the utopian vis-à-vis historical materialist ideas that inform Latin@ SFF.

Pursuant to a preliminary reassessment of the ideologies of Latin@ SFF, I will map the theories of labor, status of the machine and technology, and theories of revolutionary praxis in two Latin@ dystopian/utopian texts: Peruvian American filmmaker Alex Rivera's feature film *Sleep Dealer* (2008), and Chicana authors Rosaura Sánchez and Beatrice Pita's jointly authored novella *Lunar Braceros, 2125–2148* (2009). *Sleep Dealer* is set in a not-too-distant future along the US-Mexico border and focuses on a trio of Latina and Latino border dwellers who attempt to escape from the dystopian carceral web. In this new world, technology has fused with biology to enable the weaponizing of people's bodies and minds, the mining of memory, and the teleporting of bodily energy as profit-producing labor in remote sites. Similarly, *Lunar Braceros* narrativizes the climax in the consolidation of global capitalism, when monopolies have formed confederations that supersede the power of the nation-state. A small band of revolutionaries seeks to subvert this power and challenge their exploitation through direct action on the moon and on earth. The rebellion, which temporarily fails, is facilitated through the dissemination of underground information across place, space, and time via nanochips, a future form of miniature computer flash drives.

These texts offer stunning visual special effects and clever narrative devices that render cyborgs believable, carceral states familiar, and teleportation and moon travel mundane. The texts also introduce meta-narratives in the form of interactive websites and nanochips that add to the postmodernist aura of the narratives in which time, place, and space are continually presented and navigated out of sequence. Yet these texts resist the nihilist impulse of most postmodernist narratives. Fredric Jameson (1992) has argued that postmodernist disjunctions and transtemporal conjunctions, which he proposes as the governing cultural logic of late capitalism, also involve the fragmentation of the subject and the flattening of identity into schizophrenic superficiality. These flattened subjects are unmoored from the mechanics of alienation or even simple anomie, making the development of an oppositional consciousness, as well as rebellion and outright revolution, all the more difficult. The postmodern subject, Jameson argues, has not kept up with the technological mutations of the object, such as architecture, which houses subjects in vessels that fuse past and present, old and new, in confusing assemblages. The mystifying power of the technologically enhanced simulacrum, he suggests, is so overbearing that it even threatens our ability to theorize the present. Yet Jameson cuts through the mystifying haze of the form of postmodernism by noting:

> I want to avoid the implication that technology is in any way the "ulti-mately determining instance" either of our present-day social life or of our cultural production: such a thesis is, of course, ultimately at one with the post-Marxist notion of a postindustrial society. (1992, 37)

Jameson's critique of the postmodern fetish on and fear of technology, which is co-terminal with the purported death of the subject heralded in postmodern theory, reminds us of the salient but still radically undertheorized archetype of the Latin@ cyborg (and cyborgesque Latin@) and particularly of its relationship to the means of production. This topos animates both *Sleep Dealer* and *Lunar Braceros*. That is, despite their postmodern trappings, in which dystopic forces appear to overwhelm increasingly fragmented subjects, these two texts offer deliberate didactic discourses on the science of revolu-tionary resistance to capitalism and its multiple forms of alienation. But it is their postmodern trappings—and particularly the truncations of subjectivity and agency effected by technology—that ultimately distinguish these two texts in ways that illuminate the problem of ideology in the Latin@ specula-tive arts. One offers a theory of revolutionary praxis predicated upon a naive neo-Luddite philosophy; the other seeks to narrativize a historical materialist revolutionary theory of praxis that accounts for, without fetishizing, fearing, or dismissing, the value of machines and technology.

All Cyborgs Are Not Created Equal: Political Dissensus in Latin@ Cyborg Paradigms

Donna Haraway's (1991) pioneering work on the socialist potential of feminist cyborgs is intertwined with a reductive postmodernist reading of

Latina interstitial subjectivities as irreparably fragmented, an interpretation that Paula L. M. Moya (2002) has soundly critiqued. In contrast, Latin@ artists have refashioned the Latin@ cyborg (and less technologically mediated cyborgesque subjects) into potent symbolic forces in speculative film, television programming, and literature. From space operas (*Battlestar Galactica*) to quasi-steampunk (*El Mariachi*, 1992) to dystopian futurism (*Elysium*, 2013) to fantasy (*Spy Kids*, 2001), Latin@ mestizaje is synthesized into post-apocalyptic, technologically mediated cyborgs and quasi-cyborgs. Significantly, they lead the way out of the dystopian postmodern morass by either becoming machines or mastering them, albeit in a multiplicity of ideological directions that offer as many frustrations as utopian possibilities.

The ideological indeterminacy of the Latin@ cyborg is present from its inception. The first Chican@ cyborg appears in what may be considered the earliest Chican@ science fiction film, *Los Vendidos* (The Sellouts). The film is based on Teatro Campesino's agitprop satirical play by the same name (Valdez 1990), first performed in 1967 and recast as a filmed stage performance in 1973. The protagonist is a purportedly "vendido" robot, Eric Garcia, who in reality is a subversive mechanical Chicano cipher who betrays the Hispanic buyer who sought to exploit him as a "brown face in the crowd" for a political function with former California Governor Ronald Reagan. This first Chicano cyborg thus afforded audience members the opportunity to meditate on Chican@ identity and ideology, the overdetermination of archetypes, and urgent local political struggles of the era, as well as metaphysical interrogations of the species-being. As a result, the cyborg in *Los Vendidos* certainly is contrapuntal, but he still exists within a civil rights framework in which Chican@s were militating for inclusion within US settler colonialist and capitalist society. That is, the first iteration of a Chican@ cyborg is a medium for the unwitting performance of ideological ambivalence disguised as counterhegemonic critique and revolutionary agency.

Other prominent Latin@ cyborgs similarly fail to actualize an alternative political praxis that poses a material (and materialist) challenge to the capitalist regimens of exploitation they illuminate. For instance, Robert Rodriguez's neo-picaresque motorcycle-wandering eponymous protagonist in *El Mariachi* (1992)—who later morphs into a swashbuckling hero in prequels and sequels—is a cyborg permutation of the tired trope of the tragic mestizo. After his Pyrrhic victory against evil drug lords, he is reduced to pursuing his dream of making music with a mechanical strumming hand. In Eric Hobsbawm's (1965) topography, El Mariachi is merely an individual (and individualist) rebel who never even becomes a social bandit, much less a revolutionary who poses a coordinated challenge to power. An even more politically problematic Latin@ cyborg appears in Reyes Cárdenas's 1975 speculative serialized novella, *Los Pachucos y La Flying Saucer*, which intersects with a prominent strain of Latin@ speculative fiction that involves soft porn signifying of exoticized, racialized female Others. This story features two pachucos who "enter" into a cyborg female spaceship they use to travel across time as they wage war with a series of villains, with interspersed episodes in which the two pachucos suckle at the female spaceship's huge mechanical breasts. This masculinist iteration of Latin@ cyborg and cyborgesque paradigms also is evident in Hogan's fetish for Asian American sexbots and Mexican American lesbians and bisexual women in *Smoking Mirror Blues*, a scopophilic rendering that Bachran notes "simultaneously erodes women's claims to authorial agency and relegates women to accoutrements of men's art" (2014, 231). This scopophilia serves as a backdrop for the equally problematic expression of a proto-Luddite expression of Chican@ ambivalence to the specter of the postmodern machine, particularly computers and the Internet. The narrative revolves around a Chican@ computer game designer who conjures a malevolent Aztec god who seeks to control the world until thwarted by the gamer, who retakes control of the computer hyper-demon he helped create.

Ramírez poses alternatives to these masculinist speculative discourses by redefining the category of "cyborg" as a counterhegemonic woman-of-color praxis for black women and Chicana authors:

> Through the figure of the cyborg, [Gloria] Anzaldúa and [Judith] Butler also theorize a woman-of-color feminism. . . . Indeed, their subjects are cyborgs because they interrogate the stability of social categories, such as "woman," "American," and "human," and because they exemplify the construction of coalitions based on position and affinity, as opposed to identity and essence. However, Butler's black heroines and Anzaldúa's queer *mestiza* subject differ from a more generic cyborg because they also emphasize very particular New World histories (African American and Chicana, respectively). (2002, 394)

While these iterations of Latin@ cyborgs are by no means exhaustive, they illuminate important differences and a profound dissensus with respect to the definition, function, and political resonance of the Latin@ cyborg. By explicating the radically different cyborgian discourses in *Sleep Dealer* and *Lunar Braceros*, I propose to illuminate the need for a greater critical skepticism of the Latin@ speculative arts, particularly as regards the theories of power and counterpower that undergird the myriad texts that fall into this category. As Peruvian Marxist theorist José Carlos Mariátegui (2011) warns in the epigraph to this essay, the speculative arts—especially various "futurisms"—must be appraised based on their intertwined aesthetics, poetics, and political affinities lest we be deluded into thinking that all "new" art is actually new and revolutionary.

Specters of the Machine in Alex Rivera's *Sleep Dealer*: Revolutionary Ruptures or Neo-Luddite Spectacle?

Alex Rivera's rendering of the Latin@ cyborg in his speculative film *Sleep Dealer* affords and demands an interrogation of the ideological subtexts of the Latin@ speculative arts. *Sleep Dealer* is set in the near future when the United States has completely sealed the US-Mexico border, thereby preventing what Americans call "illegal" immigration. As a solution to the paradox of a bigoted, anti-immigrant society that still relies on Latin@ immigrant labor for its economic vitality, technological innovations now enable emigrants to teleport to distant job sites through special electrical nodes implanted in their forearms and backs. These cyber-braceros, or cyber-workers, also are known as "sleep dealers," and their trance-like pantomimed work exacts a potentially lethal toll on their bodies and minds (figs. 1, 2).

The brilliant plot revolves around three intersecting storylines. Memo Cruz works as a sleep dealer in a Tijuana cyber-factory after fleeing his rural town in Oaxaca, Mexico, which was reduced to a desert by a multinational corporation that has monopolized all water in the area. Chicano Rudy Ramirez is a newly minted drone pilot for this same multinational corporation. His first mission was to destroy the small home where Memo, a ham radio operator, had been regularly hacking into drone communications; Memo's father died in the inferno. Waitress Luz Martinez sells her memories through a memory-dealing website, "True Node." Luz tells her new friend Memo how to contact a "coyotek" (or virtual coyote/smuggler) to get cheap black market implants necessary for work in this new cyber-labor world. The already exploitative maquiladoras of old are now much more lethal, as these nodes enable factories to literally suck energy out of the workers. These three Latin@ cyborgs (and quasi-cyborgs, whose integration into machines varies in type and intensity) come together to fight the militarized multinational corporations whose power has supplanted all national governments. I submit that the film illuminates the complexities and potential

Figure 1. Scene from Sleep Dealer (2008) by Alex Rivera. Courtesy of Alex Rivera and Starlight Film.

Figure 2. Scene from Sleep Dealer (2008) by Alex Rivera. Courtesy of Alex Rivera and Starlight Film.

ideological contradictions of Latin@ SFF by presenting victory, liberation, and dis-alienation as being accessible only through the complete rejection of modern machines and postmodern technologies.

Ramírez's claim that "good science fiction re-presents the past or present, albeit with a twist" (2008, 185–86) is inversely true in this film. Written and produced at the height of the war on terror, the film is a chilling manifestation of the simulacrum effect that Jean Baudrillard (1994, 1995) identified in the First Gulf War. In the never-ending war on terror, US soldiering is overdetermined as a technologically mediated subjectivity and activity that involves remote-controlled drones, flexible body armor, specialized optics that increase vision beyond 20/20, and instrumentation that responds to bodily functions such as eye movements, making the weapon an extension of the human bearer. That is, the differences between the past human and future cyborg are indiscernible in the present. These transtemporal depictions of the technologically mediated soldier body raise serious questions about whether the machine is inherently violent, and whether it can be reclaimed and transformed into something other than violence. This is a particularly urgent inquiry since the cyborg has become more than a metaphor: it is a very real subject of history who embodies a unique materiality as a violently mediated interspecies techno-subject. Rivera's film, which responds to the incessant US xenophobia and war on terror that continually lead to new technological innovations, proposes to synthesize a way out of this dystopian morass. However, I believe the film does so in ways that may not necessarily offer a liberatory materialist synthesis of the evils of multinational monopoly capitalism that it so successfully explicates and indicts.

In Rivera's film the machine is not just a medium for exploitation; it is the actual manifestation of evil, and this ultimately hampers its potential use in counterhegemonic interventions. The exploitation of sleep dealers illuminates the multiple levels of labor alienation, which for cyber-braceros involves bioelectric fusions with machines that physically deplete them and can even lead to sudden death through reverse power surges. Technology also invades deep into the species-being: Luz's nodes, for instance, enable her memories to be bought and consumed in a rapacious manner that leaves her emotionally and physically exhausted after each memory upload session. It is a form of psychological exploitation and alienation, since the panoptic software can discern when an uploader is inventing memories or, alternatively, withholding true memories about real experiences. It thus constantly pushes her to open up the cyber-bracero equivalent of a pornographic money shot (fig. 3).

Figure 3. Scene from Sleep Dealer *(2008) by Alex Rivera. Courtesy of Alex Rivera and Starlight Film.*

All of these Latin@ cyborg characters are brought together when the cyber-pilot Rudy Ramirez sees the scenes of his own inaugural drone bombing flight while trolling the True Node website, where Luz had been uploading memories of her new friend Memo. Rudy subsequently commissions Luz to find out more about the family of the man he killed, and this inevitably brings him into contact with Memo in a tense scene that eventually leads to rapprochement. In the film's denouement, the three Latin@ cyborgs plot to enable cyber–*soldado razo* Rudy Ramirez to both use and rid himself of his cyborg self by destroying the dam he once protected for its corporate owner. This will release the life-giving water to the destitute farmers of Memo's home village and strike a devastating blow against the multinational corporation that Rudy resents for turning him into a killer of innocent civilians in defense of corporate profit. The film ends with the two males parting ways; Luz disappears following a devastating argument with Memo, who remains distrustful of her because he realizes she had been plumbing his mind for memories to sell to the man who killed his father.

While Memo and Luz apparently have satisfying, intense cybersex because of the nodes (showing how technology brings people together), and Rudy is able to blow up the dam because of his cybernetically weaponized body and his training as a drone pilot, the film nonetheless betrays a fear of the postmodern machine-human, or cyborg. The male-centered, dystopian, and neo-Luddite vision is consolidated in two final scenes that take the film into the realm of steampunk fusions of old and new technologies and, ultimately, toward a complete rejection of all machines. Despite the fact that Memo's village is restored to life by water flowing freely after the dam has been destroyed, he remains in Tijuana to tend his garden, watering maíz seedlings with a tin coffee can punched with holes out of which the sacred liquid drips to give life. The Edenic agrarian trope is paired with a now-redundant lesson offered by Rudy Ramirez, the ex-*soldado razo* who went native in a replay of Daniel Cano's (1990) "shifting loyalties": after Ramirez's defiant act of sabotage, he is pictured boarding a rickety bus that takes him "south," to an undisclosed place in Mexico or beyond, off the grid, and far away from the reaches of the militarized multinational corporation and industrialized postmodern society.[1] Both Memo's and Rudy's post-cyborg lives thus offer a semi-pacifist neo-Luddite antithesis to discourses that celebrate cyber-technology as the always already present future (yet another important strain in SFF).

It is true that this film provides a "twist" in its rendering of the past and future, as Ramírez expects "good science fiction" to do, but more important, the ideological tenor of the speculative twist in *Sleep Dealer* is not revolutionary: it does not involve the transformation of society or even the intimation of the need to destroy the ruling capitalist class beyond one act of revenge. While the film presents a visually luscious and prescient rendering of the alienation of labor through its exposé on the psychological and physical dimensions of cyber-estrangement, it leaves no room for harnessing technology as part of a coordinated revolutionary struggle; after all, the three friends go their own ways. The film's denouement suggests that we should simply smash the machine, the same response advocated by the early nineteenth-century English textile artisans known as Luddites, who protested the introduction of mechanization that threatened their livelihood at the dawn of the Industrial Revolution. In *Sleep Dealer*, the protagonists' anti-technology rebellion involves their destruction of the hydroelectric dam and their refusal to plug into the networks that would reactivate their de facto cyborg subjectivities (since their nodes remain implanted). The solution to the alienating and mystifying power of the simulacrum effect is simply to reject it, with the only alternatives being a return to the land to grow corn in isolation, an escape ever further south, or a decision simply to disappear into the Tijuana lumpenproletariat, as does Luz. The film emphasizes an anti-technology agrarian society that at best models a primitive communitarianism where water is freely shared. No attention is paid to the fact that this nostalgic individualist paradigm might be possible only after the world system completely collapses, bringing about devastation that would likely result in the extinction of all human beings. That is, the vision in *Sleep Dealer* is not just utopian and unscientific, as Marx notes in juxtaposing historical materialism and utopianism, but also fundamentally dystopian, defeatist, and naïve. No coordinated rebellion is possible within its neo-Luddite paradigm; the only option is mere survival as individuals. Everyone is left to fend for themselves. At best, they may engage in acts of sabotage that Hobsbawm (1965) would correctly call primitive rebellion, with no hope of effecting the type of systemic change that would eliminate the base cause of oppression: capitalism.

Towards a XicanIndi@ Communist Glocalactic Synthesis in Sánchez and Pita's *Lunar Braceros, 2125–2148*

In contrast to the persistent scopophilia, nostalgic indigenist discourses, and ideologically inchoate cyborg paradigms in the Latin@ speculative arts, Rosaura Sánchez and Beatrice Pita's 2009 novella, *Lunar Braceros, 2125–2148*, offers a more cogent, theoretically sophisticated, and ideologically consistent Marxist speculative intervention predicated on a cyborg proletarian revolution. *Lunar Braceros* is set in the mid-twenty-second century, when the earth has undergone a hegemonic realignment that began with a power grab by the New Imperial Order—made up of the ten dominant multinational consortia—which allied with US fascists to execute a coup in the United States. The new world power of the Cali-Texas Confederation is based in North America and several parts of the Pacific, all of Africa, and Chinese "colonies." The narrative focuses on multiple groups of multiracial rebels who are resisting this extreme yet logical evolution of international capitalism. A liberated indigenous zone in the Amazon region of South America temporarily provides refuge to other rebels who were once industrial cyborg moon workers, or lunar braceros, and dwellers of lumpenproletarian reservations on earth resembling concentration camps.

Within this dystopian geopolitical landscape, Sánchez and Pita introduce a subaltern, queer, cholo-inflected, indigenous-centered, and collectivist synthesis of the Latin@ speculative project: they repackage popular culture and genre fiction that breaks down complex politico-economic theories of labor alienation vis-à-vis new technologies in the cyber age. More important, they offer a theory of praxis for revolutionary struggle that is historically informed, scientific, and pragmatically unrestrained. That is, *Lunar Braceros* recasts cyborgs—who range from astronauts to nanochip recordings of now-dead people to a multiracial cast of characters who take control of space ships, weapons, and other technology—as an always already complexly racialized and gendered revolutionary cadre. This cadre has not disavowed technology or any mechanisms or means, including armed struggle, for effecting a structural transformation of the world, which necessarily involves the working class taking power and using it.

Sánchez and Pita's speculative synthesis of a revolutionary, multiracial, anti-capitalist insurgency has an important locus in the majority-indigenous commune of Chinganaza, which is organized along ancient and simultaneously modern principles of communalism. In this twenty-second-century dystopian future, in which multinational capitalist fascist monopolies have taken over the world, Chinganaza serves as a utopian agrarian refuge and way station for earth-based peasant and lumpen revolutionaries as well as for space proletarian rebels. This place, which corresponds to an actual location in the southeastern part of present-day Ecuador, is described in one dialogue among characters:

> Strictly speaking, the Commons in Chinganaza does not follow the Incan model. All the land here is held in common and all those dwelling here contribute to the subsistence and maintenance of the commons in some way. All of us have duties and each one of us, both men and women, has to spend part of the day working in the fields. (Sánchez and Pita 2009, 20)

In Chinganaza, no class, or racialized gendered class segment, is privileged; all coalesce as a subaltern counterhegemonic workforce that is also a coordinated fighting force.

Their enemy is the New Imperial Order, which controls much of the world and the moon. Within this dystopian universe, a competing Ruso-Chinese Confederation is an ally to the globally dominant Cali-Texas Confederation; this makes resistance even more difficult, as power truly has become a postnational global and intragalactic phenomenon. There also are nonaligned Amerindian confederations, such as the Southern Confederation of South American countries and the Andean Confederation, both of which are less rapacious and imperialist than the other confederations but also distinct from the communist liberated zone of Chinganaza, with which they engage in small-scale trade.

The New Imperial Order also operates the reservations, which contain a surplus labor pool of homeless and unemployed (13). Their only opportunities to leave the reservations are as bodies used for experiments by biolabs seeking to create artificial organs (14), or as "tecos," also known as lunar braceros, or moon laborers. Tecos sign work contracts for moon tours to run the robotics for mining operations, or to work as waste disposal laborers who handle dangerous toxic detritus since the over-polluted earth can no longer accommodate its own refuse. "Reslifers," as reservation dwellers are called, can escape their carceral life if a family member deposits a sufficient amount of money in a bank account to buy their freedom. This is an almost impossible prospect, since it requires years of work under bleak and often lethal conditions, provided one can even obtain a job in this high-tech world that requires educational resources usually beyond the reach of reservation dwellers. In an allusion to the surplus labor pool of large segments of the Chican@ population, the Fresno Reservation is located in the agricultural community of present-day Fresno, California.

The novella's plot focuses on eighteen-year-old Pedro's attempt to reconstruct the insurgent lives of his parents using nanotexts, which his biological mother Lydia left for him before disappearing into the underground. We learn through these nanotexts that Pedro's biological father Gabriel was assassinated by agents of the multinationals he was fighting, with his body unceremoniously dumped on a roadside in Brazil. We also learn that Lydia previously had been a reslifer born on the Fresno Reservation and eventually joined her brother Ricardo in the resistance movement. Faced with a literal prisoner's dilemma after having been incarcerated for their subversive activities, Lydia took a job on a lunar waste disposal unit in exchange for early release. Using their nanotexts, in addition to information added by his uncle Ricardo and other rebels, Pedro essentially travels through time and space in a dialogue with his now-dead father and disappeared mother. It is through one nanotext that Pedro discovers the socially symbolic truth about his birth and rearing. His parents fertilized and froze Pedro's embryo before they became sterile as a result of their nuclear disposal work on the moon. The quasi-cyborg fertilized egg was later brought to term by his parents' trusted friends and fellow rebels: Leticia bore Pedro and raised him with her lesbian partner, Maggie, and a host of other revolutionaries, many of whom help fill in the dialogic narrative. In this dystopian world where the protagonists are fighting for a materialist egalitarian resolution, collective parenting removes the primacy of biology in the construction of family, which underscores the revolutionary collectivist paradigm operative in the book.

Like its model of parenting and child rearing, the jointly authored novella is itself a collective dialogic enterprise, in which the idea of a protagonist also is collectivized through the cybernetic polyphony enabled by nanochips. Chinganaza becomes a metonym for a collectivist revolutionary paradigm that fuses an agrarian utopia with hyper-technological realities. In a rejection of the naive utopian discourses and Luddite impulses that define much of dystopian SFF, the narrative in *Lunar Braceros* includes one nanochip description of Chinganaza as a "commune, where we work together; here the land belongs to those who work it; everything is shared and there are no bosses," with the added proviso: "but we're not fooling ourselves; we are a tiny bubble in a turbulent world" (119). As Gabriela Nuñez notes in her essay in this anthology, food scarcity, and the low quality of food available on the reservations, becomes a site of struggle: the rebels engage in alternative collectivized organic food production not just for sustenance, but as indigenous-centered egalitarian political praxis. The didacticism of this description of communal living is complemented in other scenes where the authors describe Pedro's rearing and socialization as a socialist, which also serves to underscore the authors' own socialist realist aesthetic. Indeed, *Lunar Braceros* is imbedded with didactic Marxist discourses delivered through nanochips, which become veritable protagonists themselves. In yet another symbolically significant and highly didactic nanotext passage, for instance, the rebel parents offer their yet-to-be-born son a lesson about the complex and ever-evolving nature of place, space, and subjectivity:

> Space is formative, and when you grow up and become an astronomer, Pedro, you will need to remember this alternative space in which you were born and recall always that space is a product of social relations. Right, you're right, I am talking about a different kind of space. Here, not outer space. You'll undoubtedly be involved in the production of new spatial relations, maybe—hopefully—even in outer space, on another planet, but I want you never to forget this particular place, our commons, and that it represents a rejection of everything that is hegemonic and dominated by capital relations. (25)

The authors, who are Marxist theorists and veteran activists, responsibly temper the socialist realist romanticism of this passage by noting that Chinganaza later is invaded and the inhabitants scattered throughout the world. Pedro relocates to Mexico as he tries to reconnect with other rebels to continue what essentially is defined as a permutation of Mao Tse Tung's paradigm of "permanent revolution." That is, like the open-ended nature of testimonio that serves as a clarion call to readers to join in the struggle at hand, this narrative refuses to deliver an easy nostalgic or romantic resolution to the fight against capitalism's incessant, exploitative onslaught against people, earth, and the cosmos.

The main conflict in the plot (conveyed through nanochips) arises when Lydia and other lunar braceros discover a shipping container with the bodies of tecos they replaced, ominously signaling the fate planned for them. Some of them naively had believed that work would set them free. The tecos subsequently plot a rebellion and take over a spaceship, forcing the pilots at gunpoint to take them back to earth, where they escape their lethal labor bondage and join other rebels. This armed insurrection becomes linked to other coordinated actions against capitalists and their agents; the rebellion is designed not just to escape the alienating servitude of moon labor, but as a class war waged by subalterns against the forces buttressing capitalism. In contrast to the neo-Luddite rebels in *Sleep Dealer*, the protagonists in *Lunar Braceros* are revolutionaries who engage in theorizing and actualizing armed revolutionary insurrection pursuant to a strategic equilibrium in which the state is fought to a stalemate that eventually will lead to set-piece final battles that in turn result in a new order, not just in the liberation of individuals to tend private gardens, as it were.

A unique dimension of the theory of revolutionary praxis narrativized in *Lunar Braceros* is its synthesis of a Marxist XicanIndi@ paradigm that resists naive agrarian utopias bequeathed to SFF by Thomas More's (2003) paradigmatic 1516 tract, *Utopia. Lunar Braceros* instead is informed by current social movements and insurgent populations, particularly indigenous people in the Americas and the southern hemisphere, while simultaneously accounting for the future in its reclamation of technology, the machine, and a revolutionary cyborg. Indeed, the authors add an intergalactic extension to the productive neologism "glocal," which has been used to explicate how the local and glocal are intertwined: *Lunar Braceros* takes place in a local, global, and intergalactic—or glocalactic—space. The cover art and images interspersed throughout the novella by muralist Mario A. Chacon reiterate this new synthesis of seemingly incompatible Maoist and Trotskyite paradigms of revolution, packaged in a neo-cholo aesthetic characteristic of popular Chican@ mural art that is set both on earth and in outer space. The cover and interspersed drawings serve as a supplemental plot map that features key scenes and underscores the subaltern racialized hybrid cholo indigeneity of the space proletarian tecos. This hybridity is foregrounded in the cover image, in which oxygen tubes flow out of a teco's spacesuit helmet like a regal headdress made of the turquoise green, blue, and yellow feathers of the revered Quetzal bird, albeit without the feudal overtones; this particular teco also wears work gloves and space boots adorned with indigenous imagery. Significantly, his left fist is raised in a defiant gesture of counterpower, while his open right hand hails the viewer as if in a call for solidarity. Despite being an alienated worker reduced to a *calavera*, or skeletal frame, the teco is not defeated (fig. 4).

Figure 4. Cover art for Lunar Braceros, 2125–2148 *(Calaca Press, 2008). Reprinted courtesy of authors Rosaura Sánchez and Beatrice Pita and artist Mario A. Chacon.*

Lunar Braceros is not just a XicanIndi@ futurist tale, but a XicanIndi@ revolutionist allegory about the technologically saturated present and the changing nature of human—or rather cyborg—subjectivity. It illustrates how social relations continue to be shaped by one's relationship to production in new, yet fundamentally familiar, contexts of labor exploitation. The authors, as Marxists, center the machine and industrialization alongside agriculture and the human disposition to collectivities by historicizing the uses and misuses of technology and human labor. In the authors' exposé of rapacious moon mining, labor alienation in cyberspace, intragalactic space, and genetic engineering on earth, the nanochip serves as a synecdoche:

it locates the story simultaneously in the future and the present, in a transtemporal space where technology assumes a greater role in human society to the point that the machine almost eclipses—and at times even embodies—this new subject and society. In an unpublished interview, the authors note:

> We think that the interspecies/cyborgs of the future will necessarily need to be included in any transformative project. We've been thinking along these lines for *LB2* [*Lunar Braceros 2*] since Lydia and Pedro will be involved in genetic manipulation and the market for "choice genes."[2]

The authors thus introduce a radical alternative and Marxist challenge to cultural workers engaged in the Latin@ speculative arts: Cyborgs of the world, unite!

Notes

1. An important subplot in Daniel Cano's 1990 novel *Shifting Loyalties* focuses on rumors that a Chicano draftee defected from the US army and joined the Viet Cong out of potential ideological sympathies with subaltern anti-capitalist and anti-imperialist revolutionaries.

2. Interview by author, November 18, 2013.

Works Cited

Bachran, Daoine S. 2015. "From Code to Codex: Tricksterizing the Digital Divide in Ernest Hogan's *Smoking Mirror Blues*." *Aztlán: A Journal of Chicano Studies* 40, no. 2: 221–38.

Baudrillard, Jean. 1994. *Simulacra and Simulation*. Translated by Sheila Faria Glaser. Ann Arbor: University of Michigan Press.

———. 1995. *The Gulf War Did Not Take Place*. Bloomington: Indiana University Press.

Cano, Daniel. 1990. *Shifting Loyalties*. Houston: Arte Público.

Cárdenas, Reyes. 1975. *Los Pachucos y La Flying Saucer*. Reprinted in *Reyes Cárdenas: Chicano Poet, 1970–2010*. San Antonio: Aztlán Libre, 2013.

Haraway, Donna. 1991. "A Cyborg Manifesto: Science, Technology, and Socialist-Feminism in the Late Twentieth Century." Chap. 8 in *Simians, Cyborgs, and Women: The Reinvention of Nature*. New York: Routledge.

Hobsbawm, Eric. 1965. *Primitive Rebels: Studies in Archaic Forms of Social Movement in the 19th and 20th Centuries*. New York: W. W. Norton.

Hogan, Ernest. 2001. *Smoking Mirror Blues*. La Grande, OR: Wordcraft of Oregon.

Jameson, Fredric. 1992. *Postmodernism, or, the Cultural Logic of Late Capitalism*. Durham, NC: Duke University Press.

Mariátegui, José Carlos. 2011. "Art, Revolution, and Decadence." In *José Carlos Mariátegui: An Anthology*, edited and translated by Harry E. Vanden and Marc Becker, 423–26. New York: Monthly Review. First published 1926.

More, Thomas. 2003. *Utopia*. New York: Penguin. First published in 1516.

Moya, Paula L. M. 2002. *Learning from Experience: Minority Identities and Multicultural Struggles*. Berkeley: University of California Press.

Ramírez, Catherine S. 2002. "Cyborg Feminism: The Science Fiction of Octavia E. Butler and Gloria Anzaldúa." In *Reload: Rethinking Women + Cyberculture*, edited by Mary Flanagan and Austin Booth, 374–402. Cambridge, MA: MIT Press.

———. 2004. "Deus ex Machina: Tradition, Technology, and the Chicanafuturist Art of Marion C. Martinez." *Aztlán: A Journal of Chicano Studies* 29, no. 2: 55–92.

———. 2008. "Afrofuturism/Chicanafuturism: Fictive Kin." *Aztlán: A Journal of Chicano Studies* 33, no. 1: 185–94.

Rivera, Alex, dir. 2008. *Sleep Dealer*. Maya Entertainment.

Rodriguez, Robert, dir. 1992. *El Mariachi*. Los Hooligans Productions.

Sánchez, Rosaura, and Beatrice Pita. 2009. *Lunar Braceros, 2125–2148*. San Diego: Calaca.

Valdez, Luis. 1990. *Los Vendidos*. In *Luis Valdez—Early Works: Actos, Bernabé, and Pensamiento Serpentino*. Houston: Arte Público.

Machete Don't Text
From Genre Textualities to Media Networks in *Machete*

William Orchard

Released in September 2010, Robert Rodriguez and Ethan Maniquis's film *Machete* tells a complicated story about its eponymous hero, played by Danny Trejo. On the one hand, the movie is a revenge fantasy in which Machete, a former member of the Mexican Federal Police, must kill Torrez (Steven Seagal), the drug lord who beheaded Machete's wife and drove him out of Mexico and into hiding in Texas. While the revenge plot is set up before the credits roll, a second crime drama begins when Machete, who becomes an immigrant day laborer while on the lam, is hired by a man who frames him for the attempted assassination of a right-wing Texas Senate candidate (Robert De Niro) running on a vehement anti-immigration platform. In the course of trying to exact revenge on Torrez and expose a conspiracy that links Torrez to the senatorial candidate, Machete enlists the assistance of Agent Sartana Rivera (Jessica Alba), a US Immigration and Customs Enforcement (ICE) agent who first tracks Machete and then allies with him, and Luz (Michelle Rodriguez), a pivotal figure in the Network, a clandestine immigrant aid movement. Upon the film's initial release, reviewers noted that *Machete* continued Rodriguez's work of mixing popular genres. For instance, Stephen Holden (2010) of the *New York Times* described the film as a "live-action comic book, with roots in the pungent swamp of 1970s B movies," while *Variety* declared it an "overstated mashup" (Leydon 2010). This assessment was justified by the movie's obvious nods to 1970s exploitation films in its rough production values, narrative investments in socially marginalized groups, and genre depictions of men as violent and virile and women as a sexual objects for male consumption (Brayton 2011, 277–78).

Additionally, reviewers were prepared to receive the film in this way because *Machete* first appeared as a mock trailer in *Grindhouse* (2007), Rodriguez's double-feature collaboration with Quentin Tarantino that deployed B-movie conventions.

A second trailer that appeared closer to the film's release encouraged a different reception. Referred to as the "Arizona trailer," it debuted on Cinco de Mayo 2010 and begins with Machete staring into the camera and saying calmly, "This is Machete, with a special Cinco de Mayo message." After a short pause, the camera rapidly zooms in on Machete's face, which contorts in anger as he punctuates his statement, "to Arizona." As Zachary Ingle notes, "for those not part of the subculture already aware of *Machete* through *Grindhouse*, the film's controversial 'Arizona' trailer brought the film to the attention of a wider audience" (2015, 159). Machete's growl gives the otherwise kitschy film a political thrust, offering the movie as a statement on current debates about undocumented immigrants. Indeed, it succeeded in provoking both ends of the political spectrum, building an audience of those who were sympathetic to the plight of immigrants in the Southwest and inspiring a flurry of right-wing media responses that used the film to reinvigorate a "Latino threat" narrative (Ingle 2015, 163–65; also see Chavez 2013). This trailer, then, prepared critics and reviewers to read the film in the context of SB 1070, a measure passed by the Arizona state legislature three months before the film's release that forces immigrants to have required documents in their possession at all times.

As a result, scholars have viewed the film as a fantasy response to the political persecution of Latin@s, one in which the film's hero fulfills the wish for justice through spectacular acts of violence (Brayton 2011; Ingle 2015). However, if we limit our analysis to the genre of revenge fantasy, we would not only pursue predictable genre conventions but also connect the fulfillment of justice to the familiar, although in this instance cartoonish, warrior-hero of the corrido tradition. Ramón Saldívar (1990) presented this figure as the central protagonist of Chicano resistance narratives. Responding to powerful feminist critiques by Norma Alarcón, Gloria Anzaldúa, and Sonia Saldívar-Hull, among others, Saldívar concedes in his later work that the "*corrido* expresses a specific construction of male mastery, articulating ideologies of resistance and historical agency with ideologies of masculinity. This articulation privileges and enforces male dominance" (2006, 176). Saldívar-Hull notes that this privileging erases Chicanas from history, and she develops a feminist methodology from Anzaldúa's work "for a new consciousness based on recovering history and women's place" in it (2000, 63).

In this essay, I pursue a different path for recuperating women and other protagonists as agents in the quest for justice by shifting the terms of analysis from genre to medium. This shift involves attending to the role that nonhuman objects—especially various technologies—play in the formation of Latin@ assemblages. It also exposes how the film is not simply a wish-fulfilling fantasy but also a reflection on the ways in which Latin@s must critically utilize new media technologies to form collectivities that can supplement the singular heroism of figures like Machete. My turn toward media is inspired by N. Katherine Hayles's call for "medium-specific" analyses. Hayles reminds us that texts are always embodied and that the "materiality of those embodiments" factors into our interpretations (2002, 31). Film studies have long practiced this method, scrutinizing the role of the camera or spectator in our understandings of the medium. Although Hayles reminds us to attend to the materiality or "objectness" of any particular work, Bruno Latour's recent writing helps us understand how objects can also be agents that shape social formations. Drawing upon Latour's ideas, Rita Felski considers the objecthood of literary works in terms that invest them with agency. Instead of looking at a work's ideological content or historical context, Felski asks, "Why do we need . . . to overlook the multifarious ways in which they weasel themselves into our hearts and minds, their dexterity in generating attachments?" (2011, 582). Extending this question to *Machete*, we can ask: given that the hero is seemingly out of date and encased in a narrative that continuously invokes a sexist era and its politics, why does the film still attract and animate a Latin@ public?

In order to understand how the film-as-object operates on the publics it rallies, we need to probe more deeply into how the film itself explains the relation of objects to the formation of Latin@ communities. Latour calls for scholars to not take social context for granted as something that is easily discerned. Instead, he presents actor-network theory as an alternative that he describes as a "sociology of associations" (2005, 11). Actor-network theory (ANT) takes an ant's view of the world, carefully mapping the associations that attach different nodes of a social network. Latour's theory is distinctive in its insistence on seeing human and nonhuman actors as equally capable of "modif[ying] a state of affairs by making a difference" (Felski 2011, 582). However, it is important to note that, as Heather Love explains, "extending the same treatment to objects and people does not mean elevating objects to the status of humans but rather putting humans '*on par*' with objects" (2010, 376, emphasis in original). While Latour decenters the human from our conceptions of the social, Rodriguez is more focused on humans—not in order to articulate a clear form of social justice, but to produce *feelings* of justice based on a spectacularized punishment of inchoate oppressors, which provides viewers with a lulling sense that scores have been settled by film's end. If we perform a genre reading of the film, Machete is the hero-agent who solves both his problems and the problems related to undocumented immigrants who are absorbed into his plots. However, attending to human and nonhuman actors in the ways that Latour proposes, we can discern on the surface of this film a set of connections that don't offer a distinct politics but suggest the ways in which media, objects, and humans might come into connection to unlock the political possibility that resides in Latin@ social formations.

Because socially marginalized groups like the undocumented have been dehumanized—whether through denial of citizenship rights or simple refusal of empathy—Latour's theory allows us to view them not as abject but as agential. *Machete* locates this latent agency in objects that are cast off as obsolete but nonetheless retain efficacy. In its valorization of the subversive potential that resides in the discarded thing, *Machete* indulges a rasquache sensibility, which Tomás Ybarra-Frausto defines as "an underdog perspective—a view from *los de abajo*, an attitude rooted in resourcefulness and adaptability." This involves "making do with what is at hand" by repurposing it in creative and unexpected ways that express a stylized vernacular (1991, 155, 160). As much as the film delights in these startling transformations, it sees them as not enough: political action requires combining the possibility inherent in these old objects with the potentiality of new media. In this way, the film is also consistent with "Chicanafuturism," which, as Catherine S. Ramírez defines it, "explores the ways that new and everyday technologies, including their detritus, transform Mexican American life and culture" (2008, 187). Although the film finally sees new technologies as necessary for Latin@ political mobilizations, it also recognizes that these must be coordinated with old-fashioned objects, mapping the uneven mediascape on which contemporary Chican@ and Latin@ politics rest.

Persistent Obsolescence in the Latin@ Mediascape

Arjun Appadurai coined the term *mediascape* to describe both "the distribution of the electronic capabilities to produce and disseminate information

. . . [and] the images of the world created by these media" (1997, 35). This definition contains the ideas that cultural groups will connect differently to media technologies and that this affects how each group imagines itself. *Machete* comprehends this difference and further shows how the heterogeneous media competencies that exist among Latin@s function to separate as much as bring together different segments of *latinidad*. The film begins to map this uneven distribution of media competencies when Machete speaks one of its most famous lines: "Machete don't text." This moment occurs midway through the film, when ICE Agent Rivera is waiting for Machete to return from an information-gathering mission. The scene opens with Rivera anxiously biting her lips and repeatedly checking her cell phone for missed text messages. When Machete finally arrives, Rivera shouts, "Where the fuck have you been? You could have at least texted." Machete responds, "Machete don't text." On the DVD's audience track, this line receives one of the most audible responses from filmgoers, and fan bloggers repeatedly cite the line as a favorite. One blogger links the line to what he interprets as the film's anti-technology stance: "Machete leads the revolution against too much oppressive technology in our lives" (Hayden 2010).

Understanding "Machete don't text" as a line about resisting technological advances and preferring a simpler past accords with readings of Rodriguez's earlier films. In the feature that established his reputation, *El Mariachi* (1992), Rodriguez laments the intrusion of technology as something that dehumanizes Mexicans. As El Mariachi explains, "Technology has crushed us, robbed us of our culture, turning us into machines." This transformation is most evident when the mariachis are replaced by an electronic keyboard player who renders them obsolete. However, the intrusion of technology's corrupting influence is also apparent in the depiction of gangsters who are equipped with cell phones and spy with surveillance cameras. Charles Ramírez Berg argues that the film associates this technology with the United States, "whose relentless technology and ruthless market system have combined to destroy Mexican culture" (2002, 236–37).

Berg's reading may reinforce the tendencies to see Mexican culture as premodern, tendencies that Ramírez (2008) challenges in her discussions of Chicanafuturism, but these anti-technological views were also promoted in accounts of Rodriguez's early filmmaking career. The title of his memoir about filming *El Mariachi*, *Rebel Without a Crew* (1996), underscores how Rodriguez improvised stylish cinema without the advanced technologies that would necessitate a full crew. If his inventiveness with limited tools was part of the lore that built around Rodriguez as *El Mariachi* attracted the attention of larger audiences, it is a narrative that Rodriguez himself has cultivated rather than dispelled. Although *El Mariachi* was produced for a slight sum, it benefited from post-production wizardry before being released to US audiences by Miramax. As Rodriguez's career progressed, he maintained his renegade persona as he became an early adopter of technologies like 3D and digital video. In this way, Rodriguez adopts a rasquache veneer while increasingly incorporating cutting-edge technology into his production processes.

Although there are reasons to read "Machete don't text" as an anti-technology statement, within the larger narrative of the film the line points to how Machete's form of singular heroism is troubled less by technology than by the connections that technology enables. After Machete delivers the famous line, he adds, "Machete gets evidence," and proceeds to hand over a stack of CDs to which he has transferred the encrypted computer files of Michael Booth (Jeff Fahey), the man who is trying to frame Machete for the attempted assassination of the senator. To add insult to this injury, Machete leaves in Booth's office a digital camera containing footage of Machete having sex with Booth's wife and daughter (Lindsay Lohan). These moves suggest that, although he might be enamored of a simpler past, Machete understands the usefulness of technology in achieving the forms of revenge that orient his heroism in the present. He also capably uses high-tech devices to promote his sexual virility and extend his male privilege. The phrase "Machete don't text," then, signals a problem not with technology but with attachment. In this particular scene, attachment and connection are gendered: the female agent is figured as needy and ensnaring, as a threat that constrains the male hero. At this moment Rivera and Machete are beginning to see themselves as part of the Network, an immigrant aid movement coordinated by Luz. Machete is still incapable of seeing himself as part of the weave of a network, instead seeing himself as an exceptional individual who might make use of the Network but who also stands apart from it.

The Network is a key character in the film, although it is not embodied in any one person. Sianne Ngai notes that networks are "especially challenging to traditional character systems" (2013, 383) because they are "organized around the principle of perpetual inclusion" and are "reconfigurable in new ways and at all scales" (here she quotes Galloway and Thacker 2007, 60–61). The problem that network's pose for character systems may be one of the things that makes the Network well suited for representing a movement that includes the undocumented. On the one hand, the indeterminate nature of a network in a standard character system mirrors the uncertain position of the undocumented subject, whose denationalization inhibits the assertion of rights. The network, in this instance, is always on the verge of receding. On the other hand, a network's capacity for inclusion and expansion expresses a utopian hopefulness to alter its composition as it moves toward its political aim. While the film's Network is its own entity, it is most associated with the taco truck owner Luz, a character whose name, meaning "light," functions both as a beacon and as a way of illuminating a set of social relations.

The Network becomes most visible through different media forms. The first of these is "Shé," a figure who is represented on a poster that features a silhouetted woman standing against a bright red background. The woman wears a sombrero and holds a rifle, her chest crisscrossed with bandoliers. The poster evokes two familiar revolutionary figures: La Adelita, the Mexican *soldadera* who both cared for and fought with the soldiers in the Mexican Revolution, and Che Guevara, a leading figure in the Cuban Revolution. This image, then, connects the Network with larger utopian projects in the Americas while also embodying these in the women whose covert operations sustain political activity even as their role is often unacknowledged. When Machete asks Luz whether she is Shé, Luz responds, "Shé is someone I made up to lead the Network. Shé brings hope. Shé inspires." Shé, therefore, stands in for the potentiality of a group networked for a particular political end. Shé marks the space for reassembling the social by allowing for a politically efficacious group to be imagined. However, the Shé poster also registers the fragility of any networked system: by appropriating the Che and Adelita images to signal a new progressive political project, the Network must also recognize that it might be appropriated in ways that extend beyond and even contradict its intentions.

If the Network is rendered vulnerable by its unpredictability, it also becomes vulnerable when visible in public spaces. This aspect of the Network is highlighted in the scene that follows the opening credits. In contrast to the prelude to the credits, which is hyperbolic and cartoonish, the opening scene is realistic. The sequence opens with sounds of the Texas Tornados' "(Hey Baby) Que Paso?" and a shot of Mexican day laborers being hired by a man passing by in a pickup truck. The soundtrack is quickly overtaken by the voice of a radio journalist who is interviewing the deputy director of the local ICE office on the topic of border security. As the deputy director explains that the office is working to improve patrols, the camera cuts to young men congregating in front of Luz's taco truck and then to Agent Rivera sitting in her parked BMW, capturing these images with a camera's telephoto lens. Conceding that the patrols are ineffective, the deputy director contends that ICE must "attack the problem at its source" and that this source is a "whole support network that not only helps illegal aliens get across but is also helping them get settled once here." He then announces ICE's goal: "We need to uncover and dismantle this network." As he describes the Network, Agent Rivera captures an image of a young man handing a sheet of paper to Luz. Seen from the ICE agent's point of view, the paper appears to be a covert missive that may reveal something about the Network's operations.

However, the film interrupts the agent's gaze to provide the viewer a glance at the paper as Luz sees it, a close-up beyond the reach of ICE's surveillance. The paper contains nothing incriminating, but is merely a pencil portrait of Luz. In contrast to the Shé poster, which repurposes familiar iconography to recruit supporters into the Network while also exposing it to those, like ICE, who would seek its demise, the portrait of Luz reveals the affective connections and forms of attachment that sustain the Network. The opening scene also tells us something about the types of media that bind the Network. In contrast to the high-tech cameras and mass media used by ICE, the Network makes use of low-frequency media—forms like handmade posters, drawings, and collages as well as niche broadcast media and cell phones. Indeed, the two moments in which the Network becomes visible involve the latter two technologies.

In the first instance, we receive a glimpse of the various people who participate in the Network as a Latina anchorwoman broadcasts reports of the senator's shooting. Although she delivers her report in English, the reporter works for a fictional network called Exactamundo, which evokes the names of Spanish-language US media networks such as Telemundo. Significantly, these kinds of broadcast media report news relevant to Latin@s that major networks often deem insignificant to their mainstream audiences. As the Exactamundo anchorwoman reports that the "gunman may have been of Mexican descent," we receive images of Latinas in their workplaces, watching the broadcast. The camera cuts from the newscaster to a kitchen prep area where workers eye the television screen, then proceeds to a pair of women working in a laundry facility, and ends with a housekeeper cleaning a hotel room. These familiar images connect Latina workers (ostensibly undocumented) through the arduous labor—cooking, washing, cleaning—that they perform for the maintenance of everyday life. By placing the television screen in the various sites where this labor is performed, the film links these figures in a new way through the consumption of media and through the suggestion of a developing political consciousness about the treatment of immigrants. The television, a seemingly old-fashioned object in the era of broadband, on-demand media consumption, becomes an actor that constellates a social group and enables a political consciousness.

This brief survey of immigrant labor reveals how the attachment to low-tech media is not nostalgia for a simpler past, but relates to a question of access. In a 2010 survey on Latin@s and digital technology, the Pew Hispanic Center reports that Latin@s have comparatively limited access to the Internet and home broadband connection, but also that Latin@s are more likely to maintain social networks using cell phones than using a computer (Livingston 2011). Although cell phones may seem to be the newest horizon in media technologies, the media landscape was different a mere five years ago, when the film was made. Broadband and on-demand access were the media gold standard then, in part because they are connected with living in a stable location. In contrast, the cell phone is associated with mobility and uprootedness and lacks the computer's range of technological capabilities. However, the film repeatedly shows that, while cell phones may be out of date in the dominant culture's view, they play crucial roles in connecting diverse individuals as they navigate a world of uneven access. As Luz explains, the Network includes not only undocumented immigrants but also "all types, all races . . . lawyers, priests, doctors, homeboys." Luz presents the Network as an alternative to a "system" that is broken. The knowledge that constitutes this "alternative" flows in part from an assemblage that is enabled by these seemingly antiquated technologies. In a recent examination of Theodor W. Adorno's attachment to out-of-date technologies, Joel Burges notes that "the outmoded can prompt counterhistorical thinking: it engages the obsolete as a resource for an alternative to the present" (2013, 75). In *Machete*, superannuated technology connects the marginalized to a resource and establishes a well of utopian desire that is instrumental to imagining an alternative to a "system" that regards these forms of technology and those attached to them as things to be left behind. Yet, as the second moment when the Network becomes visible and active suggests, the film also shows how the knowledge generated in these social formations must combine with other media competencies if it is to effectively confront the system it seeks to disable.

Gender and Genre in the Networked Imaginary

Gender is etymologically linked to genre: both derive from the Old French word for "kind, sort, or class." It makes sense that genre and gender would be closely bound, and that a revenge fantasy centering on a warrior-hero and privileging masculinity would produce problematic representations of women as it executes the genre's conventions. However, the counternarrative of the actor-network provides us a description that reveals gender functioning in a different way. Here, women emerge as key agents and are aligned with new media. The film's Chicanafuturism depends upon linking the attachments we have to old-fashioned objects like the warrior-hero narrative to new media capabilities and to women who play crucial roles in political mobilizations. We can track this complicated interplay between gender, genre, and a networked imaginary by attending to the film's representations of action and passivity.

When the film first represents the Network through the consumption of television news reports, it deploys a familiar trope used to think about Latin@s: the representation of them as a sleeping giant that is passive and difficult to mobilize (Beltrán 2010, 2). Of course, this sleeping giant is mobilized, and it turns out to include many more people than the immigrant laborers typically represented. Significantly, the Network is activated in the film by a text message, but before this happens Machete himself enters the text-messaging fold. He sends the message late in the film after his brother (Cheech Marin), an ex-Federal and Roman Catholic priest, is killed by Booth, the man who is framing Machete for shooting the senator. Booth crucifies the priest on a church altar. After gazing at his dead brother's body, Machete pulls a cell phone from his pocket and, fumbling with it, asks Agent Rivera, "How do you text with this thing?" Rivera responds, "I thought Machete don't text," to which he replies, "Machete improvises."

The substitution of "improvise" for "text" highlights how Machete has been improvising throughout the movie. He improvises weapons out of a number of ordinary everyday objects, from surgical knives and skull scrapers to weed whackers and hedge shears to kitchen knives and corkscrews. When he repurposes these objects, he unlocks the subversive potential of objects that are associated with immigrant labor. Far from being tools of abjection, they emerge as potential weapons and suggest the threat that percolates beneath an outward veneer of docility. The term "improvise" here also signals Machete's willingness to alter his identity in an attempt to avenge the deaths of his wife and brother. In this case, improvising means shifting from being the lone warrior hero to becoming one node in the Network. The exchange of "text" for "improvise" also underscores the ways in which texting, which we normally associate with its semantic content, is also an *action*.

Thinking of texting as a form of action is one way to view the emergence of the Network as more than just the waking of a sleeping giant, although the film does provide us with the satisfaction of viewing this awakening. The text message that activates the Network is sent from an unidentified member of the group, suggesting that the Network can be mobilized by any member, not simply by purported leaders like Luz or Machete. We see the text message ring on the phones of a number of Latino laborers. These men answer the message and then move into action, abandoning their positions in the labor economy for the more urgent work of the Network. By using men to represent the active Network and women to represent the passive sleeping giant, the film demonstrates how networks, despite their seeming horizontality, reproduce hierarchies. While some theorists of the network as an activist formation address this concern, I want here to retain Latour's focus on description and, below, to consider how this gendered representation of action is one way the film capitulates to the genre conventions it sets in motion.

Although the film's final showdown between the Network and its various interconnected nemeses is conveyed with the abandon typical of comic book violence, it is important to note that those who come to embody the Network are also those who have the highest stake in remaining invisible: the undocumented. The coming-into-visibility of the noncitizen in order to pursue immigrant justice is not a fantasy of the film but actually happened in 2006, when thousands of immigrants and their allies took to the streets of US cities in response to HR 4437, the Border Protection, Antiterrorism, and Illegal Immigration Control Act of 2005. HR 4437 contained "several notably harsh provisions: the bill declared that simply being undocumented constituted a felony and criminalized any offer of nonemergency assistance to undocumented workers and their families" (Beltrán 2010, 130). Cristina Beltrán argues that thinking of these demonstrations in terms of economics, naturalization, or public policy obscures "one of the demonstrations' most significant aspects: their power as a moment of *initiation* and an inaugural performance of the political. By taking to the streets and claiming spaces and rights, immigrants and their allies created relational spaces of freedom and common appearance where none existed previously" (132, emphasis in original). To cast this in Latour's terms, the events of 2006 revealed our understanding of the social context to be erroneous by revealing a new network of associations.

In the film, the Network represents this potential to bind individuals in configurations where they can imagine new social and political ways of being. If out-of-date technologies function as resources for imagining alternatives to the present, the film suggests that this thinking requires other media competencies in order to gain political traction. The completion of the circuits of information needed to disrupt another network ("the system") that persecutes immigrants requires the hi-tech media competency of Agent Rivera, who is incorporated into the Network when she recognizes immigration policy as a set of unjust laws. Her conversion to the Network's cause demonstrates that hi-tech competencies in and of themselves are not sufficient for the kinds of political action she later helps initiate. In the opening surveillance scene, hi-tech equipment is figured as obscuring Rivera's view of what is actually happening at the taco truck. She is converted to the Network's cause only after she is convinced by the arguments emanating from the Network's low-tech discoveries. After this conversion, Rivera redirects her hi-tech skills to interpret Booth's computer files and makes use of the priest's surveillance tapes, bringing both to the Exactamundo reporter in order to expose publicly how the anti-immigration senatorial candidate is being bankrolled by the Mexican drug lord so that the cartel can control the paths into the United States after a border fence is built. By tracing the way in which different objects and technologies are used in the network—graphic art, drawing, televisions, niche media, computers, and surveillance—we see how *women* bring together different segments of *latinidad* to resolve the story's plots.

While Rivera could be read as a statement on the need for new media competencies in the formation of Chican@ and Latin@ networks, her character also shows that collective action need not reduce to homogeneity. Rivera, Machete, and the Network discover a common opposition to the immigration laws proposed by the senatorial candidate and the border vigilantes with whom he cavorts. But they have varying ideas about the forms that immigrant justice might take. Beltrán notes a similar pattern in the 2006 demonstrations: the demonstrators all opposed the criminalization of undocumented workers but disagreed about what "justice" would entail. Some sought amnesty, while others advocated a guest worker program. Still others called for enhanced border security (2010, 147). In *Machete*, this heterogeneity within the Network is noted in the final moments of the film, when Rivera tells Machete that she pulled strings at ICE to get him papers. He refuses, saying, "Why be a real person when I'm already a myth." The refusal of documentation may be another way that "Machete don't text," but this does not mean that he eschews technology in favor of collectivist politics. By insisting on a mythic individuality, he insists upon remaining an exceptional hero who is available for the sequels that the genre demands.

When he chooses to remain a myth, he also elects to be a thing rather than a man, a story that will bring together different people into new assemblages that can be activated for political ends. Machete's declaration that he doesn't text is a fantasy, like the film itself. By remaining a myth, he is encoded in text. But if the film is an object that forges attachments, its genre and hero are, like some of the outdated technologies that produce the Network, also superannuated. This near obsolescence is indicated in the casting of a sixty-seven-year-old actor as the warrior hero. Machete and the genres that he is attached to are in their twilight moments. As Maria Cotera notes, challenging scholars of Chican@ literature to invent new interpretative practices, the resistant warrior hero of the corrido paradigm—epitomized in Gregorio Cortez—no longer provides the field with ideological cohesion. She sees the contemporary moment as one heralded

> by a host of new protagonists: injured aristocrats, migrant souls, queer bodies, and postmodern subjects who have entered a literary universe once populated almost exclusively by rebellious warrior-heroes and working-class saints. These new protagonists and the literary works that they produce and populate demand that we read texts and even traditions in different ways. (2007, 158–59)

Machete's links to the corrido hero are clearly drawn in Rodriguez's film. Machete's birth name is Isador Cortez, and in Rodriguez's film universe, he is the older brother of Gregorio Cortez (Antonio Banderas) in the wildly popular *Spy Kids* franchise. If we attend only to genre in our analysis, we could easily lose track of the emergent protagonists that Cotera enumerates. By focusing on media—here composed of technologies and material objects that aid in the production of social formations—we see the significance of several other actors in contemporary political mobilizations, including women, the undocumented, cell phones, and television. We also see how the mediascapes Latin@s inhabit are always varied, comprising technologies that are cutting-edge and those that are seemingly obsolete. The turn toward media here is a new interpretative strategy that answers Cotera's call. *Machete*, though, teaches us that attending to Chican@ and Latin@ studies' new protagonists need not require abandoning the figures that once gave the field coherence. It may simply require reading them in new ways.

Works Cited

Appadurai, Arjun. 1997. *Modernity at Large: Cultural Dimensions of Globalization*. Minneapolis: University of Minnesota Press.

Beltrán, Cristina. 2010. *The Trouble with Unity: Latino Politics and the Creation of Identity*. New York: Oxford University Press.

Berg, Charles Ramírez. 2002. *Latino Images in Film: Stereotypes, Subversion, Resistance*. Austin: University of Texas Press.

Brayton, Sean. 2011. "Razing Arizona: Migrant Labour and the 'Mexican Avenger' of *Machete*." *International Journal of Media and Cultural Politics* 7, no. 3: 275–92.

Burges, Joel. 2013. "Adorno's Mimeograph: The Uses of Obsolescence in *Minima Moralia*." *New German Critique* 40, no. 1: 65–92.

Chavez, Leo. 2013. *The Latino Threat: Constructing Immigrants, Citizens, and the Nation*. 2nd ed. Stanford, CA: Stanford University Press.

Cotera, María. 2007. "Recovering 'Our' History: *Caballero* and the Gendered Politics of Form." *Aztlán: A Journal of Chicano Studies* 32, no. 2: 157–72.

Felski, Rita. 2011. "Context Stinks!" *New Literary History* 42, no. 4: 573–91.

Galloway, Alexander R., and Eugene Thacker. 2007. *The Exploit: A Theory of Networks*. Minneapolis: University of Minnesota Press.

Hayden, Erik. 2010. "'Machete Don't Text': 11 Reasons Why Robert Rodriguez's Machete Is the Sweetest Film Thus Far This Year." *The Film Doctor* (blog), September 5. http://filmdr.blogspot.com/2010/09/machete-dont-text-11-reasons-why-robert.html.

Hayles, N. Katherine. 2002. *Writing Machines*. Cambridge, MA: MIT Press.

Holden, Stephen. 2010. "Growl, and Let the Severed Heads Fall Where They May." Review of *Machete*. *New York Times*, September 3, C4.

Ingle, Zachary. 2015. "The Border Crossed Us: *Machete* and the Latino Threat Narrative." In *Critical Approaches to the Films of Robert Rodriguez*, edited by Frederick Luis Aldama, 157–74. Austin: University of Texas Press.

Latour, Bruno. 2005. *Reassembling the Social: An Introduction to Actor-Network-Theory*. New York: Oxford University Press.

Leydon, Joe. 2010. Review of *Machete*. *Variety*, September 6, 36.

Livingston, Gretchen. 2011. *Latinos and Digital Technology, 2010*. Washington, DC: Pew Hispanic Center.

Love, Heather. 2010. "Close But Not Deep: Literary Ethics and the Descriptive Turn." *New Literary History* 41, no. 2: 371–91.

"Machete—Arizona Trailer." 2010. YouTube video, December 15. https://www.youtube.com/watch?v=If3GRbAMkCc.

Ngai, Sianne. 2013. "Network Aesthetics: Juliana Spahr's *The Transformation* and Bruno Latour's *Reassembling the Social*." In *American Literature's Aesthetic Dimensions*, edited by Cindy Weinstein and Christopher Looby, 367–92. New York: Columbia University Press.

Ramírez, Catherine S. 2008. "Afrofuturism/Chicanafuturism: Fictive Kin." *Aztlán: A Journal of Chicano Studies* 33, no. 1: 185–94.

Rodriguez, Robert. 1992. *El Mariachi*. Culver City, CA: Columbia Pictures. DVD.

————. 1996. *Rebel Without a Crew: Or How a 23-Year-Old Filmmaker with $7,000 Became a Hollywood Player.* New York: Plume.

————. 2010. *Machete.* Beverly Hills, CA: Twentieth-Century Fox Home Entertainment. DVD.

Saldívar, Ramón. 1990. *Chicano Narrative: The Dialectics of Difference.* Madison: University of Wisconsin Press.

————. 2006. *The Borderlands of Culture: Américo Paredes and the Transnational Imaginary.* Durham, NC: Duke University Press.

Saldívar-Hull, Sonia. 2000. *Feminism on the Border: Chicana Gender Politics and Literature.* Berkeley: University of California Press.

Ybarra-Frausto, Tomás. 1991. "Rasquachismo: A Chicano Sensibility." In *Chicano Art: Resistance and Affirmation, 1965–1985,* edited by Richard Griswold del Castillo, Teresa McKenna, and Yvonne Yarbro-Bejarano, 155–79. Los Angeles: Wight Art Gallery, University of California.

Girl in a Coma Tweets Chicanafuturism
Decolonial Visions, Social Media, and Archivista Praxis

Michelle Habell-Pallán

> The future will belong to the mestiza.
> —Gloria Anzaldúa, *Borderlands/La Frontera*

> The Internet helps us in re-imagining identity beyond notions of nation, community, pueblos, gender, and sexual orientation. Today, computer technologies are affecting your sense of identity; shaping your identity; affecting the way you interact with family, friends, colleagues.
> —Gloria Anzaldúa, *Light in the Dark/Luz en Lo Oscuro*

> Picture me away / Are we alright now? / Something's gonna happen / You're staring off now to the sky / We're staring off now / . . . We are the stars that light up the night.
> —Girl in a Coma, "Clumsy Sky"

"Super proud!" exclaims a tweet by San Antonio–based punk trio Girl in a Coma, posted on September 10, 2009, while they viewed the exhibition *American Sabor: Latinos in US Popular Music* at the Museo Alameda in San Antonio (fig. 1).[1] The message included a photo of the wall panel that described the band:

> Influenced by their conjunto musician grandfather, Selena, and Chicana punks of the '70s and '80s, these rocker grrrls represent the cutting-edge millennial voice of Tejanas and Chicanas who are citizens of the new Latina bohemia.

> Influenciadas por su abuelo—músico de conjunto—por Selena y por las chicanas punk de los '70s and '80s, estas chicas rockeras representan la

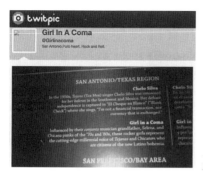

Figure 1. Girl in a Coma's "super proud" tweet post.

voz milenaria vanguardista de las tejanas y chicanas ciudadanas de la nueva bohemia latina.

American Sabor is the first traveling bilingual exhibition to demonstrate the profound combined influence of the rhythms and instruments of Afro-Caribbean and Mexican-origin communities on early rock 'n' roll and US pop music.[2] It represents the eclecticism of Latinx and Chicanx musical traditions in the United States. As a curator of *American Sabor*, I was surprised and thrilled that musicians interacted with the exhibition and shared it with their fans. This caused me to reflect that although the new generation of Chicanx musicians and cultural producers vigorously wield new media and social technology to create a digital presence that expands their communities of listeners, this innovation has been rarely acknowledged in recent scholarship. Focusing on Girl in Coma's engagement with Chicanafuturism, this chapter uses the metaphor of a feedback loop to demonstrate the interchange between *American Sabor*, Girl in a Coma, and the collective archivista praxis of Women Who Rock (WWR). The WWR Digital Oral History Archive is an open-access networked archive that uses new media platforms to bring together "scholars, musicians, media-makers, performers, artists, and activists to explore the role of women and popular music in the creation of cultural scenes and social justice movements in the Americas and beyond."[3] By exploring the interchange between these three entities, this essay suggests that Chicanx music serves as a resource to speculate on how new media can transform Chicanx scholarship in its production and delivery.

Girl in a Coma's tweet, their wielding of social media generally, and their 2007 "Clumsy Sky" music video animate an aesthetics and practice of Chicanafuturism that deserves attention. As a band that started off with few material resources, yet is rich in creative initiative, Girl in a Coma

161

makes innovative use of social media to claim their space within alternative music's past, present, and future. This approach is decidedly Chicanafuturist, as defined by cultural historian Catherine S. Ramírez, who was inspired by the speculative work of Gloria Anzaldúa's decolonial critique. According to Ramírez, Chicanafuturism is Chicana cultural production that "attends to cultural transformations resulting from new and everyday technologies (including their detritus); that excavates, creates, and alters narratives of identity, technology, and the future; that interrogates the promises of science and technology; and that redefines humanism and the human" (2004, 77–78). Although Chicanafuturism "questions the promises of science, technology, and humanism for Chicanas, Chicanos, and other people of color" (Ramírez 2008, 187), recognizing that the result has often been dystopic realities, the movement is willing to experiment with new technologies to harness their emancipatory potentials. Chicanafuturism renarrates the past, present, and future of subjects colonized in the borderlands, those who negotiate cultural, ideological, and spiritual mestizaje. Like Afrofuturism, Chicanafuturism seeks a future that rehumanizes those aggrieved by the logic of colonialism. As Chicanafuturism reframes the past through new communication technologies, the potentials of new presents and futures are born.

Girl in a Coma's development as a band coincides with the rise of social technology. Their conscious use of new social media and communication devices demonstrates how members of this generation, still in their twenties, mine stories of technologies past, present, and future to bring into being music and media representations of more free and just futures, à la Ramírez. As the band reconfigures human relationships between musicians and fans, they bend the arc of social technology away from military and corporate intelligence and toward decolonial ends.

The mestiza band members' engagement with Chicanafuturism resonates with Anzaldúa's speculation that "the future will belong to the mestiza" (1999, 102). This future will be shaped by the mestiza subject's use of the Internet for "re-imagining identity beyond notions of nation, community, pueblos, gender, and sexual orientation" as she experiments with new technologies that provide new ways of interacting "with family, friends, colleagues" (Anzaldúa 2015, 188). Understanding the band's music as speculative and decolonial prompts my driving question: Can their deployment of social technology to share their music, create online intimacy with fans within and beyond la frontera/the borderlands, and critique anti-immigrant legislation enrich Chicanx studies with new methods of imaging decolonial futures through music?

Girl in a Coma's tweet about *American Sabor* exemplifies the cultural feedback loop between Latinx music and US popular culture. By feedback loop, I refer simply to a situation where part of the output or a sound is returned as new input. In the case of amplified guitar, the sound that comes out of an amp goes back in, creating a cycle that feeds back into itself, strengthening upon each return. Part of the work of *American Sabor* is to represent the eclecticism of Lantinx and Chicanx musical traditions in the United States. Girl in a Coma is one example in a long legacy that is represented in the exhibition. The fact that Girl in a Coma uses their social network to reroute the history of *American Sabor* represents a positive feedback loop in a way that contributes to the collective work of archivista praxis. Collective archivista process, with an ear to the future, resounds in the WWR Digital Oral History Archive. Coming full circle, Girl in a Coma's oral history is now preserved in this online archive, projecting their presence into the future with the support of the University of Washington Libraries infrastructure.

Who Is Girl in a Coma?

Girl in a Coma is composed of San Antonio–born sisters Nina and Phanie Diaz and their childhood friend Jenn Alva. Their self-conscious cultural use of trans-American musical influences like Tejano, country and western, punk, and pop, as well as British subcultural styles aligns with a long tradition of "Chicano rock," one that resonates with the mainstream, even as it is deeply misunderstood. Influenced by their grandfather's conjunto music, Tejana singer Selena, and Chicana punk godmother Alice Bag (Alicia Armendariz), Girl in a Coma represents Chicana/Tejana millennial voices.[4] My collaborators and I featured these self-taught musicians in *American Sabor* for many reasons. Foremost was their "badass" musicianship: Nina's powerful, anguished-yet-fierce vocals paired with her impressive guitar shredding, distorted and feedback-rich, and combined with Phanie's precision percussion and Jenn's insistent bass distortion. What sets them apart from earlier forms of Chicanx rock is their embrace of queer subjectivity, their status as an "all-girl" band, and their early adoption of social technologies and new media. As I argue, these technologies permit them, and their collaborators, to fashion visual and sonic representation within decolonial imaginaries and to create communities of affiliation beyond their San Antonio home base. As the band deploys social technology to create bi-directional intimacy online and in live performances, with fans both within and beyond the US-Mexico borderlands, and to mobilize opposition to Arizona's anti–Mexican immigrant legislation, Catherine Ramírez's conceptualization of Chicanafuturism comes alive. Embodying Gloria Anzaldúa's dream of Chicanafuturism, these musicians engage in cultural subversion of strictly defined market-driven industry genres. Equally important, they create community and alternative worlds with limited resources. Doing this by means of their creative expression aligns with the longer tradition of eclecticism within Chicanx cultural production.

Though the band is now appreciated by music critics—their release *Exits and All the Rest* made NPR Music's 50 Favorite Albums of 2011—their ethos is still deeply misunderstood. One reviewer loved the CD, stating on NPR, "The songs here showcase . . . an enormous range of influences, from the slithery twang of 'Sly' to the Morrissey-esque new wave of 'Smart'" (Brown 2011). Yet the same reviewer also critiqued the release for its "stylistic inconsistency," thereby missing the point of Chicanx rock and Chicanx aesthetics of borderlands mestizaje, which have always mixed, blurred, and reinvented musical genres from across the Américas. Phanie Diaz, the band's drummer, explains their influences and listening practices, defining borderlands mestizaje in the process:

> A mix of everything, you know: not only did we grow up listening to Tejano, but my mom played a lot of Beatles, a lot of Patsy Cline, Ritchie Valens, and then we started to mix on our own. Nina and I got into Riot Grrrl, punk rock. I still listen to that. . . . Nina loves Jeff Buckley so it's just a mix of all kinds of genres. I think that's why that record kind of itself explains a lot of things. You have a rockabilly song and then a straight-up punk song, and then a ballad. We just go into every genre 'cause we listen to it all. (Diaz 2010)[5]

Chicanx scholars, fans, and musicians have long understood what Diaz notes: Chicano rock exists as an approach, a way of listening and playing, rather than as a genre (Gonzalez 2012, 107; Little Willie G. 2008). Its most powerful effect has been to unfix categories across the social spheres of Chicanx studies, the academy, and music markets. The band takes it one step further: we hear what Chicanafuturism sounds like from a queer Tejanx/Chicanx perspective. Their lyrics incorporate queer desires and imagine another, freer world not threatened by their existence. The band's eclectic listening practices permit them to mix and match from the archive of

Tejano, country and western, rock, and punk to make their own new sound. In the feedback between these sounds, they tap into a speculative energy.

Rock the Speculative

Inspired by Anzaldúa's love of sci-fi that infuses her creations of decolonial alternative worlds, Ramírez suggests a provocative path of inquiry when she asks, "What happens to Chicana/o texts when we read them as science fiction?" (2008, 190). She introduces a new analytic for understanding the speculative nature of such texts, especially as Chicanafuturism engaged in dialect with Afrofuturism. Propelled by Ramírez's productive query, I ask what happens to Chicanx music when we hear it as speculative. Notably, Ramírez asserts, "Many black writers, artists and musicians, such as . . . the band Earth, Wind & Fire, insert Africans and/or African Americans into what [Greg] Tate describes as 'a visionary landscape.'" Ramírez describes this landscape as "sci-fi-esque—that is, it is one of computers, spaceships, alien creatures and intergalactic travel" (2002, 374).

I observe that the sci-fi-esque and the speculative were encoded early on in Chicanx rock, especially in its expression of what is now considered early punk. In the early 1960s, Question Mark and the Mysterians, sons of Tejano workers who migrated to Michigan, named their band after a Japanese science fiction film (Carson 2005, 85).[6] Their quirky sensibility inspired another Michigan-rooted band, Iggy and the Stooges, who then inspired David Bowie and the Spiders from Mars—an early punk feedback loop (Ambrose 2009). Critic Shelley Streeby (2015) demonstrates how the long-running graphic novella series *Love and Rockets*, first published by Jaime Hernandez in 1981, plays upon this connection between sci-fi and Chicanx punk. In some ways, Girl in a Coma is an incarnation of one of *Love and Rockets*'s fictional bands, led by Esperanza Leticia "Hopey" Glass, one of the series' most beloved characters. I suggest that Girl in a Coma's music adds another dimension to Chicanafuturism's visionary landscape, a landscape deeply informed by the decolonial imaginary.

Anzaldúa reminds us that "we can transform our world by imagining it differently" (2015, 20). Her visionary, decolonial story crafting, like the "visionary fiction" of Octavia Butler and the Octavia's Brood collective, moves toward "building new, freer worlds from the mainstream strain of science fiction, which most often reinforces dominant narratives of power" (Imarisha 2015, 4). In visionary fiction, the "arc [is] always bending toward justice" (4). Anzaldúa also emphasizes that the decolonial is a transformative state, a process rather than a point of arrival. Through her body of speculative story crafting, Anzaldúa demonstrates that decolonial transformation means, in part, "unlearning consensual 'reality'" (2015, 44). What happens when we move this speculative story crafting across a variety of media and platforms, including music, social media, museums, and archives? Girl in a Coma's "Clumsy Sky" version of Chicanafuturism, in its lyrical and video visionary story-crafting formats, provides a clue. For certain, it mines the potentials of the here and now and presents a queer altermundo in contrast to the status quo heteronormative fantasy story crafting of fellow San Antonio filmmaker Robert Rodriguez.

"Clumsy Sky"

"Clumsy Sky" is a compelling example of what Chicanafuturism sounds like.[7] The term *Chicanafuturism* might seem to imply the eerie squeaks and wails of a theremin, cold new wave synth sounds by the likes of Kraftwerk or Zapp & Roger, or unfamiliar, technologically rendered beats and rhythms. Those sounds are not audible in "Clumsy Sky," nor in Girl in a Coma's music generally. Their version of Chicanafuturism is generally synth-absent and sounds familiar because it incorporates beats and rhythms from rock and punk's past into the present and future, a past that Latinxs and Chicanxs helped build in the first place. With this incorporation, the sound completes a feedback loop, but with a twist. "Clumsy Sky" depicts the band making music the "old-fashioned" way, with drum, bass, and guitar. The song begins with Nina's sparse yet clear guitar chords marking the intro's time signature. Her voice is rendered in a slow, almost lullaby way, building yet restraining the excitement to create an anticipatory mood. Her lyrics open with an invitation to envision and speculate: "Picture me, away." The song continues slowly: "Are we alright now? / Something's gonna happen / You're staring off now to the sky / We're staring off now." With unique phrasing, the song asks us to envision somewhere "away," in a different place or time from the here and now. "Away" is evocative because of its temporal and spatial connotations, and because it also means "in a safe or secure place." We are asked to imagine ourselves somewhere where outcasts are alright. We know it is future tense, because Nina sings "something's going to happen." "We are staring off at the sky" again suggests an astral or "outer space" reality, perhaps some "intergalactic travel" in the style of Afrofuturism. She asks, "Are we alright now?," the "we" indicating a relationship, either romantic or collective. Just after Nina sings "we are looking up at the sky," the anticipatory emotion of the music cannot be contained. With her command "hush heart just play dumb," the tempo speeds up and the sound becomes heavily layered with bass guitar and drum. Nina's distorted guitar feedback propels the music into a new sonic dimension and the song takes off. The phrase "you are waiting for my sign" leads to more images of secret codes and whispered language. Sociologist Deborah Vargas explains that "the song was written by lead singer Nina Diaz, who composed the lyrics based on a coded language" that she used to communicate with a partner (2012, 224).

Vargas eloquently writes that "Clumsy Sky" is a straightforward love song that bends time and love toward the arc of the social world of the cantina. Complementing Vargas's reading, I suggest that the song captures the sensation of a decolonial potentiality where subjects such as the band and their fans imagine and live in a time where their realities are valued and centered. It is a love song to collective, potential futures, especially since it ends with astral imagery: "we are the stars that light up the night." This imagery is searching for a new world, a new heaven, with new relationships of earth to stars. Turning to Girl in a Coma's video of "Clumsy Sky," with its embedded codes of Chicanafuturism, we are able to look at this phenomenon in a medium in which the visual augments the music, providing a fuller sound.

From *Pretty Vacant* to "Clumsy Sky"

The "Clumsy Sky" music video is the result of Girl in a Coma's collaboration with independent filmmaker Jim Mendiola. Mendiola's encounter with the band was meant to be. His 1996 film *Pretty Vacant* is a form of speculative story crafting. It is a mockumentary about a day in the life of Molly Vasquez, a Tejana artist in a punk band and an undercover archivista, who also happens to be a Sex Pistols superfan. As a prototypical borderlands subject, Molly lives between worlds even as she creates a new world through her art making, music, and critical practices.[*] Molly might be the first speculative Tejana rock critic! I argued in *Loca Motion* that she adjusts punk's genealogy so that its framing includes the incorporation of Tejano music (Habell-Pallán 2005). Molly's fictional adjustment foreshadows that made by Girl in a Coma in the "Clumsy Sky" video.

The band renders Chicanafuturism in video format, illustrating how the past, present, and future of Tejano and rock collide in their onstage performance.[9] In the video, filmed in the historic Lerma's Nite Club in San Antonio, the girls pay tribute to the conjunto music legends that have rocked that stage for over fifty years. Steeped in Tejano and Chicanx culture, and with its atmospheric setting, Lerma's was also used as a location shot for the 1997 movie *Selena*. Set designers for the film created and left behind a larger-than-life painting referencing Mexican artist Jesús Helguera's 1950 *Amor Indio*, which looms over the band on the stage's back wall (fig. 2). Featuring the legend of Popocatépetl and Ixtaccíhuatl, the painting is an iconic love scene reproduced on countless Mexican *panadería* (bakery) calendars (Esquibel 2003, 298). It is a nostalgic and stereotypical image of Mexican indigeneity, often referenced in Chicanx movement art to reclaim indigenous pasts. It also exemplifies heteropatriachal gender binaries. The queerly raucous band on the stage stands in stark contrast to the painted limp body of an Aztec princess, cradled by her warrior, for whom she died.

The video intersperses crowd shots of audience members collectively using their cell phones to take photos, document the event and themselves, and light up the stage (fig. 3). In the final section of "Clumsy Sky," a hand disrupts the received trajectory of Tejano music by posting a Polaroid photo

Figure 2. Amor Indio, *featuring Popocatépetl and Ixtaccíhuatl, in back of the band in "Clumsy Sky."*

Figure 3. Documenting the scene in "Clumsy Sky."

of the band within a constellation of photos of Lerma's conjunto stars. This is an ironic contrast of old and new media. Six photos are arranged in the shape of Texas. The hand, presumably belonging to one of the band members, posts their photo and completes the shape of the state, visually ushering in another kind of state within and beyond Texas, beyond nation and borders: the future, alternative, and queer states of being. The last sounds in the video are the amp shutting off Nina's feedback—it is very audible—calling attention to the technology of sound amplification and Nina's expert wielding of it. Vargas interprets this ending as demonstrating that "Girl in a Coma's music moves within and through Tex-Mex sound— literally and symbolically surrounding the band's cultural milieu—but is not necessarily of it, thereby enabling an alternative racialized gendered sensibility of what constitutes Tex-Mex music" (2012, 218). It is a visionary Tex-Mex, inspired by Anzaldúa's borderlands imagery. Equally important, the final scene, in which the band members insert themselves in an expanded formation of conjunto, serves as a metaphor for the process of archivista praxis (fig. 4).

Reading "Clumsy Sky" through the lens of Chicanafuturism provides insight into the way cultural production of the "connected age" negotiates

Figure 4. Archivista praxis in "Clumsy Sky."

the aesthetics of nostalgia that characterizes earlier forms of Chicanx cultural production. It also advances imaginaries that support a decolonial futurity that rehumanizes the damned of colonialism by claiming hidden pasts as resources for new futures. If the received trajectory of conjunto music doesn't recognize the band, the band's sound and video produce an alternative trajectory of conjunto in which they are audible.

The "Clumsy Sky" music video opens with a profile of Nina singing into a vintage microphone. As the tempo picks up, the visual mimics the sound of Nina's guitar feedback loop. The camera moves back and forth from the band playing and expertly handling musical technology on stage (electric guitar, amps, and gear) to shots of the venue and the crowd. Vargas explains, "The close-up shot of a wall splashed with photos of Tex-Mex conjunto accordionists such as Narciso Martínez, Valerio Longoria, and Flaco Jiménez suggests the sound that has emanated from Lerma's for decades" and matches the dizzying sensation feedback produces (2012, 224). A bumper sticker in support of Julian Castro promotes his campaign for mayor of San Antonio and portends his eventual appointment to head the US Department of Housing and Urban Development. A young man with a mohawk and (possibly) his grandfather are "staring off," sitting in the cantina united by music. Perhaps they are whispering codes of survival. Shots of the band playing and the crowd responding suggest that the cantina stage is the portal of transmission to alternative worlds, if only temporarily. The idealized heterosexual couple rendered through the Popocatépetl and Ixtaccíhuatl image on the wall behind the band is contrasted with a shot of a queer couple holding hands. During the song's bridge the video cuts to a choreographed community dance, with the audience dancing in sync. The shot implies that social movement can emerge from communal joy. The community dance represents a form of *convivencia*, a collective and intentional creation of autonomous social space where "the deliberate act of being with each other, and of being present to each other" takes place (Gonzalez 2014). Again, the video contains the speculative, inasmuch as anything could happen, but this is grounded in material reality since these communities actually do exist. In this way, the band embeds the codes of Chicanafuturism into the present. In contrast to the fictional fans of Aztlan-a-Go-Go, the band of Mendiola's Molly character in *Pretty Vacant*, the fans of Girl in a Coma exist in the here and now, again gesturing toward a Chicanapresentism where the lines between now and then are blurred.

These visuals of "Clumsy Sky" disrupt what queer performance scholar José Esteban Muñoz (2009, 22) identifies as "straight time" and nonnormative futurity. Muñoz proposes a new relationship between past, present, and future. By accepting the here-and-now present of reality, we reproduce cultural logics of "capitalism and heteronormativity" (12), which he calls straight time. Muñoz suggests that we can draw on an alternative past, or that which is "no-longer-conscious" (84), to create a future defined outside the confines of straight time, a future that I suggest moves to the rhythm of decolonial time. Within this audio and visual representation of queer time, Girl in a Coma's video references iconic symbols and sounds that mark the Tejano borderlands. The video recognizes the Tex-Mex conjunto music past, but it does not engage in nostalgic longing for a community built on patriarchal privilege as do some early forms of Chicanx literature, according to scholar Curtis Márez (1996). Instead we are talking about a platform that opens "the realm of potentiality," a potentiality that Chicana theorist Anzaldúa imagined in her emancipatory *Borderlands/La Frontera* (1999) and that is embodied by Girl in a Coma's music. In this way, the band's music resonates with Anzaldúa's *pensamiento fronterizo*, mestiza consciousness, and *conocimiento nepantla* as she urges us to delink from both hegemonic and marginal fundamentalisms. In fact, literary critic José D. Saldívar (2012) argues that Anzaldúa's border thinking, what he understands as transmodernity, presents decolonial alternatives to the present world-system.

Cultural production has been a place for counter-responses and aesthetics that detach from the logics of coloniality. The "Clumsy Sky" video represents mestiza subjects deploying technology, playing with normative codes, imagining altermundos. In fact, Muñoz's notion of a "concrete utopia" may be useful in explaining how the sounds of Chicanafuturism and Chicanapresentism are grounded in material reality and possibility. He explains, "Concrete utopias are relational to historically situated struggles, a collectivity that is actualized or potential" (Muñoz 2009, 3). The case of Lerma's is a material example of such situated and contentious struggle. About five years ago the city of San Antonio planned to shut down this beloved venue due to safety concerns. Community members and activists fought off demolition and pushed the city to declare the site as historically significant.[10] This building, which embodies Chicanx music history (Vargas 2012) and yet was almost demolished, became digitally archived through the "Clumsy Sky" video. Lerma's is the concrete site from which Girl in a Coma and their community of fans launch their speculative vision and concrete utopia.

Muñoz also asserts that "queerness is essentially about the rejection of a here and now and an insistence on potentiality or concrete possibility for another world" (2009, 1). Girl in a Coma's insistence on another world shapes the impact of their cultural work. For example, the band participated in the Sound Strike, an artists' boycott of Arizona to protest SB 1070, a controversial state law whose draconian provisions included requiring all suspected immigrants to carry documentation of their legal status at all times. The boycott, intended to "limit [Arizona's] ability to function and implement the law" (Kraker 2010), resonates with Muñoz's "insistence . . . for another world" (2009, 1) when understood in the context of the heated debates about the criminalization of Latinx immigrants and bans on the teaching of Chicanx studies. Such mobilization aligns with cultural historian Gaye T. Johnson's assertion that "marginalized communities have created new collectivities based not just on eviction and exclusion from physical places, but also on new and imaginative uses of technology, creativity, and spaces" (2013, x). As Girl in a Coma participates in a movement of artists that insists on the reality of a new world now, they change the present to transform the future.

Social Media, Girl in a Coma–Style

"Clumsy Sky" speaks to the politics of self and of collective representations at many levels; it also speaks to the reality of Latinx lives in relation to the adoption of new media technology. In fact, I first learned about Girl in a Coma through Mendiola's blog *Ken Burns Hates Mexicans*.[11] Impressed by the band, I thought they'd bring a fresh voice to *American Sabor*. While the exhibition was traveling, I organized a panel with Girl in a Coma for the 9th Annual EMP Pop Conference in Seattle in 2010. The band addressed the conference theme, "The Pop Machine: Music and Technology," by dialoguing about the ways bands and fans utilize social media such as Twitter, Facebook, and MySpace. Twitter wasn't yet as popular as it is now, and the band members were early adopters. Phanie Diaz turned the panel into a mini-workshop on how to use social media:

> We actually heard about Twitter during the last SXSW [South by Southwest music and media festival and conference]. Amanda Palmer was talking about how much she used it. We all had done an interview together. We got into it and asked what was it about. It was truly helpful for us as a band. The good thing about it is, for instance, if a show is being canceled . . . we can just tweet "sorry, everybody," like instantly, kind of a live feed of what is going on. . . . [Fans] ask you questions on Twitter, in Twitter you can answer them right back, you can keep them informed of what is happening at the moment with the band. And we can also have contests and giveaways the day, the night of the show, and just, like, first person to come to the door and say banana or something [*laughs*] . . . they get in and it keeps you very connected with everybody. . . . Besides Twitter there's MySpace, Facebook. That's a good way for us to put up videos using YouTube. [Fans] see what's going on with the tour, we make a video . . . a quick edit of what is happening. Instead of us just blogging about it, they [fans] can visually see what we are seeing, what is happening to us. So, obviously, it keeps us very intimate and keeps everyone in tune. . . . Sometimes a fan would tweet, "I could not get into your show tonight because I'm . . . missing three bucks," so a guest system, like that, that's a good way of taking care of our fans. . . . How we got onto the Tegan and Sara tour was I simply sent a MySpace message, saying that we were fans of their music. I didn't think that they would read it . . . and we end up exchanging emails because she was a fan of ours and then asked us to go on tour with her. So, we met a lot of bands that way, just by sending messages and saying "oh we are fans of your music." (Diaz 2010)

As Diaz explains, social media collapses the distance between Girls in a Coma and the bands they love. Diaz was surprised that Tegan and Sara, a more established queer band, invited them to tour after Diaz left a fan message on their MySpace page. For a band with few resources, new platforms such as YouTube also collapse the distance between them and their own fans, allowing them to document life on the road through short videos, providing a richer visual and aural experience for fans than blogging alone can provide. They utilize YouTube as an unofficial archive. Twitter also collapses distance, informing fans in real time about tour information and generating excitement through mini-contests. Fans even message Girl in a Coma if they don't have enough funds to cover their show tickets. This willingness to take care of fans who are struggling demonstrates that the band's use of technology goes beyond creating a fan base to build a sense of community and collectivity. This process of community building using social media also helped mobilize their fans in support of the Sound Strike boycott in Arizona. Their participation is a form not only of decolonial aesthetics, but of decolonial practice.

Such mobilizations resonate with Anzaldúa's musings that online communications open possibilities to recast identity in terms of relationality outside the restrictive concepts of "nation, community, pueblos, gender, and sexual orientation" (2015, 188). Diaz's experiences align strikingly with Anzaldúa's recognition that "computer technologies are affecting your sense of identity; shaping your identity; affecting the way you interact with family, friends, colleagues" (188). Diaz's experiences and Girl in a Coma's effective use of social media align with national trends. According to a Pew Research Center study, "86% of Latinos say they own a cell phone. . . . Fully 84% of Latino internet users ages 18 to 29 say they use social networking sites such as Facebook and Twitter, the highest rate among Latinos" (Lopez, Gonzalez-Barrera, and Patten 2013). This study found that young Latinxs are early adopters of new media and that their range of use is significant. Before her untimely death, Anzaldúa predicted such technological intimacy and used sci-fi imagery to do so: "People's mass movements across neighborhoods, states, countries, and continents, as well as the instant connection via satellites, Internet, and cell phones, make us more aware of and linked to each other. Soon our consciousness will reach other planets, solar systems, galaxies" (2015, 69–71). The "Clumsy Sky" video demonstrates that the use of new communication technology, like cell phones, has become embedded in young Latinxs' lives in moments of collective pleasure, confirming Anzaldúa's foresight.

Archivista Praxis

With so many Latinxs using social media to communicate, we as scholars are called to imagine new ways of teaching, archiving, and sharing information via new online platforms.[12] We are asked to consider new digital platforms that feature sound media to create new possibilities of popular music studies within Chicanx studies and vice versa. Can scholars use these platforms toward decolonial ends? Can we transform knowledge production and its delivery through a Chicanafuturism lens to create an altermundo? Can they help us experiment with creating a decolonial humanities?

New platforms do provide an opportunity to produce, deliver, and archive knowledge in mushrooming digital and networked formats. But in our neoliberal era marked by privatization of higher education, these methods of creating scholarship also create an opportunity to ask these questions: To what end do we produce and archive new knowledge and scholarship, and in whose service? Is it possible to take the very tools that have been developed through technologies that support military and corporate ends and use them in the service of those subjects who have been pushed out of archives—"the prohibited, the hybrid, the queer, and/or the colonized" (Ramírez 2002, 393)? Do these technologies hold potentials for emancipatory scholarship? Chicanafuturism compels us to ask these questions to make sure that Chicanx and other aggrieved communities are part of a freer future and are not absented by these very technologies.

To answer these questions let's retrace the feedback loop discussed earlier. Girl in a Coma's use of sound-based social media to share their visionary story crafting led to their inclusion in *American Sabor*. Their tweet inspired me and my WWR collaborators to think deeply about the scholarly and pedagogical potentials of social media tools. Such models helped envision a collective praxis of digital archiving that leverages sound-based media (Habell-Pallán, Retman, and Macklin 2014).[13] This collective praxis was used to develop the digitally born WWR archive. Coming full circle, Girl in a Coma's oral history is now preserved in this archive. Through this feedback loop, Girl in a Coma's Chicanafuturism has inspired me and my colleagues not only to "comment *about* technology and media" but also to participate more actively in constructing knowledge *in and through* our objects of study (McPherson 2009).

Girl in a Coma's "Clumsy Sky" video narrative serves as a metaphor for doing scholarly work, specifically archivista praxis, using a Chicanafuturism approach—one that engages social technology and new media to forge a decolonial vision. Archivista praxis and digital archiving resists the colonizing impulse of academic frameworks and processes that tend to push away mestiza presence. We are talking about the how as well as the whom of knowledge curation, but the discussion must also include the where.

Returning to Ramírez's argument that Chicanafuturism reflects colonial and postcolonial histories, the difficult flows of power, displacement, and culture that empire building activated, I suggest that the spirit of Chicanafuturism aesthetics resonates with Anzaldúa's (2015), Emma Pérez's (1999), and Walter Mignolo's (2006) call for an epistemic shift in consciousness among scholars in the humanities. These critics call on us to question and remake our praxis of knowledge production within the university. Before her passing, Anzaldúa observed, "Many are witnessing a major cultural shift in their understanding of what knowledge consists of and how we come to know, . . . a shift away from knowledge contributing both to military and corporate technologies and to the colonization of our lives by television and the Internet" (2015, 119). Anzaldúa's recognition informs Mignolo's exhortation to scholars in the humanities to delink from the coloniality of knowledge. Pointing out the powerful humanities scholarship emerging from "women's studies, gender and sexuality studies, gay and lesbian studies, Afro-American studies, ethnic studies, Latino/as studies" (Mignolo 2006, 328), not to mention indigenous and American Indian studies, Mignolo recognizes scholarly sites that counter "the rhetoric of modernity and the logic of coloniality" by introducing "new justification of knowledge: knowledge not at the service of the church, the monarch, or the state, but knowledge for liberation; that is, for subjective and epistemic decolonization" (328). Mignolo emphasizes the fundamental role that decolonial humanities must play in the process to decolonize "knowledge" and "being." He calls for a methodological shift in terms of the process of producing knowledge in the academy—a fashioning of new methods that value embodied knowledge and are produced in collectivity, delinked from the logic of coloniality.

Attempting to create scholarship *en convivencia* that delinks from the logic of coloniality allowed us to tap into the possibility of networked digital formats within an academic context. Within the larger collective cultural and epistemological shift Anzaldúa and Mignolo call for, WWR developed a collective process that created

> an archive not in the service of the state, but rather to catalyze emancipatory dialogues, alternative histories, and feminist futures. We aim to decolonize the archive by creating it through a collective process and archivista praxis, ensuring that it is freely accessible online at no cost,

and providing long-term preservation for artists and activists who are documenting their own scenes and have been excluded or pushed out from "official" archives. Scholar Emma Pérez's *Decolonial Imaginary: Writing Chicanas into History* provides a method that reframes the past in order to imagine different presents that disrupt the idea of an inevitable colonial future. The WWR archive does not simply cast back retrospectively to tell a static story of scenes and movements past; it also documents scenes and movements as they unfold in the present. In assembling the archive, we have created our own scenes, our own fluid community of inquiry. This living archive both reflects and generates alternative communal and creative networks and genealogies. The archive's collection will continue to expand as we continue to conduct more oral histories, generate more programing, and create new media and scholarship in coming years. (Habell-Pallán et al., forthcoming)

WWR pulls on Emma Pérez's (1999) understanding of the archive's relation to the decolonial imaginary. The decolonial imaginary appropriates the archive, and in the process it negotiates, contests, and transforms archival discourses. For Pérez, the creation of alternative pasts is more useful than relying on official ones. Pérez reminds us that third space feminism permits "a look to the past through the present always already marked by the coming of that which is still left unsaid, unthought. Moreover, it is in the maneuvering through time to retool and remake subjectivities neglected and ignored that third space feminism claims new histories" (127).

WWR archivista praxis serves as one of many examples of this collective rethinking of archival processes. WWR seeks to continue this decolonial epistemic shift in the unlikely place of music analysis through the building of a collective archive that is easily accessible to scholars, artists, students, and the general public at no cost. At its most hopeful, this WWR archivista praxis seeks to serve as an epistemological intervention within the humanities (Habell-Pallán, Retman, and Macklin 2014). Its potential comes, in part, from the feedback loop I've traced through this chapter. Archivista praxis responds to the call of Chicanafuturist aesthetics and attends to Anzaldúa's, Pérez's, and Mignolo's call for methodological shifts in knowledge, production, and interrogation of the archive.

The evocative final image of the "Clumsy Sky" video provides a visual that exemplifies archivista praxis (see fig. 4). As the band places the Polaroid image of themselves within the visual genealogy of conjunto players, Vargas asserts that their act "is less a gender reappropriation of the cantina space and more precisely a piercing echo of the working-class femininities and sexualities that have long populated the soundscape of cantina culture" (2012, 224). "Clumsy Sky" then creates an alternative genealogy of women who rock Tejano and Chicanx music, activating the past as a zone of possibility, not a genealogical inheritance. They rock the archive. Girl in a Coma and Mendiola's video, like the story crafting of the borderlands sci-fi writers about whom literary critic Lysa Rivera writes, is motivated by a desire for a "future with a past" (Rivera 2012, 431). Girl in a Coma and Mendiola join a continuum of borderlands artists who create music and media that "value cultural recovery but also underscore the vitality of speculation" (431). In this way, they mirror the cultural work of contemporary Afrofuturism, based on a futurity that rehumanizes those aggrieved by the logic of colonialism.

Conclusion

Working on *American Sabor* confirmed the importance of a Chicanafuturist perspective. Without it, Chicanas are often erased from the past and excluded from the future. It also confirmed the importance of experimenting with new modes of scholarly work. Experimenting with analog and digital platforms built for sound media constituted a strategy for opening up the museum to queer sounds of mestizaje. It also became apparent how important it was to include Girl in a Coma, given that the band knew how to reach and engage a younger, social media–savvy generation. The band's tweet about *American Sabor* created a positive feedback loop that sparked this essay. Their "Clumsy Sky" video artfully captures the documenting and archiving of those usually pushed out of official archives.

Thinking about that exclusion, I collaborated with colleagues and graduate students to develop the WWR Digital Oral History Archive to preserve the stories of women who rock but are normally left out. We included an oral history with Girl in a Coma, completing the positive feedback loop–enabled digital platforms. Like the "Clumsy Sky" video, the WWR project seeks to create an archive not in the service of the state, but in the service of emancipation.

Chicanafuturism takes hold of the tools of decolonial humanities to engage archivista practices, not just to advance Chicanx studies into the future but also to advance digital humanities via Chicanx studies as well. Digital platforms that deliver sound-based media allow for decolonial experimentation, with one foot in the institution and the other in community. Both *American Sabor* and WWR produce, document, and preserve alternative pasts, alternative genealogies, in order to support alternative futures. Developed through the method of *convivencia* and Chicanafuturist aesthetics, the archive is now a resource for feminista media production, curriculum and new scholarship, and exhibitions. The online presence of *American Sabor* and WWR illustrates the potential of digital new media archives. With a focus on music, media, and social justice, this archiving practice "excavates, creates, and alters narratives of identity, technology, and the future" as it "interrogates the promises of science and technology"—completing, in the process, a Chicanafuturism feedback loop. As Ramírez cautions, we are aware of the ways technology has been used against us. But we use technology to experiment with knowledge production and sharing from a Chicanafuturism perspective, knowing "something's gonna happen."

Notes

Special thanks to Maylei Blackwell, Vivi C. H., Jaime Cardenas, Angie Chabram, Sergio de la Mora, Julia Fogg, Girl in a Coma, Carlos Jackson, Roshanak Kheshti, Tiffany A. Lopez, Cathryn Merla-Watson, B. V. Olguín, Wilfried Raussert, Sonnet Retman, Alicia Schmidt Camacho, and Deborah Wong, as well as the writing women of Mediating Difference: Sights and Sounds. I am grateful for invaluable support from the University of Washington's Royalty Research Fund, Simpson Center for the Humanities, and H. R. Whiteley Center.

1. The tweet can be seen at https://twitter.com/Girlinacoma/statuses/ 3895767156. View the photo at http://twitpic.com/h8b0n.

2. *American Sabor: Latinos in US Popular Music* was created by the Experience Music Project (EMP) in partnership with the University of Washington. I served as guest curator with Marisol Berríos-Miranda, Shannon Dudley, Jasen Emmons, Francisco Orozco, and Robert Carroll. Within the context of intense anti-immigrant politics and nativist sentiment, the exhibit attempts to shift discussions about national culture. It does so by reframing mainstream narratives about rock 'n' roll to demonstrate that Latino communities in the United States have long played crucial roles in the making of what some consider to be the quintessential form of American national culture. The exhibit asks audiences to rethink the "American" in American popular music culture, showing that American pop music has been and is more Latinx than is generally recognized. For an extended review, see Ovalle (2009). *American Sabor* opened in 2007 as a 5,000-square-foot exhibit at the EMP Museum in Seattle and toured nationally until 2010. Under the auspices of the Smithsonian Institution's Traveling Exhibition Service (SITES), *American Sabor* was then repackaged as a smaller, two-dimensional exhibit that traveled from 2011 to 2015. SITES currently hosts an online digital exhibit at americansabor.org.

3. Introductory text on the Women Who Rock: Making Scenes, Building Communities Digital Oral History Archive, University of Washington Libraries, http://content.lib.washington.edu/wwrweb/.

4. Listen to their voices in a Women Who Rock oral history mini-doc, "Girl in a Coma (at a Zoo in Seattle)," in which I interview the three band members. Video by Scott Macklin, filmed August 2011, available on YouTube, https://www.youtube.com/watch?v=GC8SI4S3dQ0_.

5. Diaz spoke at a roundtable I organized, "Girl in a Coma Tweets Chicana-Futurism," at the 9th Annual EMP Pop Conference in Seattle on April 17, 2010. Transcript forthcoming in the WWR Oral History Archive.

6. For more on Question Mark and the Mysterians and their Tejano influence on early punk, see Habell-Pallán (2005).

7. Girl in a Coma, "Clumsy Sky," on the album *Both Before I'm Gone* (Blackheart Records, 2007).

8. For an extended analysis see "¡Soy Punkera, Y Que?": Sexuality, Translocality, and Punk in Los Angeles and Beyond," chap. 5 in Habell-Pallán (2005).

9. The "Clumsy Sky" music video is on YouTube, http://www.youtube.com/watch?v=N0gJ5iiEBp0.

10. More information about the campaign to save Lerma's is available at http://www.savelermas.org.

11. No longer being updated, but archived posts through 2012 are available at http://brownstate.typepad.com.

12. Routing sound studies through Chicanx and women of color feminist theorizing allows me to account for the ways in which Girl in a Coma allows us to "hear" or "listen to" Chicanafuturism and decolonial imaginaries through their deployment of archivista practices and their engagement with social technology. New developments in sound media have transformed the band's relation to the delivery and sharing of their music, as well as their relationship to audiences. These same developments profoundly shape the ways we as scholars in Chicanx/Latinx studies can deliver, share, and archive knowledge embedded in sound-based media. Michele Hilmes suggests that sound's "ephemerality has always presented a considerable barrier to study; now the new digital materiality of sound presents us with an opportunity to recognize this considerable lacuna in our research" (2013, 178). My focus is on "how the visual augments sounds . . . how popular music works as media" (Coates 2008, 128), or how the visual helps us hear a fuller sound. More specifically, what kind of collective praxis can be developed if we focus on sound-based media within the context of exhibitions and collective archive building? For as sound studies scholar Jennifer Stoever-Ackerman argues, "Sound is not merely a scientific phenomenon—vibrations passing through matter at particular frequencies—it is also a set of social relations" (2010, 61).

13. *American Sabor* and Women Who Rock are "disruptive"/decolonial in the sense that they combine Chicana and black feminist theorizing and digital media platforms to challenge received narratives about the production of popular music in the United States and to present new bodies of evidence that create forgotten genealogies. Women Who Rock harnesses the power of digital platforms to call attention to material realities of inequity. WWR's goal is to leverage digital technology to create social infrastructure.

Works Cited

Ambrose, Joe. 2009. *Gimme Danger: The Story of Iggy Pop*. London: Omnibus.

Anzaldúa, Gloria. 1999. *Borderlands/La Frontera: The New Mestiza*. San Francisco: Aunt Lute.

———. 2015. *Light in the Dark/Luz en Lo Oscuro: Rewriting Identity, Spirituality, Reality*. Edited by AnaLouise Keating. Durham, NC: Duke University Press.

Brown, David. 2011. "Girl in a Coma, 'Exits and All the Rest.'" 50 Favorites: From Frank Ocean to June Tabor: E–J. NPR Music's 50 Favorite Albums of 2011. http://www.npr.org/2011/12/05/142906513/50-favorites-from-e-j.

Carson, David A. 2005. *Grit, Noise, and Revolution: The Birth of Detroit Rock 'n' Roll*. Ann Arbor: University of Michigan Press.

Coates, Norma. 2008. "Sound Studies: Missing the (Popular) Music for the Screens?" *Cinema Journal* 48, no. 1: 123–30.

Diaz, Phanie. 2010. "Girl in a Coma Tweets ChicanaFuturism." Presented at 9th Annual EMP Pop Conference, "The Pop Machine: Music and Technology," Seattle, April 17.

Esquibel, Catrióna Rueda. 2003. "Velvet Malinche: Fantasies of 'the' Aztec Princess in the Chicana/o Sexual Imagination." In *Velvet Barrios: Popular Culture and Chicana/o Sexualities*, edited by Alicia Gaspar de Alba, 295–307. New York: Palgrave Macmillan.

Gonzalez, Martha. 2012. "Chican@ Artivistas at the Intersection of Hope and Imagination." In *El Mundo Zurdo 3: Selected Works from the 2012 Meeting of the Society for the Study of Gloria Anzaldúa*, edited by Larissa M. Mercado-López, Sonia Saldívar-Hull, and Antonia Castañeda, x–xx. San Francisco: Aunt Lute.

———. 2014. "Mixing in the Kitchen: Entre Mujeres (Among Women) Translocal Musical Dialogues." In *Performing Motherhood: Artistic, Activist, and Everyday Enactments*, edited by Amber E. Kinser, Terri Hawkes, and Kryn Freehling-Burton, 69–87. Bradford, Ontario: Demeter.

Habell-Pallán, Michelle. 2005. *Loca Motion: The Travels of Chicana and Latina Popular Culture*. New York: New York University Press.

Habell-Pallán, Michelle, Sonnet Retman, and Angelica Macklin. 2014. "Notes on Women Who Rock: Making Scenes, Building Communities: Participatory Research, Community Engagement, and Archival Practice." *NANO: New American Notes Online*, no. 5. http://www.nanocrit.com/issues/5/notes-women-who-rock-making-scenes-building-communities-participatory-research-community-engagement-and-archival-practice.

Habell-Pallán, Michelle, Sonnet Retman, Angelica Macklin, and Monica De La Torre. Forthcoming. "Women Who Rock: Making Scenes, Building Communities: Convivencia and Archivista Praxis for a Digital Era." In *The Routledge Companion to Media Studies and Digital Humanities*, edited by Jentery Sayers. New York: Routledge.

Hilmes, Michele. 2013. "On a Screen Near You: The New Soundwork Industry." *Cinema Journal* 52, no. 3: 177–82.

Imarisha, Walidah. 2015. Introduction to *Octavia's Brood: Science Fiction Stories from Social Justice Movements*, edited by Walidah Imarisha and adrienne maree brown, 3–5. Oakland, CA: AK Press.

Johnson, Gaye Theresa. 2013. *Spaces of Conflict, Sounds of Solidarity: Music, Race, and Spatial Entitlement in Los Angeles*. Berkeley: University of California Press.

Kraker, Daniel. 2010. "'Sound Strike' Targets Arizona Immigration Law." NPR Music, July 23. http://www.npr.org/templates/story/story.php?storyId=128720832.

Little Willie G. 2008. Interviewed in *Chicano Rock! The Sounds of East Los Angeles*, directed by Jon Wilkman. PBS Home Video.

Lopez, Mark Hugo, Ana Gonzalez-Barrera, and Eileen Patten. 2013. *Closing the Digital Divide: Latinos and Technology Adoption*. Washington, DC: Pew Research Center.

Márez, Curtis. 1996. "Brown: The Politics of Working-Class Chicano Style." *Social Text* 48 (Fall): 109–32.

McPherson, Tara. 2009. "Introduction: Media Studies and the Digital Humanities." *Cinema Journal* 48, no. 2: 119–23.

Mignolo, Walter D. 2006. "Citizenship, Knowledge, and the Limits of Humanity." *American Literary History* 18, no. 2: 312–31.

Muñoz, José Esteban. 2009. *Cruising Utopia: The Then and There of Queer Futurity*. New York: New York University Press.

Ovalle, Priscilla Peña. 2009. "Synesthetic Sabor: Translation and Popular Knowledge in American Sabor." *American Quarterly* 61, no. 4: 979–96.

Pérez, Emma. 1999. *The Decolonial Imaginary: Writing Chicanas into History*. Bloomington: Indiana University Press.

Ramírez, Catherine S. 2002. "Cyborg Feminism: The Science Fiction of Octavia E. Butler and Gloria Anzaldúa." In *Reload: Rethinking Women + Cyberculture*, edited by Mary Flanagan and Austin Booth, 374–402. Cambridge, MA: MIT Press.

———. 2004. "Deus ex Machina: Tradition, Technology, and the Chicanafuturist Art of Marion C. Martinez." *Aztlán: A Journal of Chicano Studies* 29, no. 2: 55–92.

———. 2008. "Afrofuturism/Chicanafuturism: Fictive Kin." *Aztlán: A Journal of Chicano Studies* 33, no. 1: 185–94.

Rivera, Lysa M. 2012. "Future Histories and Cyborg Labor: Reading Borderlands Science Fiction after NAFTA." *Science Fiction Studies* 39, no. 3: 415–36.

Saldívar, José David. 2012. *Trans-Americanity: Subaltern Modernities, Global Coloniality, and the Cultures of Greater Mexico*. Durham, NC: Duke University Press.

Stoever-Ackerman, Jennifer. 2010. "Splicing the Sonic Color-Line: Tony Schwartz Remixes Postwar *Nueva York*." *Social Text* 28, no. 1: 59–85.

Streeby, Shelley. 2015. "Reading Jaime Hernandez's Comics as Speculative Fiction." *Aztlán: A Journal of Chicano Studies* 40, no. 2: 147–66.

Vargas, Deborah R. 2012. *Dissonant Divas in Chicana Music: The Limits of La Onda*. Minneapolis: University of Minnesota Press.

PART III

Latin@ Horror and the Politics of Monstrosity

#rapetreesarereal
Chican@futurism and Hybridizing Horror in Christopher Carmona's "Strange Leaves"

Cynthia Saldivar

All along the United States–Mexico border there have been reports of women's undergarments sighted on trees. Commonly referred to as "rape trees," these mark the sites where immigrant smugglers sexually assault migrant women and adorn the surrounding trees with their victims' undergarments. The stark contrast of the delicate garments against the harsh Texas sun constructs a surreal setting where the intimate collides with the public, attesting to the terrifying experiences—the very stuff of horror—that Central American migrant women endure in hopes of crossing into the United States. Dominant media coverage of these rapes and rape trees largely demonizes the perpetrators, the smugglers known as coyotes, obscuring the systemic root causes of undocumented immigration from Central America and the complex struggles, negotiations, and identities of Latina immigrants. Much of this coverage portrays the borderlands and immigrants as backward and primitive, regurgitating racist stereotypes and tropes dating back to the nineteenth century. However, South Texas Chicano author Christopher Carmona gives a more intimate and complex glimpse into the lives of Latinx immigrants in his 2014 award-winning short story "Strange Leaves." As I will show, his perspective is decidedly Chican@futuristic in scope: it refuses binaries of the primitive and technological, unveiling the dynamic, complex, and even contradictory ways in which Latinx immigrants and allies exert agency.

"Strange Leaves" is a modern-day short story set in South Texas and centering on the plight of a teenage Guatemalan immigrant, Shi. Shi is found in the middle of the night, somewhere south of the Sarita checkpoint, by Haldon, a middle-aged divorced man who lives in McAllen.

Found stripped of her clothing, Shi is evidently the victim of a sexual crime. Haldon takes her to the Border Patrol, who release her with an appointment to see a judge. She takes a bus to McAllen, where she ends up once again in the care of Haldon. "Strange Leaves" is written from the perspectives of these two main characters.

To give legibility to the harrowing experiences of Latina immigrants, Carmona harnesses, hybridizes, and radically revises the generic conventions of domestic and body horror even as he collapses and refuses putative distinctions between horror and terror. While domestic horror plays on our fears of the family and the familiar turning into the monstrous, body horror often depicts direct and graphic violence upon the body. Intertwined in both are temporal elements—in terror, the moment of anticipation, and in horror, the moment when fear becomes reality. To accomplish this dual task, one that requires rejecting colonial binaries endemic to the horror genre, Carmona, I suggest, adopts a more holistic and inclusive perspective. His outlook is based on mestiza consciousness and, in particular, on Chicanafuturism, which Catherine S. Ramírez defines as "Chicano cultural production that attends to cultural transformations resulting from new and everyday technologies (including their detritus); that excavates, creates, and alters narratives of identity, technology, and the future; and that redefines humanism and the human" (2004, 77–78).

As Latin@ speculative studies scholars Cathryn Merla-Watson and B. V. Olguín underline, horror is "a mode of reading that enables us to access nuances in established genres" (2016, 144). Through his use of hashtags as section titles, Carmona adapts the genre of horror as a collective call to action against the systematic oppression that plagues the Latinx community. Fusing technology and horror further erases colonial interpretations of the horror genre. Challenging binary classifications, Carmona refuses to follow the traditional conventions of horror and instead creates a new subgenre that speaks to the materiality of this text.

(Re)fusing Horror

Cyborgs are a hybrid of man and machine, a work of science fiction. Chela Sandoval examines how the US labor sphere is filled with repetitive work found in "warehouses, assembly lines, administrative cells, and computer networks that run the great electronic firms of the late twentieth century" (1999, 248). The workers who perform these tasks are disproportionately people of color who "know the pain of the union of machine and bodily tissue, the robotic conditions, and in the late twentieth century, the cyborg conditions under which the notion of human agency must take on new meanings" (248). Sandoval argues that colonized people have already developed the cyborg skills necessary for survival. Building on Donna Haraway's notion of the cyborg, Sandoval argues that technologies can "generate the forms of agency and consciousness that can create effective forms of resistance under postmodern cultural conditions" (249). Haraway redefines the term "cyborg" as "a cybernetic organism, a hybrid of machine and organism, a creature of social reality as well as a creature of fiction" (1991, 7). She extends the cyborg to propose a new theoretical framework, "cyborg feminism," which represents plurality and positionality. Sandoval builds on cyborg feminism to create cyborg consciousness, "the technological embodiment of a particular and specific form of oppositional consciousness . . . U.S. third world feminism" (1999, 248). Cyborg consciousness challenges white patriarchal systems. Sandoval also examines how survival makes it necessary to enter into a "cyberspace-of-being" that is "now accessible to all human beings through technology" (259). Cyberspace allows for subjugated populations to renegotiate their positionality using the same tools and technology that have become vital to first world cultures.

Cyberspace shapes communication, community, and identity in today's society. Gloria Anzaldúa recognized the role that cyberspace plays in decolonizing identity: "the Internet helps us in re-imagining identity beyond notions of nation, community, pueblos, gender, and sexual orientation" (2015, 188). Participating in online communities, people have the freedom to explore aspects of themselves that may be socially taboo. Technology is decolonizing identity labels by allowing computer users to substitute "representations of reality for the real" (188) and to create various online identities and communities; this allows for identities to be fluid rather than fixed. Technology also promotes rapid communication, which Anzaldúa credits for changing the nature of activism. She cites the email petition "Latinos Speak Out against War: An Action for Peace and Social Justice," which connected more than 200,000 people in a "virtual march" against the US war in Iraq in 2003 (188). Technology is a tool that can be used to challenge heteronormative patriarchal systems and create social change.

Catherine S. Ramírez (2002) examines the manner in which technology shapes Mexican and Mexican American identities. She connects Haraway's cyborg feminism with Anzaldúa's mestiza consciousness because both celebrate hybridity and pluralism. Gloria Anzaldúa's mestiza consciousness is born contesting binaries: "in attempting to work out a synthesis, the self has added a third element which is greater than the sum of its severed parts" (1999, 80). Both cyborg feminism and mestiza consciousness represent a synthesis of binaries that fuses the past with the future. Ramírez examines how cyborg identity is based on positionality and creates coalitions that are based not on identities but on essence. For example, "the term 'woman of color' forges links between women from distant and disparate locations (both geographic and socioeconomic) by positioning them—and recognizing that they have been positioned—within particular histories of exclusion, oppression and resistance" (Ramírez 2002, 384). She concludes by recognizing how science fiction, a genre long considered the domain of white, middle-class males, is now being transformed into a politicized space for the disenfranchised. Ramírez's concept of Chicanafuturism is one such example. Chicanafuturism explores the ways that technology, both old and modern, transforms Mexican/Mexican American identity. Chicanafuturism "articulates colonial and postcolonial histories of *indigenismo, mestizaje,* hegemony, and survival" by using the tools of the present to remember the past (Ramírez 2008, 187). Chicanafuturism is the new twenty-first-century mestizaje as it combines old and modern technologies to bridge the past and the present and ultimately reimagine Latinx identity.

Although Ramírez, Anzaldúa, and Sandoval envision technology as a means to connect, decolonize, and gain access to information, visual studies scholar Lisa Nakamura counters this by reminding us that not everyone has access to the Internet. For those who do, the degree to which they have control over the medium varies. Nakamura states, "Internet users all engage with interfaces over which they have more or less control, experience more or less comfort or alienation, more or less immediacy, more or less ability to create or produce, more or less investment in the interface's content and forms of representation" (2008, 95–96). She examines how racial and gendered representations reinforce white privilege and set up "distinct roles for particular races, and distinct ways of conceptualizing the racialized body as informational property for use in dataveillant state apparatuses" (97). The Internet has also become a forum for personal reinvention through avatars and simulated online communities that create isolation and work against human connection. Nakamura examines how films and commercial advertisements continue to portray minorities as "objects rather than . . . subjects" (203), and she reminds us that "being permitted to exist is not the same as equal representation" (206). Digital representation is a commodity that must be seized by those who would otherwise not be given full access.

Horror, History, and Hashtags

"Strange Leaves" is a nonlinear, fractured account of Shi's journey to the United States and the immediate aftermath. Carmona incorporates new and old technology through the use of hashtags, cellphones, and an iTelegram. By juxtaposing the ancient, indigenous name Shi with images of cutting-edge technology, Carmona "disrupt[s] age-old racist and sexist binaries that exclude Chicanas and Chicanos from visions of the future" (Ramírez 2008, 189). In addition to her name, Shi's limited understanding of Spanish signals her indigenous background. Her character thus represents a racialized past that has been excluded from the modern capitalist world. However, Carmona disrupts this representation by immersing Shi in a technological landscape. Each section begins with a hashtag that serves as both a section title and a call to action, immediately signaling that this is a modern story. The first section is titled #immigrationshuffle, to highlight the way the system handles immigrants. Told from Shi's perspective, it begins in the middle of her journey as she arrives at the Sacred Heart Catholic Church shelter in McAllen.

Carmona illustrates how recent advances in communication technology, particularly social media, have made computers vital to human connection. Twitter, on its help center Web page, defines the hashtag as a means to mark topics in a tweet and states that it was organically created by Twitter users to categorize messages. Sauter and Bruns examine the hybridity of the hashtag "as both topical marker and discursive technology" (2015, 49), noting that hashtags materialize out of shared experiences and have an impact on social and political reality. One use of the hashtag is to connect people from various nationalities, races, genders, and socioeconomic backgrounds and mobilize them for collective action. Recently, hashtags such as #feelthebern and #blacklivesmatter have infiltrated US politics to spark or consolidate social movements. Carmona uses a hashtag at the beginning of each section of his story to explore the power relations between the characters. The use of hashtags throughout the story contributes to its complex hybridity and brings together multiple identities, histories, and peoples.

However, hashtags have also been overused by social media devotees as a means of self-promotion or to verbalize the mundane. Hootsuite.com published a blog post explaining the dos and don'ts of using hashtags (LePage 2014). It makes clear that hashtags are not supposed to be too specific, as they are a means to connect social media users and engage them with a common theme. When users deploy hashtags that are too individualistic, they are essentially disengaging with fellow social media users. By incorporating these types of individualized hashtags into the story, Carmona is highlighting the unique experience that Latinx immigrants face.

The hashtag #refugeegirlatmydoorstep is an example of one instance in which Carmona uses a unique hashtag to illustrate the duality of social media. The section features a phone call from Haldon to his friend Ronnie. Haldon has just taken Shi in and needs support, so he reaches out to the same person he contacted when he first found Shi. Ronnie voices doubts about Haldon's action: "Because you're a 35-year-old man. Recently divorced. With an underage immigrant girl in your apartment." Ronnie is concerned that society will judge Haldon negatively, assuming that he has ulterior motives for helping. However, at the end of the conversation Ronnie asks Haldon to "hit me up on Facebook. Give me progress report pics." Facebook encourages users to highlight the best parts of their lives, creating the appearance that life is perfect. As a result, it has become a platform for narcissistic behavior such as posting selfies and constant status updates. Yet it is also a way to show support for various causes. For example, the Ice Bucket Challenge, which began as a dare in 2014, raised money for research on amyotrophic lateral sclerosis, or ALS. The Ice Bucket Challenge was a social media sensation, as it allowed people to star in videos while supporting a cause. Similarly, by asking Haldon to send progress pictures, Ronnie participates in a double-faced social media culture that allows users to engage in self-promotion while also helping others. Shi is an immigrant who has been abandoned by a system that refuses to adequately provide for her physical and mental needs. The "progress report pics" connect Shi to the world but will not foster the support she needs to overcome her trauma. Her exposure on Facebook thus serves as another means of exploitation.

Collective movements have invaded social media platforms. One of the most marketable of these is the breast cancer awareness movement, with its trademark pink ribbon. According to Sulik (2012), "pink ribbon culture" unites sentimentality, support, and self-transformation, the promise of medical technology, and the denigration of death and the dying. She argues that the movement has impeded the fight against breast cancer because it promotes the profit-making cancer industry. Pink ribbon culture also reinforces gender norms with the image of "the she-ro . . . a feminine hero with the attitude, style, and verve to kick cancer's butt while wearing 6-inch heels and pink lipstick" (2012, 16). The she-ro is a stark contrast to the young Guatemalan immigrant whom Haldon finds wearing "no pants, no panties, just a pair of sandals and a white shirt with a pink ribbon on it." The fact that a shirt reading "Help End Breast Cancer" has found its way onto Shi is a commentary on the multi-billion-dollar breast cancer industry and marketplace that has infiltrated all aspects of American life. Although it started as a means to connect, unite, and support breast cancer survivors, the movement has created a disconnect between participants—"who walk or run for a cure every year donning smiling faces and pink paraphernalia" (Sulik 2012, 12)—and the harsh realities of those who are sick with and fighting breast cancer. Indeed, the hypervisibility of the breast cancer movement renders invisible the reality of breast cancer and the multiple forms of exploitation and abuse that women face. Carmona makes visible these lived experiences by juxtaposing the image of the pink ribbon against the exploited and abused body of Shi.

Rape Trees Are Real

As demonstrated above, not all hashtags operate in the same manner. While some are "mainly used as paratextual markers akin to emoticons or punctuation marks" (Sauter and Bruns 2015, 48), other hashtags are created as a means to spur collective action. As Sauter and Bruns state, "An important subset of all hashtags . . . are used to mark out a specific discursive territory and facilitate the coming together of participants with shared thematic interests" (48). Carmona creates the hashtag #rapetreesarereal as a call for a new social movement that will bring to light the reality of Latinx exploitation in the borderlands.

This section of the story is written in the form of an iTelegram, a telegram ordered online and delivered on paper to the recipient's door—a modern twist on an old technology. In 1844 Samuel Morse sent Alfred Vail the first telegraphic message. The telegram thus became popular in the same decade that the United States adopted the notion of Manifest Destiny, the belief that Anglo America had the right to take over lands from coast to coast. It was also the decade of the US-Mexican War and the signing of the Treaty of Guadalupe Hidalgo. These historical moments are significant because they marked turning points in the bloody and brutal history of the borderlands. Carmona incorporates a telegram, sent by Haldon to his friend Ronnie, as a means to connect this time period of extreme border violence to the present day; yet by using an iTelegram rather than the old-fashioned kind, Carmona is using the tools of the present to link to the past and renegotiating technology as a means to reimagine the future. The hashtag #rapetreesarereal issues a call for social change that will end the brutal violence of the borderlands, thus imagining a future that is no longer marred by the atrocities of the past.

Traditional telegrams used the word STOP at the end of each sentence, and Carmona uses the same device to format the iTelegram. The use of the caesura creates a suspenseful tone that is reminiscent of a horror tale being shared around the campfire. This tension is amplified by the use of language: "I heard a strange sound when I was on the road {stop} . . . heard a woman scream {stop} . . . deep down I knew it was something horrible {stop}." Each line incorporates descriptive text that anticipates the horrors that are about to be confronted. Carmona introduces a haunting element: "At first I thought I saw the shadow of three people run across the darkened brush {stop} Maybe it was the ghosts of immigrants that never quite made it {stop}." As the story continues it becomes evident that this is more than a spiritual haunting: "But I knew better {stop}." This statement makes clear that what Haldon is about to confront is not spiritual but material.

The iTelegram continues its suspense as Haldon states, "What I saw, bro, was worse than anything I could have imagined {stop} First I saw a tree with strange leaves {stop}." This is the first reference to the rape trees, and there is no other description of the act of rape. "The woman was lying on the ground wearing only a shirt {stop} No pants, no panties, just a pair of sandals and a white shirt with a pink ribbon on it {stop}." Typically, body horror relies on the visual, especially graphic depictions of violent attacks on the body. Carmona, however, merely implies that a rape has occurred. As Sarah Projansky asserts, "The male gaze and women as objects-to-be-looked-at contribute to a culture that accepts rape, and in which rape is one experience along a continuum of sexual violence that women confront on a daily basis" (2001, 9). In this rape culture, graphic rape scenes become akin to pornography. By choosing to exclude such a scene, Carmona refuses to serve up the Latina body to the male gaze.

As the story continues, the strange leaves are finally revealed: "She hung her bra and panties from a tree . . . I turned to look one last time {stop} Too many bras, too many panties, too many strange leaves {stop}." This is the moment of the story where the historical traumas of the past collide with those of the present. It is "an allegorical moment, an instant in which an image of the past sparks a flash of unexpected recognition in the present" (Lowenstein 2005, 14). "Strange leaves" is a direct reference to "Strange Fruit," a poem written in the 1930s by Abel Meeropol after he saw a photo of a lynching. The poem later became famous as a Billie Holiday song. Like the rape in "Strange Leaves," the lynching is not described as it happens, but the implication is impossible to miss:

> Southern trees bear a strange fruit
> Blood on the leaves and blood at the root
> Black bodies swingin' in the Southern breeze
> Strange fruit hangin' from the poplar trees

As documented by Angela Y. Davis (1981) and others, during 1865–95 over ten thousand lynchings were recorded. As noted above, this is the period when the telegram was popular. Carmona continues to connect this moment in history to the present day to highlight the continued horrors being afflicted upon marginalized bodies. Davis states that in order for lynching to become popularly accepted, its violence and savagery had first to be deemed justifiable. She argues that the "myth of the black rapist" was born as a justification for lynching and as a means to silence the systematic rape of African American women by slave masters and other white men. In the narrative that demonized African American men as rapists, white women became virginal, white men become saviors, and African American women were seen as harlots (Projansky 2001, 6). A similar mentality shapes the discourse surrounding the rape trees found along the US-Mexican border. By connecting a historical African American symbol of fear to the rape of the Latinx immigrant, Carmona illustrates the historical materialism that binds the cultural experiences of both.

The hashtag #rapetreesarereal brings to light the horrific atrocities that are occurring throughout the Mexican-US borderlands and connects the histories of African American and Latino lynching. Carmona's choice of this phrase also makes direct reference to the recent media coverage of rape trees. Conservative bloggers have used these trees to demonize Mexican immigrant men as rapists, which resonates with the past. One such blog post is titled "Donald Trump Was Right . . . Rape Trees Found along US Southern Border" (Hoft 2015). To validate the outrageous title it quotes another blog post, this one on Latina.com. "'rape trees' are places where cartel members and coyotes rape female border crossers and hang their clothes, specifically undergarments, to mark their conquest" (Rosario 2009). This narrative uses the rape tree as a symbol of the brutality of the Mexican male and suggests that lynching would be fit punishment. As one commenter posted on another blog, "Why not hang the coyotes in the same tree NEXT to the undergarments???" Such commentary illustrates how the past is present, as allegations of Mexican rapists, most famously by Republican presidential candidate Donald Trump, have fueled the anti-immigrant sentiment sweeping the nation. For their part, liberal bloggers have questioned whether rape trees are real, claiming that the scenes have been staged by ranchers living on the Mexican-US border. What is missing from this discourse is the victim's perspective. This silencing of the victim further ignores the real-life trauma that is continuously occurring throughout the borderlands.

Domestic horror plays on the spaces where we should feel safest, such as the home. However, domestic horror reconfigures these spaces so that the walls that are meant to serve as protection become the walls that confine. For many immigrants, crossing into the United States promises a "better life"; the hardships and exploitation that they endured in their homelands will be eradicated upon crossing the border. This dream is immediately shattered when they reach the US borderlands. After crossing the border, Shi is raped in the very place where she was supposed to find her salvation. The rape tree symbolizes the merging of domestic horror with body horror, exposing the complex hybridity within the two genres.

Implications of body horror permeate "Strange Leaves." Because of the intimate assaults that immigrant women endure, when they face horror it is the norm, not the exception. When Shi arrives at the refugee shelter and explains to a volunteer why she does not have undergarments, her story is met with a "horrified" look. However, Shi lets the volunteer know that it is "OK" because she "took pill before. No baby." Shi is indicating that as long as there is no pregnancy, the rape is tolerable. It is the unavoidable price that she had to pay to cross into the United States. As the story continues, Shi's country is described as "no place for indias bonitas. No place for young girls like Shi. Not anymore." Even if Shi had stayed in Guatemala, it is implied, she would have encountered similar violence at the hands of the townsmen who had begun to notice her "growing breasts on chest. Ass being shaped by growing hips. Thinning face and fuller lips." By fragmenting the description, Carmona is criticizing the reduction of women to their body parts. Shi was considered sexually available even though she was, in years, still a child: "Now when body aging faster than mind. Now Shi is woman." Again body horror fuses with domestic horror as we realize that Shi was not safe in her hometown. She was forced to leave the one place she was familiar with in order to stay safe.

Rape is the manner in which the body is assaulted in "Strange Leaves," and it occurs in two pivotal scenes. The most obvious is the rape that

Shi endures when crossing into the United States. However, much as Shi must pay the price for entering the country, so must her mother. The section marked by the hashtag #journeybeginswith5thousandbucks reveals the true price that Shi's mother has paid for her daughter's journey. The coyote tells the mother that he can get Shi into the United States and she can be free in America, but "he also wants $5,000 American and a night with Mama." As Shi's mother eventually consents to these terms, she is coerced into having sex with the same man who will eventually violate her daughter. Furthermore, it is implied that this may not be the only man who exploited the mother's desperation to ensure her daughter's future in the United States. "Don't know how Mama gets money to pay coyote. When asked, Mama refuses to tell. Has something to do with man who owns restaurant where Mama works." Both instances of rape stem from the patriarchal systems that allow Latina bodies to be sexualized and discarded. Without a husband to protect her and Shi, Mama is reduced to using her body as a means to generate income and ensure a better life for her daughter. Simplifying the hashtag to focus on the monetary price that was paid actually highlights the sexual exploitation that occurs throughout the section. Carmona anticipates Shi's experience of sexual violence and desperation by pointing out that Mama may very well know what is in store for Shi, but she does not allow that thought to invade, as she truly believes that this is her daughter's only way out of the misery of her community.

In two key scenes, tears convey a sense of helplessness. They are reminiscent of the Trail of Tears in the early 1800s, when Native Americans in the southeastern United States were forced to leave their homes and trek west, thousands dying along the way. Migrants of today face many of the same hardships that were endured during the Trail of Tears: exhaustion, hunger, disease, and violence mark both of these trails. For many who come to the United States, the journey is also a forced migration. Again Carmona alludes to the atrocities of the past to expose the brutal violence of the present. Although Shi clearly does not want to make the journey—"Shi doesn't want to leave Mama. Mama is all Shi has left"—she has no other choice.

The tears are shed by the two motherly characters in the story. Benita Gomez-Santander is a woman who is also migrating to the United States, and she prepares Shi for the rape that she is about to endure. "Benita looks at her and smiles again. This time the way a mother looks at daughter knowing that something terrible is coming and she can't stop or protect her." Benita forces Shi to think about the horrors that are about to come. Benita holds Shi for the rest of the journey, and when the van stops, forces her to take the pill that will prevent pregnancy. "Benita hugs one last time and says, 'No baby. Not for you.' She feels hot tear trickle down Benita's cheek and onto her forehead." This is the only means of protection that Benita has to offer Shi.

Shi's Mama is also doing the only thing she can do to protect her daughter and offer her a better life. However, this decision is not made blindly, and it is apparent that Mama realizes what Shi will have to endure. "Don't know how Mama will protect when Shi is on road with him. Don't know if Mama lets that thought invade. Don't think she wants it to. She cries all night before truck showed up, 4 a.m." Tears are shed to mark the start of Shi's journey. Mama tries to remain strong as Shi gets on the truck to depart. "But just before truck pulls away Shi sees single tear fall from corner of Mama's eye glistening in moonlight." It is no coincidence that the tears shed in this story are by the motherly figures. La Llorona is a Mexican folktale about a mother who kills her children and spends eternity crying and desperately searching for them. The mothers in this story are similar to La Llorona in that they both know the harm that Shi is going to endure yet are helpless to prevent it from occurring.

Conclusion

Chicanx horror calls for collective action to rectify historical atrocities that still plague the Latinx community. William Calvo-Quirós defines Chican@ speculative production as a means by which a community can interpret the present through the lens of history to develop "collective epistemological tactics for survival even as it envisions a future free of oppression" (2016, 156). At the core of Chican@ speculative productions, Calvo-Quirós argues, is the tension of colonial hauntings and the need for change. Carmona utilizes Chicanafuturism to fuse old and modern technologies as a means to merge colonial and postcolonial histories. The 2016 presidential race, under way as this essay was written, has shown that bigotry and hateful rhetoric are still very much present in US society today.

Carmona sheds light on the Latinx immigrant experience and demands that we unite to combat the systemic oppression that drives the atrocities presently occurring in the borderlands. Throughout "Strange Leaves," Carmona merges the body and domestic horror to create a new Chicanx codex where the atrocities of the past collide with the monstrosities of the present. Examining "Strange Leaves" through the lens of Chicanafuturism exposes the multiple layers of meaning and symbols that give voice to the Latina immigrant experience. Chicanafuturism fuses both old and modern technologies as a means to reimagine the future. Deconstructing the binary mode of analysis allows for a holistic approach that exposes the materiality of the violence that connects past and present. Carmona utilizes elements of Chicanafuturism as a collective call to action against the current sexual violence that Latina immigrants endure. Chicanafuturism creates an understanding of the subjectivity and lived experiences of Latinas in the borderlands.

Works Cited

Anzaldúa, Gloria. 1999. *Borderlands/La Frontera*. San Francisco: Aunt Lute.

———. 2015. *Light in the Dark/Luz en Lo Oscuro: Rewriting Identity, Spirituality, Reality*. Edited by AnaLouise Keating. Durham, NC: Duke University Press.

Calvo-Quirós, William A. 2016. "The Emancipatory Power of the Imaginary: Defining Chican@ Speculative Productions." *Aztlán: A Journal of Chicano Studies* 41, no. 1: 155–70.

Carmona, Christopher. 2014. "Strange Leaves." *Texas Observer* short story contest finalist, published on the *Texas Observer* website, September 29. https://www.texasobserver.org/short-story-contest-christopher-carmona. Forthcoming in *The Road to Llorona Park*, by Christopher Carmona. Nacogdoches, TX: Stephen F. Austin State University Press.

Davis, Angela Y. 1981. *Women, Race, and Class*. New York: Vintage.

Haraway, Donna. 1991. *Simians, Cyborgs, and Women: The Reinvention of Nature*. New York: Routledge.

Hoft, Jim. 2015. "Donald Trump Was Right . . . Rape Trees Found Along US Southern Border." *Gateway Pundit* (blog), July 4.

LePage, Evan. 2014. "The Do's and Don'ts of How to Use Hashtags." *Hootsuite* (blog), August 27.

Lowenstein, Adam. 2005. *Shocking Representation: Historical Trauma, National Cinema, and the Modern Horror Film*. New York: Columbia University Press.

Merla-Watson, Cathryn Josefina, and B. V. Olguín. 2016. "From the Horrific to the Utopic: Pan-Latin@ Speculative Poetics and Politics." *Aztlán: A Journal of Chicano Studies* 41, no. 1: 143–54.

Nakamura, Lisa. 2008. *Digitizing Race: Visual Cultures of the Internet*. Minneapolis: University of Minnesota Press.

Projansky, Sarah. 2001. *Watching Rape: Film and Television in Postfeminist Culture*. New York: New York University Press.

Ramírez, Catherine S. 2002. "Cyborg Feminism: The Science Fiction of Octavia E. Butler and Gloria Anzaldúa." In *Reload: Rethinking Women + Cyberculture*, edited by Mary Flanagan and Austin Booth, 374–402. Cambridge, MA: MIT Press.

———. 2004. "Deus ex Machina: Tradition, Technology, and the Chicanafuturist Art of Marion C. Martinez." *Aztlán: A Journal of Chicano Studies* 29, no. 2: 55–92.

———. 2008. "Afrofuturism/Chicanafuturism: Fictive Kin." *Aztlán: A Journal of Chicano Studies* 33, no. 1: 185–94.

Rosario, Mariela. 2009. "'Rape Trees' Found along Southern US Border." Latina. com, March 11.

Sandoval, Chela. 1999. "New Sciences: Cyborg Feminism and the Methodology of the Oppressed." In *Cybersexualities: A Reader in Feminist Theory, Cyborgs and Cyberspace*, edited by Jenny Wolmark, 247–63. Edinburgh: Edinburgh University Press.

Sauter, Theresa, and Axel Bruns. 2015. "#auspol: The Hashtag as Community, Event, and Material Object for Engaging with Australian Politics." In *#Hashtag Publics: The Power and Politics of Discursive Networks*, edited by Nathan Rambukkana, 47–59. New York: Peter Lang.

Sulik, Gayle. 2012. *Pink Ribbon Blues: How Breast Cancer Culture Undermines Women's Health*. New York: Oxford University Press.

Contesting Monstrosity in Horror Genres

Chicana Feminist Mappings of de la Peña's "Refugio" and Hamilton's Anita Blake, Vampire Hunter Series

Luz María Gordillo

> I have debated on whether to share the real reason that there are not more African American or dark-skinned vampires in my books. I can't decide if it's politically correct to say it here. The truth is that all vampires are paler as vampires than they were as live people, thus someone of African American descent would be paler. But how pale? I was pretty sure that if I had characters that were African American but paled them all out that I'd be accused of trying to literally white-wash them.
> —Laurell K. Hamilton, *Ardeur*

> [Science fiction is] potentially the freest genre in existence. . . . A science fiction writer has the freedom to do absolutely anything. The limits are the imagination of the writer. There are always blacks in the novels I write and whites.
> ——Octavia Butler, "Black Women and the Science Fiction Genre"

US mainstream cultural productions of science fiction and fantasy, horror, and gothic genres confabulate and create alternative and futuristic worlds that are predominantly white and heterosexist. Dominant narratives in the speculative arts are raced and gendered; they identify tropes of magical domination and technological advancement of and for straight white maleness. The lack of powerful queer women of color as protagonists in narratives that promise utopian/dystopian futuristic advancements and alternative worlds of fantasy illustrates the heterosexism and racism plaguing these popular narratives.

The representation of women as powerful witches and vampires, common from the 1960s through the late 1980s, transformed in the late twentieth century when heterosexist male vampire narratives took the lead in the horror/gothic/fantasy realm. Author Anne Rice may have initiated this barrage of male-centered vampire narratives with her novel *Interview with the Vampire* (1976). Rice also published a three-book series, The Mayfair Witches, in 1990–94, in which witches retained most of their magical powers and used these powers to challenge their male vampire counterparts. Gradually, however, during the last decades of the twentieth century female witches were left behind as vampire narratives increasingly reflected "straight white male ontologies" (Winnubst 2003, 11).

Today, mainstream cultural productions of sci fi and horror/gothic/fantasy represent the epitome of white patriarchal heterosexist cultural bias, with misogynist meta-texts imbued in many of these popular narratives. Horror/gothic/fantasy narratives tend to disseminate heteronormative, racist, and classist cultural propaganda that influences the realm of the imaginary. Catherine S. Ramírez comments, "Like black people, especially black women, Chicanas, Chicanos, and Native Americans are usually disassociated from science and technology, signifiers of civilization, rationality, and progress" (2008, 188). It is interesting, therefore, to consider two speculative fiction texts that have strong female protagonists who challenge male-dominated narratives but that reflect very different approaches to representations of monstrosity. Chicana Terri de la Peña's short story "Refugio," published in 1996, features a Mexican immigrant lesbian vampire, while Euro-American Laurell K. Hamilton debuted her half-Mexican kick-ass vampire slayer in the series Anita Blake, Vampire Hunter, in 1993.

Hamilton's Anita Blake series offers an example of how white heterosexist hierarchies in vampiric texts are popularized and prioritized. Even though sci fi is "potentially the freest genre in existence" (Butler 1986, 14), Hamilton problematizes race when she asks herself "how pale" she should make her African American characters. Pondering this, she justifies ontologies of white sociopolitical domination: "I'd be accused of trying to literally white-wash them" (2010, 135). Moreover, the protagonist Anita Blake, with one or two minor exceptions, has strictly heterosexual if polyamorous relationships.

In contrast to the wide acclaim given Hamilton's work, productions featuring women of color, such as de la Peña's short story "Refugio," have been nearly ignored by critics. With contrasting rhetorical and analytical structures, "Refugio" functions as a subversive metatext to restrictive white vampiric narratives, condemning their overt heterosexist racism. I argue below that de la Peña's Mexican immigrant, shape-shifting lesbian vampire disrupts mainstream hetero-racist narratives with alternative signifiers grounded in politico-cultural resistance. Authors of color like de la Peña, who produce unique work in sci fi and horror/gothic/fantasy genres, evade Euro-American feminist cultural critics. Most academic work involved in theorizing the construction of a horror/gothic/fantasy genre and published by mainstream scholarly presses does so within a white landscape only.

Commenting on vampire narratives produced by women, Carol Siegel characterizes some as feminist. She concludes,

> The *feminist* side of the spectrum culminates in Hamilton's sex-radical feminism, unrestricted pleasure as political duty that costs one the respect of the conservative majority, a place in mainstream culture, and the possibility of traditional domestic bliss, but offers, in addition to delightful sexual adventures, counterculture fellowship, a family made through loving connections, emotional fulfillment, and self-respect. (2011, 265, my emphasis)

There is no doubt that Hamilton turned sexist patriarchal paradigms upside down by presenting a strong kick-ass female protagonist who cares about her "monster" family. However, her work also exemplifies how white authors and academics have continued to ignore the construction of theoretical frameworks by women of color. These frameworks have engaged race and sexuality as important and inseparable discursive and performative components of work by women of color.[1]

By considering and challenging the lack of literary space allotted to speculative cultural productions by Chicanas, we can place the production by women of color at the center of theoretical articulations that incorporate race, class, gender, and sexuality. Such a framing challenges white feminists' limited and constricted analyses of horror/gothic/fantasy genres. Chicana feminist and lesbian Terri de la Peña threads into her fantasy world the sociopolitical and transnational experiences of Mexican immigrant women and women of Mexican descent in the United States. Her text places Mexican immigrants, Mexican Americans, and Chican@s at the center of a narrative in which the barrio functions as a social refuge (*refugio*) where political strategies that denounce social/racial/sexual oppression are contested and negotiated. Building on this feminist Chicana framework, de la Peña's "Refugio" offers a countercultural alternative to a social order whose racist, separatist, and nativist rhetoric continues to be disseminated through US mainstream popular culture.

The Politics of Race and Sexuality in Hamilton

Laurell K. Hamilton published her first book in the Anita Blake, Vampire Hunter series, *Guilty Pleasures*, in 1993. *Dead Ice*, the twenty-fourth book in the series, appeared in 2015. Over the course of two decades the series has sold over 6 million copies, and Hamilton reached the *New York Times* bestseller list with *Obsidian Butterfly* in 2000 (fig. 1). The latter title is of interest not only because of the literary recognition it has achieved but also because for the first time in her series, Hamilton examines and confronts head on—albeit through a very racist lens—her young, pale-skinned protagonist's biracial background.

Anita Blake is a twenty-seven-year-old vampire slayer and necromancer living in St. Louis. Her deceased mother was Mexican and her father is white. Encouraged by her Mexican grandmother, a voodoo priestess, Anita rejects her Mexican background and identifies only with her paternal white heritage. Blake inherits her maternal grandmother's powers as a necromancer who can raise the dead, and she works as an animator for Animators Inc., a firm that charges to

Cover of the 2001 edition of Laurell K. Hamilton's Obsidian Butterfly. *The cover was created by Judith Murello and Erika Fusari. Image courtesy of Penguin Random House.*

raise the dead. Anita also serves as a licensed vampire executioner for RPIT, a marginal police division that investigates preternatural crimes. Anita falls in love with Jean-Claude, the feared vampire Master of the City, and with Richard, the leader of the werewolf pack. Blake states, "I'd been virtuous for so long, but when I lost it, I lost it big time. [I went] from celibacy to fucking the undead" (Hamilton 1998, 247). Toward the end of the series, Anita Blake is unable to stop having sex, even when she's violently abused by some of her lovers.

Hamilton emphasizes both her protagonist's Latina identity—her Otherness—and her ability to pass for white. The author justifies her selection of a Hispanic protagonist: "I'm so white-bread, if you cut me I'd bleed bleached flour! I have no ethnicity to me, and I've always wanted some" (Hamilton 2000a). In the series, the Mexican American female body is rejected and devalued by Euro-American standards. Blake's fiancé, the "epitome of WASP breeding" (131), abandons her after having premarital sex because of her mixed race—in the Hamiltonian universe biracial bodies are unacceptable.[2] On the other hand, although Blake is partly of Mexican descent, she has "skin so pale, it's almost white" (Hamilton 1997, 47). In 2000, when Hamilton published *Obsidian Butterfly*, anti-Mexican sentiment was prevalent in the Euro-American imaginary, with Mexican immigrants equated to domestic terrorists (Gordillo 2009, 149). In this political environment, Hamilton's half-Mexican, half-white protagonist states firmly, "I'm not passing, Bernardo. I am white. My mother just happened to be Mexican" (Hamilton 2000b, 131).[3] This racial/ethnic whitewashing gives her unearned socioeconomic and cultural privileges that a woman of color in the United States would not otherwise have.

The lack of characters of color, in particular African Americans, in the Anita Blake series is obvious even though much of the series takes place in St. Louis, where, according to 2010 census data, the total population is 49.2 percent black or African American and only 43.9 percent non-Hispanic white. *Obsidian Butterfly* is set in Santa Fe, which, according to 2013 census data, is 47.3 percent Hispanic or Latino and only 39.4 non-Hispanic white.[4] Hamilton's justification for this racist ahistorical and discriminating absence is that she fears being "accused of trying to literally white-wash" African American characters; however, Hamilton has no racial/ethnic guilt about whitewashing Anita Blake. Mikhail Lyubansky comments that Hamilton "generously shared with me her inspiration for Anita's full assimilation into Whiteness" (2010, 146). To which Hamilton responds, "Since I get a lot of Hispanic fans loving the fact that Anita is half-Hispanic, I could argue that, but that she looks white seems to be his point. That I can't argue with" (2010, 135). Hamilton claims the right to construct notions of race and ethnicity through a narrow, subjective lens that allows her to pick and choose those who can be assimilated/whitewashed and those who, by contrast, have no opportunities to belong in her Hamiltonian world.

Though Anita Blake is of mixed racial background, Hamilton places her vampire slayer within a white experience. Because of her skin tone Blake enjoys white privilege. Moving in and out of contested sociopolitical and cultural spaces for people of color, Anita Blake has sex with vampires and monsters because Blake is monster and executioner of monsters at the same time; she breaks laws with impunity while working for the police and consulting with the FBI. Simon the killer asks Blake, "How many vampire kills you got, bitch?" After much hesitation Blake responds, "Most of the fifty are sanctioned kills" (Hamilton 2000b, 488). Her confidence, then, stems from her privilege and ability to operate with ease within the realm of the legal as well as the illegal, and within private and public spaces alike.

Acting as an insider/outsider, executioner/monster, good girl/bad ass cop, all in an ethnic/racial body, Anita Blake shows contempt for her own cultural background when she tries to erase the existence of her Mexican grandmother and mother. Although she owes all of her magical powers—and consequently her career success and her ability to sleep with the monsters she loves—strictly to her maternal line, she accepts the need to sever herself from her Mexican roots:

> Grandmother Flores had told me that I was a necromancer. It was more than being a voodoo priestess, and less. I had a sympathy with the dead, all dead. It was hard to be a vaudun and a necromancer and *not be evil.* . . . She had encouraged my being *Christian. Encouraged my father to cut me off from her side of the family. Encouraged it for love of me and fear for my soul.* (Hamilton 1994, 50, emphasis added)

To Blake, the demon/enemy/monster part of her is her Mexican ancestry. Her magical powers are what define her as "Other." Consequently her race/ethnicity is not only demonized, but rendered invisible. Although "much of the most intense conflict in the novel is fueled by Anita Blake's determination to distance herself from her magical abilities and from the monsters" (Holland-Toll 2004, 176), thus cutting herself off from tropes of Otherness and Mexicanness, the politics of race are completely ignored. Supporting a color-blind political agenda represented by a melting pot rhetoric that "whitewashes" certain minorities through complete assimilation, Hamilton's Anita Blake in *Obsidian Butterfly* viciously turns against all things Mexican. The text and its popularity illustrates how even semi-feminist mainstream vampiric narratives posit racist and heterosexist discourses that demonize the representation, subjectivity, and sexuality of Latinas.

The Politics of Identity and Violence in de la Peña

In stark contrast to Hamilton's "pale" half-Mexican vampire slayer is the Mexican immigrant lesbian vampire featured in Terri de la Peña's short story "Refugio" (1996).[5] "Refugio" takes place in el barrio, a socially and politically contested location in Los Angeles where the award-winning author, a Chicana lesbian of Mexican immigrant and Mexican American background, examines the politics of gender, sexuality, and identity.

Refugio Torres, a female lesbian vampire and shape shifter, looks fifty-seven but is almost 600 years old. She has chosen not to be immortal because she is tired of battling against abuses of her Mexican immigrant/Mexican American/Chicana community. When she turns 600, Refugio decides, she will "[call] it quits. That's why I look the way I do; I really am aging" (de la Peña 1996, 174). Refugio is a powerful vampire/shape shifter. With a "dagger's cold blade" (167) she makes her mark, transforming Chican@ gang members into social activists who protect their community. Refugio lives in the barrio and works as a nurse in a hospital a few blocks away. Her partner and female lover is shape shifter Noche (Night), who prefers to stay out of sight and in dog form most of the time. Refugio and Noche have been together for many decades, and because Noche could appear to be young and incredibly beautiful, while Refugio looks much older, she and Refugio decided she should assume the form of a black wolf-like dog in public spaces.

When de la Peña published "Refugio" in 1996, the sociopolitical environment for Mexican immigrants, Mexican Americans, and Chican@s was contentious. Immigration policies like Operation Gatekeeper implemented on the San Diego–Tijuana border in 1994 had increased deaths of Mexican immigrants while promoting anti-Mexican sentiment in the United States (Gordillo 2009, 162). While Hamilton sidesteps racial/ethnic conflicts, de la Peña introduces into this hostile sociopolitical context a subversive transnational monster. Noche exclaims to Refugio, "You're the only affirmative action vampire I know, esa" (de la Peña 1996, 173), when she finds out that Refugio wants Mario, a newly converted vampire/shape shifter, to take the life of the white supremacist who killed him. Refugio has selected Mario to head the protectorate that will look after the barrio when Refugio and Noche leave.

De la Peña surrounds Refugio with symbolic transcultural tropes that confer power while also keeping Refugio and her lover Noche safe and warm. Refugio's Oaxacan blanket is such a strong totem of safety and security that only Noche, her lover/partner/friend/wife, in an intimate moment may nudge "through the red-and-black Oaxacan blanket to [Refugio's] buried cuerpo" (165), evoking a metaphorical coffin. Described as a "woolen cocoon" (165), the blanket also serves as a force field that protects Refugio's and her lover's bodies from harm. The Oaxacan blanket stands out, claiming its historical space. The colors red and black, tropes of working-class solidarity, convey transnational understandings of revolutionary strikes both in Mexico and in the United States. More recently, they suggest the black, red, and white logo of the United Farm Workers (UFW), a symbol of working-class struggle, resistance, and victory.

As a Mexican immigrant and transnational worker, Refugio juggles two nations at the same time—Mexico and the United States. She and her lover also inhabit two worlds, those of the living and the undead. Within this contested duality, de la Peña offers a rhetorical manifesto that mirrors

Gloria Anzaldúa's declaration in her highly influential monograph *Borderlands/La Frontera*: "I will have my voice: Indian, Spanish, white. I will have my serpent's tongue—my woman's voice, my sexual voice, my poet's voice. I will overcome the tradition of silence" (1987, 59). In bed with her lover, when lines are sometimes blurred between the real and the fantastic, Refugio thinks to herself, "Yo estaba dormida como una muerta"—I was sleeping like the dead (de la Peña 1996, 165). In a strong Anzaldúan strategic move, de la Peña uses Spanish within the narrative as a revolutionary tool to destabilize racial/ethnic structures of power in the United States that have historically devalued languages like Spanish and condemned communities who speak it. Once the rhetorical and linguistic challenge has been posed (among other examples, the word *Oaxaca*, of Mixtec origin, is almost impossible for many Euro-Americans to pronounce) and the codes laid out, Refugio sets out into the world where "more trouble—a gang fight, a shooting, maybe a driveby" may be lurking and her superpowers needed. "Noche, no te apuras. . . . I know it's almost time for me to go" (165–66). Intercultural language debates have also driven a wedge between Hispanophone communities in the United States, which may disagree on such matters as the use of Spanglish. Mexican immigrant Refugio's semiotic and linguistic approach indirectly assures "no te apuras" rather than "no te apures" because, according to de la Peña, it's irrelevant and absurd to have the colonizer's language continue to harm Latin@ communities in the United States.

Conjuring up another symbolic cultural force field, Refugio protects herself from the chill of the night, and also from the police, "wrapped in [her] full-length hooded Guatemalan poncho" (166). The poncho, a trope of *latinidad*, shields her against all metaphorical enemies, like the "increased police presence at the barrio's edges" (166). Refugio denounces police brutality and the historical abuse of Mexican immigrants and people of Mexican descent by government officials and restrictive immigration laws in the United States:

> In my time, I had dealt with bigots of all types: conquistadores, revolutionaries, Texas Rangers, the U.S. border patrol, the LAPD, to name a few. Didn't Belen Gomez realize that brown people—Aleuts, Native Americans, Mexicans, Latin Americans, South Americans—were indigenous to this continent? No matter what anyone called us, we were *not* immigrants; we were here already. We met the boat, so to speak. (171)

Challenging notions of white privilege and foreignness/Otherness, as well as conceptualizations of legality and law and order, de la Peña is explicit in identifying the enemies of communities of Mexican immigrants, Mexican Americans, and people of color in general. Her construction of the barrio as fantastic and dangerous does not derive from Euro-Americans' restrictive racial classifications and hegemonic divisions of urban space; rather, the barrio is depicted as place of danger for Latin@s, who may be spied on ("No wonder la Noche was agitated. I heard helicopters—several—whirling through the twilit barrio") and worse, shot at (165–66). Refugio exposes the fantastic/danger when on her way to work, "I hurried along . . . Small and round, I did not want to be mistaken for a roaming muchacho. How would a helicopter pilot recognize my scurrying figure as a gray-haired mujer, not a baggy-pants, shorn-headed gang-banger?" (166). It is clear that those whom Refugio fears may act without scruples, common sense, or reason toward people of color living in el barrio.

De la Peña highlights conflicts in the barrio that have to do not only with race but also with gender, sexuality, and nationality in a shared and contested space. Refugio comments, "Belen and others like her [light-skinned Mexican Americans] in the barrio considered me an eccentric old woman . . . in the midst of a traditional Mexican-American community, my independent nature could arouse distrust" (171). This marginalization causes Refugio to leave the place she loves: "Far too many times in the past, I had had to move on, to leave a place where I had settled, because I no longer could fit in" (171). Consequently, Refugio embraces her ethnic/racial background, challenging at the same time intraethnic differences: "Why do you listen to that pendejo talk show, eh? All those hateful people . . . All you hear on this damn show are anti-Mexican call-ins. All about taggers and gangs and 'illegal' immigrants." Belen, nurse and co-worker, defends her own ethnic/racial disassociation: "People who call in are anti-*immigrant*, not anti-Mexican." Refugio warns, "I'm vieja and seen a lot, Belen. Trying to be a 'good Mexican' like you, trying to blend in, walking around with blinders on, won't guarantee you a damn thing" (170–71). During the Great Depression in the 1930s, Mexican Americans, Chican@s, and Mexican immigrants were indiscriminately deported to Mexico just because they "looked" Mexican. Many people of Mexican descent who were deported were US citizens who did not speak Spanish and had never been to Mexico (Gordillo 2010, 94–95). Rather than simply turning the paradigm upside down and glorifying or victimizing people who live in el barrio—a place Refugio loves and calls home—de la Peña also presents the intracultural conflicts that challenge gender and ethnic/racial divisions of labor.

Refugio exists within urban marginal spaces. Rather than making these places ahistorical, de la Peña underlines the oppressive systems that leave communities of color with limited options in terms of how to organize their lives around social spaces and what place to call home. Moreover, de la Peña's Refugio queers at the same time the spaces that she and Noche inhabit every day. According to Mary Pat Brady, "The production of space involves not simply buildings, transportation, and communications networks, as well as social and cultural groups and institutions, . . . it also involves the processes that shape how these places are understood, envisioned, defined, and variously experienced" (2002, 6). Refugio then redefines alternatives for her people—Mexican Americans, Mexican immigrants, and Chican@s—on how to work together in the barrio and its discursive spatiality to stay safe and redeem the youth who are joining gangs and "tagging" the barrio. De la Peña eroticizes and sexualizes her lesbian relationship with Noche in intimate spaces, as when Refugio narrates, "I drew nearer, ending her mirth when I covered her red mouth with mine" (de la Peña 1996, 169). In a bold rhetorical move, she also links queerness, sexual practices, and existing as a lesbian as being one with the urban environment, normalizing their relationship and their existence as parts of the barrio. In one of the most sensual and sexual scenes in the story, de la Peña has her three protagonists—Refugio, Noche, and el barrio—engage in a vampire-wolf-barrio ménage à trois: "Through the misty dawn I witnessed her approach, her topaz eyes piercing the foggy air. Gaining momentum, her ebony body sleek and supple, she hurled herself over the cemetery fence to welcome me. In her exuberance, her throaty voice punctuated the silent street. She nearly toppled me" (167). Noche, Refugio, and el barrio then are the rulers, seducers, and protectors of this socially constructed urban space, linking people of color. They are not detached from nature; rather, their naturalness co-exists within urban spatiality, at home within their own historicity.

In an attempt to normalize the demonization and criminalization of el barrio, Refugio's co-worker, Euro-American Dr. Sorensen, spews out to her, "Why you live in the middle of that war zone, I'll never understand" (169). Refugio, knowing that the barrio belongs to her as much as she belongs there, defiantly retorts, "I belong there" (170). Refugio warns her fellow Mexican American co-worker: "Listen Belen, tu sabes que I was born in Mexico. No me gusta oir esa cochinada. I don't like hearing people say we're all a bunch of criminals" (171). De la Peña constructs social urban cartographies that explain how Chicana literature "implicates the production of space in the everyday, in the social . . . for understanding the intermeshing of the spatial and the social. And Chicana literature argues for and examines the relevance of race gender, and sexuality—as well as class—to the making of space" (Brady 2002, 5). De la Peña's powerful and sensual triad—vampire, wolf/night, barrio—dismantles and counterattacks the simplistic assumptions that construct the barrio as fantastic and dangerous and its people, by default, as embodying and engendering social pathology.

In Terri de la Peña's vampiric world, discursive elements in the story redefine monstrosity through the prism of intersectionality: race, class, gender, sexuality, and nationality. De la Peña challenges traditional processes of "Othering" by appropriating the undead body and transforming it into a paranormal transnational revolutionary and metaphorical Adelita/Zapata, who protects their space—el barrio. Refugio's "violence" transforms her victims into vampire/shape-shifter social activists who commit their powers to the betterment of the community while embracing all forms of Mexicanness or *latinidad* among Mexican immigrants, Mexican Americans, Chican@s, and Latin@s in general. At the same time that de la Peña embraces social cartographies that need Refugio's help and the help of the community, she condemns the cultural borders embedded in this social spatiality that engender violence. Even though Santa Monica College's main campus is only blocks away from el barrio and thus should welcome students of color, it is so white that when Mario, a gang member, is mercilessly shot by a Euro-American vigilante, the assailant is able to hide on the college campus: he "sprint[ed] across Pico toward the community college. . . . He must have blended in with the evening students because the police found no trace of him" (de la Peña 1996, 176). Education, a mainstream trope of both social egalitarianism and capitalist exclusiveness, is another realm where spatial boundaries mark urban spaces that are meant to keep people of color out. The college—privileged space—is transformed to signify danger, a place where institutional racism and discrimination is rampant. The student body provided the perfect cover for the violent murderer—whiteness.

Mario is taken to the hospital. As he dies, Refugio turns him into a vampire/shape shifter, deciding that Mario will avenge his death by killing his murderer. As an act of resistance, De la Peña's narrative allows the oppressed—like the young gang member—a space and a moment to "destabilize the real" (Halberstam 1993, 199) by inverting structures of power and violence, as when Mario kills the vigilante: "His horrified eyes bulged when Mario began his attack. The stranger's screams split the night. Only la Noche's barking obscured it" (de la Peña 1996, 177). Theorist Jack Halberstam asserts,

> Imagined violence . . . is the fantasy of unsanctioned eruptions of aggression from "the wrong people, of the wrong skin, the wrong sexuality, the wrong gender." We have to be able to imagine violence and our violence needs to be imaginable because the power of fantasy is not to represent but to destabilize the real. Imagined violence does not stop men from raping women but it might make a man think twice about whether a woman is going to blow him away. (1993, 199)

It is these very intersections that allow "the wrong people, of the wrong skin," gender, and sexuality to use imagined violence to destabilize the real. The white supremacist who wants to "clean up [the] streets, get rid of all the fuckin' Mexican trash around here" is the enemy, while the Mexican ex-gang member is redeemed and granted a second chance (172). Turning racial and social structural maps upside down and inside out, de la Peña complicates issues of ethnicity, sexuality, racial categories, spatiality, and violence. She does so not by creating binary oppositions but by conjuring a world where "Othered" fantastic creatures—the Mexican immigrant and lesbian vampire—are normalized, while racist and heterosexist mainstream US culture is problematized and demonized in the bodies of white Dr. Sorensen and the white supremacist murderer and "gun enthusiast" Stan Maxwell (178).

Conclusion

Terri de la Peña's Mexican immigrant heroine, Refugio, represents an (alter) Native counternarrative of subjectivity in which fantastic configurations allow her to protect her resilient community. Laurell K. Hamilton, by contrast, in order to perform as "Other," and in the tradition of blackface, allegorically co-opts a brown body. In *Obsidian Butterfly*, in particular, she (mis)appropriates and possesses Anita Blake's mixed ethnicity and uses it as a vehicle to demonize, dehumanize, and criminalize Mexican Americans, Mexican immigrants, and Chican@s in general. That this racist performance has escaped the scrutiny of white feminist cultural critics suggests the need to deepen the theoretical conversation between radical white feminists and feminists of color.

De la Peña does not take the monster out of Refugio but brings Chicana/Mexicana feminism into the Mexican immigrant lesbian monster. The author provides a new (alter) Native world where violence against members of the dominant white majority is justified while racial/ethnic and sexual minorities have more sociopolitical options available to them. Moreover, as a Mexican immigrant and lesbian vampire, Refugio invokes the dark beast within and without as an appropriation of power and ethnic pride in relation to white culture. In her relationship to Noche, her lover, warrior, bitch, protector, and defender, Refugio appreciates that which is dark and integral to her universe—the brown body and the darkness of night.

Appropriating the historical markers of working-class strength, solidarity, and victory, Refugio and Noche shape-shift into ravens and "together, [they take] . . . flight, soaring over the vast farmlands, heading in the direction of Delano." Their flight summons the imagery of Dolores Huerta, the "dragon lady," who allegorically soars on the black eagle of the UFW. This is a political reminder that these communities of Mexican descent will continue to demand fair distribution of social and economic resources, in particular for Mexican immigrants in the United States. Their presence in imaginary worlds of fantasy and science fiction makes it imperative to counterbalance the invisibility of people of color among authors and critics of the speculative arts. Octavia Butler, lesbian feminist of color, affirms this in an interview conducted in 1986: "A science fiction writer has the freedom to do absolutely anything. The limits are the imagination of the writer. There are always blacks in the novels I write and whites" (16). Terri de la Peña's "Refugio" and her Mexican immigrant lesbian vampire and shape shifter, Refugio Torres, function as destabilizing tropes and as subversive texts and metatexts. In so doing they challenge mainstream hegemonic horror/gothic/fantasy narratives, whose heterosexist and racist discourses have long been woven into the speculative arts.

Notes

1. Linda J. Holland-Toll comments, "As a young woman in college, Anita Blake surrendered her virginity to her fiancé only to be abandoned by him when his family thought her *not quite up to high St. Louis society*" (2004, 183, italics added). In fact, Blake was abandoned because she was half Mexican; thus Holland-Toll disregards Anita's real experience of racial discrimination.

2. Full quote: "I was engaged once until his mother found out my mother had been Mexican. He was blond and blue-eyed, the epitome of WASP breeding. My future-in-law didn't like the idea of me darkening her family tree."

3. Mikhail Lyubansky states, "I actually must confess that I missed Anita Blake's Mexican background entirely in my own reading" (2010, 146).

4. US Census Bureau, State and County QuickFacts, http://quickfacts. census.gov/qfd/states/35000.html.

5. De la Peña also published "Territories" (2008), a short story that won the 1992 Chicano/Latino Literary Prize, as well as the novels *Margins* (1992), *Latin Saints* (1994), and *Faults* (1999).

Works Cited

Anzaldúa, Gloria. 1987. *Borderlands/La Frontera: The New Mestiza.* San Francisco: Aunt Lute.

Brady, Mary Pat. 2002. *Extinct Lands, Temporal Geographies: Chicana Literature and the Urgency of Space.* Durham, NC: Duke University Press.

Butler, Octavia. 1986. "Black Women and the Science Fiction Genre: Black Scholar Interview with Octavia Butler." *Black Scholar* 17, no. 2: 14–18.

de la Peña, Terri. 1992. *Margins.* Seattle: Seal.

———. 1994. *Latin Saints.* New York: Djuna.

———. 1996. "Refugio." In *Night Bites: Vampire Stories by Women,* edited by Victoria A. Brownworth, 165–78. Seattle: Seal.

———. 1999. *Faults.* New York: Djuna.

———. 2008. "Territories." In *The Chicano/Latino Literary Prize: An Anthology of Prize-Winning Fiction, Poetry, and Drama,* edited by Stephanie Fetta, 215–28. Houston: Arte Público.

Gordillo, Luz María. 2009. "The Bracero, the Wetback, and the Terrorist: Mexican Immigration, Legislation, and National Security." In *A New Kind of Containment: "The War on Terror," Race, and Sexuality,* edited by Carmen R. Lugo-Lugo and Mary K. Bloodsworth-Lugo, 149–66. New York: Rodopi.

———. 2010. *Mexican Women and the Other Side of Immigration: Engendering Transnational Ties.* Austin: University of Texas Press.

Halberstam, Judith. 1993. "Imagined Violence/Queer Violence: Representation, Rage, and Resistance." *Social Text* 37: 187–201.

Hamilton, Laurell K. 1993. *Guilty Pleasures.* New York: Ace.

———. 1994. *The Laughing Corpse.* New York: Ace.

———. 1997. *The Killing Dance.* New York: Ace.

———. 1998. *Burnt Offerings.* New York: Ace.

———. 2000a. "Death and Sex." *Locus Magazine,* September. http://www.locusmag.com/2000/Issues/09/Hamilton.html.

———. 2000b. *Obsidian Butterfly.* New York: Jove.

———, ed. 2010. *Ardeur: 14 Writers on the Anita Blake, Vampire Hunter Series.* Dallas: Smart Pop.

———. 2015. *Dead Ice.* New York: Random House.

Holland-Toll, Linda J. 2004. "Harder than Nails, Harder than Spade: Anita Blake as 'The Tough Guy' Detective." *Journal of American Culture* 27, no. 2: 175–89.

Lyubansky, Mikhail. 2010. "Are the Fangs Real? Vampires as Racial Metaphor in the Anita Blake Novels." In Hamilton 2010, 137–48.

Ramírez, Catherine S. 2008. "Afrofuturism/Chicanfuturism: Fictive Kin." *Aztlán: A Journal of Chicano Studies* 33, no. 1: 185–93.

Rice, Anne. 1976. *Interview with the Vampire.* New York: Knopf.

Siegel, Carol. 2011. "The Twilight of Sexual Liberation: Undead Abstinence Ideology." In *The Sexuality Curriculum and Youth Culture,* edited by Dennis Carlson and Donyell Roseboro, 261–75. New York: Peter Lang.

Winnubst, Shannon. 2003. "Vampires, Anxieties, and Dreams: Race and Sex in the Contemporary United States." *Hypatia* 18, no. 3: 1–20.

Colonial Pasts, Utopian Futures
Creative and Critical Reflections on the Monstrous as Salvific

Linda Heidenreich

> It's not enough to be queer sexually, but we have to be queer in the way
> we think and the way we see the world. We have to be queer because
> queer is always at odds with the status quo. Instead of buying in as
> lesbians that we're just like all the other guys, we're just folks, the only
> difference we have is our sexual preference, we have to say that we are
> not normal and we don't want to be normal. Who wants to be normal?
> Normal is those fuckers that are polluting the world, the oppressors. We
> have to "queer" the world in a lot of different ways.
> —Gloria Anzaldúa, *ColorLines* interview

> May your skulls remain as thick as they were when you awoke this morning,
> May your members shrivel each time you tell a lie,
> May your children learn the truth about this court and this day,
> May your nights remain sleepless until your final rest.
> And please, remember to turn my body over to my friends for a decent burial,
> Adiós, Señores
> —Josefa of the Most Precious Blood, *Vampiric Memories, Volume One*

From the colonial era to the present, citizens of empires have built their
identities through the construction of the other as monstrous. With the
1776 Declaration of Independence affirming that "all men are created
equal" except for the "merciless Indian Savages," the United States is a
paradigmatic example of this dynamic. Building on the work of Antonia
Castañeda, Nina Auerbach, and others, I argue that today's monsters
are not new but are part of this very old tradition of imperialist binaries,
which, historian Castañeda argues, can be traced at least as far back as the
colonial myth of Calafia. A nation's monstrous tales tell us much about its
relationship to the colonized—that is, its constructed other. I argue that the

213

current portrayals of monsters, particularly popular tales in which vampires fall in love with mortals while embracing the nation-state, should be read against the celebratory grain, as these tales remain predicated upon the construction of subaltern humans as monstrous. Moreover, for those of us figured as monstrous, it is critical that we mobilize our differences—that is, our monstrous selves—to challenge the nation-state and its binary logic of exclusion. And so I close with an alternative narrative: a Chicana vampire tale in which two Chicana vampires, Josefa and Jesusa, survive colonial violence, become immortal, and live to tell the tale that rejects the nationalist logic of exclusion.

It all begins with Calafia.

According to the 1510 novel by Spaniard Garcí Rodríguez Ordóñez de Montalvo, Calafia was a tall and powerful warrior, ruling the island paradise of California, which was depicted as an island populated almost exclusively by women. These women, according to Vicente Blasco Ibáñez, "had a slightly dark skin, tolerated no men in their midst, and lived much like the Amazons of antiquity" (1924, 59). They tamed griffins and had their way with male captives taken in their frequent raids. Thus they were able to reproduce each new generation of women warriors. Yet, as in all stories of ancient monstrous women, this paradise also had to come to an end. One day, after coming to the aid of infidels in their assault on Constantinople, Calafia fell in love with Esplandián, a Christian knight. She left her people in hopes of marrying him, but he married another, and "Queen Calafia, once the terror of the battle-fields, [became] but a poor broken-hearted woman" (Ibáñez 1924, 71). Her rejection and the subsequent removal of the threat to the patriarchal paradigm of nation that she embodied ultimately enabled the restoration of patriarchal order.

As noted by Castañeda, the story of Calafia played a critical role in the colonization of the Americas. She is one of the Western world's first monsters. Indeed, long before there ever was a Dracula, Calafia emerged as a female "New World Monster" who led an army of Amazons against male invaders but was ultimately "subdued, tamed, dominated" (Castañeda 2014, 67). Despite their radically different contexts and genealogies, I submit that there is a strong discursive filiation between Calafia and Dracula that revolves around fear of the other, specifically a fear that constructs the other as a threat to the nation. Until recently, most novels and movies about vampires depicted them as threats to be destroyed. With the advent of the WB television network's *Buffy the Vampire Slayer* (1997–2003), however, there was a return to the Calafia-type narrative and specifically to the discourse positing that the monster/vampire must be tamed and assimilated to consummate the colonial project. After all, *Buffy the Vampire Slayer* features a storyline in which Buffy takes as her sidekick and lover the vampire Angel, who allies himself with humans in their fight against vampires and eventually regains his human soul.

Drawing upon Antonia Castañeda's (2014), Nina Auerbach's (1995), and Eric Kwan-Wu Yu's (2006) feminist postcolonial critiques of monstrosity and monsters, this essay provides a brief overview of the historical construction of monsters, especially vampires, as threats to the Western settler colonial nation. I map how today's politicians and the popular press construct immigrants as threats and how this fear is then addressed through popular culture with an increase in vampire-themed movies, television shows, and more. With the recent development of what I term assimilationist vampire texts (television, film, novels), the issue of difference remains critical to our understanding of the centrality of monstrosity and monsters in neocolonial discursive battles.

Assimilationist vampire texts insist that the salvation of the monster and the nation is possible only if the monster suppresses or rejects any traits that might challenge the stability of the nation. For instance, in texts such the *Twilight Saga* (2008–12), not all vampires are to be exterminated; those who seek assimilation as docile and contained vampires can be saved. While earlier iterations of the assimilationist vampire, such as the character Angel in the *Buffy* series, left open the possibility of some disruption, the new iteration of vampires clearly does not. A creation of Joss Whedon (who also wrote *Firefly* and *Agents of S.H.I.E.L.D.* for television), *Buffy* featured a strong blond teenager who, with a community of friends, kept her suburban town of Sunnydale safe from monsters. Yet Buffy was not uncritical of the place and time in which she lived, and once Angel regained his soul, he too was able to view Sunnydale through a critical lens. In contrast, as will be discussed below, the vampire members of *Twilight*'s Cullen family are so white they literally sparkle in sunshine, and they protect the status quo as if their lives depend upon it. Originally a young adult novel conceived by Stephenie Meyer, *Twilight* expanded into a four-volume series, plus spin-offs and five films. In contrast to Buffy, *Twilight*'s human protagonist, Bella, lacks direction in her life until she meets Andrew Cullen, a son in the Cullen family. For the next four years viewers witness Andrew protect the young Bella, willing to give his own life in order to save her. This narrative trajectory of tamable/assimilable monsters is especially dangerous for people of color, queers, and Southern hemisphere subalterns whose difference is simultaneously marked and figured as a threat. In today's popular television culture, monsters are to be tamed as part of the colonial project, and full-blown imperialisms, that continue to devastate peoples, places, and the entire planet.

Such narratives call to mind Gloria Anzaldúa's admonition, "Who wants to be normal? Normal is those fuckers that are polluting the world, the oppressors," and her corollary call to "'queer' the world" (1999). Rather than reject difference as an epithet or embrace the containment arising from the assimilationist discourse of difference-as-sameness, we should refuse to have our monstrosity tamed; the future survival of queer subaltern and still colonial communities and our ability to enact critical cultural change may very well depend on it. Following Anzaldúa's call and speculative interventions into the logic of coloniality, and in the tradition of Jewelle Gomez and Mario Acevedo, who reimagined vampires as black, and brown, and disruptively countercultural, I offer my own creative critical intervention into the colonialist discourse on monsters. I both map the colonization of monstrosity and performatively intervene in this process through a brief story—"Poison Men: A Chicana Vampire Tale"—in which Josefa and Jesusa, two Chicana vampires, strive to decolonize California pursuant to a queered, and queer, utopia.

Count Dracula as a Borderlands Subject

Many of today's modern vampire tales are based on Bram Stoker's classic novel *Dracula*, written in 1897 and constructed, at least in part, as a response to the crisis in late-nineteenth-century England. It was a time when the emerging middle and upper classes feared the loss of empire and their attendant privileges, a threat that was personified by the presence of the other in their midst. For citizens of England, that other was embodied by colonized people from places such as India. While Indians from the South Asian subcontinent had been exoticized in the West for well over a century, many South Asians were now crossing class and social lines established by the colonizer by attending British schools, becoming ordained as Anglican priests, and speaking out against their subordination through political activities (Misra 1984, 14–21; Young 2010, 71–72). Ironically, their rejection of colonial rule was fed and bolstered by liberal ideologies of assimilation. In 1813 the first Anglican bishop of Calcutta was named, followed by missionary excursions to convert India to Christianity (Chatterton 1924). Two decades later Lord William Bentinck brought a

216

political era of Westernization and assimilation to the colony, opening up administrative positions to Indians, making English the dominant language in education, and Westernizing the curriculum (Bearce 1956, 238; Seed 1952). But then as now, the colonized refused containment. While the goal of "modernizing" India and assimilating its people was colonial and necessarily exploitative, eventually those who attended British schools, including both Gandhi and Chandra Bose, would insist on national sovereignty (Pelinka 2003, 31–55). They began by challenging discriminatory laws that were predicated on characterizations of Indians as exotic, primitive, and in some cases, outright monstrous.

The English empire's fear entailed not just a fear of the other but a fear of mestizaje, a mixing of blood and culture that theorists such as Anzaldúa (1987) have argued not only constructs a fluid geopolitical and culturally hybrid borderlands but also deconstructs the binary paradigm that undergirds oppressive constructs like the nation-state. As Eric Lott argues, the Dracula archetype in vampire literature was a "sort of one-man miscegenation machine" (quoted in Winnubst 2003, 7). Significantly, Bram Stoker placed Dracula's castle in nineteenth-century Transylvania, on the borderlands of European civilization, where society barely resembled that of late Victorian England. Count Dracula, as the monstrous other, moved from the outskirts of civilization to the metropolis, where he adopted the mannerisms of the male colonizer, passed as human, and sucked the blood out of unsuspecting citizens. Stoker's narrative filled a need for the British public, articulating a popular fear of the increasingly more familiar other. Moreover, within the same text, he assured upstanding English men and women that the empire was safe by dramatizing how these invading imposters could be discovered, hunted down, and destroyed through ritualized public violence. Once rid of vampires and others posing as true Englishmen, Britain could continue to build her empire (Auerbach 1995; Yu 2006).

A closer look at Stoker's text, however, reveals that for him the threat of Dracula was not merely one of singular imposters among the English masses, but the danger that such imposters could reproduce and overwhelm the nation. Stoker's Dracula held the ability to reproduce himself, multiplying like "ripples from a stone thrown in the water" (1992, 230). In this way, the fear of the other in late-nineteenth-century English horror literature foreshadows European and American fears of immigrants in the late-twentieth- and early-twenty-first-centuries and, especially, of their ability to reproduce more rapidly than the middle and upper classes of their new host countries.

The flourishing of American vampire movies, television shows, and print media, from the turn of the twenty-first century to the present, therefore should not surprise us. Today, Americans are bombarded with images of vampire invaders, from the *Twilight* series to the film *Abraham Lincoln: Vampire Hunter* to a passel of less well known young adult and adult novels. In February 2015 Amazon.com listed 44,354 titles as new "vampire books" (filtering out all titles only available as used). A search of the Scholastic website showed 248 vampire-themed books for children in grades 1–8. Again, this outpouring of vampire tales takes place at a time of crisis, when the cultural composition of the nation is again changing. Specifically, the transformation involves citizens of Mexico—a country traditionally exploited by US capital, whether through the land grab of 1848, US investment during the Porfiriato, or more recently NAFTA—who now reside within US borders. While some decry the threat of the invading other, population studies tell a different story. According to historian Mary E. Odem, the perception of a threat from "new immigrants" stems from the realization that Latina/os are already an integral part of the US economy and society (2008, 359). A 2014 study by the Pew Research Center confirmed that natural increase—that is, births—accounts for over 75 percent of Latina/o population growth in the United States (Brown 2014). One of the racist metaphors associated with this demographic trend is the term "anchor babies," which posits that unauthorized immigrants purposely give birth in the United States to enable them to remain with their children, who are US citizens by virtue of their birth.

As recently as 2014, the country experienced another convergence of vampiric discourse and anti-immigrant rhetoric when a wave of Central American children fled their homelands and sought refuge in the United States. With an increase in violence against citizens in Mexico, El Salvador, Guatemala, and Honduras, many families felt they had no choice but to send their children north, and false rumors circulated that they would be granted accelerated asylum (UNHCR 2014, 4–7, 23–49). Anti-immigrant sentiment directed at the arriving children was swift and brutal. In California, angry protestors blocked a school bus of immigrant children, yelling xenophobic slurs as the bus driver tried to maneuver them to safety (Gurulé 2014, 11). The anti-immigrant narrative initially reflected earlier vampiric discourse describing immigrants as a monstrous threat, an invading army threatening the nation. In a report in *La Voz Bilingüe*, journalist Ernest Gurulé (2014) noted:

Texas' Louie Gohmert has likened them to Nazi soldiers who invaded France in World War II. Georgia Congressman Phil Gingrey . . . has warned that the U.S. should be prepared for outbreaks of swine flu, tuberculosis and the almost always deadly Ebola virus.

The root causes of the children's flight in 2014, like the flight of so many children before them, were tied to US policies: counterinsurgency wars funded by US tax dollars, US policies that have fueled the rise of the drug cartels, and sociopolitical and economic vacuums created by draconian trade agreements such as NAFTA (Quintana 2014; Ruiz-Marrero 2014, 15).[1] Children were crossing into the US borderlands because of the policies of empire. While previous generations of Latinas/os were tolerated only if they could be colonized, absorbed, and assimilated into the practice of empire, these new young immigrants remained a monstrous specter in the popular media as the purportedly unassimilable other.

Yet amid the media frenzy, a shift in discourse took place. The plight of the children resulted in a discursive tug-of-war between anti-immigrant forces and immigrant rights activist communities. While the anti-immigrant activists threatened schoolchildren with xenophobic language and metaphors, local and national immigrant and human rights organizations adopted the language of welcome and inclusion. Surprisingly, it was Republican George Will who made headlines when he introduced the language of assimilation: "My view is that we have to say to the children, 'Welcome to America. You're going to go to school and get a job and become Americans'" (Gurulé 2014). In so doing, he mediated the xenophobic discourse of monstrosity with a seemingly compassionate alternative that, I submit, was deceptively destructive in its deracination of difference in the service of the US empire.

This discursive contest between those proposing to exclude immigrants (or, in the case of some border militias, hunt them down) and immigrant rights groups advocating that immigrants be welcomed and assimilated as "Americans" returns us to foundational colonial narrative of Calafia, whom Rodríguez de Montalvo, over five centuries ago, constructed as the quintessential monstrous feminine. As Castañeda points out, Calafia was not unique, but instead exemplary of the empire's female other found throughout the romance *novelas* of the time, which revolved around the archetype of the "infidel queen." As previously noted, Calafia's threat to empire is ultimately contained as she "converts to Christianity and offers herself—body, soul, and worldly goods—to the hero-object of her desire, even though he rejects her" (Castañeda 2014, 67). Beth Berila argues that the fear of the other that drives such imperialist narratives is in part rooted in a refusal to see the nation as "multiple, relational, and contestatory." Indeed, the Calafia narrative dramatizes an effort to exclude different bodies from the nation, and in a violent quest for the stability of the nation, to also destroy any difference those bodies might have possessed (Berila 2005, 122).

While a minority of twenty-first-century vampire narratives, such as *Abraham Lincoln: Vampire Hunter*, continue to portray the monster as an evil threat that must be destroyed, most narratives, from *Twilight* to the television series *True Blood* and *Vampire Diaries*, argue that vampires hold the potential to be just like humans; they also intimate that, with a little bit of loving, vampires can become upstanding citizens and assimilate into the dominant culture. Even in *Abraham Lincoln: Vampire Hunter*, not all the vampires are beyond redemption. While slave-holding rebels who embody the vampiric must be destroyed, there is one fictive vampire worthy of redemption: Henry Sturges, who convinces Lincoln that he needs to save the Union (Grahame-Smith 2010). In the case of *Twilight*, the vampiric protagonists are not only assimilable, but stand in for a nostalgic American past with reproductive nuclear families and daughters who wait until marriage before having sex. Commenting on the vampire family in *Twilight*, Anna Silver notes that "the Cullens as a group stand for the ideal family of a mythic past" (2010, 122). In such narratives, where vampires are more committed to a mythic domestic past than the average mortal American, the possibility of any structural critique, where the monsters might decide that normal is unworthy of their difference, is elided. They can be incorporated into the nation if they assimilate, leaving any disruptive differences behind. There are palpable benefits for the assimilated other, but negating their difference also has emotional, psychological, and existential costs, which never really go away.

Perhaps what is needed in this context where problematic vampire/ monster narratives persist as imperialist palimpsests, then, is a new vampire narrative, one in which the other is not destroyed but is able to survive without assimilation, without becoming like those whom Gloria Anzaldúa calls "normal . . . fuckers . . . who are polluting the world." Black and Latina/o authors have started to point the way. At present we have vampire narratives such as Jewelle Gomez's *Gilda Stories* and Mario Acevedo's *Nymphos of Rocky Flats*, which provide two examples of how we might use vampire narratives to imagine a different world, one where monsters survive, even if they may not exactly thrive. As discussed below, both texts recall Anzaldúa's argument that the "normal" is destructive. In these dystopian narratives, it is by embracing the monstrous and rejecting the normal that the protagonists will ultimately save themselves and their communities. For instance, in the *Gilda Stories*, we are presented with a black lesbian vampire who, as a girl, barely survived the violence of slavery. Welcomed into a community of vampires who feed on mortals but do not kill them, she is eventually turned into a vampire herself. With the gift of vampire immortality she then moves through time: the era of US slavery, the post–civil rights era, and into the future, where, having failed to learn from their mistakes, mortals suck the planet dry. Throughout the novel, the vampires walk among humans but maintain a community and culture of their own. The author thereby segues with nativist Dracula and Calafia discourses but immediately turns them onto themselves by framing the monstrous disruption as potentially redemptive.

Acevedo's *Nymphos of Rocky Flats* takes a different approach to challenging nativist narratives, presenting a protagonist who investigates government cover-ups and eventually lives to tell the tale of a violent police state and bloodthirsty proto-fascist vampire hunters. Acevedo's Felix Gomez is an Iraq war veteran who was turned into a vampire after killing innocent women and children during the second Gulf War. Upon returning to the United States, he is hunted by the *vânători*, vampire hunters who tear the fangs out of vampires before killing them. Eventually he meets other supernatural beings and slowly finds ways to survive as the other. While this text offers a less disruptive resolution than the *Gilda Stories*, it nonetheless illuminates the evil of the normal that has turned society into a police state.

Both the *Gilda Stories* and *Nymphos of Rocky Flats* are texts that inspire reimaginings of the past, present, and future through a postcolonial queer lens that offers monstrously hopeful endings—that is, futurities in the Muñoz sense of the word (2009). Both novels stand as exemplars of the radical possibilities for reclaiming monster narratives as empowering spaces for queers, Chicanas/os, and other racialized bodies who refuse to disappear. Perhaps equally important, both novels are rooted in historical reality in the manner in which they draw attention to the destructiveness of the normal: *Gilda Stories* opens with the violence of the US slave state and ends with the environmental devastation of the planet; *Nymphos of Rocky Flats* opens with a battle scene where US soldiers mistake women and children for combatants and slaughter them. Normal, in both of these novels, results in violence and destruction of horrific and epic proportions, all of which is grounded in real episodes of US history as a nation founded on slavery and an empire perpetuated through never-ending wars.

Can a vampire narrative build upon the legacies of Gomez and Acevedo to take the monstrous one step further so that the other remains the other, but also works to shift the larger "normal" structures of the surrounding society? That is, can monsters flourish without being wedded, bedded, and assimilated? Pursuant to this inquiry, I offer an excerpt from my vampiric tale "Poison Men: A Chicana Vampire Tale." The story opens in late-nineteenth-century California, and the central characters are two vampires, Josefa and Jesusa, both in their mid-twenties, who grew up together on the land when it was still Mexico. Jesusa is a fictive character with no specific historical antecedent. Like Emma Pérez's Micaela Campos in *Forgetting the Alamo*, she emerges from the need to remember a history not yet written—that of queer Chicanas (Esquivel 2006, 112–29; Pérez 2009). Josefa, on the other hand, is a historical person: a woman who held her own during the California gold rush and refused the destructive narratives of Euro-American settlers, resulting in her death. In 1851, the historical Josefa, also known as Juanita, of Downieville, California, killed a white man in self-defense and was lynched by a mob of white men; she has recently been reclaimed as a Chicana who resisted (Castañeda 1990, 225; Murguía 2002). Like Antonia Castañeda and Alejandro Murguía before me, I write in part to honor her life and her resistance to empire through her reclamation of the monstrosity that was mapped onto her, to lethal ends.

Josefa's resistance to white patriarchal privilege by settler colonialists in nineteenth-century California, and much of her larger life story, has been distorted or lost through years of colonial discourse. However, we do know that she lived and worked in Downieville with her husband or partner, José. As noted by Murguía, "By mid-1851, the once plentiful Sonorans were rare in the Sierra foothills. So for Josefa, or any Mexican woman, to have reached the gold country, she had to be resilient, brave, and determined" (2002, 46). On the night of the fourth of July, a miner by the name of Joe Cannon and his friends were drunk and knocking on doors. When they reached the house of Josefa and José, they broke the door down. Cannon returned to the house the next day and had words with the couple; when he came into their home Josefa stabbed him and he died. The town held a kangaroo court where José was banished from the town and Josefa was sentenced to hang. She was hung that same day, as 2,000 men stood watching. (Hurtado 1999, 134–36; Levy 1993, 84–88; Murguía 2002, 38–56; Pitt 1999, 73–74). At her death she stated that if she found herself in the same circumstances, she would again defend her honor; she then asked that her body be turned over to her friends for a proper burial (Levy

1993, 88). While Josefa most probably lived in California long before her accusers, it was she who was painted as an invader, and she who was labeled a monster in need of containment or destruction. Here is my alternative history of Josefa . . .

Poison Men: A Chicana Vampire Tale

Josefa lay still in the cold night air, coughed and spat and pulled air into her lungs. Yes, they were still her lungs. She was still Josefa. And she was still alive. She felt the rough boards beneath her and the night air above. She was in a wagon, alone.

This was not heaven, or she would not be alone, and her throat would not feel as if it were on fire. But it was not hell either: the air was too clean, and somehow she was at peace—at peace in the back of this wagon, parked amid the forsaken dead, thieves and prostitutes and people just too plain poor to be buried anywhere else. So much for a decent burial.

Her mind wandered back to better times, girlhood times, before the gringos came—or at least when there were fewer of them. She and Jesusa running through her uncle's fields, chasing sheep until old man Diego lost patience with them and shooed them off.

She tried to hold the good memory, but this morning's memory replaced it. They had killed her—"hung by the neck until dead"—isn't that what the "judge" said?

She knew she had to move, but her body ached, her throat remained on fire and her head pounded, worse than when she had put on that big drunk to celebrate her fifteenth. An hour and a half of Mass, dancing with boys and old men and her sisters, and then an evening with Jesusa, a bottle of whiskey and the bliss that only two girls can find when left in peace in their 'buelito's barn. The joy in her grandparent's eyes and the joy in Jesusa's eyes merged—then the pounding in her head brought Josefa back. "This is not a hangover, this is because they tried to kill me."

Still too tired to face bad memories, she listened in the silence. Somehow, she knew the answers were there. She listened to the air pull into her body, push out of her body, and slowly the burning slowed. Her mind cleared—sifted through memories and then pushed her with a mighty thrust into the present. She had to get out of here.

She thought she heard Jesusa's voice, not in her ears but in her head. Like St. Joan, she had gone mad. Old man Diego would say, "That's what happens to little girls who run the hills dressed like boys, chasing sheep."

But she was no longer a little girl. And she did hear Jesusa's voice, laughing with that nervous tic of hers. Josefa tried to reach out to her but it did not work; maybe she was just trying too hard.

Josefa sat up slowly, and then quickly; she felt blood course through her veins, oxygen and blood and something else. Her eyes burned and then focused and she could see through the night, see as if it were day—better than if it were day. She laughed. The smell of sanctity surrounded her: jasmine and lavender.

Jumping from the wagon she marveled at her own agility. She had never been weak, slow or awkward, but this was different. She felt as if she could run forever, reconquer California for herself—herself and Jesusa and José, and then move on to the rest of the world.

She listened.

Then she moved quickly, hoping to retrieve her disguise from her house. Would the house be guarded? Would a miner already have moved in? Taken what they had come to take anyway? They took her life, or so they thought; what was left was her house, her precious house, bought with the savings of her precious Jesusa. But now was not the time to remember.

She fled to the house, moving from shed to shrub to outhouse, cursing the day they had ever left Yerba Buena and praying her voices were true—that Jesusa was indeed somehow somewhere still alive. Her speed quickened, she moved fast as air and angels, she flew from shadow to shadow.

She hoped José would be gone. Rumors had started long before this week that he was a "pretty boy"—they were not married. The kangaroo court had found him "not guilty," but banished him anyway. Would he flee south? She did not have time to dwell on the thought.

Night. She did not see anyone. And she could see, clear into the dancing shadows that played under towering oak trees, along her path and at her door—her door without a door because the drunken Bob Cannon had kicked it in. Quietly she entered, saw the moon lighting her bed, the one piece of furniture that she had brought when they moved. Then she saw him—José María, asleep on her bed. A slow anger began to build inside her: she had told him to flee. The gringos had ordered him to leave.

Looking at his face she noticed a lingering dampness on the pillow—and her anger waned. She moved to wake him, and then thought better of it. If he did not grieve her loss, the others might suspect something amiss—remember their accusations of his softness. And with her body gone from the wagon it was best he grieved. And so she left an unsigned note: "you said you would go south. For the memory of Josefa y su Jesusa—go."

Quickly and quietly she moved to the trunk and opened it. The smell of cedar and memories of five good years filled the room. Her "disguise" was still there: hat, pants, shirt, boots, and a neckerchief with J.M.J. embroidered in deep green. Her "boy-girl attire" is what Jesusa and José called it. Josefa abandoned her dress and assumed the attire of her boy-girl self, grabbed the neckerchief, blew José María a silent kiss and then headed for the saloon. She knew that she would find at least one of her horses there—and who knows, if she was as strong as she felt, she might even take back her rifle.

* * *

Downieville. She knew where to find them. Approaching the saloon she could smell them, the lot of Cannon's friends. Lawrence was there. He was just as bad as Cannon. She should have stabbed them both, made the streets safe for women to walk down at night—or by day for that matter. And here he was. While still a block away she could hear him, smell him as he moved out of the saloon to the alley. Dirty pig was still pissing in alleys instead of using an outhouse.

She flew to the alley, waited for him to finish and move away from his own waste, then moved in and pulled up his chin. He was startled and smiled, a stupid shit-eating grin, like he had just won at Monte; then he passed out. Again the smell of lavender and jasmine, so strong that the alley no longer smelled of white men and piss. Her voices pulled her. Thrusting her teeth into his neck she drank deeply, until her veins felt as if they would explode—until his pulse weakened. Then she entered his mind, just walked right in: gold, horses, and fucking—and not just two-legged mortals. Her mind moved away from his and she laughed, leaned back against the alley wall and laughed until tears poured down her face, mixing with Lawrence's blood. This was better than dancing in springtime. She was a god. Taking her neckerchief from her pocket she wiped the thick-salty-sweet blood from her mouth and neck and tried to wipe it from her shirt. Her voices told her she was not a god but she chose to ignore them.

Then something went wrong, she knew something was wrong, a wave of dizziness pushed her against the rails. She needed to focus. Months later she would learn about *speat*, a disease vampires contracted by mixing with bad seed, but tonight all she knew was that something was wrong. She was no longer a god. She needed to get out of Downieville.

Josefa quickly went through Lawrence's jacket and found four gold coins, then found her yegua with Cannon's saddlebags—and her rifle. It would be faster to travel without Calafia, but somehow she could not get herself to leave the mare behind. And so she left—left old Lawrence passed out in the alley, his willie still flaccid from too much liquor. Soon it would be rotting from speat, but that is another story.

* * *

Josefa's voices brought her south to the desert of Mexicali and the monastery of the Most Precious Blood. Seriously, the Most Precious Blood. She collapsed outside the exterior gates and was collected by two novices wearing what seemed to be work habits: simple linen tunics reaching to just above their ankles, red aprons, and beige veils tied back behind them. And riding boots. Years later she would remember moving in and out of consciousness, hearing women's voices, and seeing those boots. That was when she knew she was safe.

Lucia and Scholastica gathered her up and brought her inside the gates (two sets of gates) and then into the infirmary. Mother had told the community she would be coming, as she had followed her in her dreams. And they knew Josefa was ill, very ill, from taking in bad blood. If it was any consolation, by now the unholy beast who had infected her would also be suffering gravely. A vampire could survive speat if treated promptly, but for mortals it was a death sentence—not because there was no cure, but because they never slowed down enough to see the cure.

Mother looked down at the child, so bold in her riding britches and a flannel shirt, and despite her pain, a smile. Mother clasped her hands behind her scapular and breathed deeply. They would have to educate her as quickly as possible, teach her enough to survive the cleansing, and then make sure she never did anything that reckless again. California could still be saved, but not with the young bloods spreading speat throughout the community. Generation after generation of male mortals, sprouting sores in their groins, mouths, and just about any area of the body capable of producing moisture. Eventually their organs would fall away, and that was not the end of it. But they were not her concern. She worried for her own kind. Six centuries in the life and six centuries of watching the young ones make rash decisions: play god, get themselves sick, get themselves healed. Even then some of them went back to reckless living, driven by pride, anger, or revenge—or perhaps a blend of all three.

Isi, their infirmarian, knew the drill, but Mother spoke to her anyway. "We will be needing limpias for Lucia and Scholastica and quarantine for this one"—nodding down toward Josefa—"with daily baths of hoja santa, cuachalalate, árnica amarilla, and coahuilote. Restrict her to a diet of consecrated wine and blood from the sisters." Isadora nodded, her sharp eyes looking out from behind a pair of wire-framed glasses she did not need, then turned so quickly her scapular flew out just a bit, and exited to the back room where she stored the precious herbs.

Mother returned to her office, sat and closed her eyes. In the morning Josefa's lessons would begin. In the morning they could tell her about her Jesusa. Yes, she was alive, but now was not the time to see her.

* * *

Six months passed. Six months of study, in her cell, alone. Daily checking in with Isi: Isadora of the Toluca Valley, whose keen dark eyes could see right through her. Isadora had survived waves of the peste and years of working in a leper's colony. She towered above most other vampires and mortals in both physical and moral stature. Centuries after her own resurrection she was immune to most mortal and immortal diseases. With centuries of studying all that the earth and the heavens had to offer, she could cure almost anything. She was fierce and brilliant and practical all at the same time. Josefa had come to crave her touch—the only personal contact she was allowed while in recovery.

Theothane came and tutored her in the afternoons but she did not enter the room. Instead she sat outside the door, reciting histories—and insisting that Josefa repeat them back.

> Xochitl studied at Texcoco
> learned the wisdom of Nezahualcoyotl
> Xochitl had the gift of song
> sang our stories into flower
> from Xochitl we learn of beginnings
> and how to cure the peste . . .

It was easier to remember things than before her resurrection, but Theothane assured her it would be even easier once she was well. She tried to remember how she felt after she awoke in the pauper's field, but that seemed a distant past. Mother said it was nothing. "Focus on the present, to see the seconds moving by, even while looking across the longer expanse of time. Practice after meals each day, when your energy is at its fullest." But Josefa did not yet know enough of the past to see the long expanse. And so she passed the days alone, bathing and memorizing, slowly growing stronger, waiting for the day of the cleansing, waiting for human contact.

* * *

The day finally came, three years later. Josefa had learned the history of the community from the Olmecas to the Toltecas, the cure for speat, and for depression. Not that speat caused depression, but both ran rampant after the arrival of the settlers, and both could be fatal to both mortals and the community. And so Josefa learned their cures, and she learned the complete works of Nezahualcoyotl, Xochitlcoytl, and Huehuecoyotl; she learned to read in Spanish and was learning to read in Latin. Mother had said all this knowledge was nothing, a drop in the bucket. Once she was clean they would attend to the bucket—but Josefa reveled in the breadth and depth of it all.

Now she followed Mother to the chapel, not the public chapel where the sisters went to Mass during the day, but a smaller chapel. Images of saints she did not recognize lined the entrance. Most wore the habit of the order, with eyes that seemed to look into the present and speak to her heart. The sisters helped her undress and wrapped her in a warm blanket, placing her arms outside their swaddling, and then moved back, leaving space for Mother to work. Mother entered the space in silence, discalced, bearing two large chalices. The sisters lifted Josefa's shoulders and head so that she could drink half the contents of the chalice; the other half would be reserved for the next day. She chewed coca leaves and then joined the sisters as they intoned three Madre Nuestras: "Madre Nuestra, quien nos da la vida . . ." Their raised voices filled the room, washing over her like hopeful dreams.

And then there was silence.

The cut was swift, skillfully opening her radial artery. Mother caught the contaminated blood in the second chalice and bled her until the cup was full. Lucia ran to empty the chalice and then returned. As Mother began the second letting Josefa felt herself drift away. No one tried to stop her, and so she fell into a heavy yet restless sleep. Voices pulled her into a dream that was not a dream.

"Move quickly."

"She is doing well."

"Has she been asking after her amante?"

"Focus hermanas, this is not the time for idle chatter."

"Josefa. Josefa!" It was the voice of Mother. "Josefa, you must concentrate. Focus your energy on healing, healing your body, your mind, your spirit: these are one. Mija, remember your prayer."

Josefa pulled her mind to focus and prayed, "Sana mi cuerpo, sana mi mente, sana mi espíritu. Sana mi cuerpo, sana mi mente . . . ," then faded from consciousness once again.

The next morning she awoke, still too weak to move. The blanket, now soaked in blood, yet still strangely warm, had been pulled back from her. She lay still, listening to the world around her. The sisters were there, Mother was there. There were three eggs on her chest. She could not open her eyes to see them, but she could feel them. They pulled energy from her. Somehow she knew it was not good energy. It was energy that needed to go. This was the end. This would make her clean. She breathed slowly. Again Mother intoned the Madre Nuestra; too weak to join them, Josefa listened, and then just as quickly as she had felt the knife cut her wrist the evening before, the eggs were pulled from her chest. Lucia ran with them from the chapel. The sisters gathered Josefa in their arms and brought her back to her cell. That was the last she remembered of the cleansing—that and her own private vow never to drink from a poison man again.

That day she dreamed clean dreams and she saw into the long expanse of the future. She had work to do, young immortals to save, and perhaps a couple of mortals too, if they proved worthy of salvation. There would be training, but with others like herself. She would never be alone again, unless by choice. Together they would reconquer California, make the world safe from the likes of Cannon and Lawrence. But first she had to find Jesusa. They had to have a talk.

Notes

I would like to thank Nishant Shahani, the best writing partner ever, for his patience in critiquing this article as it developed, and Adelina Anthony for naming Josefa's yegua.

1. In December 1988 the Subcommittee on Terrorism, Narcotics and International Operations of the Senate Committee on Foreign Relations published *Drugs, Law Enforcement and Foreign Policy*, which examined links between drug trafficking and the Contras, US-backed rebels fighting to overthrow the Sandinista

government of Nicaragua. The subcommittee found "involvement in narcotics trafficking by individuals associated with the Contra movement; participation of narcotics traffickers in Contra supply operations through business relationships with Contra organizations; provision of assistance to the Contras by narcotics traffickers, including cash, weapons, planes, pilots, air supply services and other materials, on a voluntary basis by the traffickers; payments to drug traffickers by the U.S. State Department of funds authorized by the Congress for humanitarian assistance to the Contras, in some cases after the traffickers had been indicted by federal law enforcement agencies on drug charges, in others while traffickers were under active investigation by these same agencies" (US Senate 1988, 36).

Works Cited

Anzaldúa, Gloria. 1987. *Borderlands/La Frontera: The New Mestiza*. San Francisco: Aunt Lute.

———. 1999. "With Heart in Hand/Con Corazon en la Mano: An Interview with Gloria Anzaldúa." By Monica Hernández. *ColorLines*, October 20.

Auerbach, Nina. 1995. *Our Vampires, Ourselves*. Chicago: University of Chicago Press.

Bearce, George D., Jr. 1956. "Lord William Bentinck: The Application of Liberalism to India." *Journal of Modern History* 28 no. 3: 234–46.

Berila, Beth. 2005. "Reading National Identities: The Radical Disruptions of *Borderlands/La Frontera*." In *Entre Mundos/Among Worlds: New Perspectives on Gloria E. Anzaldúa*, edited by AnaLouise Keating, 121–28. New York: Palgrave Macmillan.

Blasco Ibáñez, Vicente. 1924. *Queen Calafia*. New York: E. P. Dutton.

Brown, Anna. 2014. "U.S. Hispanic and Asian Populations Growing, but for Different Reasons." *Fact Tank: News in the Numbers*, Pew Research Center, http://www.pewresearch.org/fact-tank/2014/06/26/u-s-hispanic-and-asian-populations-growing-but-for-different-reasons/.

Castañeda, Antonia. 1990. "The Political Economy of Nineteenth-Century Stereotypes of Californianas." In *Between Borders: Essays on Mexicana/Chicana History*, edited by Adeleida R. Del Castillo, 213–36. Los Angeles: Floricanto. Reprinted in *Three Decades of Engendering History: Selected Works of Antonia I. Castañeda*, edited by Linda Heidenreich, 37–63. Denton: University of North Texas Press, 2014.

———. 2014. "Malinche, Calafia y Toypurina." In *Three Decades of Engendering History: Selected Works of Antonia I. Castañeda*, edited by Linda Heidenreich, 65–88. Denton: University of North Texas Press. First published in *Feminism, Nation, and Myth: La Malinche*, edited by Rolando Romero and Amanda Nolacea Harris. Houston: Arte Público, 2005.

Chatterton, Eyre. 1924. *A History of the Church of England in India since the Early Days of the East India Company*. London: Society for Promoting Christian Knowledge. http://anglicanhistory.org/india/chatterton1924/.

Esquivel, Catrióna Rueda. 2006. *With Her Machete in Her Hand: Reading Chicana Lesbians*. Austin: University of Texas Press.

Garcí, Rodríguez Ordóñez de Montalvo. 1510. *Las sergas de Esplandián*. Seville.

Grahame-Smith, Seth. 2010. *Abraham Lincoln: Vampire Hunter*. New York: Grand Central.

Gurulé, Ernest. 2014. "Children at the Border." *La Voz Bilingüe* (Denver), July 29.

Hurtado, Albert L. 1999. *Intimate Frontiers: Sex, Gender and Culture in Old California*. Albuquerque: University of New Mexico Press.

Levy, JoAnn. 1993. *They Saw the Elephant: Women in the California Gold Rush*. Hamden, CT: Archon.

Misra, Udayon. 1984. "Nineteenth Century British Views of India: Crystallisation of Attitudes." *Economic and Political Weekly* 19 (January): 14–21.

Muñoz, José Esteban. 2009. *Cruising Utopia: The Then and There of Queer Futurity*. New York: New York University Press.

Murguía, Alejandro. 2002. *The Medicine of Memory: A Mexica Clan in California*. Austin: University of Texas Press.

Odem, Mary E. 2008. "Subaltern Immigrants: Undocumented Workers and National Belonging in the United States." *Interventions* 10, no. 3: 359–80.

Pelinka, Anton. 2003. *Democracy Indian Style: Subhas Chandra Bose and the Creation of India's Political Culture*. Piscataway, NJ: Transaction.

Pérez, Emma. 2009. *Forgetting the Alamo, or, Blood Memory*. Austin: University of Texas Press.

Pitt, Leonard. 1999. *The Decline of the Californios: A Social History of the Spanish-Speaking Californians, 1846–1890*. Berkeley: University of California Press. First published 1966.

Quintana, Victor M. 2014. "How NAFTA Unleashed the Violence in Mexico." Center for International Policy Americas Program, Mexico City. http://www.cipamericas.org/archives/11427.

Ruiz-Marrero, Carmelo. 2014. "Contras and Drugs, Three Decades Later." *Louisiana Weekly*, November 10, 15.

Seed, Geoffrey. 1952. "Lord William Bentinck and the Reform of Education." *Journal of the Royal Asiatic Society of Great Britain and Ireland*, no. 1/2: 66–77.

Silver, Anna. 2010. "*Twilight* Is Not Good for Maidens: Gender, Sexuality, and the Family in Stephenie Meyer's *Twilight* Series." *Studies in the Novel* 42 (1/2): 121–38.

Stoker, Bram. 1992. *Dracula*. New York: Barnes and Noble. First published 1897.

UNHCR (United Nations High Commissioner for Refugees). 2014. *Children on the Run: Unaccompanied Children Leaving Central America and Mexico and the Need for International Protection*. Washington, DC: UNHCR.

US Senate, Subcommittee on Terrorism, Narcotics and International Operations of the Committee on Foreign Relations. 1989. *Drugs, Law Enforcement and Foreign Policy*. Washington, DC: US Government Printing Office. http://nsarchive.gwu.edu/NSAEBB/NSAEBB113/north06.pdf.

Winnubst, Shannon. 2003. "Vampires, Anxieties, and Dreams: Race and Sex in the Contemporary United States." *Hypatia* 18, no. 3: 1–20.

Young, Richard Fox. 2010. "Holy Orders: Nehemiah Goreh's Ordination Ordeal and the Problem of 'Social Distance' in Nineteenth-Century North Indian Anglicanism." *Church History and Religious Culture* 90, no. 1: 69–88.

Yu, Eric Kwan-Wu. 2006. "Productive Fear: Labor, Sexuality, and Mimicry in Bram Stoker's Dracula." *Texas Studies in Literature and Language* 48 (Summer): 145–80.

PART IV

From the Dystopic to the Utopic

The Future of Food?
Indigenous Knowledges and Sustainable Food Systems in Latin@ Speculative Fiction

Gabriela Nuñez

The pairing of food discourses and futurity is ubiquitous, and in this combination Latin@ labor is often a missing ingredient. The liberal food movement activist sees genetically modified food as frightening and futuristic. The corporate biotech behemoth Monsanto, for its part, claims it will solve future ecological and food scarcity problems through knowledge and technology.[1] Journalist Julianne Hing links the future of urban space to Latin@ influence when she says, "In Los Angeles we can experience the *future 'New America'* through the city's emerging food culture." That New America, involving "the imminent browning of the United States," is "so real you can taste it" (Hing 2013, emphasis added). Hing emphasizes that Latin@s are 48 percent of Los Angeles, a sign of the diversity coming to the United States in the near future.

Anticipating this understanding, celebrity chef Roy Choi's food truck "revolution" began with his Korean taco truck and evolved from his own futuristic visions. In his talk "A Gateway to Feed Hunger: The Promise of Street Food," Choi (2013) says:

> I had no idea it was gonna be a revolution, man. I had no idea. We were just trying to make some ends, make some money, get paid, have some fun, you know. But, the moment I stepped behind that wheel, it was like, I knew my whole life was going to change. I felt like I had locked into a portal, and I could see things that didn't exist in the present time. I saw these people. It was weird, it was like I could see these people on the street, but they weren't there yet.

In this futuristic narrative, Choi's truck, Kogi, acts as a time/space portal and the conduit to his visions of feeding people lined up on Los Angeles streets. His visions quickly materialized, as Choi's truck and his tweets helped launch the broad popularity of gourmet food trucks during the mid-2000s, despite a much longer history of Latin@ food and taco trucks in Los Angeles. Choi's use of technology and the cool urban aesthetic he infused into his delicious Korean-Mexican street food helped trigger a shift in the mainstream perception of the Mexican taco truck. Once known as "roach coaches," popular with construction workers, food trucks became part of a new, young, and hip foodie culture.

Narratives connected to food systems reflect the tropes of futurity indicative of speculative fiction (SF), an umbrella genre often equated to science fiction but also encompassing "soft" science fiction such as fantasy, horror, and the gothic (Bahng 2008, 140). However, as part of these discourses of futurity, the role of Latin@s remains a digestible ethnic experience marked by an absence of Latin@ labor. If, as Hing suggests, Los Angeles represents the future of a New America through its Latin@ food, then what roles will Latin@s have within future systems for the production, processing, transport, and consumption of food? I suggest that some Latin@ SF provides an answer.

By focusing on the novels *Atomik Aztex* (2005), by Sesshu Foster, and *Lunar Braceros: 2125–2148* (2009), by Rosaura Sánchez and Beatrice Pita, I argue that Latin@ SF presents an intimate relationship between nature and technology in which futuristic "progress" often comes at the expense of natural resources and sustainable food systems for Latin@ communities. These novels consider how indigenous epistemologies might be politically transformative in the present by imagining speculative and futuristic scenarios of how food systems affect the daily lives of Latin@s. *Atomik Aztex* and *Lunar Braceros* both grapple with Mesoamerican ideologies in their imaginings of Latin@ speculative futures, yet they do so in different ways.

The ecological disaster created by the negative effects of progress is what Laura Barbas-Rhoden (2011, 143) calls "ecocide via modernization." The dystopic Central American novels she reviews feature modern, mostly urban settings afflicted with disease, pollution, and poverty, which are the result of sick societies locked in exploitative relationships with the natural world. Despite the dystopias these novels portray, "the endings of each novel suggest the possibilities of regeneration anchored in the rich history of Mesoamerian societies," (144) suggesting that the practices and belief systems of Mesoamerican culture provide a hopeful antidote to social ills. Jonathan Tittler asserts a similar idea with a concept he calls "eco-indigenism," which involves

> entering into a fertile relationship with non-Western cultures—ones that were not technologically advanced, not globalized, not conspicuous consumers of the diminishing natural resources of our biosphere—in order to learn from them what our limited perspective does not allow us to see. (2010, 30)

Lunar Braceros privileges indigenous knowledges, or eco-indigenism, about the land and in turn about food, demonstrating that cooperative living in harmony with the human and nonhuman environment can counter environmental destruction wrought under the guise of progress. The novel's protagonists are trapped in a labor peonage system in which they work in exchange for harmful processed foods and basic necessities. Cooperative farming and communal land provide a sustainable alternative to this system, but the novel presents such eco-indigenism as requiring constant protection in light of the capitalist imperative to develop land and excavate natural resources in a world growing ever more toxic.

Atomik Aztex refutes the possibility of eco-indigenism, suggesting that Aztec knowledge, as a remedy for ecocide via modernization, doesn't exist outside of a superficial aesthetics or consumable notion of Aztec culture as a commodity. Through a cyclical and parallel narrative structure, *Atomik Aztex* presents grueling and dangerous labor conditions for undocumented workers in Los Angeles's urban slaughterhouses as the defining aspect of the city's dystopian hell. The violence in the slaughterhouses connects the experiences of animals in food production to the dire exploitation of Latin@ workers. The novel remains critical of indigenous alternative worlds, however, highlighting the constant co-optation of indigenous ideologies and the incessant violence endemic to global consumerism and contemporary food systems.

"We're in the future!" The Importance of Latin@ Futurities

In a 2008 interview with the Paley Center for Media about Latin@s in science fiction, Edward James Olmos explains his responsibility as the only Latino on *Battlestar Galactica*, a show representing the few survivors of humanity in a futuristic setting. He tells of a twelve-year-old Latino fan who cried with joy as he said, "We're in the future, we're in the future, I saw *Battlestar Galactica* and we're in the future!" (also quoted in Tatum 2013, 808). This emotional reaction to Olmos's character underscores the historical absence of Latin@ characters from speculative futures. Given census projections of a consistent increase in Latin@ population and the continuing growth of Latin@ communities throughout the United States, it should be difficult to imagine a future *without* Latin@s. Contemporary novels, if not television shows, are finding science fiction, and speculative fiction more broadly, to be a means to address social issues that affect Latin@ communities.

Recent scholarship has addressed the use of futurity in Latin@ SF as a way to critique economic, environmental, and political crises in the present and as a way to recognize that hegemonic discourses of technological and scientific "progress" can be devastating for communities of color. Catherine S. Ramírez proposes Chicanafuturism, which "explores the ways that new and everyday technologies, including their detritus, transform Mexican American life and culture" and articulates "colonial and postcolonial histories of *indigenismo, mestizaje,* hegemony, and survival" (2008, 187). In her reading of borderland SF texts, Lysa Rivera (2012) argues that the genre offers critical visions of globalization both today and in the near future but also insists on reading late capitalism as a troubling and enduring extension of colonial relations of power between the United States and Mexico. Rivera's analysis examines the future as a return to the colonial past in neoliberal economic form, rather than as a vision of progress for Latin@s. According to both authors, SF warns that without viable alternatives, these futures promise to repeat the worst of colonial histories along the US-Mexico border (Ramírez 2008, 185; Rivera 2012, 416). These scholars and others illuminate the claim that provides a foundation for this essay: that Latin@ SF provides a way to retell colonial and postcolonial histories and imagine alternatives to neoliberal economic hegemony.

Food and Futurity in Literature

Food studies have recently gained currency within US ethnic literary studies.[2] For example, Anita Mannur uses anthropological and philosophical food studies as a springboard to articulate her reading of food in South Asian diasporic literature. Mannur asserts that food discourses reaffirm ethnic and cultural identity, and her work interrogates the relationship between ethnic and racial identities and the nostalgic representation of food in literature (2010, 12). Other scholars also suggest that food plays an integral role in one's identity in relation to race/ethnicity, gender, sexuality, and socioeconomic status (Abarca 2006; Herrera 2010; Gabaccia 1998;

Rebolledo 1995; Soler and Abarca 2013). For instance, Jennifer Ann Ho and Christina Herrera analyze food in ethnic US literature as a marker of both compliance with and resistance to Americanization (Hererra 2010, 244; Ho 2005, 3). Ho states, "People define themselves against the consumption habits of others: we are who we are because of what and how we eat, and they are different because of what and how they eat" (2005, 12). Therefore, the edible can encode ethnicity and cultural "authenticity," or "Americanness," or, often, a combination of both (Dalessio 2012, 3).

Scholars of Chicana literature have used food studies to make important feminist and queer interventions. The major debates in the field focus on food preparation and consumption as feminist and decolonial practices, analyze the social space of the kitchen, and highlight food tropes that connect women's food preparation with the radical act of writing, or hunger with women's intellectual, spiritual, and sexual needs (Rebolledo 1995, 133). Meredith E. Abarca asserts that culinary epistemologies, or *sazón*, place the body as the center of knowledge and challenge the privileging of the senses of sight and hearing over taste and smell (2006, 77). Sarah Wald (2011, 567) calls attention to the production side of the food system by reading Helena María Viramontes's novel *Under the Feet of Jesus* (1995) as a corrective to Michael Pollan's nonfictional text *The Omnivore's Dilemma* (2006), arguing that the novel humanizes its farmworker characters and represents the foundation of a food justice movement that embodies workers' and immigrants' rights.

Current scholarship in Latin@ SF and literary food studies provides a lens to consider the role of food in the everyday lives of Latin@s and how their relationship to food articulates larger social problems related to food justice and health. It also illuminates decolonial knowledge related to food systems. I would add that the treatment of food systems in Latin@ SF is also an indication of the value of indigenous epistemologies, social justice, and viable alternatives that imagine healthier lives for future Latin@s.

"Chinganaza" as a Site of Utopian Food Systems

In the novel *Lunar Braceros*, food systems in earthly barrios and on the moon exemplify gross injustices against working-class Latin@s, African Americans, and poor whites and Asians (Sánchez and Pita 2009, 116), while food systems in the utopic space of Andean indigenous lands called Chinganaza portray a desirable and sustainable alternative. *Lunar Braceros* tells the story of future Latin@ workers through the memoirs of the protagonist, Lydia. These are recorded as electronic nanotexts that she leaves for her son Pedro when she joins a clandestine resistance network, a class-based struggle to end the pervasive system of peonage labor. In Sánchez and Pita's conception of the future, Latin@s make up the majority of service workers as futuristic janitors called trash-techs. As in the *bracero* system of the past (1940s–60s), trash-tech work is based on a seasonal contract: workers complete a three-year term on the moon while their employers deposit their wages into a bank account for them on earth. They never collect these deposits, however, as their employer poisons their last meal prior to their scheduled return to earth (18). Trash-tech work is one of the few alternatives to living on corporate-run reservations on earth, where the unemployed, especially poor people of color, are rounded up and forced to work for housing, food, and minimal medical services, but no wages. Resembling contemporary barrios, the reservations are organized by housing projects, and complex systems of surveillance cameras, panoptic-style architecture, and razor wire confine the "reslifers" to their neighborhoods. Any delinquency is punishable with more unpaid labor, and there is no access to nature or even empty space (35). The nanotexts describe Lydia's experiences growing up on a reservation, becoming a trash-tech, and raising Pedro in Chinganaza until she separates from him.

The militaristic control of reslifers is directly connected to food systems on the reservations. In a nanotext Lydia explains the system of work for food and as punishment:

> As we got to the mall, I could see two of Ricardo's friends working at one of the burger places; they had to work on the weekends because their father had tried to escape from the reservation and their mother couldn't get enough hours of work to meet their needs . . . that is, to work off what they consumed. (35)

Lydia's description portrays reslifer teenagers working in a fast-food restaurant to help support their family's consumption on the reservation. Their father's delinquency, or rather his attempt to escape the reservation, leads to his death, and their mother cannot get enough hours of work to pay off the family's consumption debt. Lydia also recounts a memory to Pedro about taking her sister out for the day, lamenting, "I kept thinking about how long it was going to take my dad to work off the two ice creams we had just had" (36). The lack of clear compensation for labor on the reservations extends to food consumption and living expenses, creating a system of debt that the reslifers will never be able to entirely work off.

Taken together, the examples also show a pattern of characteristically unhealthy foods on the reservations. Although these processed foods do not in themselves necessarily make a diet unhealthy, the reslifers do not have access to fresh fruits and vegetables, even though the reservations are located in California's central valley, known for its agriculture prior to the ecological devastation in the novel. Lydia leaves her parents behind in the reservation when she goes to work on the moon, determined to use her wages to free them and help her father realize his dream of leaving the reservation in order to live with his wife, meet his grandson Pedro, and tend to his garden (46). The garden represents the opportunity to produce food outside the jaws of corporations, with the harvest coming into a reslifer's own hands, a dream that is unrealizable for Lydia's father unless she can rescue him from the reservation.

Lunar Braceros presents the communal Andean land of Chinganaza as a utopic alternative to the reservation and the lunar colony, especially in relation to its food systems, because residents employ indigenous approaches to agricultural living and communal farming. Chinganaza is reclaimed land in the southeastern section of Ecuador where Lydia and her fellow trash-techs start raising children once they escape death by poisoned food on the moon. This land is populated by displaced indigenous tribes who practice traditional communal agricultural techniques on their ancestral homeland, knowledge that Lydia passes on to her son in hopes of a more sustainable future (115). In his essay in this collection, Ben Olguín reads Chinganaza as collectivist revolutionary space in its communal structure of farming, parenting, child rearing, and socialist didactic lessons in insurgent theory. As Lydia explains,

> Gardening, as you know, isn't the only task assigned by our commons committee. Some of us have other duties as well, like teaching or working in the nursery or helping with the arts and crafts that are then taken by one of our agents and sold in the marketplace of nearby towns. Our surplus fruit is also taken to be sold but grain and other goods are kept in mountain caves that are much like the cellars and keep the provisions fresh. What we get for the crafts and other surplus is used to buy cloth, shoes, medicines and sugar. As you know we grow our own coffee and that is a lifesaver. . . . We also grow our own tobacco and coca leaves, which we use for tea and for medicine. (20)

The philosophy of working the land cooperatively to grow thriving biodiverse crops, based on farming practices that are specifically suited to the topography of the area, extends to all necessities. This way of living represents a healthy and sustainable alternative to life on the reservations and on the moon. At the same time, the novel is careful not to romanticize indigenous cultures, and it avoids situating indigenous epistemologies as "premodern" or as somehow preceding technological advances. Lydia explains to Pedro that Chinganaza is not outside of the structures that have destroyed other parts of the earth: the tributaries that lead to the land are all contaminated, and the remaining protected gas and oil reserves in the area are attractive to transnational corporations (13). In fact, the novel ends with a nanotext written by now eighteen-year-old Pedro, who follows in his mother's activist footsteps when life in Chinganaza becomes no longer sustainable. An influx of "thousands of new settlers in the Andean region" is destroying its biodiversity in their search for uncontaminated land (120). Pedro represents a new generation of eco-activists needed to protect an indigenous way of cooperative living and growing food.

Food-Industry Labor in *Atomik Aztex*

While *Lunar Braceros* avoids romanticizing indigenous epistemologies, *Atomik Aztex* directly questions romantic representations of indigenous culture. The novel presents a society that situates ancient culture as a style or aesthetic for consumption, rather than as a viable alternative to contemporary exploitation of food-industry workers. The novel suggests that those in power will always abuse their positions and that the capitalist imperative of speeding up the line for higher profits reflects a dystopic future for human and nonhuman life. The slaughterhouse and the military battleground become reflections of each other, where soldiers, food-service workers, and animals are all sacrificed for the bottom line.

The narrative form of *Atomik Aztex* reflects on history and futurity outside of teleological and linear time. The protagonist occupies various spaces, including Mexico City, Los Angeles, and Stalingrad, in a cyclical time pattern. Two narrative threads representing the ancient past and the contemporary moment run alongside each other, at times crossing, crashing, and intersecting, and eventually blending into one. The novel speculates an alternative history, one in which the Spanish never conquered the Aztecs. Instead, the protagonist Zenzontli, a celebrated Aztec warrior, lives in an alternate reality in which the Aztek Socialist Imperium has defeated the Spanish. Zenzontli lives in Mexico with his family, circa 1943. He owns a compound with lush tropical gardens that house his pet jaguar Bobo and nameless, caged Spanish slaves, and he uses the most modern technologies to keep his menageries clean. Despite his seeming self-importance, he has many problems. He barely has a relationship with his wife and children. His Clan Elder takes his life savings, then sends Zenzontli and his soldiers to Stalingrad, Russia, to fight the Nazis during World War II, a mission that guarantees high casualties and probably death. Furthermore, Zenzontli suffers from an affliction—a series of nightmarish visions of himself in the future as Zenzo, an undocumented worker living in East Los Angeles who cannot afford a car, has an estranged ex-wife and children, and slaughters pigs for a living.

These visions of himself make up the second and parallel narrative thread of the novel. In it, the protagonist named Zenzo narrates a harrowing border-crossing experience from Mexico to Los Angeles, where he lands a job slaughtering pigs for the Farmer John Meat Company. He works tirelessly and secretly to unionize his fellow workers and is constantly under the watchful eye of his boss and nemesis, Max, who looks for any reason to fire Zenzo. Like Zenzontli, Zenzo has anachronistic visions of Mexico's ancient past.

With its bunker-like walls, the Farmer John slaughterhouse represents the most nightmarish aspect of the novel. Foster based it on an actual slaughterhouse by the same name in the industrial city of Vernon, California, just southeast of downtown Los Angeles. Hormel Foods, which acquired the slaughterhouse in 2005, has been called out for anti-union practices, exploitation of undocumented Latin@ labor, environmental degradation, abuse of animal welfare, contamination of the food supply, and extremely dangerous workplace conditions (Genoways 2014).

Atomik Aztex emphasizes that violence in the food industry affects both undocumented workers and the animals being slaughtered. Zenzo is a model food worker who excels at skillfully slaughtering pigs, most likely because his life depends on his efficiency. He maintains his focus even though Max, as plant manager, is constantly looking to make him fail by overscheduling him to exhaust him and by tampering with his already dangerous workspace. Zenzo describes a normal workday inside the slaughterhouse.

> You had to . . . keep your wits about you—you couldn't get too chilly or tired or slow, otherwise you might get hit. You don't want to get body-slammed by a 350-pound hog and fall on your knife or the spinning circular saw with its yellow spring-coiled electric cord, or bump somebody else with the knife or saw. . . . Each broadback hog descends toward the kill floor through a chute with its huge head first. . . . I reach my left arm around the hog's shoulders and I lean into its girth, the warm, grizzly skin

> prickling worse than your old man's two day stubble, I give it the last firm
> goodbye hug, pressing the knife into its throat at the same time, drawing
> it diagonally down, slicing the carotid with one motion, then on out the
> other side. The blade comes back at me soft as sliced cornbread. It's a
> one-two movement, that dance step. (Foster 2005, 6–7)

Zenzo's description of the kill floor shows his vexed relationship with the
hogs. On the one hand, it is an intimate relationship in which he gives
the animal a "goodbye hug" as he "press[es] the knife into his throat." The
reference to a dance step suggests the hogs are his dance partners. However,
if he doesn't stay focused, the hog becomes a deadly threat, especially in
relation to the technology that makes it possible for Zenzo to kill the
hog—the electric knife or the spinning circular saw. The physical demands
of the exhausting job make Zenzo vulnerable to the same technologies he
uses to kill the hogs. Zenzo is another cog in the meat-production line. A
careless move would cause injury to both Zenzo and a co-worker.

Ironically, the outside of the Farmer John slaughterhouse building tells
a much different story, depicting happy pastoral hogs while erasing Latin@
workers and dangerous labor practices from the food system. The wrap-
around mural "Hog Heaven" depicted in the novel is based on the actual
mural surrounding the real-life factory, which depicts a manicured farmland
of happy pigs grazing on green grass, sitting in mud, flying airplanes, taking
walks, and smiling.[3]

Even though the city of Vernon is far from a utopic pastoral farmland
of health and happiness, the characters do become more human when
they're outside the slaughterhouse. This is seen most clearly when they're
enjoying food from the taco truck parked outside the factory. Even Max's
sinister personality takes a turn when he's eating. Zenzo explains:

> Who would've known? You saw him out in the yard, standing out by the
> roach coach, eating tacos de carnitas with the workers, joking with the
> health & safety inspectors. Just another one of the boys, you might think.
> Later, you saw him stalking thru the plant with his clipboard, scowling
> like he'd just woken out of a nightmare, hunched over in his white coat
> as if whipped by a furious unhappiness of some sort. (48)

While outside the plant at the taco truck, eating pork tacos with the
workers and the safety inspectors, Max builds rapport with them. Inside
the plant, by contrast, Max becomes angry and goes from being "one of the
boys" and "everybody's buddy" (49) to taking on animal-like characteristics
as he stalks and "prowls" (49) the plant as if searching for prey. He growls

at Zenzo and screams lectures at other workers about their work infractions, bringing some workers to tears and punishing others with exhausting double shifts (51). The convivial humanness Max demonstrates toward others is immediately lost within the walls of the slaughterhouse as Max takes out his intense unhappiness on the workers. His ability to connect with others on a human level over tacos underscores the dehumanizing effects that violence has on everyone, workers and bosses alike, inside the slaughterhouse.

While at first Zenzontli, Zenzo's indigenous counterpart, lives in a far less nightmarish world, Foster avoids romanticizing the indigenous past. Zenzontli is not confined to a slaughterhouse, but he is a dispensable military worker at the mercy of any leader who has more power than he does. Sascha Pöhlmann (2010) has noted how *Atomik Aztex* problematizes romantic notions of the ancient indigenous past as remedy for contemporary social problems. For instance, Pöhlmann emphasizes Zenzo's pride about the Aztecs' superficial style of violence:

> Aztec dominance comes about not only through their supreme insight into the energies released by human sacrifice, but also through their knowledge about the importance of aesthetics. Their warriors are success-ful because they are cool; they are "sneaky, tough, hardened, intelligent, good looking, all around nice guys, studded with all type of metaphysikal dekorations, war paint, spiritual jewelry studs sticking out of our faces, stern, determined brows, quetzal feathers and plumes of rare vanishing species of the rainforests." (2010, 228)

Pöhlmann suggests that the novel criticizes any group in power that asserts violence over others, citing as examples the Aztec imperative for human sacrifice, Spanish slave ownership as status symbol for Aztecs, and the Clan Elder's disregard for Aztec soldiers' lives (including Zenzontli's). He interprets Zenzontli's attention to the details that make Aztec warriors "cool" as Foster's darkly humorous suggestion that one culture will always justify colonizing another by claiming the barbarity of the other, as reflected in arbitrary signs.

Ultimately, Foster suggests that humanity is difficult to attain within the context of colonization and violence. At the novel's end Zenzo asks, "What is it to be a man?" (Foster 2005, 202). In this rhetorical question he laments his inability to feel fully human. Just as Zenzo asserts an intimate relationship with the hogs he slaughters, he feels spiritually connected to other animals: "I mean, sometimes I sense a monkey spirit. I could be mistaken. That's the trouble with one's inner life. Monkeys could be playing around with it" (203). The reader might reasonably question this humanity when Max disappears, as he may have left town—or Zenzo may have pushed him into the meat grinder inside the Farmer John plant. At the novel's end, Boy Scouts at the baseball stadium eating Dodger Dog hot dogs, a lady's poodle in Pasadena, and celebrities at Pink's hot dog stand all suffer from stomachaches, projectile vomiting, and poisonous farts, perhaps because they are eating Max's body. Zenzo, on the other hand, enjoys the idea of consuming Max: "In my freezer I keep a stash of packages of hot dogs dated to the exact date they say Max disappeared, which I may consume with relish & lick my fingers" (200). With this plot point Foster implicates eaters and consumers who are complicit in the system of violent destruction of both workers and animals.

What the two novels have in common is their refutation of an anthropocentric future as healthy or desirable. In *Atomik Aztex*, the violent killing of animals in the slaughterhouse has direct negative impacts on the Farmer John workers, as it crushes their humanity and leads to unhappiness and alienation. Slaughtering pigs is also physically exhausting, draining, and dangerous labor; thus the novel connects the experiences of animals in food production to the dire exploitation of Latin@ workers on the kill floor. In *Lunar Braceros*, Chinganaza is a utopic space because of its protected status, which shields it—at least for a time—from development and extraction by transnational corporations that have destroyed the livable environment. Both novels call for a more ecological everyday practice in which respect for nonhuman life would help create sustainable food systems for contemporary and future working-class Latina@ communities.

Notes

1. Monsanto co-opts keywords from the environmental movement such as "sustainability" and "conservation," declaring on its website: "At Monsanto, we're focused on working with others to deliver sustainable agricultural solutions that address our biggest challenges—things like climate change and resource conservation—while sustaining the environment" (http://discover.monsanto. com/sustainable-farming). The term *sustainability* invokes the future of an ongoing biological system. However, small farmers, the target of Monsanto's genetically modified seed patent infringement lawsuits, assert that the biotechnological corporation is destroying the future of farming. See the documentary *The Future of Food* (2004) by Deborah Koons Garcia. For a more complete definition of the term

sustainability see *Our Common Future* by the World Commission on Environment and Development (1987).

2. See monographs such as *Consumption and Identity in Asian American Coming-of-Age Novels* (Ho 2005); *Culinary Fictions: Food in South Asian Diasporic Culture* (Mannur 2010); *Hunger Overcome? Food and Resistance in Twentieth-Century African American Literature* (Warnes 2004); *Black Hunger: Soul Food and America* (Witt 2004); and *Racial Indigestion: Eating Bodies in the 19th Century* (Tompkins 2012); as well as edited collections such as *Rethinking Chicana/o Literature through Food* (Soler and Abarca 2013); and *Eating Asian America: A Food Studies Reader* (Ku, Manalansan, and Mannur 2013). Also of interest are journals such as *Gastronomica: The Journal of Food and Culture*; *Alimentum: The Literature of Food*; and *Food, Culture & Society*.

3. The mural was started by Hollywood movie set painter Les Grimes, who died in the 1960s before finishing the project. It has since been completed and retouched by painter Arno Jordan and other artists through the years. http://www.lataco.com/taco/farmer-johns-hog-wild-mural-vernon.

Works Cited

Abarca, Meredith E. 2006. *Voices in the Kitchen: Views of Food and the World from Working-Class Mexican and Mexican American Women*. College Station: Texas A&M University Press.

Bahng, Aimee. 2008. "Extrapolating Transnational Arcs, Excavating Imperial Legacies: The Speculative Acts of Karen Tei Yamashita's 'Through the Arc of the Rain Forest.'" *MELUS* 33, no. 4: 123–44.

Barbas-Rhoden, Laura. 2011. *Ecological Imaginations in Latin American Fiction*. Gainesville: University of Florida Press.

Choi, Roy. 2013. "A Gateway to Feed Hunger: The Promise of Street Food." Presentation to MAD Symposium, Copenhagen, 25–26 August. http://www.madfeed.co/video/a-gateway-to-feed-hunger-the-promise-of-street-food/.

Dalessio, William R. 2012. *Are We What We Eat? Food and Identity in Late Twentieth-Century American Ethnic Literature*. Amherst, NY: Cambria.

Foster, Sesshu. 2005. *Atomik Aztex*. San Francisco: City Lights.

Gabaccia, Donna R. 1998. *We Are What We Eat: Ethnic Food and the Making of Americans*. Cambridge, MA: Harvard University Press.

Garcia, Deborah Koons. 2004. *The Future of Food*. Mill Valley, CA: Lily Films.

Genoways, Ted. 2014. *The Chain: Farm, Factory, and the Fate of Our Food*. New York: Harper Collins.

Herrera, Christina. 2010. "'Delfina, ¡más tacos!': Food, Culture and Motherhood in Denise Chávez's A Taco Testimony." *Food, Culture, and Society* 3, no. 2: 241–56.

Hing, Julianne. 2013. "L.A. Food Culture Offers a Glimpse into 'The New America.'" *Colorlines: News for Action*, April 26. https://www.colorlines.com/articles/la-food-culture-offers-glimpse-new-america.

Ho, Jennifer Ann. 2005. *Consumption and Identity in Asian American Coming-of-Age Novels*. New York: Routledge.

Ku, Robert Ji-Song, Martin F. Manalansan IV, and Anita Mannur, eds. 2013. *Eating Asian America: A Food Studies Reader*. New York: New York University Press.

Mannur, Anita. 2010. *Culinary Fictions: Food in South Asian Diasporic Culture*. Philadelphia: Temple University Press.

Olmos, Edward James. 2008. "Battlestar Galactica: We're in the Future." Paley Center for Media, July 29. https://www.youtube.com/watch?v=FCgTH-z58w4.

Pöhlmann, Sascha. 2010. "Cosmographic Metafiction in Sesshu Foster's 'Atomik Aztex.'" *Amerikastudien/American Studies* 55, no. 2: 223–48.

Pollan, Michael. 2006. *The Omnivore's Dilemma: A Natural History of Four Meals*. New York: Penguin.

Ramírez, Catherine S. 2008. "Afrofuturism/Chicanafuturism: Fictive Kin." *Aztlán: A Journal of Chicano Studies* 33, no. 1: 158–94.

Rebolledo, Tey Diana. 1995. *Women Singing in the Snow: A Cultural Analysis of Chicana Literature*. Tucson: University of Arizona Press.

Rivera, Lysa. 2012. "Future Histories and Cyborg Labor: Reading Borderlands Science Fiction after NAFTA." *Science Fiction Studies* 39, no. 3: 415–36.

Sánchez, Rosaura, and Beatrice Pita. 2009. *Lunar Braceros 2125–2148*. San Diego: Calaca.

Soler, Nieves Pascual, and Meredith E. Abarca, eds. 2013. *Rethinking Chicana/o Literature through Food: Postnational Appetites*. New York: Palgrave Macmillan.

Tatum, Charles, ed. 2013. *Encyclopedia of Latino Culture*, vol. 3, *From Calaveras to Quinceañeras*. Santa Barbara, CA: Greenwood.

Tittler, Jonathan. 2010. "Ecological Criticism and Spanish American Fiction: An Overview." In *The Natural World in Latin American Literatures*, edited by Adrian Taylor Kane, 11–36. Jefferson, NC: McFarland.

Tompkins, Kyla Wazana. 2012. *Racial Indigestion: Eating Bodies in the 19th Century*. New York: New York University Press.

Viramontes, Helena María. 1995. *Under the Feet of Jesus*. New York: Plume.

Wald, Sarah D. 2011. "Visible Farmers/Invisible Workers: Locating Immigrant Labor in Food Studies." *Food, Culture, and Society* 14, no. 4: 567–86.

Warnes, Andrew. 2004. *Hunger Overcome?: Food and Resistance in Twentieth-Century African American Literature*. Athens: University of Georgia Press.

Witt, Doris. 2004. *Black Hunger: Soul Food and America*. Minneapolis: University of Minnesota Press.

World Commission on Environment and Development. 1987. *Our Common Future*. New York: Oxford University Press.

Narrating the Right to Health
Speculative Genre in Morales's *The Rag Doll Plagues*

Andrew Uzendoski

Human rights are speculative principles. They project an ideal baseline for the treatment of individual humans. As defined by Lynn Hunt, human rights require three qualities: "rights must be *natural* (inherent in human beings); *equal* (the same for everyone); and *universal* (applicable everywhere). For rights to be *human* rights, all humans everywhere in the world must possess them equally and only because of their status as human beings" (2007, 20). However, universal human rights have yet to be standardized and secured across the globe, and in this sense the concept of human rights remains a speculative fiction. I explore this speculative nature of human rights in my analysis of Alejandro Morales's *The Rag Doll Plagues* (1992). Throughout his speculative text, Morales recognizes the right to health as a universal human right. By examining how Morales employs conventions of speculative fiction to advocate the right to health, I will demonstrate how the genre uniquely enables authors to promote and protect human rights ideals.[1]

Morales uses the unpredictable spread of viral pathogens as a narrative device to mark universal characteristics that connect people across North America. National and racial differences do not stop the transmission of infectious diseases across the continent; epidemics caused by aggressive viruses reveal biological vulnerabilities shared by diverse populations. Organized in three acts, *The Rag Doll Plagues* depicts how three distinct pandemics ravage three North American populations in three different eras (the eighteenth, twentieth, and twenty-first centuries). In addition, the novel anticipates that corporations will supersede nation-states as the principal agents that control health care systems around the globe. Morales targets for-profit hospitals and transnational pharmaceutical corporations as the primary threats to securing universal access to health care.

If the universal realization of human rights remains a speculative fiction, Morales teaches his readers how speculative fiction can promote human rights ideals through the interaction between protagonists in the final two acts of his novel. To represent the productive relationship between writing and reading speculative fiction, Morales generates a posthumous dialogue between a deceased man and his grandson when the grandson reads his grandfather's unpublished speculative novel. The resulting intergenerational dialogue between grandfather and grandson instigates the speculative process of cognitive estrangement. The theory of cognitive estrangement was developed by Darko Suvin to address how speculative genres productively juxtapose "an imaginative alternative" to the reader's own "empirical" or "naturalistic" experiences (1979, 7–8). As a result of this process of juxtaposition, cognitive estrangement both denaturalizes contemporaneous social and political systems and confronts the reader with alternative systems and epistemologies. Presuming economic and social systems as conditional and therefore changeable, cognitive estrangement encourages readers of speculative fiction to critique systematic prejudices and conceptualize structural change.

In his self-referential narrative, Morales simultaneously produces and models cognitive estrangement. Throughout the entire novel, he challenges the reader to recognize the right to health as a universal human right held by everyone at the end of the twentieth century. In the third act, Morales specifically demonstrates how cognitive estrangement can develop critical thought and political agency. Reflecting the overarching political aims of *The Rag Doll Plagues*, the grandfather's (fictional) speculative novel motivates the grandson to enter politics and protect the health of the poorest citizens in North America during the middle of the twenty-first century. Therefore, while the novel's third and final act is set in a dystopian future, Morales expresses optimism that dystopian prophecies can help readers materialize political reform in the present. By employing cognitive estrangement in his speculative novel, Morales prompts his reader to reconceptualize what qualifies as a universal human right.[2]

Cognitive Estrangement

In *Metamorphoses of Science Fiction* (1979), one of the first volumes that posited a literary theory of science fiction, Darko Suvin explains the concept of cognitive estrangement. Through the process of estrangement, speculative genres reimagine common concepts and objects as uncommon, making the known seem alien. Elaborating on how Suvin conceptualizes this process, Isiah Lavender III explains that in speculative fiction, "the ordinary world is defamiliarized; it is presented in a way that is exceedingly, and perhaps eerily, different from our own experience" (2011, 28).[3] Ultimately, estrangement marks existing hegemonic systems as products of particular cultural and political histories. Neither inevitable nor monolithic, such systems are therefore amendable.

Cognitive critique is what distinguishes how estrangement is specifically employed in speculative genres. The concept of cognition "implies not only a reflecting of but also on reality. It implies a creative approach tending toward a dynamic transformation rather than toward a static mirroring of the author's environment" (Suvin 1979, 10). Cognitive estrangement both historicizes a given moment's normative social structures—opening up space for the articulation and critique of underlying ideologies—and exploits the contingencies of economic and legal systems. That speculative fiction "sees the norms of any age, including emphatically its own, as unique, changeable, therefore subject to a cognitive view" is a result of a dynamic interaction between estrangement and cognition, formally expressed by "an imaginative framework alternative to the author's empirical environment" (7–8). Through cognitive critique, the reader assumes an active role in the meaning making and world building of speculative fiction, resulting in new and unexpected epistemological transformations.

Samuel Delany celebrates this ability of the genre to represent multiple epistemologies within a single text. "If s-f is affirmative," he argues, "it is not through any obligatory happy ending, but rather through the breadth of vision it affords, through the complex interweave of these multiple visions of human origins and destinations" (2009, 27). Speculative fiction is an "affirmative" genre when it prompts the reader to conceptualize the reformation of existing social and political systems from a variety of distinct yet interrelated perspectives. The global hegemony of a single political or social system is rejected by speculative fiction. In the process of imagining other worlds, speculative texts produce literary spaces where multiple epistemologies coexist.

Juxtaposing multiple worldviews, cognitive estrangement serves as the mechanism in speculative fiction that spurs the reader to interrogate the dominance of existing social and political systems. "Like the postmodern culture with which it emerged," Sherryl Vint writes, "speculative fiction critiques and rethinks the discourses by which we understand commonplace reality. It is thus not merely a fiction about the difference between the fictional world

251

and our own, but one in which the ontology of 'reality' itself is unstable" (2014, 90). Therefore, to understand how *The Rag Doll Plagues* activates cognitive estrangement, we must identify how the novel critiques Eurocentric epistemologies while recognizing the material ramifications of epistemological transformations. For example, the reconceptualization of what constitutes a universal human right—such as the human right to health—can have direct implications for health care policies at national and local levels.

Representing the full transformative potential of cognitive estrangement, the protagonist in the third act of *The Rag Doll Plagues* leads a political movement to empower marginalized and disenfranchised peoples after reading his grandfather's speculative novel. Thus, by the novel's conclusion, Morales frames speculative literature as a decolonial tool that can critique settler-colonial institutions and empower colonized populations. And by promoting the right to health as a universal human right, Morales's speculative novel centers the right to health as a vital component of decolonization.

Narrating the Right to Health

The narrative structure of *The Rag Doll Plagues* facilitates the process of cognitive estrangement. The novel is organized into three acts. In each act, Morales describes how different settler-colonial governments respond to pandemics (or "plagues") in three different centuries: the Spanish empire in the eighteenth century, the US government in the twentieth century, and a future confederation of settler-colonial states known as Lamex in the twenty-first century. This juxtaposition denaturalizes each empire's claim to territory in North America. Spain, the United States, and Lamex are each contextualized as but one of many settler-colonial states jockeying for the control of indigenous peoples and lands. Indeed, the novel's structure posits the United States as a finite settler-colonial state; it will exist no longer than the Spanish empire.

The first act is set in eighteenth-century Mexico City. Doctor Gregorio has been sent by royal officials in Madrid—the colonial metropole—to find a cure for a mysterious plague named "La Mona." For months the plague has been killing indiscriminately, its victims both indigenous and European. Gregorio fails to find a cure, but the virus eventually disappears after ravaging the population for years. At the end of the section, Gregorio breaks off the engagement with his Spanish fiancée and chooses to remain in Mexico for the rest of his life. Like the acts that follow, the first act effectively historicizes a distinct manifestation of settler-colonial logic—in this case, Spanish political and social policies. In addition, the discriminatory medical system developed by the Spanish government for Mexico in the eighteenth century will be mirrored in the second act by the US health care system in the 1980s. Similarities between the two settler-colonial governments contextualize US political and social systems within a longer history of colonization of the Americas. When understood as extensions of European settler-colonial policy, US political and social institutions are neither inevitable nor fixed; rather, they are historical and amendable. Therefore, the first act sets the conditions for cognitive estrangement in the second act.

Set in the United States during the 1980s, the second act offers the contemporary reader a seemingly identifiable setting—one that the reader will soon feel alienated from via cognitive estrangement. The protagonist of the novel's second act, Gregory, is a champion of universal access to health care. Dedicated to serving poor and marginalized populations, Gregory staffs the Santa Ana Medical Clinic in his Los Angeles barrio called Delhi. While the clinic addresses inequalities within the US health care system, Morales recognizes that health is determined by social and economic factors. Indeed, Gregory's barrio is named after the Delhi Sugar Factory because the community first emerged as the marginalized labor force for an international agricultural corporation.

Early in the act, Morales presents a dynamic assessment of the many factors that have produced a health crisis in the barrio. Gregory identifies his patients at the clinic as "the beautiful faces marked by the history of young and old Chicanos who worked, studied, loved, hated and helped each other in times of need, and just as easily shot each other to watch a brother or sister bleed to death on the pavement" (Morales 1992, 71). He recognizes the contradictory emotions that motivate the seemingly random acts of violence that have afflicted the community in Delhi. As the passage continues, Gregory references various reasons that assailants use to justify their violent behavior: "For revenge, for the reputation of my sister, for a bad drug deal, for pride, for the honor of family, for their *barrio*, the homeboys and homegirls would explain as they lay dying from a huge hole made by a 357 magnum bullet fired from a cruising car at eleven-thirty at night, just when the party was underway" (71). He goes on to list numerous explanations for the recent rise in violence. Familial, economic, personal, communal, political, and national interests are interlinked in brief acts of aggression and anger. Thus, Gregory understands both his duty as a health care worker and the escalating violence in Delhi in relationship to broader structures. For example, he underscores the social impact of drive-by shootings: "if the person died, I couldn't deal with what he or she left behind. The toughest part was when I had to face the family. In their faces I saw my mother, father, brothers and sisters" (71). Just as the name Delhi evokes a legacy of agricultural labor exploitation, each individual patient at the clinic references larger constellations of social, economic, and political structures.

Significantly, Gregory's words anticipate legal approaches to health as a human right that would emerge at turn of the twenty-first century. To fully appreciate and defend the right to health, as Paul Farmer argued in 1999, we must conceptualize "public health and access to medical care [as] social and economic rights; they are every bit as critical as civil rights" (1487). Elaborating on the social aspect of health in 2005, Alicia Ely Yamin asserted that "because rights must be realized inherently within the social sphere, this formulation immediately suggests that determinants of health and ill health are not purely biological or 'natural' but are also factors of societal relations" (1159). By contextualizing *The Rag Doll Plagues* alongside recent developments in health and human rights, we can identify how Morales innovatively captures the complexities of recognizing health as a human right.[4]

To further establish his protagonist's ethos, Morales contrasts Gregory's ideals with the economic interests of Termolino N. Trompito, the director of a nearby for-profit hospital where Gregory works when not at the clinic. Gregory identifies Trompito as "arch enemy" to the "concept of indigent care in the County." In contrast to Gregory's work ethic and devotion to Delhi, Trompito practices "a convenient, power-hungry politics which in the long-run always supported his fellow cronies and above all made him look good" (Morales 1992, 86). He is even described as a "little Hitler" (87). This relationship between Gregory and Trompito symbolizes the different approaches to health care practiced by Gregory's local clinic and Trompito's corporate hospital. In contrast to Trompito's incessant monetization of every aspect of health care, Gregory's approach draws from multiple sources of knowledge and privileges local organizations over national and transnational institutions.

In the novel, Gregory marries a Jewish actress named Sandra. While Gregory recognizes "Hitler" in Trompito, Sandra's figure reminds Gregory of "the victims of the holocaust" (77). However, Sandra has hemophilia. After receiving a blood transfusion, she contracts HIV. Much of the second act of the novel narrates how Sandra struggles to receive adequate treatment in US hospitals while also contending with prejudice both from her colleagues and from medical staff. For example, while visiting the Orange County Theater, where she previously starred in a wildly successful Chicano staging of Federico García Lorca's *Blood Wedding*, she is treated as an "unpredictable, contaminated animal" (108). When she asks the director of the theater if she can audition for parts in the upcoming season, the director tells Sandra through a half-closed door, "You just don't know about this sickness. Nobody wants to endanger their lives by working with you" (109). He then closes the door on Sandra.

Sandra receives even worse treatment at the hospital. Gregory details her experiences at a University of California, Los Angeles (UCLA), medical center: "Several doctors and nurses absolutely refused to be in the same room with her . . . they considered Sandra a human scourge, a Pandora's box filled with diseases capable of destroying humanity" (112). Gregory painfully observes that the doctors value Sandra more as an object to be experimented on than as a human to be cured. "Sandra was simply a research case, a human disease puzzle to be solved," he writes. "The endocrinologist and the hematologist saw her as a job risk. Their complaint was that they did not get combat pay for endangering their lives with scum like her" (112). Not only do the staff at the university hospital dehumanize Sandra, they view her illness as a mandate for monetary compensation. The scene underscores how public-funded institutions are being transformed by corporatization and privatization. Again, Morales juxtaposes Gregory's actions against the actions of other doctors. If Gregory's commitment to his community's health is reflected in how humanely he treats individual patients, the impersonal approach practiced by the staff at the UCLA hospital represents the disinterest of the growing health care industry in serving poor and marginalized communities. Decisions by the staff are driven by financial concerns, not health care needs.

The content of act 2, especially Sandra's narrative, anticipates and raises the profile of recent debates on human rights and health. Paul Hunt, a United Nations special rapporteur, wrote in 2006 that the right to health includes freedoms ("such as the right to be free from discrimination and involuntary medical treatment") and entitlements ("such as the right to essential primary care"), a framework endorsed by the World Health Organization. Moreover, Hunt stresses that the right to health "has a particular concern for the disadvantaged, the vulnerable and those living in poverty" and therefore "requires an effective, inclusive health system of good quality" (604). In *The Rag Doll Plagues*—published in 1992, a decade before Hunt was named the first-ever UN special rapporteur on the right to health—Morales dramatizes violations of the right to health in terms of both freedoms and entitlements. Sandra is a victim of discrimination and an object of experimentation, and adequate health care for patients from the barrio of Delhi is never guaranteed. Crucially, as Gregory fails in his individual attempts to meet the health needs of his community and of his wife, Morales's narrative demonstrates that structural change is necessary to ensure effective health care—and that non-Eurocentric epistemologies are vital resources for developing alternative health care systems and practices. Thus, Morales's speculative novel can be located at the forefront of human rights advocacy for the human right to health.

Rejected by the hospital at UCLA, Sandra and Gregory travel to Mexico to seek better medical treatment. In the following scenes, set in the Mexican village of Tepotzotlan, Morales casts indigenous Mexico as a site of healing and positions indigenous medical practices in opposition to the corporatization and monetization of US health care. Sandra is warmly welcomed by her indigenous doctors. She ingests a medication called "Nahaultzin's nourishment," she participates in "the celebration of the energy of Tepoztecatl," and she partakes of a *nahuatl* healing therapy conducted by a local *curandera* while in Tepotzotlan (Morales 1992, 120–23). The indigenous medicine has a positive effect on Sandra. However, while in Mexico, she is diagnosed with Kaposi's sarcoma, and she must return to the United States to acquire necessary medication to treat the illness. Within weeks, Sandra dies at home in Los Angeles with Gregory and her parents at her side. It is only after Sandra's death that Gregory begins to write the speculative novel that will influence his grandson a half century later, allowing the grandson to build upon his grandfather's experiences and knowledge.

Lamex and the Political Ascendancy of Multinational Corporations

In act 3 of the novel, the perpetrator of human rights abuses is not a single nation-state but a conglomeration of states named Lamex. Within the borders of Lamex, citizenship is distinguished by three different ranks: Lower Life Existence, Middle Life Existence, and Higher Life Existence. Each tier of citizenship affords access to particular territories across the continent; the most desirable land is home to the class categorized as Higher Life Existence. The ranking also determines what type of health care a citizen can access: the higher the citizenship, the better the health care the citizen receives. Lamex was formed by an economic agreement between Mexico,

Canada, and the United States, an agreement referred to in the novel as the Triple Alliance. This alliance is allegorical; Morales's novel was published in 1992, the year the North American Free Trade Agreement (NAFTA) was signed by the same three countries. Lamex can be read as a speculative embodiment of NAFTA as a transnational economic organization that has transcended the sovereignty of each nation-state in North America. The novel reminds us that nation-states are not the only antagonists to universal human rights.

In this dystopian future, manmade pollution dumped into the Pacific Ocean has had a catastrophic consequence: the pollution has produced a virus that kills its host within days. The protagonist of the third act is the grandson of the second act's protagonist. He is a prestigious Lamex doctor who specializes in contagious illnesses, and like his grandfather, he is also named Gregory. However, unlike his grandfather, the younger Gregory discovers a cure for the new plague. By transfusing into the veins of plague victims blood extracted from poor mestizo citizens, who have lived in the polluted environment of Mexico City all their lives and are therefore immune to a pollution-borne disease, Gregory is able to heal his patients. Tragically, this treatment demands blood from the most impoverished communities on the continent. Soon, every rich family on the West Coast literally buys impoverished citizens from Lower Life Existence living in Mexico City in order to have ownership of (and thus easy access to) their restorative mestizo blood. A cure produced from the blood Lower Life Existence citizens only benefits citizens of Higher Life Existence.

Through this narrative of forced migration and breeding to provide health care for the most privileged citizens, Morales marks the economic interests that drive medical research and treatment in a world system dominated by transnational corporations. As noted by Michael Hardt and Antonio Negri, in such a world system "government and politics come to be completely integrated into the system of transnational command" (2000, 307). In our current moment, such transnational command is represented by trade agreements such as NAFTA, CAFTA (Central America Free Trade Agreement), and TRIPS (Agreement on Trade-Related Aspects of Intellectual Property Rights).[5] In the future envisioned by Morales, transnational command is symbolized by Lamex, a transnational organization (created by the Triple Alliance of Mexico, the United States, and Canada) that has divided the continent into economic zones.

The conclusion to the third act does not see the economic inequalities of Lamex resolved. Instead, the class divisions of the dystopian organization are inadvertently amplified by Gregory's discovery of a cure: the poorest citizens of the state become slaves in the homes of the wealthiest. Families are broken up when individual citizens of Lower Life Existence from Mexico City are forced to move across the country and breed in accordance with specific genetic models to produce children with the blood type most effective at curing (wealthy) victims of the new plague. Because citizenship is not standardized across the nation-state, citizenship in Lamex does not confer universal human rights. Advanced medical procedures and treatments developed in Lamex are only available to Lamex citizens in the upper class. In the future, poor citizens of Lamex receive mediocre health care, if any, and are readily expendable when a pandemic breaks out across the continent.

Cognitive Estrangement and the Politicization of the Reader of Speculative Fiction

The plot in the third act not only produces cognitive estrangement, it demonstrates how the process of cognitive estrangement can politicize the reader. Act 3 of *The Rag Doll Plagues* features a self-referential employment of cognitive estrangement. While developing a cure for the plague in his grandfather's library, Gregory begins to read speculative novels written by his grandfather. Commenting on the appeal of these explicitly speculative texts, Gregory reflects that it was a "thrill and challenge to read the literary creations of my grandfather, a writer of novels who posited his vision of the future world" (Morales 1992, 141). His grandfather's speculative writing will transform Gregory. While reading it, Gregory begins to question the social and legal hierarchies that structure life in Lamex. The speculative fiction motivates Gregory to imagine alternative social and legal systems, leading him to seek political agency. Thus, an intergenerational dialogue between grandfather and grandson, instigated solely by reading and writing speculative fiction, activates the process of cognitive estrangement. By the end of the novel, Gregory decides to become a political leader and to defend the rights of Lower Life Existence citizens across the continent.

Signaling the transformative potential of cognitive estrangement, Gregory notices that reading his grandfather's novels alters the way he conceptualizes traditional conventions of literary genres: "I concentrated on history and fiction and discovered very little difference in this oppositional binary that resisted separation" (141). This reconceptualization of speculative fiction is an early sign of how his grandfather's writing instigates cognitive critique. Former conceptions of genre—that fact and fiction are neatly separated by genre categories; that genre fiction is for entertainment—are upended. Gregory explains, "I grasped my inability to discern fact from fiction. Grandfather Gregory's novel became a history. I began to read exclusively for the pleasure of information and not for the pleasure of entertainment nor for psychological avoidance" (159). As the value of speculative fiction shifts from receiving entertainment to acquiring information, Gregory changes from a passive to an active reader.

Gregory is affected by one speculative novel in particular. Written by his grandfather, this novel offers numerous critiques of medical practices at the turn of the twenty-first century. This text shares the name of Morales's novel: it is titled *The Rag Doll Plagues*. His grandfather's own *Rag Doll Plagues* confronts Gregory with the ethics of treating sick populations, especially those that have been marginalized by racist or homophobic policies. From his own perspective in the middle of the twenty-first century, Gregory grapples with the political arguments that underwrite his grandfather's speculative text. After finishing the novel, Gregory will be tasked with implementing new policy informed by his grandfather's writing.

In one section of the novel, his grandfather critiques the US health care system when he describes the testing of an experimental synthetic chemical on 1,000 patients with cancer. The chemical is surprisingly successful, and within hours many of the terminally ill patients feel cured. However, as news of the cure spreads across the hospital, demand for the chemical becomes overwhelming. "Every severely ill patient, regardless of whether he suffered from terminal cancer or not, wanted the cure," Gregory's grandfather writes. "At nine o'clock, the city police and county sheriffs arrived to face a full-fledged riot" (158). Some patients are able to escape the hospital and share the news of the miracle cure with the public. Cancer patients from all across the United States begin traveling to the hospital where the experiment was conducted. Demand for the drug sets off widespread violence, and numerous doctors lose their lives when they are unable to obtain the chemical. Soon counter-reports that the drug does not actually work begin circulating in the news, but such reports do not dampen public demand. Gregory's grandfather writes:

> The citizenry aggressively accused the government and the multinational drug producers of withholding chemicals in certain parts of the world in order to maintain profit margins and in other areas of the globe to control population. As a whole, the population was convinced that cancer had

259

been cured, but political and economic factors out of their control resulted
in the medications not being released to save lives. (159)

The passage presents a tragic vision of the economic interests of multinational drug companies trumping the health of a national citizenry.

In response to his grandfather's novel, Gregory is shocked—and he
begins to change his perspective on the ethics of medical experimentation
and access to health care. Gregory's politicization is the result of cognitive
estrangement that occurs as he reads his grandfather's speculative fiction.
Thus, Gregory models how the reader might become politicized as a result
of Morales's novel. Indeed, his interaction with his grandfather's novel
begins to change his valuation not only of speculative fiction but also of
health care practices across the continent. As the "novel" transforms into
"history"—and prophecy becomes fact—Gregory questions the medical
ethics that he has been taught as a doctor and a citizen of Higher Life Existence. The more he reads from his grandfather's library, the more critical he
becomes of the class hierarchies that divide the citizenry of Lamex. As the
third act develops, and Gregory reads more of his grandfather's speculative
fiction, he becomes outspoken against the segregation of sick/poor patients.
Colleagues caution him that he may lose his position if he continues to
critique the economic and social policies of Lamex. At one point, needing
his research but fearing his political commentary, administrative agents of
Lamex sequester Gregory away from other health workers.

In another speculative plot that addresses the tragic consequences of
failing to protect the right to health, Gregory's grandfather writes about
an "AIDS camp" constructed in 1999 on University of California property
located in Asilomar, California. The camp is established in response to
a riot that breaks out in San Francisco when "the citizenry" protested
the use of public funds to support AIDS patients. Gregory's grandfather
describes the scene: "Without warning, the outside community attacked
and brutally dragged out to the street every AIDS victim in the Moribundus
Support Houses and systematically massacred them" (160). In the wake
of the riot, the California state government mandates that the University
of California—"which donated [the land] for the right to conduct experiments on AIDS"—relocate all the state's AIDS patients to a single site in
Asilomar. Soon, "the other states followed suit and arranged to help finance
a national AIDS settlement at Asilomar," writes the grandfather. "In one
year, almost all the AIDS patients were housed at Asilomar. Those who
went underground were given one month to surrender or face the death

penalty. The logic behind this concentration camp alternative was that it was the only way to control the AIDS plague" (160). Gregory's grandfather then concludes this (speculative) history of the AIDS pandemic in the United States with a striking image: "By the year 2003, Asilomar cremated its last experimental AIDS patient" (160).

Referring to the AIDS settlement as a concentration camp, and describing the systematic cremation of AIDS patients, Morales once again employs symbols of the Holocaust to describe atrocities at the turn of the twenty-first century. With these references to the Holocaust—along with earlier references to Hitler and to Jewish victims of the Nazis—Morales invokes the human rights paradigm, as the Universal Declaration of Human Rights is frequently contextualized as a historical response to World War II and specifically the Holocaust. Three events are therefore framed as systematic human rights abuses in the novel: the medical treatment of AIDS patients in the 1980s, cancer research and the distribution of medicine in the 1990s, and the quarantine of AIDS patients at the end of the 1990s and beginning of the 2000s.

While at first Gregory struggles to process this narrative, his initial skepticism vanishes after he finishes his grandfather's novel. "I tried to convince myself that I was reading fiction," he writes. "Nonetheless, according to Grandfather, these were actual interviews preserved in the University of California library" (160). And while we, the readers of Morales's novel, also do not know the "accuracy" of his grandfather's speculative novel, we do know the prejudice that he witnessed against his wife Sandra. In addition, we are well aware of the medical disadvantages that faced the Chican@ community of Delhi. Thus, we know that his grandfather's political and social critiques are grounded in experiences—working for a clinic that served a Chican@ community and caring for a wife who was diagnosed with AIDS. Ultimately, his grandfather's speculative novel provides Gregory with an effective epistemological framework in which to understand the social and political inequalities of Lamex's health care system. Contextualizing Lamex's failure to provide adequate health care for each citizen—regardless of class or citizenship status—from the perspective of his grandfather's own experiences, Gregory recognizes that the structural change of Lamex's political system is necessary to secure the right to health for everyone. At the end of the novel, he quits his position as a medical researcher for Lamex and assumes leadership of a nascent political movement.

261

Conclusion

Morales's novel promotes cognitive estrangement as a decolonial tool. In the final passage, Gregory describes how reading his grandfather's speculative fiction transformed his worldview. Surrounded by his grandfather's library, Gregory remarks: "I am no longer me. I am transfigured into all those that have gone before me: my progenitors, my hopeful ever-surviving race. From the deepest part of my being there rushes to the surface of my almond shaped eyes an ancient tear" (200). His grandfather's novel has successfully instigated the process of cognitive estrangement and has persuaded Gregory to imagine a social system alternative to the hierarchal structure of Lamex. At the end of act 3, Gregory becomes the director of the political and paramilitary sectors of El Mar de Villas, a sector of Lamex dedicated to the dismantling of the Triple Alliance and the representation of poor Mexican citizens.

Morales does not give *The Rag Doll Plagues* a happy ending. The structural inequalities of Lamex's health care system are not resolved at the end of act 3. Instead, we must appreciate the narrative arc of the novel for its historicization and exploration of multiple epistemologies. After all, the climax of the third act is Gregory's epistemological breakthrough, not his discovery of a cure for the new plague. The conclusion of *The Rag Doll Plagues* is a testament to the process of cognitive estrangement. Gregory's politicization represents the novel's ideal effect on potential readers. Thus, *The Rag Doll Plagues* models how authors can use speculative texts as imaginative forums to propagate and defend alternative epistemological frameworks.

Notes

1. In comparison to contemporaneous Chican@ novels, *The Rag Doll Plagues* is unique in how it defends the right to health as a universal right. However, the novel is similar to *The Heirs of Columbus* (1991), by Native American author Gerald Vizenor (Anishinaabe). In Vizenor's speculative novel, a group of Anishinaabe storytellers create a new indigenous nation in the Pacific Northwest that offers free health care to anyone, regardless of whether they are indigenous or nonindigenous.

2. As María Herrera-Sobek writes, "an underlying theme of the novel is the various protagonists' epistemophilic desire. All three male protagonists explicitly state their love for books, for reading" (1995, 107). While Herrera-Sobek and

Manuel M. Martín-Rodríguez (1995) have stressed the importance of the fact that all three protagonists are voracious readers and prolific writers, no study has yet focused on the role played by speculative genres in their writings, especially Morales's celebration of speculative fiction in the final act of the novel.

    3. In part, Suvin grounds his understanding of estrangement in the work of Bertolt Brecht, who wrote that "a representation which estranges is one which allows us to recognize its subject, but at the same time makes it seem unfamiliar." This move cites the performative aspects of Brecht's theatric work while grounding Suvin's own work in existing literary theory (Suvin 1979, 6).

    4. For further examples of conceptualizing the right to health in the context of social and economic rights, see Inoue and Drori (2006), Persaud (2010), and Forbath (2005).

    5. TRIPS imposes a minimum requirement for the protection of intellectual property rights on member states of the World Trade Organization. First drafted in 1994, the agreement significantly favors the rights of multinational corporations over those of nation-states. As Matthew Flynn writes, "The TRIPS agreement undoubtedly increases the structural power of capital by establishing an overarching international legal code and juridical structure that favors the interests of transnational firms with large intellectual property portfolios" (2012, 4–5).

Works Cited

Delany, Samuel R. 2009. *The Jewel-Hinged Jaw: Notes on the Language of Science Fiction*. Middletown, CT: Wesleyan University Press. First published 1977.

Farmer, Paul. 1999. "Pathologies of Power: Rethinking Health and Human Rights." *American Journal of Public Health* 89, no. 10: 1486–96.

Flynn, Matthew. 2012. *From Structural to Symbolic Dimensions of State Autonomy: Brazil's AIDS Treatment Program and Global Power Dynamics*. Rapoport Center Human Rights Working Paper 2/2012. Austin: Rapoport Center for Human Rights and Justice, University of Texas.

Forbath, William E. 2005. "Social Rights, Courts and Constitutional Democracy: Poverty and Welfare Rights in the United States." *Democratization* 12, no. 5: 725–48.

Hardt, Michael, and Antonio Negri. 2000. *Empire*. Cambridge, MA: Harvard University Press.

Herrera-Sobek, María. 1995. "Epidemics, Epistemophilia, and Racism: Ecological Literary Criticism and The Rag Doll Plagues." *Bilingual Review/La Revista Bilingüe* 20, no. 3: 99–108.

Hunt, Lynn. 2007. *Inventing Human Rights: A History*. New York: W. W. Norton.

Hunt, Paul. 2006. "The Human Right to the Highest Attainable Standard of Health: New Opportunities and Challenges." *Transactions of the Royal Society of Tropical Medicine and Hygiene* 100: 603–7.

Inoue, Keiko, and Gili S. Drori. 2006. "The Global Institution of Health as a Social Concern: Organization and Discursive Trends." *International Sociology* 21, no. 21: 199–219.

Lavender, Isiah, III. 2011. *Race in American Science Fiction*. Bloomington: Indiana University Press.

Martín-Rodríguez, Manuel M. 1995. "The Global Border: Transnationalism and Cultural Hybridism in Alejandro Morales's The Rag Doll Plagues." *Bilingual Review/Revista Bilingüe* 20, no. 3: 86–98.

Morales, Alejandro. 1992. *The Rag Doll Plagues*. Houston: Arte Público.

Persaud, Roshni D. 2010. "Rights-Based Approaches and Health Disparities in the United States." In *Rights-Based Approaches to Public Health*, edited by Elvira Beracochea, Corey Weinstein, and Dabney Evans, 31–68. New York: Springer.

Suvin, Darko. 1979. *Metamorphoses of Science Fiction: On the Poetics and History of a Literary Genre*. New Haven, CT: Yale University Press.

Vint, Sherryl. 2014. *Science Fiction: A Guide for the Perplexed*. New York: Bloomsbury.

Vizenor, Gerald. 1991. *The Heirs of Columbus*. Middletown, CT: Wesleyan University Press.

Yamin, Alicia Ely. 2005. "The Right to Health Under International Law and Its Relevance to the United States." *American Journal of Public Health* 95, no. 7: 1156–61.

"Waking the Sleeping Giant"

Mestizaje, Ideology, and the Postcyberpunk Poetics of Carlos Miralejos's *Texas 2077*

José R. Flores

Every US election cycle brings renewed discussions of how the "Latino vote" may influence the upcoming elections. As Cristina Beltrán highlights, "This enduring depiction of Latinos as untapped potential is intrinsically linked to an impression of Latinos as politically passive and difficult to mobilize: the giant that seemingly *cannot* be roused from its slumber" (2010, 4). However, Beltrán is less concerned with how to awaken the sleeping giant than with analyzing who exactly constitutes this colossal body. In other words, do we understand the "Latino vote" as a unified bloc that shares a common political agenda? That seems very unlikely at present. However, looking to the future, what if Latinos reached a point of political consolidation that made them a coherent and powerful electoral force nationally? And if this were to happen, on what basis would Latinos organize, and what would be their primary concerns? Welcome to *Texas 2077: A Futuristic Novel*, where Latinos have indeed come together to usher in a new era, as it were, through the formation of a new and dominant Latino political party called New Era.

Race and politics converge in Carlos Miralejos's self-published novel, written in 1998 and set mainly in a near-future Texas. I begin my discussion by providing a brief synopsis of the novel and situating *Texas 2077* within the science fiction subgenre of postcyberpunk, an aesthetic that has a less bleak and alienated way of perceiving the world than other speculative genres, particularly cyberpunk. Following this point, I analyze how the text reinforces the trope of the Latino community as a political "sleeping giant" and discuss some of the challenges to this notion as proposed by Cristina Beltrán in *The Trouble with Unity* (2010). I conclude by turning to the concept of mestizaje to analyze *Texas 2077*'s reading of Latino racial unity in a future US society. For this, I refer back to José Vasconcelos's controversial utopian vision outlined in *La raza cósmica*, first published in 1925, and the complexities of mestizaje in Chicana/o literature and culture, which are illuminated in Miralejos's new novel.

Texas 2077 and Postcyberpunk Politics

Before venturing into the future, *Texas 2077* sets the initial four chapters in the year 1999. It introduces the emerging Latino-dominated political party New Era, which seeks to participate in the Year 2000 Time Capsule Project planned by the conservative media conglomerate C.K. Enterprises. However, Max Wizenberg, who is identified as the Jewish executive of C.K., instructs the company's marketing manager, David Szklaruk, to reject New Era's request to participate. Wizenberg, who is worried about the increasing population of Latinos, wants to hinder Latino political organizing and suppress media coverage of it. He fears that if Latinos were to move into power, "Israel would lose the U.S.A.'s support, and the Islamic nations would annihilate the state of Israel" (Miralejos 1998, 20). After this awkward if not subtly anti-Semitic attempt to situate the drama in a globalized context, the novel proceeds with Szklaruk recognizing the latest rejection of New Era's request as another deliberate attempt by C.K. Enterprises to suppress Latino visibility. He decides to leak the order to the public because "it was the right thing to do" (23). Following public backlash against C.K., New Era is invited to participate in the time capsule project, and it gains tremendous momentum in moving ahead as an independent political party with David Szklaruk as the head of its marketing department.

Fast forward to the year 2077, and New Era has become the largest political party in the United States. Originally based in San Antonio, the party had a predominantly Latino membership at the end of the twentieth century, but by 2077 its political stance has attracted people "from all ethnic groups" (123). New Era is eager to win big in the upcoming congressional elections that will set up the party's presidential candidate for victory in 2080. However, a Texas independence movement led by the state's governor emerges and threatens New Era's chances of winning. The novel's intersecting racialized ethnic conflicts set the scene for battle.

The novel centers on the life of Ernesto "Tito" Tellez, a middle-aged Tejano nuclear physicist who is chairman of the New Era party in the year 2077. In that position, he is charged with the task of working with

Democrats and Republicans to defeat a bid for Texas independence in an upcoming referendum. Meanwhile, on a visit to Cancún, Tito learns from a local indigenous community, the Itzaes, that an asteroid will collide with Earth in sixty-six years, and he is the only one who can organize the effort to destroy it. Because of his connection with the Itzaes, Tito assumes responsibility for overseeing the committee to defend the Earth. Tito moves from one problem to the next in *Texas 2077*, which prompts his best friend Rafi to assert, "You have too many problems . . . Do you realize that on one hand you're supposed to save the United States from splitting apart and, on the other hand, you're supposed to save our planet? All that while you're in the middle of a romantic affair with a married and younger lady" (121). Nonetheless, Tito remains hopeful that everything will be resolved.

In "Notes Towards a Postcyberpunk Manifesto," Lawrence Person (1998) provides a critique of cyberpunk and describes it as the bleak predecessor of the postcyberpunk novels of the early 1990s. According to Person's description of postcyberpunk fiction, the novels of this sci-fi sub-genre represent a world that is "impacted by rapid technological change and an omnipresent computerized infrastructure." Its characters are "frequently integral members of society (i.e., they have jobs)" instead of the "alienated loners" of the 1980s cyberpunk novels. Moreover, postcyberpunk is "suffused with an optimism that ranges from cautious to exuberant" and "makes fundamentally different assumptions about the future." Such is the case of *Texas 2077*, where the majority of the characters, including the protagonist Tito, hail from the upper middle class. Additionally, Person states:

> Postcyberpunk characters frequently have families, and sometimes even children. . . . They're anchored in their society rather than adrift in it. They have careers, friends, obligations, responsibilities, and all the trappings of an "ordinary" life. Or, to put it another way, their social landscape is often as detailed and nuanced as the technological one.

Texas 2077 describes in detail some of the technological underpinnings of a futuristic US society: the transcontinental shuttle that travels through vacuum tubes at 6,200 miles per hour, or the Siri-like functions of the HK (Home Keeper) computer, which can access all forms of public information, including people's locations, an early nod to present-day social media features. Yet the focus is on the quotidian (and later heroic) activities of Tito in his personal and professional lives. Tito and his wife Marta have grown apart over time and he gradually initiates an affair with a younger, married Anglo woman, Jenny. He explains that things were "much better when I was younger and building up a family. But now that the children had grown and left home, I felt a deep void in my relationship with Marta" (Miralejos 1998, 78). In an odd turn of events, Marta is killed by members of a satanic cult; soon thereafter, Tito resumes his affair with Jenny and they eventually marry. Professionally, Tito enjoys a considerable amount of success in his career as chairman of the national executive committee of New Era.

Lawrence Person has observed that "cyberpunk characters frequently seek to topple or exploit corrupt social orders." Postcyberpunk characters, by contrast "tend to seek ways to live in, or even strengthen, an existing social order, or help construct a better one." The characters in *Texas 2077* fit the latter pattern. The novel attempts to envision a society in which "the various social, political, and economic ills of the real world have been solved, leaving an ideal realm of justice and tranquility" (Booker and Thomas 2009, 75). The rise of New Era exemplifies the desire to improve conditions for the Latino community in the United States. Unity among Latinos is emphasized as a first step in enabling New Era to enact positive changes in American society. By bringing Latinos together on the basis of a shared cultural and ethnic background, New Era seeks to create a united front that will remain in the public eye and counter perceptions of Latinos as foreigners who are deprived of political representation and power.

Alternative Histories/Future Possibilities: La Raza Unida Party as Essentialist Specter

In some ways reminiscent of La Raza Unida party of the 1970s, the New Era political party in *Texas 2077* shares a similar perspective on uniting Latinos as a political bloc in which race and ethnicity are essential components of political action and mobilization. New Era seeks to garner support from the US Latino population, believing that group unity is necessary for Latino advancement. However, before achieving their goal of unity, the delegates of New Era recognize the need to "reduce to a minimum the infighting among the different nationalities within our Hispanic group" in order to present a "united Latino front" (Miralejos 1998, 47). Only then can New Era claim a share of political power and awaken the Latino sleeping giant. The symbol of the "giant," according to Cristina Beltrán, "represents the long-standing desire to be seen as a vital and inescapable part of the national political landscape"—as a constituency that has "earned its right to both representation and recognition" (2010, 5). Moreover, the giant "functions as a symbol of *presence*, a figure whose size makes it impossible to ignore and whose growing influence will surely impact every aspect of American cultural and political life" (5). The novel in many respects reinforces the idea that the growing Latino demographic will translate into a Latino political party striving for a common agenda. Yet the novel's futuristic vision fails to foresee some of the essentializing pitfalls of fashioning political unity on the slippery identity concept of *latinidad* and a presumed collective consciousness.

The idea of *latinidad* and the trope of the sleeping giant as its political embodiment raises critical issues that concern the blurring of the lines between the distinct Latino subgroups and wide-ranging ideological trajectories that have always existed among Latinos. As Beltrán suggests, the sleeping giant notion "implies a certain homogeneity—the belief that in some way crucial way, Latinos perceive themselves as part of some larger whole . . . with shared interests and a common policy agenda" (2010, 4). The discourse of Latino unity and the aspiration of mass mobilization can be ambiguous, given the inexistence of a consolidated Latino political group with a collective political conscious and will. In addition, all-encompassing identification markers like "Latino" or "Hispanic" do little to specify the subjects in question. As Beltrán notes:

> When referring to "Latinos in the United States," it is far from immediately clear whether the subjects under discussion are farmworkers living below the poverty line or middle-class homeowners, urban hipsters or rural evangelicals, white or black, gay or straight, Catholic or Jewish, undocumented Spanish monolinguals or fourth-generation speakers of English-only. (6)

This is not readily seen as a problem in the New Era political party, or in the novel as a whole. In the beginning chapters, delegates representing states with significant Latino populations (California, Arizona, New Mexico, Texas, New York, and Florida) convene in San Antonio and recognize that "infighting" among the different Latino groups must stop if they aspire to gain any political power. This compromise suggests that in order to become present in the national political arena, New Era must subscribe to the homogenizing concept of *latinidad* and "[mobilize] around a recognizable set of issues . . . to both secure federal resources and gain national exposure" (Beltrán 2010, 7). In fact, except for the first point demanding linguistic freedom of expression, the basic tenets under which New Era has organized make no mention of demands that address "Latino community" issues exclusively.[1] Seemingly, the early compromise between New Era delegates at the turn of the millennium yielded favorable results and made New Era the largest political party, with a number of constituents outside of the Latino community.

There are subtle indications in *Texas 2077* that the unifying effect of *latinidad* is less likely to influence first-generation Latinos than Latinos whose families have lived in the United States for generations. This comes to light during a strategizing session to attack a separate proposal to annex Texas to Mexico. Ruben, Tito's New Era colleague, affirms that while "many of our citizens are first generation Mexican-American . . . a great number of them would be happy to see Texas incorporated into Mexico" (Miralejos 1998, 85). Ruben's recognition of generational differences illustrates the complexities of pursuing unity based on race and ethnicity. Moreover, the generational divide brings to the forefront an equally important consideration that will be discussed later on identity and the connection to physical landscapes, in this case the US Southwest, and particularly Texas.

The novel highlights the fear produced by the notion of an awakening Latino giant and its potential to enact enduring changes to US society and culture. As mentioned before, the opening of *Texas 2077* portrays a Jewish organization's worries about "the power acquired by Hispanics in recent years" and the adverse effects this may have for "American-Jewish relations" (41–42). It is assumed that once in power, this homogenous Latino group with Catholic inclinations will cease all support for the Jewish state of Israel. Such a homogenizing depiction of Latinos disregards the cultural nuances and distinctions among them. In this the novel mirrors real life, where the rapid growth of the Latino population is understood by some Americans as a threat that will "undermine the country's unity and civic values" (Beltrán 2010, 7). Over a decade ago, Samuel P. Huntington warned in *Who Are We? The Challenge to America's National Identity* that the country is moving toward a "culturally bifurcated Anglo-Hispanic society with two national languages" (2004, 221). In large part, Huntington casts the blame on immigration trends:

> Mexican immigration is leading toward the demographic *reconquista* of areas Americans took from Mexico by force in the 1830s and 1840s, Mexicanizing them in a manner comparable to, although different from, the Cubanization that has occurred in southern Florida. It is also blurring the border between Mexico and America, introducing a very different culture, while also promoting the emergence, in some areas, of a blended society and culture, half-American and half-Mexican. Along

with immigration from other Latin American countries, it is advancing Hispanization throughout America and social, linguistic, and economic practices appropriate for an Anglo-Hispanic society. (221)

As Beltrán (2010, 7) notes, Huntington's "dystopian vision" of the Hispanization and gradual splitting of American society is based on the amalgamation of all Latino subgroups as a cohesive political entity with a common agenda. The fear that the sleeping giant will wake and tear the country apart is a prime example of how Huntington "both accepts and then deploys the logic of *Latinidad*" in order to "fan the flames of xenophobia" (8). Furthermore, Huntington puts forward the idea that mass immigration from Latin American has "reduced the incentives for cultural assimilation" (2004, 253). With respect to Mexican Americans, he asserts that they

> no longer think of themselves as members of a small minority who must accommodate the dominant group and adopt its culture. As their numbers increase, they become more committed to their own ethnic identity and culture. Sustained numerical expansion promotes cultural consolidation, and leads them not to minimize but to glory in the differences between their culture and American culture. (253)

Once more, Huntington refers to Latino cultural values as threatening to the Anglo-Protestant values on which the country was founded. Latinos are still perceived as "foreign" and as marked by certain traits that are not conducive to functioning successfully within modern American society. Yet the misguided views of Huntington and his denunciation of immigrant values as negative also contribute to the very outcome that he opposes: the consolidation of the Latino community. In other words, Beltrán writes,

> The internal logic of *Latinidad* is . . . also emotive and experiential. *Latinidad* is a historical practice constituted through the homogenizing effects of racism experienced by Latinos and other people of color. . . . Latino pan-ethnicity has been fostered by a climate of xenophobia in which the regional and cultural history of all people of Latin American descent has been erased. . . . Given this type of broad-based discrimination, it is unsurprising that *Latinidad* emerged as a productive response to prejudice and racial stereotyping. (2010, 7)

While the New Era party in *Texas 2077* attempts to incorporate a multicultural membership, it is still Latino-dominant and is predicated upon a nostalgic view of *latinidad* as more unified and less heterogeneous than it has ever been.

Postcyberpunk Mestizaje and La Raza Cósmica Redux

The cultural and racial dichotomy that Samuel P. Huntington envisions as the future of US society takes on a different dimension in *Texas 2077*. Whereas Huntington fears the bifurcating of language, culture, race, and the economic apparatus, *Texas 2077* depicts a dynamic cultural and racial syncretism. The speculative nature of *Texas 2077* makes "New Era" less a political party name than a signal of the inevitable changes that American society will undergo. In many ways reminiscent of José Vasconcelos's visionary text, *La raza cósmica*, and his theory of mestizaje, *Texas 2077* suggests that racial unity that transcends nationalisms will usher in a new epoch in American society, one that will afford Latinos a greater degree of political agency and a key role in determining the country's direction. This racially based utopian strategy for the unification of mestizo bodies is in harmony with Vasconcelos's own speculative ideas of mestizaje. Moreover, *Texas 2077*'s push for a utopian vision of unity brings to the forefront the many valences of mestizaje and shows how Chicano/Latino identity is embedded "within systems of asymmetrical power relations" that suggest "mutability as mestiza and mestizo bodies enact new relational subjectivities arising from a history of racial conflict" (Pérez-Torres 2006, 7). Accordingly, it is important to return to Vasconcelos's concept of mestizaje in order to analyze *Texas 2077*'s reading of Latino racial unity in future US society.

The end of the Mexican Revolution set the stage for the country to define a national identity. The Mexican intellectual José Vasconcelos (1882–1959) exemplified the educational aspirations of the revolutionary government; he was appointed first as chancellor of the National University (1920) and shortly thereafter as minister of education (1921–24). In his popular and controversial essay *La raza cósmica* (1925), Vasconcelos put forth his vision of a future civilization forged and inhabited by a "cosmic race" that is a synthesis of the world's major races. In the essay, the concept of mestizaje refers to the process of cultural and biological mixing of all "races" in the creation of the "mestizo."[2] As a result, the national mestizo identity exalts the indigenous origins of the country and subsequent Spanish influence, though it pointedly does not embrace Mexico's African heritage. This newly formed national identity was welcomed by many Mexicans, particularly those in larger cities.

Vasconcelos's utopian vision in *La raza cósmica* extended beyond Mexico's borders. He saw all of Latin America as the site of synthesis of the mestizo, a transcendent figure and the future heir to modern civilizations.

However, before Mexico could reach that point, according to Vasconcelos, it was imperative that "inferior races" be educated by "superior" ones and "integrated" into the larger society. This is the most controversial aspect of his essay, as he suggests that mestizaje not only unifies the country but also directly subsumes the distinctions or traits of people of indigenous and African descent. Vasconcelos's mestizo ideology favored the rapid integration of all ethnic communities: it was an attempt to unify the people of Mexico based on a shared indigenous past and modernize the marginalized communities that are categorized as inferior in order to incorporate them into society. This was to be done in part by state-sponsored educational projects known as cultural missions. Claude Fell (1989, 149) writes that Vasconcelos perceived the cultural missions' socializing function as providing the provinces an escape from their lethargy or "cultural numbness" (*adormecimiento cultural*) and gradually incorporating them into national society. Although the ideology of mestizaje was seen as a way to break ties with a strictly European worldview, the term perpetuated an ideology that favored the "whitening" of indigenous and Afro-Mexican communities by state action.

In the section titled "Mestizaje," Vasconcelos draws from pseudo-scientific racial theory and exalts "Anglo" science as an essential tool in the creation of the cosmic race. Yet in his introduction to the bilingual edition of *La raza cósmica*, translator Didier T. Jaén writes that one of the reasons Vasconcelos's text is constantly criticized is due to the misreading of the essay as scientific or sociological in nature (Vasconcelos 1979, xiii). Jaén states that *La raza cósmica* should be evaluated for its vision of a new era of humanity and as an inspired call to the nations of Latin America to take the lead in creating the cosmic race (xiii). In addition, he stresses that science was not the means to develop Vasconcelos's vision; rather, the "spiritual" factor would be the vehicle of this cosmic movement. Along the same lines, Enrique Krauze writes that "*La raza cósmica* is not a utopia. It does not propose a clear social structure, rules for social harmony . . . and perpetual peace. It is, in the biblical sense of the term, *a vision*" (1984, 41; my translation, my emphasis).

Although Vasconcelos insists on a mestizo ideology, he looks with great admiration upon the technological advances of North American civilization and believes that this will have a major role in the final synthesis of the cosmic race (Vasconcelos 1979, 23). The favoring of a particular type of "knowledge" over another is clearly seen in his essay. In creating his vision, Vasconcelos opts for a Western philosophy that exalts science as a beneficial tool. Similarly, Vasconcelos advocates for North American contributions as fundamental, without considering the contributions of marginalized nonwhite communities:

> Latin America owes what it is to the white European, and is not going to deny him. . . . However, we accept the superior ideals of the Whites but not their arrogance. We want to offer them, as well as to all other peoples, a free country where they will find a home and a refuge, but not a continuation of their conquests. (Vasconcelos 1979, 23)

While reaffirming "white superiority," Vasconcelos decides, ironically, not to accept the white man's "arrogance." His racial theory is not a mere scientific methodology but, according to him, a moral action for the elimination of racial hierarchies such as those observed in the United States (Vasconcelos 2011, 100). Vasconcelos believed that his racial theory of mestizaje, the process of cultural and biological mixing, contrasted favorably with racial segregation practices in Mexico's northern neighbor. Citing Catholic influences, he argued that the Spanish treated the indigenous and African populations more humanely than ethnic minorities were treated in the United States, and he believed that racial mixing in Mexico would eliminate prejudice and racial hierarchies. However, his proposal for mestizaje suggests another purpose as well, namely to eliminate racial traits that he considered inferior and an obstacle to the synthesis of his cosmic race:

> The lower types of the species will be absorbed by the superior type. In this manner, for example, the Black could be redeemed, and step by step, by voluntary extinction, the uglier stocks will give way to the more handsome. Inferior races, upon being educated, would become less prolific, and the better specimens would go on ascending a scale of ethnic improvement. (Vasconcelos 1979, 30)

In promoting his project of mestizaje, Vasconcelos remained hopeful that the positive aspects of each race would be accentuated and the negative would be erased. However, the idea that certain characteristics of the races would be visible and others suppressed problematizes Vasconcelos's intention to create a population where everyone is equal. Vasconcelos was not a "prophet" in terms of race relations. He was, however, a visionary who saw the future according to his present circumstances, which were those of someone with a relatively high social position. During the reconstruction of Mexican society, Vasconcelos wanted to universalize all races in Mexico without distinction of diversity. Yet there was an undeniable favoring of Western ideals and technology in his vision that disminished the importance of alternative forms of knowledge, especially indigenous epistemologies.

A close reading of *Texas 2077* reveals numerous echoes of the ideas put forth in *La raza cósmica*, though it is unclear whether this is an intentional nod to Vasconcelos by the author.[3] At the opening of the novel, the New Era delegates who convene in San Antonio respond to allegations that Latinos can also discriminate:

> Latinos are the least racist of all the ethnic groups making up this society. A Latino or Hispanic person could be of practically any race or mix of races, our identity is based on a multitude of characteristics, like language, country of origin, Spanish heritage, and surname. A Latino could be white and of European extraction, could be Black, could be Amerindian, or could be of Asiatic extraction. (Miralejos 1998, 46)

The claim that a Latino can encompass all "races" situates these characters within the notion of the "cosmic race." These New Era delegates believe that through their united efforts they will not only change the course of US politics but create a society in which Latinos become key players in the future of the country. Indeed, the New Era becomes the largest political party by 2077 by building an alliance between all members of the Latino community, transcending cultural and national origin differences. Essentially, unity is created by the mere fact of being "brown." Even though Latinos have become the largest ethnic group in the country, however, there is still push-back from non-Latino community members who continue to perceive Latinos as foreigners regardless of their citizenship status. For instance, at one point in the novel, Tito is held hostage in Mexico by an Anglo gang lord, Maxwell, who asks, "Aren't you glad to be in your native country?" (Miralejos 1998, 199). Tito responds by affirming his many generations of Texas heritage, but Maxwell retorts, "Sure, all the Chicanos say the same thing. I don't trust any of you . . . You will never be one of us. You aren't American, you're a fucking Mexican. Nothing but dirt" (200). Another example of the anti-Latino sentiment is surely the Texas independent movement led by the governor, who is not pleased with the direction of the Union. Ironically, Texas has always had a significant Latino presence, and unless the governor were to seek their expulsion, Texan independence would not necessarily resolve his racial anxiety. In other words, the Latinization of the United States in the novel has provoked reactionary efforts to retain at any cost the Anglo-Protestant values that Samuel P. Huntington fears will one day disappear.

As it turns out, the unification of Latinos has also positively affected transnational relations with Latin America. The transnational alliances of this new era are illustrated by the relatively effortless way in which New Era members engage and partner with Mexicans, including the president of Mexico. There is an underlying mutual respect as a result of a shared racial and historical background. In fact, when the fictional President Carvajal of Mexico is courted by a group of Chicano entrepreneurs to accept the proposal for the return of Texas to Mexico through annexation, he respectfully declines, because although regaining Texas would heal a grave historical wound, he sees no need to jeopardize the relationship between the two countries. Furthermore, the Mexican president shares the historical perspective of the journey that Chicanos/Mexicanos have taken to get to this point in time. He tells his guests that

> it took a long time, and the sweat and perseverance of countless Mexican peasants to produce what you are. You, and millions like you, are the product of a historical event of giant proportions. For more than two centuries the Mexican people have endured discrimination in our own land, we have been ignored as if we never existed, we had worked hard and long for meager salaries. Now, at the end of our journey, we cannot afford to be in a hurry. (Miralejos 1998, 74)

President Carvajal thus not only reaffirms the unity between the two groups of mestizos but also signals that Chicanos/Latinos have reached the "end" of their journey, in other words, the end of their struggle. The way that he traces the journey of the mestizo body reminds us of how the "racialized body in Chicano/a culture evokes a kind of historical consciousness. The body is the physical manifestation of a long, difficult, and constantly evolving colonial history" (Pérez-Torres 2006, 197). At this point in *Texas 2077* it would seem as though Vasconcelos's utopian visions of mestizaje have been realized.

Another element of *La raza cósmica* in Miralejos's novel that points to the science fiction nature of the text is the role of technology. Yet rather than focus on the mundane technological applications in Tito's life, the novel shows how the syncretism of Western technology and Indohispanic spiritualism come together to save the Earth from an apocalyptic event. According to Jacinto, an Itzae on the Yucatan peninsula, an asteroid eleven miles across, named the Golden Phoenix, is on a collision course with Earth and will strike in sixty-six years. Jacinto recounts that the Golden Phoenix came close to colliding with Earth in 2523 BC but that this time it will definitely do so. Tito reluctantly asks what he can do to help and is told that he must convince the leaders of the United States to organize a campaign to "shoot it down" (Miralejos 1998, 109). This scene evokes Vasconcelos's admiration for the technological advances of North American civilization and his belief that it would have a major role in the final synthesis of the cosmic race. The mestizaje that occurs between Western technology and Indohispanic spiritualism signifies here the salvation of the planet and further represents the power in the processes of mestizaje.

As Rafael Pérez-Torres writes, "Mestizaje finds its very power in its evo-cation of historical and social conditions in which Chicanos and Mestizas in the Americas live. More, it is those conditions *lived in the body* that make mestizaje such a powerful trope in understanding Chicano and Chicana culture and identity" (2006, 70, emphasis in original). Vasconcelos's utopian visions of unity and mestizaje in *La raza cósmica* come with their own set of controversial ideological positionings, and they are a reminder that unity and race among Latinos is not as clear-cut and simple as it is represented in *Texas 2077*. However, Carlos Miralejos's speculative text does contribute to discussion of the transformative power of mestizaje as a path toward unity. Moreover, in opting for a speculative style, *Texas 2077* recasts important issues of colonialism and postcolonialism, as well as Chicano/Latino his-torical processes of mestizaje, as survival tactics. All are experiences that need to be told, especially within science fiction. While this genre has not traditionally been the preferred mode of expression for Chicano/Latino authors, they are now increasingly expanding its limits.

Notes

1. The following are the basic tenets of the New Era political party: "(1) The Government can't force anyone to speak a specific language. (2) The Govern-ment can't force anyone not to smoke or drink. (3) Tax rate on liquor or tobacco products can't be different from the general sales' tax rate. (4) The Government can't apply adult laws and court procedures to minors. It doesn't matter how heinous the crime. And, we believe that the laws and procedures applicable to minors must be overhauled. (5) The age of adulthood must be the same for all states and must apply to all privileges, obligations, and penalties. (6) Cloning can't be prohibited. But any clone creation procedure must be reported ahead of time. All clones must be registered. Criminals can't be cloned. (7) Cyborgs are citizens, robots are not. (8) Media reporters must pay for answers! Answers should be copyright protected" (Miralejos 1998, 124; numbering added).

2. According to seventeenth-century caste system and its racial categories, a mestizo person was of "mixed Spanish and Indian descent." There were also a variety of categories for people of African descent: *negro, mulato, morisco, lobo, coyote, chino.*

3. I made numerous efforts to contact the author to ask about his intentions, but had no luck in finding any contact information beyond the P.O. box supplied for ordering the novel. It is not even certain whether "Carlos Miralejos" is his real name or a pen name, one whose literal meaning ("looks far") would fittingly describe the speculative style of his texts.

Works Cited

Beltrán, Cristina. 2010. *The Trouble with Unity: Latino Politics and the Creation of Identity.* New York: Oxford University Press.

Booker, M. Keith, and Anne-Marie Thomas. 2009. *The Science Fiction Handbook.* Malden, MA: Wiley-Blackwell.

Fell, Claude. 1989. *José Vasconcelos: Los años del águila (1920–1925).* Mexico City: UNAM.

Huntington, Samuel P. 2004. *Who Are We? The Challenges to America's National Identity.* New York: Simon & Schuster.

Krauze, Enrique. 1984. "El caudillo Vasconcelos." In *José Vasconcelos: De su vida y su obra,* edited by Álvaro Matute and Martha Donís. Mexico City: UNAM.

Miralejos, Carlos. 1998. *Texas 2077: A Futuristic Novel.* Daytona Beach, FL: Outer Space.

Pérez-Torres, Rafael. 2006. *Mestizaje: Critical Uses of Race in Chicano Culture.* Minneapolis: University of Minnesota Press.

Person, Lawrence. 1998. "Notes Towards a Postcyberpunk Manifesto." *Nova Express,* no. 16. Reposted on Slashdot.org, October 9, 1999.

Vasconcelos, José. 1979. *The Cosmic Race/La raza cósmica.* Translated by Didier T. Jaén. Los Angeles: Centro de Publicaciones, Department of Chicano Studies, California State University, Los Angeles. Originally published as *La raza cósmica: Misión de la raza iberoamericana: Notas de viajes a la América de Sur.* Paris: Agencia Mundial de Librería, 1925. Citations refer to the 1979 edition.

———. 2011. "The Race Problem in Latin America." In *José Vasconcelos: The Prophet of Race,* edited by Ilán Stavans, 91–111. New Brunswick, NJ: Rutgers University Press.

Engineering Afro-Latina and Mexican Immigrant Heroines

Biopolitics in Borderlands Speculative Literature and Film

Isabel Millán

> Under biopolitics, life itself becomes the object of political governance,
> and political governance becomes the practice of steering the
> biological life of individuals and species.
> —Sherryl Vint, "Introduction: Science Fiction and Biopolitics"

If steering biological life is an example of political governance, can science fiction become a space in which to envision life as resilience? Catherine S. Ramírez theorizes science fiction as a "creative and politicized 'space' for the articulation of the pasts, presents, and possible futures of the 'aliens' and passport-less of the New World" (2002, 375). She popularized Chicanafuturism by tracing its intersections with and divergences from Afrofuturism, noting that "while Afrofuturism reflects diasporic experience, Chicanafuturism articulates colonial and postcolonial histories" (Ramírez 2004, 78). Despite Ramírez's productive distinctions between Chicanafuturism and Afrofuturism, I am interested in merging them in my comparative analysis of Afro-Latina and Chicana heroines in science fiction and fantasy.

Specifically, I compare Jacqueline Carey's speculative fiction character Loup Garron with cinematic figure María Isabel "Isa" Reyes in order to gauge their resonance and potential impact within broader Afro-Latin@, Latin@, and Chican@ speculative narratives. While Loup Garron may be read as Afro-Latina, queer, and lacking the ability to feel fear, Isa Reyes is depicted as a Mexican immigrant whose abilities include merging her dream world with reality. In her fantasy fiction novels *Santa Olivia* (2009)

279

and *Saints Astray* (2011), Carey challenges readers to question the US values that necessitate a humanist retort. The plot is set in Outpost No. 12, a near-future dystopia geographically located on the US-Mexico border. Garron's DNA has been genetically altered and kept secret by the US military. In contrast, José Néstor Márquez's science fiction film *ISA* (2014) depicts Reyes with an implanted chip in one side of her brain. She is one of many individuals monitored and exploited by billion-dollar corporations. Both youths seek answers about their pasts and about those responsible for engineering them into their current forms. I suggest that the engineering and potential disposability of Chicana/Latina/Afro-Latina heroines as noncitizens within these border dystopias parallel current US-Mexico bio/border politics of displacement, violence, and dismissal.

Embedded within the seemingly absurd or idiosyncratic storytelling of speculative fiction is a means to center counternormative characters such as Garron and Reyes, who challenge contemporary border politics. I use *speculative* as an umbrella term for science fiction, fantasy fiction, and other fictions that blur the lines between what we may consider plausible or impossible. It encompasses, specifically, Catherine Ramírez's term *Chicanafuturism*, which builds on and is always already entangled in productive ways with Afrofuturism (2002, 2004, 2006, 2008). In her survey of Afrofuturism, Ramírez (2002, 2008) highlights the instrumental work of Octavia Butler, including *Kindred* (1979), *Wild Seed* (1980), *Dawn* (1987), and *Parable of the Sower* (1995). Although many of the earlier works now considered at the root of Afrofuturism were published in the 1980s, cultural critic Mark Dery (1993, 736) coined the term in the early 1990s (see also Womack 2013, 16). Afrofuturist texts "use science fiction themes, such as abduction, slavery, displacement, and alienation, to renarrate the past, present, and future of the African diaspora" (Ramírez 2008, 186). An expanded survey of Chican@futurism can encompass Marion C. Martinez's circuit board art that Ramírez so deftly explicates, as well as Rosaura Sánchez and Beatrice Pita's 2009 novel *Lunar Braceros, 2125–2148*, Alex Rivera's film *Sleep Dealer* (2008), and Juan Felipe Herrera's picture book for children, *Super Cilantro Girl/La Superniña del Cilantro* (2003). Each deals with major themes such as alienation and exploitation. Within popular media, there is a plethora of images of whiteness on screen, while people of color are relegated to the margins, women are commonly depicted as passive or victims, and queer characters are often humiliated and bullied. In this context, characters such as Loup and Isa become all the more vital and urgently needed as protagonists.

In relationship to Afrofuturism and Chicanafuturism, I view Loup Garron and Isa Reyes as examples of Ramírez's paradigmatic characters who interrogate "the promises of science and technology" by redefining "humanism and the human" (Ramírez 2004, 78). Afrofuturism, as further theorized by Alondra Nelson, "reflect[s] African diasporic experience and at the same time attend[s] to the transformations that are the by-product of new media and information technology" (2002, 9). These byproducts may include technological waste that the nation-state finds disposable, such as Loup, who is a technological byproduct of government experimentation on her father, Martin, and the rest of the Lost Boys. They may also include new commodities such as Isa, who becomes of value to an unnamed transnational corporation once she is rediscovered as a youth. These protagonists represent many of the marginalized individuals who are exploited, subjected to experimentation, or disposed of after their use value is extracted. Such practices in the real world have included medical apartheid and forced sterilizations as well as ongoing femicides across the Americas, in which bodies marked as feminine, of color, indigenous, queer, poor, differently abled, or undocumented become targets of institutional violence.[1] Within their speculative dystopian worlds, Loup Garron and Isa Reyes succeed in seeking out justice; they provide the possibility of freedom or escape and transformation, along with the prospect that those responsible will eventually be held accountable. Beyond their individual actions and unique abilities, they reflect a broader critique of biopower, where "biopolitics deals with the population, with the population as political problem, as a problem that is at once scientific and political, as a biological problem and as power's problem" (Foucault 2003, 245). Loup and Isa become "power's problem" through embodiment and through the spaces they navigate.

Engineering (Bio)Powers

Within science fiction and fantasy, a living organism engineered or altered into existence usually holds a contentious relationship with its creators, especially if the organism is imprisoned or exploited against its will. Popular examples include Alice of the video game and film series *Resident Evil* (Anderson 2002), or Sarah Manning of the television series *Orphan Black* (Manson and Fawcett 2013). Similarly, both Loup Garron and María Isabel Reyes exist in their current forms because powerful entities such as states and corporations experimented on humans. These entities exert their dominance in the form of global power or global wealth. The "governmentalities" described by Michel Foucault as practices associated with the "gradual, piecemeal, but continuous takeover by the state" (2008, 77) can also be extended to corporations, because like the state, corporations also wield power and exploit their labor force. Loup Garron and Isa Reyes threaten these regimes of power by actively mobilizing against them in their efforts to unmask their biological origins and the attendant servitude and exploitation.

In Jacqueline Carey's first speculative novel featuring Loup Garron, *Santa Olivia* (2009), Loup is depicted as different not solely because of how she is racialized, gendered, or sexualized, but because of her supernatural abilities. In "La Prieta," Gloria Anzaldúa writes, "The whole time growing up I felt that I was not of this earth. An alien from another planet—I'd been dropped on my mother's lap. But for what purpose?" (1981, 199). Similarly, Loup Garron realizes that she does not quite belong in Outpost No. 12. She stands out among those around her because of her inability to feel fear, along with her overwhelming strength and agility. Loup, after all, is a hybrid or offspring of a human and a GMO—a genetically modified organism (Carey 2009, 22). As a result of government experimentations, which I will discuss below, Loup's father Martin and other GMOs are unable to experience fear even as they exhibit extraordinary strength, speed, and endurance. While fearless soldiers may be beneficial to those who engineered them into existence, fear is also a survival mechanism, and these GMOs must make up for the lack of it by learning how to be "extra careful" in order to properly decipher their surroundings in anticipation of possible danger (23).

Based on passages in the book, I read Loup Garron as Afro-Latina and queer. We might also describe her as Afro-Chicana or Mexican American and Haitian, and as bisexual or lesbian. Loup's race or ethnicity is never explicitly stated, however, and the only images of her in the novels are the book cover silhouettes (figs. 1, 2). From conversations between Loup's parents, Carmen and Martin, readers discover that Carmen is Mexican American and bilingual in English and Spanish. Martin was born on a barren island, La Gonâve, in Haiti, and is unlike anyone Carmen had ever met. Carmen initially reads Martin as African American until he speaks with an unrecognizable accent. She asks, "Where do you come from and where are you going? Where were you even born? 'Cause I know it's not America. I can hear it in your voice, man. I've heard a hundred thousand different soldiers' accents, and yours isn't one of them" (20). Carmen and Martin's time together is short-lived, as he has to flee once he is discovered by the Outpost military. Before his departure, he requests that Carmen name

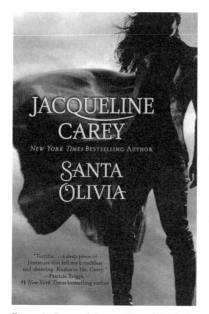

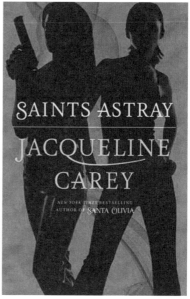

Figure 1. *Cover of* Santa Olivia *(2009), by Jacqueline Carey.*

Figure 2. *Cover of* Saints Astray *(2011), by Jacqueline Carey.*

the baby Loup, French for wolf. Her full name, Loup Garron, resembles the French term for werewolf, *loup-garou*. I also read Loup as a play on Lupe, short for Guadalupe, which invokes the Virgin of Guadalupe.

Martin passes on his genetic alterations to Loup. Even her birth is unusual. She is born on Santa Olivia day, the annual festival in celebration of the town's patron saint, Santa Olivia, a child-saint who allegedly ended a prior war. Without warning, Carmen Garron's water breaks, and with the assistance of Sister Martha, Carmen gives birth to Loup in the middle of the town square. Loup is described in the novel as

> a cute baby with caramel-colored skin, a thatch of black hair and black eyes like her father. . . . It wasn't until her eyes began to focus that Carmen was sure. In her round cherub's face, those eyes were as steady and fearless as the effigy of Santa Olivia the child-saint, just like her father's had been. (42)

Unsure of how much the infant will resemble her father, Carmen murmurs, "Loup Garron. . . . What are you gonna be, wolf-cub?" (42).

Loup stands out more as she grows older: "While Loup was between the ages of two and five, the differences that marked her grew more pronounced.

She was an agile, darting child, curious and fearless; and yet when she was still, it was an unchildlike stillness" (43). Loup's older brother Tommy becomes responsible for teaching her to be careful. Their bond fills Carmen with "secret pride and hidden fear. She adored her responsible son and her strange, fearless daughter with a deep, aching ferocity" (43). Yet this also frightens her: "She was terrified that word would get out that she'd borne a daughter to a man who wasn't wholly human, a man the government wanted to catch" (43–44). Indeed, unlike her daughter, Carmen is overwhelmingly fearful—that someone will "unearth her secrets . . . that one day there would be soldiers on their doorstep to take her baby away to a laboratory" (44).

Loup is nationless both because her mother is a denizen of Outpost and because her father is property of the US government. If discovered, Loup also runs the risk of being stripped of her humanity and becoming US-government property. Loup's older brother, Tommy, adds another layer of complexity to this family. He is named after his father, Tom, who was a solider stationed at Outpost No. 12. Tom was white, had blond hair, and grew up as a farm boy in Minnesota. Tom's strong desire to marry Carmen after they discovered she was pregnant posed a threat to this military space because it was illegal for soldiers to marry locals. His sudden death caused Carmen to suspect that he was murdered by the military. Carmen eventually gave birth to a baby boy with blue eyes and named him Tommy. He is seven years older than Loup, and despite all their differences, the siblings remain close up until Tommy's death.

Similar to those who lack recognizable citizenship, queer bodies pose a threat to power when they cannot be confined within homonormativity. In her synthesis of biopolitics, Jasbir K. Puar argues that "queerness as automatically and inherently transgressive enacts specific forms of disciplining and control, erecting celebratory queer liberal subjects folded into life (queerness as subject) against the sexually pathological and deviant populations targeted for death (queerness as population)" (2007, 24). Puar's formulation serves as an apt prism through which to read Loup's deviant embodiment. As Loup Garron matures, she begins to explore her body and becomes curious about others. Her muscles do not feel like those of others around her. Hers seem to generate something equivalent to an electrifying pulsation. She notices that some individuals are deeply repelled by her while others are uncontrollably drawn to her. She also discovers that, like her mother's attraction to her father, her own GMO abilities include sexual agility and the ability to evoke an overpowering sexual response from others.

Her inability to experience fear also makes her unusually oblivious toward the potential prejudices of others, including homophobia, allowing her to fall in love with another girl, Pilar Ecchevarria. Pilar, who had only dated boys or young men, suddenly finds herself unable to resist Loup.

While Loup Garron is born with her genetic alterations, Isa Reyes is altered as a child. Initially Isa has no recollection of her childhood. "Do you remember stuff when you were little? Like when you were three or four years old?" she asks her best friend Nataly Gómez. "Some stuff," Nataly replies. Isa sighs, "I don't remember anything. Not one thing." Isa does not remember in part because a portion of her childhood was stolen from her by those who encapsulated her in order to exploit her dreams. The audience is unaware of the full duration of Isa's capture; however, she was five years old when discovered and released by her father. Isa likely also has PTSD (post-traumatic stress disorder): her body's incubation period was followed by an abrupt awakening to the sight of a man slashing a machete in her direction, after which she was given to coyotes to embark on a journey across the Mexico-US border.

Isa does not discover her abilities until high school, when she is accidently hit by a car while jogging. As she lies in the middle of the street unconscious, with her eyes closed but visibly moving back and forth under her eyelids, and with her earphones still in place, the audience catches a glimpse of her cellphone, which reads, "PAIRED. CONNECTING." Meanwhile, the film cuts, first to an image of a little girl holding someone's hand, then to a man waving a machete, and then to a series of radio and cell towers, ending with one overlooking a building surrounded by a vast forest. Two men monitoring desktop computers become alarmed as an unknown input, "input seven," momentarily connects to their program. Isa gains consciousness in a hospital, where a CT scan reveals an unusual pattern on the right side of her brain: "Did the patient say she had an implant?" asks one of the doctors. "No, why is that flickering?" "I don't know. It looks like radio interference." Moreover, the doctors notify Isa that the scar behind her right ear could not have resulted from a car accident, as her aunt and uncle had led her to believe. Upon hearing the news, Nataly teases Isa, "It all makes sense. The way you are always so good at math and stuff. This whole time. It's that thing in your brain. You're a mutant!"

Isa's accident has alerted her makers to her existence and potential financial benefits. Dedál, the lead scientist, discovers that Isa is one of her former test subjects: "Input seven must be seventeen by now. She was stolen when she was five. She appears to remember nothing, but she's searching, digging around. The chip is reaching out; interfacing with the system. I have to find my way back in; a weakness, a fear." Dedál's reference to Isa's being "stolen" does not correspond to the moment her project kidnapped Isa from her biological parents, but rather the moment her father found and freed her from the scientist's experiment. Dedál also discovers Isa's ability to merge her dream world with her reality:

> A normal child learns to distinguish between dream and reality by the age of four. Input seven must lack that ability. She doesn't understand the difference. The chip processes everything. Conscious and unconscious. Dream and reality. That's why it's so powerful. It can't last. The chip is going to burn out. I have to capture the output before it does.

Dedál continues, "The code on the chip has evolved. It could corrupt the system. But the new system, the one that survives, will be better. Progress requires sacrifice." Dedál's scientific endeavors in the name of progress require the literal sacrifice of bodies deemed disposable, whose dreams can be exploited across a global electronic trading platform. Yet, Isa is also discovering her abilities, and she attempts to share her knowledge of them with Nataly:

> ISA: The thing the doctor showed me. That thing that's inside my brain. I think it's doing something to me. It's not bad, it's not bad, okay. I've been having these amazing dreams, Nataly. They're not dreams. They're more like memories. Like, there's this program and I'm rewriting it as it runs. I can change it. I can make things happen. Real things. I made this. It's encoded. These are the coordinates.
>
> NATALY: We should go.
>
> ISA: Go where?
>
> NATALY: To the hospital. To make sure everything's okay.
>
> ISA: They're not going to believe me. I wouldn't believe me!
>
> NATALY: But you could be bleeding, or worse!
>
> ISA: I'm not, I'm better!

Nataly's initial disbelief leaves Isa no choice but to proceed on her own. If her own best friend did not believe her, it is unlikely anyone else will. Instead, she tells Nataly, "I love you," and walks away. Isa's tech-savvy skills lead her through a maze of questions surrounding her unknown birth parents, her place of birth, and the scar behind her right ear, which reveals the presence of a hidden chip implanted in her brain. With the eventual help of Nataly and rebellious Officer Jaime Díaz, Isa combats the scientists and global corporations responsible for engineering her and the other entrapped children who are being monitored and whose dreams are extracted for profit.

While readers of the *Santa Olivia* series are primarily guided by the textual descriptions of the literary character Loup Garron, the audiovisual elements within *ISA* provide additional details about Isa Reyes and the rest of the cast (fig. 3). Isa's own understanding of herself is convoluted. The story her Tía María and Tío José had told her about her parents was not true. Isa and her parents were not from Arizona, and they did not die in a car accident when she was a child. She discloses to Nataly, "My tío said that I was, that I was brought over by immigrants. I wasn't born here. He says that's all they know." While the publicity for *ISA* markets the protagonist as an "All-American Girl," we might also view this as a centering of Mexican and indigenous immigrant experiences, depending on how we read Isa or her biological parents. Moreover, her character is played by Jeanette Samano, whose profile on IMDb (Internet Movie Database) lists her as "Latin/Hispanic, Mixed, Native American."[2] What is clear from the backdrop is that Isa lives in a working-class Chican@ neighborhood in Los Angeles. Her aunt and uncle primarily speak to her in Spanish although they understand her when she responds in English. Isa's aunt is blind, which provides an additional avenue for communicating, since being blind is not depicted as an impairment within the film; on the contrary, her aunt teaches Isa to read

Figure 3. Isa Reyes in a dream sequence. Film still from ISA *(2014), directed by José Néstor Márquez. Reproduced by permission of Fluency Films.*

Braille, which becomes an asset that will help her decipher a code leading to Mexico. Their home also includes several references to Catholicism, such as images of la Virgen de Guadalupe in Isa's room. Finally, Isa's peers were cast in order to reflect LA's diverse multicultural backgrounds. For example, Nataly Gómez is played by Sabi, a Salvadoran and African American singer and actor. Within the film, viewers catch a glimpse of stickers on her notebook that say "El Salvador" or depict the Salvadoran flag. She is also bilingual in English and Spanish, challenging anyone who may have initially read her as African American but not Latina. Additional friends include Big Boy, played by Filipino American actor Timothy DeLaGhetto.

The states and corporations behind Loup Garron's and Isa Reyes's current abilities will not be content until both protagonists are once again under their control. They engineered each of them for a particular purpose. Within the *Santa Olivia* series, GMOs were meant to serve as advanced military soldiers, while in *ISA*, children's dreams were harvested as a way to gain economic global power. Loup and Isa were meant to be commodities, disposable once their exploitation was complete and their use value exhausted. Instead, they prove to be potent obstacles for those who originally engineered them.

Geopolitics: The Malleability of Borders and Intangibility of Space

Defining a space usually includes setting parameters or borders. These are rarely permanent, often porous, and can shift over time. Juana María Rodríguez suggests:

> It is the time-space matrix that is most useful to an analysis of site-specific practices. Such an understanding requires an analysis of the relationships within and between different localized discursive sites, different disciplines, different sites of knowledge production. (2003, 32)

In what follows, I map out critical spaces within the *Santa Olivia* book series and the film *ISA* that shape each protagonist, yet are also molded or bent out of shape by Loup Garron and Isa Reyes. "Biopolitics' last domain," according to Foucault, "is control over relations between the human race, or human beings insofar as they are a species, insofar as they are living beings, and their environment, the milieu in which they live" (2003, 244–45). This control of mass populations is facilitated through the control of space, where borders become militarized and border crossers—such as Loup and Isa—become enemies of those in control.

Loup Garron's personal history is influenced by the political climate prior to her birth: the world was at war, and uncontrollable sickness and death erupted in waves all around the globe. Specifically, the United States was at war with China. The Chinese government had created a scientific laboratory in Haiti where they experimented on the Haitian population in an attempt to manufacture genetically modified soldiers. Scientists succeeded in spawning twenty genetically modified boys from this lab. When the boys were approximately eight years old, US forces raided the lab, taking the boys into custody, only to further imprison, study, and train them to be soldiers during the next ten years. The boys eventually managed to escape from the US government, plotting to reunite in Mexico. Loup's father and the other GMOs were referred to in the tabloids as the "Lost Boys"; they were described as "artificial werewolves spawned in secret laboratories" and as "an army of ravening wolf-men poised at America's back door" (Carey 2009, 22). However, despite rumors of their existence, the US government publicly denied any knowledge of these men.

Simultaneously, the United States was also at war with Mexico and blamed Mexico for spreading the disease epidemic. As a result, the US government did two things. First, it built a permanent wall on its southern border with Mexico. This episode evokes the political rhetoric and panic that erupted in our own world only a few years ago in response to H1N1 influenza, or "swine flu," a discourse that Sherryl Vint describes as conflating the "management of borders, disease vectors and agricultural trade with speculative fantasies about invader species and zombie plagues" (2011, 161). And second, the US government created pockets along this wall to function as military buffer zones or outposts, such as Outpost No. 12, which was once a border town in Texas named Santa Olivia. Upon the military's arrival, their highest in command, General Argyle, gave the citizens of Santa Olivia the choice to stay or leave. However, many were poor, ill, and dying, with nowhere else to go, so most remained. Not until the wall was being constructed did the military announce:

> "We are at war! This is no longer a part of Texas, no longer a part of the United States of America! You are in the buffer zone! You are no longer American citizens! By consenting to remain, you have agreed to this! The town of Santa Olivia no longer exists! You are denizens of Outpost No. 12!" (Carey 2009, 2)

At the center of Outpost No. 12 is the town square. It is surrounded by homes and businesses, as well as a gym and a church. The military base within Outpost No. 12 occupies an additional buffer zone between these marginal spaces and US territory. All of these spaces prove integral to the plot, establishing a set of hierarchies between characters, where Loup oscillates between being invisible, marginalized, or hypervisible.

Within Outpost, there are two semiautonomous spaces where Loup will spend considerable time in order to challenge the military. The first is the gym. Originally a family fitness center called Unique Fitness, it was turned into a boxing club after the military arrived (46). It is managed by "the Coach," Floyd Roberts, who is the "only guy in Outpost who didn't have to stay if he doesn't want" (46). He trains residents of Outpost who want to fight against General Argyle's men. Anyone who wins one of these prize fights is promised two tickets out of the military buffer zone. No one, however, has ever won, since it is said that the general chooses Olympic champions to fight on his behalf. However, the residents of Outpost do not know that the general also uses GMOs to fight more promising boxers. Below the coach in the gym's hierarchy is Miguel Garza, a resident who shows great potential as a prizewinning boxer but lacks commitment to his training. Below him are the older fighters who have fought and lost against the general's men. And below them in this hierarchy are the younger men in training who hope to one day win their way out of Outpost. This is Tommy's greatest desire as well, and since Loup was expelled from school the very first day for challenging the teacher, they spend their time at the gym instead.

At this point in the narrative, Tommy is thirteen, and his sister Loup is six years old. However, she is already stronger and faster than anyone around her. Her solid gaze tends to attract a lot of attention, as does her physicality. Moreover, anyone who touches her can literally *feel* that she is different. Out of concern, Tommy continues to teach her how to be careful, how to not draw attention to herself, and how to hide from others when necessary. The gym is also significant because Tommy's training ultimately qualifies him for a boxing match against one of the general's men. Loup tries to warn her brother that he is fighting against another GMO, Johnson, but she is unsuccessful, and Johnson accidentally kills Tommy in the boxing ring.

The second semiautonomous space in Outpost No. 12 is the church. Loup Garron calls it her new home after her mother dies. At the church of Santa Olivia, Loup joins the other orphans, or Santitos. This church is unique in that Father Ramon Perez is not actually a priest, nor is Sister Martha Stearns an actual nun. Everyone in Outpost knows and chooses to ignore this, along with the intimate relationship between the two, because of the services they provide, including mass, a free clinic, and free meals. In time, we also discover that Father Ramon and Sister Martha live in a polyamorous relationship with a third person, Anna, who is the teacher at the orphanage. It is at the church that Loup begins to impersonate Santa Olivia by doing good deeds throughout Outpost with the help of the other Santitos. These deeds directly challenge the military because they begin to instill hope into the local residents who feel abandoned by the outside world.

As the first novel reaches a crescendo, the military, the gym, and the church collide in a final boxing match. Loup, who has trained with the help of the Coach and Miguel Garza, is now ready to box against Johnson, the person responsible for her brother's death. Although she is only a teen, Loup fights and wins. Instead of awarding her a ticket out, however, General Argyle arrests and interrogates her. Johnson eventually betrays the general by helping Loup escape. Overall, Loup's GMO status poses a direct threat to the US military because she has renewed hope in the people as a result of winning the fight and, later, escaping the militarized buffer zone.

While the imaginary world of *Santa Olivia* is a near-future dystopia geographically situated on the US-Mexico border, the sequel, *Saints Astray* (2011), ventures out into a triad of geographic spaces as Loup and Pilar navigate through Mexico, Europe, and finally the United States. Loup completes her heroic arc by eventually exposing the truth about the existence of outposts and the genetic experimentations and exploitation of GMOs within US territory. Within the Santa Olivia series, the speculative becomes the vehicle to critique scenarios that are all too real today.

Space and time work differently in *ISA*, given Isa Reyes's unique abilities. Consciously manipulating her dreams, she occupies distinct spaces simultaneously. When she is dreaming, she occupies the physical space where she fell asleep, such as her bedroom, but she also inhabits the dream world. At the same time, she occupies space within the corporation's software. Thus, with the simple act of falling asleep, Isabel Reyes transcends the boundaries of space, navigating from the reaches of her physical body to those of her mind through memories and dreams.

One of her most striking dream sequences includes a reunion with her parents. She never sees them face to face; however, she does manage to speak with her mother. Isa and her parents are in a car. The radio plays a song by Los Payos, "María Isabel" (1969): "La playa estaba desierta / El mar bañaba tu piel / Cantando con mi guitarra / Para ti, María Isabel." Isa attempts to gain answers from her parents:

ISA: Mom? Dad?

MOTHER: Yes, Isa?

ISA: I love you.

MOTHER: I love you, too.

ISA: Where are we going?

MOTHER: Home, we're going to live together now.

ISA: But I'll miss the summer course.

MOTHER: Mr. Degrasse said not to worry.

ISA: Can Nataly come?

MOTHER: Of course, Isa.

ISA: Mom, what happened to me in the accident?

MOTHER: There was no accident.

This realization is momentarily shattered by another discovery. What began as a conversation with her parents as she sat in the back seat of their car suddenly becomes the realization that she is outside, in the middle of a desert. Her parents are no longer physically in the same space with her. Instead, they have become a mere billboard image (fig. 4). She is puzzled by their disappearance and by a new riddle. What lies within the hidden compartment behind the billboard? Deciphering this is significant because the crystal bug-like object she finds within her dreams remains in her hands, even upon awakening.

Isa Reyes also exists on a digital level, within advanced computer software created by Dedál. The digital world can often appear mysterious unless one is knowledgeable about software and hardware (such as servers located within data centers). While the scientific laboratories and the corporations funding them are elusive throughout *ISA*, they have tangible effects on Isa Reyes and the surrounding characters. Therefore, even when Isa and viewers do not yet know where Dedál's headquarters are located, Dedál knows how to locate Isa and further exploit her: "Soon, very soon, we will . . . open her up. And everything will come out. The chip. The key." The chip within Isa's brain is an earlier version of one implanted in hundreds of other children who were captured and "hardwired," connected to hardware

Figure 4. Isa's dream sequence with biological parents. Film still from ISA *(2014), directed by José Néstor Márquez. Reproduced by permission of Fluency Films.*

that uses software to extract their dreams while they remain in a permanent state of "sleep," similar to an induced coma. The children's bodies are enclosed or wrapped within pod-like body bags, giving the appearance of a cocoon-like entrapment (fig. 5). However, unlike a caterpillar that will eventually become a butterfly, their bodies will lie dormant while their imaginative "labor" is extracted, until they are eventually disposed of by the corporation. In this manner, the laboratories become the physical links between the exploited labor force (the children) and the employers (the corporation). A significant exception is the one child located within

Figure 5. Children in laboratories. Film still from ISA *(2014), directed by José Néstor Márquez. Reproduced by permission of Fluency Films.*

Dedál's headquarters. His face is uncovered and he appears asleep, similar to a patient in a hospital (fig. 6). Viewers are left wondering who this child is and why Dedál appears emotionally attached to him. Regardless, all of these laboratories are funded by Mr. Gross, a mysterious character who represents an equally elusive corporation that is never named.

The corporation is willing to go to any lengths for financial profit. One of the assassins it employs is Borroso, whose name literally translates to blurry, unclear, or opaque, but can also be read as a play on the Spanish verb *borrar*, to erase. He is tasked with erasing or eliminating any potential threats to the corporation, and he accomplishes this through his omnipresence on screen—his ability to go anywhere by blending in and avoiding detection or interrogation. For example, he murders Isa's teacher, Mr. Degrasse, and then impersonates a substitute teacher in order to gain access to Isa's classroom and peers. He eventually kidnaps Isa in an attempt to extract the information from her chip, and he would have killed her had friends not interfered.

Isabel Reyes's final dream sequence allows her to manipulate not only her own reality but also the scientific laboratories and corporate reality on the other side of the software, hundreds of miles away. What begins as a fear sequence, in which Isa is chased by a man in a sombrero with a machete, becomes an emotional reunion with her biological father. "Papá?" she questions. He caresses her and then becomes upset at the sight of a red wire attached to her, chopping it off with his machete. Isa suddenly remembers a similar childhood memory: her father is not slashing her, he is slashing

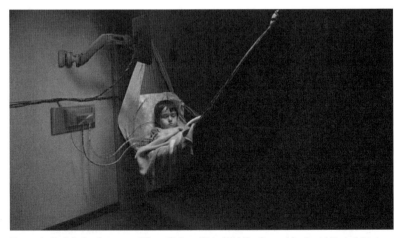

Figure 6. Dedál's headquarters. Film still from ISA *(2014), directed by José Néstor Márquez. Reproduced by permission of Fluency Films.*

at the red wires attached to her. This is followed by another memory: her father is sending her away, across the border, and into the care of two people whom she will grow up to refer to as her tía and tío. Isa returns from her memory and reenters her dream sequence with her father, who disappears soon after. But he has left his machete behind, which Isa takes into her hands and uses to slash all the red wires from the computer program, thereby freeing herself and the other children worldwide. We hear, "System down." Isa awakes, frees herself from Borroso, and exits along with Nataly, Officer Diaz, and a kaleidoscope of monarch butterflies.

Conclusion

The counterhegemonic resonance of the *Santa Olivia* series and the film *ISA* comes from the characters, settings, and plots of these dystopic borderlands texts. However, a reader's or viewer's interaction with Loup Garron and Isa Reyes is also mediated by a wider network of authors, illustrators, editors, filmmakers, actors, and publicists invested in the works' creation and distribution. They are often operating within genre-specific categories of niche marketing geared to, for example, Latina/o science fiction enthusiasts. These marketing tactics often incorporate contemporary political discourse around issues of representation (e.g., race/ethnicity, gender, sexuality, citizenship) or border and immigration debates.

The speculative worlds created by Jacqueline Carey and José Néstor Márquez recenter two heroines, Loup Garron and Isa Reyes, who most likely would be marginalized in other mass market books and film productions. These characters may have been engineered into existence by states or corporations, but they refuse to be subjugated and subjected to further injustices. With the help of their loved ones, both characters expose the atrocities inflicted on them and on others in similarly exploitative conditions. Loup and Isa also mark ongoing efforts to center bodies traditionally marginalized within speculative fictions. Perhaps readers and viewers who identify with them might even be inspired to create their own speculative fictions and engineer alternative realities that also pose a threat to structures of power.

Notes

1. The history of medical apartheid has been documented by Washington (2006). For more information on forced sterilizations, see Stern (2005); on feminicides, see Smith (2005) and Belausteguigoitia and Melgar (2007).

2. The content on the Internet Movie Database (IMDb) is usually submitted by filmmakers, actors, or agents and may include subscription fees. Jeanette Samano's page includes a resume likely uploaded by her manager, Anthony Topman of LA Management (http://www.imdb.com/name/nm5031380/resume?ref_=nm_ov_res). For information about IMDb, see the "Press Room" (http://www.imdb.com/pressroom/?ref_=ft_pr).

Works Cited

Anderson, Paul W. S., dir. 2002. *Resident Evil*. Constantin Films.

Anzaldúa, Gloria. 1981. "La Prieta." In *This Bridge Called My Back: Writings by Radical Women of Color*, edited by Cherríe Moraga and Gloria Anzaldúa, 198–209. New York: Kitchen Table: Women of Color Press.

Belausteguigoitia, Marisa, and Lucía Melgar, eds. 2007. *Fronteras, violencia, justicia: Nuevos discursos*. Mexico City: Programa Universitario de Estudios de Género, UNAM.

Butler, Octavia. 1979. *Kindred*. New York. Doubleday.

———. 1980. *Wild Seed*. New York: Warner Aspect.

———. 1987. *Dawn*. New York: Warner Aspect.

———. 1995. *Parable of the Sower*. New York: Warner Aspect.

Carey, Jacqueline. 2009. *Santa Olivia*. New York: Grand Central.

———. 2011. *Saints Astray*. New York: Grand Central.

Dery, Mark. 1993. "Black to the Future: Interviews with Samuel R. Delany, Greg Tate, and Tricia Rose." *South Atlantic Quarterly* 92, no. 4: 735–78.

Foucault, Michel. 2003. *"Society Must Be Defended": Lectures at the Collège de France, 1975–1976*. Edited by Mauro Bertani and Alessandro Fontana. Translated by David Macey. New York: Palgrave Macmillan.

———. 2008. *The Birth of Biopolitics: Lectures at the Collège de France, 1978–1979*. Edited by Michel Senellart. Translated by Graham Burchell. New York: Palgrave Macmillan.

Herrera, Juan Felipe. 2003. *Super Cilantro Girl/La Superniña del Cilantro*. Illustrated by Honorio Robledo Tapia. San Francisco: Children's Book Press.

Manson, Graeme, and John Fawcett, creators. 2013. *Orphan Black*. BBC America.

Márquez, José Néstor, dir. *ISA*. 2014. Fluency Films.

Nelson, Alondra. 2002. "Introduction: Future Texts." *Social Text* 71, vol. 20, no. 2: 1–15.

Puar, Jasbir K. 2007. *Terrorist Assemblages: Homonationalism in Queer Times.* Durham, NC: Duke University Press.

Ramírez, Catherine S. 2002. "Cyborg Feminism: The Science Fiction of Octavia E. Butler and Gloria Anzaldúa." In *Reload: Rethinking Women & Cyberculture,* edited by Mary Flanagan and Austin Booth, 374–402. Cambridge: Massachusetts Institute of Technology Press.

———. 2004. "Deus ex Machina: Tradition, Technology, and the Chicanafuturist Art of Marion C. Martinez." *Aztlán: A Journal of Chicano Studies* 29, no. 2: 55–92.

———. 2006. "El fantasma en la maquina: El arte chicanafuturista de Marion C. Martinez y la descolonización del futuro." In *Suturas y fragmentos: Cuerpos y territorios en la ciencia ficción,* 54–65. Barcelona: Fundació Antoni Tàpies.

———. 2008. "Afrofuturism/Chicanafuturism: Fictive Kin." *Aztlán: A Journal of Chicano Studies* 33, no. 1: 185–94.

Rivera, Alex, dir. 2008. *Sleep Dealer.* Maya Entertainment.

Rodríguez, Juana María. 2003. *Queer Latinidad: Identity Practices, Discursive Spaces.* New York: New York University Press.

Sánchez, Rosaura, and Beatrice Pita. 2009. *Lunar Braceros, 2125–2148.* National City, CA: Calaca.

Smith, Andrea. 2005. *Conquest: Sexual Violence and American Indian Genocide.* Boston: South End Press.

Stern, Alexandra Minna. 2005. "Sterilized in the Name of Public Health: Race, Immigration, and Reproductive Control in Modern California." *American Journal of Public Health* 95, no. 7: 1128–38.

Vint, Sherryl. 2011. "Introduction: Science Fiction and Biopolitics." *Science Fiction Film and Television* 4, no. 2: 161–72.

Washington, Harriet A. 2006. *Medical Apartheid: The Dark History of Medical Experimentation on Black Americans from Colonial Times to the Present.* New York: Random House.

Womack, Ytasha L. 2013. *Afrofuturism: The World of Black Sci-Fi and Fantasy Culture.* Chicago: Chicago Review Press.

Decolonizing the Future Today
Speculative Testimonios and Utopian Nepantlerx Futurisms in Student Activism at the University of California, Davis

Natalia Deeb-Sossa and Susy J. Zepeda

> We must never settle . . . we must dream and enact new and better
> pleasures, other ways of being in the world, and ultimately new worlds.
> —José Esteban Muñoz, *Cruising Utopia*

This collaborative essay takes the utopian theoretical interventions of José Esteban Muñoz (2009) and Gloria E. Anzaldúa (2002a) as a point of departure for reimagining the hierarchical US university system as a potentially decolonial feminist site of empowerment and future possibility. Student activism and outright rebellion on university campuses is not new. This essay, however, focuses on a recent case study that shows how testimonio, or personal testimony, can promote healing and rejuvenation in the face of fatigue, anger, and *coraje*, or frustration. Instead of only expressing the anger arising from multiple grievances—a necessary yet exhausting form of activism—student activists at the University of California, Davis (UC Davis) enacted a utopian future by creating a decolonized present where the multiplicity of their voices, experiences, and wounds could be seen, heard, and honored. As black lesbian feminist visionary Audre Lorde (1997) reminds us, "Anger expressed and translated into action in the service of our vision and our future is a liberating and strengthening act of clarification." When Lorde theorizes that "anger is loaded with information and energy" (280), she guides us to find creative ways to express and release this anger as a step toward redress and healing. In the case of the Davis students, their anger stemmed from intergenerational trauma that had been provoked by the university and its structures of power, which were intertwined with forms of white supremacy and settler colonial logics (Ferguson 2012; Morgensen 2011). In this utopian moment at UC Davis, nepantlerx students—that is, students whose subjectivities and identities are at the intersections of multiple paradigms and who propose egalitarian politics—deployed speculative testimonios as a central method in the long path of seeking justice and an egalitarian world.

UC Davis has a long history of student protests and actions in response to tuition hikes and other complaints against the University of California administration. In recent years, issues have included the failure of university regents and the state of California to honor commitments made in the California Master Plan for Higher Education; 81 percent tuition increases for students; mandatory furloughs, including for tenure-track professors; firings of lower-ranking workers, especially those working directly with students; and well-publicized raises for the highest-paid administrators. In November 2011, several hundred student activists rallied on the main quadrangle at Davis to protest proposals for increased tuition fees due to draconian state budget cuts (Golden 2011a). State funding to UC Davis was cut by 40 percent, and the campus faced a $130 million deficit in 2011 (Golden 2011b). Students felt they were being forced to bear the brunt of the pain that came from poor leadership at the state and university levels.

On November 18, 2011, during an on-campus Occupy movement demonstration, Lt. John Pike, a university police officer, pepper-sprayed a group of peaceful demonstrators who were seated on a paved path. The students were nonviolently protesting tuition hikes to defend their right to an affordable education (fig. 1). The incident was captured on video, and in the audio one can hear the fear and desperation in the voice of a young protestor who yells, "Protect yourselves!" "Close your eyes!" (BBC News 2016). It was a dystopian moment that has since become iconic. Officer Pike and other campus police were armed with riot gear and out in full force. This militarized police force sought to disrupt the protests by spraying students with chemical weapons, which for the protestors and witnesses recalled colonial legacies of police brutality and militarized violence against indigenous, black, and border-crossing communities of color. This moment, a display of the university's continuing role in hegemony, became an open wound and a trauma, especially for the nepantlerx students and communities of the university campus. It also signaled a need for activists to respond to other needs that sometimes are deemphasized in the heat of direct action: caring for the individual and collective self and refusing to allow perpetrators to efface the evidence of their crimes. This was especially

Figure 1. Police officer pepper-spray attack on students, University of California, Davis, November 18, 2011. Image in public domain.

important given that senior university administrators sought to obliterate the assault on students from institutional and public memory.[1]

The message sent to students and the public was clear: the university administration would "secure" the campus by enacting and enforcing militarized forms of police power against political protest and intellectual dissent. In the era of the war on terror, this fit with the discourse that posits draconian police measures as "protecti[on]" against those categorized as "terrorist" (Chatterjee and Maira 2014; see also Maira and Sze 2012). The university became a dystopian space where fear bred anxiety and mistrust, producing an atmosphere that was disproportionately harmful to marginalized, gendered, racialized, and otherwise nonnormative, otherized people. This fear was heightened through the persistent application of settler-colonial logics, which were supported by homeland security rhetoric. Rojas Durazo (2014) argues, "In the post 9-11 [era], [the] increasingly militarized university campus [and] intensified surveillance of communities of color has led to heightened abuses of police power and police violence" (191). The militarization and surveillance of academic settings is not unique to the University of California, Davis, nor is it something new; on the contrary, the targeting of student activism that disrupts state agendas is a destructive colonial legacy and long-standing practice in public institutions (Ferguson 2012).

In the aftermath of these events at UC Davis, the student response included the use of utopian testimonial discourse to address important needs among nepantlerx activist communities. Our analysis of these developments is rooted in the histories of critical ethnic studies and in the struggle for feminist studies, which open possibilities to reimagine a utopian present.[2] We draw from decolonial feminisms that urge and enable us to trace the colonial roots of the university structure as a means of finding liberation in the present through "women of color" knowledge formations (Lugones 2010; Mendez 2015; Santa Cruz Feminist of Color Collective 2014). We are inspired by the UC Davis Mellon Research Initiative "Social Justice, Culture, and (In)Security," which was established in 2012 as a result of a proposal co-written by the chairs of the departments and programs in African and African American studies, Chicana/o studies, Native American studies, and gender, sexuality and women's studies. The social justice initiative created an avenue for dialogue and activism to critically address the violence of the November 2011 pepper spray incident in relation to other disparities on campus and beyond.[3] As a methodology for reimagining the fabric of the university, each iteration of the social justice initiative contributed to a collective dreaming of a utopian institution that would be decolonial, anti-imperialist, antiracist, antisexist, antihomophobic, and antifascist in design and operation. To be in congruence with decolonial women of color knowledge formations—which we are calling nepantlerx visions—the university would need to be horizontal and communal in structure in order to counter hegemonic national and heteronormative settler colonialist discourses that intersect with domestic "terrorism" discourses in the ongoing war on terror.

The first major public event held to launch the social justice initiative was the Angela Y. Davis Teach-In, titled "Social Justice in the Public University of California: Reflections and Strategies," held on February 23, 2012. Angela Davis began by honoring the original people of the land upon which the UC Davis campus is located. The university, a land grant institution, has a legacy of inequality that is rooted in the theft of this land.[4] In her talk, Davis challenged the UC Davis community to critically imagine transformation through a "feminist university," one that "teaches students, and faculty, and workers alike to develop intellectual habits that allow us not only to challenge what is, but to challenge those tools that we use to apprehend and analyze what is." She challenged us to go deeper into critical thought and to trace and reimagine the structures within which we teach, think, organize, and exist. Davis asked, "How might we as students and faculty link our teaching, our research, our learning to . . . radical social transformation?" (2012). Davis's reference to "radical social transformation" intersects with the discourse of the Santa Cruz Feminist of Color Collective, which proposes critical shifts in the university power structure that could make possible a decolonized feminist university.[5] This would be a space where nonlinear, vulnerable, undocumented, and ancestral stories, pedagogies, and knowledges are centered, a site where utopian desires are possible.

Talking Circles: Nepantlerx Interventions into the Dystopian US University

It was from these urgings to imagine a decolonial feminist university that we began organizing a student-centered social justice initiative event, one that would offer a nepantlerx intellectual lens and praxis. We had already formed social justice initiative talking circles, which were horizontal formations that included undergraduates, graduate students, community members, staff, and faculty. Drawing on our collective reading of Linda Tuhiwai Smith's (1999) "Twenty-Five Indigenous Projects," the organizing committee framed the next event as a decolonized political space of healing and rejuvenation by building on Smith's articulations of "testimonio" and "storytelling" (144).[6] In relation to the land and its original people, we asked how our current geography reflects forms of settler colonialism and how we might build or imagine a "queer decolonized" space (Pérez 1999, 2003). In particular, we wondered how we could create such a space while working within the academy, where white supremacist forces and dominant forms of knowledge erase indigenous peoples (Morgensen 2011; A. Smith 2006). Indigenous scholars Waziyatawin Angela Wilson and Michael Yellow Bird (2005, 3) have suggested that the "praxis" of decolonization is the act of "working toward our own freedom to transform our lives and the world around us," and this idea became central to our organizing.[7]

Our commitment to the praxis of decolonization meant a search for new ways to create knowledge and action outside preexisting paradigms that perpetuated hegemony. Chilisa (2011) defines decolonization as "a process of centering the concerns and worldviews of the colonized Other so that they understand themselves through their own assumptions and perspectives" (13). The processes of decolonialization, as defined by Laenui (2000)—mourning, dreaming, and action—were evident as we planned the event and in the event itself. Mourning refers to the process of "lamenting the continued assault on the historically oppressed and former colonized Other's identities and social realities" (Chilisa 2011, 15). Dreaming is the phase when the colonized Other theorizes and imagines other possibilities (16). Action is the last phase of the process of decolonization, when dreams translate into social transformation and empowerment, and the colonized Other finds solutions, takes action, makes demands, and works toward improvement (17).

As our talking circles continued, we were inspired to ask several questions: How do we collectively imagine and live a decolonial queer future? How do we present the voices of nondominant students and consider their lived experiences, which are informed by intertwined yet forgotten historical legacies of genocide, enslavement, and colonization, as the basis for imagining this utopian future? How do we create organizing spaces that address inequalities and illuminate injustices to shift the terrain of social consciousness in our society to one of justice and healing? Moreover, what is justice for us? What forms of healing do we need, how do we apply them, and how might this also be part of the utopian political praxis we are pursuing? It all began with dialogue.

After about a year of intriguing programming, on May 28, 2014, students, staff, faculty, and community members affiliated with the social justice initiative collaborated across disciplines, positions, and interests to create an evening event, "Decolonizing Communities and Geographies at UC Davis and Beyond: Spoken Word, Performance and Activism." The impetus was to create a space where students could express their distress and trauma, with the goal of rejuvenation, in response to their exhaustion in dealing with a militarized, settler-colonialist, and capitalist institution. Students had grown tired of constantly doing the activist work of promoting and teaching antiracism, antisexism, and antihomophobia without seeing transformative structural change or healing from these forms of violence. Students—especially nepantlerx students—felt anger and frustration, *coraje*, at being regarded as merely a statistic, token, or source of funding. When would their stories matter? When would their life experiences matter? That evening we came together to imagine justice at the university. We created a space of genuine caring designed to build relations and connections. We were driven by a clear understanding that revised methods were needed to restore students holistically so they could continue doing the important work of necessary political dissent. Muñoz's critical methodology of hope was central to our effort (2009, 3). Our vision was to create a regenerative space where students would once again feel inspired to believe in justice and a utopian future.

In preparation for the "Decolonizing Communities" gathering, an email invitation was circulated to "all poets, wordsmiths, lyricists, spoken word artists, storytellers, and performers," along with a flyer created by artist Gilda Posada of Taller Arte del Nuevo Amanecer (TANA) (fig. 2).[8] We created an open space where undergraduate students, in particular, could creatively and "safely" speak out against police brutality, university injustices, Islamophobia, homophobia, and other forms of linked oppressions both on campus and in their/our worlds. We chose to come together in the Art Annex, a one-story building with three main classrooms used primarily for cinema and digital media courses, art courses, and humanities events. We arranged the main room to fit one hundred people comfortably. To the right we had a sign-up table, and behind it were tables with light snacks. Most of the social justice initiative events are held in this space, as it accommodates people with allergies and other physical disabilities. Our emcee, Sarita Hernandez, a queer of color undergraduate scholar, kept

Figure 2. Event poster for "Decolonizing Communities and Geographies at UC Davis and Beyond: Spoken Word, Performance and Activism," May 28, 2014. Courtesy of Natalia Deeb-Sossa and Susy J. Zepeda.

the flow of presentations going, and she helped maintain the energy of the space by, for example, offering resources to students who might feel upset by the testimonios. Also central to the gathering was queer US-born Costa Rican visual artist Pamela M. Chavez, who created a live painting during the performances, inspired by the testimonios of nepantlerx students.

That evening we heard from students who are usually silenced or hypervisible, criminalized, racialized, and/or tokenized in society and the university. Mainly students of color, they included queer, two-spirit, and feminist students who were in search of a decolonized healing space where they could be heard and seen as whole beings in all their complexities and differences. Students from Movimiento Estudiantil Chicano de Aztlán (MEChA) read a collaborative statement of solidarity with the community of Salinas, California, where police had fatally shot three Latino men in the three months prior to the event (fig. 3). A woman of color described her

Figure 3. MEChA student presentation at "Decolonizing Communities and Geographies at UC Davis and Beyond: Spoken Word, Performance and Activism," May 28, 2014. Courtesy of Natalia Deeb-Sossa and Susy J. Zepeda.

body as a "site of violence" and dedicated her statement to her daughter in the audience; in a spoken word piece titled "Refugee," a genderqueer Asian American student recalled the trauma her family had suffered as a result of the Cold War. That night, students came together, just as they had during the nights leading up to the event, and decolonized the university space for each other; they fought back through their words and love and prepared collectively to liberate other institutional spaces, that is, to start creating the feminist university Angela Davis challenged us all to imagine. The evening was full of political words that were critical of multiple forms of capitalism, misogyny, and racism, expressed through song, poetry, art, laughter, tears, movement, and otherworldly narratives. All the participants spoke of injustices and traumas, touching and opening wounds for the purpose of healing: it was a *limpieza*, a cleansing, through *palabras* and testimonio. The students were decolonizing their world, as Cherríe Moraga

(1993) has written in "Queer Aztlán: The Re-formation of Chicano Tribe," by decolonizing their minds, bodies, and spirit.

A cadre of brilliant and courageous students drew upon radical discourses and decolonizing practices to manifest a "queer aesthetic," speaking to what Muñoz (2009) calls "concrete utopias." These are collective utopias that are grounded in and arise from the historical traumas and immediate needs of specific communities, offering visions of healing:

> Queerness is a structuring and educated mode of desiring that allows us to see and feel beyond the quagmire of the present. The here and now is a prison house. We must strive, in the face of the here and now's totalizing rendering of reality, to think and feel a *then and there*. Some will say that all we have are the pleasures of this moment, but we must never settle for that minimal transport; we must dream and enact new and better pleasures, other ways of being in the world, and ultimately new worlds. (2009, 1)

The students' imaginings, storytelling, and collective demands emerged as a contemporary manifestation of Catherine S. Ramírez's (2008) theory of "Chicanafuturism," a site that "articulates colonial and postcolonial histories of *indigenismo, mestizaje*, hegemony, and survival" (187). The students' stories layered together the structural dimensions of inequity with the individually lived experiences that manifest those inequities. Ramírez notes that "Chicanafuturist works disrupt age-old racist and sexist binaries that exclude Chicanas and Chicanos from visions of the future" (189). The "queer aesthetic" proposed by Muñoz, which he argues often "contains blueprints and schemata of a forward-dawning futurity" (2009, 1), extends Ramírez's formulations of Chicanafuturism. It builds on her redefinition of "science fiction" as "not simply escapist fantasy, but a creative and politicized 'space' for the articulation of the pasts, presents, and possible futures of the 'aliens' and passport-less of the New World" (C. Ramírez 2002, 375).

That evening in May 2014 became a space where activist students attempted to perform their desired future in the present. Through their performances, the students created their own strategies of decolonization, similar to those that Linda Tuhiwai Smith (1999) has identified: retelling their stories, envisioning the future, creating a space of self-determination, and giving voice to the marginalized that moves away from a deficit-based orientation. "Intrinsic in story telling," Smith suggests, "is a focus on dialogue and conversations amongst ourselves as indigenous people, to ourselves and for ourselves" (1999, 145). This involves the need to come home for healing that sharpens the critique and understanding of external forces that disrupt inner harmony and peace (Thich Nhat Hanh 1992). As time travelers and healers of the present, the students created a reality similar to those that have been imagined by Latina/o speculative artists, especially Latina/o queer cultural workers like Gloria Anzaldúa (1987), Rosaura Sánchez and Beatrice Pita (2009), multigenre artist Adelina Anthony, and filmmaker Aurora Guerrero, to name only a few.[9] By the end of the evening, students had harnessed their revolutionary force by collectively drafting a set of demands for the UC Davis administration, with the vision of creating a decolonized university.

This student movement at UC Davis thus centered testimonios as a speculative utopian discourse. Students used testimonios to create a glimpse of their vision of a decolonial feminist university in direct challenge not only to the racism and marginalization they experienced within academia but also to the corporatization of the university and to the militarized forces that attack marginalized students like them—poor, queer, students of color.

Decolonizing Communities and Geographies: Testimonio as Speculative

Prior to the pepper spray incident, UC Davis was not widely known for student activism. However, the institution has a long, vibrant, and diverse history of campus protests against discrimination toward students and faculty of color, tuition hikes, and increasing student debt, all of which have contributed to the very low retention and recruitment rates for under-represented students. For example, over twenty-five years ago, in May 1990, four students went on a five-day hunger strike to protest discriminatory practices in the Spanish department and the low retention rates of students of color and faculty of color (Ruiz 1993, 245).[10] Activists have opposed the corporatization of the university (as illustrated by US Bank's contract with the institution) and have called for support for the lowest-paid workers on campus, such as food service workers employed by Sodexo (Maira and Sze 2012). Despite this history of constructive protest and some achievements, UC Davis is now known, since the 2011 incident, as the "pepper spray university" (Chatterjee and Maira 2014; Maira and Sze 2012).

With this historical memory in mind, the "Decolonizing Communities" organizing committee had a vision to create a grounded dialogue that would gather voices and spirits in a collective effort to activate the past in the present in order to imagine and move toward a utopian queer future. This included building a feminist university space that could also argue for decolonial transformation of geographies, spaces, and movements beyond campus. In planning the May 2014 event, we focused on the method of testimonio to help us meditate on students' spoken word performances as embodied sites of collective storytelling and shared imagining of new egalitarian futures. That is, we invoked the utopian speculative dimensions of testimonio. As Walidah Imarisha suggests, "Whenever we try to envision a world without war, without violence, without prisons, without capitalism, we are engaging in speculative fiction" (brown and Imarisha 2015, 3). As in much of the speculative fiction literature, film, and visual arts that comes from communities of color and queer visionaries—Octavia Butler, Gloria Anzaldúa, Debora Kuetzpal Vasquez, and Mujeres y Cultura Subterránea, to name but a few—we insisted that the fictional utopias could be made real.[11] From the dystopian space of the neoliberal US university system, we were determined to reimagine and rebuild.

Testimonios, especially in Latin America, have been used as a mode of resistance, what Craft calls "resistance narrative" (1997, 3). Testimonios take many forms, but they generally involve a written narrative in the first person by someone who is also the protagonist or witness of the events s/he is sharing (Beverley 2004). Often though not always by women, testimonios document collective struggle by using individual voices to underscore the intense repression of marginalized communities. In this way, notes Kathryn M. Smith (2011), testimonio "deliberately blurs the line between 'the personal and the political' to give the women (and men) in the margins a voice" (30). Latin Americanist cultural critic John Beverley (2004) also emphasizes that testimonios are polyvocal compositions that speak to the circumstances of an entire community. Rigoberta Menchú's *I, Rigoberta Menchú* (1984) and Alicia Partnoy's *The Little School* (1986) are examples of testimonios by Latin American women who experienced and resisted governmental repression (in Guatemala and Argentina, respectively).

As chronicles of survival, testimonies provide guidance to readers on how to continue resisting repression and building new realities. Dandavati (1996), in her study of the Chilean women's movement under the Pinochet regime, writes,

> Women struggled to become independent agents involved in determining the direction in which their country would move. They not only protested the political, economic and socio-cultural domination of the military regime, but also sought to transform the existing situation and offered an alternative vision of society based on democracy, equity and horizontal social relations. (6)

Dandavati notes that the Chilean women's movement was "more than a reaction to the cultural model of domination and authoritarianism envisaged by the regime": it involved "a process of creation as well" (8). One of the major interventions made by Catherine S. Ramírez's recovery and reframing of Chicana lesbian authors such as Gloria Anzaldúa within the genealogy of the speculative arts is to recenter testimonio as a millenarian utopian form and discourse. Moreover, Ramírez underscores that writers like Anzaldúa actually believe that a new future—one without violence—is possible. Student activists at UC Davis actualized this sentiment in their own reclamation of their collective utopian testimonial voice.

As feminist of color scholars, we look to the Latina Feminist Group (2001) anthology *Telling to Live: Latina Feminist Testimonios* as a touchstone for mapping the unique nuances of testimonio in US contexts. The Latina Feminist Group, an editorial collective composed of Chicana and Latina feminist scholars, theorizes testimonio as "a form of expression that comes out of intense repression or struggle," adding that it is "an effort by the disenfranchised to assert themselves as political subjects through others, often outsiders, and in the process to emphasize particular aspects of their collective identity" (13). These scholars demonstrate that testimonios are worth recording and writing about because they reveal dynamics of power, creative imaginings, and forms of resistance and protest that are not often recorded in official histories or narratives. Moreover, other Chicana feminist scholars have considered testimonio as a space or *sitio* (Pérez 1991, 161–62) from which to theorize gender as well as cultural, economic, and political borders (Bañuelos 2006; Burciaga and Tavares 2006; Delgado Bernal 2006; Holling 2006).[12] Like Latin American permutations of testimonio, Latina feminist redeployments of testimonio always gesture toward a material and materialist intervention: they seek to transform the oppressions that they so lucidly and painfully catalog.

The student activism at UC Davis that both preceded and followed the police attack on November 18, 2011, was critically reflected in the testimonios of nepantlerx students and performed in a public space. These narratives can be understood in relation to the Latina Feminist Group's perception of testimonio as "a crucial means of bearing witness and inscribing into history those lived realities that would otherwise succumb to the alchemy of erasure" (Latina Feminist Group 2001, 2). Students' distrust of and challenges to official histories and white supremacist structures, of the university administration and the society at large, would be forgotten or silenced dissident narratives unless they were documented or remembered in some form that could be shared. This is part of the vision of this essay: to document stories and subaltern accounts of inequalities and liberation (Zavella 2001). That is, we are documenting their testimonial acts of resistance and performance of a utopian Chicanafuturism in the present.

With the students' permission, we collected and recorded their testimonios, then did follow-up interviews with a select few for this article. In an effort to extend the circle of allies, the students offered their narratives as a call for solidarity and also as an offer of solidarity to intersecting movements, as earlier forms of testimonio have also done. Their always already speculative utopian testimonios narrate how as students and as social actors, they negotiate political, social, historical, and economic realities that constrain their lives and world. Their narratives constitute a challenge to and transgression against these constraints. The testimonios capture what Hurtado (2003) has called "conversations with power," which shed light on and offer language to critique how "authority" has been imposed on students on a daily basis and the ways in which students have resisted those barriers, including by organizing to create awareness of injustices (33). The testimonios situated the students as participants as they "work[ed] to recognize and validate [their] existence and experiences . . . as subjects" (Holling 2006, 81) or within the framework Sandoval (1991, 2000) calls "tactical subjectivity."[13]

Our main purpose in organizing the gathering was to honor, remember, enact, and reenvision radical opposition to a militarized campus and police state. Tellingly, what emerged were testimonios as speculative texts in search of healing from sexual assault and interconnected histories of displacement and war. Their imaginings of change were inspired by Octavia Butler (1993, 3):

> All that you touch
> You Change.
> All that you Change
> Changes you.
> The only lasting truth
> Is Change.

The testimonios shared that evening embody Muñoz's "queer aesthetics" and were akin to what Muñoz calls "concrete utopias," which he astutely suggests are relational to historically situated struggles, a collectivity that is actualized or potential. . . . Concrete utopias can also be daydream-like, but they are the hopes of a collective, an emergent group, or even the solitary oddball who is the one who dreams for many. Concrete utopias are the realm of educated hope. (2009, 3)

Muñoz's formulation emerges from his argument and vision of a queer future that is yet to arrive: thus the need to imagine another world or other worlds with decolonial or critical methods. These methods include his own methodology of hope as well as Linda Tuhiwai Smith's (1999) paradigm of storytelling. Muñoz assists us in grounding the queer aesthetic or dimensions of the students' political performances that actively and collectively imagine new visions for the future. We argue that testimonios are a central part of Chicanx and Latinx speculative aesthetics—and, as Catherine S. Ramirez has proposed, auto-historias such as Gloria Anzaldúa's classic text *Borderlands/La Frontera* (1987)—and perhaps may even be foundational to the speculative arts. After all, in her potent essay "now let us shift . . . the path of conocimiento . . . inner work, public acts," Anzaldúa (2002a) leads the reader through a synergistic seven-stage process in which the *etapas*, or spaces, are cyclical and nonlinear.[14] The second stage, nepantla, is theorized as "torn between ways," as a site of transformation and questioning. It is "the zone between changes where you struggle to find equilibrium between the outer expression of change and your inner relationship to it" (548–49).

Nepantlerxs: Toward a New Testimonio-Based Student Movement For Decolonizing the University

Building on Gloria Anzaldúa's concept of nepantla and social justice–centered pedagogy, as well as Catherine S. Ramírez's (2008, 190) innovative suggestion to reread Anzaldúa's *Borderlands* as a speculative fiction text, we see students' testimonios as a reflection of the nepantla state. Occupying an "in-between space," fed up with the restrictive cultural scripts and ideologies that bind them, nepantleras "facilitate passages between worlds," formulating methodologies based on their negotiations of distinct structures and spaces (Anzaldúa 2002b, 1). Nepantlera students—whom we identify as nepantlerx, with the "x" signaling intersectional, gender nonconforming, and transgender identities—used their views from these cracks between worlds to reimagine "interconnectivity" (Anzaldúa 2002a, 570). As Anzaldúa states, "By moving from a militarized zone to a roundtable, nepantleras acknowledge an unmapped common ground: the humanity of the other" (570).

For extensive analysis in this article, we choose to focus on two nepantlerx students who offered their testimonies at "Decolonizing Communities" event in May 2014 and later voluntarily sat with us to tell their stories in more detail. In their testimonios and storytelling, the two students, Edra and Iris (pseudonyms), questioned the normalization of gendered violence in the "academic industrial complex" while simultaneously reimagining transformation and healing in the university setting and beyond.

Edra started at UC Davis as an animal science major but faced intense racism in this department; she then transferred to and graduated from the Department of Chicana/o Studies. She observed that "Chicana/o studies at Davis is more radical on retention" in comparison to other units on campus. Edra's critical perspective makes visible the struggle to retain students through a holistic approach grounded in a social justice–centered Department of Chicana/o Studies and provides background to the 2015 emergence of the student-centered #MovimientoDeRetencion.

In her 2014 testimonio, Edra, a survivor of sexual assault, speaks to the prevalence of sexual violence on campuses and within subaltern communities such as the Chicana/o community. She offered two pieces at the "Decolonizing Communities" gathering: one was in collaboration with Natalia Deeb-Sossa, to protect Edra's anonymity, and the other was a spontaneous open-mic testimonio that she read after her attacker had left the event.[15] Her testimonio brought attention to the fact that one in four women in college experience the trauma of rape, and despite the fact that there is another rape on a US college campus every twenty-one hours, only 10 percent of survivors report the rape.

Deeb-Sossa's reading of Edra's piece was a profound gesture of solidarity and retention. Edra wanted her story to be heard and her pain to be expressed publically, yet the vulnerability of exposing her sexual assault to an audience of peers so soon after the violation was too difficult for her. Reading the piece without naming its author, Deeb-Sossa served as an intermediary—respecting Edra's autonomy, protecting her survivor status, and ultimately creating a healing space for her, and for all the survivors in the room, by validating this lived experience. In many ways, this moment illuminates the possibilities of a decolonized feminist university, where social actors across positions and experiences have a platform for horizontal collaboration, and where action and healing are grounded in a heart-mind connection that draws upon intellect, emotion, and spirit to help create another world free of violence.

All too often, students do not report rape because of how universities respond to sexual violence on campus. Students found responsible are typically not suspended or expelled, but receive probation and educational sanctions.[16] University administrators often explain such light penalties by saying that "campus proceedings are educational" and "the process is not punitive." For cisgender female students who experience rape and other forms of sexual assault on campus, the fact that less than a third of college students found guilty of such violations are expelled from school means that survivors live in constant fear for their safety and the safety of other women and gender-nonconforming people on campus. The threat of repeat offense is ever-present. In this context, Edra shared her testimonio, titled "FALSE questioning," in which she recalls being sexually assaulted by two men during her last year at school. Here we offer excerpts:

> It's *your* fault they say, *you* wanted it they say
> They make me believe the lies till this day . . .
>
> Did you say no?
> How drunk were you again?
> How much do you remember?
> *So you don't* remember saying no?
> Did they touch you?
> Where and how did they touch you?
> So you were drunk, *but did you fight back?*
> Why didn't *you* fight back?
>
> What happened after?
>
> Now I am paying the consequences
> The police report written wrong, they don't believe me
> Invalidating what really happened!
> Giving the "men" back the power
> Trying to silence me and keeping me in fear . . .
>
> Too many people asking why I don't seem the same?
> Fighting the struggle of accepting me and my body and that we are survivors
> Trying to sleep without nightmares
> fighting off the flashbacks
> understanding what PTSD really means
> Being shameful of my history and that I am broken in pieces,
> looking at the pieces, wondering

if I want to put the pieces back together to be myself once again
But I hate those pieces of me, and I ask why?
I want to get rid of those pieces, and I cry?
I know they are a part of me now. . . .

Courageously, Edra challenges those who doubt her account of rape, reminding us that sexual violence is an expression of unequal power and as such has been a core practice of colonization (A. Smith 2005). Most people still equate rape with the act of being forcibly violated in a dark alley, at gunpoint or knifepoint, by a stranger. This societal conception allows those who question survivors to dismiss sexual assaults that occur in college dorms on a weekend night, or after a date or party where alcohol is abused, by denying that they are rape or sexual violence. Edra's testimonio interrogates university structures to actively deconstruct the presence of a rape culture that valorizes and normalizes violent masculinities and heteropatriarchal privilege that are performed by punishing, dominating, and humiliating nondominant people. On many campuses, this work is left to the LGBTQ and women's resource centers: always under threat of budget cuts, they are nonetheless expected to provide stable support systems for students who experience traumas, including sexual violence.

In their interactions with Edna, campus officials questioned whether what had happened was actually rape. They called it a "student conduct violation," and no further investigation was done. Her experience is a clear though not surprising example of the lack of accountability within dominant university structures with respect to sexual violence. A decolonial feminist university would draw explicit interconnections between the destruction of land and peoples by colonial powers, violent acts committed during war, and violence against bodies in other settings, such as on campus. As argued by feminist scholar and activist Simona Sharoni (2015), "In the case of campus rape, for survivors there is a dominant view fortified by rape culture asserting that 'she asked for it.' Rape on the battlefield is a crime against humanity. But the same act on the college campus is viewed as a misunderstanding, a miscommunication." We ask: why normalize rape and suggest to survivors that they merely need to be more alert, as sexual assault is something that "just happens"? Only perpetrators of violence benefit from silence—an unreported rape is a rape that never happened. That is why an official university policy that encourages survivors to speak up about their experiences, as a step toward accountability, is rare. The "Decolonizing Communities" event sought to change this culture of impunity by reclaiming the university as site for consciousness raising and collective action geared to a utopian paradigm that is nothing less, and nothing more, than equality.

Despite the imposed silence Edra experienced as a rape survivor, she wrote and shared her truth that evening with the support of Deeb-Sossa. In an interview after the event, Edra noted that sharing her testimonio was a "good way to process what happened and begin to heal the pain that I feel. . . . When they heard my spoken word and saw my screen prints they never doubted me, they in fact thanked me for speaking up about such incidents that happen on campus." Her courage led to healing: when Edra broke into scattered pieces while remembering the violence, it allowed a transformation of energy, from pain to *sanación*. She began healing herself, her ancestors, and the community. Edra is a nepantlerx, an agent of "awakening" and seeker of a path to a new utopian paradigm. She challenged all those present that evening to gain "deeper awareness, greater *conocimiento*" of sexual assault on campuses and gender-based violence in our society, particularly for indigenous women of color. Her truth telling became a site of liberation, a means to reimagine "community accountability."[17]

Another nepantlerx student who rose that evening is Iris, a fourth-year with a double major in gender, sexuality, and women's studies and English. This genderqueer student chose to speak about the brutal homicide of six students on the University of California, Santa Barbara (UCSB) campus in May 2014. The violator left videos and written manifestos saying that he was seeking to violently take the lives of sorority women and others at the university as revenge for the way women had rejected him. The white-passing (part Vietnamese) cisgender male posted a detailed video of his horrific vision on YouTube prior to his violent outburst that left the community in a traumatized state. In response, Iris, who prefers the gender-neutral pronouns they, them, and their, shared their memory of a "lived experience," a wound that was reopened with this atrocity. Iris publicly testified to their own truth, using humor and sarcasm in a spoken word testimonio:

> The thing that disturbs me the most about the UCSB killings, other than everything about it, is that it reminds me of my ex . . . He embodied all of this hurtful rage, including rape culture and masculinity and et cetera, because he was suffering and trying to find a place that would accept him and validate him, and the racist, sexist masculinity gave him what he wanted. It's a breeding ground that allows men to learn hateful attitudes against women are okay.
>
> This is probably one of the first times I've ever spoken publicly about this . . . I suffered heavily from daily abuse and microaggressions for several

years, which included "owing him love and respect because he did so much for me," and being unsure of how to empower myself and navigate until I broke out of the relationship and found feminism and queerness. I tried to mold myself so that I could give him what he wanted, so he wouldn't feel so inadequate about his masculinity, so that he wouldn't be so violent and destructive. FUCK THAT SHIT. . .

. . . I'm tired of living in silence, and I'm still in near constant concern of daily acts of violence that can happen for no reason due to unexamined violent dynamics . . . I know a little too closely that it is wrong to pathologize shooters and glorify them, when there is so much systematic oppression that gets validated.

We can prevent this—by having individuals take responsibility for perpetuating systems of violence that destroy everyone of all genders, and having conversations to interrupt that violence. . . . I've had to work really hard to deprogram learning, and I'm still deprogramming, abusive violent models of relationships with others and to the world. . . . [I] would appreciate some love my way please.

Iris courageously shared the abuse they endured from their ex to bring attention to the "crisis of masculinity," which is the normalization and glorification of violent masculinity (Katz and Jhally 1999). That is, masculinity and success are equated to dominance, violence, and aggression. In the US, cisgender boys and men are socialized into violent heteronormativity that rationalizes a dominant form of masculinity, which is reflected in the legacies of patriotism, US imperialist war, and military service. The Santa Barbara perpetrator and Iris's ex both constructed their heterosexual "manhood" through violence. Men may turn to violence especially when their manhood is threatened, they fail at performing their one-dimensional masculinity, or they are called out of the heteronormative structure—that is, when they are rejected by women or called "feminine" or "a fag" in efforts to denigrate them. Gloria Steinem (1999) notes that in our patriarchal, racist, and homophobic society, privilege is given to white heterosexual men. They have become addicted to the "drug of superiority," and they will do whatever it takes to maintain their privileges and assert dominance over other groups.

Exactly a year later, as part of their senior thesis, Iris designed "speculative fiction workshops" inspired by black science fiction author Octavia Butler. This was a step toward Iris's healing and emerging formation as a nepantlerx. Demonstrating resilience and faith in creating a decolonial future, Iris asked participants "to individually work on creating story worlds, including oppression work"—that is, critical analysis that sets the stage for analyzing interconnected systems of domination such as capitalism, slavery, genocide, and colonization. Iris, who shares a birthday with Butler, was influenced to design these workshops after encountering and reading adrienne maree brown and Walidah Imarisha's innovative anthology *Octavia's Brood* (2015), which imagines alternative empowering futures through science fiction writing based upon Butler's legacy. In a moment of empowering clarity during office hours with Susy J. Zepeda, Iris discussed their close read of this anthology and declared, "I am a writer too!" Following this self-reflective epiphany, Iris ventured to create decolonized feminist spaces on campus where people could participate in what they named "world building" and "creating story worlds," where "oppression work" and feminism were central dimensions. The world building proposed by Iris, as well as Iris's performance, makes it possible to imagine a future without capitalism and a world without racism, sexism, or any form of heteropatriarchal violence. That is, through speculative testimonio praxis, including storytelling and writing full of radical hope—utopian *esperanza*—Iris and other students not only indicted the normalization of oppression in US universities, which sometimes even thrives in the guise of diversity, but also authorized themselves to create new futures today, a decolonized feminist university, *un nuevo mundo*.

Demands: By Way of a Conclusion

Here we have taken a leap of faith and time to be in conversation with sci-fi and speculative fiction scholars to show how nepantlerx student testimonios are an integral element of Chicana/o speculative fiction praxis.[18] Nepantlerx students have been deeply wounded by the "academic-industrial complex" and by capitalism, colonialism, and heteropatriarchy more broadly, and their testimonios envision and call for decolonized spaces in which to live, create, and imagine justice. Nepantla, as Anzaldúa envisioned, reflects the praxis of decolonization. The students therefore strive to develop political, cultural, social, and spiritual consciousness as a means of living in harmony with creation and the cosmos. In this way students come to recognize themselves as healers, *curanderxs*, of their own paths and communities.

At UC Davis, through political performance and testimonios, students called for radical social transformation as they came together and co-created a politics of resistance, or what Muñoz calls "concrete utopias," within the academy. They encouraged one another through their valor, speaking truth, telling stories, offering strategies of survival, sharing their creativity, and revealing critical histories, all to challenge current systems of structural domination. Muñoz (2009) offers "hope as a critical methodology" that "can be best described as a backward glance that enacts a future vision" (4). In many ways, this is what was created on that evening in 2014, which offered a sense of hope, community, and belonging. It led to the renewed experiences of the nepantla state, providing a social space that was simultaneously fixed yet focused on the horizon, a space that is still arriving, for the formation of collective transformation, healing, imagining, and actualizing new realities.

Together, nepantlerx students envisioned their healing and survival and harnessed their revolutionary force through a set of demands to the UC Davis administration, with the vision of creating a more just and equitable university and world. This list of collective demands was created by students during the evening of the "Decolonizing Communities" event in May 2014. It articulates the desires of these nepantlerx students in relation to their lived experiences and their visions of decolonizing the politics of the US academy. We offer this list of demands as a testament to our belief in the possibility of testimonio as a central part of Chicanx speculative aesthetics and corresponding utopian politics.

- Pass a divestment resolution, otherwise known as BDS (Boycott, Divestment, and Sanctions), throughout the University of California system.
- Divest from gun manufacturing and the military industrial complex.
- Reconsider the Greek system by engaging in dialogue regarding privileges, support, and lack of awareness of distinct peoples, genders, class formations, etc.
- Create an environment that works to eliminate forms of racism, sexism, heterosexism, misogyny, ableism, and transphobia.
- Revise the protocol for reporting sexual assault to take into consideration the challenges of speaking up, create more spaces of dialogue with survivors, and make administration more accountable. Reimagine processes of reporting so police are not the only source of public record.
- Increase funding for the gender, sexuality and women's studies program, for the ethnic studies departments, and for other feminist and queer entities on campus dedicated to decolonization, critical race and ethnic studies, Indigenous studies, and feminist studies.
- Remove the threat of defunding that faces the women's center (WRRC) and LGBTQIA center.

- Address police brutality as an issue on our increasingly militarized campus and acknowledge racial profiling of men and women of color, in particular.
- Decolonize ideas of free speech, hateful speech, land, and sovereignty.
- Retain Native American, Indigenous, African American, Chican@, Latin@, and other underrepresented students.
- Create increased funding opportunities for undocumented students.
- Employ compassionate forms of social justice, including meditation spaces for everyone.
- Transform classrooms into spaces that give students the opportunity to imagine and create curriculum focused on critical people of color speculative literature in the humanities, arts, and cultural studies division.
- Increase research and curricular links between spirituality and science.
- Interrogate how "Chicanafuturism" opens a path for spirituality, *curanderismo*, time travel, and soul retrieval in speculative discourses and beyond.

Notes

1. Toward the end of the thirty-six-day sit-in by student activists at Mrak Hall (the administration building), the university made efforts to erase the memory of the pepper spray violation and "clean" the reputation of administrators, in particular Chancellor Linda Katehi, "the pepper spray chancellor" (Parvini 2016). UC regents president (and former US secretary of homeland security) Janet Napolitano placed Katehi on administrative leave (Watanabe 2016).

2. Ferguson (2012) suggests, "The history of the U.S. ethnic and women's studies protests presents the transition from economic, epistemological, and political stability to the possibility for revolutionary social ruptures and subjectivities" (5).

3. A central vision of the Social Justice Initiative was to create an interconnected dialogue across distinct communities battling injustices within and beyond the university and searching for transformative methods of social justice. The co-directors of this interdisciplinary initiative were professors Amina Mama (women's studies), Inés Hernández-Avila (Native American studies), and Yvette Flores (Chicana/o studies). For more information on the Social Justice Initiative, see http://socialjusticeinitiative.ucdavis.edu.

4. In 2009, a Native American Contemplative Garden was created in Davis to honor the original people of the land, the Patwin people. Given the legacy of

genocide and the violence that continues in the present, it was a significant yet insufficient response. But it was a gesture of reclamation and the start of our attempts to create a space—indeed multiple spaces—of healing.

5. For discussion of "radical social transformation," see Santa Cruz Feminist of Color Collective (2014).

6. The organizing committee was made up of undergraduate students from across campus and from distinct organizations. They worked in collaboration with Alberto Valdivia, a graduate student in geography; Naomi Ambriz, in gender, sexuality and women's studies; and the authors, Natalia Deeb-Sossa, an associate professor who is an active co-creator of the University of California at Davis Race Project (http://ucdraceproject.org), and Susy Zepeda, who held a visiting assistant professorship with the newly launched Social Justice Initiative.

7. Also see Alexander (2005) for discussions of colonization, decolonization, the psychic, and the sacred.

8. TANA is a community-based art center in Woodland, California, that operates as a wing of the Chicana/o Studies Department at UC Davis. See http://tallerartedelnuevoamanecer.com.

9. A list of Anthony's works is available at http://www.adelinaanthony.com. An interview with Aurora Guerrero, writer/director of independent feature-length films, can be found at http://www.indiewire.com/2012/07/interview-with-aurora-guerrero-writerdirector-of-mosquita-y-mari-211018/.

10. The protest resulted in agreements to launch an official investigation into alleged racism in the Spanish Department, establish an on-campus ethnic and cultural center, and increase the number of full-time faculty members in the African and African American, Asian American, Native American, and Chicana/o studies programs, among other things.

11. See, for example, Butler (1986), Anzaldúa (1987), and chap. 18 in this volume by Vasquez. For Mujeres y Cultura Subterránea, see http://mujeresyculturasubterranea.blogspot.com.

12. Saldívar-Hull (1991) points out that we must "look in nontraditional places for our theories: in the prefaces to anthologies, in the interstices of autobiographies, in our cultural artifacts, our *cuentos* [stories], and if we are fortunate to have access to a good library, in the essays published in marginalized journals not widely distributed by the dominant institutions" (206).

13. Sandoval (1991) theorizes "US third world feminism" in relation to decolonizing worldwide movements that rely on "tactical subjectivity": "a political revision that denies any one ideology as the final answer, while instead positing a *tactical subjectivity* with the capacity to recenter depending upon the kinds of oppression to be confronted."

14. In "now let us shift," Anzaldúa (2002a) gives us a template for self-awareness, which she denotes as *conocimiento*. *Conocimiento* shares a sense of affinity with all things and advocates mobilizing, organizing, and sharing information, knowledge, insights, and resources with other groups. The seven stages are: (1) the rupture: fragmentation, which is both an ending and a beginning; (2) nepantla: a site of transformation and questioning; (3) the Coatlicue state: the cost of knowing and a "desire for love and connection" (551); (4) the call to action: longing for your

potential self; (5) re-membering Coyolxauhqui: releasing, repairing, healing, and rewriting new personal and collective stories; (6) the clash of realities: reframing, accepting ambiguity; and (7) spiritual activism: "shifting realities . . . acting out the vision or spiritual activism" (568), acting with compassion, neutrality, advocating a "'nos/otras' position—an alliance between 'us' and 'others'" (570).

15. The authors learned at the actual event of the presence of Edra's attacker.

16. According to the National Sexual Violence Resource Center's "Statistics about Sexual Violence" (2015), "more than 90% of sexual assault victims on college campuses do not report the assault." http://www.nsvrc.org/sites/default/files/publications_nsvrc_factsheet_media-packet_statistics-about-sexual-violence_0.pdf.

17. Rojas Durazo (2010) offers a transformative way to deal with sexual violence on a university campus through "community accountability." Also see Bierria, Kim, and Rojas (2010) and Kim (2010).

18. We agree with Cathryn Josefina Merla-Watson and B. V. Olguín, co-editors and visionaries of this anthology, who write in the introduction, "It is imperative to recognize that Chican@ and Latin@ studies scholars have long theorized and provided complex theoretical models for interpreting the differential experiences of the horrific and fantastic as well as the dystopic and utopic."

Works Cited

Alexander, M. Jacqui. 2005. "Remembering *This Bridge*, Remembering Ourselves." In *Pedagogies of Crossing: Meditations on Feminism, Sexual Politics, Memory, and the Sacred*, 257–86. Durham, NC: Duke University Press.

Anzaldúa, Gloria. 1987. *Borderlands/La Frontera: The New Mestiza*. San Francisco: Aunt Lute.

———. 2000. *Interviews/Entrevistas*. Edited by AnaLouise Keating. New York: Routledge.

———. 2002a. "now let us shift . . . the path of conocimiento . . . inner work, public acts." In *This Bridge We Call Home: Radical Visions for Transformation*, edited by Gloria E. Anzaldúa and AnaLouise Keating, 540–78. New York: Routledge.

———. 2002b. "(Un)natural Bridges, (Un)safe Spaces." In *This Bridge We Call Home: Radical Visions for Transformation*, edited by Gloria E. Anzaldúa and AnaLouise Keating, 1–5. New York: Routledge.

Bañuelos, L. Esthela. 2006. "Here They Go Again with the Race Stuff': Chicana Negotiations of the Graduate Experience." In Delgado Bernal et al. 2006, 95–112.

BBC News. 2016. "Pepper Spray University UC Davis 'Hid Search Results.'" April 15.

Beverley, John. 2004. *Testimonio: On the Politics of Truth*. Minneapolis: University of Minnesota Press.

Bierria, Alisa, Mimi Kim, and Clarissa Rojas, eds. 2010. "Community Accountability: Emerging Movements to Transform Violence." Special issue, *Social Justice* 37, no. 4: 1–11.

brown, adrienne maree, and Walidah Imarisha. 2015. *Octavia's Brood: Science Fiction Stories from Social Justice Movements*. Chico, CA: AK Press.

Burciaga, Rebecca, and Ana Tavares. 2006. "Our Pedagogy of Sisterhood: A *Testimonio*." In Delgado Bernal et al. 2006, 133–42.

Butler, Octavia. 1986. "Black Women and the Science Fiction Genre: Black Scholar Interview with Octavia Butler." *Black Scholar* 17, no. 2: 14–18.

———. 1993. *Parable of the Sower*. New York: Four Walls.

Chatterjee, Piya, and Sunaina Maira. 2014. *The Imperial University: Academic Repression and Scholarly Dissent*. Minneapolis: University of Minnesota Press.

Chilisa, Bagele. 2011. *Indigenous Research Methodologies*. Thousand Oaks, CA: Sage.

Craft, Linda J. 1997. *Novels of Testimony and Resistance from Central America*. Gainesville: University Press of Florida.

Dandavati, Annie G. 1996. *The Women's Movement and the Transition to Democracy in Chile*. New York: Peter Lang.

Davis, Angela. 2012. "New Visions of the University." Speech delivered at "Teach-In: Social Justice in the Public University: Reflections and Strategies," University of California, Davis, February 23.

Delgado Bernal, Dolores. 2006. "*Mujeres* in College: Negotiating Identities and Challenging Educational Norms." In Delgado Bernal et al. 2006, 77–79.

Delgado Bernal, Dolores, C. Alejandra Elenes, Francisca E. Godinez, and Sofia Villenas, eds. 2006. *Chicana/Latina Education in Everyday Life: Feminista Perspectives on Pedagogy and Epistemology*. Albany: State University of New York Press.

Ferguson, Roderick. 2012. *The Reorder of Things: The University and Its Pedagogies of Minority Difference*. Minneapolis: University of Minnesota Press.

Golden, Cory. 2011a. "Katehi, Chief Huddled with 13 on Decision to Remove Camp." *Davis Enterprise*, December 11, A1.

———. 2011b. "UCD Rally Ties Tuition Fight to Occupy Movement." *Davis Enterprise*, November 16, A1.

Holling, Michelle A. 2006. "The Critical Consciousness of Chicana and Latina Students: Negotiating Identity amid Socio-cultural Beliefs and Ideology." In Delgado Bernal et al. 2006, 81–94.

Hurtado, Aida. 2003. "Theory in the Flesh: Toward an Endarkened Epistemology." *International Journal of Qualitative Studies in Education* 16, no. 2: 215–25.

Katz, Jackson, and Sut Jhally. 1999. "The National Conversation in the Wake of Littleton Is Missing the Mark." *Boston Globe*, May 2, E1.

Kim, Mimi E. 2010. "Moving beyond Critique: Creative Interventions and Reconstructions of Community Accountability." *Social Justice* 37, no. 4: 14–35.

Laenui, Poka. 2000. "Processes of Decolonization." In *Reclaiming Indigenous Voice and Vision*, edited by Marie Battiste, 150–60. Vancouver, BC: UBC Press.

Latina Feminist Group. 2001. *Telling to Live: Latina Feminist Testimonios*. Durham, NC: Duke University Press.

Lorde, Audre. 1997. "The Uses of Anger: Women Responding to Racism." In "Looking Back, Moving Forward: 25 Years of Women's Studies History," special issue, *Women's Studies Quarterly* 25, nos. 1–2: 278–85. Keynote address to the National Women's Studies Association, Storrs, CT, June 1, 1981.

Lugones, María. 2010. "Toward a Decolonial Feminism." *Hypatia: A Journal of Feminist Philosophy* 24, no. 4: 742–59.

Maira, Sunaina, and Julie Sze. 2012. "Dispatches from Pepper Spray University: Privatization, Repression, and Revolts." *American Studies Association* 64, no. 2: 315–30.

Menchú, Rigoberta. 1984. *I, Rigoberta Menchú: An Indian Woman in Guatemala.* London: Verso.

Mendez, Xhercis. 2015. "Notes Toward a Decolonial Feminist Methodology: Revisiting the Race/Gender Matrix." *Trans-Scripts* 5: 41–59.

Moraga, Cherríe. 1993. "Queer Aztlán: The Re-formation of Chicano Tribe." In *The Last Generation: Prose and Poetry*, 145–74. Boston: South End.

Morgensen, Scott. 2011. *Spaces between Us: Queer Settler Colonialism and Indigenous Decolonization.* Minneapolis: University of Minnesota Press.

Muñoz, José Esteban. 2009. *Cruising Utopia: The Then and There of Queer Futurity.* New York: New York University Press.

Partnoy, Alicia. 1986. *The Little School: Tales of Disappearance and Survival.* San Francisco: Midnight.

Parvini, Sarah. 2016. "UC Davis Spends $175,000 to Sanitize Its Online Image after Ugly Pepper Spray Episode." *Los Angeles Times*, April 14.

Pérez, Emma. 1991. "Sexuality and Discourse: Notes from a Chicana Survivor." In *Chicana Lesbians: The Girls Our Mothers Warned Us About*, edited by Carla Trujillo, 159–84. Berkeley, CA: Third Woman.

———. 1999. *The Decolonial Imaginary: Writing Chicanas into History.* Bloomington: Indiana University Press.

———. 2003. "Queering the Borderlands: The Challenges of Excavating the Invisible and Unheard." *Frontiers* 24, nos. 2–3: 122–31.

Ramírez, Catherine S. 2002. "Cyborg Feminism: The Science Fiction of Octavia E. Butler and Gloria Anzaldúa." In *Reload: Rethinking Women + Cyberculture*, edited by Mary Flanagan and Austin Booth, 374–401. Cambridge, MA: MIT Press.

———. 2008. "Afrofuturism/Chicanafuturism: Fictive Kin." *Aztlán: A Journal of Chicano Studies* 33, no. 1: 185–94.

Rojas Durazo, Ana Clarissa. 2010. "In Our Hands: Community Accountability as Pedagogical Strategy." *Social Justice* 37, no. 4: 76–100.

———. 2014. "Decolonizing Chicano Studies in the Shadows of the University's 'Heteropatriarchal' Order." In Chatterjee and Maira 2014, 187–214.

Ruiz, Vicki L. 1993. "'It's the People Who Drive the Book': A View from the West." *American Quarterly* 45, no. 2: 243–48.

Saldívar-Hull, Sonia. 1991. "Feminism on the Border: From Gender Politics to Geopolitics." In *Criticism in the Borderlands: Studies in Chicano Literature, Culture, and Ideology*, edited by Héctor Calderón and José David Saldívar, 203–20. Durham, NC: Duke University Press.

Sánchez, Rosaura, and Beatrice Pita. 2009. *Lunar Braceros, 2125–2148.* National City, CA: Calaca.

Sandoval, Chela. 1991. "U.S. Third World Feminism: The Theory and Method of Oppositional Consciousness in the Postmodern World." *Genders* 10 (Spring): 1–24.

———. 2000a. *Methodology of the Oppressed.* Minneapolis: University of Minnesota Press.

Santa Cruz Feminist of Color Collective. 2014. "Building on 'the Edge of Each Other's Battles': A Feminist of Color Multidimensional Lens." *Hypatia: A Journal of Feminist Philosophy* 29, no. 1: 23–40.

Sharoni, Simona. 2015. "Why Feminists Should Care about the Israeli-Palestinian Conflict." Interview by Aviva Stahl. *The Establishment,* April 13. http://www.theestablishment.co/2016/04/13/why-feminists-should-care-about-the-palestine-israeli-conflict.

Smith, Andrea. 2005. "Sexual Violence as a Tool of Genocide." In *Conquest: Sexual Violence and American Indian Genocide,* 7–33. Boston: South End Press.

———. 2006. "Heteropatriarchy and the Three Pillars of White Supremacy: Rethinking Women of Color Organizing." In *Color of Violence: The INCITE! Anthology,* edited by INCITE! Women of Color Against Violence, 66–73. Boston: South End Press.

Smith, Kathryn M. 2011. "Female Voice and Feminist Text: Testimonio as a Form of Resistance in Latin America." *Florida Atlantic Comparative Studies Journal* 12, no. 1: 21–38.

Smith, Linda Tuhiwai. 1999. "Twenty-Five Indigenous Projects." In *Decolonizing Methodologies: Research and Indigenous Peoples,* 142–62. London: Zed.

Steinem, Gloria. 1999. "Supremacy Crimes." *Ms. Magazine,* August–September, 45–47. Reprinted in *Women's Voices, Feminist Visions: Classic and Contemporary Readings,* edited by Susan M. Shaw and Janet Lee. Boston: McGraw-Hill, 2004.

Thich Nhat Hanh. 1992. *Touching Peace: Practicing the Art of Mindful Living.* Berkeley, CA: Parallax.

Watanabe, Teresa. "UC Davis Chancellor Placed on Leave as Officials Launch Probe into Alleged Misconduct." *Los Angeles Times,* April 27.

Wilson, Waziyatawin Angela, and Michael Yellow Bird, eds. 2005. *For Indigenous Eyes Only: A Decolonization Handbook.* Santa Fe: School of American Research Press.

Zavella, Patricia. 2001. "Silence Begins at Home." In Latina Feminist Group 2001, 43–54.

PART V

Charting Chican@futurist Visual Art

Juventino Aranda and Chican@futurism

Margarita E. Pignataro

Chicano artist Juventino Aranda, a native of Washington State, works primarily in sculpture, painting, video, and performance, and secondarily in photography and printmaking; his art incorporates Chican@ themes bridging past, present, and future (fig. 1). Aranda is one of 296 artists who submitted proposals to the Tacoma Art Museum in Tacoma, Washington,

Figure 1. *Juventino Aranda,* Don't Let My Glad Expression Give You the Wrong Impression (After Jasper Johns), *2015. Pendleton wool selvage, gingham tablecloth, and latex paint, 108 × 78 inches. Photography by Rachel Smith.*

for the exhibition *Northwest Art Now @ TAM 2016*. Along with twenty-three other finalists, he exhibited at the show, which ran from May through September 2016. In May 2016 he traveled to Spokane to take part in an exhibition at Saranac Art Projects that dealt with romanticizing the west.

Aranda welcomed me to his Walla Walla, Washington, studio on March 7, 2016, for an interview in which he shared insights on how his art can be seen through multiple lenses, including the speculative Chican@futurist lens. At first glance, Aranda's artwork—some pieces consist of blankets, barricades, and barbed wire—arouses the spectator's curiosity with its isolated spatial stillness of readily identifiable objects. However, after speculation and discussion, one recognizes various Chican@futurist messages—the connection to memories of struggles associated with these familiar and iconic, yet out-of-context and reappropriated, symbols. The reappropriation of objects with Chican@ themes contributes to the Chican@futurist art world and provides a foundation for the speculative viewing of Aranda's work.

In our time together, Aranda spoke about how he draws from, and is inspired by, Afrofuturism and Chican@futurism and utopian/dystopian themes. He also touched on the influence of Guillermo Gómez-Peña on his politics and art; on themes of resistance and freedom; and on how he repurposes iconic objects and images and uses technology in his work. Our discussion focused in part on two Aranda pieces in which underlying Chican@ themes and a futuristic perspective subtly emerge. Both are sculptures: *All Is Not Quiet on the Southwestern Front*, created in 2011, and *The Neo-Middle Passage*, created in 2010.

Afrofuturism and Chican@futurism

On a visit to New York City in 2013, Aranda visited the Studio Museum in Harlem to see *The Shadows Took Shape*, a show organized by the museum's assistant curator Naima J. Keith and independent curator Zoe Whitley. The website for the show describes it as "a dynamic interdisciplinary exhibition exploring contemporary art through the lens of Afrofuturist aesthetics." Afrofuturism, as the website states, is a term coined by writer Mark Dery in his essay "Black to the Future: Interviews with Samuel R. Delany, Greg Tate, and Tricia Rose." In the essay, included in his edited book *Flame Wars: The Discourse of Cyberculture* (1994), Dery writes that "the notion of Afrofuturism gives rise to a troubling antinomy: Can a community whose past has been deliberately rubbed out, and whose energies have subsequently been consumed by the search for legible traces of its history, imagine possible futures? Furthermore, isn't the unreal estate of the future already owned by the technocrats, futurologists, streamliners, and set designers—white to a man—who have engineered our collective fantasies?" (180).

Thus, our conversation began with a discussion of Aranda's knowledge of Afrofuturism and a mention of Catherine S. Ramírez, who compares Afrofuturism to Chicanafuturism: "And like Afrofuturism, which reflects diasporic experience, Chicanafuturism articulates colonial and postcolonial histories of *indigenismo*, *mestizaje*, hegemony, and survival" (2008, 187). Although Ramírez notes that the concept of Chicanafuturism is "indebted" to Afrofuturism (187), and she draws from Alondra Nelson's definition of Afrofuturism (Ramírez 2004, 76–78), she also mentions the inspiration of New Mexican artist Marion C. Martinez's sculptures and wall hangings at the show *Cyber Arte: Tradition Meets Technology* in Santa Fe in 2001 (2008, 187–88). Ramírez defines Chicanafuturism as "Chicano cultural production that attends to cultural transformations resulting from new and everyday technologies (including their detritus); that excavates, creates, and alters narratives of identity, technology, and the future; that interrogates the promises of science and technology; and that redefines humanism and the human" (2004, 77–78).

The reconceptualization of images shapes the body of work that Aranda presents, and the result is an imagery beyond the theorized: a space other than the box in which Chican@s are at times placed by hegemonic standards that stereotype populations. I ask Aranda how his work reflects Chican@futurism.

ARANDA: My work tends to deal more with the dystopia side of Chican@futurism: when I create this work I look to the past, but I also look to the future, and the future is bleak. My work definitely deals with the negative, the "no hope for the future." But at the same time there's a utopia in my work. It is the image of a future with a Chicano consciousness, all inclusive, Chicano and Chicana.

I did a performance piece with my partner Rachel Smith entitled *No You Shave* at Modern Art 2014 at the Modern Hotel in Boise, Idaho. We were in a hotel room and it was a gender-neutral or all-gender-inclusive consciousness where the woman, Rachel, shaved her face, and the man, me, shaved the legs. The clothing we chose to wear also reflected gender swapping. That's part of my non–sexual binary approach to the future.

329

My futuristic approach also includes the use of electronic devices in my work, for example, electronic megaphones instead of the older bullhorn that cheerleaders would use in the 1960s. In one piece I use a controller from the Nintendo 64 video game console. They came up with the number 64 to refer to how powerful 64 bits were, and it was important to me because I was playing video games on that console and reading *Lowrider* magazine. To me, the 1964 Chevrolet Impala lowrider was appealing, being sleek and sexy and also comfortably accommodating a family. So those things, the console and the lowrider, were iconic, and I use this concept in my piece *Rollin' in Peace (R.I.P.)*.

So, looking to the future I see Raza as powerful because we are increasing in numbers, but the political system of the country is the same. So I reappropriate iconic United States symbols with a Chicano/Chicana consciousness, striving to empower and represent La Raza in all my mediums.

Political Activism and the Influence of Guillermo Gómez-Peña

Aranda grew up in Walla Walla and studied at Eastern Washington University in Cheney, which has, as he describes it, a "full devoted Chicano studies program." There he was exposed to the work of noted Chicano performance artist and activist Guillermo Gómez-Peña, whose street theater influenced Aranda's politics as well as his art.

PIGNATARO: Could you tell me about your early life and how you developed your political consciousness?

ARANDA: Growing up in eastern Washington in this town of Walla Walla, which was not necessarily ultra-conservative or all-conservative, I never felt that I was—and maybe I was just being naïve, but I didn't feel that I was targeted or that there was a lot of negative stigma happening. It wasn't until later on, when I went to college, that I experienced this. However, a little history [that came to my mind] recently with David Bowie's passing: I had never, until I was about seventeen years old and a junior in high school, heard anybody speak out against the government. At a barber shop, the owner, a white man, was cutting my father's hair, and it was interesting to hear him speak out about the impending war that was being drummed up in Iraq [after 9/11]. It's one of those memories that I'll always remember: to hear this person talking against the government and listening to Bowie's album *The Rise and Fall of Ziggy Stardust and the Spiders from Mars*, an album that came out around the very end of Vietnam, 1973. [In the barbershop that day] was the first time that I heard David Bowie and the song "Space Oddity" on the self-titled album *David Bowie* [which came out in 1969], the first time I ever heard music that really would change my way of thinking. [It was also the first time that I specifically heard] someone speak out against the government. I always thought that that was grounds for—thinking back to Winston and the book *1984*, the thought police were going to be everywhere. I had read that book and I was like, "Oh my gosh, this man is going to get in trouble."

And even with my parents, it was always, "Don't speak out against the government. It's great here in America. Don't speak about its injustices when it has treated you so well." That was never told to me [directly], but in a roundabout way, that's the way it felt to me: "Don't speak out [against the United States] because it's great." Which is true, because America here is like . . . it's like a fantasy to me. And I am grateful for this fantasy that I live, but I know that at any moment this is going to be gone tomorrow or I might close my eyes and it was just a dream. I know that there is reality, or what I perceive to be reality, but things kind of feel not real sometimes, and I feel that living in America is quite a dream, no pun with the American Dream. I feel that I still wake up and sometimes I'm kind of still dreaming.

PIGNATARO: You mention Guillermo Gómez-Peña in your artist's statement. Could you elaborate on his influence on your art?

ARANDA: Early on, I immersed myself in what it was to not only be Chicano, but Chicano in the Northwest. It was in an art and humanities course that I took my freshman year in college, without even deciding on an art major yet, that I was exposed to Gómez-Peña and Roberto Sifuentes. Both were doing these performances they called street theater. This later on influenced me to become a performance artist as well—some of my works have been exhibited as multichannel videos or performance work.

At the time that I learned about Gómez-Peña, I was part of demonstrations and experiencing this dissidence. I would come back from college and help organize demonstrations in the high schools. During the nationwide protests against HR 4437, a bill that dealt with "illegal" immigration, the largest demonstration, about 500,000 people, was in Los Angeles. Around the same time, the last week of March 2006, school walkouts were happening in Washington State, in Wenatchee and Pasco, and I directly helped organize the one in Walla Walla. What happened was that a group of us from Eastern Washington University went to the 2006 National MEChA

Conference at Northern Arizona University in Flagstaff. The demonstrations in LA and Seattle, and all over the United States, inspired us to organize demonstrations locally. I remember helping plan the high school walkouts, waiting a block away from the high school for the students so we could join them and continue marching through downtown Walla Walla. Bringing that movement consciousness from Eastern Washington University and the MEChA conference to Walla Walla was part of my political involvement.

We were talking about Gómez-Peña and his street theater—yeah, political demonstrations are real heavy with Gómez-Peña's work, but he makes it palatable for everyone to view, even though it's in your face when you see his performances and demonstrations.

Now, working forty hours a week and maintaining my art practice, I haven't been involved in demonstrations as much as when I was in college. I feel that my work as a practicing artist resonates with the political climate and that is my contribution, I would say.

All Is Not Quiet on the Southwestern Front

The sculpture *All Is Not Quiet on the Southwestern Front* was created in 2011 and exhibited in the show *Territory: Generational Triptychs* at the Northwest Museum of Arts & Culture in Spokane. The artist uses pine, OSHA safety blue enamel, stainless steel fasteners, and sand, and the work measures 216 × 96 × 108 inches (fig. 2).

The work was created the same year that Arizona congresswoman Gabrielle Giffords suffered a head wound in an assassination attempt in Tucson. The artist was aware of this incident and of the intense anti-Raza sentiments swirling in Arizona, where two state laws passed the preceding year (SB 1070 and HB 2281) had imposed draconian anti-immigrant measures and prohibited Mexican American studies, even banning some books.

PIGNATARO: *All Quiet on the Western Front* is the title of Erich Maria Remarque's 1929 novel about a soldier's experience in World War I, as well as the title of the 1930 movie adaptation. Could you comment on the title of your piece, *All Is Not Quiet on the Southwestern Front?*

ARANDA: *All Quiet on the Western Front* was required reading in my high school. I created my piece right around the same time that Gabrielle Giffords was shot. Giffords was a representative from Arizona during a time

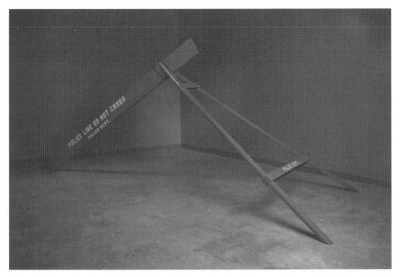

Figure 2. Juventino Aranda, All Is Not Quiet on the Southwestern Front, *2011. Pine, OSHA safety blue enamel, stainless steel fasteners, and sand, 216 × 96 × 108 inches. Photography by Eric Galey.*

when Chicano studies courses were being eliminated and books banned in an area with predominantly Chicano students. It was a modern-day—I don't want to say brainwashing, because that doesn't seem right, and not acculturation, but there were all these efforts to erase history going on at that time. The Southwest is a hotbed of immigration, with many immigrants dying in the Southwestern desert. So, these events in the news really drew my attention to the Southwest, to Arizona.

A lot of the images I use are iconic, manipulated through repeat exposure in the mass media and cultural institutions—for example, museums. The imagery of the barricade in my sculpture evokes the iconic image of antitank barricades used on Normandy Beach on D-day during World War II.

The Neo-Middle Passage

The Neo-Middle Passage was created in 2010 and presented at the exhibition *This Is How Big I Was When I Was Little: Eastern Washington University Undergraduate Senior Show* at the Gallery of Art, Eastern Washington University, Cheney. Aranda used galvanized steel, steel, barbed wire, and vinyl privacy slats to make the 180 × 96 × 3 inch sculpture (fig. 3). The

Figure 3. Juventino Aranda, The Neo-Middle Passage, *2010. Galvanized steel, steel, barbed wire, and vinyl privacy slats, 180 × 96 × 3 inches. Photography by the artist.*

artist discusses the Chicano movement of the 1960s and says that now, in 2016, a revival or repeat of history is under way as we move into the future.

ARANDA: In my work, I also view a repeat of history that is not for the better. It's just going to get worse, and it does terrify me. I get scared of the themes and ideas that I project in my work. We have come so far and accomplished so much, yet we still are not at the point where we need to be. There is always this level of—I don't want to say stagnation, but it kind of feels like one step forward and ten steps back, though it's not necessarily ten steps back. It's always just one step forward, and those steps forward never really seem like they are advancing to a utopia.

PIGNATARO: Could you explain the birth of the piece *The Neo-Middle Passage?*

ARANDA: *The Neo-Middle Passage* was conceptualized and created at Eastern Washington University, on campus. It is a location in front of the arts building and I chose that specifically. One day I saw a path; if you look closely at the picture, there's a path of rocks, stepping-stones, that appeared in front of the building because people were too lazy to walk around when a straight line is the closest and fastest way between two points. People were cutting across the grass and creating this trail, and so the groundskeepers put those stones there, and I decided to take advantage of that and conceptualize this piece. I felt that there was this middle passage happening within that building, not that those students crossing through were the exact people I was thinking of when I created that work, but there was this path created. [It was because of] this path, and how it was always green and lush, and a path always taken, that I decided to create that piece.

It is a fence that is six feet high and has barbed wire across the top. It's brown to go along with the brown color of the border, and black in some places, sometimes rusted in others. To me that was iconic of South Texas, where my mom is from. So I created a piece revolving around the term "middle passage." The middle passage was traveled by Africans coming to America. So, the piece shows how in America, coming across the border in your own land can cause tension, and from one country to the next, there's more of a tension. That tension is drawn down into the earth, like a fence trampled down in the middle. If you envision the piece without that pathway in the middle it would be like a sprung-up fence, normal, straight across, but I pulled it down so that it's like assistance, like the underground railroad. It's like America telling you, "Yes, come in. Come and help and be a part of this great country. But we're not going to really accept you. And we're not going to really treat you like you should be treated, but yes, please come in." So, that's like the country pulling the fence down to help you in. So there is that neo-middle passage that happens for immigrants from Central and South America.

Resistance and Freedom

Editors Scott L. Baugh and Víctor A. Sorell state in the introduction to *Born of Resistance: "Cara a Cara" Encounters with Chicana/o Visual Culture* (2015), "It may be most useful to suggest that Chicana/o visual culture was *born* of resistance and what it has since grown into is open to interpretation and negotiation" (5, italics in original). In *All Is Not Quiet on the Southwestern Front*, Aranda uses the image of a barricade that is not standing fully upright, as a New York City street barricade, for example, would be. And in *The Neo-Middle Passage*, the fence is pulled down, parted in the middle, again not the norm. These images seem to propose a futuristic, fantastical world where there are no obstacles to overcome, no resistance, though his images are open to interpretation. Barricades could keep one safe and isolated, with no entry from outside, or they could keep one from advancing. There is freedom to roam, or resistance, from one side or both. Fences have much the same significance, delineating boundaries, a route, or control passages. When opened, they serve as a way to enter and leave. The future is borderless, just as Gómez-Peña represents it, transgressing earthly spaces and announcing possibilities. Thus my question to Aranda concerns resistance and freedom.

PIGNATARO: In *The Neo-Middle Passage* you demonstrate the pulling down of a metal fence by, as you mentioned in one of our previous conversations, "a force underground." Would you consider your art as portraying resistance and/or freedom?

ARANDA: There is a resistance in my work. When [Juan Roselione-Valadez, one of the jurors for *Northwest Art Now @ TAM 2016*] pointed out that my work was playful, I realized that I do make work that is palatable in the iconic imagery that I create, but at the same time I want it to be resisted. I want people to feel uncomfortable, to get a sense of feeling what it is like to be Chicano in America and to strive for a utopia when really it's a dystopia. My work sets me free, and I hope that the message behind it sets other people "free" to create a resistance against the atrocities that are happening in America. For me, as a Chicano here in America, where I am not an immigrant but from a family of immigrants, it is a struggle to identify not as one or the other, but to find a happy medium, and Chicano is that happy medium. But I still feel American. I still feel Mexican, but not Mexican American. I can't live in Mexico.

Technology

In addition to interviewing Aranda in person in Walla Walla, I emailed the artist to inquire about two additional pieces that reflect a technological aspect of his work. *In Search of . . .* is a 2010 sculpture made from pine, Minwax Early American wood stain, steel, gold enamel, and megaphones, with dimensions of 96 × 24 × 54 inches (fig. 4). It was presented at Eastern Washington University in the 2010 undergraduate senior show, *This Is How Big I Was When I Was Little*. A 2011 sculpture, *Rollin' in Peace (R.I.P)*, is constructed with a Radio Flyer wagon and Nintendo 64 game console controller, measuring 36 × 33½ × 44½ inches (fig. 5). It was presented at the Northwest Museum of Arts & Culture as part of the show *Territory: Generational Triptychs* in 2011. The following are excerpts from Aranda's written responses to my questions.

PIGNATARO: Reflecting on the Chicanafuturism definition that Ramírez offers in her articles, how do you incorporate technology, Chicano themes,

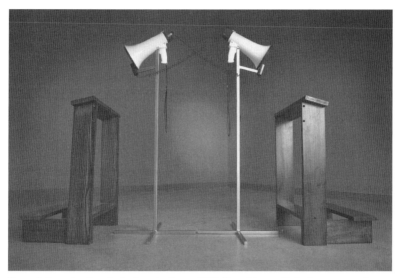

Figure 4. Juventino Aranda, In Search of . . . , 2010. Pine, Minwax Early American wood stain, steel, gold enamel, and megaphones, 96 × 24 × 54 inches. Photography by Eric Galey.

Figure 5. Juventino Aranda, Rollin' in Peace (R.I.P.), 2011. Radio Flyer wagon and Nintendo 64 game console controller, 36 × 33½ × 44½ inches. Photography by Eric Galey.

and futuristic notions in your artwork? Also, how would you define your purpose in including technology?

ARANDA: I have found it quite complex to identify how I work, as well as why and how I combine the themes and ideas that I incorporate into my work. No one theme or material is always the entire piece; it's more about how I edit the conglomeration of ideas and materials while approaching or finishing a new piece. For example, in all my works that include technology, the technology has primarily been used as a material or element rather than as a theme. For example, if this were the 1960s, when access to technology was more of a luxury, I most likely would have used another iconic American image/tool that is used to deliver messages loudly to the masses, an analog bullhorn, like those used by cheerleaders at sporting events. As for the use of a video game controller or its equivalent, this element of the Radio Flyer wagon piece would definitely have been omitted, but I would keep the lowrider imagery. Now, had this piece been portrayed as being told in or about the future, the video game console controller I imagine would be cordless or even hands-free, and [there might even be] no wheels on the wagon. No wheels, because the cult classic film *Back to the Future II* made it seem that all cars would be flying by the year 2015.

PIGNATARO: Could you elaborate on the inspiration for your pieces *In Search of . . .* and *Rollin' in Peace (R.I.P.)*?

ARANDA: Concerning *In Search of . . .*, the indoctrination into Catholicism in my upbringing was nowhere near that of many Chicanos or even others in my family. It is these stories, both personal and at large, that I wanted to bring out. Divide and conquer, westward expansion, submission/subservience, miscommunication, and wealth/wage gap are all themes in this piece. Concerning *Rollin' in Peace (R.I.P.)*, the naivety of youth is so wonderful. When I hear the term "simpler times," I think of my youth. Everything was magical, like a fairy tale. The news in all forms of media did not resonate as reality. The things happening to me that directly affected me were cuts, scrapes, bruises, and the occasional chastisement from pushing the limits, that would then result in slight punishment. This yesteryear when life was new and exciting will never be again, yet to chronicle what I felt the future was going to be still brings me great joy amid the chaos that is now reality.

All of my works deal with Chicano themes that span the generations, since the inception of Chicanismo and before. These Chicano themes that I visit over and over again are ones I cull from the Chicano experience, from the time of Cortés to the present. So to speak specifically to the works *In Search of . . .* and *Rollin' in Peace (R.I.P.)*, these two pieces happen to deal with Catholicism, speaking up/out, as well as death/loss and unity. Even though I tend to portray and foresee a bleak future, I do so in a playful way while remaining hopeful, with subtle ironic humor.

Postscript

Viewing Juventino Aranda's art, we can see the Chican@futurist aspect: a futuristic, resilient Chican@ realm where fences or barricades are overcome. In his artist's statement, Aranda says, "I am at the intersection of Mexican and American. Not Hispanic, not Latino, and definitely not Spanish, even though every day I live with the consequences of their conquest. It is these struggles for self-identity that have greatly influenced my process." He represents Chican@s through artistic media, defending and displaying his culture and history in a playful and educational manner. His social-political awareness raises consciousness in those who gaze at and ponder his art as he migrates through temporal spaces past, present, and future.

Images of artworks by Juventino Aranda are available on the artist's website: juventinoaranda.com.

Works Cited

Baugh, Scott L., and Víctor A. Sorell, eds. 2015. *Born of Resistance: Cara a Cara Encounters with Chicana/o Visual Culture*. Tucson: University of Arizona Press.

Dery, Mark. 1994. "Black to the Future: Interviews with Samuel R. Delany, Greg Tate, and Tricia Rose." In *Flame Wars: The Discourse of Cyberculture*, edited by Mark Dery, 179–222. Durham, NC: Duke University Press. First published in *South Atlantic Quarterly* 92, no. 4 (1993): 735–78.

Ramírez, Catherine S. 2004. "Deus ex Machina: Tradition, Technology, and the Chicanafuturist Art of Marion C. Martinez." *Aztlán: A Journal of Chicano Studies* 29, no. 2: 59–92.

———. 2008. "Afrofuturism/Chicanafuturism: Fictive Kin." *Aztlán: A Journal of Chicano Studies* 33, no. 1: 185–94.

For Those Seeking Signs of Intelligent Life
Xicana Chronicles of the Original Alien Ancestors

Debora Kuetzpal Vasquez

My age is a mystery, even to me. My mamitas did not celebrate my birthdays like other moms. But then again, they, or rather we, are not like others. I am the birth child of two mujeres. My mamita Ixchel is a Xicana artist and a curandera of Mayan descent with clairvoyant abilities. As an artist, she paints Mayan history integrated with her visions of a world beyond the stars, just as her people have always done. As a curandera she heals with herbal concoctions, sobadas, and spirit. My mami Koyol is a mujer from the Orion constellation, as it is known by most of the Western world, but the Maya called it Ak' Ek', which means Turtle Star (fig. 1).

I was constantly asking mami Ixchel to tell me the story about how they met. Every time mami Koyol was gone, we would cuddle up in colchas drinking tecito de canela and she would tell me how my familia's beautiful love story began . . .

After having various duplicitous partners, Ixchel called into the Universe for a mujer who was sincere, fierce, and benevolent. On a visit to Teotihuacan, she felt compelled to climb the pyramid of the moon at nightfall. As she stood on top of the pyramid gazing at the moon, she called out for her true love. She didn't know how this mujer would manifest, but what occurred she would have never imagined. A great rolling light flashed through the clouds and an aircraft hovered down and landed on top of the pyramid of the sun. The small sleek spaceship was lit up like an exquisite lowrider sports car. A mujer bathed in light exited the craft and radiated toward Ixchel. She was stunning: dark striking features surrounded by an aura of gold and silver flecks. Their minds spoke and in a flash they knew

Figure 1. *Debora Kuetzpal Vasquez, Ak' Ek'–Orion Constellation. Acrylic on canvas. Image courtesy of the artist.*

everything about each other. They kissed passionately, and as mami Ixchel says, "it was out of this world"; then she laughs, "cliché, I know." They fell in love. This space woman asked her if she wanted to take a ride, and mamita Ixchel agreed. They made love in that flashy lowrider spaceship floating among the stars. I was conceived that night and they named me Citlali (fig. 2). Mamita called this mujer Koyol, short for Koyolxauki, Mexica Diosa de la Luna, since the moon had answered her desire.

Mami Koyol lived with us. She would leave every so often for months at a time, but she would always come back. When she was gone, mami Ixchel and I would make art and learn about our gente in museums and in art and culture books. We have always connected with the star beings in Ak' Ek', and our ancestors recorded it in the codices and in sculptures thousands of years ago. Mamita and I loved to make barro replicas of the extraterrestrial astronauts from Mayan cultura. Artists from other cultures also reflected spaceships in their work. One of my favorites is *The Crucifixion* (1350), a fresco that hangs above the altar at the Visoki Decani Monastery. Two spaceships with humanlike navigators are seen hovering above the crucifixion. I really like the one on the right with the star insignias. He appears to be looking back at the other ship. My favorite from our (Mayan)

Figure 2. Debora Kuetzpal Vasquez, Interstellar Love: The Conception of Citlali, *2015. Acrylic on canvas. Image courtesy of the artist.*

cultura is in the Madrid Codex, K'inich Janaab' Pakal, the Mayan rocket man. Mami Koyol says it's a pretty accurate depiction, with some artistic license taken, of course.

I would also pass the time swinging on tires, reading, and going to the tiendita with my primitos, and before I knew it, she was back. Lots of the kids in our barrio only had mom(s), so I wasn't any different than them. My huelit@s and tí@s lived in our barrio so they were always around.

When I passed from childhood to womanhood, mami Koyol was away, but we celebrated it with a mujer temazkal. That afternoon, as I was stripping the banana leaves from their ribs to place on the floor of the temazkal, I felt sad that mami Koyol wouldn't be here. At dusk, the five lava rocks were pulled out of the fire and placed in the center of the temazkal, one in each of the four directions and one in the center. We entered the darkness of the temazkal. My huelita entered first to be next to the door, then my tías and primas by descending ages. All went around the hearth clockwise like the passing of time. I was last with the exception of mami Ixchel, who was the temazkalera. She pushed in the big pot of water and closed the door behind her. It was pitch-black except for the low light of the hearth. Mami poured water on the rocks and the steam indicated the beginning of the rounds. Each person has the opportunity to make wishes for the universe, share the story of her passage into womanhood, and lastly specify what she desired for my future; taking a sip of water from the jarrito and passing it indicated to the next person that it was her turn to speak if she so wished. As my eyes adjusted, it was amazing to see the radiance of the hearth barely lighting the faces of the mujeres of my familia. Mami Ixchel went out of the temazkal, which was unusual. When the door reopened, mami Koyol entered! I was soooo happy to see her! Mami Koyol explained that she had come to take me on a special journey. I was excited and a little scared. I looked at mami Ixchel for approval and she gave me a big smile and a wink. I took mami Koyol's hand and she began to speak.

As she spoke I felt myself rise out of my body and go through the ceiling of the temazkal. I looked down; I saw the temazkal in transparent luminosity and mamita Ixchel's smiling face looking up at me. Effortlessly we flew through the moonlit clouds, "ay que bonito es volar . . ."

Mami Koyol watched me to see if I was digging the ride, then continued her story as we soared toward space. "Ixchel's gente and my people have had a connection since the creation of the earth, because we are the same people. This is why you hear of very few alien abductions involving native people. We're just visiting back and forth. When the earth was created, a group from Ak' Ek' came down to help populate the earth. I find it entertaining when experts theorize that the Maya were not intelligent enough to have built their great pyramids. Of course they were intelligent enough: the beings from Ak' Ek' are the same beings now known as the Maya. It's true that they have developed differently over time. Our people on earth have been colonized by many ruthless people who have disempowered them, while those on Ak' Ek' have been allowed to develop intellectually and humanistically without coercion." She paused, switched hands, and put her arm around me. "We are approaching the first wormhole. Don't be afraid, our gente have traveled through wormholes for centuries."

She smiled and said, "Ready? Keep your hands inside the ride." We began to fall, not straight down but like the incline of a steep slide. It was fast and it took turns that swerved left and right, then dropped like a roller coaster, only we were floating on a bed of stars and it wasn't scary, it was energizing. The atmosphere was cool and warm at once. The heat from the tunnel of stars kept us warm from the cold darkness of space. A cool, airy breeze escaped from the openings between the clusters of stars. Every once in a while I would look over at mami to make sure everything was okay. She would smile and say, "Enjoy the ride." We passed from one wormhole to another for a total of three. The last one was different than the other two: it was slower, larger, straighter, and we could see glimpses of Ak' Ek' ahead (fig. 3).

I didn't know if it was because mami Koyol had described it to me so many times that it felt as if I had done this before. As we approached Ak' Ek', she pointed out La Madre Creadora and the three stars on her belt that are her children, Los Niños. "In various parts of the earth you will find these exact stars replicated in the landscape by pyramids, crop circles, or stones, as in Teotihuacan where I met your mami. They are left to remind her children on earth where they come from and where they will return. As soon as we get closer, you will be able to see the three stones of the hearth. Ak' Ek' is depicted by the Maya as a turtle glyph. The turtle is the symbol for mother in many Indigena cultures because of its protective shell,

Figure 3. Debora Kuetzpal Vasquez, Citlalita Approaching Ak' Ek'. *Acrylic on canvas. Image courtesy of the artist.*

and the three tun (stones) placed in a triangle represent the hearth. The hearth is extremely important to the Maya because it is the foundation of the Mayan home. As the legend goes, before the earth was created and the sky was lifted, the hearth was located in both earth and sky because they were one. You can see them now—they're right below the Niños Belt. That hazy little nebula in the center of the hearth is K'ak, the flame. Its haziness is the smoke coming from the flaming hearth. It appears toward dawn on August 13, the night of creation, when the sky was lifted and the hearth remained on the earth to feed and warm Mother Earth's children."

Before reaching Ak' Ek', we were blinded by a flurry of stars whizzing by. Suddenly, it cleared. On the other side of the stars was another planet that looked like earth. I was confused: "Mami, are we going home?" "Yes, but it's your other home." As we got closer, I began to make out the landscape. It looked like earth but without the buildings, bridges, and roads. We touched down in a field of soft green grass and a covey of quail burst into flight. The air was crisp and clean and there were all kinds of animals—monkeys, giraffes, zebras, lions—running around and coming up to us to be petted.

I asked mami why the animals were so friendly. She explained that no one there desires to consume meat, not even the animals, so the animals do not hunt each other or the beings. The animals and the beings are safe and secure, so they are friendly. "We cannot devour animals, especially if they are being treated badly, and we never really know how they are treated unless we raise them ourselves. The key to peace is being conciente of all living things. Everyone here lives in perfect harmony because we care for each other."

What was this remarkable place, was it like this everywhere? Apparently this is what the earth would look like if it were untouched by human greed. There were no cars, trains, or planes, and hence no pollution. We transported ourselves with our minds. Wherever we wanted to go, we just wished ourselves there.

We went to the mountains, the rain forests, the deserts, and my favorite place, the beach. The night beach glowed like a million stars, on the sand and floating on the water. The rolling waves were luminescent and strangely eerie and romantic. The day beach looked more like the beaches I visited in Mexico, only more surreal, perfect in a way. The white sands were covered with exquisite shells and crystal clear turquoise waters.

Mami directed me over to a little open-air kitchen where the most striking people I had ever seen were hanging out enjoying each other's company. Their faces were a deep olive with large dark eyes. They hugged me as if they had known me all my life. I could picture mami Ixchel making tortillas in this kitchen in space. Mami walked me over to my nanita, a little viejita sitting on a bench. Her silver hair glistened in a blue tone and her eyes were a soft golden brown. She stretched her arms out to me: "Ven, siéntate aquí. You don't remember, but you've come here several times before. The first time you were a baby. Actually we've seen you grow up. Your mamita Ixchel has come here too. You two stole my Koyol's corazón, so sometimes she's here and sometimes she's there." I felt like I had taken something from her, so I apologized, "I'm sorry nanita, you must miss her." She laughed and wrapped her arms around me. "No, Citlalita, time is different here. When she's gone it just feels like she's on a little vacation." I told Nanita that I loved it there and asked her if mamita Ixchel and I could come to live with her and mami Koyol. "Not yet," Nanita said, adding that I had a lot to do on earth. She assured me that one day I would come here to stay. Until then I could continue to come and visit her. She gave me another little hug and sent me to play with my primitos.

While mami Koyol and I were floating in the ocean, I asked her why she would have ever left this extraordinary place. Mami said she fell head over heels in love with mamita Ixchel and me. Here or on earth, our gente were the same people, after all. She said she couldn't live there happily without any worries if our gente were suffering on earth. How could we be completely happy? She reminded me that we also have these beautiful places on earth, in the Bahamas, in Maldives, and in Mexico. It angers other extraterrestrial species that the people on earth are not caring for these places, or the animals, or the people. So we still need to keep making our gente aware of the importance of taking care of Madre Tierra and the animales. She also reminded me that it only takes one person to begin that shift in consciencia. We go back to earth now and eventually we will all return here. When we get the materialism and hate out of our hearts, then we can come home.

Mami Koyol and I had been gone a long time; I became concerned for my familia. Were they still in the temazkal? Were they okay? In an instant we were back in our bodies. I opened my eyes and there was my family smiling at me. We had been gone only minutes. My huelita went out first and we followed in the same clockwise movement. The mujeres who stayed outside covered our nude bodies with fresh, clean blankets as we emerged from the temazkal, the womb that on this occasion was the channel that transported me through time and space. They brought us a jarrito of te de siete azares and we fell into a deep sleep.

After our nap, mami Koyol and I climbed up to my treehouse and sat looking at the night sky. It was different somehow. Not better or worse, just different. I longed to be in that place. I finally asked mami Koyol the question that I had been afraid to ask. "Mami, is there any hope for our gente here on earth?" She answered, "One day our gente on earth will recognize who they are and reexamine where real power comes from. This is why the powers that be fear them and all extraterrestrials. They are afraid that if intelligent life inhabits the earth, they will consider humans inferior and enslave them, just as the powers that be have done with every culture they have encountered. They are afraid that this will be their day of reckoning. They should be more afraid of their own self-destruction. Their greed has led them to make an exchange with other extraterrestrials, and the military industrial complex utilizes this knowledge to gain power in the world. The earth is a teatro with the powers that be setting the stage and writing the dialogue. Those with eyes wide open, who do not allow themselves to be placed on that stage, will make change. So will those hippie-like beings that people make fun of because of their crazy notions of love, peace, and caring for animals and Mother Earth. Mujeres who do not need the approval of men will rewrite the dialogue needed to save the earth. One day our gente will realize they do not need the materialistic society this government has built to smokescreen what is really happening. Until that day comes, the people of Ak' Ek' will watch vigilantly over our descendants, ready to intervene should the ties the government has with the present aliens prove destructive.

"Our gente will survive as they always have, either here or there. Remember the words of your madrina Gloria:

"Here we'll still be, like the horned toad and the lizard, relics of an earlier age, survivors of El Quinto Sol. Perhaps we'll be dying of hunger as usual, but we'll be members of a new species, skin tone between black and bronze, second eyelid under the first with the power to look at the sun through naked eyes. And alive mijita, very much alive."

I moved to sit between her legs and she wrapped her arms around me. I felt protected in her arms, as I always have (fig. 4).

Mami Ixchel taught me about José Vasconcelos, a Mexican philosopher. He published an essay in 1925, "La Raza Cósmica," about the cosmic race that embraced the idea that Mexicans and their descendants would transcend because they carried the blood of Europeans, Asian-descended Natives, and Africans. Mami Koyol feels that "it's a beautiful concept, but we are La Raza Cósmica because we come from the cosmos, to which one day we will return."

De Todo Corazón,

Citlali,

La Xicana Superhero

c/s

Figure 4. Debora Kuetzpal Vasquez, A Mis Doce Annos. Acrylic on canvas. Image courtesy of the artist.

The Mission Manifesto
Project MASA

Luis Valderas

The MeChicano Alliance of Space Artists (Project MASA), established in San Antonio, Texas, in 2005, is a network of Chicano artists who are inspired by the American space race and the Royal Chicano Air Force of Sacramento. Members of the network are spread throughout the nation and are linked by a shared experience of culture and a fascination with science and outer space (fig. 1).

In an effort to provide meaningful and enduring sociopolitical commentary, Project MASA artists are working to convey to new generations of Chicanos the issues of identity and social justice. The inter-generational makeup of the network presents opportunities for dialogue and mentorship. It is by engaging in modern culture that Chicano artists of the new millennium will enrich the discourse of future generations. Strands to be addressed include:

- The Chicano identity, past-present-future
- Chican@ gender roles in the new millennia
- Art, space, science, and the new Chican@
- *La raza cósmica*—our elders and us

The Chicano identity, past-present-future, is in constant evolution. The intermingling of cultures in a more tolerant society is the future of the Chicano family. Adaptation and transformation require a foot in the past and present, a familiarity with transitions between borders, and a flexibility that is conducive to a reimagination of realities. For the Chicano identity to step into the future, the shared experiences that are the glue in our culture must be transmitted to all. It is time, in this new millennium, to jettison outdated and oppressive gender roles, allowing for a more equitable representation and treatment of our mothers and sisters. A new Chican@ will lead the way, and it is through art and science that *la raza cósmica* will enter the future that awaits us.

Project MASA has engaged in exhibition, public relations, and networking of artists. While the group has been largely inactive since 2007, Luis Valderas continues to produce work within the same spectrum (figs. 2, 3).

Figure 1. Project MASA logo.
Image courtesy of the artist.

Figure 2. Luis Valderas assembling his solo exhibition The Sky Is Brown in 2014. Photograph courtesy of the artist.

Figure 3. Luis Valderas, Black Dream Place, *2015. Photograph courtesy of the artist.*

(Trans)Mission Possible
The Coloniality of Gender, Speculative Rasquachismo, and Altermundos in Luis Valderas's Chican@futurist Visual Art

Cathryn Josefina Merla-Watson

> of other planets I am
> dreaming
> of other ways of seeing
> this life.
> —Cherríe Moraga,
> "Dreaming of Other Planets"

Launched by visual artist and arts educator Luis Valderas in the early 2000s, Project MASA—an ironic acronym for "MeChicano Alliance of Space Artists"—is an ongoing collaboration of diverse Chicana/o artists mainly concentrated in San Antonio, Texas. Its formation was a direct response to post-9/11 xenophobia and racism as evidenced in the heightened militarization of the US-Mexico border; the rise of the Minutemen militia and other vigilante groups; the Border Protection, Antiterrorism and Illegal Immigration Control Act of 2005; and Arizona Senate Bill 1070, considered the strictest anti-immigration legislation in the country. Project MASA's mission continues to be to "establish an awareness of outer space as an integral part of the Chicano(a) modern mythos/reality/iconography."[1] While on the surface this mission may appear comical for its otherworldly allusions, its politics are firmly grounded in material realities and discursive practices that influence these realities. In creating what they term a "Chicano(a) modern mythos" for the twenty-first century, for instance, Project MASA "space artists" refuse the dichotomies of coloniality by combining Mesoamerican iconography—the "primitive"—with images of outer space and science fiction tropes—the "modern." In this way, Project MASA exemplifies what

Catherine S. Ramírez (2004) calls "Chicanafuturism," which unearths objects, images, symbols, and mythos associated with the primitive and the past and recombines them with those associated with the present and the future, thereby re-seeing colonial distinctions between the past and the future, the human and the nonhuman, the technologically advanced and the primitive. As a visionary enterprise, Chicanafuturism—and, I would add, an expanded Chican@futurism by multigender groups such as Project MASA—radically discombobulates and reshapes Western epistemology and ontology (Ramírez 2008, 189).[2]

This group's "project," as it were, seeks to proliferate and conjoin multiple ways of seeing, as playfully embodied in the group's title, a triple (at the very least) entendre. While *masa*, or dough (usually corn), evokes the tamale and the Mesoamerican spiritual significance of maize, it is also regional Chican@ slang for "shit," eliciting abjection and the seeming detritus of the past.[3] In addition, *masa* homophonically suggests NASA—the government agency created amid Cold War paranoia to compete with the Soviet Union in space—recalling images of progress and teleology, the secular and the empirical, what can be seen, known, and controlled. The group's title hence juxtaposes and melds the primitive or abject with the modern or technologically advanced, demonstrating the collaborative's focused engagement with Eurocentric binaries through visual mediums.

As decolonial philosophers have illuminated, colonialism in the Américas was not solely a physical act of terrorism but also an epistemological project aimed at infecting knowledge production itself. Shifting attention to colonialism's purchase on epistemology and ontology reveals the insidious nature of its legacies and, more pointedly, shows how it continues to shape the lifeworlds of Latin@s and people of color. The modus operandi of coloniality, moreover, is a binary visual logic that severs subject from object, self from racialized other, primitive from modern, in addition to reifying these as organizing categories of social life. This colonial optic or imaginary unremittingly, though anxiously, seeks to see, classify, know, and control the other and to produce and maintain the proper spaces in which these visual mechanisms occur (Mignolo 2000, 16). Gloria Anzaldúa (1999), whom I also consider a decolonial philosopher, underscores the stakes and potential of challenging the dualistic thinking that informs coloniality: "A massive uprooting of dualistic thinking in the individual and collective consciousness is the beginning of a long struggle, but one that could, in our best hopes, bring us to the end of rape, of violence, of war" (102).

In this article, I explore how the Chican@futurist collaborative Project MASA directly assaults colonial regimes of the visible, occluding their binary gaze. Paying specific attention to Luis Valderas's representative India ink drawing on paper titled *Semilla* (2006) (fig. 1), I demonstrate how Valderas's drawing works within and against neocolonizing semiotics. I submit

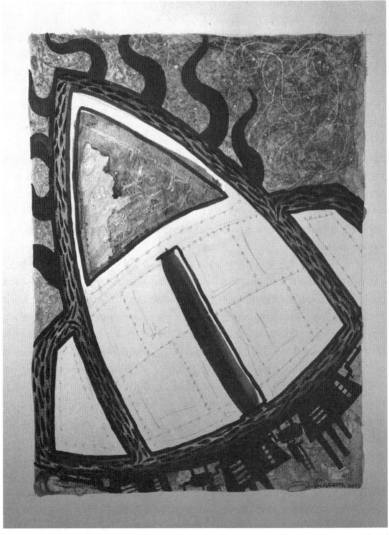

Figure 1. *Luis Valderas,* Semilla, *2006. India ink drawing on paper, 20 × 16 inches. Reproduced by permission of the artist.*

that he mobilizes the defamiliarizing power of science fiction in tandem with the disordering "underdog perspective" (Ybarra-Frausto 1991, 156) of a speculative rasquachismo that stems from a working-class Chicana/o sensibility of creative recycling or "making do" (156). In doing so, Valderas and the Project MASA collective reconstruct what I term *altermundos*, a collective visionary politics that both dislodges and peers beyond binaries buttressing the architecture of colonial epistemologies.[4]

In particular, I analyze how Valderas's *Semilla* enacts a playful and speculative rasquache sleight of hand to bring into relief the optics of the modern/colonial gender system, foregrounding the colonial visual apparatus itself. According to María Lugones, the "modern/colonial gender system," or the "coloniality of gender," refers to how coloniality instated and worked through racial categories and also is mutually constitutive of categories of gender and sexuality. The coloniality of gender violently imposed (and continues to impose) Eurocentric notions of biological sexual dimorphism and attendant normative gender roles and sexualities, "the patriarchal and heterosexual organizations of relations" (Lugones 2008, 2). Through an ambiguous and multivalent "avocado seedpod/rocket," Valderas's *Semilla* fuses Mesoamerican deities and iconography as well as la Virgen de Guadalupe with evocative images of San Antonio and South Texas that represent the technologically advanced. For Valderas, definitions of the primitive and the modern are not only fundamentally raced but also gendered and sexualized.[5]

I propose that Valderas's multivalent works, along with the myriad works of Project MASA, collectively engender altermundos, decolonizing "third space"[6] visions that are at once grounded in concrete realities while looking toward the decolonial and the utopian.[7] My neologism is inspired by the utopian spirit of the global justice movement's "altermondialism" and by Alicia Gaspar de Alba's (1998) "AlterNative" and Laura Pérez's (2007) "altarity," both of which index decolonizing aesthetic practices. Echoing Cherríe Moraga's meditation in the epigraph, Project MASA's altermundos propose "other ways of seeing this life," which force the viewer to see beyond staid Western dualisms and embrace more holistic perspectives. Significantly, though, Project MASA's altermundos are not divorced from this world but are firmly positioned within it—while also keeping an "Other" world within sight. Valderas's *Semilla*, as I demonstrate here, exemplifies how Chican@futurist visual art intervenes within the ocular and material logics of coloniality and unlooses horizons of possibility that have been tightly fastened by dualistic seeing and thinking.

Project MASA: Scrapping the Coloniality of Gender in the Mission City

In rendering altermundos, Project MASA seeks to transform actual space and place—namely, the cityscape of San Antonio—by creatively recycling its place-based and global histories of coloniality, unveiling how the past inflects the present and the future and redefining the binary category of the primitive and the modern. To date, Project MASA has held three gallery shows, in 2001, 2006, and 2007, in the Gallista Gallery on the Mexican American Southside, and in Centro Cultural Aztlan, located northwest of downtown. The former venue has functioned for nearly two decades as a vital hub for fostering Chicana/o cultural arts, such as art shows, spoken word events, and fundraisers, and the latter was founded in the late 1970s by Chicana/o community organizers to promote culturally relevant programming. These venues provide alternatives to the elite white art institutions that attest to the enduring aesthetic legacy of coloniality. They also bring together the Chicana/o community and its allies in a shared space to facilitate dialogue and incite political action.

Yet to more fully address the nuanced ways in which Project MASA's altermundos dismantle the coloniality of gender, it is imperative to view this art and the exhibition spaces as nodes in a larger network of coloniality and to understand the broader context of San Antonio, which has always been ground zero for colonialism and neocolonialism in the Americas. As San Antonio author and Rhodes Scholar John Phillip Santos (1999) writes in his creative memoir, "San Antonio is a palimpsest of erasures . . . a hidden-away Mexican city where a lot of old accounts are still being settled, where blood memory runs deep" (149). San Antonio's social and political geography is carved out by overlapping and mutually informing layers of colonialism and internal colonialism: first the Coahuiltecans were colonized by the Spanish, and then the Tejana/os were subject to US imperialism and Western expansion.

Now the seventh-largest city in the United States, San Antonio is home to five missions founded by Spanish Franciscan monks in the early 1700s, the largest constellation of missions in North America. Similar to missions throughout the Southwest, those in San Antonio have been sanitized and romanticized, repackaged for tourist consumption, recasting the subjugation and disappearing of American Indians as part of the natural order. By the early nineteenth century, when the missions became secularized, much of the American Indian population—which the Spanish

Franciscan monks referred to collectively as the Coahuiltecans—had been decimated by disease or assimilated within the Mexicana/o population. In addition to rendering invisible American Indian labor, culture, and presence in the region, the missions, and especially the Alamo, symbolically solidify and reflect a new social hierarchy that emerged from the modernization of Texas in the 1880s to early 1920s, during which time the Tejana/o ranching elite was displaced by a largely white "industrial and agricultural social complex" (Flores 2002, xvii). Anthropologist Richard Flores (2002) has demonstrated how the Alamo functions as a "master symbol" that reinforced Anglo superiority and Mexican inferiority within the US imagined community. Examining both local politics and popular film in the twentieth century, Flores traces how the Alamo is transmuted into a jingoist, hypervisible icon encapsulating an invented past as well as a racialized and gendered mythos of Texan and US individualism, freedom, and liberty. The missions continue to stand as both discursive and physical testimony to the ongoing colonization of native peoples and the subjugation of Mexican@s and Chican@s, as well as a more general coloniality of knowledge and power.[8]

The missions also signal the way in which coloniality ossifies intersections of race, class, and gender. Currently, scant scholarship details the gendered and sexualized dynamics animating Spanish colonialism in South Texas or the treatment of Coahuiltecans by Spanish priests and soldiers during the mission period of San Antonio. Although she focuses on a different geographic context, namely the Alta California missions, Deborah Miranda (2010) in her brilliant study of "*joya* gendercide" documents the "murder, renaming, regendering, and replacement" (267) of third-gender indigenous peoples such as the Chumash. Miranda highlights the centrality of gender and sexuality to coloniality—the brutal imposition of sexual dimorphism and heterosexual patriarchy—and she radically challenges romanticized and nostalgic imaginings of indigenous life within Spanish Franciscan missions.

In an attempt to denaturalize San Antonio's enduring racialized, gendered, and sexualized legacies of colonialism, many artists in Project MASA play upon and dramatize the peculiar juxtaposition that shapes the social geography of the Mission City, where the seemingly antiquated or romanticized—the "feminine"—exists alongside the modern and technologically advanced—the "masculine." San Antonio has been prominently figured through Spanish heritage fantasies, visible in the Spanish Colonial Revival architecture of business and residential areas and the European promenade-style "River Walk" along the San Antonio River that winds through downtown. Yet, since the nineteenth century San Antonio has simultaneously been imagined as an anachronistic zone of hedonism, unbridled sexuality, and otherness, evident in the Anglo fascination with the fandango dances (Peña 1999), the fetishization of the Chili Queens, and the infamous Red Light District located in the downtown area in the early twentieth century, all of which are associated with "exotic" and "spicy" Latina sexuality (McMahon 2013). As Anne McClintock (1995) has argued, the colonial imaginary figures land or territory as "feminized and spatially spread for male exploration" (23). It is within this erotized as well as gendered and sexualized colonial terrain that Project MASA stakes out the sites for its visual interventions.

Further sparking the colonialist erotic imagination was San Antonio's mixed-race and multicultural population. In fact, during the mid-1800s, after visiting San Antonio and encountering its mestiz@, black, and American Indian population, travel writer and landscape architect Frederick Law Olmsted (1857) described the city as a place inhabited by a strange "jumble of races," emanating "an odd and antiquated foreignness" (113). Olmsted here regurgitates the racist and sexualized stereotypes of his era that pertain to racial intermixing, casting people of color as primitive and uncivilized. He also manufactures a romanticized image of San Antonio as a quaint and remote outpost of empire, a profoundly heteronormative and gendered "seductive hallucination" (Nericcio 2007) projected by his white male gaze.

At the same time, due to its concentration of military and ancillary industries—concrete byproducts of colonialism and US imperialism—San Antonio is also associated with progress and the modern—the ostensibly "masculine." With early infrastructure built to support military operations surrounding the Alamo, San Antonio was well positioned to become what is now one of the largest military-industrial complexes in the country, boasting four active installations and earning its sobriquet, "Military City USA." More recent additions include Boeing Aerospace Operations, Lockheed Martin Aeronautics, and Fortune 500 companies related to the oil and gas industry. Enhancing San Antonio's modern image is its relative proximity to NASA in Houston and the SpaceX private launch site in Brownsville, presently under construction. Ironically, despite such modernizing forces, Mexican Americans continue to face persistent structural inequality. While the industries, corporations, and government entities based in San Antonio and in the surrounding region contribute to and profit from global warfare and environmental degradation, Mexican Americans in San Antonio and in Texas at large experience some of the highest rates of poverty, infant mortality, disease, school dropout, and incarceration in the country.

Project MASA's altermundos intervene within the neocolonial logics molding this stark disparity by playfully repurposing and re-visioning the gendered racialized binary of the primitive and the technologically advanced. Inspired by such predecessors as the California-based art collective Royal Chicano Air Force (RCAF) and the Texas-based art collective Con Safo, Project MASA, along with other Chican@futurist visual art, marshals a uniquely speculative rasquachismo to recompose altermundos.[9] While rasquachismo has traditionally denoted the tacky or funky, Tomás Ybarra-Frausto (1991) reappropriated the term to describe a unique working-class "Chicano sensibility" of utilizing and recycling what is available in one's immediate material surroundings to create aesthetic beauty or pleasure, as demonstrated in everyday barrio practices such as yard art, lowriders, or self-presentation. Encompassing an arsenal of "coping strategies you use to gain time, to make options, to retain hope," rasquachismo is a place-based aesthetic revelatory of Chican@ knowledges, social practices, and political desires (Ybarra-Frausto 1991, 157). However, while what I refer to as a "speculative rasquache" retains the aspects of hope and "making do," it also indexes the explicitly visionary praxis of reusing, melding, and refunctioning of images, icons, or significations associated with the primitive and the modern. Marshalling a speculative rasquache sensibility enables Project MASA's Chican@futurist visual art to conduct "thought experiments" of revolutionary vision energized by a "continual creative motion" (Anzaldúa 1999, 79–80). These altermundos cleave and disintegrate sedimented binaries—the bulwark of colonial ordering—and simultaneously reassemble a utopian outlook grounded in the here and now.

(Con)fusing the Coloniality of Gender in *Semilla*

Enlisting a speculative rasquachismo in his representative sixteen-by-twenty-inch India ink drawing *Semilla*, or "Seed," Valderas visually denatures categories of the primitive and the modern and foregrounds how they thoroughly infuse the modern/colonial gender system in the Mission City and beyond. A cursory glance at *Semilla* finds a rocket bursting into a starry night sky rendered through nearly imperceptible white, black, and blue scribble lines. However, a closer examination of the drawing unveils a dynamic and multivalent form, an avocado seedpod/rocket, that requires an agile and intuitive optic. The avocado seedpod/rocket blends and (con) fuses various symbolically suggestive forms, including a seed, a rocket ship, and la Virgen de Guadalupe, to explore connections between the persistent binaries of the primitive and the technological, the celestial and the earthbound, the masculine and the feminine. Valderas hence manipulates perspective and actively engages the viewer through this multivalent form.

For Valderas, the avocado seed functions as "a station to which other ideas may be linked," activating "visual connections with other icons." The artist explains that his avocado seedpod/rocket does not follow a set course but affords him visual exploration through space and time, enabling him to recursively reconnect the past, present, and future. Accordingly, what he has called an "earthbound unifier of collective memory" engenders and anchors multiple and seemingly contradictory perspectives. In fact, this multidimensionality is reinforced through Valderas's use of symmetry, which enables and prompts a viewing of *Semilla* from multiple vantage points since what appears to be the top of the drawing may also be perceived as the bottom.[10] Valderas elaborates this visionary third space politics and praxis, the rendering of altermundos:

> As with most of my work, the viewer is required to refocus in order to see the big picture. You have to look at the depth of the field in the composition to recognize and wear it, placing yourself between these two places and observing. I want the viewer to become that space traveler.[11]

Eschewing semantic closure or fixity, Valderas constructs open-ended and shifting constellations of significations, inviting viewers to participate in the genesis of meaning. Through such decolonizing borderlands semiotics—a veritable "methodology of the oppressed" (Sandoval 2000) or, rather, "optics of the oppressed"—Valderas strains operative binaries informing the modern/colonial gender system, opening up other altermundos or vistas of possibility.

In concert with his use of form, Valderas employs color—India ink—to etch out multiple perspectives and ostensibly unrelated significations. In a meta-discursive fashion, Valderas uses India ink to reference the mechanism or socially constructed nature of vision itself. In various shades of blue and black, India ink as a medium refuses a singular way of seeing and embodies chromatic plurality.[12] It is also used by ophthalmologists for corneal tattooing to improve vision, and by NASA scientists as a polishing agent to enhance the optical properties of certain metals. In addition, India ink brings to mind contradictory signifying or linguistic systems, as it is associated both with British colonial cartography and with Aztec codices

destroyed by Spanish conquest. Finally, India ink gestures toward a "counterhegemonic Chicana/o prisoner subjectivity" (Olguín 2010, 29), since
it references the ink illicitly concocted by Chican@ prisoners for *pintas*,
or tattoos. Valderas's use of color in conjunction with the seedpod/rocket
therefore constitutes a decolonizing chromatic discourse, or "aesthetic color
intervention," that resists the mono-logic of coloniality and the Eurocentric
conquest of color (Calvo-Quirós 2013, 81).

The seedpod/rocket encases and yokes together seemingly opposed
images of the masculine and the feminine as well as the primitive and the
modern. In one view, the phallic rocket represents the pinnacle of Western
civilization and technological progress, recalling the atomic age and the
Cold War space race. The rocket also becomes tethered to masculinity as it
conjures the penetration of unknown frontiers, echoed in the introduction
to the original series *Star Trek*: "To boldly go where no *man* has gone before."
In another view, the avocado seed is linked to the "primitive," evoking
Mesoamerican culture and lifeways. A source of nourishment in the Mayan
diet, the avocado has been a staple food in Mexico as well as Central and
South America since 500 BCE. Furthermore, while avocado, or *aguacate*, is
the Aztec name for testicle, and "seed" more generally is slang or vernacular
for semen, seeds are also considered the female part of a plant. In merging
the primitive and the modern, the masculine and the feminine—as well as
transposing these polarized binary categories—Valderas's avocado seedpod/
rocket concurrently visualizes how the modern/colonial gender system's
imposition of sexual dimorphism shapes and entwines such categories. In
(con)fusing these categories, Valderas consequently dissolves them. Thus,
rather than *pitting* itself against that which is projected by the coloniality
of knowledge and power as opposed and disparate, the seedpod/rocket
cultivates new connections and imaginaries, gesturing toward how indigenous knowledges are indeed technologically advanced and at the same
time toward the exclusionary and porous parameters—and "barbarous"
nature—of the modern. In this light, Valderas's seedpod/rocket encapsulates
the germinal or the potential for a third (outer) space perspective.

The seedpod/rocket challenges the modern/colonial gender system
most centrally by juxtaposing and merging the figure of the rocket with
that of la Virgen de Guadalupe. In fusing these seemingly disparate figures,
though, the artist foregrounds unexpected visual resonances. While the
triangular shape of the seedpod/rocket alludes to the general figure of Guadalupe, the dark wavy lines emanating from the top half of the seedpod/
rocket suggest the rays of light surrounding Guadalupe and the rocket's

fiery exhaust. Additionally, the stars in the background of the upper half of the drawing intimate Guadalupe's starry mantle, and the urban scene on the bottom resembles both the fin of a rocket and the angel who uplifts her figure. Many Chicana artists, including Ester Hernandez, Alma López, Yolanda López, and Isis Rodriguez, among notable others, have refashioned Guadalupe as an agentic feminist cultural icon. Valderas traces a slightly different, though parallel, trajectory by repurposing her figure to interrogate and expose how the heart of coloniality pulsates in sexual dimorphism and heterosexual patriarchy. To that end, Valderas limns Guadalupe's inherently antibinary constitution, exploring her cultural syncretism and visual mestizaje, a blending of European and Aztec religious iconography. To be sure, Guadalupe's image has not circulated untethered from hegemonic powers, for since her inception in New Spain she has functioned as a vehicle of accommodation and oppression in addition to resistance and subversion. However, as Jeanette Peterson (1992) points out, during the nineteenth and twentieth centuries Guadalupe's figure was commandeered to provide ideological support for revolutionary movements in Mexico, and it has functioned, too, as a Chicana feminist icon. Valderas's rendering of Guadalupe takes its cue from these subversive genealogies, especially as he foregrounds her cultural hybridity, which he poses as antibinary.

Many scholars such as María Josefina Saldaña-Portillo and Joshua Lund have rightly critiqued postmodern discourses of mestizaje for their unintentional reification of racial purity and their reinforcement of racial binaries and categories. Valderas's employment of mestizaje in his allusion to Guadalupe, however, functions as a "representational practice" (Davalos 2001) that enables what Anzaldúa calls a "new mestiza consciousness." In *Borderlands/La Frontera*, Anzaldúa describes this new mestiza consciousness as flexible and tolerant of ambiguities, ambivalences, and contradictions, embodying "divergent thinking, characterized by movement away from set patterns and goals toward a more whole perspective, one that includes rather than excludes" (1999, 101). While she "operates in a pluralistic mode" (101), the new mestiza is more than the sum of her parts: she is a novel, evolving, and indeterminate synthesis. Because of her ability to adapt and transform, as Anzaldúa provocatively claims, *"En unas pocas centurias, the future will belong to the mestiza"* (102).[13] Valderas's figuration of Guadalupe is emblematic of the new mestiza consciousness, for she functions as a shifting interface between multiple spaces, temporalities, and significations that elude Western binaries and teleology. She is indeed an icon in flux, an ongoing cultural composition.

Valderas draws out Guadalupe's association with seeds and fertility, invoking Mesoamerican spirituality, memory, and history. Guadalupe's figure appropriates and binds together iconography culled from Our Lady of the Immaculate Conception and a pantheon of indigenous mother earth deities.[14] Much of Our Lady's iconography resonated with Mesoamerican religious beliefs that were grounded in agriculture and the natural world. According to accounts, Guadalupe first appeared on December 9, 1531, on the Hill of Tepeyac, near the northern part of present-day Mexico City, to a Christianized Native, Juan Diego. She requested in the Aztec language of Nahuatl that a church be built in her honor. Not incidentally, the Hill of Tepeyac was a place of worship for the Aztec goddess Tonantzin, or Coatlaxopeuh. For this reason, in some regions of Mexico today Guadalupe is called Tonantzin, "Mother of Seeds," who is also known as Coatlicue. In *Semilla*, Valderas excavates this Aztec mother earth or seed goddess from within Guadalupe's form. Defying binary logic, Coatlicue possesses the capacities for both creation and destruction. A central figure and guiding metaphor in Chicana feminist thought, Coatlicue, Anzaldúa explains, represents "duality in life, a synthesis of duality, and a third perspective— something more than mere duality or a synthesis of duality. . . . *Coatlicue* depicts the contradictory . . . she is a symbol of the fusion of opposites" (1999, 68–69). Similarly, the allusion to Guadalupe in *Semilla* functions as a multidimensional, hybrid vision that confuses and rescripts the sacred and profane, the male and female, and disidentifies with a colonizing figure that advanced the coloniality of knowledge and power.

Valderas also blurs gendered Eurocentric binary vision by tethering Mesoamerican deities Quetzalcoatl and Ometeotl to Guadalupe's figure. The shapes suggesting an industrial, post-apocalyptic cityscape located in the bottom right-hand portion of the drawing additionally index Guadalupe's cloak or mantle as well as Quetzalcoatl, the "feathered serpent" deity. In traditional renderings of Guadalupe, based on the "miraculous" appearance of her life-size imprint in Juan Diego's cactus-fiber *tilmatli*, or cloak, positioned underfoot are a crescent moon and an angel. Some believe the angel to be representative of Quetzalcoatl, a synthesis of snake and bird, the earthly and the celestial. A contrast is further construed between primitive and modern in that the post-apocalyptic cityscape mimics the fiery "plume" of a rocket, recalling, too, the plumes or feathers associated with Quetzalcoatl. Moreover, the starry cosmos that encapsulates the seedpod/rocket connotes Guadalupe's mantle, which in turn elicits "the luminous skirt wrapped about the feminine aspect of Ometéotl" (León-Portilla 2012,

50), a "dual, bisexual god" (Miller and Taube 1997, 127) who combines feminine and masculine energies.

Yet another visually striking way in which Valderas intervenes within the coloniality of gender through the seedpod/rocket qua Virgen de Guadalupe is by highlighting her yonic valences. The triangular shape of the nose cone or control module and the wavy rays of light emanating from it in the upper left quadrant suggest the clitoris and pubic hair, while the fin and wings in the lower quadrant imply the labia minora and majora. Valderas here takes a lead from and extends an established corpus of Chicana/o art, which, in refashioning Guadalupe into a more empowered and sexually agentic being, has visually brought to the fore "in her overall silhouette the elongated, flower-like shape of the vagina" (L. Pérez 2007, 262). This can be seen in the work of Alma López, Yolanda López, and Alfred Quiroz, among others (see also Gaspar de Alba and López 2011). These synecdochic renderings transform Guadalupe from a passive object of heteronormative and patriarchal projection into an active agent guided by her own bodily desire and memory. Laura Pérez (2007) explains:

> If our sexuality, and our genitalia specifically, have been eroticized through the projection of titillating evil upon them by Western patriarchal culture as the gateways to a deadly carnality and sin . . . , then by necessity the uncovering of the dignity of each and every body that Mother Mary's and Jesus's incarnations symbolize must contest rather the "sin" in demeaning representations of these, and perhaps even the idealist belittlement of and violence against a body that is unavoidably the temple of embodied being. (262)

In a similar vein, Valderas fleshes out Guadalupe through the sexually evocative hybrid form of the seedpod/rocket that occupies most of the drawing, unapologetically confronting viewers and visually encouraging them to recognize Guadalupe's sexual and generative powers. And though Valderas employs relatively abstract and malleable forms, *Semilla* is anything but disembodied. On the contrary, the seedpod/rocket disputes and denaturalizes the virgin/whore dichotomy that haunts and braids together the subjectivities of Mexicanas, Chicanas, and Mexican indigenous women.

Valderas "reenergizes" Guadalupe's form by merging it with the shape of a rocket. Guadalupe has been historically depicted as an icon of female passivity, and she is one of the most visible icons informing the virgin/whore dichotomy, through which her figure is antithetically linked to La Llorona and Malinche. Anzaldúa (1996) elucidates, stating that "after the Conquest, the Spaniards and their Church continued to split *Tonantsi/Guadalupe*. They desexed *Guadalupe*, taking *Coatlalopeuh*, the serpent/sexuality, out of her" (53). By yoking together Guadalupe's figure with the shape of a rocket, Valderas combines what is perceived as passive and as active, thereby diffusing their categorical boundaries and reactivating Guadalupe. In addition, doing so reveals Guadalupe's latent energies—her potential to evolve or change—insofar as Tonantzin is associated with the "four winds," or the cardinal directions, for she is the mother of all the gods who rule over each quadrant. These winds or directions, moreover, are associated with natural cycles and agriculture. Through this inductive visual logic, Valderas elicits resonance among heretofore disparate semantic frequencies, reenergizing Guadalupe's figure—that is, rendering her *sexually active*. This erotic and multidimensional portrayal of Guadalupe brings to mind the words of Sandra Cisneros (1996), a formerly San Antonio–based author who describes her sexual awakening, which is aroused by "My *Virgen de Guadalupe*": "My sex, dark as an orchid, rubbery and blue purple as *pulpo*, an octopus, does not look nice and tidy, but *otherworldly*" (50–51; final emphasis added). By teasing out Guadalupe's erotic and sexually active inflections, Valderas effectively recasts her within a decolonial perspective, projecting her toward a cosmos irrevocably tied to the past and present.

Valderas's seedpod/rocket qua Virgen, finally, works as a connecting and mediating force. Like the "new mestiza," Guadalupe is "a synthesis of the old worlds and the new of the religion and culture of the two races in our psyche, the conquerors and the conquered. . . . She mediates between humans and the divine, between this reality and the reality of spirit entities" (Anzaldúa 1996, 54). *Semilla* emphasizes her synesthetic quality in the way she occupies the center of the drawing, intimately entwining the cosmos and the utopian with the dystopian and earthly matters, the nourishing and the psychically depleting. In this view, the rays of light resemble the spines of maguey, recollecting Guadalupe's alternative indigenous identity, the "Mother of Maguey," who was associated with fertility and healing (Taylor 1987, 19). The post-apocalyptic cityscape at the bottom of the drawing further recalls Guadalupe's more colonizing aspect, given that the creator of the Guadalupe icon was inspired by common portrayals of Our Lady of the Immaculate Conception that were based upon an engraving of the Apocalyptic Woman described in the Book of Revelation during the mid-sixteenth century (Peterson 1992, 40). In these ways, Valderas's avocado seedpod/rocket brings together the seemingly contradictory and rejects the binary logic endemic to coloniality.

Codex: (Trans)Mission Possible!

Harnessing the power of speculative rasquache tactics, Valderas generates altermundos that break down binaries between the seeming past and present, sacred and profane, male and female, primitive and technologically advanced. In doing so, he re-fuses the coloniality of gender, of knowledge, and of power and concatenates new outgrowths, potentially new ways of seeing and being, that have previously lain dormant in the lag between the colonial and postcolonial (E. Pérez 1999). Project MASA creates lines of sight in which other ways of being and becoming take shape, pushing the viewer beyond convenient dualisms upon which Eurocentrism relies and into altermundos—multidimensional and more complex semiotic universes.

Through the rendering of altermundos, moreover, Valderas makes visible and works within, against, and *beyond* gendered colonial legacies germane to San Antonio, as emblematized by the city's constellation of missions that concretely stand as the natural order. *Semilla* visually propels the (trans)mission of subaltern memory, history, and knowledge in all its vibrant difference into the present and future "like endless fishbones: slowly, steadily wounding the consuming body" (L. Pérez 1999, 20). Thus, while the first part of my title, "(Trans)Mission Possible," gives a cheeky nod to *Mission: Impossible*—a 1996 action spy film and American television series from the 1960s and early 1970s that incorporated aspects of science fiction through its focus on advanced technology—my play on the phrase has less to do with Cold War paranoia about the menacing Other and everything to do with how Chicana/o artists mobilize the speculative to intervene within gendered and sexualized legacies that still shape the "Mission City." As I have shown here, San Antonio and the borderlands offer Project MASA critical sites from which to pressure coloniality as well as to envision and launch altermundos that connect the local to the global and universal.

As I finalize this article during the fall of 2014 and winter of 2015, I am continually assailed by news events unbelievably horrific and otherworldly, the very stuff of dystopian fiction: police brutality and the systematic targeting and brutal extinguishing of people of color. I am haunted by names such as Michael Brown and Eric Garner, and the names of myriad other men and women of color. I am also troubled by news of the defunding of Planned Parenthood, a principal provider of basic health care to poor women—women who, in the Rio Grande Valley, one of the most impoverished regions of country, where I now live and teach, are overwhelmingly Mexicana or Chicana. These are women who toil in the fields with their families and whose invisible labor supplies this nation's produce. Such are the tangible traces of the modern/colonial gender system in the borderlands, where lives hang in the balance at the shifting intersections of race, class, gender, sexuality, and citizenship. I realize that in our neocolonial social system in which black and brown lives are devalued and delimited in advance, it would be too easy to capitulate to what Joy James (2007) calls "tragedy fatigue" and dismiss the role of the visual or aesthetic in contemporary politics. But as Anzaldúa (1987) prophetically reminds us, "Nothing happens in the 'real' world unless it first happens in the images in our heads" (109). Carmen Tafolla (2005), former poet laureate of San Antonio, echoes this in a recognition of Valderas's art: "Now especially, in this time of words and an Orwellian 'Truth is Lies' usage of words, we have need of his images, his art, which even in the insanity of war, abuse and lies, helps us see the big picture, the huge pattern."

As Valderas and Project MASA powerfully demonstrate, to set into motion the now perhaps politically evacuated slogan "another world is possible" is to begin to (re)see it, to reimagine our collective futures. Yet "Masanauts" do not follow a set course; altermundos engendered by Project MASA and other Chican@futurist cultural production do not guarantee ready-made blueprints for futures to come, but rather sketch out decolonial desire and gesture toward the *ganas* to move beyond convenient dualisms into uncertain borderlands and third (outer) spaces. This "final frontera" is not some remote and unrealizable utopia or "no-place," but rather assumes form as multiple altermundos grounded in earthly matter, the lived experiences and histories of Chican@s. These altermundos, fashioned through a speculative rasquachismo, enlarge the visual scope of possibility of our collective life-worlds beyond white heteronormative and patriarchal futurity and generate new insights that hopefully will prompt revolutionary action—that make *do*.

Notes

1. Project MASA's website is no longer extant, but more information about the work of Valderas is available on the Art to the Third Power (ART3) website of Luis Valderas and Kim Bishop, www.arttothethirdpower.com.

2. In using the "@" or "at sign," I highlight Chicana/os' relationship to digital and advanced technology as well as how Chicana/o culture has always already been "advanced," thereby collapsing binaries of primitive and modern. In addition, I take a cue here from Sandra Soto's (2010) "queer performative Chican@," which she describes as "a *rasquachismo* that at first sight looks perhaps like a typo and seems unpronounceable" and disrupts normative gendered signs of "a" and "o" (2–3).

3. For example, as in "talking masa" or "talking shit." See the definition of "masa" in the online *Urban Dictionary*, http://www.urbandictionary.com/define. php?term=masa.

4. Miguel López-Lozano (2008) in *Utopian Dreams, Apocalyptic Nightmares* similarly discusses how Mexicano and Chicano writers at the turn of the millennium confront various inhering structures and forces of coloniality, such as "industrial development, urbanization, and environmental damage" (1), by incorporating science fiction techniques.

5. Luis Valderas, e-mail to author, May 16, 2007.

6. My use of "third space" is informed by third space Chicana feminism, such as the work of Gloria Anzaldúa, Cherríe Moraga, Emma Pérez, and Chela Sandoval, who define the term as an interstitial or liminal space that permits decolonial imaginaries (E. Pérez 1999). As well, in an e-mail on May 16, 2007, Valderas foregrounds his engagement with Chicana third space feminism. Of the development of Project MASA, he states, "It is very much in the middle of things (particularly with Anzaldúa and Border Theory, Emma Pérez—*Decolonial Imaginary* . . .)."

7. My understanding of the utopian is inspired by José Muñoz's (2009) notion of queerness. Drawing on Ernst Bloch's "concrete utopia," Muñoz defines queerness as "an insistence on potentiality or concrete possibility for another world" (1).

8. The descendants of the Coahuiltecans are not federally recognized, since many of them were "Christianized" during the mission period. This not only has affected tribal status, blocking them from important federal and state resources, but has also instated de facto cultural genocide.

9. On Con Safo, see Cordova (2009).

10. Quotations in this paragraph are from an e-mail by Luis Valderas to author, May 16, 2007.

11. Ibid.

12. It also important to note here that color is not inherent to objects; rather, we see colors that are reflected—and not absorbed—by the object. The production of color, in other words, pertains to how we perceive wavelengths. In this way we might say that color is a human construction.

13. Mikko Tuhkanen further explains that Anzaldua's "mestiza metaphysics" eschews notions of purity and is animated by the indeterminate evolution of being or "ontology of interconnectedness and becoming" (2011, 270).

14. See Granziera (2004) for a fuller discussion of the various earth mother deities incorporated into and inspiring Guadalupe's figure and iconography.

Works Cited

Anzaldúa, Gloria. 1999. *Borderlands/La Frontera: The New Mestiza*. 2nd ed. San Francisco: Aunt Lute.

———. 1996. "Coatlalopeuh, She Who Has Dominion Over Serpents." In *Goddess of the Americas/La Diosa de las Américas: Writings on the Virgin of Guadalupe*, edited by Ana Castillo, 52–55. New York: Riverhead.

Calvo-Quirós, William A. 2013. "The Politics of Color (Re)Significations: Chromophobia, Chromo-Eugenics, and the Epistemologies of Taste." *Chicana/Latina Studies* 13, no. 1: 76–116.

Cisneros, Sandra. 1996. "Guadalupe the Sex Goddess." In *Goddess of the Americas/ La Diosa de las Américas: Writings on the Virgin of Guadalupe,* edited by Ana Castillo, 46–51. New York: Riverhead.

Cordova, Ruben C. 2009. *Con Safo: The Chicano Art Group and the Politics of South Texas.* Los Angeles: UCLA Chicano Studies Research Center Press.

Davalos, Mary Karen. 2001. *Exhibiting Mestizaje: Mexican (American) Museums in the Diaspora.* Albuquerque: University of New Mexico Press.

Flores, Richard R. 2002. *Remembering the Alamo: Memory, Modernity, and the Master Symbol.* Austin: University of Texas Press.

Gaspar de Alba, Alicia. 1998. *Chicano Art Inside/Outside the Master's House: Cultural Politics and the CARA Exhibition.* Austin: University of Texas Press.

Gaspar de Alba, Alicia, and Alma López, eds. 2011. *Our Lady of Controversy: Alma López's "Irreverent Apparition."* Austin: University of Texas Press.

Granziera, Patrizia. 2004. "From Coatlicue to Guadalupe: The Image of the Great Mother in Mexico." *Studies in World Christianity* 10, no. 2: 250–73.

James, Joy. 2007. Foreword to *Unmaking Race, Remaking Soul: Transformative Aesthetics and the Practice of Freedom,* edited by Christa Davis Acampora and Angela L. Cotton. Albany: State University of New York Press.

León-Portilla, Miguel. 2012. *Aztec Thought and Culture: A Study of the Ancient Nahuatl Mind.* Translated by Jack Emory Davis. Tulsa: University of Oklahoma Press. First published 1963.

López-Lozano, Miguel. 2008. *Utopian Dreams, Apocalyptic Nightmares: Globalization in Recent Mexican and Chicano Narrative.* West Lafayette, IN: Purdue University Press.

Lugones, María. 2008. "The Coloniality of Gender." *Worlds and Knowledges Otherwise* (Center for Global Studies and the Humanities, Duke University) vol. 2, dossier 2. https://globalstudies.trinity.duke.edu/wko-v2d2.

McMahon, Marci R. 2013. "The Chili Queens of San Antonio: Challenging Domestication through Street Vending and Fashion." In *Domestic Negotiations: Gender, Nation, and Self-Fashioning in US Mexicana and Chicana Literature and Art,* 27–48. New Brunswick, NJ: Rutgers University Press.

McClintock, Anne. 1995. *Imperial Leather: Race, Gender, and Sexuality in the Colonial Contest.* New York: Routledge.

Mignolo, Walter D. 2000. *Local Histories/Global Designs: Coloniality, Subaltern Knowledges, and Border Thinking.* Princeton, NJ: Princeton University Press.

Miller, Mary Ellen, and Karl Taube. 1997. *An Illustrated Dictionary of the Gods and Symbols of Ancient Mexico and the Maya.* London: Thames & Hudson.

Miranda, Deborah A. 2010. "Extermination of the Joyas: Gendercide in Spanish California." *GLQ: A Journal of Lesbian and Gay Studies* 16, nos. 1–2: 253–84.

Moraga, Cherríe. 1993. "Dreaming of Other Planets." In *The Last Generation: Prose and Poetry by Cherríe Moraga,* 33. Boston: South End Press.

Muñoz, José Esteban. 2009. *Cruising Utopia: The Then and There of Queer Futurity.* New York: New York University Press.

Nericcio, William Anthony. 2007. *Tex[t]-Mex: Seductive Hallucinations of the "Mexican" in America*. Austin: University of Texas Press.

Olguín, B. V. 2010. *La Pinta: Chicana/o Prisoner Literature, Culture, and Politics*. Austin: University of Texas Press.

Olmsted, Frederick Law. 1857. *A Journey through Texas; or, a Saddle Trip on the Southwestern Frontier*. New York: Dix, Edwards.

Peña, Manuel H. 1999. "Music of the Nineteenth Century: An Overview." In *Música Tejana: The Cultural Economy of Artistic Transformation*. College Station: Texas A&M University Press.

Pérez, Emma. 1999. *The Decolonial Imaginary: Writing Chicanas into History*. Bloomington: Indiana University Press.

Pérez, Laura E. 1999. "*El desorden*, Nationalism, and Chicana/o Aesthetics." In *Between Woman and Nation: Nationalisms, Transnational Feminisms, and the State*, edited by Caren Kaplan, Norma Alarcón, and Minoo Moallem, 19–46. Durham, NC: Duke University Press.

———. 2007. *Chicana Art: The Politics of Spiritual and Aesthetic Altarities*. Durham, NC: Duke University Press.

Peterson, Jeanette Favrot. 1992. "The Virgin of Guadalupe: Symbol of Conquest or Liberation?" *Art Journal* 51, no. 4: 39–47.

Ramírez, Catherine S. 2004. "Deus ex Machina: Tradition, Technology, and the Chicanafuturist Art of Marion C. Martinez." *Aztlán: A Journal of Chicano Studies* 29, no. 2: 55–92.

———. 2008. "Afrofuturism/Chicanafuturism: Fictive Kin." *Aztlán: A Journal of Chicano Studies* 33, no. 1: 185–94.

Santos, John Phillip. 1999. *Places Left Unfinished at the Time of Creation*. New York: Viking.

Soto, Sandra K. 2010. *Reading Chican@ Like a Queer: The De-Mastery of Desire*. Austin: University of Texas Press.

Tafolla, Carmen. 2005. "MesoMorphine: PAX AMERICANA and Other Myths: A Critique by Carmen Tafolla." Latina/o Art Community. http://latinoartcommunity.org/community/EducationalRes/Vistas/Tafolla-MesoMorphine.html.

Taylor, William B. 1987. "The Virgin of Guadalupe in New Spain: An Inquiry into the Social History of Marian Devotion." *American Ethnologist* 14, no. 1: 9–33.

Tuhkanen, Mikko. 2011. "Mestiza Metaphysics." In *Queer Times, Queer Becomings*, edited by E. L. McCallum and Mikko Tuhkanen, 259–94. Albany: State University of New York Press.

Ybarra-Frausto, Tomás. 1991. "Rasquachismo: A Chicano Sensibility." In *Chicano Art: Resistance and Affirmation, 1965–1985*, edited by Richard Griswold del Castillo, Teresa McKenna, and Yvonne Yarbro-Bejarano, 155–62. Los Angeles: Wight Art Gallery, University of California.

Mundos Alternos
A Skylab for Speculative Curation

Robb Hernández

Although the study of Latina/o speculative aesthetics is gaining momentum within cultural discourses of literature, film, and graphic arts, its consequence for contemporary art history and performance is little known. Because live art actions and exhibition displays are temporary, the audience's capacity to see and experience the work narrows. As a result, the venue itself performs an important function by mediating between artist, art practice, and arts laboratory. The outcomes of these momentary actions, visual interventions, and performances intensify our attention to and experience of space. For example, while Vargas-Suarez Universal's installation for the Rubin Center for the Visual Arts, *Search for Life: Aliens, Water and Surveillance* (2008), compared the "alien" terra firma of Mexico and Mars, Pedro Reyes's *Pirámide Flotante/Floating Pyramid* (2004) is a site-specific installation of utopian environmental design set on water.[1] A part of the second annual *Trienal Poli/Gráfica de San Juan*, Reyes's Styrofoam sculpture drifts on the Caribbean Sea, monumentalizing the multidimensional force of the Bermuda Triangle, where earthly maritime borders interconnect extraterrestrial portals. The two works show how Latino and Latin American artists propose a speculative geography that reimagines the borderlands through a transplanetary orientation of earth and sea. So too, a plethora of works reflect creative expression inspired by the sky, suggesting an important visual discourse that animates another vision for *latinidad*, one that defies border, gravity, and citizenry by looking skyward. This aerial relation to Latino subjectivity is nowhere more evident than in the science fiction (SF) impulse of contemporary Puerto Rican art.

As a result, a "skylab" emerges, opening onto an alternate world, a world undergirding the curatorial schema of the exhibition *Mundos Alternos: Art and Science Fiction in the Americas*. Set to open on September 30, 2017, at the University of California, Riverside ARTSblock, *Mundos Alternos* is part of the Getty Foundation's ambitious arts initiative *Pacific Standard Time*. With forty-six exhibitions at major museums and cultural institutions, *Pacific Standard Time: LA/LA* is framed around the interconnections of Los Angeles with Latin America ("LA/LA"), interpreting this linkage through different time periods, art movements, themes, and artist monographs. Though many of these shows focus on the past, *Mundos Alternos*, curated by Tyler Stallings, Joanna Szupinska-Myers, and me, takes up the future.

Visiting six nations in Latin America and the Hispanophone Caribbean (Argentina, Brazil, Chile, Cuba, Mexico, and Puerto Rico), as well as ten US cities (Austin, Chicago, Houston, Los Angeles, Miami, New York, Phoenix, San Antonio San Francisco, and Santa Fe), the curatorial team assessed over 300 artists. This resulted in the selection of thirty-five artists for ARTSblock, an 8,000-square-foot space with the distinction of being the third-largest art museum in the University of California system. Inspired by what Latin American curator Mari Carmen Ramírez (2000, 15) calls "constellations," and organizing works through a synecdochical approach based on "luminous points," we drew from a range of media and genres: paintings, graphite drawings, cinematic props, mixed-media sculptures, video projections, site-specific installations, costume design, and a smaller exhibition within the exhibition. *Mundos Alternos* engineers "alternate worlds" in immersive media environments, challenging the earth-bound sites from which citizenship, borders, and national bodies are traditionally viewed in Latino, Latin American, and American studies.

From the outset, the rich terrain, profusion of artworks, and regional SF imaginaries underlying an exhibition of this type posed other lines of inquiry for the curatorial team. What constitutes a Latino and Latin American "science fiction" art practice? Is it based on a recognizable set of generic SF tropes like time travel, space exploration, alien contact, utopic world building, or cyberpunk? Is it a question of legible iconographies that rely on narrative figuration, like OVNIs (*objeto volador no identificado*, or UFO in English), extraterrestrials, spaceships, or unexplainable paranormal phenomena? Or is it about SF as a mode of analysis, unsettling what was unimaginable in Latina/os' past and replacing it with a futurist vision?

Rather than rehearse an object checklist, with studied evaluations of specific works organized in an overview of the show, this essay explicates curating as a translation of interpretive processes. By thinking through three key areas undergirding *Mundos Alternos*—exhibition precedents, arts fieldwork, and aesthetic qualifiers—I underscore the difficult process of fashioning a curatorial framework for this show. Toward this end, I reflect on my experiences in a site little regarded within Latino/Latin American science fiction studies: Puerto Rico. My findings challenged our curatorial approach, magnified a SF vernacular in the everyday life of el Caribe, and expanded the visual definition of science fiction within contemporary art of the Americas overall.

Curating Alternate Americas

Although the field of Latin American science fiction is well represented in the literature and cinema of Mexico, Argentina, and Brazil, its art history is undefined in the context of speculative and futurist aesthetics. Astronomy, space exploration, celestial imagery, pre-Columbian cosmologies, and lunar lifecycles recur throughout twentieth-century Mexican art and modernism. Lithographs by influential draftsman José Guadalupe Posada demonstrate his fascination with Halley's Comet, seen as an omen of the impending Mexican Revolution in 1910.[2] Such "pessimistic" visions of cosmic light streaking across the Mexican night sky "helped to revive ancient fears related to comets" (Köhler 2002, 2). Surrealist painter and printmaker Rufino Tamayo applies space iconography and astronomical imagery in his works *Terror cósmico* (1954), *El astrónomo* (1954), and *Perro ladrando a la luna* (1942).[3] Diego Rivera's mural *Man at the Crossroads* expresses tropes closely aligned with science fiction generic structures: humanism/ machinery, dystopia/utopia, and natural ecology/scientific hegemony (Coffey 2012, 35). As art historian Mary Coffey notes, Rivera "strikes a balance between celebrating the liberatory potential of mass communication and cautioning against its potential use for evil" (37). The mural's portrait of Russian Communist revolutionary Vladimir Lenin displeased its patron, Nelson Rockefeller, and angered the US public. This, in part, motivated Rivera's decision to destroy the mural before its completion at the RCA tower in New York City's Rockefeller Center; it was later re-created as *Man, Controller of the Universe* in 1934 in Mexico City.

While these early art strategies may suggest the entry of science fiction into Latin American art history, it fits uncomfortably as a genre, and SF remained unnamed in Latin America until the 1960s. As a result, according to Rachel Haywood Ferriera (2011), there is a drive to "retrolabel" early literature engaging the fantastic, magical realist, speculative, and prophetic, uncovering another SF genealogy in its complex expression. *Mundos Alternos* confirms Haywood Ferriera's claim that "science fiction has been a global genre from its earliest days and that Latin America has participated in this genre using local appropriations and local adaptations" (1). However, her emphasis on literature does not fully embrace the ways in which art historical and curatorial theories might function in this milieu. This is especially true of contemporary art, where an emphasis on postmodern aesthetics and media-like appropriation, video art, pop art, sound collage, kinetic sculpture, and experimental modes of performance art expands science fiction's visual repertoire. In deciding what to "retrolabel," we must challenge not only the ways we read science fiction but also the ways we see it (1).

For the *Mundos Alternos* curatorial team, there were few exhibitions that could serve as precedents, especially on this size and scale. The most notable were found in the realm of Chicano art and drawn from Southern California, mostly within the last two decades. Perry Vasquez curated some of the earliest SF shows, which emphasized social satire. In San Diego, *Plan 9 from Aztlán* (1995) at Centro Cultural de la Raza and *Alien Attack: Outer Visions in Popular Art* (1996) at Virus Gallery were among cultural responses to the racist and xenophobic discourse surrounding California's Proposition 187, a ballot initiative championed by Republican governor Pete Wilson in 1994.[4] The campaign to pass the measure, which sought to deny public services to undocumented immigrants, maximized fear by warning of "illegal aliens" invading California. Wilson's analogy riffs on nativist anxiety about immigrants encroaching on the country by land across the US-Mexico border and even by sky. His dual-meaning usage of "alien invasion" drew derisive responses from Latino cultural activists. As syndicated columnists Roberto Rodriguez and Patrisia Gonzales (1994) observed, "While the anti-immigrant fervor sweeping the country is causing many to suspect that every Latino is an alien, it is also giving Latino comics great material."

For an exhibition titled *Chorizo of the Gods?* (1994), *Pocho Magazine* coeditors Lalo Alcaraz and Esteban Zul staged a visual parody replete with a silver sombrero suspended from the gallery ceiling like a flying saucer and a mock tabloid magazine cover exposing Pete Wilson's long-concealed "alien" heritage shared with his *primo*, Mordok (Goodwin 2013, 144). In his excellent assessment, Matthew David Goodwin contends, "While Alcaraz is responding to the derogatory correlation of the alien and immigrant, he is also responding to the hysteria of the citizenry that imagines itself as the victim of colonization" (71). As a cartoonist, Alcaraz imbues the exhibition with a searing political commentary in contrived artifacts, false documents, and humorist texts, mocking the absurdity of Prop 187. By confronting Wilson's racist ideology, he unmasks the "white cube" that lures the public into a false state of belief under the guise of historical accuracy and museum authority. Like Vasquez's exhibitions, Alcaraz's curatorial intervention exemplifies science fiction's biting social commentary and unsettles the "legitimate" citizen-subject. Shows like *Chorizo of the Gods?* and *Plan 9 from Aztlán* are important models for SF exhibitions in Latino cultural spaces. While their kitschy register constitutes an undeniable visual archive, these shows are removed from the restrictive nomenclatures and discursive organizations of contemporary art history.

Science fiction's entry into an institutional art-museum cultural complex would unfold more than a decade later. Following *The Shadows Took Shape* (2013) at the Studio Museum in Harlem, an influential exhibition on Afrofuturist aesthetics, contemporary art curators seemed to find the speculative a compelling resource for social commentary and a locus for artistic innovation. In 2015, Sarah Montross, a Mellon postdoctoral curatorial fellow at the Bowdoin College Museum of Art, organized *Past Futures: Science Fiction, Space Travel, and Postwar Art of the Americas*. Whereas *The Shadows Took Shape* presented sixty artists over a span of twenty-five years, *Past Futures* was more focused, examining space age technological advancements, the boom in science fiction as a recognizable genre in the United States, and creative responses to new scientific knowledge about space exploration and the moon landing. Her curatorial vision is anchored in the postwar period of the 1940s through 1970s (see Keith and Whitley 2013). Montross observes that the show "combines the empirical with the imaginary" and notes how "these contemporary artists are revisiting the well-trodden territories of science fiction and space travel to create entirely new meanings, which suggests that artistic practice and historical reexamination engaging these themes will continue to expand toward new frontiers" (2015, 30).

These "new frontiers," however, are limited by SF's visual archive. *Past Futures* makes no claim to be comprehensive, but emphasizes well-known artists from Chile, Argentina, and Mexico, including Juan Downey, Gyula Kosice, and Roberto Matta (US-based artists Nancy Graves and Robert

Smithson also make appearances). Foregrounding artists recognized within the Latin American art establishment, *Past Futures* shows a curatorial predisposition for the "creative styles" of Latin American avant-gardes (Montross 2015, 16), effectively jettisoning the sardonic humor and kitsch deployed by Lalo Alcaraz and Perry Vasquez in Chicano art. *Mundos Alternos*, by taking up SF imaginaries emerging within the Hispanophone Caribbean, Central America, and in particular US *latinidad*, negotiates both exhibition styles by fusing the political satire of artists responding to anti-immigrant furor with the creative ingenuity arising from space exploration and futurist technologies as a consequence of Latin American modernism.

In Search of a Speculative Caribbean

In fact, both curatorial models reshaped the scope of our fieldwork practice. With a generous research grant from the Getty Foundation, the arts research team of *Mundos Alternos* cultivated a transnational advisory board with scholars and specialists in complementary fields. In Ciudad de México, Miguel Ángel Fernández Delgado, a historian and collector of Spanish-language science fiction, and Itala Schmelz, author of *El futuro más acá: Cine mexicano de ciencia ficción* (2009), supported artist studio visits, contributed expertise, and provided rare ephemera and books to the show's archive. Alfredo Luiz Suppia, a film professor at Brazil's Universidade Estadual de Campinas and author of *The Replicant Metropolis: Constructing a Dialogue between Metropolis and Blade Runner* (2011, in Portuguese), facilitated the team's travels throughout the Southern Cone. Contributions by art history professor Kency Cornejo emphasized the decolonial aesthetics of indigenous technologies. Her work raised the profile of Central America in the project, contributing to a more hemispheric expanse of SF visuality within a "transisthmus" topos.[5]

The initiative of contemporary art curator Rebeca Noriega Costas was key to our effort to identify little-known SF creative works in Puerto Rico. A society ravaged by US neocolonial occupation, corporate pharmaceutical experimentation, and economic deprivation, Puerto Rico has produced a strikingly decolonial SF visual vocabulary. Noriega compiled an important registry of established and emergent artists who are responding to the ways in which invasive technologies, military surveillance, and scientific laboratories have marked the island's landscape. Because of its geopolitical and strategic position in the Caribbean, Puerto Rico is what Manuel Aviles-Santiago calls a "technological embodiment of colonialism," where new technologies intended to control colonial subjects have been confronted and subverted through political dissidence against machines (2015, 1). This postindustrial built environment also reflects SF reimaginings of technology that contains portals to alternate realms, like the Arecibo radio telescope, the world's largest sonic radar for extraterrestrial sound. A house designed like a flying saucer, high on a hillside in the town of Juana Diaz, emits the key tones of the mother ship from Steven Spielberg's *Close Encounters of the Third Kind* (1977) (Wadler 2012).

Such blurred borders between techno-science, fiction, and environment took our project team from established art institutions in Santurce, a district of San Juan, to the rural hillsides of Lajas in the island's southwest corner. Our fieldwork on the island went far beyond the traditional artist studio visit or portfolio review, sometimes involving extensive stays and daylong excursions to observe the "alien" expressions dotting the cultural landscape. From my earliest moments of field research in Puerto Rico, I became aware of a SF vernacular that seemed to pervade everyday life. From the public consumption of "UFO blanco" beer, its bottle embellished with a motif of Saturn's rings encircling an orange wedge, to the street art adorning Caribbean architecture, walking the streets invited "otherworldly" encounters.[6]

For example, a chance discovery on the exterior façade of a Spanish colonial building in Viejo San Juan demonstrates the subtle but ubiquitous presence of OVNI visuality (fig. 1). Illustrated on the wall in pencil graphite, the mimetic alien figure is more than a vandal's mark, as it symbolically articulates a broader metaphorical commentary about Puerto Rico's political situation. The unexplainable zigzag movement of the flying saucer evokes the island's path to self-governance—jagged, unrealized, and speculative. Like an alien sighting, Puerto Rican national autonomy is widely doubted,

Figure 1. *Ovni street art in Viejo San Juan, 2014. Digital photograph. Collection of the author.*

377

though glimpsed long enough to suggest that "we are not alone," a reassuring position for those willing to believe that it was there in the first place.

More than a commentary on the neocolonial status of the island, the OVNI is also a link to airborne phenomena that have played a role in Puerto Rican political history. During World War II and the decade that followed, US labor shortages in manufacturing and agriculture and high unemployment on the island resulted in the migration of approximately 760,000 Puerto Ricans to New York (Padilla 1958, vii). In Elena Padilla's aptly titled anthropological study *Up from Puerto Rico*, she recognizes that "the monumental expansion of air transportation" had far-reaching consequences (vii). Traveling via "la guagua aérea" (the air bus), Puerto Ricans transited what Alberto Sandoval Sánchez calls a "figurative border zone float[ing] above the ocean" (1997, 198). This resulted in an identity formation predicated on an aerial borderland and a "floating nation" (199). Aeronautical engineering made possible the "creation of a bicultural/ transcultural interstitial zone where identity is but oscillation, flux, fusion, elusiveness, ambivalence, ambiguity, and contradictions" (198)—contradictions that place Puerto Rican border space in a vertical arrangement between future utopic promise of air travel and present dystopic reality of US empire building and the untenable financial situation of the island.

Aerial technology's entanglement with Puerto Rican cultural and national identity undergirds Sofía Gallisá Muriente's dual-screen projection *Lluvia con nieve* (fig. 2). Recovering rare film footage from Paramount Newsreel, which styled itself the "eyes and ears of the world," Gallisá Muriente (2014) exposes a speculative moment in US military occupation. She unearths forty seconds of film documenting an Eastern Airlines flight dropping two tons of New Hampshire snow on the island in 1955, a sensational ploy by the San Juan mayor, Doña Fela, to give Puerto Rico a "real" American Christmas. Arriving by way of a specialized silver capsule launched through the sky, the artificial snowfall in a baseball stadium altered the Caribbean landscape momentarily. It also created an orgiastic political spectacle that distracted *puertorriqueños* from the March 1954 attack by Puerto Rican nationalists, including Lolita Lebrón, who stormed the US Capitol building screaming "¡Viva Puerto Rico Libre!" to demand independence for the island from US military occupation (Aviles-Santiago 2015, 8). Through slow-motion speeds, languishing zooms, and studied frames, Gallisá's installation sets a disturbing tone as it scrutinizes US atmospheric technology deployed with colonializing intent. "Snow" in Puerto Rico occurred four times between 1952 and 1955—a demonstration of US aeronautical mastery

Figure 2. Sofía Gallisá Muriente, Lluvia con nieve, 2014. Video installation with publication on newsprint. Image courtesy of the artist.

over the Caribbean that is another example of technological advancement making the island landscape strange, of colonial discord coming from the sky.

So it came as little surprise when retired schoolteacher Reynaldo Ríos Ayala, president of Ovni Internacional, proposed construction plans for an "ovnipuerto" (UFO port) on the mountainous hillside of the Sierra Bermeja in Lajas, where over a hundred UFO sightings have been reported since the 1980s (see Cruz 2008, 5–6). Ríos found an unlikely ally in Mayor Marcos "Turin" Irizarry, who was elated by the possibility of building on an extraterrestrial tourism industry and rebranding Lajas as the Roswell, New Mexico, of the Caribbean (Olson 2005). Ríos Ayala's architectural design proposed a landing strip, pyramidal control tower, and observation deck for OVNI night vigils. The sensationalized publicity surrounding plans for the world's first ovnipuerto was a popular topic during my artist studio visits, among other tales of paranormal phenomenon, US military conspiracy theories, and alien abduction on the island.

This linkage of Puerto Rico with the extraterrestrial motivated mixed-media artists Adál Maldonado and José Luis Vargas to organize a road trip with Rebeca Noriega and me in pursuit of the ovnipuerto. Traveling to the southern side of the island, we met uncanny obstacles. Frustrated by the lack of clear signs and a confused GPS—"Must be the ovnis toying with

379

our instruments," José Luis remarked—we stopped off at a roadside *piña* stand. Adál's sincere request for directions to the ovnipuerto was nothing short of SF performance enacted through ordinary street talk, as though his search for the OVNIs were an everyday happening on the island, as though they walked among us. Once we were redirected, signs and building façades hinted we were close. Walls displayed alien figures embellished with Boricua signifiers: one alien sold *pinchos*, a favorite roadside meat kabob, while another drank Medalla, a popular island beer. If we were expecting evidence of an OVNI crash site, spacecraft, or futurist architectural structures, though, our findings came up short: what we encountered was a city-approved road sign designating Ruta Extraterrestre PR 303.

Undeterred, Adál began snapping photographs. If the ovnipuerto did not exist physically, it might exist conceptually. In a moment of impromptu performance, we staged our own confrontation with *extraterrestre* in Lajas. With hands pointed skyward, we embodied what contact might look like. Our physical gesture added yet one more speculative record of the ovnipuerto, another "encounter" in the repertoire of sensationalized accounts bolstering popular folklore about unexplainable phenomena like the orbs of light above the nearby Laguna Cartagena. Using another artistic measure to broaden a Caribbean speculative existence, Adál appropriated this performance documentation and created a digital postcard of the event, a piece of what he terms "mind fiction" that blends camera-based evidence with tourist photography, B-movie film still, and experimental narrative (fig. 3). Citing the multiple hoaxes played on Puerto Ricans, ranging from the illusory promise of self-governance to the distraction of airborne visual spectacularity—where, according to Guy Debord (1995, 17), "the spectacle philosophizes reality, and turns the material life of everyone into a universe of speculation"—Adál's inscription of this digital postcard puts Puerto Rico squarely under a SF lens, declaring, "The truth is out there."

Figure 3. Adál, Sightings: UFOS Sobre Ovnipuerto/Ruta Extraterrestre Lajas, 303, Lajas, Puerto Rico, 2015. *Digital photograph. Image courtesy of the artist.*

Existing in a neocolonial state, one marked by the recurrent experience of looking skyward, Puerto Rico has lived moments of technological invasion and aerial distortion throughout its political history. Based on our curatorial fieldwork, we made necessary adjustments to the aesthetic qualifications for our show to bring the historicist practice of Gallisá into productive dialogue with the speculative archive of Adál. Because Latino and Latin American artists reimagine their cultural circumstances, transgress the fixed borders between nation-states, and confront futurist technologies through a SF lens, *Mundos Alternos* presents works giving visual coherence and material expression to the state of "alienation" that characterizes an immigrant and *transfrontera* border ethos.[7] More than this, fashioning world-building possibilities from the ruins of inflammatory anti-immigrant rhetoric allows *Mundos Alternos* to undercut the racialized logic that has historically constituted SF as a hegemonic colonial genre that reenacts First World conquest over extraterrestrial lands. Our curatorial practice reverses this logic and implicitly urges Latina/o cultural studies to reconsider its orientation of borders, identities, and places through a vertically aligned transplanetary *latinidad*, of which Puerto Rico is exemplary.

Notes

The author would like to thank the editors of this volume, the *Mundos Alternos* curatorial team, the contributing artists, and, in particular, Adál, Mary Coffey, Sofía Gallisá Muriente, Matt Goodwin, Aidan Lopez Linehan, Rebeca Noriega, and Tatiana Reinoza for their invaluable insights, suggestions, and accompaniment across Puerto Rico's speculative landscape.

1. Vargas-Suarez Universal's piece was a part of the exhibition *Claiming Space: Mexican Americans in U.S. Cities* (2008) at the Rubin Center for the Visual Arts, University of Texas, El Paso. It was generously evaluated by the show's co-curator, Kate Bonansinga, in the exhibition catalog (2014, 89–108). For more on Pedro Reyes's floating sculpture, see Reyes (2008, 17–20).

2. See, for instance, Artemio Rodríguez (2003, 32).

3. For more on this consider Jiménez (2010) and Ryan (1987).

4. *Plan 9 from Aztlán* is a riff on Ed Wood's infamous B-film, *Plan 9 from Outer Space* (1959).

5. "Transisthmus" is Central Americanist literary scholar Ana Patricia Rodríguez's term (2009, 2).

6. UFO is a Belgian-style craft beer produced by Harpoon Brewery, which operates out of New England, another strange example of how Puerto Rico's social landscape is transformed by resources originating in the Vermont–New Hampshire

Upper Valley. The colonial implications of this relationship are seen in Sofía Gallisá Muriente's installation *Lluvia con nieve* (2014), which comments on the historic uses of New England snow and aerial technology to disarm the Puerto Rican independence movement in the 1950s. I discuss this unlikely regional connection further in this essay.

7. My thoughts here are indebted to Catherine Ramírez's (2002) observations of Gloria Anzaldúa's "alien consciousness" within the broader contours of women of color feminist theory, cyborg feminism, and SF studies.

Works Cited

Ávila Jiménez. Norma. 2010. *El arte cósmico de Tamayo*. Mexico City: Editorial Praxis/UNAM.

Aviles-Santiago, Manuel G. 2015. "The Technological Embodiment of Colonialism in Puerto Rico." *Anthurium: A Caribbean Studies Journal* 12, no. 2: 1–20.

Bonansinga, Kate. 2014. *Curating at the Edge: Artists Respond to the U.S./Mexico Border*. Austin: University of Texas Press.

Coffey, Mary K. 2012. *How a Revolutionary Art Became Official Culture: Murals, Museums, and the Mexican State*. Durham, NC: Duke University Press.

Cruz, José "Tony." 2008. "Vida Extraterrestre/Extraterrestrial Life: Ovnipuerto/Ufoport." In "Triangulo de las Bermudas," special issue, *Número Cero* 2: 5–8.

Debord, Guy. 1995. *The Society of the Spectacle*. Translated by Donald Nicholson-Smith. New York: Zone.

Gallisá Muriente, Sofía. 2014. "Lluvia con nieve." Statement on artist's website, http://hatoreina.com.

Goodwin, Matthew David. 2013. "The Fusion of Migration and Science Fiction in Mexico, Puerto Rico, and the United States." PhD dissertation, University of Massachusetts, Amherst.

Haywood Ferreira, Rachel. 2011. *The Emergence of Latin American Science Fiction*. Middletown, CT: Wesleyan University Press.

Keith, Naima J., and Zoe Whitley, eds. 2013. *The Shadows Took Shape*. New York: Studio Museum in Harlem.

Köhler, Ulrich. 2002. "Meteors and Comets in Ancient Mexico." In *Catastrophic Events and Mass Extinctions: Impacts and Beyond*, edited by Christian Koeberl and Kenneth G. MacLeod, 1–6. Boulder: Geological Society of America.

Montross, Sarah. 2015. "Cosmic Orbits: Observing Postwar Art of the Americas from Outer Space." In *Past Futures: Science Fiction, Space Travel, and Postwar Art of the Americas*, exhibition catalog, edited by Sarah J. Montross, 14–31. Brunswick, ME: Bowdoin College Museum of Art; Cambridge, MA: MIT Press.

Olson, Alexandra. 2005. "Puerto Rico Farming Town to Build UFO Landing Strip." *USA Today*, September 28.

Padilla, Elena. 1958. *Up from Puerto Rico*. New York: Columbia University Press.

Ramírez, Catherine S. 2002. "Cyborg Feminism: The Science Fiction of Octavia E. Butler and Gloria Anzaldúa." In *Reload: Rethinking Women + Cyberculture*, edited by Mary Flanagan and Austin Booth, 374–402. Cambridge, MA: MIT Press.

Ramírez, Mari Carmen. 2000. "Constellations: Toward a Radical Questioning of Dominant Curatorial Models." *Art Journal* 59, no. 1: 14–16.

Reyes, Pedro. 2008. "Fuerza Magnéticas/Magnetic Forces: Pirámide Flotante/ Floating Pyramid." In "Triangulo de las Bermudas," special issue, *Número Cero* 2: 17–20.

Rodríguez, Ana Patricia. 2009. *Dividing the Isthmus: Central American Transnational Histories, Literatures, and Cultures*. Austin: University of Texas Press.

Rodríguez, Artemio, ed. 2003. *José Guadalupe Posada: 150 Años*. Los Angeles: La Mano.

Rodriguez, Roberto, and Patrisia Gonzales. 1994. "Did You Hear the One about the Governor from Space?" *Seattle Times*, September 4.

Ryan, Judith. 1987. *Man, Sun, Space: Graphic Art of Rufino Tamayo*. Melbourne: National Gallery of Victoria.

Sandoval Sánchez, Alberto. 1997. "Puerto Rican Identity Up in the Air: Air Migration, Its Cultural Representations, and Me 'Cruzando el Charco.'" In *Puerto Rican Jam: Rethinking Colonialism and Nationalism*, edited by Frances Negrón-Muntaner and Ramón Grosfoguel, 189–208. Minneapolis: University of Minnesota Press.

Schmelz, Itala, ed. 2009. *El futuro mas acá: Cine mexicano de ciencia ficción*. Mexico City: Universidad Nacional Autónoma de México.

Suppia, Alfredo. 2011. *A metrópole replicante: Construindo um diálogo entre Metropolis e Blade Runner*. Juiz de Fora, Brazil: Ed. Universidade Federal de Juiz de Fora.

Wadler, Joyce. 2012. "Close Encounters of the Romantic Kind." *New York Times*, August 8.

PART VI

Latin@ Literary Altermundos and Multiverses

Intimations of Infinite Entanglement

Notes toward a Prolegomena for Any Future Repudiatory Postscript to *The Farthest Home Is in an Empire of Fire*

John Phillip Santos

> The favorite newscasters on DNA-TV seem unquestionably to be enormous, fluorescent serpents.
>
> Jeremy Narby, *The Cosmic Serpent*

My initiation as a writer, sometime in my early high school years, was from its inception almost immovably oriented toward a nonfiction autobiographical voice. As a poet, I was a phenomenologist of the everyday, always trying to connect the minutiae of the diurnal round to more expansive, perhaps even cosmic, sources and cycles of meaning. And implicit in this ontological tuning was a literary *compromiso* with the task of remembering, the centrality of memory in the ages-old *movida* of the creative process.

My literary mentor and erstwhile pen pal, Laura (Riding) Jackson, had put forward a challenge to all writers in her 1972 work *The Telling*: "I propose that you seek in yourselves the remembrance of the Before, and write what you find, and believe your words."

It was a literary *mandado* that I took to heart, along with her withering indictment of the artifice of poetry as a distraction from, if not outright betrayal of, the writer's fundamental obligation to tell truth.

This was long before I discovered the centrality of testimonio as a literary genre, in both fiction and nonfictional voices, to the emergent (and deeply conflicted) Chicano/a literary tradition, from Américo Paredes to Richard Rodriguez and Gloria Anzaldúa, among a host of others. I won't reflect here on the importance of this genre to this insurgent literary legacy, or on the serendipitous ways it has manifested itself in the works of a long list of writers (and artists). Instead, I want to explore the mutations of my version of "remembrance of the Before" and understand how they led me to the perhaps peculiar increasing emphasis on classical and emergent scientific discourses of the self in my own practice of autobiographical storytelling.

What was my "remembrance of the Before?"—and how did it shape the stories I wanted to tell?

The Soviet Union launched the Sputnik 1 satellite into Earth orbit on October 4, 1957, a fortnight and a day after I was born. One month later, Sputnik 2 vaulted Laika, a stray spotted terrier snatched from the streets of Moscow, into near-Earth orbit. Tragically, Laika expired a few short hours later, after the capsule's cooling system failed.

The tragic truth of Laika's precipitous demise was only revealed in 2002, but as the first Earth creature to enter into and expire in space, her unprecedented apogee, as well as her death, augured the question of the soul's ultimate destiny in zero gravity—an age-old ontological question suddenly, perhaps prophetically, shifted into the void of space.

Just four years earlier, Francis Crick and James Watson had finally deduced the structure of the DNA molecule's double helix (in a story of genius, intrigue, and deceit too fraught to go into here; suffice it to say, all praise to the too little heralded Rosalind Franklin and her *Photo 51*!). Humankind finally fathomed the algorithmic chemical substrate of heredity, the blueprint of our bodies.

That such a hereditary biological process existed, we knew.

But, as James Watson has observed, "The question was how could all the specificity be copied." The answer was gobsmacking. The molecule they revealed was both beautiful and alien, a self-replicating enigma emerging out of an only mortally bounded series of spontaneous mirrorings and duplications.

The wave of genetic information, the "raw material" of identity itself, carries forward across generations. And here was the mechanism underlying the mystic wavelengths of cultural transmission. Biologist Richard Dawkins captured it this way: "What is truly revolutionary about molecular biology in the post-Watson/Crick era is that it has become digital . . . the machine code of the genes is uncannily computer-like."

In the decades that followed, we would come to learn that our DNA also contains an exhaustive, time-coded archive of all our ancestral precursors, a failsafe litany of our origins—should we forget to record or remind ourselves of them—from the beginning of unicellular life: "an unbroken chain of copyings over four billion years," as the author Matt Ridley has described it.

Of course, these epochal events built on a time when a host of minds were discerning the nature of matter and the universe itself, with the momentous discovery of quantum mechanics and the special theory of relativity in the first years of the twentieth century.

So I was born into the New World (465 years into *that* story) in an interval between the discovery of heredity's machinic hard drive and Earth life's first faltering forays into the infinitude of space—in an age when the quantum nature of things was being gradually discerned and described to the world. Emerging narratives of genetics, space exploration, cosmology, and the infinitesimal flux of creation marked the tale of my own emergence *en medias res*. How could these developments not affect the way I would come to tell my own story? How could my sense of self not ultimately be overtaken by the radical instability of quantum flux, making everything of ourselves a wave- or particle-form of irreproducible infinitesimal events?

So much for the Imperial Self.

But what a catalytic time to become a Chicano poet (an already implicitly and multiply hedged identity), birthed into the South Texas borderlands of Greater Mexico (a hinterland of multiple empires, for a very long time indeed).

But as groundbreaking as these discoveries in the sciences were, as transforming as their new visions of our universe would prove to be for physics, cosmology, and biology, their impacts in the fields of culture, arts, and philosophy have been muted, and even more so in the still emergent Chicana/o literary tradition. Understandably, writers of this tradition brought forth their *cris du coeur*, testifying to experiences of oppression and exclusion, neglect and outright negation.

But I was also drawn to a host of prophetic writers such as Sir Thomas Browne, Thomas Traherne, Christopher Smart, and William Blake, along with artists and thinkers such as Samuel Palmer and Edgar Allan Poe, who had long ago prefigured aspects of a self marked by contradictory features of contingency and exactitude, randomness and serendipity, specific geographic origins and even mystic prescient evocations of quantum nonlocality.

A question began to take shape.

Might a proposed cultural metaphysics of the quantum self emerge out of a philosophical immanence that augurs a shape-shifting human agency, shirking boundaries of geographic borders and national cultural identities, boundlessly immediate, unpredictably located in every respect, infinitely searchable with instantaneity and ubiquity, migrating across the planet and (inevitably) beyond, ever deploying to expand the perimeter of humanity's consciousness?

In retrospect, I can see that was a question that propelled the narrative of my 2010 book, *The Farthest Home Is in an Empire of Fire*, the second book in a trilogy of "remembrances of the Before," narratives of my ancestral families and myself, begun with *Places Left Unfinished at the Time of Creation* in 1999.

Those two books would have a quarrel with each other.

The third is still to come.

The storytelling in *Places Left Unfinished* took shape out of my Santos/Garcia family's testimonios, oral histories of my elders. These were rooted in their experiences as *inmigrantes* in San Antonio, Texas, displaced from Mexico in 1914 during the upheaval of the Revolución in Coahuila—and silently carrying the mysterious legacy of my grandfather Juan Jose's death, a likely suicide, perhaps a murder. To reckon with this story I had to reach back into Mexico's origins through my own journeys deep into that land and its conflicted histories, to reconnect our *familia* tale to its sources in the indigenous world—and the mestizo aftermath of the Conquest.

As powerful as the reckonings with this genesis were, these journeys and stories took me to the horizon of a still more profound question: how far back could I reach to offer a *true* account of myself? And could it *truly* come to terms with the staggering implications of a quantum self, the self augured in the emerging science of genealogical genetics that promised the possibility of an infinite recall of each of our individual emergences, extending back to the beginning of unicellular life? My father's family told me stories of how we were shaped by the long Mexican episode of our ancestral journey.

What kind of story might get at our emergence through a millennial unfolding of the quantum flows of evolution and genetic inheritance that underlies all cultural legacy?

My six-year-old daughter recently asked me, "Daddy, how did life begin?" This was a reckoning with the boundedness of the testimonio as it has been practiced and received.

Our Mexican story was at best a five-hundred-year-old tale.

Yet I was increasingly drawn to the story of a humanity that was incalculable in its antiquity and complexity, as evidenced by the deep time contexts of genetics and cosmology—and quantum mechanics revealed just how improvisational and unique my origins in deep time really were.

What did this vast refraction into the past make of my beloved Mexicanness, previously extolled in *Places Left Unfinished?*

An illusion?

An improvisational riff on the human, at best?

Was this emerging tale still Chicano literature?

That was the beginning of the storytelling that shaped the sequel to *Places Left Unfinished*, namely, *The Farthest Home Is in an Empire of Fire.* Ostensibly, it followed the course of the first book, which chronicled my father's Santos and Garcia families. *The Farthest Home* delved into the deep histories of my mother's families, named Lopez and Velas.

But my mother's families, emerging from the Spanish narrative of New Spain, carried a much more documented history, inscribed in documents I would ultimately discover in the legendary Archivo General de Indias in Sevilla, pointing me to the family's provenance in Asturias. Soon, the deep past began to interpolate with the present and with a remembered future, as testified to me by a self-confessed *time-traveling ancestor from the future* who called himself Cenote Siete, and who shares the narration of *The Farthest Home* with me. He announced himself as my descendant, but one born into a time when it was possible to navigate time and space through the electromagnetic spectrum of genetic inheritance.

And he was not just communicating with me; he had been in contact with many of my precursors, including my Uncle Lico, my mother's brother and our family genealogy fanatic. He was an oracle of infinite ancestral entanglement, unaffected by vernacular understandings of time and space.

I'll demur from the blasphemy of auto-exegesis, but suffice it to say both Cenote Siete and I found each other mutually obsessed with the most distant stirrings of the self in deep time. But, as he revealed to me, he is unbounded by time and space, able to traverse these dimensions on the currents of genetic connection, reminding me of Jeremy Narby's observation that "the global network of DNA-based life emits ultra-weak radio waves, which are currently at the limits of measurement, but which we can nonetheless perceive in states of defocalization, such as hallucinations and dreams."

This was the vantage point from which Cenote Siete emerged to me in the storytelling for the book.

Of course, offbeat sci-fi had also provided an echo chamber of voices that were haunted by kindred uncertainties, particularly authors Jorge Luis Borges, Philip K. Dick, Ursula K. Le Guin, and Mary Doria Russell, and such films as *2001: A Space Odyssey* (1968), *Close Encounters of the Third Kind* (1977), *Blade Runner* (1982), and *Code 46* (2003).

I wondered at the possibility of *speculative nonfiction*, or as I imagined the story of *The Farthest Home*, a nonfiction narrative with a science fiction nervous system.

Suddenly, Chicano narrative presented itself as the prospect of an unflinching gaze into the emerging genetic mirror, a mystical psycho-manteum in which we can catch glimpses of the elusive quantum human expressions that lie far below the evidence of our races, cultures, nations, ethnicities. And as soon as you see it, it has transmuted into something new, as if nothing about ourselves is fixable, static, mappable, subject to any fathomable taxonomy or description.

This was finally a self in the mirror I could recognize.

"Is this really nonfiction?" readers often ask about this book.

"It is the story as I lived it," I always reply.

Becoming Nawili
Utopian Dreaming at the End of the World

Cordelia E. Barrera

> When the world ends, her life begins. Soon she'll know who she is.
> Nawili: shape shifter, the last in a line of indigenous warrior women.
> —Cover copy for *Becoming Nawili*

Becoming Nawili is a speculative Latin@ fantasy—part Aztec creation myth and part queer Latin@ bildungsroman. It takes place in the mid-twenty-first-century borderlands, on the cusp of a new world order that reaches back to an indigenous, matriarchal past to imagine a socially and environmentally just future. The first completed novel in my fully conceptualized trilogy, "The Pepa Chronicles," *Nawili* opens in a world devastated by modern-day fracking practices run amok. Following my reflections on the writing of the novel, three short selections from the text are presented below.

The story is told through three narrative voices: Pepa's, Diego Buendia's, and Maria's. Pepa is fifteen when the waters of the Río Grande rear like a radioactive cobra and swallow her whole. Under the earth for a year, her blood and body mutate and an ancient prophecy takes root. Fed a diet of warrior ways and animal traits by the mythical Spider Woman, Pepa is reborn to fulfill a quest written in the blood of an indigenous warrior bloodline. More powerful than any human on earth and intimately tied to *la tierra*, only she can bring order to the chaos above . . . but we don't know that, and neither does she. The Women who have gathered deep in the underground New Mexican desert might know. They have cultivated strange, collective powers of their own; they call to Pepa from dreams and the realm of her Aztec ancestors.

Nawili begins *in medias res*, as Pepa journeys from South Texas to New Mexico through a barren landscape "drunk on sand." Readers experience the changes in Pepa's body as a result of her earlier rebirth—nonlinearly detailed in part 2—and question the sentient landscape alongside her. Diego, her cousin, speaks through his journal; it's through Diego's voice that we learn about their life in the city of "New Laredos" before its obliteration. Maria is responsible for "calling" the Women to New Mexico. Her third-person account connects us with the Women and a collective political consciousness. Fictive documents in the form of journal entries, newspaper clippings, and radio broadcasts constitute the heart of part 1 and tether the reader to the world prior to its destruction.

In *Nawili*, the world and everything in it is devolving, caught in "the Middle," and transforming in untried ways. Many species—humans included—will mutate, but not like Pepa. Her powers were prophesied centuries ago. She commands the sand . . . and she can morph. Humanity might survive the mutations and transformations, but only if Pepa can survive the solitary journey north, and only if she can defeat the evil force that has begun to amass in the south. She is the key to the new order. If Pepa survives, so might humankind.

A central image in *Becoming Nawili* is water. In this New Adult novel, the toxic waters of the Río Grande both shelter and transform the young Chicana protagonist, Pepa. They also evoke Gloria Anzaldúa's *cenote*: "I have a topoi, a place I call *el cenote*," she writes. "In my imagination, I descend into this dreampool, sinkhole, deep well . . . access my culture's collective history." In the heterotopic space of *el cenote*, "memories collide, conflict, converge, condense and negotiate relationships between past, present and future" (1995). From the depths of *el cenote*, Anzaldúa pieces together the fragments of collective memories to rewrite spaces of power and knowledge for Chican@s. In *Becoming Nawili*, the *cenote* motif establishes a link to unexplored indigenous knowledge and ancestral dreampools encased in cyclical time. As Pepa descends into the body of the earth, she unchains a utopic terrain of apocalyptic hope.

Pepa's mid-twenty-first-century world mirrors our own, as brown workers provide much of the labor that sustains the newly formed Homeland States of America. On the surface, *Nawili* is a work of speculative fiction, an experimental novel that imagines a holistic way of living and being in the world. The lifeblood that courses through *Nawili* is primal, apocalyptic, and utopic. The fantastic heterotopic spaces that emerge from the ruins of eco-catastrophe, however, deliver more than the slim dream of survival we find in many Western post-apocalyptic works. The novel begins as dystopic but is ultimately utopian, blending social dreaming with transcendent idealism. The post-apocalyptic world of the novel mirrors the collective unconscious desires of the main characters, especially the Women, who form the backbone of its transformative political consciousness. In this sense, *Nawili* is patterned after works such as Sally Miller Gearhart's *The Wanderground: Stories of the Hill Women* (1979), Charlotte Perkins Gilman's *Herland* (1915), and the novels of Octavia Butler, texts that engage ecofeminist principles, nonviolent revolutions, the power of feminine collective energies, and the transformation of identity.

I am a product of the South Texas *monte*. Growing up in Laredo in the 1970s and 1980s, my friends and I had little use for indoor games. Our north side neighborhood dissolved into thickets of native *chaparral*, and we lived to explore monolithic plateaus of sticky brush, where we built endless forts from mesquite limbs snapped by families of wild javelinas. We prowled the *senderos* and the miles of untamed *monte* fed by natural creeks and reservoirs. But Laredo's wild spaces, like those throughout South Texas, are vanishing. The city's population has skyrocketed to over 244,000 inhabitants (not including those who live and work in the area without official residency papers), and the infrastructure is notoriously disorganized. In short, the new wealth and substructure created by NAFTA have wreaked havoc on the ecological limits of the landscape. In *Adios to the Brushlands* (1997), Arturo Longoria bemoans the systematic clearing of native *chaparral* in South Texas by large-scale ranching and dry farming practices that exploded in earnest in the 1970s and 1980s. But this was only the beginning. Today, the devastation of the *chaparral* in the name of oil and gas exploration and unbridled corporate interests is choking the lifeblood of the *monte verde* that is our sacred heritage as Tejanos. With the impending possibility of an expanded border wall and a looming, intensifying military presence, it remains to be seen how this unique biosphere will fare.

Two years ago, I found myself driving from Lubbock to Laredo almost weekly. My father was suddenly and inexplicably dead, and my mother was alone in the home our family had occupied for over forty years. The drive was surreal. The I-35 corridor, old Highway 83, and even forgotten country roads on the outskirts of unexceptional towns like Asherton, La Pryor, and Carrizo Springs were thick with semi-trailer trucks, oil tankers, groundwater treatment trucks, wastewater treatment trucks, hazmat trucks, trucks full of sand, steel pipe, drill rigs, casings, missiles . . . Methane plumes marked the escape of dangerous gases into the atmosphere. Rampant, unchecked

395

industrialization and fracking had found a home in South Texas. My life, like the *chaparral* that formed an integral part of my identity, had become a place full of holes.

It was at this time that I became haunted by Anzaldúa's *cenote*. Deep and brimming in uncanny signs, the *cenote* was the place I chose to drown. Perhaps, I thought, I could dive in, enter the serpent's belly the way Anzaldúa does in the "*sueño con serpientes*" section of *Borderlands* (1999), and emerge triumphant and transfigured from my sadness. Perhaps here, I could coalesce the lost pieces of myself, fragments of both flesh and spirit rent asunder by a profit economy in which my father was a number and my *monte* was for sale. Lost in my self-reflexive malaise, I kept my protagonist under the water for a year. Here she would triumph. I would seed her, under the earth, with the strength of the ancients—powers marked in the red and black ink of lost metaphors and primal memories. I would inject her veins with the blood of ten thousand warrior women. But she would need more if she were to emerge a *nepantlera* whose journey ushers a reconceptualized future, one where diversity and difference forge interconnections beyond Western androcentrism to include relations with the environment and other forms of life. Under the earth, where all was not lost, Pepa would unite the world of nature and the world of spirit; here she would encircle the numinous.

In *Becoming Nawili*, Pepa is puma, cephalopod, snake, deer, ant, coyote—all animals refused equal footing with humans in our socially produced and socially constructed world of despot dualities. In my anger and frustration over the exploitation of my community and beloved *chaparral*, I seeded Pepa with a powerful, transformative worldview, a consciousness rooted in communal expressions of identity. She becomes a shape shifter capable of transgressing her human form when she ingests the "seeds" of various animals that have been carefully prepared by the mythical Spider Woman, a kind of "cosmic mother" as described by Joseph Campbell in *The Hero with a Thousand Faces* (1973) and by Monica Sjöö and Barbara Mor in *The Great Cosmic Mother* (1987). Her body has the full consciousness and feelings of a human, but it holds knowledge "transmitted across the generations through ritual and imitation" (Peña 2005, 53). In this regard, Pepa is seeded with "the totality of what can be known" (Campbell 1973, 116) by the Spider Woman, who initiates her into the world of myth. Pepa's powers are magical, primal, and ego shattering, but she is also a reservoir of ancient knowledge. In her posthuman state, she becomes "the champion not of things become but of things becoming" (337). In order to ground egalitarian principles and deep ecological thinking into the fabric of her body and bones, she literally and figuratively *becomes* the earth itself; there is no difference, no dividing line. In *Nawili*, Pepa and the soil, sand, and water are *in lak ech*.

The world that emerges from the cinders of ecological catastrophe in *Nawili* embeds a kind of transformative environmentalism in which humans and animals must relearn how to relate to *la tierra* with psychic and biological energy rather than physical force. In *Nawili* the landscape becomes sentient and devolves to necessitate transformative, integrative, and participatory patterns of living. In this regard, the sentient earth in the novel is much like the imagined terrains in sci-fi classics like Stanislaw Lem's *Solaris* (1961) and J. G. Ballard's *The Drowned World* (1962). My hope was to both empty the landscape and fill it; it is emptied of any objective sense of place, but it brims with a subjective, felt aspect for Pepa, who, like all organic forms, must learn to commune with the landscape in order to survive. *Becoming Nawili*, then, seeks to place ecology within the broader context of human consciousness, and so incorporates imagery and feminist insights that recall preindustrial worldviews of the earth as a living organism and nurturing mother. The utopic impulse in *Nawili* is a direct parallel to the utopic impulses that I believe undergird the most compelling aspects of Anzaldúa's canon, ideas that serve as a "lure and bait for ideology" and an allegorical outline for a better world (Jameson 2007, 3).

The apocalyptic impulse in *Nawili* is defamiliarizing and reflects a despair that stems from historical and social disruption (Rosen 2008, xii). In this regard, *Nawili* owes much to the novels of Octavia E. Butler, works in which difference and diversity serve as a compass to redefine humanism with the goal of inaugurating a more heterogeneous notion of humanity. Like Butler's survivor heroes—disenfranchised women and men—Pepa, and indeed all humans in *Nawili*, must embrace radical change if they are to survive. *Nawili*, like Butler's Parable series (1993–98) and Xenogenesis trilogy (1987–89), insists that we can transform ourselves and our world, but only if and when we actively reshape our minds and bodies to develop alternative frameworks that explode the systematic oppressions that cage women, minorities, and racial and ethnic Others. *Nawili* maintains that it is only through a conscious effort of will that humanity might seed a sustainable future for itself and the planet.

One of my main objectives in *Nawili* is to complicate what it means to be human, not through scientific advancement but by regarding "how our myths of origin dictate the way we view our humanity" (Kerr 2010, 101). An overriding goal is also to reimagine origin myths in their organic totality, rather than with an eye toward replicating a mythology that imagines one supreme, detached male God and "men" fashioned in the image of that God. Instead, the world of *Nawili* is based upon an organic, ecocentric worldview dedicated to the principles of deep ecology. Deep ecology "places humans on an equal level with all other living things [and] supports and legitimates new social and economic directions that move the world toward sustainability" (Merchant 1992, 86). Deep ecology, I believe, is aligned with Anzaldúan thought in the sense that it presupposes "a new psychology, or philosophy of self" (86).

In a profit economy, human needs and desires are too easily subsumed by the system. For those of us on the edge, contending for dominance alongside the unearthed voices mired beneath the desecrated landscape under our feet, a prudent choice is to risk being swallowed whole by the earth's mouth, as Anzaldúa (1999, 63–73) describes in "The Coatlicue State." I completed *Nawili* at a time when everything in my world had become poisoned and sick. Taking Anzaldúa to heart, I entered the serpent's belly and took my young protagonist with me. In many ways it is an angry novel, but because it is geared to a New Adult audience, it is full of hope and builds upon a narrative that directly overturns the crushing force of global capitalism. We are all implicated in a landscape where the politics of disenfranchisement have historically been wielded as the *only* legitimizing practices of progress and knowledge. A key goal of *Nawili* is to expose the weaknesses of our profit economy and make visible the fault lines in a way that places *la tierra* at center stage. In this way, *Becoming Nawili* unravels "that which abides" (Anzaldúa 1999, 73) to suggest a cosmic unveiling that our world so desperately needs.

The following excerpts from the novel introduce readers to Pepa's world. Included here are the prologue and chapter 1, followed by an excerpt from part 2 titled "Cobra," in which we witness the destruction of Pepa's barrio via flashback. The prologue establishes the Río Grande as a source of ancestral power. Chapter 1 begins in the present, one year after the destruction of the world's infrastructure. It is during this time that the Spider Woman "seeds" Pepa's body with ancient shape-shifting powers—although Pepa retains no memory of her training. "Cobra" ends as Pepa is swallowed by the noxious waters of the Río Grande, marking her entry into the underworld.

Excerpts from *Becoming Nawili*

Prologue: On The Border

One last sputter of bloated blue catfish and gray redhorses with their meaty lips, and the River was gone. In its final days, the Río Grande—still called the Río Bravo by those who knew its soul best—put on a terrifying performance, much like what ancient Salineros to the south used to call a *jubileo*, or jubilee, a terrific die-off that remained in the tribe's bones for weeks, a spectacle of the senses.

A thousand years ago, when the River was a vast delta called Great Waters, it ran swift and long for almost two thousand miles, pulsing with minnows and shiners, chubs, and bony, scuted shovelnose sturgeons. Tattooed Comecrudos, lithe as new trees and dressed in shells, prowled the cattails and reeds of its southern banks to fish and feed off leopard frogs, red-eared sliders, spiny softshells, diamond-backed copperheads, the occasional blotched water snake, and, of course, all those tasty garters. To the north, wandering tribes of Cacalotes made feasts of black water moccasins thick as cottonwood trunks.

Two hundred years ago, the Río Bravo was Mother to a cascading water world whose center was a dance of a thousand circles of life. Then, she was guardian of *cenotes*, primordial dreampools hot with memories of ancestral Nahua ways. These were days of plenty, when the *río* wound into the people's dreams like a multicolored snake that pulsed ancient practices and memories alive in their blood. As long as the River glistened and blazed, it would nourish sleepers with the old ways, powerful treasures of forgotten worlds.

Twenty years ago, when the River became the property of Homeland NeT, it began to disappear from the people's dreams. They were Nahua descendants and their barrio had cradled the River for generations. Oh, they still dreamed of water—oceans and lakes and probably even other rivers like the Nile or the Mississippi—but the Río Bravo, or the Río Grande—whatever name one chose to call it—departed, walked out the door that opened onto the nighttime world of dreams. Of course no one would *choose* to dream about a long, noxious, toxic dumping site that had become a trickle of smoldering ooze in some places. But people don't choose their dreams. Anyway, the dreams about the River just stopped flowing, like the River itself.

By this time, the River was in transition, a time that those who survived would later call "the Becoming." Becoming Times, like clouds or dust in windstorms, are impossible to snag. The people's dreams of the *río* dwindled to quivers and gasps because it would not be owned and made captive by the chains of the voracious Homeland NeT. For the River, the Becoming Time was about biological time and biological progression, not the movements of a clock. The Becoming seeded a time zone never before known on earth and much older than humankind. Like a corpse flower, as the River appeared to die, it summoned life—life enfolded by mythic time, when animals were known to talk and people were known to listen. Just as the River de-evolved to a time when the old *cenotes* might once again sing, the earth's course began to change.

The men who wore the Homeland NeT logo on their sleeves could not see past the inconvenient black bubbles that rose to the surface of the water and *pop! pop! popped!* like boiling blisters, so they stopped being interested in the River. For them, the story of the River was over. Dead as snapped leaves dancing in the wind. But for the people who lived in the little barrio—not all of them, but some—the River's *cenotes* began to speak in little itches that teased their insides. When the men with the H NeT logo on their coats abandoned the River, the barrio people flocked to its troubled drizzles and pools to pay their respects, to remember. Sometimes they caught glimpses and snatches of little wormy tendrils of life. When they looked closely, some thought they saw tiny snakes, all aglow and writhing to life in the oily ooze that was once the Río Bravo.

A week ago, the Becoming Time compelled the River to swallow the light of myth. The Río Bravo, like an expectant mother, began her contractions.

Chapter 1: "Pepa"

I curl myself into a ball and huddle in a corner of the little chamber. The shapes on the walls sprout oily arms and hands that ripple like tentacles. The hands with their little suction cups are too terrible to look at, so I slit my eyes and focus on the Spider Woman's teeth. Two rows of perfectly shaped isosceles triangles, hundreds of little Y's pointing downward and chittering in unison, the clockwork of a forgotten world. The Dragon's Eyes chatter in song and I know she is happy. And because she is happy, I am soothed. But the feeling doesn't last. The shadows have become tentacles, and the tentacles have become hands that seize and coil and wind. I'm not sure I'm breathing anymore. I try to concentrate. I must concentrate! I must bring the words she taught me from the pit of my stomach back into my head where they're supposed to be, where I could use them to calm myself down.

It's no use. The shadows take my words. They snatch my words as they grab at my arms. Now they want my legs.

I wasn't expecting this. Not from her. Not after all that work, all that coaching! Now it's my eyes. My eyes can't possibly be working right because I watch in terror as my arms drip away to reveal scales, all gold and turquoise and aqua blue. I feel like a thing swallowed, a dumb, stunned fish boiling in the gullet of a sperm whale. Water drops echo like thunder in my ears. I can't possibly be breathing anymore. There's just too much water in my brain.

I think I'm a fish. I must be a fish. I have scales and cataracts on my eyes and I flail the bony, spiny things that I swear were arms and legs a minute ago.

What's happening to my body?

"Time is now," says Ari, the Spider Woman. "You ready."

Ready for what? Ready to be someone's supper? If only my brain still worked.

She wraps her long scarf, the finest green silk, around my spongy neck. There's a flipper where my neck used to be and I'm a little embarrassed about this, but she's an old friend and so she must understand that it's not my fault. I want to tell her this, but I just do that puckering-pop thing that fish do with their lips and then it's too late. I've forgotten. I've forgotten the really important thing I wanted to tell her.

"I always be with you," she says. She takes my flipper-hand, her tarantula fur sticky like glue now, and leads me to the pool. Months ago, she described this pool as the end of the world, maybe the beginning. It was too soon to tell, she said. Her words float into my head and I am filled with fear and expectation. Am I dead, or is this the new beginning she promised?

I am so sleepy, but I do as she asks, feeling my way by brushing my flippers along the cool wall. Darkness, and then a buzz and a fizzle: *lub dub lub dub lub dub* . . . It's not my heart or the prism of light that dances and flickers over the pool that I hear, but a breathing from somewhere that booms and whispers all at once. I stop flailing and give in to the soothing vibration of warm breath that is so strong it buoys my body up and up. Disoriented, I lose my footing and seem to float weightlessly.

"Here," says Ari, and she is no longer a spider woman but an ancient cave painting, the stick figure of a goddess that embodies some unremembered mystery of life and death. And on the circular walls are concrete rings that morph into shapes of snakes and coyotes and deer and rabbits, and they all move, as if running, in the same direction. I squint through my cataracts and I see a giant octopus, alone, and moving in the opposite direction. She has a fish name, an octopus name. Something I can't pronounce. She holds in one of her tentacled arms . . . what is that . . . a human? The image vanishes.

The wet arms hurry me and jostle me into the pool, which has begun to swell with water. The pool bubbles and pulses, squeezes and contracts. I am in a whirlpool now, spinning within a current that rises and falls in spasms and spurts. At first I am a downdraft, and then I am a gap, an opening that drops away to bottomless worlds. For a final instant, I see Ari through the water. She is clicking and rattling, speaking that ancient language reserved for creatures rather than humans. I must be a creature because I understand.

"No memory," rattles the wordless mouth through all those teethy triangles. "Memory in small bites only, like spice in pocket. Eat when time is right. Follow north." She and Baby Jessica smile and wave, four gleaming rows of Dragon's Eyes. The whirlpool, a gigantic yawning maelstrom now, seethes and breaks, and I shoot up and out like cannon fire.

From Part 1, Fire: "Cobra"

Papi has been dead for almost a month when the rest of my family is killed.

They come in through the front door with their guns, the puppets of the few men who now run our world. "It's a misunderstanding," Mami pleads. "Just a terrible misunderstanding! The wall mount is plugged in, do you not see that? The Eye has always been plugged in!"

I sit in my room at the end of the hall and listen as they bash Mami's head in with the butts of their rifles. I have been robbed of my breath, my skin, a body capable of movement and protestation. I am a tomb and I hear them beat her down and then kill Rene, who fights like a samurai against them but loses. Someone stops Rolo's wails and crying quick and clean, as easily as a knife through butter. I wait for the men to come to me: I'm craving death, tasting it, but when they enter my room they look past me. They see *right through me*, registering nothing but the wall I have become. They jeer and hiss and kick at Rene some more before they leave. They light the house on fire and walk out the door as indifferently as a breeze moves through a screen. I am a stone: my ears have left me, and so have my legs, my arms, my mind. But not my sight. I can see everything.

Now I am propped up against Maestro Jess's mesquite in the alley behind our house. I don't know how I got here and I don't care. I watch our house burn and wait for the men with guns to return. No one comes. All the houses in my barrio are burning, and although I can move now, it's like my ears have been cut or burned away because there is only silence. I find a long triangle of glass at my feet and I wait for the men to return. My desire is dim and cloudy, but a reptilian drive demands blood; I want to cut the men who did this. I want to murder them as they murdered my family. I wait, sit like a bag of rocks, for what feels like a day but no one comes, maybe because the world is on fire.

Now I am at the Blue Hole. I faintly recall that I have always been comforted by the smell of the cool spring water that bubbles up from the depths of the earth and feeds into this well. With my Third Eye, the one that Mrs. Myers taught me to find, I recall ancient, unspoken ripples that hum and hover like moist clouds over the surface of the deep water. Mami told me about this place long ago, but I remember the story. Now, the water is frantic with gurgles that insinuate a mysterious underwater monster ready to spring from the depths of Hell itself. I remember my Mama Chita, how I bent myself into the crook of her pudgy arm and belly as a kid when she told me the old stories. The earth is sky and earth and air in between, she says. But Hell is below, and we must own Hell as surely as we own sweeter earthbound dreams. I ask so many questions through her unwavering smile and the feathery touches of her paper-thin hands. I don't know how many worlds there are, she says, but there must be many that exist alongside ours. Even the world of an ancient time where the earth was the skin of a woman and the sun was a God-man still exists, she says.

The grass is gone and the once magical blue well is covered over with weeds and reeds and spray paint. The fires have suffocated the bluebonnets. I tear my eyes from the water that once meant life to my barrio and slog my way to the Río Grande beyond the spring. The river rages, and a glowing radioactive stew bubbles up from the murky mud below. Thick and soupy, the toxic ooze trickles like living threads. Up and up from the muck—bright orange, phosphorescent green, venom yellow. There are snakes here, hundreds of them, putrid multicolored leviathans of slime, gatekeepers of a hungry hell. I am compelled to look into the black eye of one that beckons me, to witness the smoke pouring from its nostrils as from a boiling pot over a fire of reeds. I turn away and vomit into the dirt.

Above me, the gray smoke drowns out the sun, and when I look up, the GoodGasS factory, the heart of the endless Maquiwell complex that defines the Southern Territory, is all on fire. My ears are back, because I hear faraway screams and blasts, but these terrible notes don't really register. Nothing does. Not the fires all around me, not the smoke, not the smell of death or the memory of what happened to Mami and Rene and little Rolo. I just stand there gaping into the inky eye of the writhing, glowing snake as if I'm waiting for the inevitable to happen.

The explosion is so loud that even the sound waves kill. Most of the people in the cities nearby will die in exploded buildings and on streets that crumble into the earth. Others will die later, in the toxic nightmare that follows; more will be swept away by rising waters and storms caused by shifts deep in the earth's crust. But me, I will not die.

The ground under my feet convulses and shakes, and the simmering bubbles rise and crest, rise and crest. The snake with the inky eye, its watery, glowing hood now the wide fan of a giant cobra, reaches up and swallows me with its gaping mouth. There's a thick *SLUURRRP!* and I'm gone. Sucked into and under the muddy, toxic waters of the Río Grande.

Works Cited

Anzaldúa, Gloria. 1995. "Theory and Manifesto." Manuscript drafts. Box 61, folder 21, Gloria Evangelina Anzaldúa Papers, Benson Latin American Collection, University of Texas, Austin.

———. 1999. *Borderlands/La Frontera: The New Mestiza.* 2nd ed. San Francisco: Aunt Lute.

Ballard, J. G. 1962. *The Drowned World: A Novel.* Reprint, New York: Liveright, 2013.

Butler, Octavia E. 1987. *Dawn.* Xenogenesis Book 1. Reprint, New York: Warner Aspect, 1997.

———. 1988. *Adulthood Rites.* Xenogenesis Book II. Reprint, New York: Warner Aspect, 1997.

———. 1989. *Imago.* Xenogenesis Book III. Reprint, New York: Warner Aspect, 1997.

———. 1993. *Parable of the Sower.* Reprint, New York: Grand Central, 2000.

———. 1998. *Parable of the Talents.* Reprint, New York: Grand Central, 2000.

Campbell, Joseph. 1973. *The Hero with a Thousand Faces.* Princeton, NJ: Princeton University Press. First published 1949.

Gearhart, Sally Miller. 1979. *The Wanderground: Stories of the Hill Women.* New York: Persephone.

Gilman, Charlotte Perkins. 1915. *Herland.* New York: Dover, 1998.

Jameson, Fredric. 2007. *Archaeologies of the Future: The Desire Called Utopia and Other Science Fictions*. London: Verso.

Kerr, Ryan. 2010. "The Father, Son, and the Holy Clone: Re-vision of Biblical Genesis in *The House of the Scorpion*." *Journal of the Midwest Modern Language Association* 43, no. 2: 99–120.

Lem, Stanislaw. 1961. *Solaris*. Reprint, New York: Mariner Books, 2002.

Longoria, Arturo. 1997. *Adios to the Brushlands*. College Station: Texas A & M University Press.

Merchant, Carolyn. 2005. *Radical Ecology: The Search for a Livable World*. New York: Routledge.

Peña, Devon G. 2005. *Mexican Americans and the Environment: Tierra y Vida*. Tucson: University of Arizona Press.

Rosen, Elizabeth K. 2008. *Apocalyptic Transformation: Apocalypse and the Postmodern Imagination*. Lanham, MD: Lexington.

Sjöö, Monica, and Barbara Mor. 1987. *The Great Cosmic Mother: Rediscovering the Religion of the Earth*. New York: Harper One.

Chicanonautica Manifesto

Ernest Hogan

I didn't think that my ethnic background was going to be an issue. All those riots and protests should have taught us by now, right? Today, I've been called the Father of Chicano Science Fiction, because I'm the first Chicano to have made a career writing science fiction about Chicano characters and culture. Yeah, I know, my surname is Irish . . . but mother's maiden name is Garcia, my father's family is from New Mexico, and I was born in East LA back in the fifties. Sci-fi came into my barrio through the airwaves, and I saw it as part of my natural environment, my heritage. When I got around to experimenting with writing about Chicano characters, they came to life, leapt off the page, like monsters from a mad scientist's lab. After all, for me, this was as Chicano as anything else I had known.

I wrote all kinds of things. Sent them to all kinds of markets, even East Coast magazines that put the word "taco" in italics. Still, the places where I got published usually had something to do with science fiction.

Why?

Probably because Chicano is a science fiction state of being. We exist between cultures, and our existence creates new cultures: rasquache mash-ups of what we experience across borders and in barrios all over the planet. As mestizos we have no sense of cultural purity. Mariachis on Mars? Seems natural to me. Even when I try to write mainstream, or even nonfiction, it's seen as fantastic. In a sense it is, but to me the fantastical is normal.

And it didn't matter that what I did was more like speculative fiction than science fiction. My imagination doesn't fit into cubbyholes of strict genre distinctions. Most people don't know what spec-fic is—in my ten years as a bookstore clerk, not one customer asked for speculative fiction—while sci-fi gets some recognition, even if most of the time it's misunderstood. And I don't expect people to understand me—they never did in the past. I just rev up my imagination and see where it takes me, and I don't worry if some critic thinks my prose style is "abominable" or an occasional reader is confused by the presence of my stories in their favorite science fiction magazine (Winnett 1990, 23).

I coined the term "Chicanonautica" for my column in *La Bloga* to try to claim my own space within the spec-fic world on my own terms (Hogan 2010). I seem to be a Chicanonaut—a Chicano who's always going out of bounds, crossing borders, trespassing new frontiers, going beyond conventional understandings of the barrio. One small step for a Chicano . . . And of course, when I am somewhere else, I bring the barrio with me. And when I come back home from my explorations, the barrio is transformed yet again.

It is my belief that when the barrio is transformed, it goes on to transform the rest of the universe.

The protagonists of my novels *Cortez on Jupiter* (1990), *High Aztech* (1992), and *Smoking Mirror Blues* (2001) are Chicanonauts, who, like astronauts, are sent out into a strange new environment, be it a futuristic LA, a space station, the Great Red Spot, revitalized Tenochtitlán, a virus-altered mindscape, or the downloaded identity of a computer-simulated god.

Like traditional astronauts, they explore, but since they carry the complex Chicano cultural baggage, they aren't cool or detached. The stories they generate crackle with conflict in the new environments. They get into bizarre kinds of trouble—the essence of drama, with a touch of that extra spice that tickles the tongue, gets the inner ears tingling, and sends sparks through the brain.

Instead of dystopic despair, a familiar feature of spec-fic and sci-fi, the resolution to my stories comes through transformation.

Or to quote Dennis Tedlock's (1985) translation of the *Popol Vuh*: "The boys accomplished it only through wonders, only through self-transformation."

It's a natural thing for a mestizo writer to do, being, by definition, part of a crazy, mixed-up, impure people. After all, purity has turned out to be a handicap when dealing with the future, and the unknown.

Being a Chicano thus was the perfect training for being a spec-fic writer!

As a result, people are impressed by my originality. Ben Bova called me "the most original voice to hit science fiction since Harlan Ellison."[1] It's easy for me because I'm drawing on the rasquache complexities of La Cultura, inspired by things that the kids from the white suburbs never saw. And I wasn't afraid of crossing borders, whether geographic, national, ideological, hemispheric, aesthetic, or whatever the chingada they may be.

Still, I wasn't considered "commercial" by the major publishers. They were afraid that all the Chicanonautica would scare away the audience, which was still perceived to be white and middle-class. But wasn't Godzilla commercial? And Bruce Lee? Santo? Blue Demon? Mil Máscaras? Cultural barriers were still in place.

I didn't care what they said. I went at it like a quixotic madman listening to the talking statue that inspired the Mexica to journey across the desert and build Tenochtitlán.

In the twenty-first century, the publishing world is being transformed by the intertwined developments of technology and society. It's making the world more Chicano—by mid-century it will look like a Chicano planet! Publishing in English is no longer centered in New York. People all over the planet are thinking about the future and revving up their imaginations. Guess where they're looking?

And the audience is global and diverse—La Raza Cósmica rides again!

I'm not interested in being puro Mexicano and only reaching the gente in the barrio. My roots embrace the planet, and reach out for the universe—the Intergalactic Barrio.

This is the time of Postcolonialism, Afrofuturism, and Chicanonautica.

We aren't talking about an isolated, unified movement. The virus is erupting all over the planet, in different forms, new recombinations. Look for it wherever people have new visions.

All this movement keeps a Chicanonaut busy, exploring new worlds and imagining what else could happen. Once people's minds are opened up, new realities become possible. And I'm not just talking about speculative fiction. It is about speculating, thinking, so that we can start doing things differently. I think the word for this is Revolution.

And rest assured that there are other Chicanonauts out there. They don't do things exactly as I do—we are diverse without trying. Difference is the new/old norm. We are the future. I can hardly wait to see how they're going to shake things up.

Because things need to be shaken up. We need never-ending revolution to keep science from becoming nothing but a corporate franchise.

Get ready for the Intergalactic Barrio, the bubbling cauldron of recombocultural imagination. Mi Raza Cósmica is blasting off again!

Notes

1. Ben Bova, personal correspondence with author, 1994.

Works Cited

Hogan, Ernest. 1990. *Cortez on Jupiter*. New York: Tor.

———. 1992. *High Aztech*. New York: Tor.

———. 2001. *Smoking Mirror Blues*. La Grande, OR: Wordcraft of Oregon.

———. 2010. "Chicanonautica: Defining New Frontiers/Borders, and Other Delusions." *La Bloga*, October 2. http://labloga.blogspot.com/2010/09/chicanonautica-defining-new.html.

Tedlock, Dennis. 1985. *Popol Vuh: The Definitive Edition of the Mayan Book of the Dawn of Life and the Glories of Gods and Kings*. New York: Simon & Schuster.

Winnett, Scott. 1990. Review of Ernest Hogan's *Cortez on Jupiter*. *Locus* 24, no. 3: 23.

Flying Saucers in the Barrio
Forty Years Ago, Chicano Students in Crystal City Created a Bowie-Inspired Speculative Rock Opera

Gregg Barrios

I was a child of the twentieth century. I was given a science book for Xmas in 1951.[1] A year earlier I had seen my first sci-fi film, *Rocketship X-M*. Outside the El Rancho movie theater in Victoria, Texas, there was a six-foot mock rocket ship that spun, and inside it, through a transparent plastic window, you could see the cast of the film going about their interplanetary business. Who wouldn't be impressed? And unlike later space-era movies, this one ended with everyone dying. It was the last frontier. For those of us growing up in Victoria's Mexican barrio, the cowboy and Indian trope made us feel like outsiders, so we played outer space games instead, pretending to go to Mars as explorers to find our very own brave new world.

On the radio, I listened to Captain Midnight and ordered a secret decoder. In theaters, I watched the fifteen-chapter serial *Captain Video: Master of the Stratosphere*, and features like *Forbidden Planet*, *The War of the Worlds*, *When Worlds Collide*, *The Thing*, etc. On TV, we watched the children's shows *Space Patrol* and *Tom Corbett, Space Cadet*. In Spanish-language cinemas, we watched *Santo contra la invasión de los marcianos* (Santo vs. the Martian Invasion). Pop novelty music added "The Flying Saucer," parts 1 and 2, and then the big hit "The Purple People Eater."

In junior high I spent a year reading speculative fiction, everything from Asimov to Ray Bradbury.[2] As a teenager I reviewed Nevil Shute's *On the Beach*. Of course, comic books were the most accessible speculative fiction. My favorite character was Captain Marvel Jr., a crippled lad who would discard his crutch whenever he said the magic words "Captain Marvel!" By the end of the sixties, I had seen *2001: A Space Odyssey,* based on Arthur C. Clarke's script. Little did I know that all this was preparation for my own work in the genre in the mid-1970s with a Bowie-inspired student production, *Stranger in a Strange Land.*

The sudden and unexpected death of David Bowie this year touched me personally. He had been more than an influence, more than an inspiration for this former high school English teacher and present-day playwright. A flood of memories took me back to a time when I taught in Crystal City, Texas, and my theater students created and produced a Chicano sci-fi space opera based on Bowie's music (figs. 1–3).

While my duties as an English IV teacher extended to supervising the school newspaper and teaching a video production class, it was the theater program that gave me the most satisfaction, for it allowed me to explore my own creativity and, just as important, share my enthusiasm for music and theater with my students. I'd often play new music for our rehearsal warm-ups.

Figure 1. *Poster from* Stranger in a Strange Land, *by Tony Flores, 1976.*

space oddity

GC: Ground Control to Major Tom
Ground Control to Major Tom
Take your protein pills
And put your helmet on.

Ground Control to Major Tom
Commencing countdown
Engines on
Check ignition and
may God's love be with you.

10-9-8-7-6-5-4-3-2-1,Liftoff!

This is Ground Control to Major Tom
You've really made the Grade
And the papers want to know whose
shirts you wear
Now it's time to leave the capsule
if you dare!

Tom: "This is Major Tom to Ground Control
I'm stepping thru the door
And I'm floating in a most peculiar way
And the stars look very different today

For here am I sitting in a tin can
Far above the world - Planet Earth is blue
And there's nothing I can do

Though I'm past one hundred thousand miles
I'm feeling very still
And I think my spaceship knows which way to go
Tell my wife I love her very much she knows."

GC: Ground Control to Major Tom,
Your circuit's dead, there's something wrong!
Can you hear me, Major Tom?
Can you hear me, Major Tom?
Can you hear me, Major Tom?
Can you...

Tom: "Here am I floating round my tin can
Far above the moon - Planet Earth is blue
And there's nothing I can do."

****

Major Tom: Eddie Treviño   Starman: Mando Fuentes
Ground Control: Rudy Maldonado   Satellite: Elsa Marquez

****
An Astronaut is sent to Mars. Due to carelessness on his part,
he finds himself stranded in space in a state of suspended
animation. Meanwhile, a starman coming to earth encounters a
similar problem. The ground control man receives a strange
signal and falls unconscious. Earth presumes the astronaut
is dead, and no one is aware that the starman is on his way
to earth or that ground control has received a strange signal.

Figure 2. Excerpt of playbill from Stranger in a Strange Land, by Gregg Barrios, 1976.

Figure 3. Crystal City High School students in stage production of Stranger in a Strange Land, photo by Gregg Barrios, 1976.

When I played David Bowie's LP *Station to Station* in early 1976, it was my theater students' first encounter with him, and it led to a discussion of his earlier LP, *The Rise and Fall of Ziggy Stardust and the Spiders from Mars*. Who was this strange, shape-shifting chameleon? they asked. Why did the songs vary from rock to folk to funk? And would the future be like George Orwell's *1984*? These were young Chicanos growing up in a rural community. They were opining and questioning with a newfound agency after a successful student walkout in Crystal City from 1969 to 1970 led to a more equitable school system for Mexican Americans. The students had boycotted school, demanding a slew of reforms—more Mexican American teachers and counselors, Mexican American studies courses, bilingual education—and their success was liberating personally as well as on social and political levels.

Post-boycott, the students were more confident about expressing their views on mainstream culture and music. Over time, as they listened to and processed Bowie's earlier music, especially "Space Oddity," we brainstormed ideas for a sci-fi rock opera, in some cases drawing from real-life experiences.

When a theater student and his family were returning from a shopping trip in Piedras Negras, Mexico, some thirty-five miles from Crystal City, a Border Patrol agent pulled them over for inspection. My student asked the officer why they had been stopped. "We're looking for aliens," the officer replied. To this our young actor retorted, "Oh, I didn't know they'd landed." After that, the students decided that our play might also explore how the Border Patrol perceived them: as aliens in their own land. A history teacher pointed out that during World War II, Crystal City had been the site of an "alien detention camp," then located across the street from our high school. Students added that they had relatives who had married into Japanese families.

Early on, one student asked how we could play English characters when we were Mexican Americans—that is, Chicanos. Brother Alexis Gonzales, a visiting theater professor from Loyola University New Orleans, came to the rescue. He said the students had every right—even an obligation—to play any parts they chose because they would bring something unique from their culture to the work and make it their own. "It's called acting and empowerment," Gonzales said, "and blind casting." (Four decades later, the hit musical *Hamilton* has Latino and black actors playing the lead roles of the white Founding Fathers.)

It became obvious that we were embarking on a marvelous theater venture into future, past, and present. We called our work *Stranger in a Strange Land*, from Robert Heinlein's sci-fi novel and from a US Commission on

Civil Rights report on Mexican Americans titled *Strangers in One's Land* (1970). The report spoke to the invisibility and alienation of Mexican Americans and the denial of their civil rights. Bowie's persona as the alien outsider fit perfectly. We also incorporated the alien detention camp into the final scenes of the play, framed by a regimented, Orwellian *Animal Farm* society.

At that time, the Nicolas Roeg film *The Man Who Fell to Earth*, with Bowie performing in his first starring role, wasn't in wide release, but our city library had a copy of the Walter Trevis novel it was based on. Thomas J. Newton is an extraterrestrial who comes to earth on a desperate mission to save his dying planet. I wrote a story line, set to twenty-one Bowie songs and with a cast including Major Tom, Ziggy, Starman, Lady Stardust, Jean Genie, and the strange Warren Peace.

In our collaborative script, Major Tom is stranded on Mars. A captive Starman from a dying planet communicates, through NASA's ground control, a message for Earth. Ultimately, these two characters and a young folk singer, Lady Stardust, set into motion a story filled with CIA and FBI spies as well as unscrupulous politicians, prophets, and profiteers. At the end, the imprisoned Starman is released and returns to his planet, streaking the skies with rainbows in gratitude.

For our dystopian tale set to a glam-rock beat, we employed Bowie's use of mime for makeup choices, aping the cover of his *Pin Ups* LP, on which Bowie and supermodel Twiggy appear in mime face. It added a touch of meta-theater to do the piece in whiteface.

We double-cast a few roles, since some of our student actors came from seasonal migrant farmworker families and it wasn't unusual for a contractor to tell families to immediately report for early harvests. Overnight, these families—and potentially our student actors—would have to board up their homes and make the long trek north.

Our student print shop published our playbill of twenty pages with the lyrics of each song and a book (libretto) of the play's action. *Stranger in a Strange Land* premiered in the Crystal City High School auditorium in May 1976. An elementary teacher said it was like attending an opera in New York City.

The production brought us media attention. The *Laredo Morning Times* ran a short notice. Friends from San Antonio drove to see the show. When the cast met the audience of receptive city folks, one of our actors suggested we send our libretto/playbill to "Mr. Bowie." It wasn't just bluster. They were justifiably proud of their accomplishment. It was more than greasepaint and cool sci-fi stuff; it was a window into a world of theater they had never imagined.

That summer I forwarded our libretto to Bowie, c/o RCA, his record label. By then, we were working on next year's production—the first-ever staging of *Evita* in the United States, which earned coverage by *San Antonio Express-News* arts critic Ben King.

I left Crystal City in late 1978. *Texas Monthly* editor Bill Broyles had asked me to write an investigative piece on Texas drug lord Fred Gomez Carrasco after seeing our student theater piece on Carrasco at the Floricanto Festival in Austin. A student who had been in *Stranger* told me of a new Bowie single, an instrumental titled "Crystal Japan." He was flummoxed. He asked about our letter and wondered whether Bowie might be giving us a nod or a wink in reply. Alas, we never learned whether that was the case. However, I resent the libretto from *Stranger* with a note about our production being an homage to his work. Bowie, who was on Broadway in the stage play *The Elephant Man*, quickly responded with a note and several 8-by-10 photos signed "Many Thanks, Bowie."

The year before his death, Bowie wrote and produced *Lazarus*, a sequel to *The Man Who Fell to Earth*. The play featured mime, dance, and multimedia as well as eighteen songs. New York critics described the plot in terms that sounded eerily familiar, in light of our own effort: the alien Newton returns to find a way to save his dying planet; he encounters intrigue and subterfuge in the process; like our Starman, he returns to his dying planet in the end, but unlike our space alien, he fails in his mission. It isn't out of the realm of possibility that we may have influenced the unbelievably talented genius just as he greatly inspired us in a small Texas town forty years ago.

Viva Bowie! Viva Cristal! Viva Aztlán!

Notes

A slightly different version of this article was published in the *Texas Observer*, June 23, 2016.

1. Jack Coggins and Fletcher Pratt, *Rockets, Jets, Guided Missiles and Space Ships* (New York: Random House, 1951). This was the first nonfiction book about manned space flight written for children, and most people agree that it started the publication of children's space flight books.

2. I later taught at Berendo Junior High in Los Angeles, a school that Bradbury attended as a young boy. Bradbury also allowed his fantasy story, "The Wonderful Ice-Cream Suit," to be adapted for an all-Latino-cast film by the same title in 1998, with Edward James Olmos. Bradbury wrote the screenplay, and he called it "the best film I ever made."

Sexy Cyborg Cholo Clownz

Joe Jiménez

"Smile now." The cyborg vato with the plastic bones and the lithium corazón whispered.

The ground shuddered.

For a week, with an air-motor drill fused to his forearm, an etching tool like a great sacred heart blooming out of the ulna, the cyborg cholo sat by the window of yellow light. Outside, fallout. Outside, the sun larger than light, ripping clouds and pushing its marred bulk into fields of sand. The echoes of chain saws, the echoes of drone fire and artillery. Outside, the timbre of wind clashed with the half-sun and lost. By the cracked retaining wall, a shell from the Old War glimmered. A smashed drone smoldered. The cholo winced from the crookedness of the light, from the flickering that pinned the sadness of his tongue to his lungs like a tail. For a week, he did this. Stared at light and wished. The war shell glinted, and he wondered how it would explode. If it would ever. If it would die there, or if he would—die, explode. And sunken-cheeked, the vow in his neck bone crushing a yawn, the cyborg vato with his lithium corazón watched his fallen camarada lie against the mud wall, the bald body impaled, still as tripas and melancholy as bricks, the botched light from the scuffed sky holding everything—the sand and the hulking sun and the artillery, the crashed drone giving up its little smoke, the horizon made of spilt cogs and long cracks—alone.

In the days after the drone came for them, in the garbled circuitry of his heart-grunt, the half-vato wondered, How can I bring him back?

The half-vato built of chrome piel and equipoise for eyes flipped his switch, and the inert gas of the arm vibrated—deliciously, it buzzed, faintly at first, but enlarging its whorl, soon, devouringly, so that the cyborg cholo clown's whole half-body, the organs agog and the alloys of the clavicle and cogs, the knee joint and the chingón thighs covered in

416

coiled dark pelo stirred again—if only he could extend this hum to flout the lance that splintered the other part of his corazón. If only he could enact this movement in the self to another, to his camarada with the pole pushed right through his chest and back. As the light in the world dimmed and spasmed, the cyborg cholo clown longed to see his pareja's smile—de nuevo, again. He longed to hold enough of his pareja's self to make something like fission or rain.

In the distance, a cadre of Old World tanks told the New World's remnants none of this would be forgiven or saved or left to itself. Once-trees scattered across the landscape, splinters and shrapnel. And the moon understood, and the once-animals—the half-tlaquache and the lechuzas unable to convert fully to whole bones, the half-coyotes, the quasi-armadillos, the rattlesnakes with scales forged from truck hulls, now mechanized, now hobbled or with their lithium hearts ripped out, bled in the sun. Not blood but something very like it—

In a corner of the clowns' little aluminum-lead hovel, beneath the fist-thick roof, away from the cyborg cholo's perch by the window full of yellow light, away from the fallen cyborg cholo clown, an Impala, which the two cholo clowns found in an arroyo, beneath a mesquite, offered its parts for harvesting. Its green-hued hood, candy-tinted, flat and preparado. Unhinged, the hood stood against the wall and quivered, its mouth open, ready to be hit.

"Cómetelo. Eat it," whispered the half-vato with the sixty-ounce fade and the eyes like canicas, not from their darkness or their smell but from their weight, a heaviness only cyborg vatos who've lost chingos and with metal-flake in their veins could know. He held his cheek close enough to the other one. In amazement, y con ancias, the half-vato opened his difficult mouth and drove its wetness, the tongue like a slow spade, toward the half-man with half his chest blown out.

"I like looking at you. Mirándote. Viendo lo que eres," he told the vato on pause, the one with the drone spike blown clear through his torso, so that longing stuck in his canica eyes and in the small hollow spaces in between his teeth.

The air combusted in his arm-tip, and it arched, the drill bit and the arm muscle caressing the long bones of the jaw. Curved and laden con ansias, it buzzed. The projectile split the chest in two, shattered the lithium casing of the half-heart, which led the stuff of the semi-hard heart to leak out slowly, deliberately, not resigned to be whittled down by drones or tanks, by the pandemic or the canon's silence-prolonging decrees.

Today is the day I draw you, the half-vato thought to his injured cama-rada, who sat against the steel shelf against the pared, the body made of metal and a rippled coraje we might call goose flesh if it was flesh indeed and not alloy and not falling apart in the light. The cyborg hung his playera on the harpoon, slathered in lith. In half-darkness, the garment quivered—the cotton as unsteady as the earth aguantando, its parts endur-ing the new round of blitzkrieg. *I will draw you*, he said. Without moving his mouth, with only pensamientos and agony riling up the eyes, he said it, this promesa that guarded the body and infused the motherboard of the halved heart with ganas:

"To love one's body like a calabaza loves its semillitas—

To love a man with the ardor of long-ago parrots, of imperiled lost conejitos digging dens, of half-coyotes losing their minds over the holiness of the entire moon."

Incompletely, the half-vato stuttered: "P-p-p-p-or vida." He said, "Still . . . I love you."

To see possibility when the whole world te dice, *Naw, guey. Fuck it. You ain't shit.*

But cyborgs do not feign tears.

And cyborg cholos do not throw down against drones and other bár-baros, unless their lives depend on it, the lives of their souls and the lives of the collective corazón, because cyborg cholo clowns have swallowed oaths. Each oath like a pill made of cielo and sangre, pandemonium and solace—

"To herald cariño," the half-vato says, now holding the fallen home-boy's hand. Stroking his big bigote against the missile-riddled raw half-flesh. "A new cariño, guey. A cariño that can grow inside us like one volcano carrying another volcano into the cold fatal snow, a cariño that will grow inside crags and gaping holes because there is brokenness and ache and song, a cariñito that can hear itself want, one that will hear any cruelty and rush to it like a tongue reclaiming the syllables that were taken from it. A cariño so that you will hear him leaning into the afternoons. A white bee. A cariño that marks the atlas of his body."

And then, the air motor, powered by its anachronistic batería, a silvery fish of a power cell, one that echoed teeth scraping across the stubble of a freshly faded scalp, began to buzz, for it knew its place in the great order of families and circuitry and tierra, for what else matters to the world of cyborg cholo clowns if not familia, circuitry, tierra?

"To belong. To belong. I'm going to tell you the story of cariño," said the cyborg cholo in full Sad Boy clown-face.

"I'm going to tell you the history of mamando.

I'm going to tell you the epistemology of entering a man and never wanting to leave.

The meaning of fire, guey—

This is my cariño for you," the half-vato pronounced, unbuttoning his trousers.

Therein, the half-vato rubbed himself to the fallen cyborg cholo's throat bone and chin, against the stunned ocular implant, the dark lashes made of tlaquache hair curling beneath the cyborg cholo's girth, pressing that heat against the long horseshoe cut of the myoelectric triceps muscle—and grunting ensued.

Inside of itself, the transhumeral flesh began to sire joy. Of both.

Inside the harpooned cyborg cholo clown, the full jutting girth was like a deer horn, the rising antler of arroyo math and hunger and mad love for those things we are not supposed to love, but do, love, enjoy, suckle, go inside, nonetheless—

But the little armadillo of the other cyborg heart could speak no words.

To detail what the mouth inflicts upon the emptiest bones of shadows, upon the tripas that line new consciousness, the throat that is a witness to resistencia or the harpsichord of the ribs, the fallen cyborg cholo clown held silently onto the place where it no longer hurt, and then, then, he tasted saliva, and he tasted nut, and yes, he tasted cariño. In the motherboard of his small lithium-deprived heart, lo dijo con su mechanical y lith-drained corazón, finally, "I am. I am. I am."

It was a cough. It was gagging. It was heaving and the body like a wrongness suddenly clamoring beyond itself, beyond the terror of carcass-strewn sand dunes and the giant hulking bulk of the fuming sun, beyond the grey smoke that ate the horizon and the drones that marked mestizos like the two cyborg cholo clowns, like the once-animals who belonged too much to belong.

And so, the two cyborg cholo clowns painted themselves in saliva and thumbprints. All dusk, biofeedback and deeply, throating of hope and tepid jolts of recomposition, nip interfaces as a thumb bone pinched and a tooth followed suit—this was nothing less and the tongue unpinned itself from the lungs.

"Fuck the Impala hood," moaned the half-vato, on his carbon fiber knees, mouthing the empty parts of the other cyborg's cleft chest.

The drone-spike in the chest stood between them. And how can you take such a thing out?

The floor on which they lay—an arena for revival, for malcriados, for maricón recomposition and bringing back consciousness, for busting a cybergenic nut in the name of survival, the cure for guilt, the remedy for emptiness—

So the two cyborg cholo clowns nuzzled their battle-worn bodies, their skins heaving from the exertion erections elicit, choosing metal and plástico and the patchwork of organic piel and dark hair in lieu of cover-ups and prosthetics and trajes that would only function to hide the loss each of them wore like a root ball of the soul, tentacled and tender, hungry and of the earth.

And so what does the cyborg say about aguantando?

And what can aguantando say about thrusting and taking it, a suffering that is the hands of gods reaching between the legs of the heart?

"I'm going to tell you the story of cariño," the cyborg cholo clown uttered into his vato's half-vato tongue.

"I'm going to the tell you the history of tragándotelo.

I'm going to ask you the epistemology of letting a man enter and never wanting him to leave."

The sky was yellow.

The drones cut the world up over the horizon.

The artillery shattered the wind.

Tanks crushed stones. The earth underneath winced.

A few parts of trees covered themselves in dust coats.

The sun was the sun.

Motorized animals hushed and more of them died, and the Impala waiting still to be harvested for parts listened to the metal point and the air motor make something fleshy of the harpoon and the suffering and the hard, yellow light.

And this was how the ache in the harpooned homeboy's blue cyborg clown belly read CARIÑO.

"C-c-cariño, guey," muttered the cyborg cholo wearing the new placazo, the syllables stumbling over his thick tongue, dribbling onto the dented chin, the giant plug inside him oozing and throbbing.

And the drill bit buzzing, the Old English as tender as loved skin—the cyborg cholo clown who deposited his love inside his camarada wiped away the harpoon dust and cleaned the newest placa, his face smearing with a little bit of teeth and grin.

He didn't know how long it would last.

"F-f-f-fuck it. Th-th-this is where w-w-w-we are from," whispered the once-fallen cyborg. And slowly, immensely, with all the lithium that was just deposited inside his half-corazón, with all the lithium load that had been given, the two vatos touched the leftover harpoon, and they smiled, and they let the now that was snared inside all of their bodies cry.

The Canción Cannibal Cabaret
A Post-apocalyptic Anarcha-Feminist
Revolutionary Punk Rock Musical

Amalia Ortiz

The Canción Cannibal Cabaret is a poetry/theater hybrid text intended to be read as a collection of prose and poems and also to be fully staged as a punk rock musical (fig. 1). The prose tells the story of a post-apocalyptic

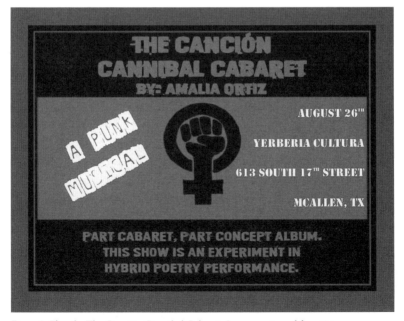

Figure 1. Flyer for The Canción Cannibal Cabaret. *Image courtesy of the artist.*

anarcha-feminist revolution fueled by the teachings of La Madre Valiente, who has "cannibalized" thoughts and rewritten them into repurposed "folk" songs from the pre-apocalyptic world. While the revolutionary figure remains in hiding, her poem songs are performed by her emissaries, Las Hijas de la Madre, in traveling propaganda rallies aimed at secretly educating and galvanizing allies into joining the Mujerista Resistance against the State.

The poetry is decidedly political and is influenced by issues of social justice that I currently feel powerless to change. Punk aesthetics and rasquachismo also inform my manuscript with their low-fi, DIY resourcefulness. Dr. Tomás Ybarra-Frausto calls rasquachismo a Chicanx sensibility born of necessity. Like punk, rasquachismo thumbs its nose at the upper classes and proudly creates something from nothing. In my manuscript, rasquachismo drives La Madre Valiente to use white, male punk "folk songs" and to radically reenvision them as intersectional feminist anthems. In doing so, she gives herself permission to be as loud and irreverent as white men have been in punk historically.

The post-apocalyptic setting allows me to defamiliarize the present to give perspective to the present. Current worldwide abuse of women and people of color is apocalyptic. The post-apocalypse can be a time of rebuilding and an opening for reenvisioning how such abuse can end. Also, for the poor and powerless in the post-apocalyptic world I describe, reading and writing are severely limited by "the State," and so rebels, fearing banishment, must communicate orally and commit illegal information to memory. It is a very current, real world of disempowered people—those who lack resources, suffer political oppression, and communicate their plight orally—that I represent in my manuscript. In my performance, the Black Bards and Red Heralds, emissaries of the revolutionary figure La Madre Valiente, are propaganda poets (figs. 2, 3). These griots of their time situate performance poetry in the future in order to make obvious its roots in the past:

> Performance Poetry is composed specifically for a presentation before a live audience . . . [It] began in pre-literate societies dating back to Homer whose traveling bards retold the stories that eventually became, in written form, the Iliad and Odyssey. Initially these poems were transmitted and recorded from performer to performer and were constructed using devices such as repetition and alliteration. Performance poetry continued through the Middle Ages when bards and wandering minstrels were the "pop" artists of their time. Today, performance poetry retains its legitimacy through singers such as Bob Dylan and Leonard Cohen. (Black and Smith 2008, 26)

Figure 2. *"Power in a Woman."*
Image courtesy of the artist.

Figure 3. *Las Hijas de la Madre. Image courtesy of the artist.*

Using the same tools as Dylan and Cohen—popular music—and performing the same function as Homer, the Black Bards and Red Heralds are important educators. They are akin to the griots of Africa, who "maintain genealogies, sing praises, compose songs, play instruments, narrate history, and serve as spokespersons" (Hale 1994, 78).

The post-apocalyptic setting also creates an interesting perspective from which to critique colonialism and imagine a world without it. As Nalo Hopkinson writes in the introduction to the postcolonial science fiction and fantasy anthology *So Long Been Dreaming*, writers of color create something unique with the genre:

> stories that take the meme of colonizing the natives and, from the experience of the colonizee, critique it, pervert it, fuck with it, with irony, with anger, with humour, and also, with love and respect for the genre of science fiction that makes it possible to think about new ways of doing things. (Hopkinson and Mehan 2004, 9)

It is my opinion that radical revolutionary changes are needed to combat the ills of capitalism, colonialism, and other oppressions such as racism, sexism, ableism, and classism. Those changes happen slowly because of opposition from those who cannot envision change or simply resist change. The apocalyptic genre, however, allows people to accept the premise of a world where civilization has suffered a complete breakdown and can now be rebuilt in a completely radical fashion. La Madre Valiente is an anticolonial, anticapitalist figure advocating an egalitarian anarcha-feminism. These concepts may seem extreme in this day and age, and the vision difficult to achieve, but in the world of my manuscript, the State is still a relatively new government existing in an unstable world, where La Madre's revolution is not only plausible but resoundingly successful. In short, the genre allows me to introduce revolution in a way that is less threatening, so that audiences will be more receptive (fig. 4).

The Pocked Eclipse, the Rise of the State, and the Birth of the Mujerista Resistance

And for many years did the civilyoungs suckle at her breasts and nest in her embrace into which she had birthed them. And she, the Great Mother, took pride in their growth and curiosity. And eventually, their independent spirits scattered the children to the four winds. And content with what she had created, the Great Mother closed her eyes for a spell of peaceful repose.

Figure 4. Black Bards and Red Heralds. Image courtesy of the artist.

And she awoke from a nightmare choking on stale air. Steel rods pierced her skin to her core and concrete corseted her. She labored to name one corner of her form that did not ache, for the entirety of her being was under attack. In her trusting slumber, she had been drugged, despoiled, violated, mutilated—and still the civilyoung ones suckled at her poisoned breasts. But now they warred against each other and hoarded more than they needed.

Heartbroken over the purity of her gift laid waste, the Great Mother released a thundering lament. Her right hand, a riotous ocean, and her left hand, colossal cliffs, curled up into fists and smashed down on her children—silencing their wars against the Great Mother and against each other.

And she returned to a feverish sleep of self-preservation, weeping hot lightening tears and coughing smoke and ash.

The civilyoung ones cried out to the Great Mother in horror. Some were humbled by her awakening. Others cursed her, and like rats on a sinking ship they trampled the bodies of the dead and continued to eat and shit their rat fill with no remorse for the fallen, weak, or ailing. The civilyoung resumed their war lording and hoarding, using the weak for sex and meat. And so existence in Nomadsland was and continues to be.

But one zone was least shaken by the fall, and on that land the State rose up to rebuild, beginning with the construction of the Grate State Gates. The Elect few born within its walls might have sat content to watch as those outside the Gates rotted—had they not been struck by breeding disease. Their new order could not overcome this curse, and needing more boots on the ground to guard the Grate Gates, the Elect allowed the entrance of fugees willing to give our children and our lives to protect the State.

Milked for our fool's blood in our appointments, we toil to provide unlimited juice to the Elect while we must be content with blackout curfews, life in the tenement yards, and restricted access to the advanced device learning that is reserved for the Elect and scholars only. Any who threaten this order are condemned to the fubar, Nomadsland.

And so warring began anew on a grand scale, with cells from Nomadsland constantly forming and plotting to breach the Grate Gates. But this time it was only the young women—the mothers—who remembered the Great Mother's rage as their own. They alone sought remedy. For years, they and their young shed the most blood and paid the highest prices to the warring and the State.

And so, mothers gathered covertly with their young after work at their appointed posts was over. And one among them, La Madre Valiente, spoke out, saying, "We will reject the curse of Eve. And we will not be cast as Lilith to birth demons to destroy us. And we will follow the Great Mother in her rage and recognize her recovery as our own. And like her, we will defend our rights to health and life. And those who threaten us will be met with *our* fists of ocean and stone."

And thus was born the Mujerista Resistance, united behind a blood-red flag reading "Mi mama me enseñó a luchar!"

La Frontera Te Llama

after "London Calling" by The Clash

La frontera te llama,
        to the north and the south
offering Flexi Compras to those living hand to mouth

La frontera te llama,
        through the bars and barbed wire
now they're fracking South Texas and the water's caught fire

La frontera te llama,
> through the internet buzz
'cause they're still ignoring Juárez, women dying just because

La frontera te llama
> yeah a black man's in charge
but incarceration's imminent for black and brown at large

the ice caps are melting, the hurricanes are near
the mass shooting madmen, the terrorists live here
the children wear targets the NRA supplies
y la frontera esta quemando and I—vivo cerca del río

La frontera te llama
> DF and DC
that kid shot dead in a hoodie, well he could've been me

La frontera te llama.
> ¿Me oyen, cartels?
take your eight-liner leeches and go straight to hell.

La frontera te llama
> Tlatelolco and Ground Zero
'cause I'm stuck in the middle and I'm looking for a hero

La frontera te llama
> you Wall Street occupiers
the government only bails out the grifters and liars

the ice caps are melting, the hurricanes are near
the mass shooting madmen, the terrorists live here
los niños sell drogas, the Golfo supplies
y la frontera esta quemando and I—vivo cerca del río

La frontera te llama,
> yeah, and I'm guilty too
'cause what they're teaching in classrooms, well, some of it ain't true

La frontera te llama
> all you locas y locos
all norteamericanos before fresa y pochos.

La frontera te llama
> Arizona and beyond
'cause when you fuck with my gente I'm sure to respond

the ice caps are melting, the hurricanes are near
the mass shooting madmen, the terrorists live here
the children carry weapons, the Zetas supply
y la frontera esta quemando and I—vivo cerca del río

Re Membering Herstory

In her domestic appointment in a home of the Elect, La Madre Valiente would slip out of her quarters at night to study a restricted device she had stolen away. This was how La Madre began to recover so many herstories lost to the State. Before the Pocked Eclipse, the learning was web-free, but those untangled herstories were burned or flooded during the fall.

It was sometime after the death of her last son that La Madre Valiente began her recitation of the old folk songs. Words on paper or the discovery of fugee use of devices is punished with expulsion from the State Gates.

And so, La Madre began to share herstories in secret. She turned to the old folk songs and repeated them among the mothers and the colored. Her campaign spread faster than violence through the tenements. Her anger gained momentum, as the dark, olive-colored, and poor women's children suffered more than others. Even the Yardie gangs set aside their fracases with one another to begin to fight for something larger—perhaps true homes instead of block corners in State yards.

The herstories La Madre loved most, those that spread quickest through the tenements, were the songs of workers and mujeres past, long before the fall—old folk songs of fugees like us long forgotten.

Rememory of Strange Fruit

> *with thanks to Abel Meeropol and Toni Morrison*

Strange fruit not hanging, but withering in crowded trucks.

Loss is expected in transport. Drivers still get paid big bucks.
Brown bodies praying for the pardon of our southern breeze,
The south still produces strange fruit, just not hanging from trees.

If the fruit survives delivery, it can be bought and sold.
Market prices double if fruit is ripe and not too old.
Dried and rotting in the desert, trampled falling off of trains,
Bondage continues in this land, though not with chains.

Growers and traffickers supply consumer-demanded yields.
There's a fortune to be made from strange fruit fertilizing fields.
Rememory of blood on leaves, rememory of blood at root,
The profits from the bitter crop outweigh our losses of our strange,
strange fruit.

50 Foot Fugee

> *after "50ft Queenie" by P. J. Harvey*

Hey!

I'm one big
Fugee.
No wall
can stop me.

Homeland
Security +
La Migra
watchin'.

Threat numb
-er one!
Second to
no one.

Checkpoint,
I'm clean.
Your walls
can't touch me.

Ask me
my name?
F-U
and C-K!

Fifty foot
fugee—
Hold back
the sea.

Biggest
woman . . .
I could birth
ten sons.

New gods!
All queens!
Fear and
walls rising.

I'm the scapegoat of the world.
You can't ignore my song.
Come on measure me.
I'm 60 million strong.

Choose one
country.
Natives
run free.

ICE raids,
barbed wire,
cheap labor
for hire,

cheap food,
cheap goods . . .
Not in

my 'hood!

Ain't got
no ID!
No wall
can stop me!

Fifty foot
fugee—
Fifty
and rising!

I'm the scapegoat of the world.
You can't ignore my song.
Dare you to measure me!
I'm 60 million strong.

Fifty foot fugee!
Fifty foot fugee!
Fifty foot fugee!
Fifty foot fugee!

The Etiology of La Madre Valiente

After the Oil Wars and the Pocked Eclipse and before the beginning of
the Great Water War, La Madre Valiente came into being in a millennium that devalued her kind. Cursed thrice, she was born poor, colored,
and female. A fugee of the Eclipse, just days old, she was abandoned
to become a ward of the State and trained in a detention camp for her
eventual appointment.

Raised without the touch of a mother or father's embrace, she was
a name and a number in the days of her indoctrination. She pledged
allegiance, memorized scriptures, and toed the line in lockstep. She began
training in the armed corps in her teen years—boots on the ground being
one of the only paths in those times to fugee emancipation.

La Madre Valiente became a true flagger—wrapped in the flag her
naked faith and trained to fight whichever wind the State demanded. So
strong was her faith—so strong, until the night before her graduation.
During the celebration, a male squad of her comrades beat and raped her, as

is often the practice by men in power these days. Infantry roughs would rub her out like the cherry of a smoke beneath a combat boot before allowing a female with that much backbone into their ranks.

That violation birthed triplets, three sons: one fair-skinned, one dark, and one her same olive color. The light child she signed over to be placed in the home of one of the childless Elect. La Madre Valiente retained visitation rights in exchange for her domestic appointment in the same home. Her other two sons grew up in the outer tenements, where La Madre Valiente did her best to keep the Yardie wolf gangs and Yard Patrol at bay. La Madre determined that her boys would rise above the gangs and escape the cruelty that the Patrol inflicted on all colored—innocent and guilty alike.

The fair child completed private device learning and was recruited for the leadership ranks of the armed corps. His Elect foster folk believed their resources and standing would shelter him, but the Water Wars took life from every zone—not equally, of course . . . But the fair child fell in the desert of a faraway region of Nomadsland.

The olive child embraced the natural arts. La Madre thought it a divine gift that flowers and fruit should bloom from his touch. He was appointed to the task of worm-working the earth. But in those early days of the Water Wars, the demand for higher yields with less water led the State to conduct experiments in modifying plants. By the time the mothers began to notice more and more of their children withering in the fields with the bone-eating epidemic, it was too late. The olive child died among those masses.

A born scholar, the dark child excelled in his early fugee training. His instructors added his name to the scholarship lottery to join the Elect in device learning. But the dark child faced all the same struggles of all dark children. His life was ended by the trigger-happy Yard Patrol one night on his return from a bodega where he had stopped to trade for a treat.

Black Men

after "People Who Died" by Jim Carroll
and "People Who Died" by Ted Berrigan

Alonzo Ashley was tased at the Denver Zoo.
Wendell Allen had weed, but he was unarmed too.
LA cops claim Ezell Ford provoked an attack,

but witnesses saw him complying when they shot him in the back.
He was only 25 when he died.
I didn't know him, but I still cried.

Eric Garner's last words were "I can't breathe!"
The asthmatic dad of six died at 43,
held in a chokehold by NYPD,
even though they banned that tactic back in 1993.
Man, I heard LAPD is sadistic,
but damn, Steven Eugene Washington was autistic.

These are black men who died, died
These are black men who died, died
These are black men who died, died
These are black men who died, died
They were all unarmed, but they still died

They didn't have a warrant when they shot Ramarley Graham.
Amadou Diallo died with his wallet in his hand.
Dante Parker was innocent. They had the wrong man.
And the Trayvon Martin verdict, I will never understand.
Trayvon, you remind me of my youngest brother.
Now you're resting in peace with all the others.

Oscar Grant was killed on New Year's Day,
handcuffed face down when they blew him away.
They're still waiting for justice in the San Francisco Bay,
but there will never be justice for Kimani Gray.
Kimani, you were a boy. You weren't even a man.
I swear, I'll never fucking understand

why.
These are black men who died, died
These are black men who died, died
These are black men who died, died
These are black men who died, died
They were all unarmed, but they still died

They only found a cell phone on Kendrec McDade,

left to die in the street without receiving first aid.
Timothy Stansbury Jr.'s last breath was in terror,
but NYPD admitted it was their "error."
Michael Brown had his hands up in the air,
but they still gunned him down. They didn't fucking care.

Patrick Dorismond, Victor Steen, Ervin Jefferson,
Sean Bell, James Brissette, Ronald Madison—
Jordan Baker, John Crawford, Aaron Campbell, Ousmane Zongo,
Sgt. Manuel Loggins Jr., and Orlando Barlow—
MLK and Malcom X are standing at your side.
I never met none of them, but I still cried.

'cause
These are black men who died, died
These are black men who died, died
These are black men who died, died
These are black men who died, died
They were all unarmed, but they still died.

These are black men who died, died
These are black men who died, died
These are black men who died, died
These are black men who died, died
I never met none of them, but I still cried.

The Self-Stimulation of La Madre

Childless, parentless—La Madre felt no connection to the past or future.
Under cover of night, she searched her stolen device for meaning.
Restricted learning, she discovered, was like Eve's apple, just another boot
at her throat.

Restricted word, restricted thought, restricted action.

As she delighted in the deviance of secret schooling, she wondered
what other delights had been restricted in order to control. Childless,
parentless, and with no faith in the State remaining—La Madre finally
belonged to herself.

With nothing to lose, La Madre gave herself permission to explore.
Deviant word, deviant thought, deviant action, deviant touch . . .

The Canción's Cannibal

after "The Cannibal's Canción" by Gloria Anzaldúa

Put rest to your relics,
as I have to communion
and Mass. There. Sunday
grins toothless. Your
teeth on my sharp skull,
you cradle sleeping nights

       with your hair. Locked
       with a fibula, I'll wear
       my heart out over

what embraces waste
my rigorous round
and finger your strings.
My wrist bone rapping
bone—your vertebrae
listening to my round
neck and jaw bones
you wear better than I—

       Blessed is cannibalism.

best tasting liver and heart
the hand, the palms, the
feet, the soles, the
vulva, the scrotum, the
nipples genitalia
swollen flesh: taboo love

       We take it
       personally
       and consume
       our customs.

Lo Juro

after "Oath" by Patti Smith
and "Gloria" by Van Morrison

Men make war for somebody's freedom but not mine.

Olla de igualdad stewing
          marked cards on the table
                    corazones sangrando
our fight our own.

          "Sisters are doin' it for themselves."

          Valientes,
we carve placas
          over cicatrices.

Adán no me embrujó.

*

I'd like to tell you 'bout me, baby.
You don't have to come around.
Just 'cause you think I'm lost,
don't mean I need to be found.

Don't you come around here.
'Cause, at just about midnight,
I can make myself feel so good. Lord!
I can make myself feel all right.

All I need is my own X-O-X-A!
'Cause, I—love my own
Xoxa!
X-O-X-A!

I'm gonna shout it all night!
Xoxa!
I'm gonna shout it every day!

Xoxa!

Van Morrison knew a girl.
Hendrix and Iggy claim they did her too.
Gloria got passed around and around.
Even Patti Smith claimed she knew what to do with Gloria.

But Gloria don't come around here.
'Cause, at just about midnight,
I can make myself feel so good. Lord!
I can make myself feel all right.

All I need is my own X-O-X-A!
'Cause I—love my own
Xoxa!
X-O-X-A!

I'm gonna shout it all night.
Xoxa!
I'm gonna shout it every day.
Xoxa!

*
So, I take full responsibility
for every culture I shock
        every cock block
for that Cyndi Lauper song I Jill off to—
        ordained or accepted,
                me vale padre.

*

Don't come a-walkin' down my street.
Don't come up to my house.
Don't you knock upon my door.
'Cause, I don't want you in my room.
I can make myself feel all right.

All I need is my X-O-X-A!
'Cause, I— love my own
Xoxa!
X-O-X-A!

I'm gonna shout it all night.
Xoxa!
I'm gonna shout it every day.
Xoxa!

*

So guys,
les doy mi despidida.
        I'm giving you the night off.
I can rub my own nub,
        or just fall asleep in my own embrace.
You can get sprung for some other, baby,
        but me,
                I'll get off just fine.

You make war for somebody's freedom, honey,
                        but not mine.

The Positive Space of La Madre Valiente

Her cisgendered but gender-nonconforming body is the opposite of what it is not.

She loves men and women equally even though they are not treated equally. Having been a parent and a child, she cares for both. She arrived in her body as we all do, through the collision of dogma and action.

Her body is a hole—a weak spot in a defensive line. A woman is a child, is a man-who-is-not-a-man, is an enemy, is a hole, is a weak spot. Her slavery-shaped skin was born through a hole in defensive lines.

Her thoughts have no shape, but are considered deadlier than her sickle-shaped breasts.

The shape of her mother's suffering is the shape of all things martyred. The family resemblance is uncanny. Eyes the color of fresh bruises. Bodies the color of bullseyes.

Tired of tasting her own blood, she fashioned her tongue, finally, into a fist and began to fight back. She will no longer trade her femininity for favors.

Tomorrow, she will awake without fear. Tomorrow, she will be free, dead, or both.

When I Was a Little Bitty Chica

after "Cotton Fields" by Lead Belly
and "Cuando Apenas Era un Jovencito" by Ramón Ayala

When I was a little bitty chica,
my momma would tell me, "Oyes Mija,
men can treat you bad, like I was treated by your dad."

When I was a little bitty chica,
my momma would tell me, "Listen Mija,
you got to love yourself, and don't rely on anyone else."

Cuando apenas era jovencita,
mi mama me decía, "Cuidado, Mija.
No aceptaras el abuso. ¡Tienes que luchar!"

"Si se encuentra con el sexismo,
mátalo con amor y feminismo.
No aceptaras el abuso. ¡Tienes que luchar!"

When I got a little bit older,
her consejos grew a little bit bolder.
She said "Who needs men? La masturbation is your friend."

"Don't you wait for no prince charming.
The patriarchy needs disarming.
You are strong, so prove the gender binary wrong."

Cuando apenas era jovencita,
mi 'Ama me decía, "Cuidate, Mija.
No aceptaras el abuso. ¡Tienes que luchar!"

"Si se encuentra con el sexismo,
mátalo con amor y feminismo.
No aceptaras el abuso. ¡Tienes que luchar!"

The Cannibal Ate Commandments and Fed Revolution

Like her spirit animal, el zopilote, La Madre Valiente ate the dead and got well, spitting up truth bones into the gullets of the hungry. One of the corpse breasts she suckled was "The Law of the Sisters of the Easy Eln." For it was legend that these sisters once pointed spears to demand their commandments be sharpied on stone.

These words of the sisters of the Easy Eln are bond:

One: Thou shalt not deny sisters the right to rock rebellion.

Two: Thou shalt not deny sisters the right to work and fair pay.

Three: Thou shalt not deny sisters the right to choose the count of babes they mother.

Four: Thou shalt not deny sisters the right to engage in tribal decisions and hold positions of the free Elect.

Five: Thou shalt not deny sisters and their babes the right to wellness.

Six: Thou shalt not deny sisters the right to learning.

Seven: Thou shalt not deny sisters the right to choose their mates.

Eight: Thou shalt not physically mistreat others. Rape and its attempt will be disciplined to the extreme.

Nine: Thou shalt not deny sisters the right to self-defense in the armed force or any rebelled position.

Ten: Thou shalt not deny sisters any freedoms or duties of the brothers.

In her domestic appointment, La Madre slipped out of bed late at night to meditate much on these commandments and contrive how to raise the Easy Eln flag from the dead.

Through the ages, the poor, and the colored, and the fugee—the women, and the young, and the weak—had been cast as emaciated children crawling desperately away from the stalking hooded vulture. La Madre now channeled the zopilote to peck instead to uncover older, buried carcasses to feed a new, angry child.

Nom de Guerre

"You think because we are women we are weak, and maybe we are. But only to a certain point . . . We can no longer remain quiet over these acts

> *that fill us with rage. And so, I am an instrument who will take vengeance."*
> *Diana, Huntress of Bus Drivers*

I eat the cries of the dead.
I am a hunter   the huntress of men.
Some people think me a monster.
For others, fantasies of vengeance I foster.

I am Diana the huntress.
We are Diana the huntress.

I wear the moon on my head.
I am a hunter   the huntress of men.
born in the barrio in a mass grave
threatening to those who hold chains to enslave

I am Diana the huntress.
We are Diana the huntress.

Hello, from the gutters of Juárez.
Hello, from the slums of Mumbai.
Hello, from the brothels of Thailand.
Hello, from sweatshops in LA.

You will know my name.
You will know my name.

Hello, Malala assassins.
Hello, Boko Haram.
Hello, from my Pussy Riot.
Hello, from my Gulabi Gang.

You will know my name.
You will know my name.

My hounds are free and unfed.
I am a hunter   the huntress of men.
My Wild Hunt's broken loose—
ghost riders crunching bones beneath their boots.

I am Diana the huntress.
We are Diana the huntress.

Join me all you who have bled.
Become a hunter   a huntress of men.
Fight corruption. Protect the powerless.
Left with no recourse, unleash your huntress.

You are Diana the huntress.
Become Diana the huntress.

Hello, from the classrooms of Yemen.
Hello, from Radical Monarchs.
Hello, my Congolese children.
Hello, Hijas de Violencia.

They will know your names.
They will know your names.

Hello, auto-defensas.
Hello, Nevin Yildirim.
Hello, my Xaltianguis Sisters.
Hello, to my Red Brigade.

And they will know your names.
They will know our name.
They will know my name.
They will know my name.

justice frozen in our crosshairs—

Black Bards and Red Heralds

La Madre knew the Elect and many brothers would consider the resurrection of these truth bones treasonous. As our numbers grew, it became increasingly challenging to keep La Madre safe. And so we, her emissaries, her Black Bards and Red Heralds, are deployed to spread her teachings and to recruit more sisters, allies, and families into the Mujerista Resistance.

Las Hijas de la Madre initially studied herstory, xeriscaping, and sustainable gardening. But quickly, we recognized a need for continued education and self-defense training.

We will not trade our femininity for favors.

in the event that you are not able to run

nose ears eyes throat temple
nose ears eyes throat temple
nose ears eyes throat temple
multiple strikes   multiple strikes   multiple

high, low, high   low, high, low   high, low, high
high, low, high   low, high, low   high, low, high
high, low, high   low, high, low   high, low, high
multiple strikes   multiple strikes   multiple

nose ears eyes throat temple
nose ears eyes throat temple
nose ears eyes throat temple
multiple strikes   multiple strikes   multiple

Don't yell help.
Yell, "Fire!"

No, don't yell help.
Yell, "Fire!"

nose ears eyes throat temple
nose ears eyes throat temple
nose ears eyes throat temple
multiple strikes   multiple strikes   multiple

#YesAllWomen are under attack.
Women and children have got to prepare.
Not all men, but the numbers are stacked.
So, you gotta beware.   You have to stay aware.

high, low, high   low, high, low   high, low, high

high, low, high	low, high, low		high, low, high
high, low, high	low, high, low		high, low, high
multiple strikes	multiple strikes	multiple	

Don't yell help.
Yell,   "Fire!"

No, don't yell, "Rape."
Yell,

"Fire!"

The Articles of Self-Defense

Las Hijas de la Madre Valiente learn tactics of war for self-defense—tools to counter the abuses their womanhood attract.

La Madre also studied *history*—man's warring—and saw a pattern of bloodshed over that-which-many-men-value-more-than-life: land, wealth, revenge, tribalism, religion, power. The claim was often made that men fought over resources, but even during the bloodiest days of the Great Water War, resources were plenty but endangered and needed protection. No, men fight over control and not always for the good of all.

La Madre was not an absolute pacifist, but she could only justify fighting as a means to preserve the peace. The articles of self-defense she deemed worth living and worth fighting for are as follows:

Freedom from Slavery

Freedom from Violence

Right to Health

Right to Education

Protection of the Great Mother

Protection of the Weak and Marginalized

To live without these precepts is to live a subhuman existence. Las Hijas de la Madre train to protect these precepts and swear an oath, "Luchamos solamente por la paz." Any directive to the contrary is a threat to humanity.

Power in a Woman

after "There Is Power in a Union" by Billy Bragg

and "There Is Power in the Blood" by Lewis Jones
and "The Battle Cry of Freedom" by George F. Root

There is power in the family, power in the home—
Power in the hands of the mother—
But we're stronger with our sisters than when we stand alone.
There is power in a woman.

All the wars of the oppressors demand innocent blood.
The mistakes of the machos, we must pay for.
From the cities and the ranchos to colonia roads of mud,
daughters divided are conquered in this man's war.

Mujeres unidas defending our rights!
Down with machismo! All women unite!
With our families and our allies, we will form a righteous clan!
There is power in a woman!

Now, I'm longing for the day when we are decolonized.
Brutality and injustice can't defeat us.
But to defend ourselves, my sisters, we must be organized,
when the patriarchy exploits and mistreats us.

Mujeres rebeldes luchando por la paz!
For every mother, we rise with our cause!
For the orphan, for the widow, lasting peace will soon be won.
There is power in a woman!

Mujeres unidas defending our rights!
Down with machismo! All women unite!
With our families and our allies, we will form a righteous clan!
There is power in a woman!

Song of the Dawn

Daylight proves problematic for La Madre Valiente. Still, mujeres whisper
anarcho-syndicalist lyrics in their lunchrooms. Their communitarian forks
tap coded beats against their metal plates, as her infectious, melodic call

for participation echoes. The hidden form of a movement has come into focus. Coordination of our opus follows.

Under cover of night, autonomous feet creep away from our appointed corners. Midnight frees us from our proletarian posts. In unison, we deconstruct our "domestication." Ages relegated to subjugation for what? And what constitutes true strength? Each ally sounds a nonhierarchical note in the canción. La Madre weaves each sharp and flat into the textile of an anthem.

Synesthetically envisioning voice as action, we taste hints of freedom and for the first time we feel hope. We can tolerate no more subordination of our discord to the Other's harmony.

Uncontrollable, a transformative chorus now intones on its own. Las mujeres prepare for a new paradigm. An egalitarian dawn breaks in the distance.

La Madre Valiente Released a Guttural Howl

She attempted to match the growling guitar with her accented and hoarse voice, wondering, "What does a revolution sound like? Harmony or discord? A chorus of angry angels *marching as to war*? A solo voice building into an army's anthem? The grinding of teeth or waving of fists in the air? Or screams silenced behind a single whisper of truth?"

She prepares our ranks to one day leave the State and reenter Nomadsland under our own rule, commanding our own agency. But to what end? To replace the patriarchy with matriarchy? To return oppression to our oppressors?

Mujeres and allies, we prepare for a new paradigm. Our egalitarian control over our individual lives now also includes control over our performance of gender. In order to decolonize gender and eradicate gender discrimination for all our children, individuals in our new society will not be reduced to gender roles but will be seen simply as humans and defined by their actions.

We will no longer perform the cultural fiction of the binary. The best of what we currently identify as masculine and feminine are open to performance by anybody. Gendered traits are simply traits and will have no bearing on how people should be treated.

Identifiable difference will be equally respected. We will enable people to be as free as possible to develop their own characteristics and ways of

thinking. Sexes will be able to develop in the absence of differential treatment during the socialization process and throughout their lives.

Together, we work toward more varied and rounded personalities than
people in gendered societies currently develop. What does *our* revolution
sound like? Our egalitarian dawn breaks on the death rattle. Join us as we
toast the last gasp of gender itself.

Gender Is Dead

after "Rock Is Dead" by Marilyn Manson

We're programming robots and brainwashing babies;
aggression for boys and submission for ladies.
The powers that be say, "Kings always trump queens."
The lords of the land rule, "There's no in between."

To be known and be loved
To be known and be loved

Gender is deader than dead.
The construct is all in your head.
The rules of your sex are all that you're fed.
Let's fuck the divisions and put them to bed.

God is gender free.

Gender is deader than dead.
The construct is all in your head.
The rules of your sex are all that you're fed.
Let's fuck the divisions and put them to bed.

One thousand fathers are prayin' for it.
We're so full of fear, and so full of shit.
We're made in God's image, and that includes me.
Seems a sin to shrink God into just "he" or "she."

To be known and be loved
To be known and be loved

Gender is deader than dead.
The construct is all in your head.
The rules of your sex are all that you're fed.
Let's fuck the divisions and put them to bed.

God is gender free.

Gender is deader than dead.
The construct is all in your head.
The rules of your sex are all that you're fed.
Let's fuck the divisions and put them to bed.

Gender is deader than dead.
The construct is all in your head.
The rules of your sex are all that you're fed.
Let's fuck the divisions and put them to bed.

Works Cited

Black, Joanna, and Karen Smith. 2008. "Inspired by the Poetic Moving Image." *Art Education* 61, no. 2: 25–29.

Hale, Thomas A. 1994. "Griottes: Female Voices from West Africa." *Research in African Literatures* 25, no. 3: 71–91.

Hopkinson, Nalo, and Uppinder Mehan, eds. 2004. *So Long Been Dreaming: Postcolonial Science Fiction and Fantasy.* Vancouver, BC: Arsenal Pulp.

Rewrite the Future!

Notes on Editing *Latin@ Rising: An Anthology of Latin@ Science Fiction and Fantasy*

Matthew David Goodwin

A great dialogue about Latin@ speculative fiction is under way among writers, critics, artists, and curators. My involvement with a forthcoming collection, *Latin@ Rising: An Anthology of Latin@ Science Fiction and Fantasy*, has allowed me to participate in that dialogue in a unique and active way. *Latin@ Rising* is the first anthology of US Latin@ literature that employs the category of speculative fiction, an overarching genre of imaginative literature that joins science fiction and fantasy. The collection features authors who have been important to the development of the field, such as Ernest Hogan, Junot Díaz, Daína Chaviano, and Ana Castillo, as well as authors who are relatively new on the scene, such as Alejandra Sanchez and Richie Narvaez. All in all, the anthology presents twenty Latin@ authors and artists along with a thrilling introduction by Frederick Luis Aldama and a haunting *El Muerto* illustration as the frontispiece by Javier Hernandez. The book is slated for release in 2017 through the San Antonio publisher Wings Press. This brief afterword provides a window on the editing of *Latin@ Rising* and on the crowdsourcing campaign that funded it.

The first question I faced in the development of the book concerned the scope. Was this to be a themed anthology or something more eclectic? Should it focus on a particular genre or subgenre? For too long, Latin@ writers, with the exception of those writing magical realism, have been directly or indirectly pushed away from publishing science fiction and fantasy. One of the functions of *Latin@ Rising* is to open a space for Latin@ authors to write without that obstacle. For this reason, I decided to design the anthology as a general speculative fiction collection that was expansive rather than restrictive. As someone who is not Latin@ and is editing a Latin@ anthology, I considered it important that the writers be involved in every step of making the book, and that included determining the content of the stories. Accordingly, the call for submissions on the website was broad: "We are taking submissions of short stories, poetry, or plays of less than 7,500 words. The general category is speculative fiction which here includes science fiction, fantasy, utopian and dystopian fiction, post-apocalyptic fiction, and alternate histories." Such a wide range of subgenres meant that the Latin@ community would have a good deal of influence in shaping the anthology. For this reason, the book works as a portrait of the community of Latin@ writers of speculative fiction and as a snapshot of this particular cultural moment, when Latin@ authors and readers are more than ever being inspired by and seeking out speculative fiction.

Authors and publishers, observing that my academic writing on Latin@ speculative fiction centered on the topic of migration, would often ask me if this was a migration-themed anthology. Prior to graduate school, I spent ten years doing immigration legal aid and organizing factory workers in the vibrant Latin@ community of northwest Arkansas. And so when I began my graduate studies, I was interested in writing about migration in Latin@ literature. I found that Latin@ speculative fiction expressed the complexity I was seeing in the community. I wanted to work with a genre that not only was full of rich aesthetic possibilities, such as the ability to extrapolate current migration trends into the future, but also was open and accessible to a wide audience. *Latin@ Rising* is the book I wish had existed at the time that I was writing my dissertation. And yet, while attention to representations of migration is important in understanding what is going on in Latin@ speculative fiction, and migration as a theme does appear intermittently in *Latin@ Rising*, I wanted the community of writers and not my personal interest to determine the scope of the anthology. Among the eighty submissions I received, the topics did in fact range widely, featuring coming-of-age stories, adventure tales, a good smattering of cyborg angst, and figures such as ghosts, space aliens, robots, and a grandmother who unwittingly saves the universe through her cooking. Reading those eighty submissions was an absolute joy, by the way, and an experience I wish readers to have, even if on a smaller scale.

The question of the scope of the anthology came up again in regard to the writers' backgrounds and connections to *latinidad*. Fortunately, there are wonderful anthologies of speculative fiction by writers living in Latin America, such as *Cosmos Latinos* and *Three Messages and a Warning* (Bell and Molina-Gavilán 2003; Jiménez Mayo and Brown 2013). But there is something unique about the experiences of those of Latin American origin, recent or distant, who are living in the United States, including those whose families lived in this region before it was the United States. A distinct anthology was merited, and so I decided that *Latin@ Rising* would exclusively feature writers living in the United States. In order to approximate the great diversity of the Latin@ community, the writers included in the anthology come from multiple regions of the United States and from eight different national heritages. Some publish their work primarily in Latin America, while others publish in the United States. Some write in Spanish, others in English. How the stories themselves connect to *latinidad* is also as diverse as possible, with many of the stories clearly enmeshed in the legacy of Latin@ literature and others using the traditional language of science fiction or fantasy. Some stories contain a lot of what would be considered Latin@ culture, weaving in Spanglish for example, while others have little or none.

The scope of the anthology and the diversity of the Latin@ community were fundamental factors in determining what would be included in the volume. The quality of the stories was equally important. This notion of quality is somewhat fraught and hard to pin down. It does not mean that I accepted only stories that were technically perfect, and indeed many that were included went through a couple of revisions. What it does mean is that the stories had to have a combination of complex characters and a strong narrative. In addition, if a work was experimental I would read it a couple of times just to make sure I could understand it as much as possible before making a decision about it. The stories also had to fit into the balance of a general anthology of speculative fiction, which needed to have a relatively equal number of science fiction and fantasy stories. Once the selection of stories was made, I used my intuition to help me order the stories in the anthology by style, tone, and genre. There is an art to creating such a collection, and the organization of the pieces is not something that can be predetermined. Anthologies can't be made by following a rule. In the end, I received many wonderful stories that theoretically could have gone into the anthology but that were not included because of limited funds and space. Because I regretted these limitations and wished that all the stories could be published, I offered to have phone conversations with the authors whose stories were not chosen. Many of the writers took me up on the offer, with the result that I met some wonderful up-and-coming writers and had a number of amazingly fruitful conversations on the state of Latin@ speculative fiction. The creation of *Latin@ Rising* was more than an editing job for me: it was a lively, Internet-mediated, multiracial, multiethnic, and multigender community event.

Coming from the academic world, I was not initially tuned into the question of payment and how it works for fiction. There was a learning curve. As authors asked about payment, I soon realized how important it is for those whose livelihood is based at least in part on their fiction. One key step I took was to apply for a "Diverse Writers Grant" from the very generous Speculative Literature Foundation, which supports projects like this one. This grant allowed me to fund a Kickstarter campaign to help pay the writers. What is important to know about Kickstarter campaigns is that they take an enormous amount of time and energy. In general, campaigns without interesting rewards for their supporters (T-shirts, posters, copies of the book to be published or of authors' other books, etc.), and without a rich multimedia advertising drive, will not be successful. Good Kickstarters do not rely just on the force of their ideas. Kickstarters are community events and the community is important. Supporters who take a risk by essentially preordering the book before it is published do not give their trust away easily. The writers were directly involved in this community as well, and many of them made promotional videos or offered signed copies of their novels as rewards.

Finally, with the help of hundreds of believers who donated time and money, the *Latin@ Rising* Kickstarter was successful in raising payment for the writers. Along the way, the campaign became a forum to discuss the book, to connect with young writers through social media, and to create a future readership for the book. It was also a way for the authors to become aware of numerous other Kickstarter campaigns that are promoting writers whose voices have gone unheard in what can be a very deaf science fiction and fantasy world. It is important to mention that the majority of book projects that raise funds through Kickstarters have a publisher tied to and supporting their campaign. The presence of an institution publicly backing the project inspires trust and reassures supporters that the book will actually come into existence. *Latin@ Rising* did not have that advantage, and the fact that the campaign was nevertheless a success attests to the widespread desire for such a book. After the Kickstarter concluded, the anthology came under the wings of Wings Press, which has a long history of publishing innovative Latin@ fiction and which picked up the book for publication.

What exactly do we gain with such an anthology? I divine that there are as many answers to this question as there are readers, but I like to think about this issue in regard to the two stories that bookend the work. In the story that opens the collection, "The Road to Nyer" by Kathleen Alcalá, the thoughtful and observant narrator visits a castle in Catalonia that is connected to her family heritage. The visit, in a style reminiscent of Kafka, rapidly becomes a dizzying adventure that is strangely intertwined with the past. Through the experience, the narrator learns important truths about her family's history. And in the closing story, Marcos Santiago Gonsalez's "Traditions," the protagonist connects to the past through the historically based virtual reality worlds that she creates. Her grandmother challenges her to make a virtual reality game about the identity crisis of Mexicans living in Japan who then migrate to Egypt. Quite a task! Though very different in genre and style, these two trips to the past through the spirit world, or virtual reality technology, provide a kind of synecdoche for speculative fiction. Latin@ speculative fiction creates imaginative spaces for contemplating culture and tradition, and yet we can only go to those spaces for a brief period of time. Eventually we must come back to the present reality. When speculative fiction is working right, we return from our journey with a deeper awareness of the contours of our traditions, and we can more creatively adapt our traditions to our lived experience. Speculative fiction is a space where we can reconcile ourselves with our own cultural background, especially when the source of that culture is far away in another country, or deep in the past.

Latin@ speculative fiction has a bright future. There are many Latin@ writers doing speculative work, and there are many more readers of speculative fiction. The art world is also opening up to speculative work. The University of California, Riverside, will stage the exhibition *Mundos Alternos: Art and Science Fiction in the Americas* in 2017, around the same time that *Latin@ Rising* will be released (see Robb Hernández's essay on curating the exhibition in this anthology). Additionally, support is coming from within the academic community, where there is great curiosity about Latin@ speculative fiction and where a number of conferences and journals are focusing on the topic. *Altermundos: Latin@ Speculative Literature, Film, and Popular Culture* is a magnificent high point in the academic response to Latin@ speculative fiction. John Morán González, in his 2010 essay "Aztlán @ 50: Chican@ Literary Studies for the Next Decade," notes that while the future of the nation has been whitewashed in the mainstream science fiction imagination, there are nevertheless a number of new Chican@ writers working in science fiction and other imaginative genres. As the future comes crashing in, it is good to remember that the legacy of speculative fiction is steeped in racism and colonialism. The authors in *Altermundos* and in *Latin@ Rising* directly challenge that legacy as they create other worlds and rewrite the future.

Works Cited

Bell, Andrea L., and Yolanda Molina-Gavilán, eds. 2003. *Cosmos Latinos: An Anthology of Science Fiction from Latin America and Spain*. Middletown, CT: Wesleyan University Press.

Goodwin, Matthew David, ed. Forthcoming. *Latin@ Rising: An Anthology of Latin@ Science Fiction and Fantasy*. San Antonio: Wings Press.

Jiménez Mayo, Eduardo, and Chris N. Brown. 2013. *Three Messages and a Warning: Contemporary Mexican Short Stories of the Fantastic*. Easthampton, MA: Small Beer.

Morán González, John. 2010. "Aztlán @ 50: Chican@ Literary Studies for the Next Decade." *Aztlán: A Journal of Chicano Studies* 35, no. 2: 173–76.

Contributors

DAOINE S. BACHRAN is a PhD candidate at the University of New Mexico, where she is studying ethnic American literature. She is currently working on her dissertation, "From Recovery to Discovery: Ethnic Science Fiction and (Re)Creating the Future," which examines ethnic science fiction's response to racism in science.

CORDELIA E. BARRERA, associate professor of English and co-director of the Literature of Social Justice and the Environment (LSJE) initiative at Texas Tech University, received her PhD from the University of Texas, San Antonio. She specializes in Latin@ literatures, the American Southwest, and third space feminism. Her publications have appeared in *Quarterly Review of Film and Video, Western American Literature,* and *Chicana/Latina Studies: The Journal of MALCS.* Her work highlights the need to disrupt mythologies of the American West by incorporating border voices and identities and concentrates on the literature of social justice and the environment. Her most current book project is an exploration of utopian forms and social dreaming on the borderlands.

GREGG BARRIOS is a playwright, poet, and journalist. He is a 2013 USC Annenberg Getty Fellow, and he serves on the board of directors of the National Book Critics Circle. He was inducted into the Texas Institute of Letters in 2015. His work has appeared in *Los Angeles Times, The New York Times, Texas Observer, Texas Monthly, Film Quarterly, San Francisco Chronicle,* and Andy Warhol's *Interview.* He is a former book editor of the *San Antonio Express-News.* He has received a CTG-Mark Taper Fellowship, a Ford Foundation Grant, and an Artist Foundation Grant for his theater work. His play *A Ship of Fools,* on Texas writer Katherine Anne Porter, premiered in San Antonio in 2015. His play *I-DJ* was published in 2016.

WILLIAM A. CALVO-QUIRÓS is an assistant professor in the Department of American Culture at the University of Michigan. He holds a PhD in Chicana/o studies from the University of California, Santa Barbara (2014), and a PhD from the Department of Architecture and Environmental Design at Arizona State University (2011). His current research investigates the relationship between state violence, imagination, and the phantasmagoric along the US-Mexico border region during the twentieth century. He looks at this region not only as a sociopolitical space of conflict and struggle but also, simultaneously, as a 2,000-mile strip of "haunted" land, inhabited by many imaginary creatures, monsters, popular saints, and fantastic tales. His other areas of interest include Chicana/o aesthetics, Chicana feminist and queer decolonial methodologies, and the power of empathy and forgiveness to formulate new racial, gender, and sensual discourses. More about his research and teaching can be found at www.barriology.com.

NATALIA DEEB-SOSSA was born in Bogotá, Colombia, and came to the United States in 1995 to continue her graduate studies and escape the violence in Colombia, which at that time was shaped by the growing drug trade. Her observations of violence eventually took her to sociology as a field of study. Deeb-Sossa is an associate professor in the Chicana/o Studies Department at the University of California, Davis. Her research interests include medical sociology, social psychology, symbolic interaction, methodology, and race, class, and gender. Her recent publication, *Doing Good: Racial Tensions and Workplace Inequalities at a Community Clinic in El Nuevo South* (University of Arizona Press, 2013), analyzes how workers at a private, not-for-profit health care center reproduce—or resist reproducing—inequalities of race, class, and gender in their interactions with each other and in their daily work with the poor, especially Latina/os. She is currently working on a co-edited book with Adela de la Torre on Chicana/o researchers' experiences when implementing community-based participatory research (CBPR).

JOSÉ R. FLORES is a PhD candidate in Spanish and Mexican American studies at Arizona State University. He received a double BA in Chicano/ Latino studies and Spanish from the University of California, Irvine. Before coming to Arizona State University, he received a Graduate Certificate in Mexican American studies and an MA in Spanish from the University of Texas–Pan American. His teaching and research interests include Chican@/ Latin@ literary studies and race politics in the United States and Latin America. He is currently working on his dissertation, "Reimaginando el discurso racial en la narrativa chicana (1970–2010)," which examines how Chican@ narratives challenge and contribute to the discussion on race formation in the United States.

MATTHEW DAVID GOODWIN is an assistant professor in the Department of English at the University of Puerto Rico at Cayey. His research is centered on the experience of migration in Latin@ literature. He is currently at work on a full-length study of Latin@ science fiction as well as editing an anthology of Latin@ science fiction and fantasy titled *Latin@ Rising: An Anthology of Latin@ Science Fiction and Fantasy* (Wings Press, forthcoming). His BA is in philosophy and his MA degrees are in philosophy of religion and English. He completed his PhD in comparative literature at the University of Massachusetts Amherst.

LUZ MARÍA GORDILLO is an associate professor and program leader in the Department of Critical Culture, Gender, and Race Studies at Washington State University Vancouver. Gordillo is the author of *Mexican Women and the Other Side of Immigration: Engendering Transnational Ties* (University of Texas Press, 2010), co-director of the film *Antonia: A Chicana Story*, and contributor of original interviews for *Three Decades of Engendering History: Selected Works of Antonia I. Castañeda* (University of North Texas Press, 2014).

MICHELLE HABELL-PALLÁN, associate professor of gender, women and sexuality studies at the University of Washington, co-directs the UW Libraries Women Who Rock: Making Scenes, Building Communities Oral History Archive—an open access and interactive digital archive (http://content.lib.washington.edu/wwrweb). Her book *Loca Motion: The Travels of Chicana and Latina Popular Culture* (NYU Press, 2005), an extended analysis of Chicana punk performance and practice, received a Modern Language Association Prize Honorable Mention. She co-edited *Latina/o Popular Culture* (NYU Press, 2002) and a recent special issue on "The 1970s" for *Women Studies Quarterly*. Her in-progress book, *Beat Migration: Sounds of Cultural Citizenship*, traces the sounds of Chicanxfuturism in punk and more. A curator of the Smithsonian Institution Traveling Exhibition Service's *American Sabor: Latinos in US Popular Music* exhibition, she jams with the Seattle Fandango Project. The Rockefeller Foundation, the UC President's Postdoctoral Award, Simpson Center for the Humanities, and Woodrow Wilson Foundation have supported her research.

LINDA HEIDENREICH is an associate professor in the Department of Critical Culture, Gender, and Race Studies at Washington State University. She is author of *"This Land Was Mexican Once": Histories of Resistance from Northern California*. Her articles have appeared in journals such as *Journal of Chicana/Latina Studies, Aztlán, Journal of Latinos in Education,* and *Journal of American Ethnic History.* Her poetry has been published in *Lean Seed, Sanctified,* and *Sinister Wisdom.* She is a co-founder of INCLSA (Inland Northwest Chicana/o Latina/o Studies Alliance) and is the book review editor for *Chicana/Latina Studies.* Her latest work, with Antonia Castañeda, Luz María Gordillo, and Deena González, is *Three Decades of Engendering History: Selected Works of Antonia Castañeda* (University of North Texas Press, 2014). Oh yes, she enjoys reading vampire novels.

ROBB HERNÁNDEZ is an assistant professor of Latina/o literary and cultural studies at the University of California, Riverside. His book project "Finding AIDS: Archival Body/Archival Space and the Chicano Avant-garde" examines alternative archive formations, curations, and collecting practices generated around the AIDS crisis in Latino artist communities in Southern California. His monographs, *VIVA Records 1970–2000: Lesbian and Gay Latino Artists of Los Angeles* (2013) and *The Fire of Life: The Robert Legorreta—Cyclona Collection, 1962–2002* (2009) were published by the UCLA Chicano Studies Research Center Press. His articles have appeared in *Aztlán: A Journal of Chicano Studies; Collections; Museum and Curatorial Studies Review; MELUS;* and *Radical History Review,* and in anthologies and exhibition catalogs, including *Art AIDS America* (University of Washington Press, 2015). He is co-curating *Mundos Alternos: Art and Science Fiction in the Americas,* which will open in 2017 at the University of California, Riverside ARTSblock. The exhibition is part of the Getty Foundation's Pacific Standard Time: LA/LA initiative.

ERNEST HOGAN is the author of *Cortez on Jupiter* (Doherty, 1990), *High Aztech* (Tor, 1992), and *Smoking Mirror Blues* (Wordcraft, 2001), and other stories that have caused some to call him the Father of Chicano Science Fiction. His mother's maiden name is Garcia. He was born in East Los Angeles. He blogs at MondoErnesto.com and LaBloga.blogspot.com.

JOE JIMÉNEZ is the author of *The Possibilities of Mud* (Kórima, 2014) and *Bloodline,* a young adult novel (Arte Público Press, 2016). Jiménez holds an MFA in creative writing from Antioch University Los Angeles. He lives in San Antonio and is a member of the Macondo Workshops. For more, visit joejimenez.net.

CATHRYN JOSEFINA MERLA-WATSON is an assistant professor in literatures and cultural studies and affiliate faculty in the gender and women's studies as well as the Mexican American studies programs at the University of Texas

Rio Grande Valley. Her teaching and research interests include Chican@ and Latin@ literary and cultural studies, and she is completing a book manuscript titled "Apocalyptic and Postapocalyptic Affects in Chicana Literature and Performance."

ISABEL MILLÁN is an assistant professor in the Department of American Ethnic Studies at Kansas State University with a PhD in American culture from the University of Michigan. She specializes in Chicana/o studies, critical ethnic studies, transnational feminist and queer theories, bilingual children's cultural productions, comics, and science fiction. Millán is currently completing her book manuscript, "(Play)Grounds for Dismissal: Niñas Raras in Transborder Children's Cultural Studies," in which she interrogates bilingual and counter-normative children's cultural productions. Her recent publications include chapters in *Graphic Borders: Latino Comic Books Past, Present, and Future* (University of Texas Press, 2016) and *The Routledge Companion to Latina/o Popular Culture* (Routledge, 2016), as well as articles in *Signs: Journal of Women in Culture and Society* and *Aztlán: A Journal of Chicano Studies*.

GABRIELA NUÑEZ is an assistant professor in the Department of Chicana and Chicano Studies at California State University, Fullerton, where she teaches courses in literature and US cultural studies. Nuñez's current research examines cultural production that depicts the intersections of food and labor and the relationship between Latinas and Latinos and the environment.

B. V. OLGUÍN is a professor in the English Department at the University of Texas at San Antonio. He is the author of *La Pinta: Chicana/o Prisoner Literature, Culture, and Politics* (University of Texas Press, 2010) and the co-editor, with Maggie Rivas-Rodriguez, of *Latina/os and WWII: Mobility, Agency, and Ideology* (University of Texas Press, 2014). He received his PhD from Stanford University.

WILLIAM ORCHARD is an assistant professor of English at Queens College, City University of New York. He is the co-editor of *The Selected Plays of Josephina Niggli: Recovered Landmarks of Latino Literature* (University of Wisconsin Press, 2007) and *Borders, Bridges, and Breaks: History, Narrative, and Nation in Twenty-First-Century Chicana/o Literary Criticism* (University of Pittsburgh Press, 2016). He is currently completing a book titled "Drawn Together: Politics, Pedagogy, and the Latina/o Graphic Novel."

461

AMALIA ORTIZ, Tejana performance poet and playwright, appeared on three seasons of *Def Poetry* on HBO and on the NAACP Image Awards on FOX. Latinostories.com named Ortiz one of "2017 Top Ten 'New' Latino Authors to Watch (and Read)." Her book of poetry, *Rant. Chant. Chisme.*, was selected by NBC Latino as one of "10 Great Latino Books of 2015," and it won the Writers' League of the Texas 2016 Poetry Discovery Prize. She was chosen to speak TEDx McAllen in 2015. She is a CantoMundo Fellow and a Hedgebrook writer-in-residence alumni, where she wrote a Latino musical, *Carmen de la Calle*. She was awarded the Alfredo Cisneros Del Moral Foundation Grant in 2002 and a writing residency at the National Hispanic Cultural Center in 2011. Most recently, she received her MFA in creative writing from the University of Texas Rio Grande Valley.

MARGARITA E. PIGNATARO is an Arizona State University alumnae. Formerly a visiting assistant professor of Spanish at Syracuse University and Whitman College, she taught courses concerning Latino/a and Chicano/a studies; Mexican American studies; gender, queer, and identity studies; Latino immigration; visual art and culture studies; media studies; and theater and performance. Her theater piece, "A Fifteen Minute Interview with a Latina," appears in *Telling Tongues: A Latin@ Anthology on Language Experience* (Calaca Press, 2007). Her work can also be found in the bilingual anthology *Déjame que te cuente* (Chiringa, 2014) and online at *Label Me Latina/o*. She currently is a faculty member in the Latina/o Studies Program at the University of Wyoming and holds the position as the Rudolfo Anaya Visiting Assistant Professor.

CATHERINE S. RAMÍREZ is an associate professor of Latin American and Latino studies and director of the Chicano Latino Research Center at the University of California, Santa Cruz. She has published on science fiction and zoot-suiters and is currently writing a history of assimilation in the United States.

SUSANA RAMÍREZ is a queer nepantlera visionary, scholar, educator, and spiritual activist living in San Antonio. *Nepantlera* is Gloria E. Anzaldúa's term, which was inspired by the Náhuatl concept of nepantla, meaning "in-between-ness," for those who facilitate passages between worlds. As part of her work as a nepantlera, Ramirez bridges many caminos, including academia, community activism, and traditional medicine. She is a first-generation PhD candidate in English, teaching women's studies and English courses at the University of Texas at San Antonio. Inspired by women of color feminisms and womanism, Ramirez has worked on various transnational art and organizing efforts, including the twenty-sixth annual San Antonio International Woman's Day March, Fandangeando con Mujeres, and UTSA's Women's History Month 2014. As her life calling, she is a practitioner of Mexican traditional medicine (MTM) and indigenous ceremony. To learn more about her work, please visit her website: www.susanaramirez.org.

LYSA RIVERA is an associate professor of English and American cultural studies at Western Washington University, where she teaches courses in Chicana/o literature, African American literature, and American cultural studies. Her research explores the political and aesthetic dimensions of Chicana/o and US black science fiction writers and visual artists. You can find some of her work in *Aztlán: Journal of Chicano Studies*, *Science Fiction Studies*, and *MELUS*.

CYNTHIA SALDIVAR is the coordinator for the First Year Experience Program at the University of Texas Rio Grande Valley, where she designs and implements culturally relevant student programming aimed at assisting first-year students transition into the university. Saldivar received a BA in communication from Bowling Green State University in 2002 and an MA in Mexican American studies with an interdisciplinary emphasis from the University of Texas Rio Grande Valley in May 2016. Her current research explores how Chicanx cultural producers redeploy conventions of horror to explore the lived experiences of Latinx, particularly in South Texas.

JOHN PHILLIP SANTOS is the University Distinguished Scholar in Mestizo Cultural Studies at the University of Texas at San Antonio. The first Mexican American Rhodes Scholar, his awards include the Academy of American Poets' Prize at Notre Dame and the Oxford Prize for fiction. His articles on Latino culture have appeared in the *Los Angeles Times*, *The New York Times*, and the *San Antonio Express-News*. He is the writer and producer of more than forty television documentaries for CBS-TV and PBS-TV, two of them Emmy nominees. He is the author of *Places Left at the Time of Creation* (Penguin, 1999), *The Farthest Home Is in an Empire of Fire* (Penguin, 2010), and *Songs Older Than Any Known Singer* (Wings Press, 2007).

SHELLEY STREEBY is a professor of ethnic studies and literature at the University of California, San Diego. She is the author of *Radical Sensations: World Movements, Violence, and Visual Culture* (Duke University Press,

2013) and *American Sensations: Class, Empire, and the Production of Popular Culture* (University of California Press, 2002). She is also the co-editor, with Jesse Alemán, of *Empire and the Literature of Sensation: An Anthology of Nineteenth-Century Popular Fiction* (Rutgers University Press, 2007). Since 2010 she has directed the Clarion Science Fiction and Fantasy Writers' Workshop and is currently working on a new book on science fiction archives and imagining the future.

ANDREW UZENDOSKI is a visiting assistant professor in the Department of English at Lafayette College, where he teaches courses on Latina/o literature, science fiction, and human rights rhetoric. In 2015 he received his PhD in English with a graduate portfolio in Mexican American studies from the University of Texas at Austin. He has published work in *Aztlán: A Journal of Chicano Studies*, *Extrapolation*, *Western American Literature*, *American Indian Quarterly*, and *Critical Ethnic Studies: An Anthology.*

LUIS VALDERAS received a BFA in secondary art education from the University of Texas–Pan American. He is a co-founder of *Project: MASA*, a national group exhibition in 2005, 2006, and 2007 that featured Latino artists and focused on Chicano identities. He is also the co-founder of 3rd Space Art Gallery, which is devoted to representing current trends in the San Antonio visual arts scene, and Art to the Third Power, a public art community engagement project. Valderas has had the opportunity to show not only locally and nationally but also internationally. His work has been exhibited at OSDE Espacio de Arte in Buenos Aires, Argentina, and the Medellin Museum of Art in Medellin, Colombia. His work was featured in the exhibitions *Chicano Art for Our Millennium* (2004) and *Triumph in Our Communities: Four Decades of Mexican American Art* (2005) and is represented in collections at the University of Texas–Pan American, Arizona State University, International Museum of Art and Science, Mexic-Arte Museum, Art Museum of South Texas, Instituto for Latino Studies/Notre Dame, and San Antonio Museum of Art.

DEBORA KUETZPAL VASQUEZ is a multi-media Chicana artist, educator, and activist. Observing the Chican@ movement through the lens of a child has shaped her life, work, and the creation of her cartoon character, Citlali, La Chicana Super Hero. Citlali combats social and political issues pertaining to women, children, and animals. Vasquez comes from a long line of curanderas/healers, but her method of healing is through her art. She received a BA at Texas Woman's University in Denton and an MFA from the University of Wisconsin Madison. She also received a certificate in traditional culture from Universidad Nahuatl in Ocotepec, Mexico. Vasquez is an assistant professor and head of the visual arts program at Our Lady of the Lake University. Her research concentration examines the artistic perception through three main foci: cultural hybridity in contemporary and global artistic approaches to Indigenous and African spiritual healing; achieving ecological balance and community health through multigenerational relationships from a feminist perspective; and bringing attention to the lack of Chicana and women's representation in the arts and the education system. She recently opened Corazones on Fire: Painting with a Cultural Edge, a painting-as-entertainment studio that focuses on healing through cultura.

Susy J. Zepeda is a queer Xicana Indígena assistant professor of Chicana and Chicano studies at the University of California, Davis. She is an interdisciplinary transnational feminist scholar interested in Chicana/Latina decolonial feminisms, critical race and ethnic studies, women of color feminisms, queer of color studies, visual culture, collaborative methodologies, and intergenerational healing. Zepeda is part of the Santa Cruz Feminist of Color Collective, which co-published "'Building on the Edge of Each Other's Battles': A Feminist of Color Multidimensional Lens" in *Hypatia* (2014). Her article "Queer Xicana Indígena Cultural Production: Remembering Through Oral and Visual Storytelling" appeared in *Decolonization* (2014). Zepeda is currently writing her first book manuscript. She received a BA in sociology and women's studies from California State University, Long Beach, and a PhD in sociology (feminist studies and Latin American and Latino studies) from the University of California, Santa Cruz. In 2013-14 she held a visiting assistant professorship with the Social Justice Initiative at University of California, Davis.

Index